•••INPUT

DIGIPRINT

DC ONE MILLION

GRANT MORRISON
DAN ABNETT
CHUCK DIXON
ANDY LANNING
RON MARZ
JAMES ROBINSON
MARK SCHULTZ
WRITERS

PRENTIS ROLLINS
JOHN DELL
DREW GERACI
BUTCH GUICE
DENNIS JANKE
PAUL NEARY
WADE VON GRAWBADGER
INKERS

JOHN COSTANZA
CHRIS ELIOPOULOS
KEN LOPEZ
BILL OAKLEY
LETTERERS

VAL SEMEIKS
BUTCH GUICE
BRYAN HITCH
GEORGES JEANTY
GREG LAND
HOWARD PORTER
PETER SNEJBJERG
PENCILLERS

CARLA FEENY
PAT GARRAHY
ROB SCHWAGER
GLORIA VASQUEZ
GREGORY WRIGHT
COLORISTS

DC ONE MILLION

Published by
DC Comics.
Cover, introduction
and compilation
copyright
© 1999 DC Comics.
All Rights Reserved.

Originally published in
single magazine form
as **DC ONE MILLION**
1-4, GREEN LANTERN
1,000,000,
STARMAN 1,000,000,
JLA 1,000,000,
RESURRECTION MAN
1,000,000, and
SUPERMAN: MAN OF
TOMORROW
1,000,000.
Copyright © 1998
DC Comics.
All Rights Reserved.
All characters, their
distinctive likenesses
and related indicia
featured in this
publication are
trademarks of
DC Comics.
The stories,
characters, and
incidents featured
in this publication
are entirely fictional.

DC Comics,
1700 Broadway,
New York, NY 10019
A division of Warner
Bros. - A Time Warner
Entertainment
Company
Printed in Canada.
First Printing.
ISBN: 1-56389-525-0
Cover illustration by
Val Semeiks and
Prentis Rollins.
Cover color by
Richard & Tanya
Horie.
Art for synopsis pages
by Pat Garrahy.

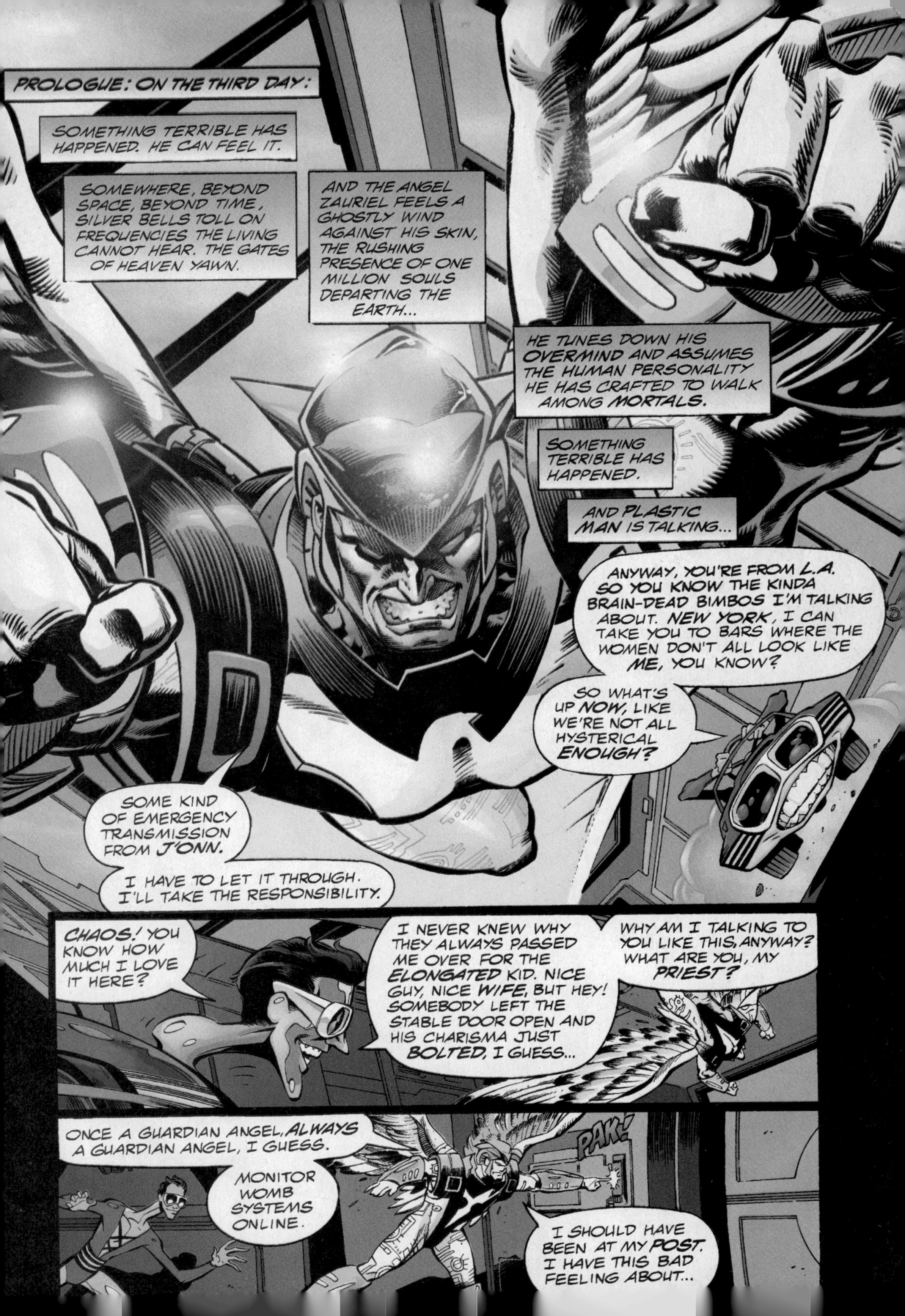
PROLOGUE: ON THE THIRD DAY:
SOMETHING TERRIBLE HAS HAPPENED. HE CAN FEEL IT.
SOMEWHERE, BEYOND SPACE, BEYOND TIME, SILVER BELLS TOLL ON FREQUENCIES THE LIVING CANNOT HEAR. THE GATES OF HEAVEN YAWN.
AND THE ANGEL ZAURIEL FEELS A GHOSTLY WIND AGAINST HIS SKIN, THE RUSHING PRESENCE OF ONE MILLION SOULS DEPARTING THE EARTH...
HE TUNES DOWN HIS OVERMIND AND ASSUMES THE HUMAN PERSONALITY HE HAS CRAFTED TO WALK AMONG MORTALS.
SOMETHING TERRIBLE HAS HAPPENED.
AND PLASTIC MAN IS TALKING...
ANYWAY, YOU'RE FROM L.A. SO YOU KNOW THE KINDA BRAIN-DEAD BIMBOS I'M TALKING ABOUT. NEW YORK, I CAN TAKE YOU TO BARS WHERE THE WOMEN DON'T ALL LOOK LIKE ME, YOU KNOW?
SO WHAT'S UP NOW, LIKE WE'RE NOT ALL HYSTERICAL ENOUGH?
SOME KIND OF EMERGENCY TRANSMISSION FROM J'ONN.
I HAVE TO LET IT THROUGH. I'LL TAKE THE RESPONSIBILITY.
CHAOS! YOU KNOW HOW MUCH I LOVE IT HERE?
I NEVER KNEW WHY THEY ALWAYS PASSED ME OVER FOR THE ELONGATED KID. NICE GUY, NICE WIFE, BUT HEY! SOMEBODY LEFT THE STABLE DOOR OPEN AND HIS CHARISMA JUST BOLTED, I GUESS...
WHY AM I TALKING TO YOU LIKE THIS, ANYWAY? WHAT ARE YOU, MY PRIEST?
ONCE A GUARDIAN ANGEL, ALWAYS A GUARDIAN ANGEL, I GUESS.
PAK!
MONITOR WOMB SYSTEMS ONLINE.
I SHOULD HAVE BEEN AT MY POST. I HAVE THIS BAD FEELING ABOUT...

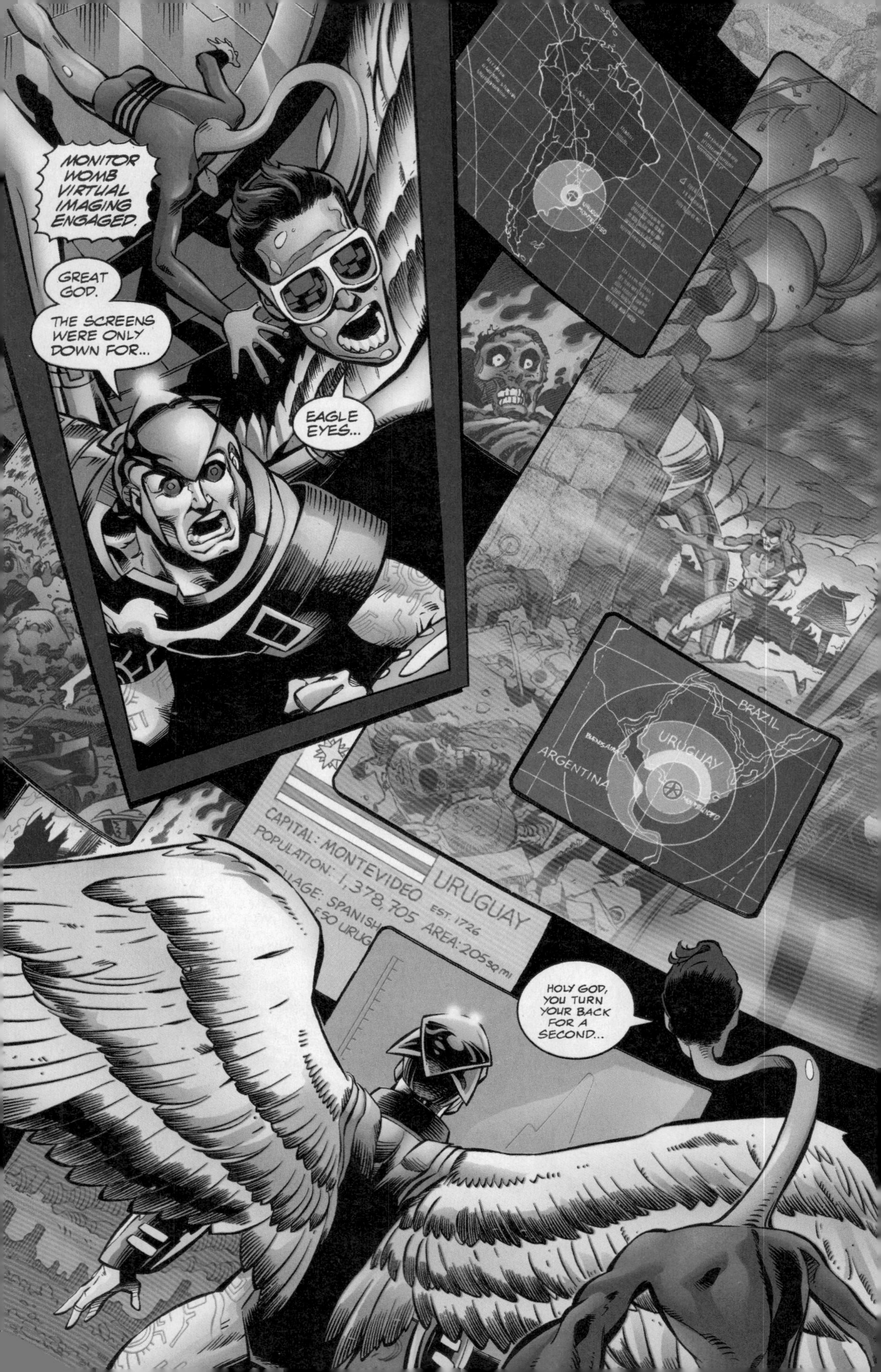
MONITOR WOMB VIRTUAL IMAGING ENGAGED.
GREAT GOD.
THE SCREENS WERE ONLY DOWN FOR...
EAGLE EYES...
BRAZIL
URUGUAY
ARGENTINA
CAPITAL: MONTEVIDEO
POPULATION: 1,378,705
EST. 1726
AREA: 205 sq mi
URUGUAY
HOLY GOD, YOU TURN YOUR BACK FOR A SECOND...

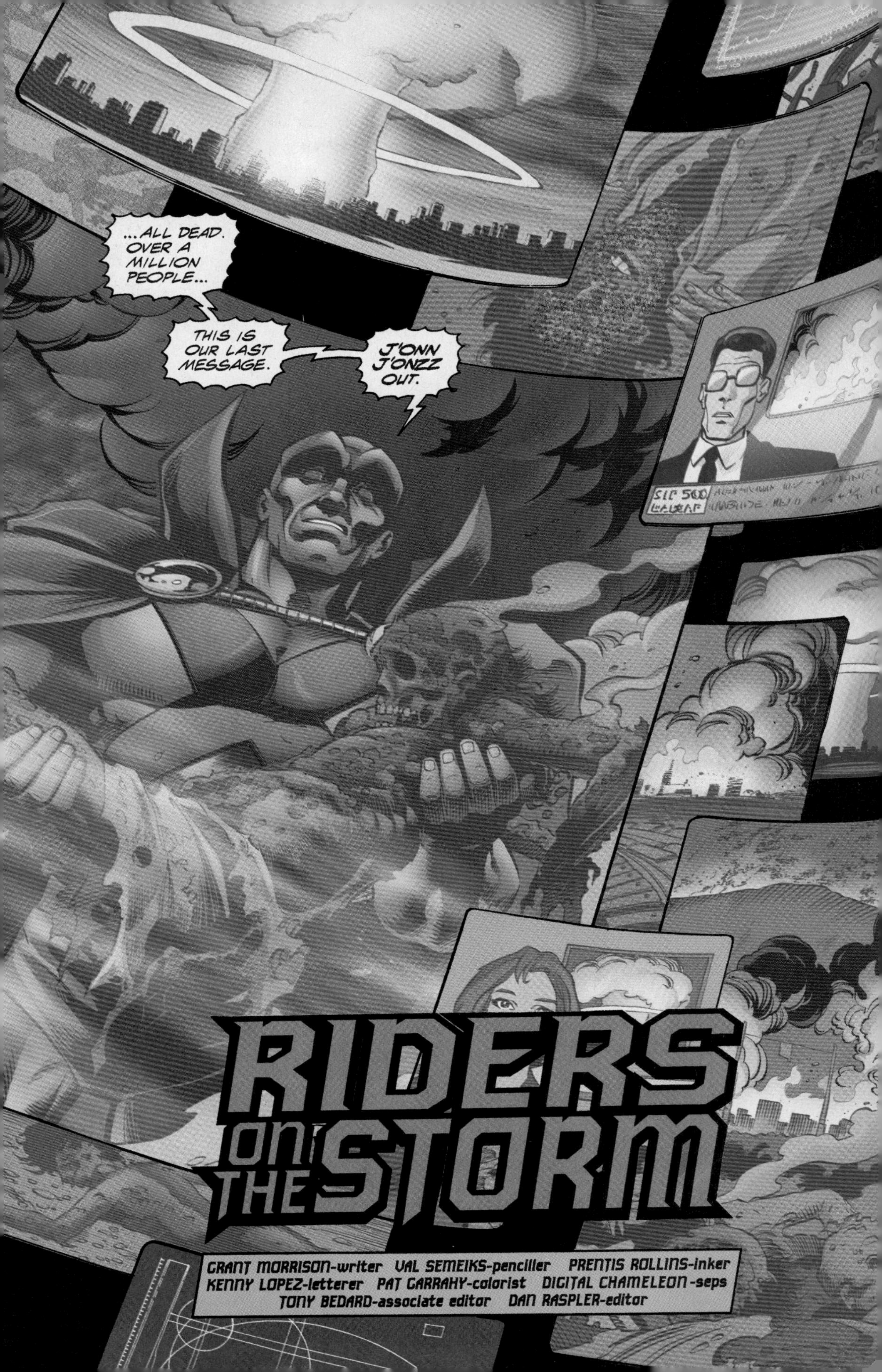
...ALL DEAD. OVER A MILLION PEOPLE...
THIS IS OUR LAST MESSAGE.
J'ONN J'ONZZ OUT.
RIDERS ON THE STORM
GRANT MORRISON-writer VAL SEMEIKS-penciller PRENTIS ROLLINS-inker
KENNY LOPEZ-letterer PAT GARRAHY-colorist DIGITAL CHAMELEON-seps
TONY BEDARD-associate editor DAN RASPLER-editor

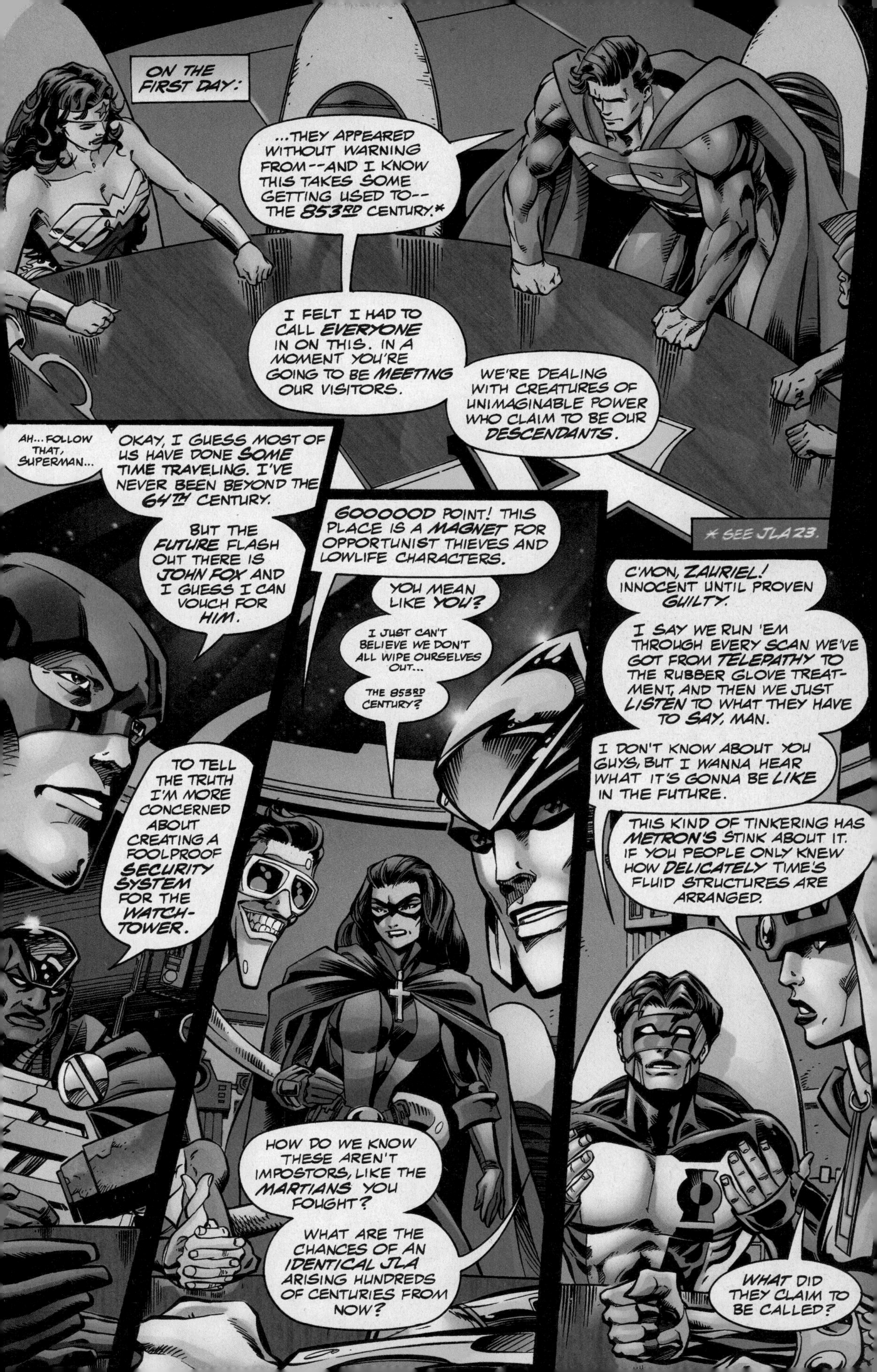
ON THE FIRST DAY:
...THEY APPEARED WITHOUT WARNING FROM--AND I KNOW THIS TAKES SOME GETTING USED TO--THE 853RD CENTURY.*
I FELT I HAD TO CALL EVERYONE IN ON THIS. IN A MOMENT YOU'RE GOING TO BE MEETING OUR VISITORS.
WE'RE DEALING WITH CREATURES OF UNIMAGINABLE POWER WHO CLAIM TO BE OUR DESCENDANTS.
AH... FOLLOW THAT, SUPERMAN...
OKAY, I GUESS MOST OF US HAVE DONE SOME TIME TRAVELING. I'VE NEVER BEEN BEYOND THE 64TH CENTURY.
BUT THE FUTURE FLASH OUT THERE IS JOHN FOX AND I GUESS I CAN VOUCH FOR HIM.
GOOOOOD POINT! THIS PLACE IS A MAGNET FOR OPPORTUNIST THIEVES AND LOWLIFE CHARACTERS.
YOU MEAN LIKE YOU?
I JUST CAN'T BELIEVE WE DON'T ALL WIPE OURSELVES OUT...
THE 853RD CENTURY?
* SEE JLA 23.
C'MON, ZAURIEL! INNOCENT UNTIL PROVEN GUILTY.
I SAY WE RUN 'EM THROUGH EVERY SCAN WE'VE GOT FROM TELEPATHY TO THE RUBBER GLOVE TREATMENT, AND THEN WE JUST LISTEN TO WHAT THEY HAVE TO SAY, MAN.
I DON'T KNOW ABOUT YOU GUYS, BUT I WANNA HEAR WHAT IT'S GONNA BE LIKE IN THE FUTURE.
TO TELL THE TRUTH I'M MORE CONCERNED ABOUT CREATING A FOOLPROOF SECURITY SYSTEM FOR THE WATCHTOWER.
THIS KIND OF TINKERING HAS METRON'S STINK ABOUT IT. IF YOU PEOPLE ONLY KNEW HOW DELICATELY TIME'S FLUID STRUCTURES ARE ARRANGED.
HOW DO WE KNOW THESE AREN'T IMPOSTORS, LIKE THE MARTIANS YOU FOUGHT?
WHAT ARE THE CHANCES OF AN IDENTICAL JLA ARISING HUNDREDS OF CENTURIES FROM NOW?
WHAT DID THEY CLAIM TO BE CALLED?

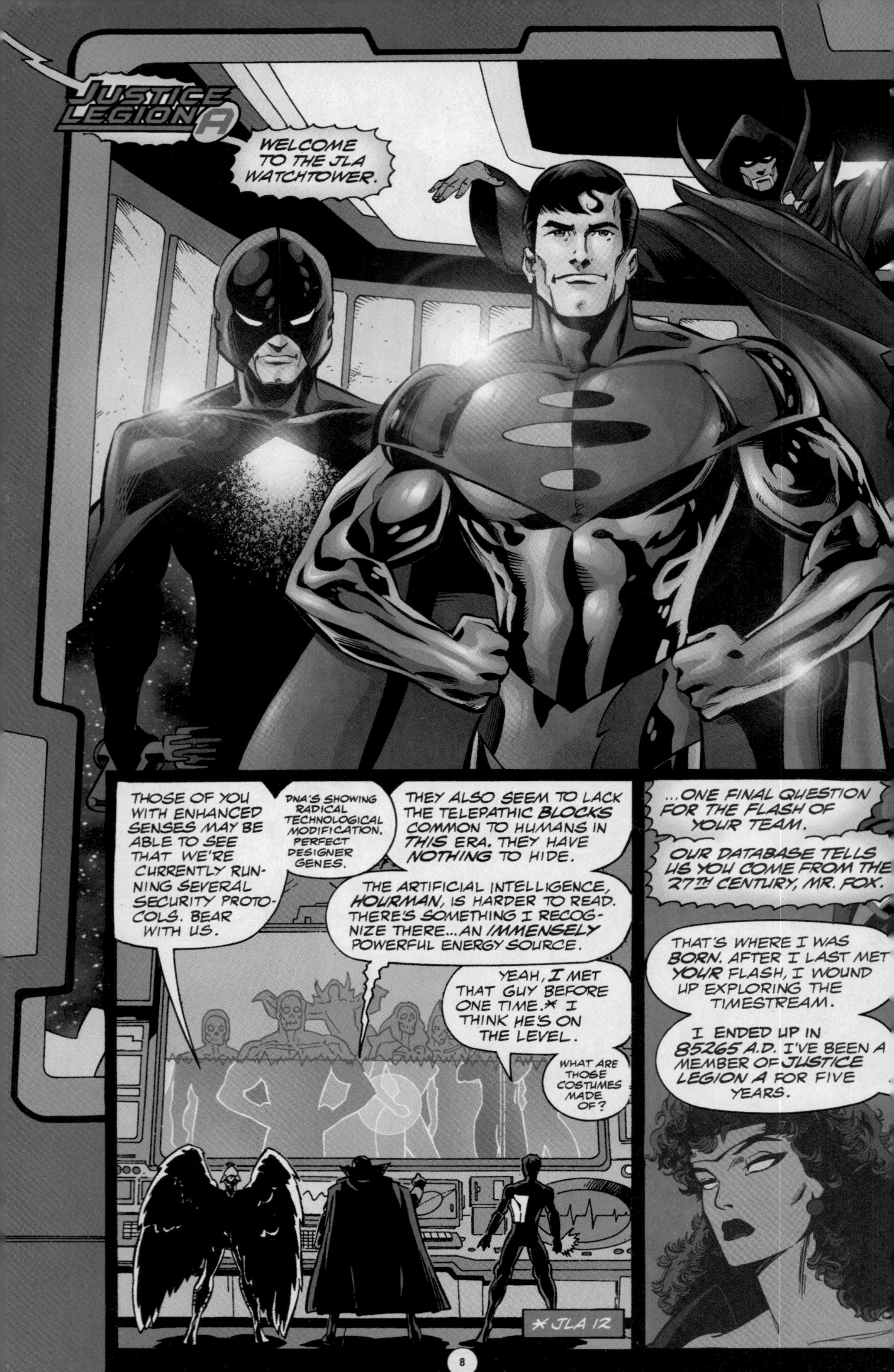
JUSTICE LEGION A
WELCOME TO THE JLA WATCHTOWER.
THOSE OF YOU WITH ENHANCED SENSES MAY BE ABLE TO SEE THAT WE'RE CURRENTLY RUNNING SEVERAL SECURITY PROTOCOLS. BEAR WITH US.
DNA'S SHOWING RADICAL TECHNOLOGICAL MODIFICATION. PERFECT DESIGNER GENES.
THEY ALSO SEEM TO LACK THE TELEPATHIC BLOCKS COMMON TO HUMANS IN THIS ERA. THEY HAVE NOTHING TO HIDE.
THE ARTIFICIAL INTELLIGENCE, HOURMAN, IS HARDER TO READ. THERE'S SOMETHING I RECOGNIZE THERE... AN IMMENSELY POWERFUL ENERGY SOURCE.
YEAH, I MET THAT GUY BEFORE ONE TIME.* I THINK HE'S ON THE LEVEL.
WHAT ARE THOSE COSTUMES MADE OF?
* JLA 12
...ONE FINAL QUESTION FOR THE FLASH OF YOUR TEAM.
OUR DATABASE TELLS US YOU COME FROM THE 27TH CENTURY, MR. FOX.
THAT'S WHERE I WAS BORN. AFTER I LAST MET YOUR FLASH, I WOUND UP EXPLORING THE TIMESTREAM.
I ENDED UP IN 85265 A.D. I'VE BEEN A MEMBER OF JUSTICE LEGION A FOR FIVE YEARS.

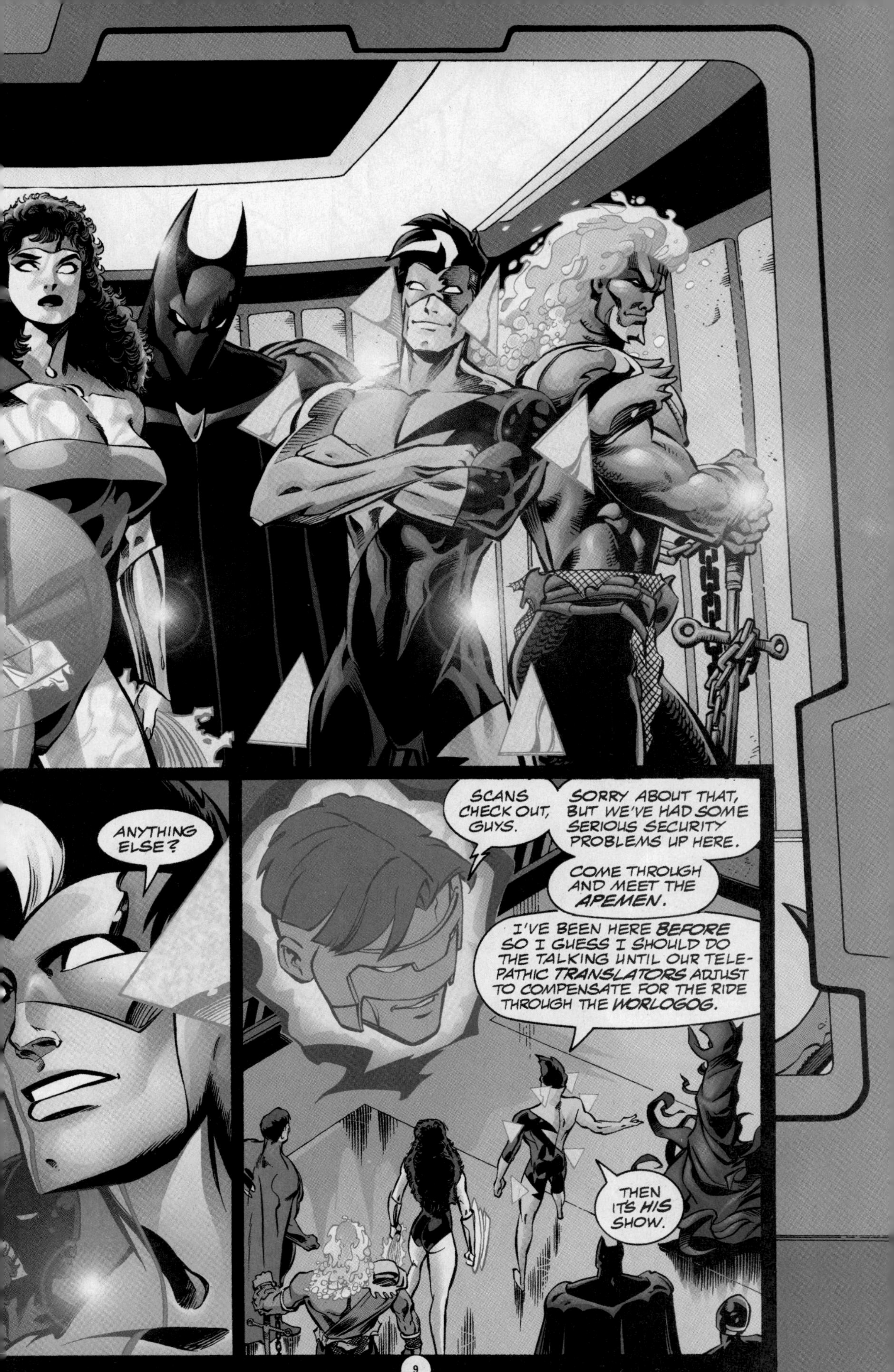
ANYTHING ELSE?
SCANS CHECK OUT, GUYS.
SORRY ABOUT THAT, BUT WE'VE HAD SOME SERIOUS SECURITY PROBLEMS UP HERE.
COME THROUGH AND MEET THE APEMEN.
I'VE BEEN HERE BEFORE SO I GUESS I SHOULD DO THE TALKING UNTIL OUR TELE-PATHIC TRANSLATORS ADJUST TO COMPENSATE FOR THE RIDE THROUGH THE WORLOGOG.
THEN IT'S HIS SHOW.

I AM HOURMAN: A TYLER CHEMOROBOTICS DIAMOND GENERATION INTELLIGENT MACHINE COLONY.

THE *WORLOGOG* IS A TIMESPANNING ENGINE BEQUEATHED TO ME BY MY TEACHER, *METRON* OF THE NEW GODS.

IT GRANTS ME MASTERY OF TIME AND SPACE. IT BROUGHT US SAFELY HERE THROUGH DEEP TIME.

METRON! DIDN'T I *SAY?*

HIS COLD FINGERPRINTS ARE ALL *OVER* THIS UNIVERSE.

SPEAKING OF NEW GODS, WHERE'S *ORION?* I MISS HIS OBVIOUS *CONTEMPT* FOR EVERYTHING I REPRESENT.

...WHY DO I LOOK AT YOU AND THINK OF MY *MOTHER,* BARDA?

I DON'T KNOW. DID YOUR MOTHER EVER THREATEN TO *DISEMBOWEL* YOU?

ORION COMES AND GOES AS HE PLEASES.

WE M[A]... NEED... HIM, BARDA

IF THE NEW GO[DS] ARE INVOLVED [IN] THIS, ORION'S FIREPOWER COULD BE VITA[L]

THIS WAS *MY* IDEA, NOT METRON'S.

I CHOSE TO COME HERE, TO ASK FOR YOUR HELP IN HONORING THE *GREATEST* HERO OF ALL TIME.

STARMAN?

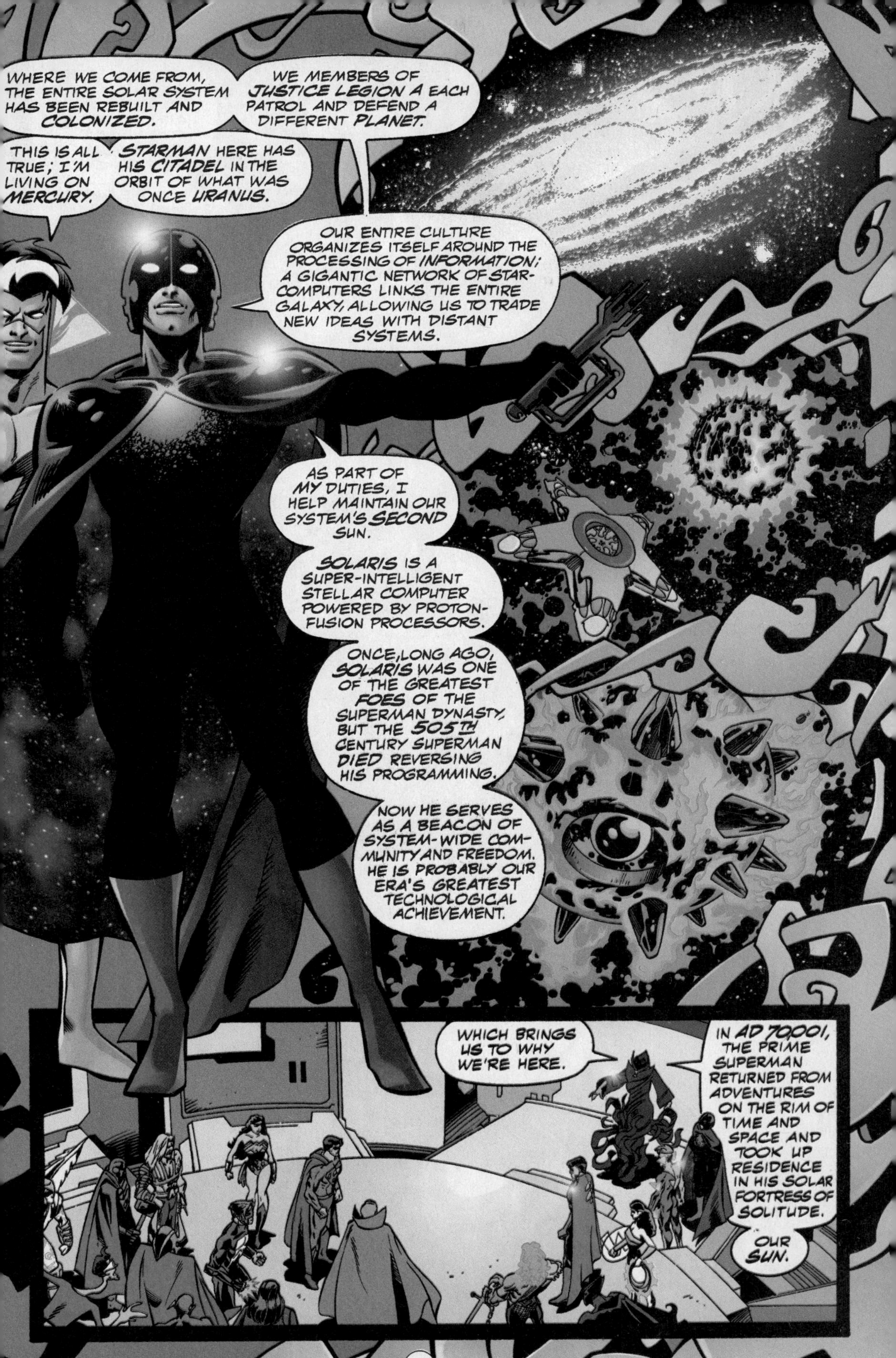
WHERE WE COME FROM, THE ENTIRE SOLAR SYSTEM HAS BEEN REBUILT AND COLONIZED.
WE MEMBERS OF JUSTICE LEGION A EACH PATROL AND DEFEND A DIFFERENT PLANET.
THIS IS ALL TRUE; I'M LIVING ON MERCURY.
STARMAN HERE HAS HIS CITADEL IN THE ORBIT OF WHAT WAS ONCE URANUS.
OUR ENTIRE CULTURE ORGANIZES ITSELF AROUND THE PROCESSING OF INFORMATION; A GIGANTIC NETWORK OF STAR-COMPUTERS LINKS THE ENTIRE GALAXY, ALLOWING US TO TRADE NEW IDEAS WITH DISTANT SYSTEMS.
AS PART OF MY DUTIES, I HELP MAINTAIN OUR SYSTEM'S SECOND SUN.
SOLARIS IS A SUPER-INTELLIGENT STELLAR COMPUTER POWERED BY PROTON-FUSION PROCESSORS.
ONCE, LONG AGO, SOLARIS WAS ONE OF THE GREATEST FOES OF THE SUPERMAN DYNASTY, BUT THE 505TH CENTURY SUPERMAN DIED REVERSING HIS PROGRAMMING.
NOW HE SERVES AS A BEACON OF SYSTEM-WIDE COMMUNITY AND FREEDOM. HE IS PROBABLY OUR ERA'S GREATEST TECHNOLOGICAL ACHIEVEMENT.
WHICH BRINGS US TO WHY WE'RE HERE.
IN AD 70,001, THE PRIME SUPERMAN RETURNED FROM ADVENTURES ON THE RIM OF TIME AND SPACE AND TOOK UP RESIDENCE IN HIS SOLAR FORTRESS OF SOLITUDE.
OUR SUN.

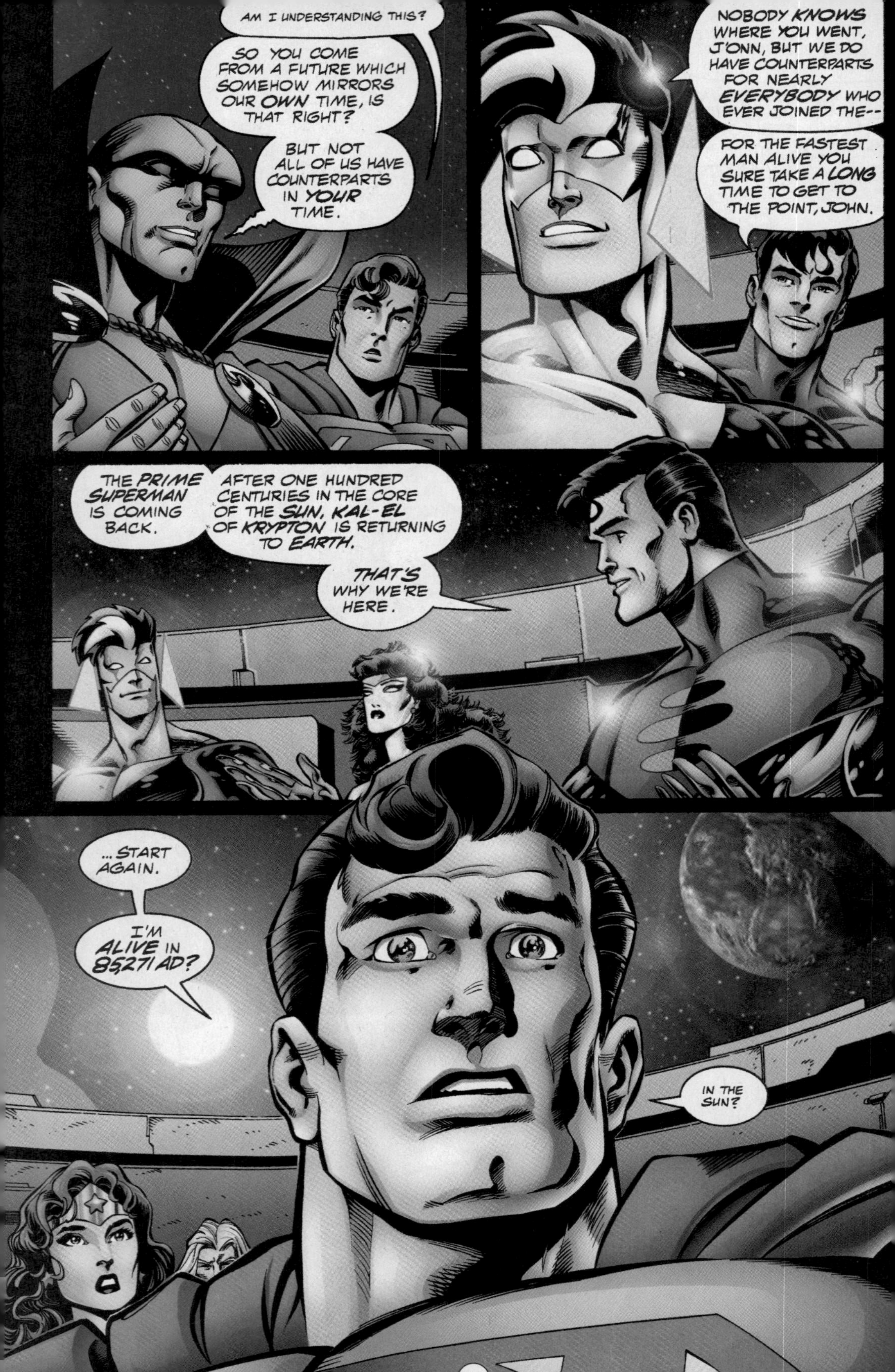
AM I UNDERSTANDING THIS?
SO YOU COME FROM A FUTURE WHICH SOMEHOW MIRRORS OUR OWN TIME, IS THAT RIGHT?
BUT NOT ALL OF US HAVE COUNTERPARTS IN YOUR TIME.
NOBODY KNOWS WHERE YOU WENT, J'ONN, BUT WE DO HAVE COUNTERPARTS FOR NEARLY EVERYBODY WHO EVER JOINED THE--
FOR THE FASTEST MAN ALIVE YOU SURE TAKE A LONG TIME TO GET TO THE POINT, JOHN.
THE PRIME SUPERMAN IS COMING BACK.
AFTER ONE HUNDRED CENTURIES IN THE CORE OF THE SUN, KAL-EL OF KRYPTON IS RETURNING TO EARTH.
THAT'S WHY WE'RE HERE.
...START AGAIN.
I'M ALIVE IN 85,271 AD?
IN THE SUN?

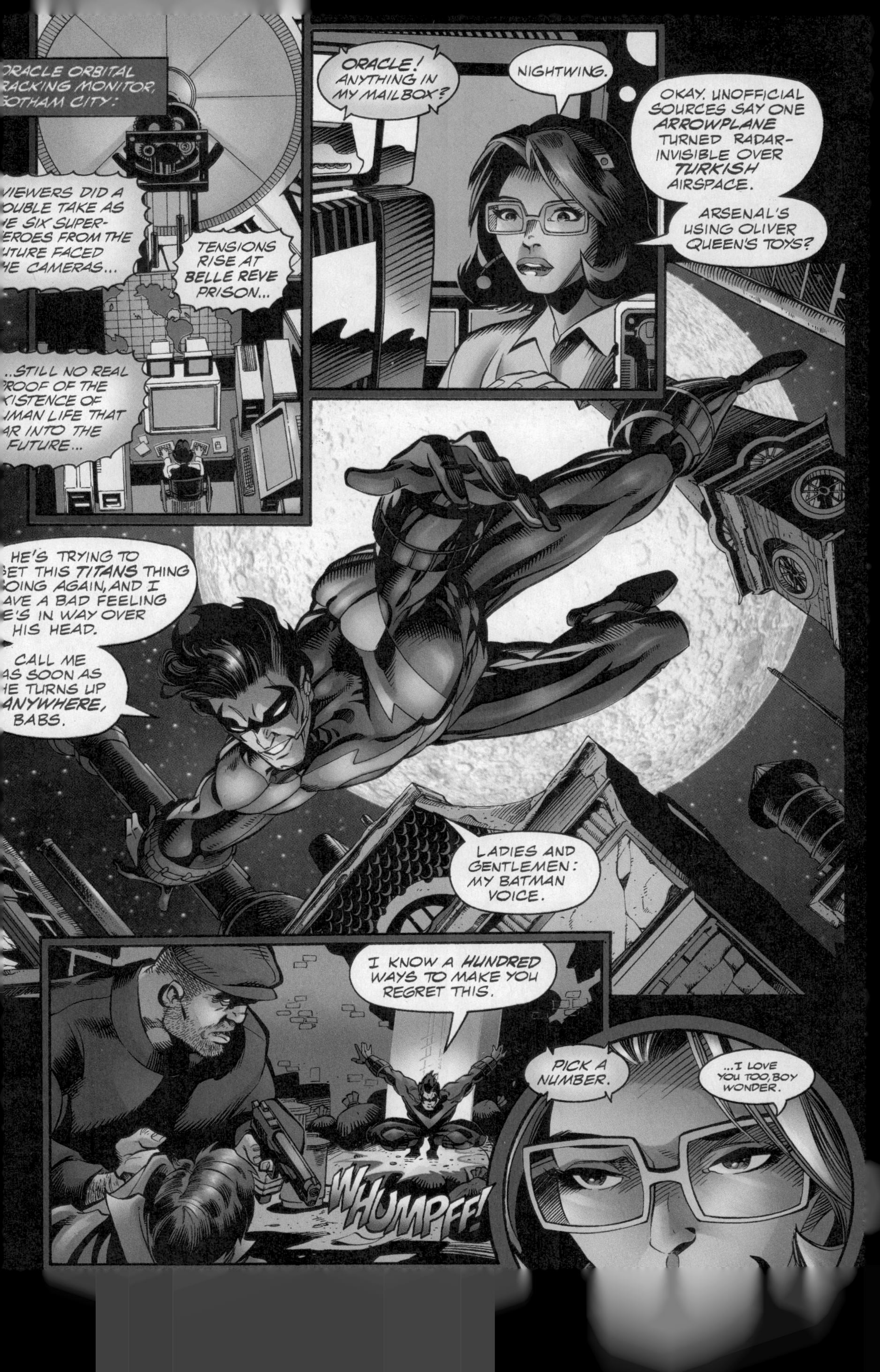
ORACLE ORBITAL
RACKING MONITOR,
OTHAM CITY:
IEWERS DID A
OUBLE TAKE AS
E SIX SUPER-
EROES FROM THE
UTURE FACED
HE CAMERAS...
TENSIONS RISE AT BELLE REVE PRISON...
...STILL NO REAL
ROOF OF THE
XISTENCE OF
MAN LIFE THAT
AR INTO THE
FUTURE...
ORACLE! ANYTHING IN MY MAILBOX?
NIGHTWING.
OKAY. UNOFFICIAL SOURCES SAY ONE ARROWPLANE TURNED RADAR-INVISIBLE OVER TURKISH AIRSPACE.
ARSENAL'S USING OLIVER QUEEN'S TOYS?
HE'S TRYING TO
ET THIS TITANS THING
OING AGAIN, AND I
AVE A BAD FEELING
E'S IN WAY OVER
HIS HEAD.
CALL ME
AS SOON AS
E TURNS UP
ANYWHERE,
BABS.
LADIES AND GENTLEMEN: MY BATMAN VOICE.
I KNOW A HUNDRED WAYS TO MAKE YOU REGRET THIS.
WHUMPFF!
PICK A NUMBER.
...I LOVE YOU TOO, BOY WONDER.

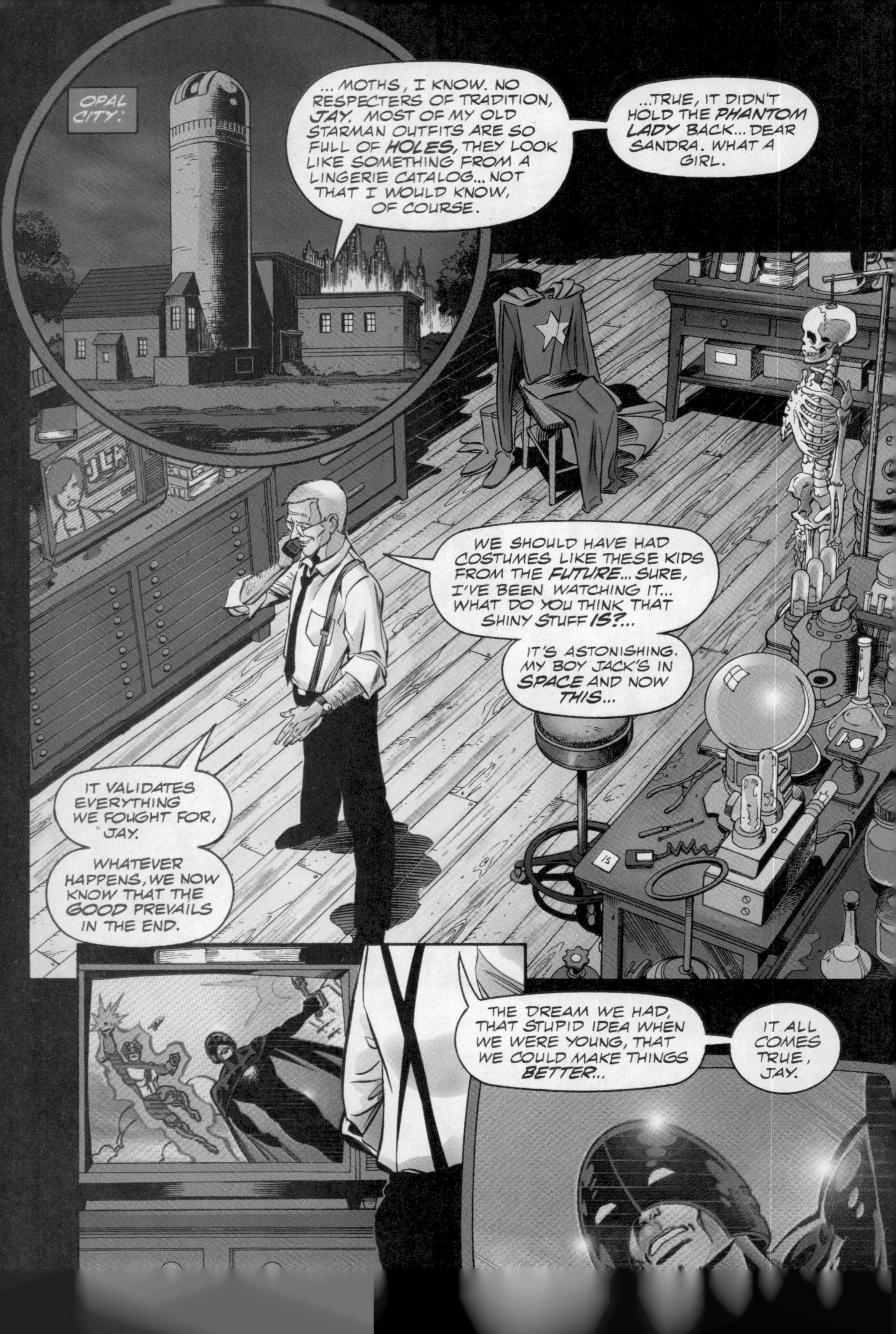
OPAL CITY:
...MOTHS, I KNOW. NO RESPECTERS OF TRADITION, JAY. MOST OF MY OLD STARMAN OUTFITS ARE SO FULL OF HOLES, THEY LOOK LIKE SOMETHING FROM A LINGERIE CATALOG... NOT THAT I WOULD KNOW, OF COURSE.
...TRUE, IT DIDN'T HOLD THE PHANTOM LADY BACK... DEAR SANDRA. WHAT A GIRL.
WE SHOULD HAVE HAD COSTUMES LIKE THESE KIDS FROM THE FUTURE... SURE, I'VE BEEN WATCHING IT... WHAT DO YOU THINK THAT SHINY STUFF IS?...
IT'S ASTONISHING. MY BOY JACK'S IN SPACE AND NOW THIS...
IT VALIDATES EVERYTHING WE FOUGHT FOR, JAY.
WHATEVER HAPPENS, WE NOW KNOW THAT THE GOOD PREVAILS IN THE END.
THE DREAM WE HAD, THAT STUPID IDEA WHEN WE WERE YOUNG, THAT WE COULD MAKE THINGS BETTER...
IT ALL COMES TRUE, JAY.

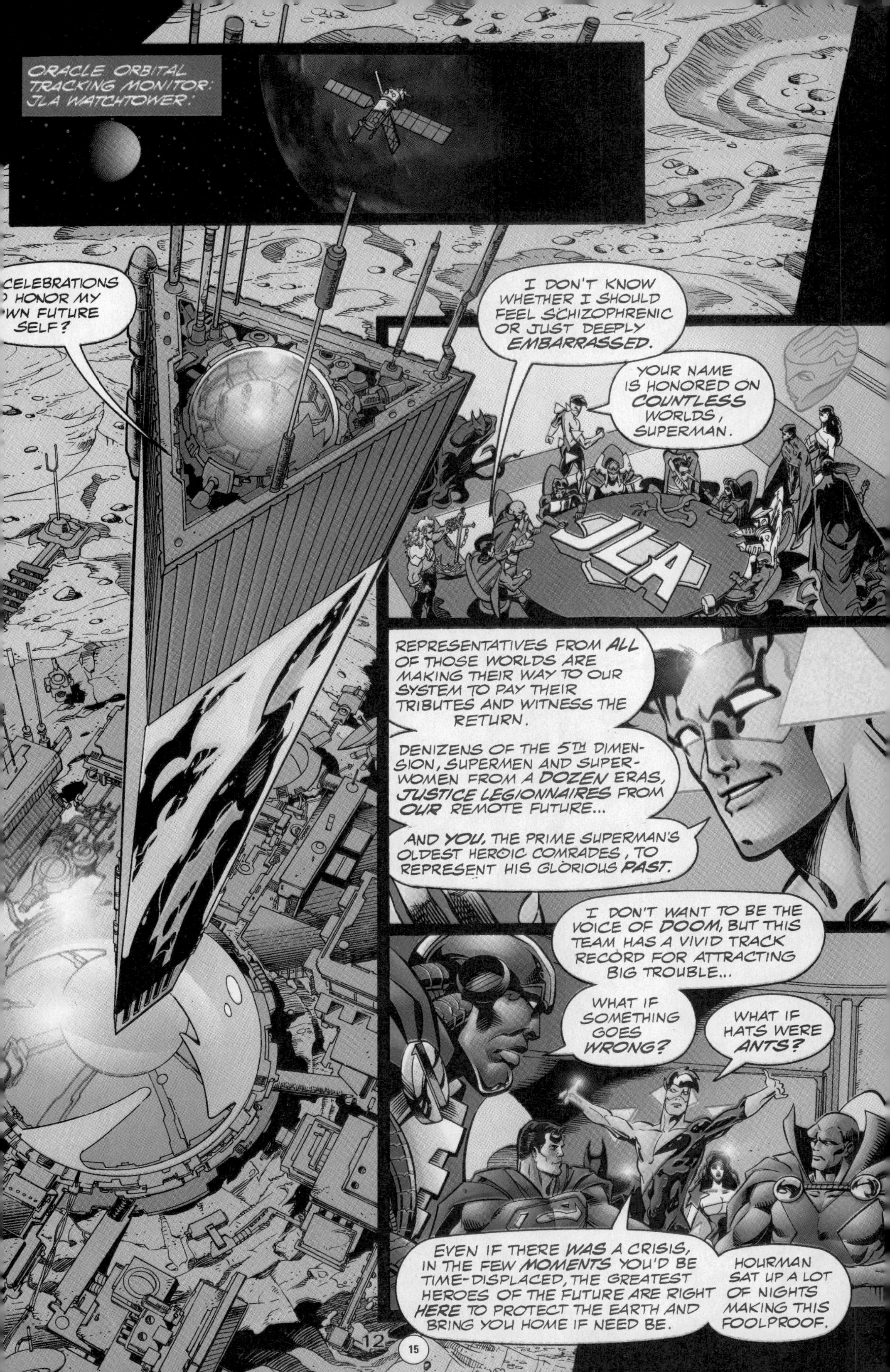
ORACLE ORBITAL TRACKING MONITOR: JLA WATCHTOWER.
CELEBRATIONS HONOR MY WN FUTURE SELF?
I DON'T KNOW WHETHER I SHOULD FEEL SCHIZOPHRENIC OR JUST DEEPLY EMBARRASSED.
YOUR NAME IS HONORED ON COUNTLESS WORLDS, SUPERMAN.
JLA
REPRESENTATIVES FROM ALL OF THOSE WORLDS ARE MAKING THEIR WAY TO OUR SYSTEM TO PAY THEIR TRIBUTES AND WITNESS THE RETURN.
DENIZENS OF THE 5TH DIMENSION, SUPERMEN AND SUPERWOMEN FROM A DOZEN ERAS, JUSTICE LEGIONNAIRES FROM OUR REMOTE FUTURE...
AND YOU, THE PRIME SUPERMAN'S OLDEST HEROIC COMRADES, TO REPRESENT HIS GLORIOUS PAST.
I DON'T WANT TO BE THE VOICE OF DOOM, BUT THIS TEAM HAS A VIVID TRACK RECORD FOR ATTRACTING BIG TROUBLE...
WHAT IF SOMETHING GOES WRONG?
WHAT IF HATS WERE ANTS?
EVEN IF THERE WAS A CRISIS, IN THE FEW MOMENTS YOU'D BE TIME-DISPLACED, THE GREATEST HEROES OF THE FUTURE ARE RIGHT HERE TO PROTECT THE EARTH AND BRING YOU HOME IF NEED BE.
HOURMAN SAT UP A LOT OF NIGHTS MAKING THIS FOOLPROOF.
12

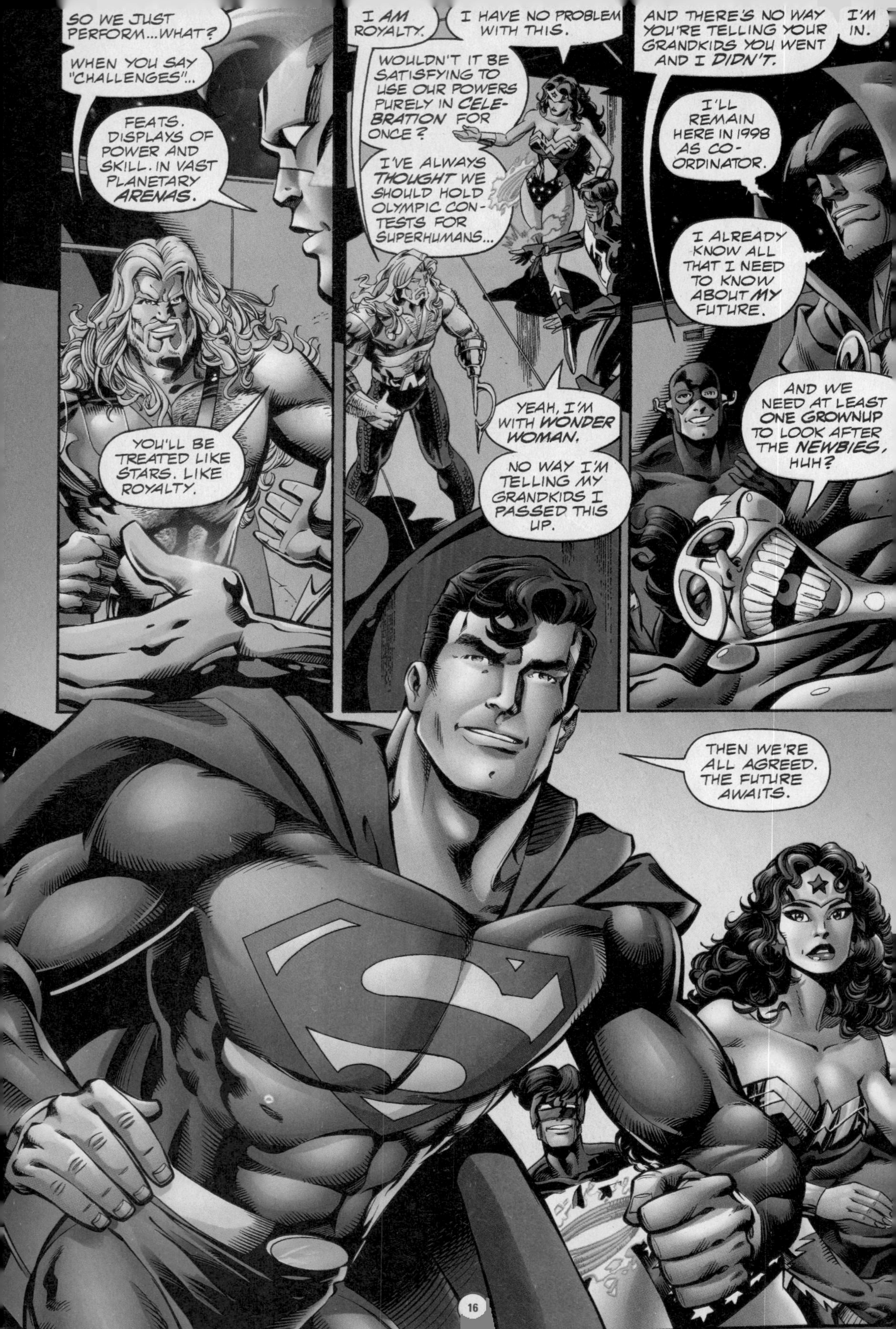
SO WE JUST PERFORM...WHAT?
WHEN YOU SAY "CHALLENGES"...
FEATS. DISPLAYS OF POWER AND SKILL. IN VAST PLANETARY ARENAS.
YOU'LL BE TREATED LIKE STARS. LIKE ROYALTY.
I AM ROYALTY.
I HAVE NO PROBLEM WITH THIS.
WOULDN'T IT BE SATISFYING TO USE OUR POWERS PURELY IN CELEBRATION FOR ONCE?
I'VE ALWAYS THOUGHT WE SHOULD HOLD OLYMPIC CONTESTS FOR SUPERHUMANS...
YEAH, I'M WITH WONDER WOMAN.
NO WAY I'M TELLING MY GRANDKIDS I PASSED THIS UP.
AND THERE'S NO WAY YOU'RE TELLING YOUR GRANDKIDS YOU WENT AND I DIDN'T.
I'M IN.
I'LL REMAIN HERE IN 1998 AS CO-ORDINATOR.
I ALREADY KNOW ALL THAT I NEED TO KNOW ABOUT MY FUTURE.
AND WE NEED AT LEAST ONE GROWNUP TO LOOK AFTER THE NEWBIES, HUH?
THEN WE'RE ALL AGREED. THE FUTURE AWAITS.

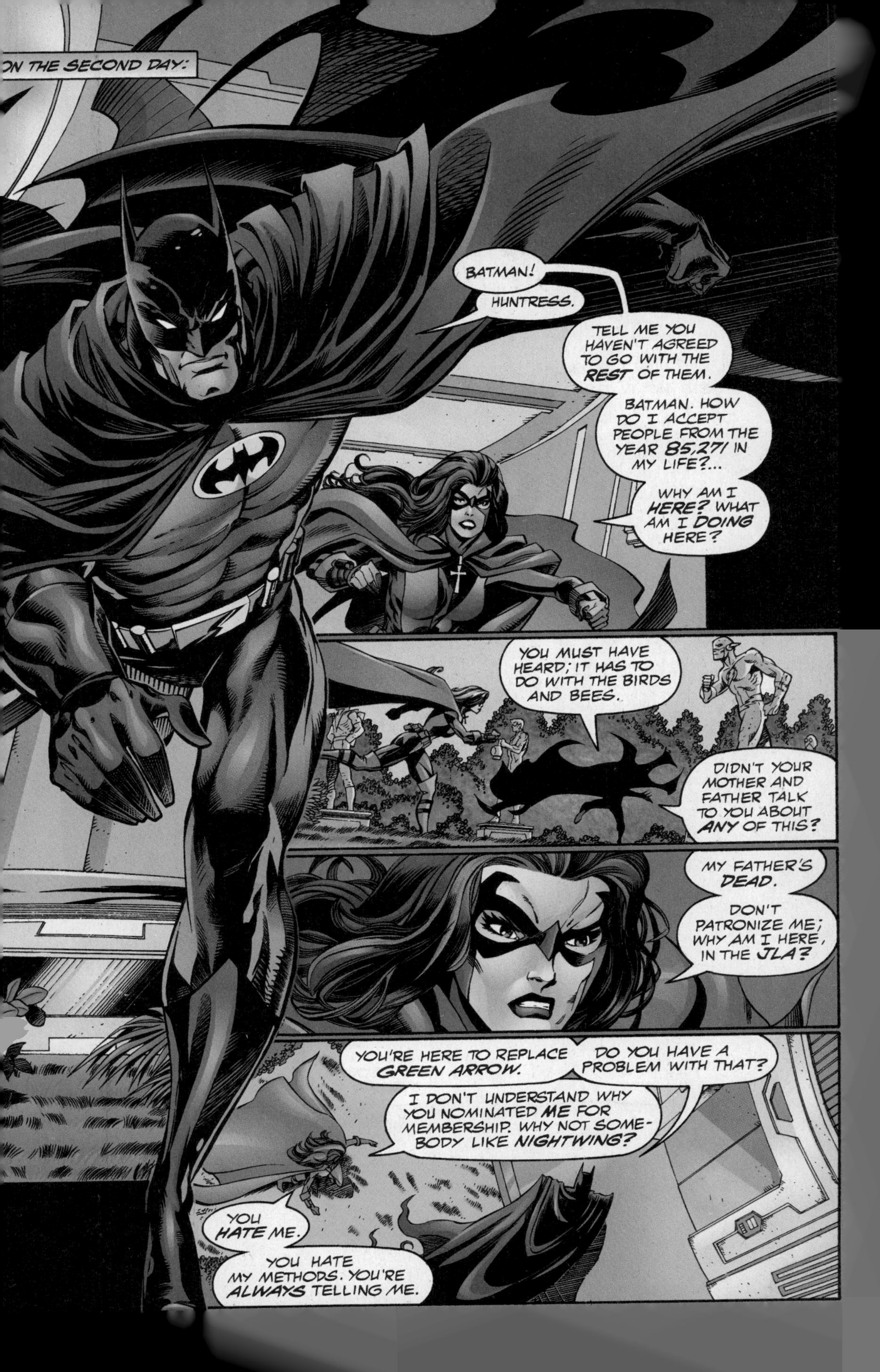
ON THE SECOND DAY:
BATMAN!
HUNTRESS.
TELL ME YOU HAVEN'T AGREED TO GO WITH THE REST OF THEM.
BATMAN. HOW DO I ACCEPT PEOPLE FROM THE YEAR 85,271 IN MY LIFE?...
WHY AM I HERE? WHAT AM I DOING HERE?
YOU MUST HAVE HEARD; IT HAS TO DO WITH THE BIRDS AND BEES.
DIDN'T YOUR MOTHER AND FATHER TALK TO YOU ABOUT ANY OF THIS?
MY FATHER'S DEAD.
DON'T PATRONIZE ME; WHY AM I HERE, IN THE JLA?
YOU'RE HERE TO REPLACE GREEN ARROW.
DO YOU HAVE A PROBLEM WITH THAT?
I DON'T UNDERSTAND WHY YOU NOMINATED ME FOR MEMBERSHIP. WHY NOT SOME-BODY LIKE NIGHTWING?
YOU HATE ME.
YOU HATE MY METHODS. YOU'RE ALWAYS TELLING ME.

THESE PEOPLE ARE SITTING HERE SERIOUSLY DISCUSSING -LIGENT STARS AND TRIPS UGH TIME TO YEARS THAT ND LIKE TELEPHONE NUMBERS!

WHY AM I HERE?

WHHKK

HIS IS THE WORLD HEY LIVE IN. OUR ORLD GETS MORE KE THEIRS EVERY DAY.

GET USED TO IT.

THAT'S NOT AN ANSWER.

I CAN'T BELIEVE YOU OF ALL PEOPLE ARE PREPARED TO TRUST THIS INSANE STORY ABOUT SUPERMAN IN THE SUN...

WE CAN'T AUTOMATICALLY ASSUME EVERYONE'S AN ENEMY.

BUT THEY USUALLY ARE, BATMAN.

§TT§

§HH§

DON'T TELL ME GOTHAM STILL NEEDS A BATMAN IN THE 853RD CENTURY.

FROM WHAT LITTLE I KNOW, GOTHAM WAS A PARADISE BEFORE IT DISAPPEARED FROM HISTORICAL RECORDS. WHERE I LIVE IS... A LITTLE MORE INTENSE.

YOUR TEAMMATES HAVE ALREADY DECIDED TO GO. WHAT ABOUT YOU?

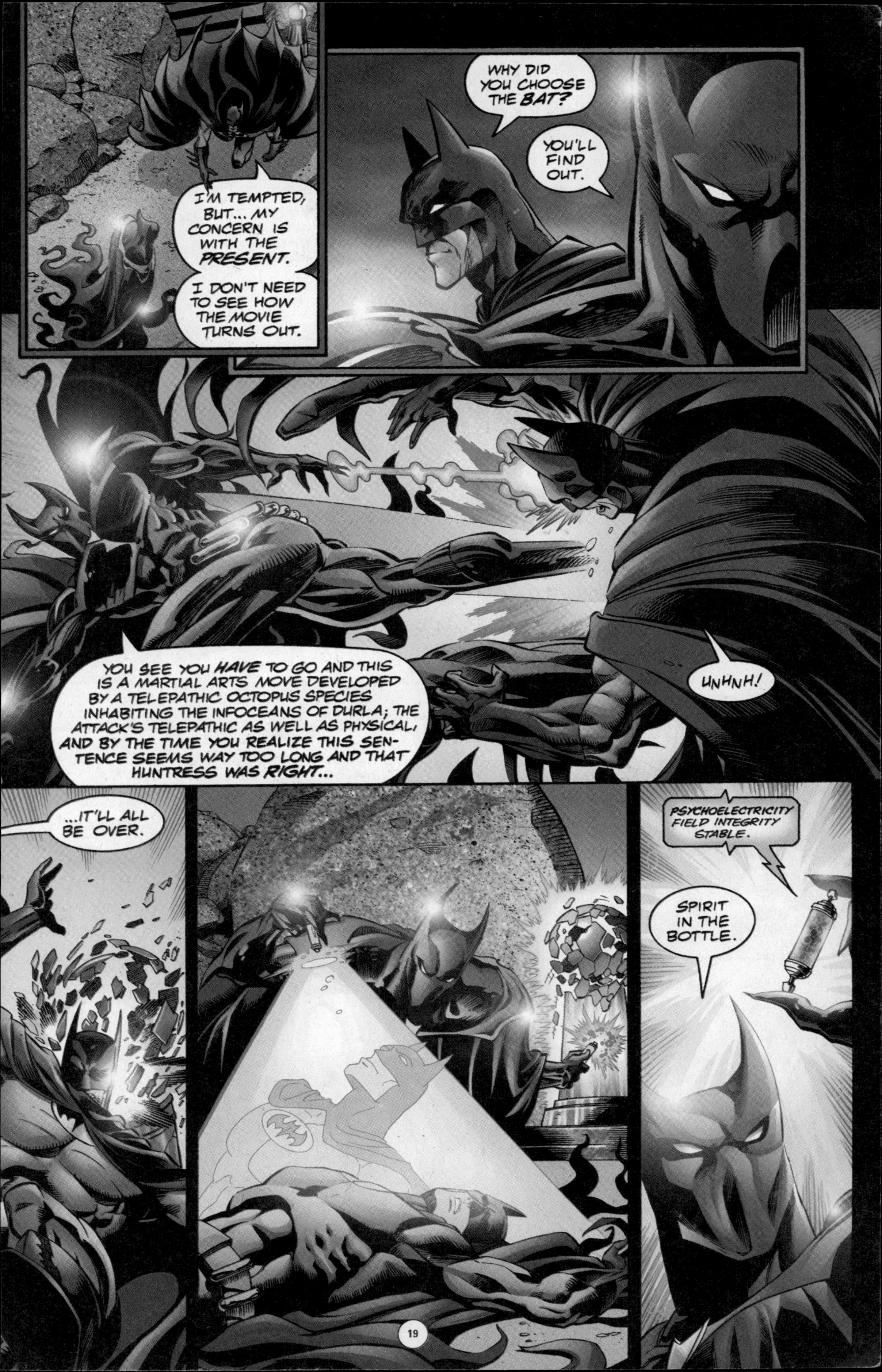

I'M TEMPTED, BUT... MY CONCERN IS WITH THE PRESENT.
I DON'T NEED TO SEE HOW THE MOVIE TURNS OUT.
WHY DID YOU CHOOSE THE BAT?
YOU'LL FIND OUT.
YOU SEE YOU HAVE TO GO AND THIS IS A MARTIAL ARTS MOVE DEVELOPED BY A TELEPATHIC OCTOPUS SPECIES INHABITING THE INFOCEANS OF DURLA; THE ATTACK'S TELEPATHIC AS WELL AS PHYSICAL, AND BY THE TIME YOU REALIZE THIS SENTENCE SEEMS WAY TOO LONG AND THAT HUNTRESS WAS RIGHT...
UNHNH!
...IT'LL ALL BE OVER.
PSYCHOELECTRICITY FIELD INTEGRITY STABLE.
SPIRIT IN THE BOTTLE.

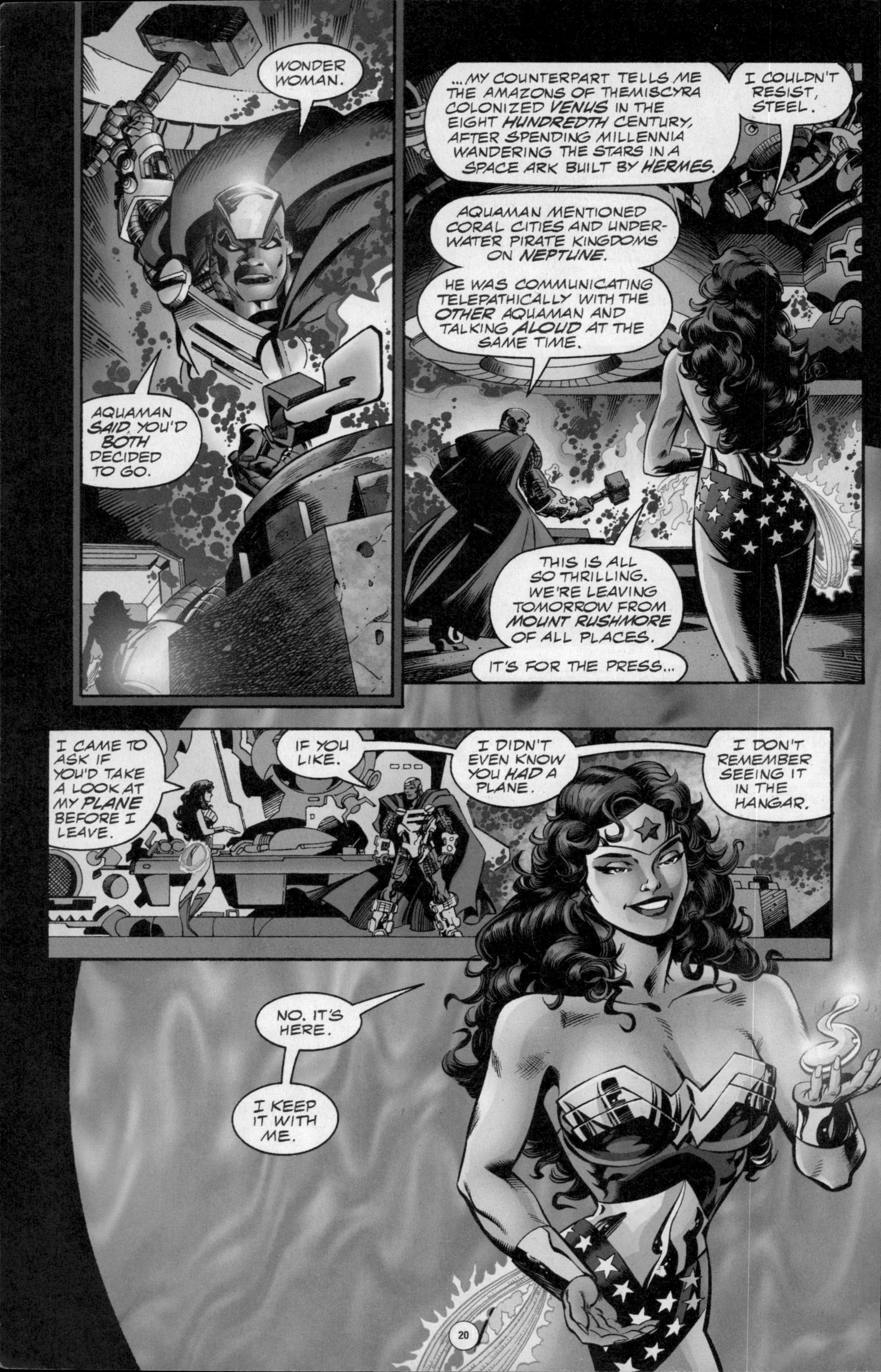

WONDER WOMAN.
AQUAMAN SAID YOU'D BOTH DECIDED TO GO.
...MY COUNTERPART TELLS ME THE AMAZONS OF THEMISCYRA COLONIZED VENUS IN THE EIGHT HUNDREDTH CENTURY, AFTER SPENDING MILLENNIA WANDERING THE STARS IN A SPACE ARK BUILT BY HERMES.
I COULDN'T RESIST, STEEL.
AQUAMAN MENTIONED CORAL CITIES AND UNDER-WATER PIRATE KINGDOMS ON NEPTUNE.
HE WAS COMMUNICATING TELEPATHICALLY WITH THE OTHER AQUAMAN AND TALKING ALOUD AT THE SAME TIME.
THIS IS ALL SO THRILLING. WE'RE LEAVING TOMORROW FROM MOUNT RUSHMORE OF ALL PLACES.
IT'S FOR THE PRESS...
I CAME TO ASK IF YOU'D TAKE A LOOK AT MY PLANE BEFORE I LEAVE.
IF YOU LIKE.
I DIDN'T EVEN KNOW YOU HAD A PLANE.
I DON'T REMEMBER SEEING IT IN THE HANGAR.
NO. IT'S HERE.
I KEEP IT WITH ME.

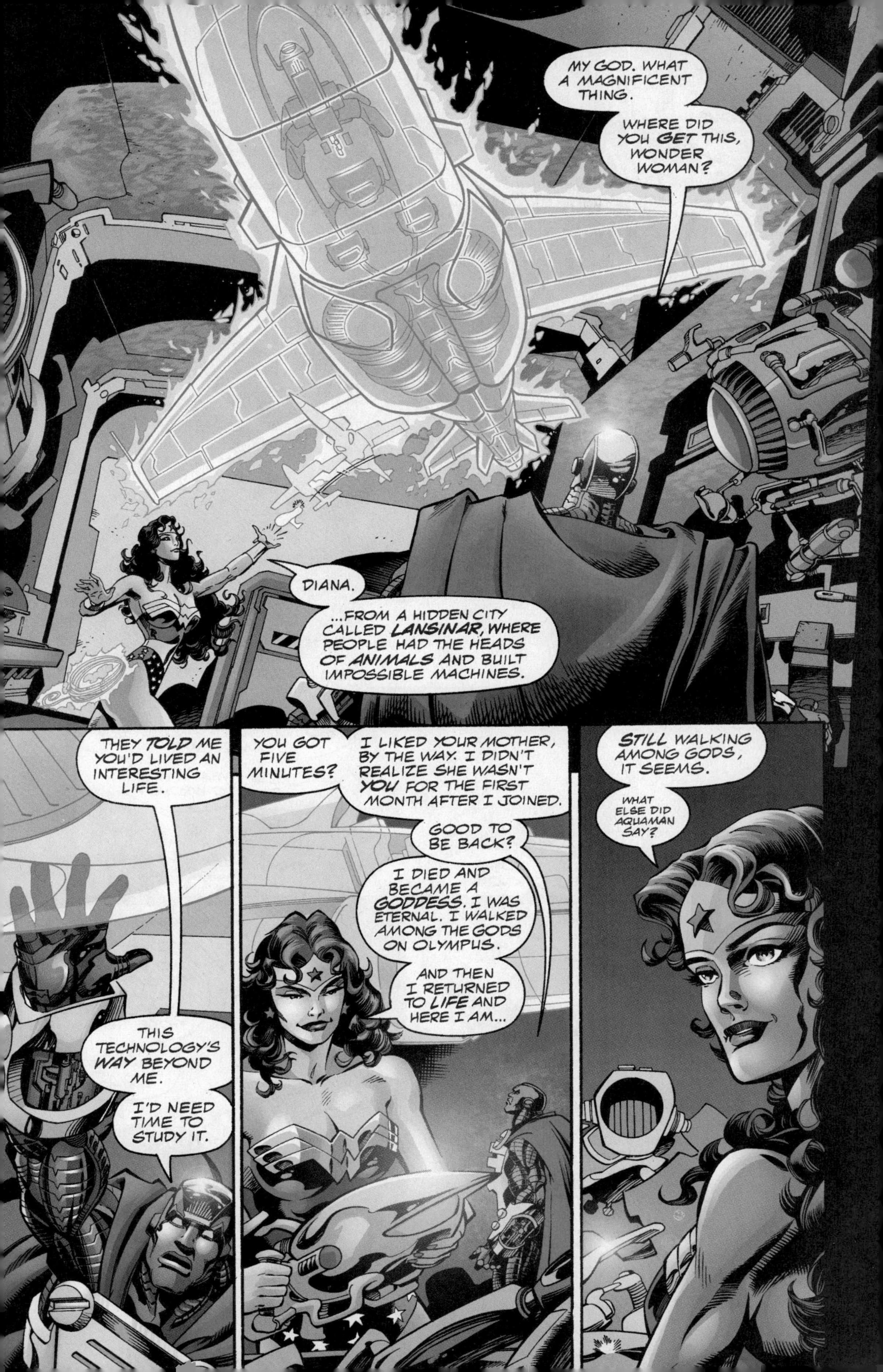
MY GOD. WHAT A MAGNIFICENT THING.
WHERE DID YOU GET THIS, WONDER WOMAN?
DIANA.
...FROM A HIDDEN CITY CALLED LANSINAR, WHERE PEOPLE HAD THE HEADS OF ANIMALS AND BUILT IMPOSSIBLE MACHINES.
THEY TOLD ME YOU'D LIVED AN INTERESTING LIFE.
THIS TECHNOLOGY'S WAY BEYOND ME.
I'D NEED TIME TO STUDY IT.
YOU GOT FIVE MINUTES?
I LIKED YOUR MOTHER, BY THE WAY. I DIDN'T REALIZE SHE WASN'T YOU FOR THE FIRST MONTH AFTER I JOINED.
GOOD TO BE BACK?
I DIED AND BECAME A GODDESS. I WAS ETERNAL. I WALKED AMONG THE GODS ON OLYMPUS.
AND THEN I RETURNED TO LIFE AND HERE I AM...
STILL WALKING AMONG GODS, IT SEEMS.
WHAT ELSE DID AQUAMAN SAY?

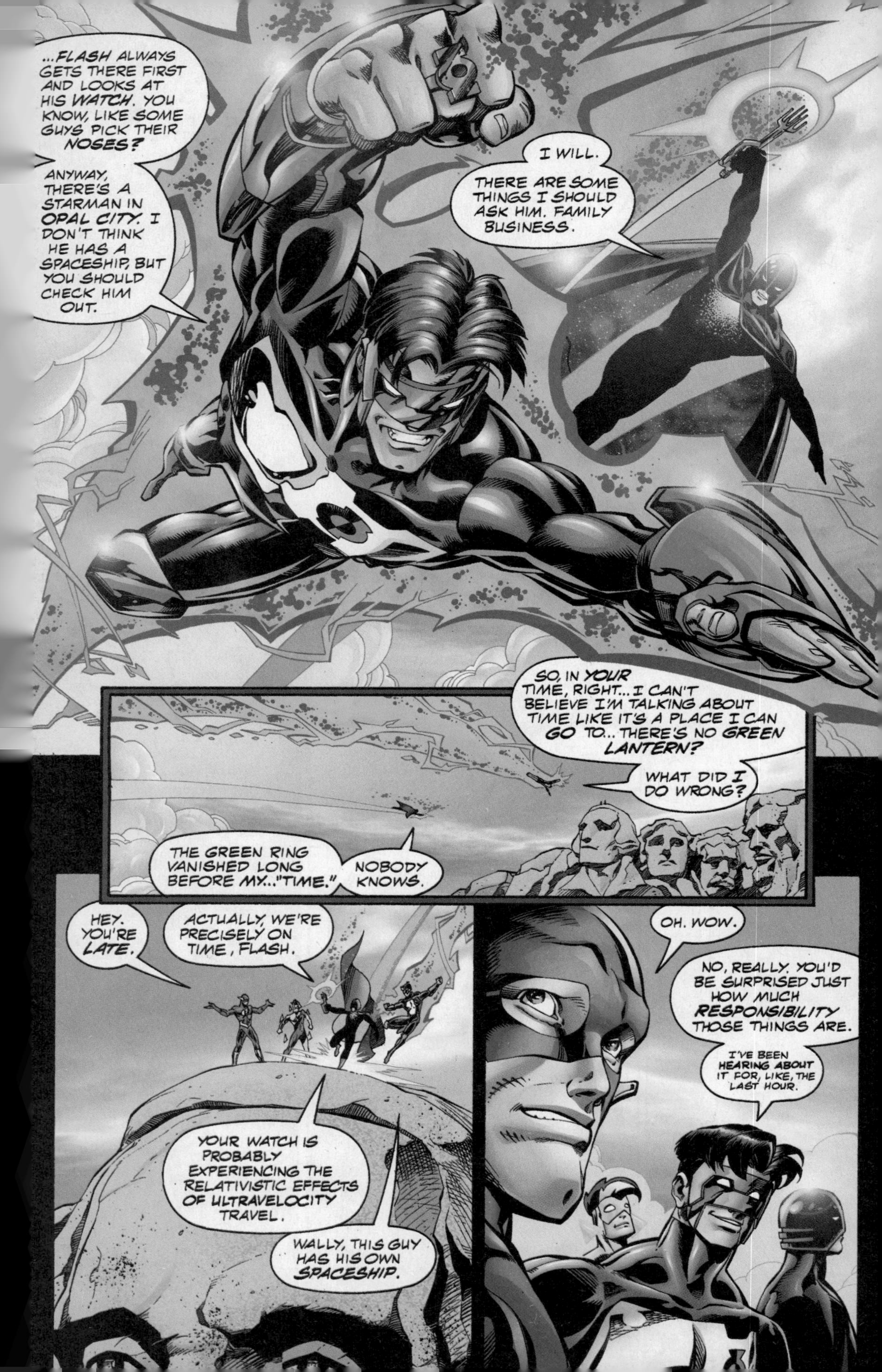
...FLASH ALWAYS GETS THERE FIRST AND LOOKS AT HIS WATCH. YOU KNOW, LIKE SOME GUYS PICK THEIR NOSES?
ANYWAY, THERE'S A STARMAN IN OPAL CITY. I DON'T THINK HE HAS A SPACESHIP, BUT YOU SHOULD CHECK HIM OUT.
I WILL.
THERE ARE SOME THINGS I SHOULD ASK HIM. FAMILY BUSINESS.
SO, IN YOUR TIME, RIGHT... I CAN'T BELIEVE I'M TALKING ABOUT TIME LIKE IT'S A PLACE I CAN GO TO... THERE'S NO GREEN LANTERN?
WHAT DID I DO WRONG?
THE GREEN RING VANISHED LONG BEFORE MY..."TIME."
NOBODY KNOWS.
HEY. YOU'RE LATE.
ACTUALLY, WE'RE PRECISELY ON TIME, FLASH.
YOUR WATCH IS PROBABLY EXPERIENCING THE RELATIVISTIC EFFECTS OF ULTRAVELOCITY TRAVEL.
WALLY, THIS GUY HAS HIS OWN SPACESHIP.
OH. WOW.
NO, REALLY. YOU'D BE SURPRISED JUST HOW MUCH RESPONSIBILITY THOSE THINGS ARE.
I'VE BEEN HEARING ABOUT IT FOR, LIKE, THE LAST HOUR.

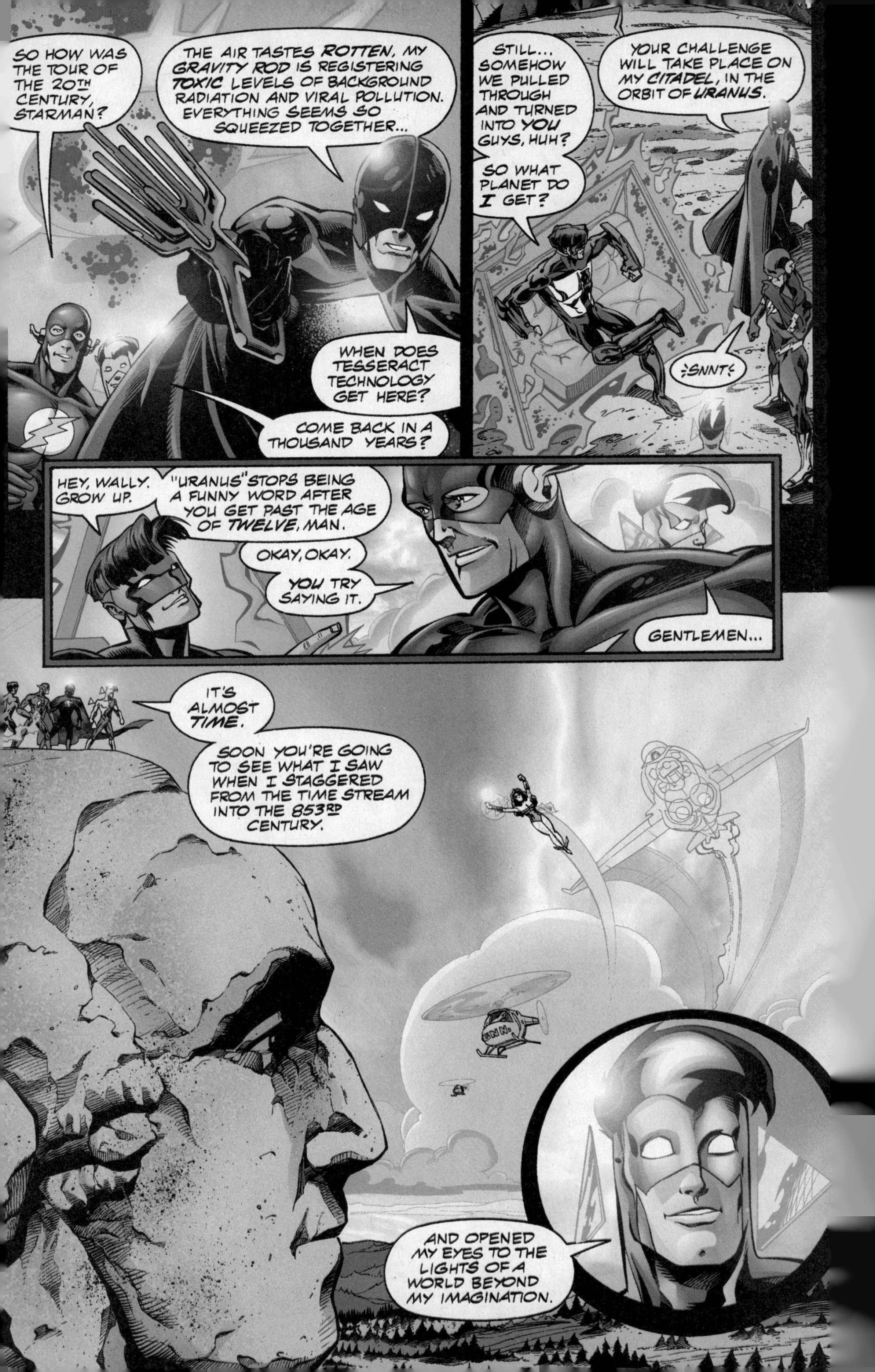

SO HOW WAS THE TOUR OF THE 20TH CENTURY, STARMAN?
THE AIR TASTES ROTTEN, MY GRAVITY ROD IS REGISTERING TOXIC LEVELS OF BACKGROUND RADIATION AND VIRAL POLLUTION. EVERYTHING SEEMS SO SQUEEZED TOGETHER...
WHEN DOES TESSERACT TECHNOLOGY GET HERE?
COME BACK IN A THOUSAND YEARS?
STILL... SOMEHOW WE PULLED THROUGH AND TURNED INTO YOU GUYS, HUH?
SO WHAT PLANET DO I GET?
YOUR CHALLENGE WILL TAKE PLACE ON MY CITADEL, IN THE ORBIT OF URANUS.
SNNT
HEY, WALLY. GROW UP.
"URANUS" STOPS BEING A FUNNY WORD AFTER YOU GET PAST THE AGE OF TWELVE, MAN.
OKAY, OKAY.
YOU TRY SAYING IT.
GENTLEMEN...
IT'S ALMOST TIME.
SOON YOU'RE GOING TO SEE WHAT I SAW WHEN I STAGGERED FROM THE TIME STREAM INTO THE 853RD CENTURY.
AND OPENED MY EYES TO THE LIGHTS OF A WORLD BEYOND MY IMAGINATION.

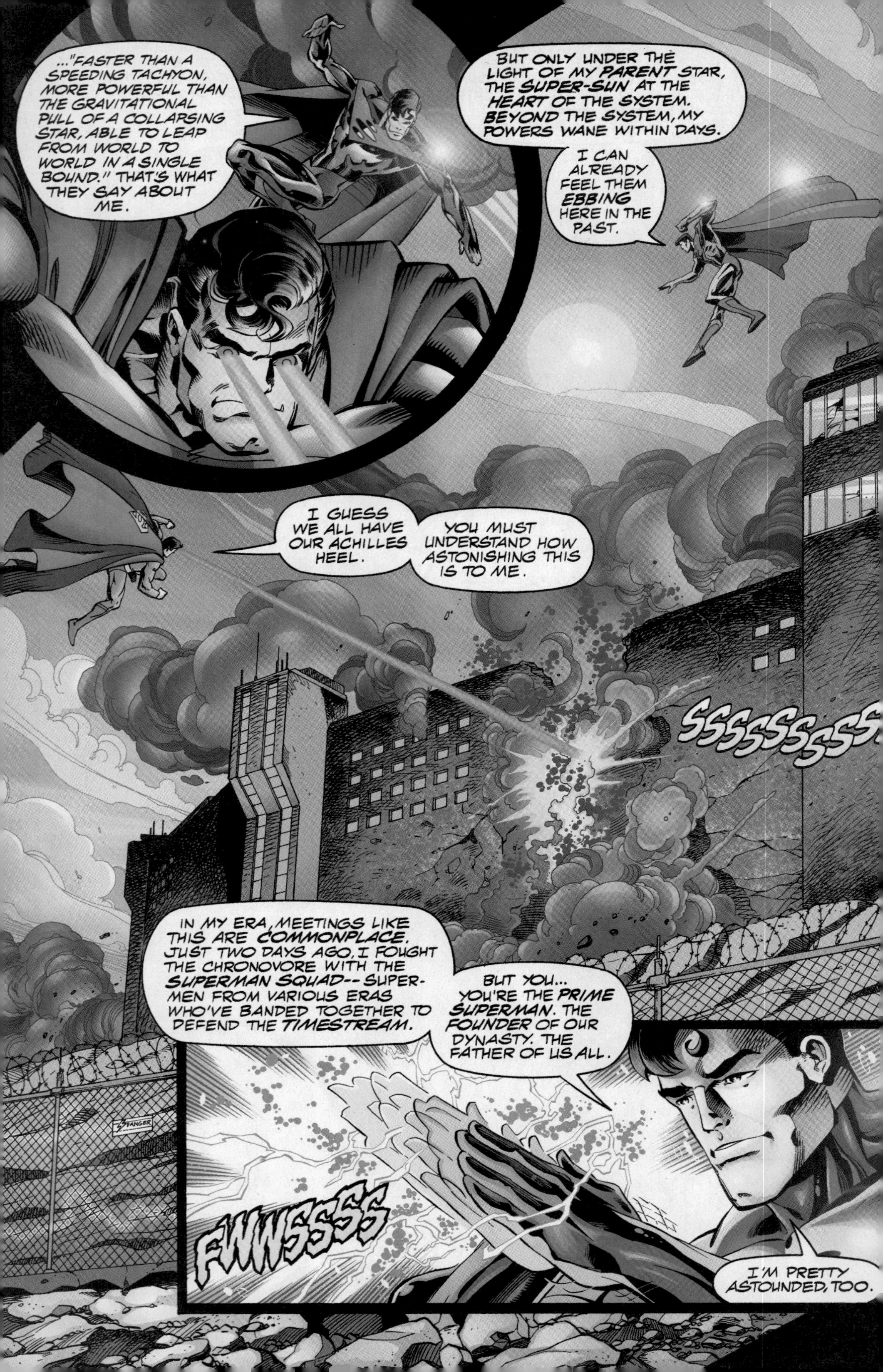
..."FASTER THAN A SPEEDING TACHYON, MORE POWERFUL THAN THE GRAVITATIONAL PULL OF A COLLAPSING STAR, ABLE TO LEAP FROM WORLD TO WORLD IN A SINGLE BOUND." THAT'S WHAT THEY SAY ABOUT ME.
BUT ONLY UNDER THE LIGHT OF MY PARENT STAR, THE SUPER-SUN AT THE HEART OF THE SYSTEM. BEYOND THE SYSTEM, MY POWERS WANE WITHIN DAYS.
I CAN ALREADY FEEL THEM EBBING HERE IN THE PAST.
I GUESS WE ALL HAVE OUR ACHILLES HEEL.
YOU MUST UNDERSTAND HOW ASTONISHING THIS IS TO ME.
SSSSSSSSSS
IN MY ERA, MEETINGS LIKE THIS ARE COMMONPLACE. JUST TWO DAYS AGO, I FOUGHT THE CHRONOVORE WITH THE SUPERMAN SQUAD-- SUPERMEN FROM VARIOUS ERAS WHO'VE BANDED TOGETHER TO DEFEND THE TIMESTREAM.
BUT YOU... YOU'RE THE PRIME SUPERMAN. THE FOUNDER OF OUR DYNASTY. THE FATHER OF US ALL.
DANGER
FWWSSSS
I'M PRETTY ASTOUNDED, TOO.

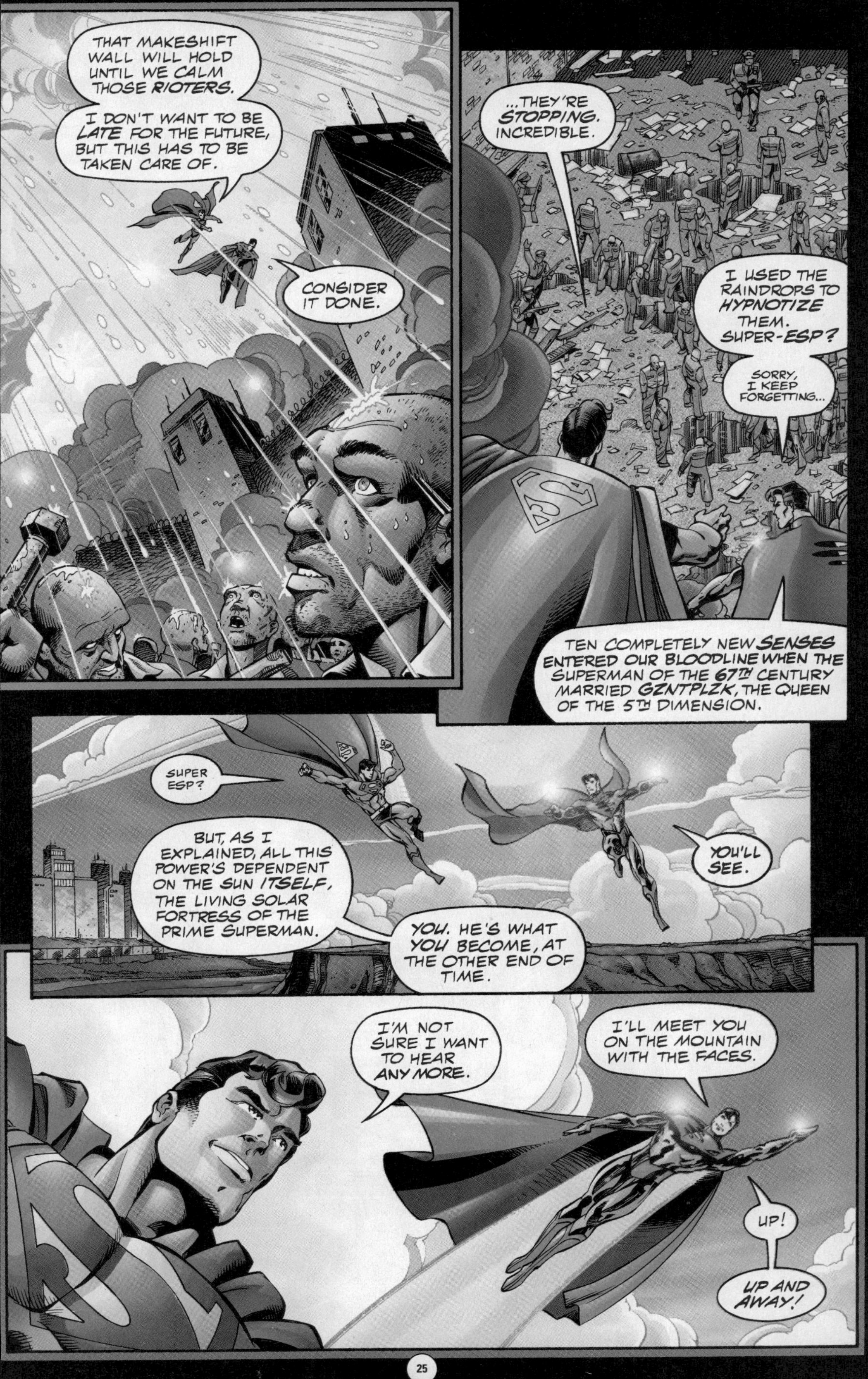
THAT MAKESHIFT WALL WILL HOLD UNTIL WE CALM THOSE RIOTERS.
I DON'T WANT TO BE LATE FOR THE FUTURE, BUT THIS HAS TO BE TAKEN CARE OF.
CONSIDER IT DONE.
...THEY'RE STOPPING. INCREDIBLE.
I USED THE RAINDROPS TO HYPNOTIZE THEM. SUPER-ESP?
SORRY, I KEEP FORGETTING...
TEN COMPLETELY NEW SENSES ENTERED OUR BLOODLINE WHEN THE SUPERMAN OF THE 67TH CENTURY MARRIED GZNTPLZK, THE QUEEN OF THE 5TH DIMENSION.
SUPER ESP?
YOU'LL SEE.
BUT, AS I EXPLAINED, ALL THIS POWER'S DEPENDENT ON THE SUN ITSELF, THE LIVING SOLAR FORTRESS OF THE PRIME SUPERMAN.
YOU. HE'S WHAT YOU BECOME, AT THE OTHER END OF TIME.
I'M NOT SURE I WANT TO HEAR ANYMORE.
I'LL MEET YOU ON THE MOUNTAIN WITH THE FACES.
UP!
UP AND AWAY!

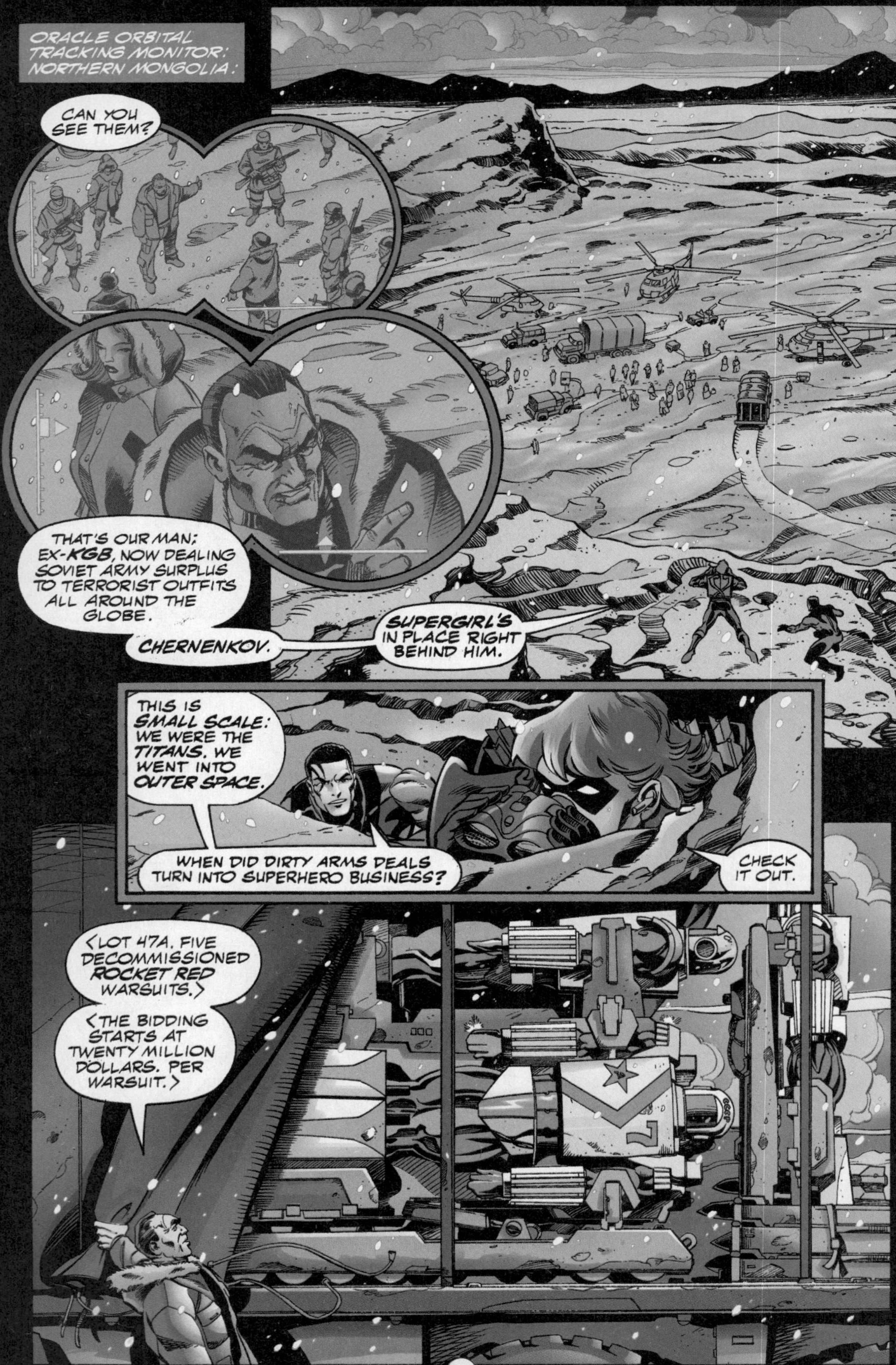

ORACLE ORBITAL TRACKING MONITOR: NORTHERN MONGOLIA:
CAN YOU SEE THEM?
THAT'S OUR MAN; EX-KGB, NOW DEALING SOVIET ARMY SURPLUS TO TERRORIST OUTFITS ALL AROUND THE GLOBE.
CHERNENKOV.
SUPERGIRL'S IN PLACE RIGHT BEHIND HIM.
THIS IS SMALL SCALE: WE WERE THE TITANS. WE WENT INTO OUTER SPACE.
WHEN DID DIRTY ARMS DEALS TURN INTO SUPERHERO BUSINESS?
CHECK IT OUT.
<LOT 47A. FIVE DECOMMISSIONED ROCKET RED WARSUITS.>
<THE BIDDING STARTS AT TWENTY MILLION DOLLARS. PER WARSUIT.>

USER-COMPATIBLE
NEURAL INTERFACE.
SMART TARGETING...>

THE IMPACT MUST
HAVE SCRAMBLED
YOUR BUG-ARROW'S
TRANSMITTER.

I CAN'T
MAKE OUT
A *WORD*.

IT'S
RUSSIAN.   SHH!

< I HEAR SIX
HUNDRED MILLION
DOLLARS.>

<THREE
BILLION
DOLLARS.>

< I'LL TAKE *ALL*
OF THEM.>

< MAKE AN
EXCUSE,
YOU.>

I DIDN'T
KNOW YOU
COULD SPEAK
RUSSIAN.

THE GUY
IN BACK. WHO
IS THAT?

< YOU KNOW
MY NAME.

< I KNEW YOUR
GREAT-GREAT-GREAT
GRANDFATHER...OR DID
I MISS A *GREAT?* IN
FACT, I'VE PROBABLY
MET *ALL* OF YOUR
ANCESTORS AT ONE
TIME OR ANOTHER.>

OH
NO.

SAVAGE.

VANDAL
SAVAGE.

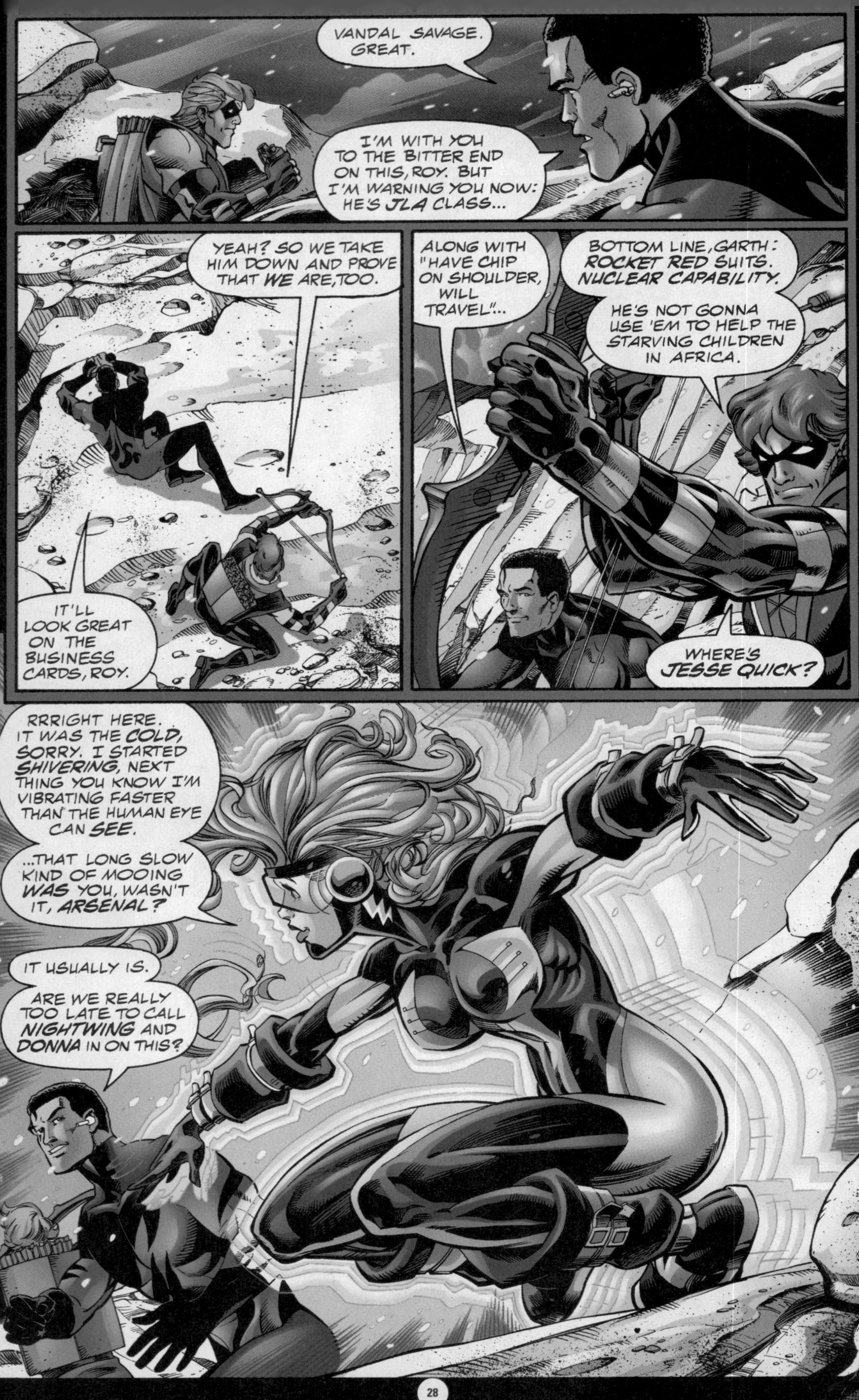

VANDAL SAVAGE. GREAT.
I'M WITH YOU TO THE BITTER END ON THIS, ROY. BUT I'M WARNING YOU NOW: HE'S JLA CLASS...
YEAH? SO WE TAKE HIM DOWN AND PROVE THAT WE ARE, TOO.
IT'LL LOOK GREAT ON THE BUSINESS CARDS, ROY.
ALONG WITH "HAVE CHIP ON SHOULDER, WILL TRAVEL"...
BOTTOM LINE, GARTH: ROCKET RED SUITS. NUCLEAR CAPABILITY.
HE'S NOT GONNA USE 'EM TO HELP THE STARVING CHILDREN IN AFRICA.
WHERE'S JESSE QUICK?
RRRIGHT HERE. IT WAS THE COLD, SORRY. I STARTED SHIVERING, NEXT THING YOU KNOW I'M VIBRATING FASTER THAN THE HUMAN EYE CAN SEE.
...THAT LONG SLOW KIND OF MOOING WAS YOU, WASN'T IT, ARSENAL?
IT USUALLY IS.
ARE WE REALLY TOO LATE TO CALL NIGHTWING AND DONNA IN ON THIS?

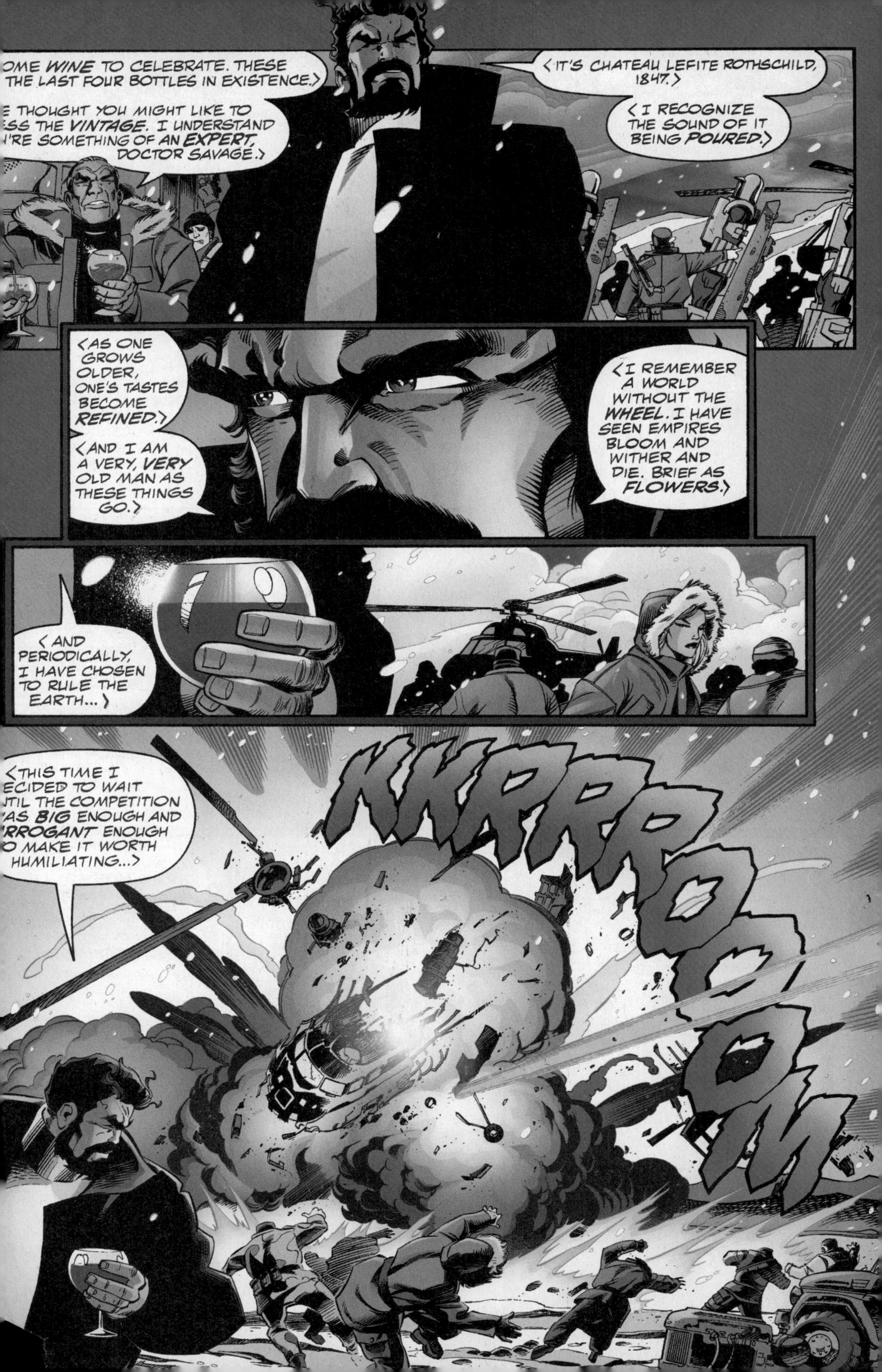
OME WINE TO CELEBRATE. THESE THE LAST FOUR BOTTLES IN EXISTENCE.>
E THOUGHT YOU MIGHT LIKE TO ESS THE VINTAGE. I UNDERSTAND I'RE SOMETHING OF AN EXPERT, DOCTOR SAVAGE.>
<IT'S CHATEAU LEFITE ROTHSCHILD, 1847.>
<I RECOGNIZE THE SOUND OF IT BEING POURED.>
<AS ONE GROWS OLDER, ONE'S TASTES BECOME REFINED.>
<AND I AM A VERY, VERY OLD MAN AS THESE THINGS GO.>
<I REMEMBER A WORLD WITHOUT THE WHEEL. I HAVE SEEN EMPIRES BLOOM AND WITHER AND DIE. BRIEF AS FLOWERS.>
<AND PERIODICALLY, I HAVE CHOSEN TO RULE THE EARTH...>
<THIS TIME I ECIDED TO WAIT NTIL THE COMPETITION AS BIG ENOUGH AND RROGANT ENOUGH O MAKE IT WORTH HUMILIATING...>
KKRRROOOM

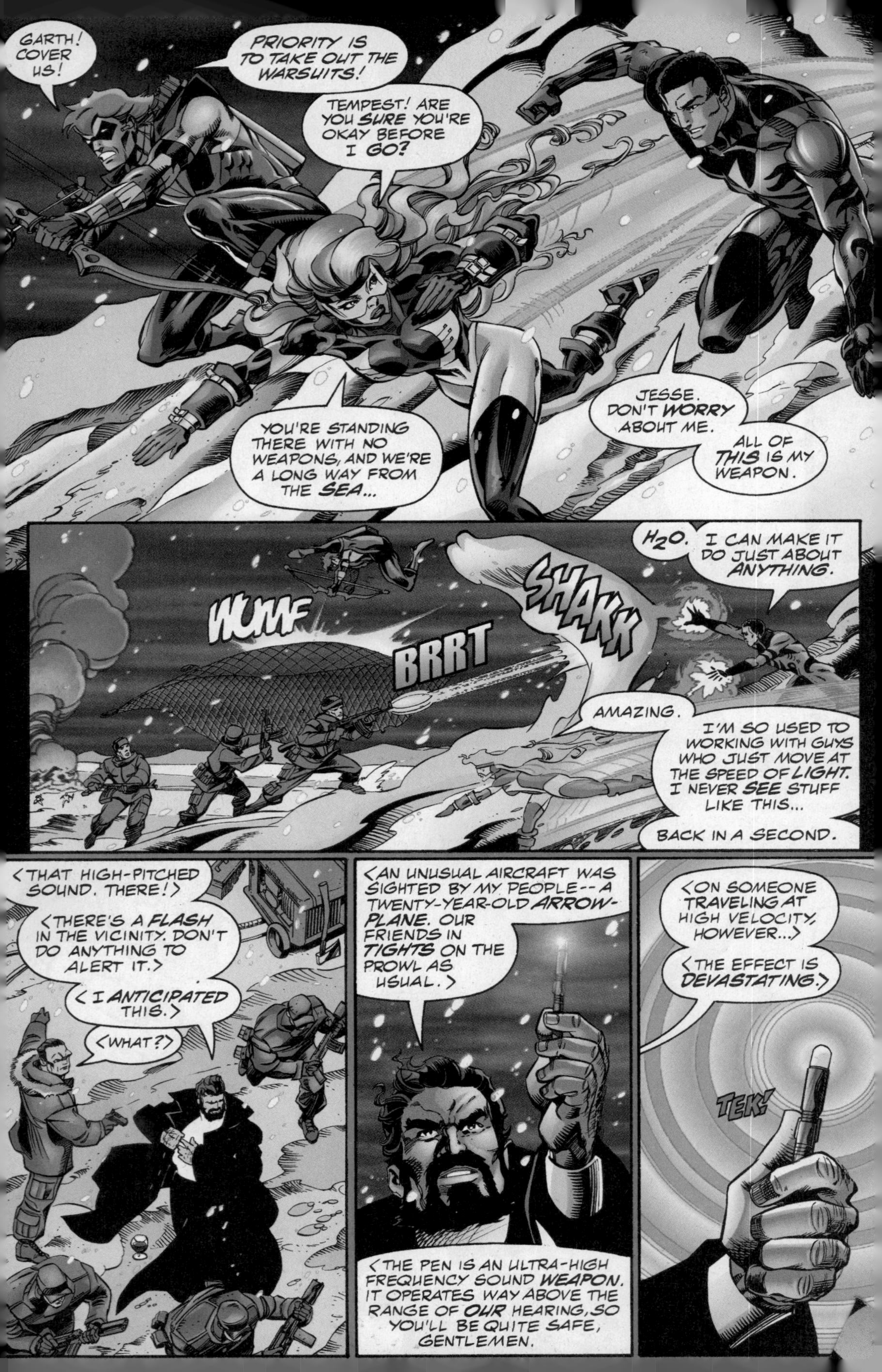
GARTH! COVER US!
PRIORITY IS TO TAKE OUT THE WARSUITS!
TEMPEST! ARE YOU SURE YOU'RE OKAY BEFORE I GO?
YOU'RE STANDING THERE WITH NO WEAPONS, AND WE'RE A LONG WAY FROM THE SEA...
JESSE. DON'T WORRY ABOUT ME.
ALL OF THIS IS MY WEAPON.
H2O. I CAN MAKE IT DO JUST ABOUT ANYTHING.
WUMF
SHAKK
BRRT
AMAZING.
I'M SO USED TO WORKING WITH GUYS WHO JUST MOVE AT THE SPEED OF LIGHT. I NEVER SEE STUFF LIKE THIS...
BACK IN A SECOND.
<THAT HIGH-PITCHED SOUND. THERE!>
<THERE'S A FLASH IN THE VICINITY. DON'T DO ANYTHING TO ALERT IT.>
<I ANTICIPATED THIS.>
<WHAT?>
<AN UNUSUAL AIRCRAFT WAS SIGHTED BY MY PEOPLE-- A TWENTY-YEAR-OLD ARROW-PLANE. OUR FRIENDS IN TIGHTS ON THE PROWL AS USUAL.>
<THE PEN IS AN ULTRA-HIGH FREQUENCY SOUND WEAPON. IT OPERATES WAY ABOVE THE RANGE OF OUR HEARING, SO YOU'LL BE QUITE SAFE, GENTLEMEN.
<ON SOMEONE TRAVELING AT HIGH VELOCITY, HOWEVER...>
<THE EFFECT IS DEVASTATING.>
TEK!

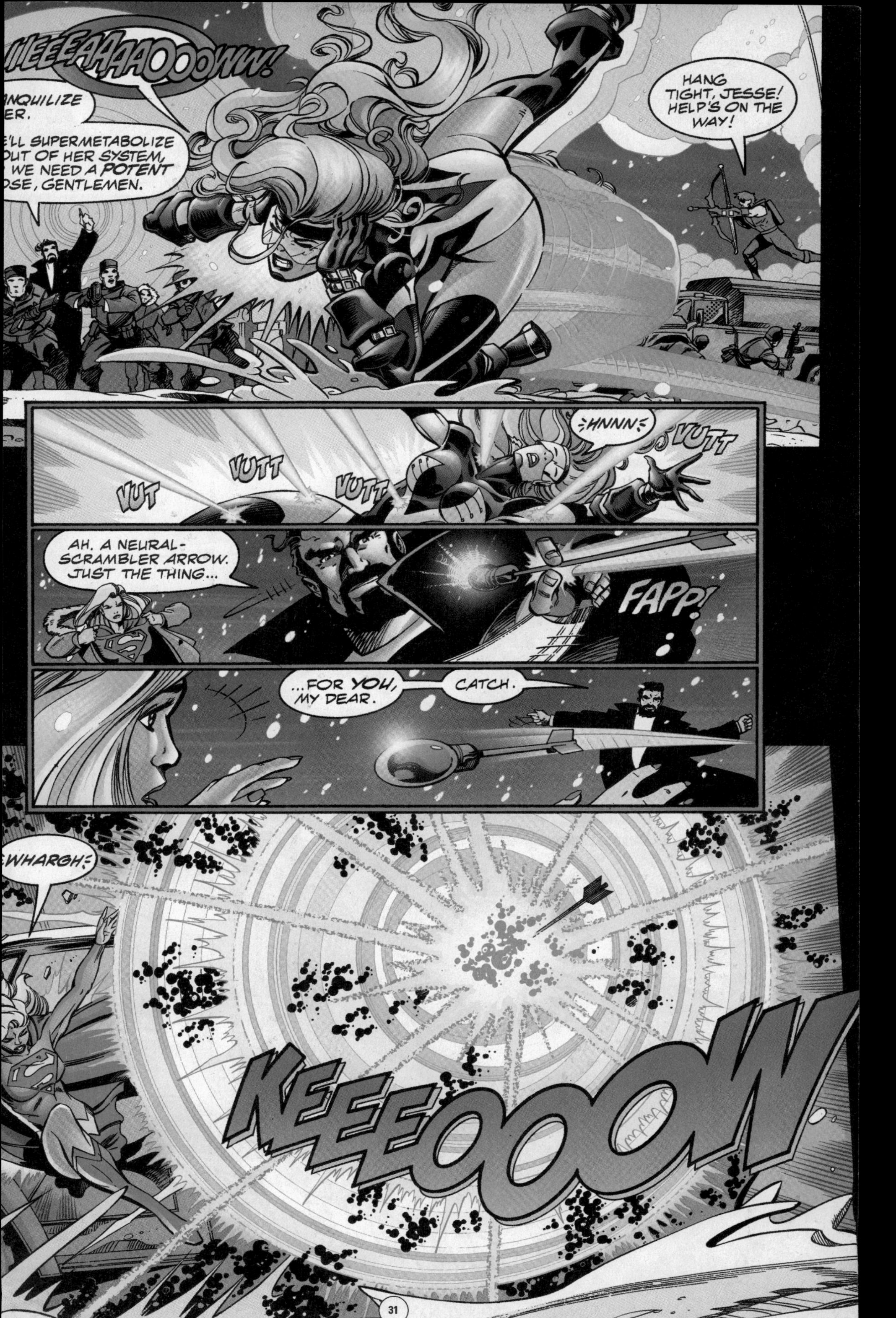

IIEEEAAAAOOOWW!
...NQUILIZE
...ER.
...E'LL SUPERMETABOLIZE
...OUT OF HER SYSTEM,
...WE NEED A POTENT
...OSE, GENTLEMEN.
HANG TIGHT, JESSE! HELP'S ON THE WAY!
HNNN
VUT
VUTT
VUTT
VUTT
AH. A NEURAL-SCRAMBLER ARROW. JUST THE THING...
FAPP!
...FOR YOU, MY DEAR.
CATCH.
WHARGH!
KEEEOOOW

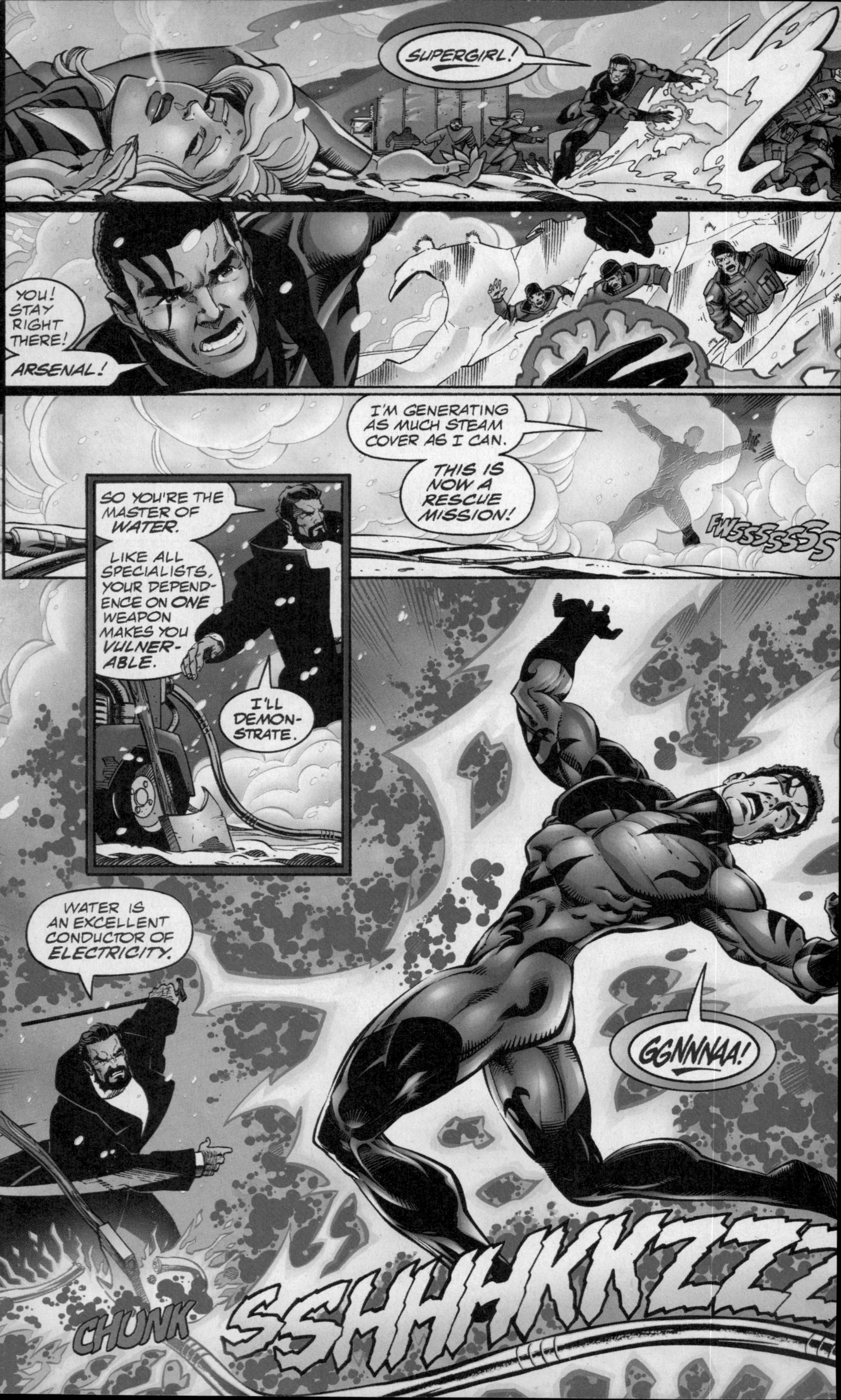

SUPERGIRL!
YOU! STAY RIGHT THERE!
ARSENAL!
I'M GENERATING AS MUCH STEAM COVER AS I CAN.
THIS IS NOW A RESCUE MISSION!
FWSSSSSSS
SO YOU'RE THE MASTER OF WATER.
LIKE ALL SPECIALISTS, YOUR DEPENDENCE ON ONE WEAPON MAKES YOU VULNERABLE.
I'LL DEMONSTRATE.
WATER IS AN EXCELLENT CONDUCTOR OF ELECTRICITY.
GGNNNAA!
CHUNK
SSHHHKKZZZ

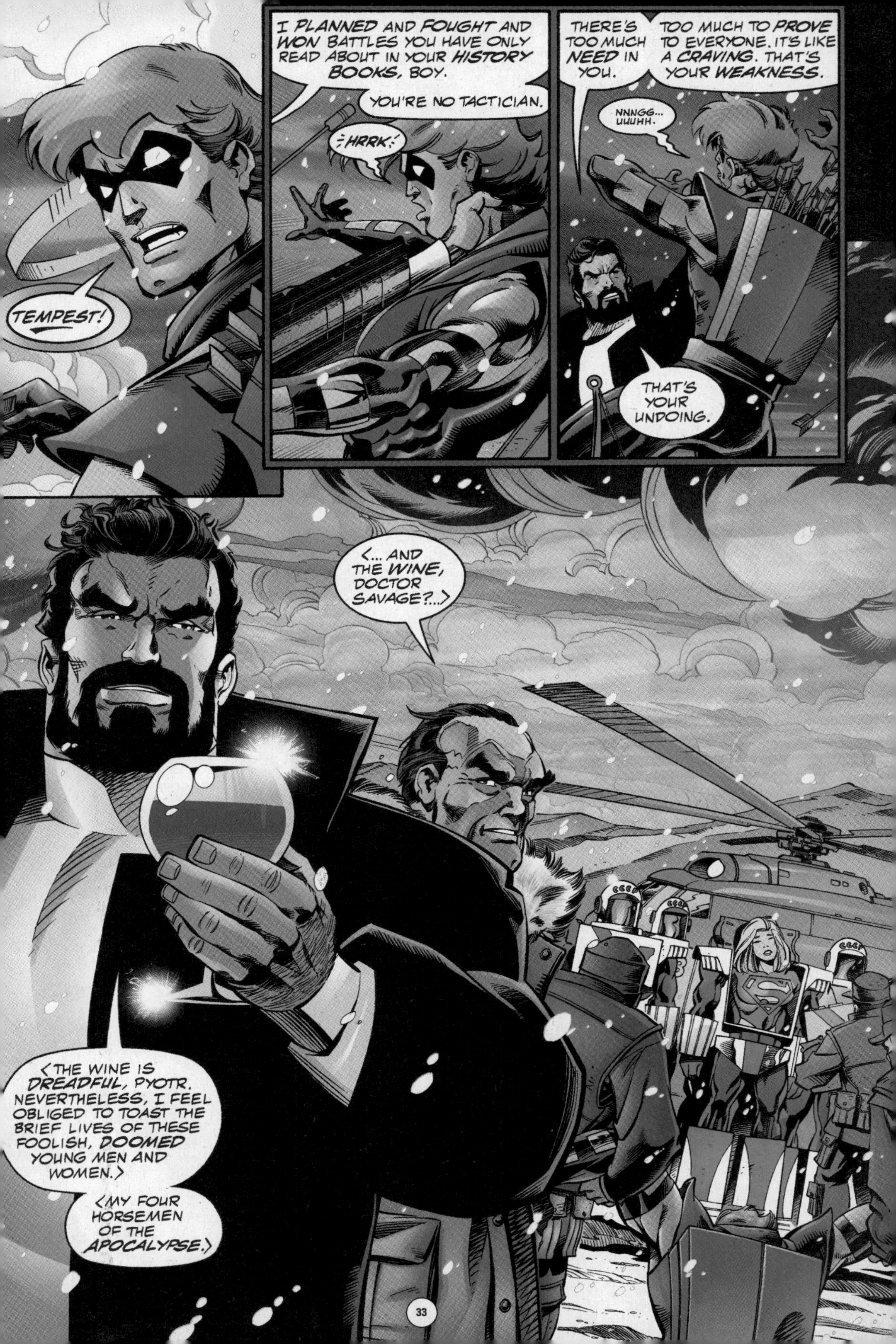
TEMPEST!
I PLANNED AND FOUGHT AND WON BATTLES YOU HAVE ONLY READ ABOUT IN YOUR HISTORY BOOKS, BOY.
YOU'RE NO TACTICIAN.
HRRK
THERE'S TOO MUCH NEED IN YOU.
TOO MUCH TO PROVE TO EVERYONE. IT'S LIKE A CRAVING. THAT'S YOUR WEAKNESS.
NNNGG... UUUHH.
THAT'S YOUR UNDOING.
<... AND THE WINE, DOCTOR SAVAGE?...>
<THE WINE IS DREADFUL, PYOTR. NEVERTHELESS, I FEEL OBLIGED TO TOAST THE BRIEF LIVES OF THESE FOOLISH, DOOMED YOUNG MEN AND WOMEN.>
<MY FOUR HORSEMEN OF THE APOCALYPSE.>

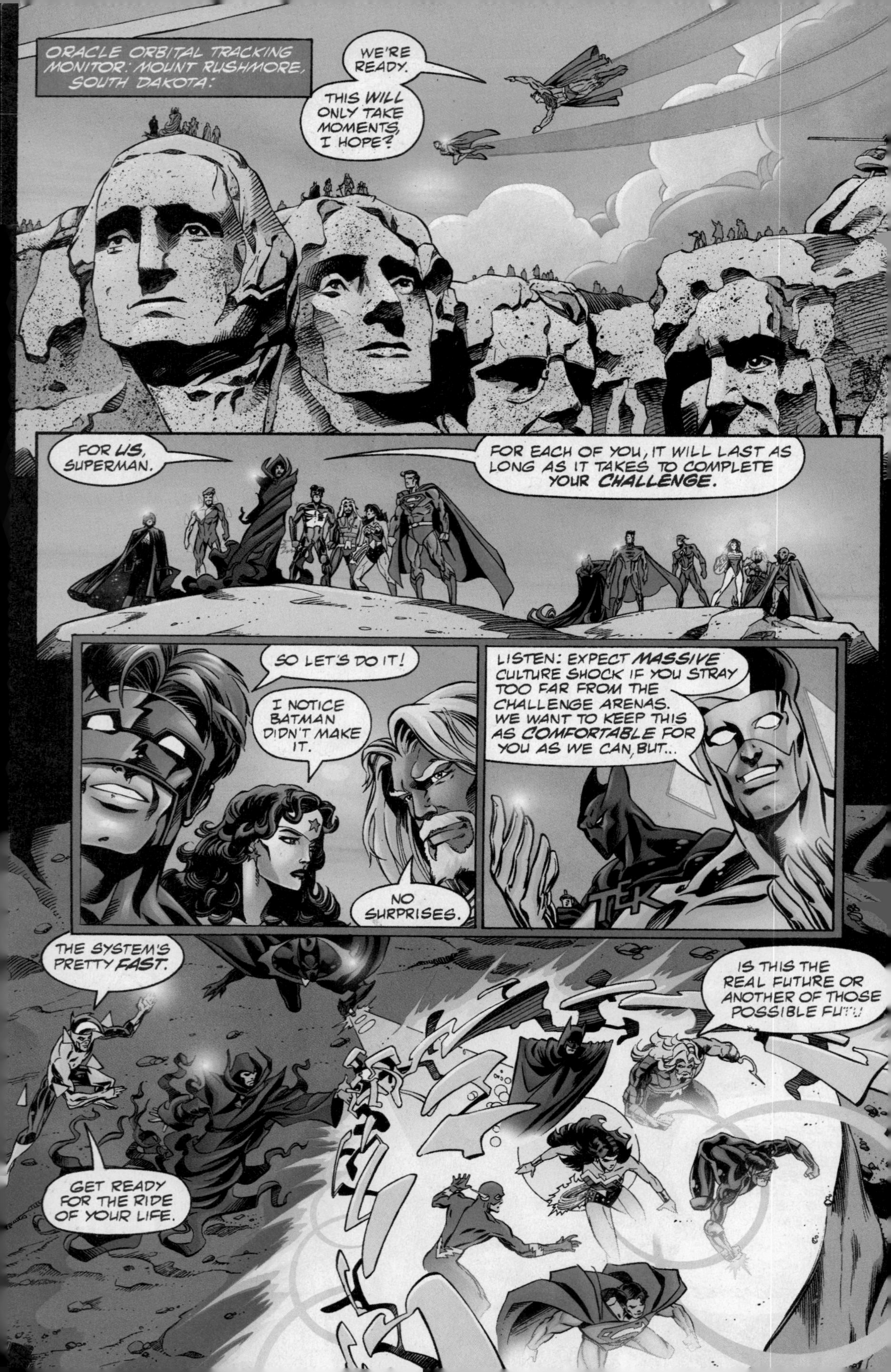
ORACLE ORBITAL TRACKING MONITOR: MOUNT RUSHMORE, SOUTH DAKOTA:
WE'RE READY.
THIS WILL ONLY TAKE MOMENTS, I HOPE?
FOR US, SUPERMAN.
FOR EACH OF YOU, IT WILL LAST AS LONG AS IT TAKES TO COMPLETE YOUR CHALLENGE.
SO LET'S DO IT!
I NOTICE BATMAN DIDN'T MAKE IT.
NO SURPRISES.
LISTEN: EXPECT MASSIVE CULTURE SHOCK IF YOU STRAY TOO FAR FROM THE CHALLENGE ARENAS. WE WANT TO KEEP THIS AS COMFORTABLE FOR YOU AS WE CAN, BUT...
TEK
THE SYSTEM'S PRETTY FAST.
IS THIS THE REAL FUTURE OR ANOTHER OF THOSE POSSIBLE FUTU
GET READY FOR THE RIDE OF YOUR LIFE.

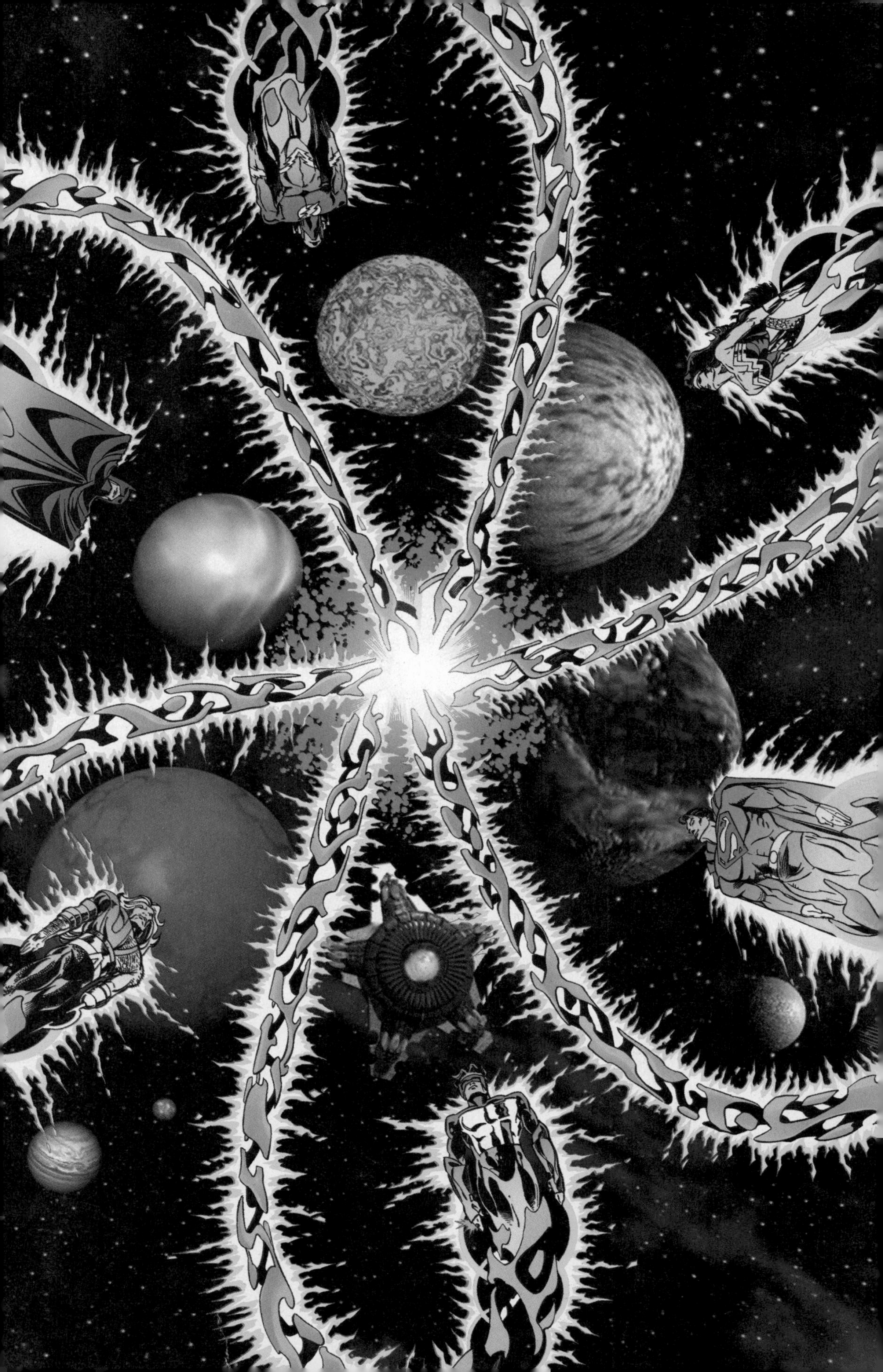

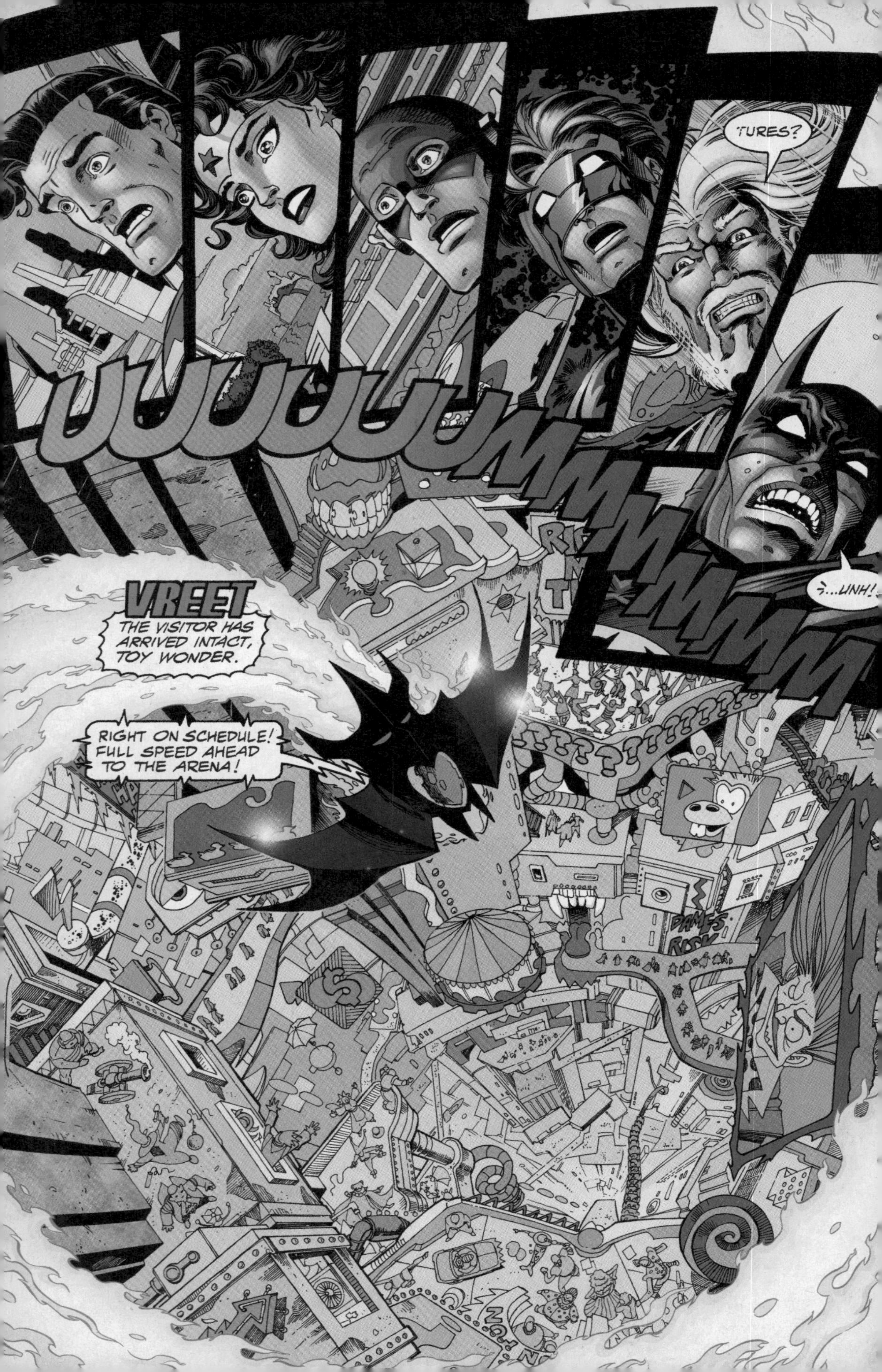
TURES?
UUUUUUUMMMMMMMMM
...UNH!
VREET
THE VISITOR HAS ARRIVED INTACT, TOY WONDER.
RIGHT ON SCHEDULE! FULL SPEED AHEAD TO THE ARENA!
DAMES RISK

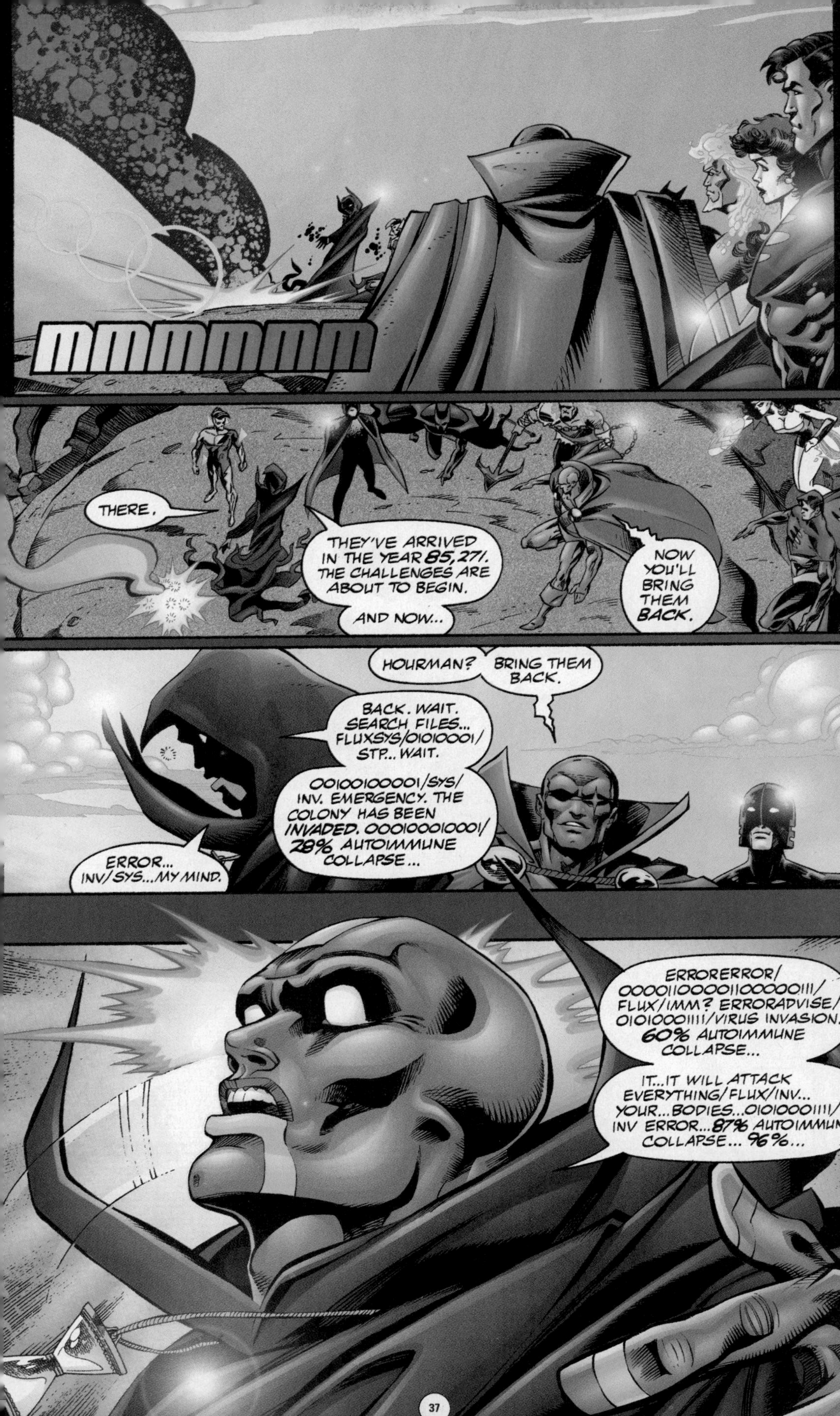
MMMMMMM
THERE.
THEY'VE ARRIVED IN THE YEAR 85,271. THE CHALLENGES ARE ABOUT TO BEGIN.
AND NOW...
NOW YOU'LL BRING THEM BACK.
HOURMAN?
BRING THEM BACK.
BACK. WAIT. SEARCH FILES... FLUXSYS/01010001/ STP... WAIT.
00100100001/SYS/ INV. EMERGENCY. THE COLONY HAS BEEN INVADED. 000100010001/ 28% AUTOIMMUNE COLLAPSE...
ERROR... INV/SYS...MY MIND.
ERRORERROR/ 000011000011000000111/ FLUX/IMM? ERRORADVISE/ 01010001111/VIRUS INVASION. 60% AUTOIMMUNE COLLAPSE...
IT...IT WILL ATTACK EVERYTHING/FLUX/INV... YOUR...BODIES...0101000111/ INV ERROR...87% AUTOIMMUNE COLLAPSE... 96%...

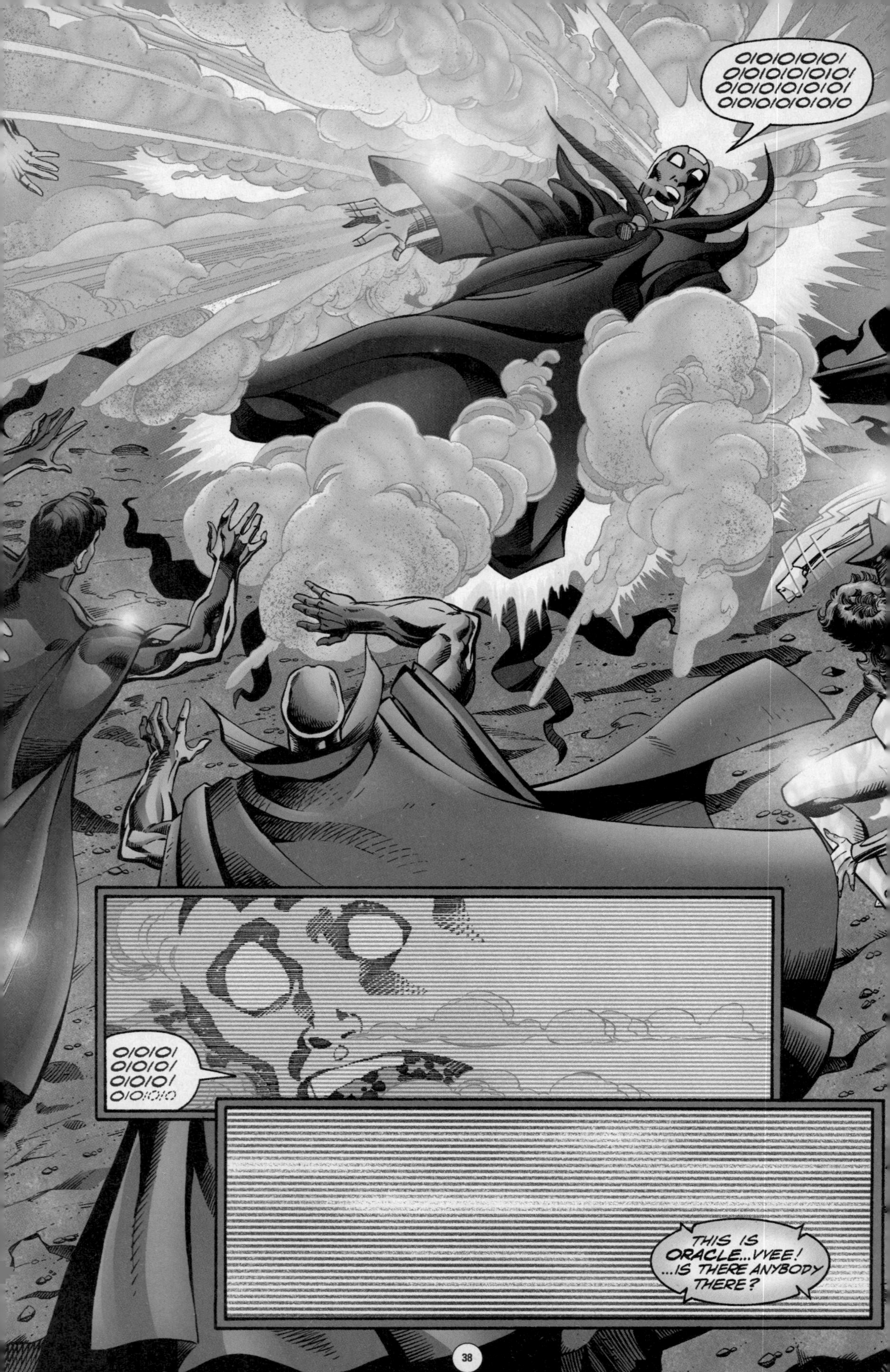

01010101010101010101010101010101010101010101010
0101010101010101010101010
THIS IS ORACLE...VVEE! ...IS THERE ANYBODY THERE?

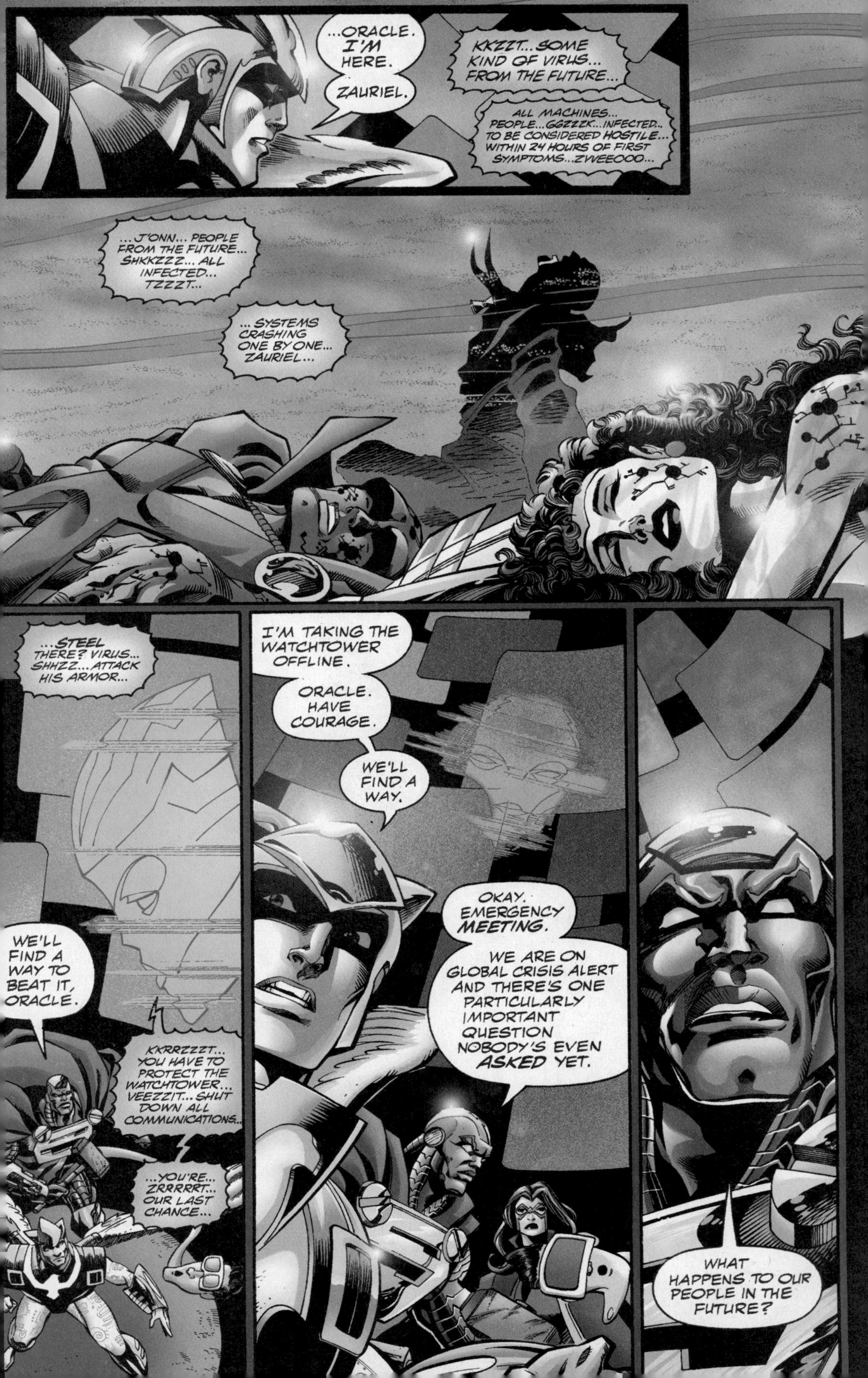
...ORACLE. I'M HERE.
ZAURIEL.
KKZZT... SOME KIND OF VIRUS... FROM THE FUTURE...
ALL MACHINES... PEOPLE... GGZZZK... INFECTED... TO BE CONSIDERED HOSTILE... WITHIN 24 HOURS OF FIRST SYMPTOMS... ZWEEOOO...
...J'ONN... PEOPLE FROM THE FUTURE... SHKKZZZ... ALL INFECTED... TZZZT...
...SYSTEMS CRASHING ONE BY ONE... ZAURIEL...
...STEEL THERE? VIRUS... SHHZZ... ATTACK HIS ARMOR...
WE'LL FIND A WAY TO BEAT IT, ORACLE.
KKRRZZZT... YOU HAVE TO PROTECT THE WATCHTOWER... VEEZZIT... SHUT DOWN ALL COMMUNICATIONS...
...YOU'RE... ZRRRRRT... OUR LAST CHANCE...
I'M TAKING THE WATCHTOWER OFFLINE.
ORACLE. HAVE COURAGE.
WE'LL FIND A WAY.
OKAY. EMERGENCY MEETING.
WE ARE ON GLOBAL CRISIS ALERT AND THERE'S ONE PARTICULARLY IMPORTANT QUESTION NOBODY'S EVEN ASKED YET.
WHAT HAPPENS TO OUR PEOPLE IN THE FUTURE?

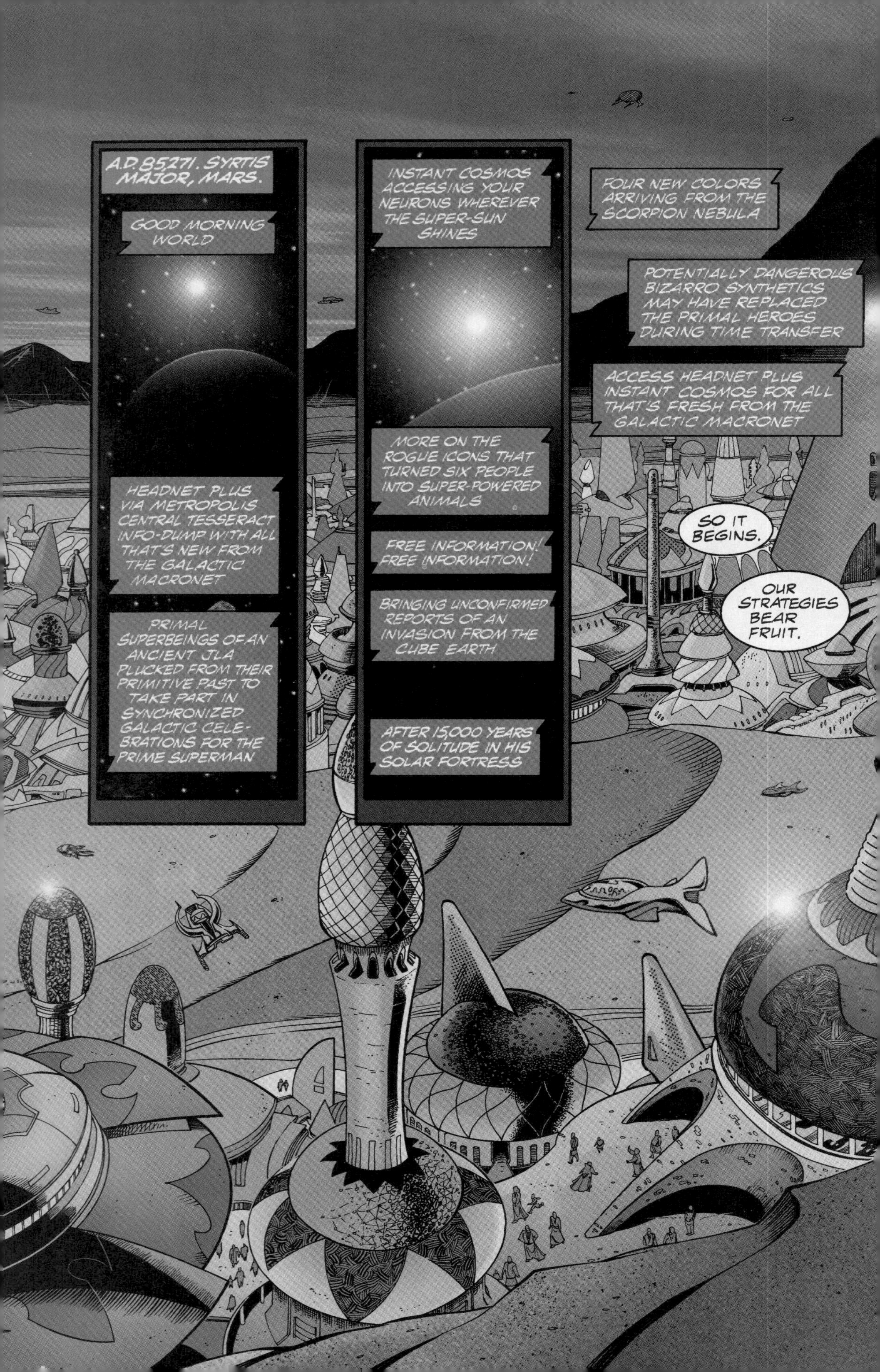
A.D. 85271. SYRTIS MAJOR, MARS.
GOOD MORNING WORLD
HEADNET PLUS VIA METROPOLIS CENTRAL TESSERACT INFO-DUMP WITH ALL THAT'S NEW FROM THE GALACTIC MACRONET
PRIMAL SUPERBEINGS OF AN ANCIENT JLA PLUCKED FROM THEIR PRIMITIVE PAST TO TAKE PART IN SYNCHRONIZED GALACTIC CELE-BRATIONS FOR THE PRIME SUPERMAN
INSTANT COSMOS ACCESSING YOUR NEURONS WHEREVER THE SUPER-SUN SHINES
MORE ON THE ROGUE ICONS THAT TURNED SIX PEOPLE INTO SUPER-POWERED ANIMALS
FREE INFORMATION! FREE INFORMATION!
BRINGING UNCONFIRMED REPORTS OF AN INVASION FROM THE CUBE EARTH
AFTER 15,000 YEARS OF SOLITUDE IN HIS SOLAR FORTRESS
FOUR NEW COLORS ARRIVING FROM THE SCORPION NEBULA
POTENTIALLY DANGEROUS BIZARRO SYNTHETICS MAY HAVE REPLACED THE PRIMAL HEROES DURING TIME TRANSFER
ACCESS HEADNET PLUS INSTANT COSMOS FOR ALL THAT'S FRESH FROM THE GALACTIC MACRONET
SO IT BEGINS.
OUR STRATEGIES BEAR FRUIT.

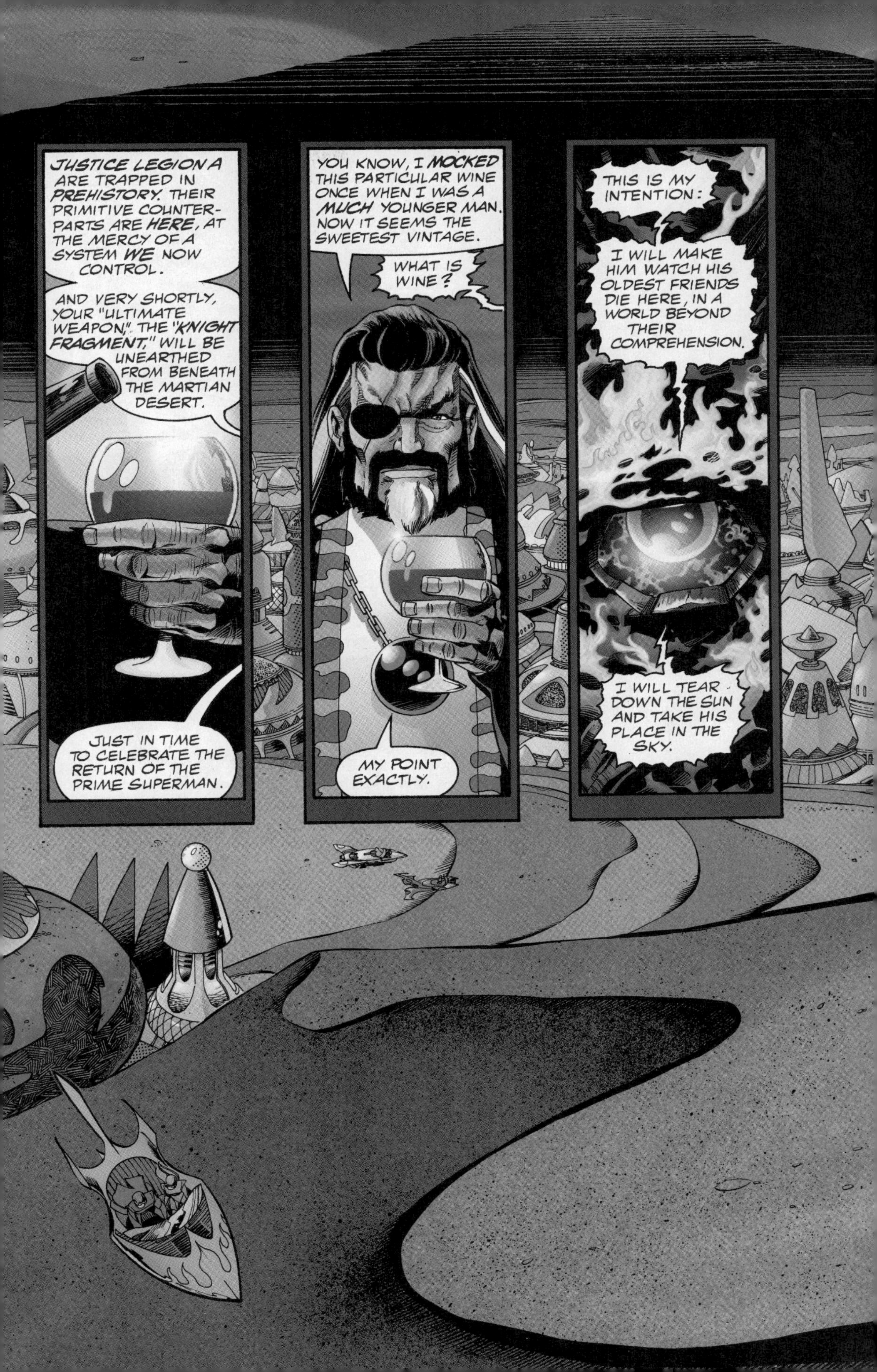

JUSTICE LEGION A ARE TRAPPED IN PREHISTORY. THEIR PRIMITIVE COUNTER-PARTS ARE HERE, AT THE MERCY OF A SYSTEM WE NOW CONTROL.
AND VERY SHORTLY, YOUR "ULTIMATE WEAPON", THE "KNIGHT FRAGMENT," WILL BE UNEARTHED FROM BENEATH THE MARTIAN DESERT.
JUST IN TIME TO CELEBRATE THE RETURN OF THE PRIME SUPERMAN.
YOU KNOW, I MOCKED THIS PARTICULAR WINE ONCE WHEN I WAS A MUCH YOUNGER MAN. NOW IT SEEMS THE SWEETEST VINTAGE.
WHAT IS WINE?
MY POINT EXACTLY.
THIS IS MY INTENTION:
I WILL MAKE HIM WATCH HIS OLDEST FRIENDS DIE HERE, IN A WORLD BEYOND THEIR COMPREHENSION.
I WILL TEAR DOWN THE SUN AND TAKE HIS PLACE IN THE SKY.

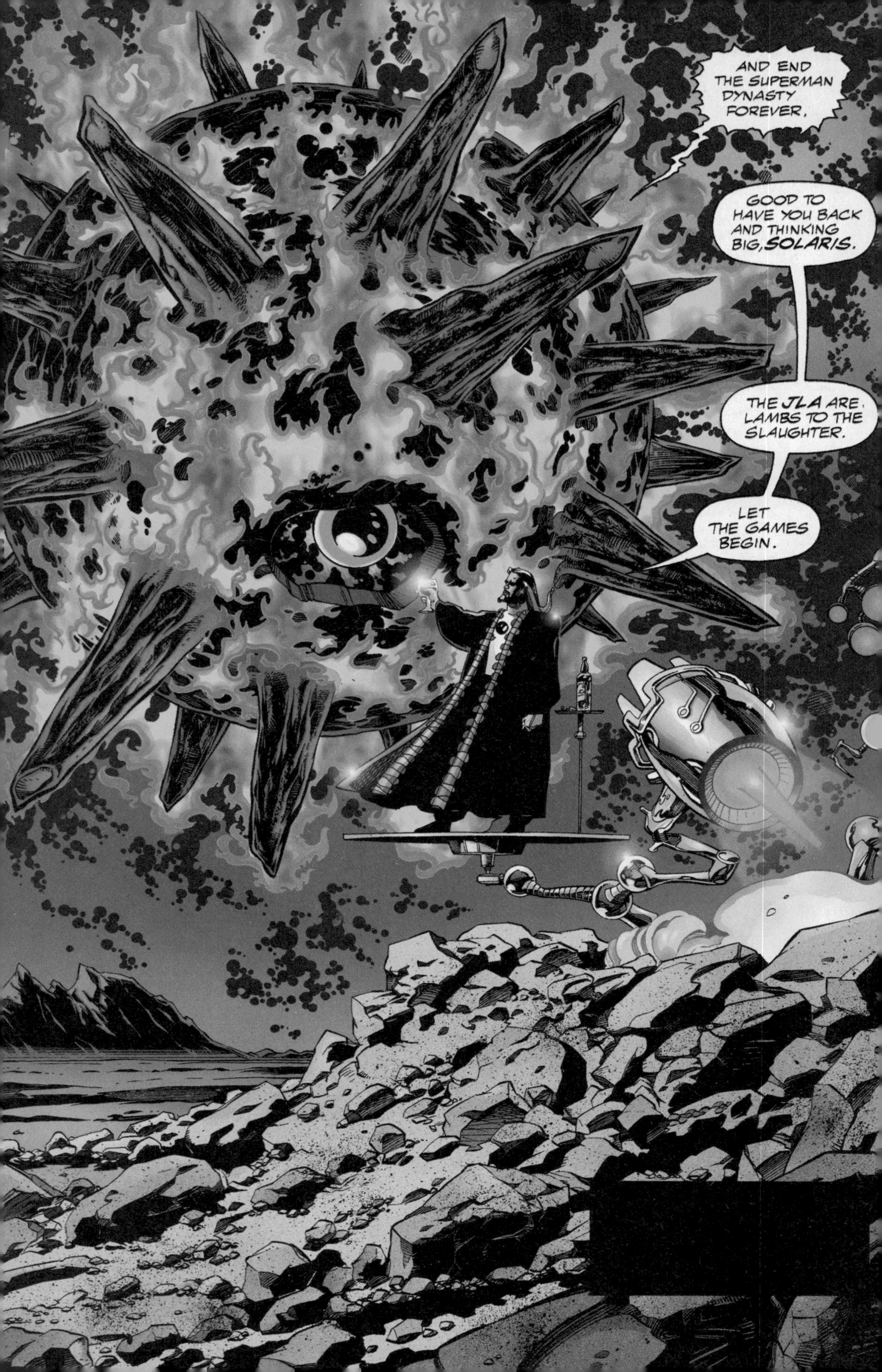
AND END THE SUPERMAN DYNASTY FOREVER.
GOOD TO HAVE YOU BACK AND THINKING BIG, SOLARIS.
THE JLA ARE LAMBS TO THE SLAUGHTER.
LET THE GAMES BEGIN.

•••INPUT

DIGIPRINT

IN THE 853RD CENTURY, THE GAMES HAD BEGUN!

WITH A TRILLION SENTIENTS IN ATTENDANCE, EACH JLA MEMBER ENGAGED IN EPIC CHALLENGES TO HONOR THE RETURN OF THE PRIME-SUPERMAN.

ON EARTH, SUPERMAN FACED THE "CHALLENGE OF THE PERFECT SOLIDS," MATCHING WITS WITH ANDROID GEOMETRONS PRIMED TO COUNTER THE MAN OF STEEL'S STRENGTH AND SKILL.

BATMAN CHEATED DEATH IN THE CAVERNS OF PLUTO, WINDING HIS WAY THROUGH A DEADLY OBSTACLE COURSE DESIGNED TO PUSH HIS AGILITY AND ESCAPE ARTISTRY TO THE LIMITS.

ON THE AMAZONS' ADOPTED WORLD OF VENUS, WONDER WOMAN SPARRED WITH HER WARRIOR SISTERS IN THE GLADIATORIAL ARENA FOR THE FIRST TIME IN OVER 800 CENTURIES.

5,000 METERS BENEATH THE OCEANS OF NEPTUNE, AQUAMAN DEMONSTRATED HIS AMAZING AQUATIC ABILITIES TO CITIZENS OF SPRAWLING CITY-SHIPS.

MEANWHILE, ON MERCURY, THE FLASH MATCHED HIS PHENOMENAL VELOCITIES IN AN EPIC FOOTRACE AROUND THE TINY PLANET.

AND PAST DISTANT URANUS, ABOARD THE SPACE CITADEL OF THE 853RD-CENTURY STARMAN, GREEN LANTERN KYLE RAYNER WILLED HIS WAY TO A POWER-RING-FUELED VICTORY IN AN INTERSTELLAR "CHARIOT RACE" AGAINST THE SOLID-LIGHT MACH TURTLE.

UNFORTUNATELY, ALL OF THEIR CHALLENGES ENDED ABRUPTLY IN CHAOS, SABOTAGED FROM WITHIN! AS THE HEROES STRUGGLED FOR THEIR LIVES AGAINST HOST-WORLDS WHO NOW BELIEVED THEM ALL MONSTROUS BIZARRO DUPLICATES, KYLE RETURNED TO STARMAN'S CITADEL TO LEARN A DARK SECRET...

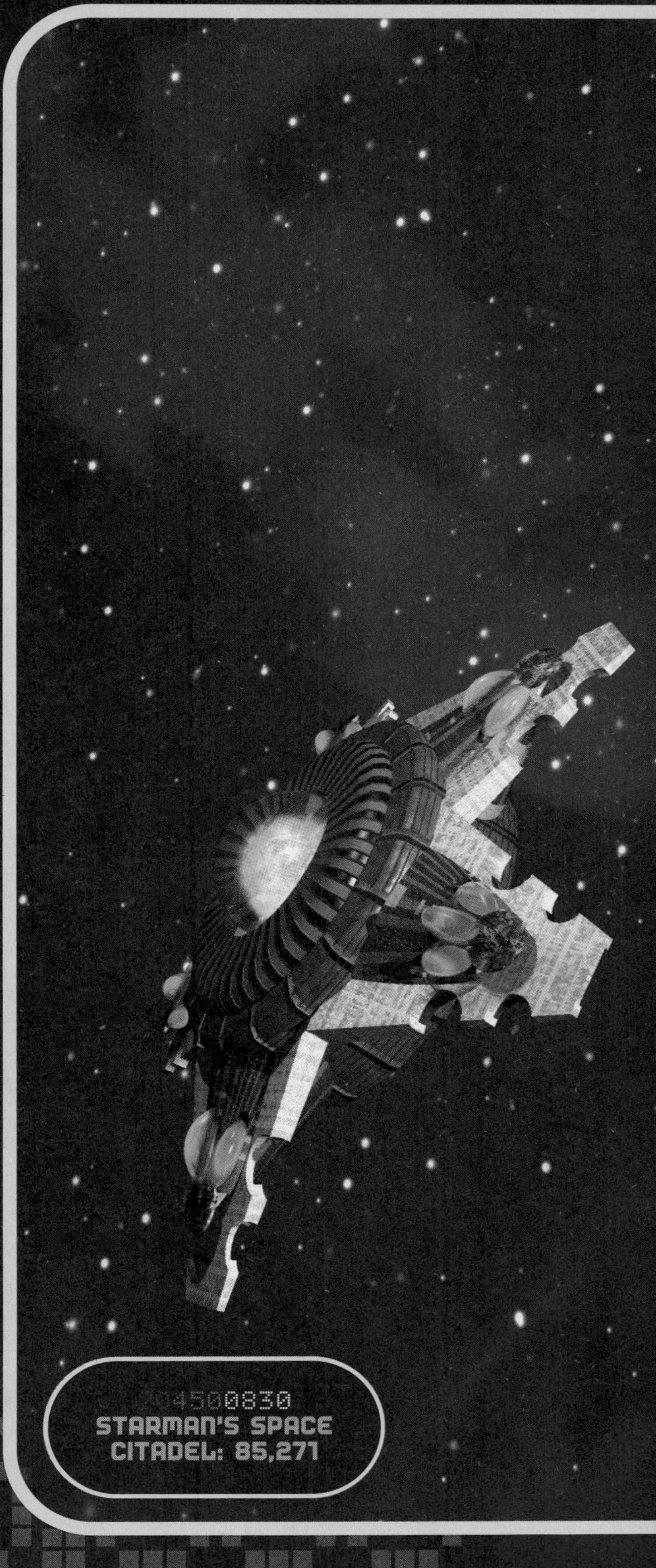
04500830
STARMAN'S SPACE CITADEL: 85,271

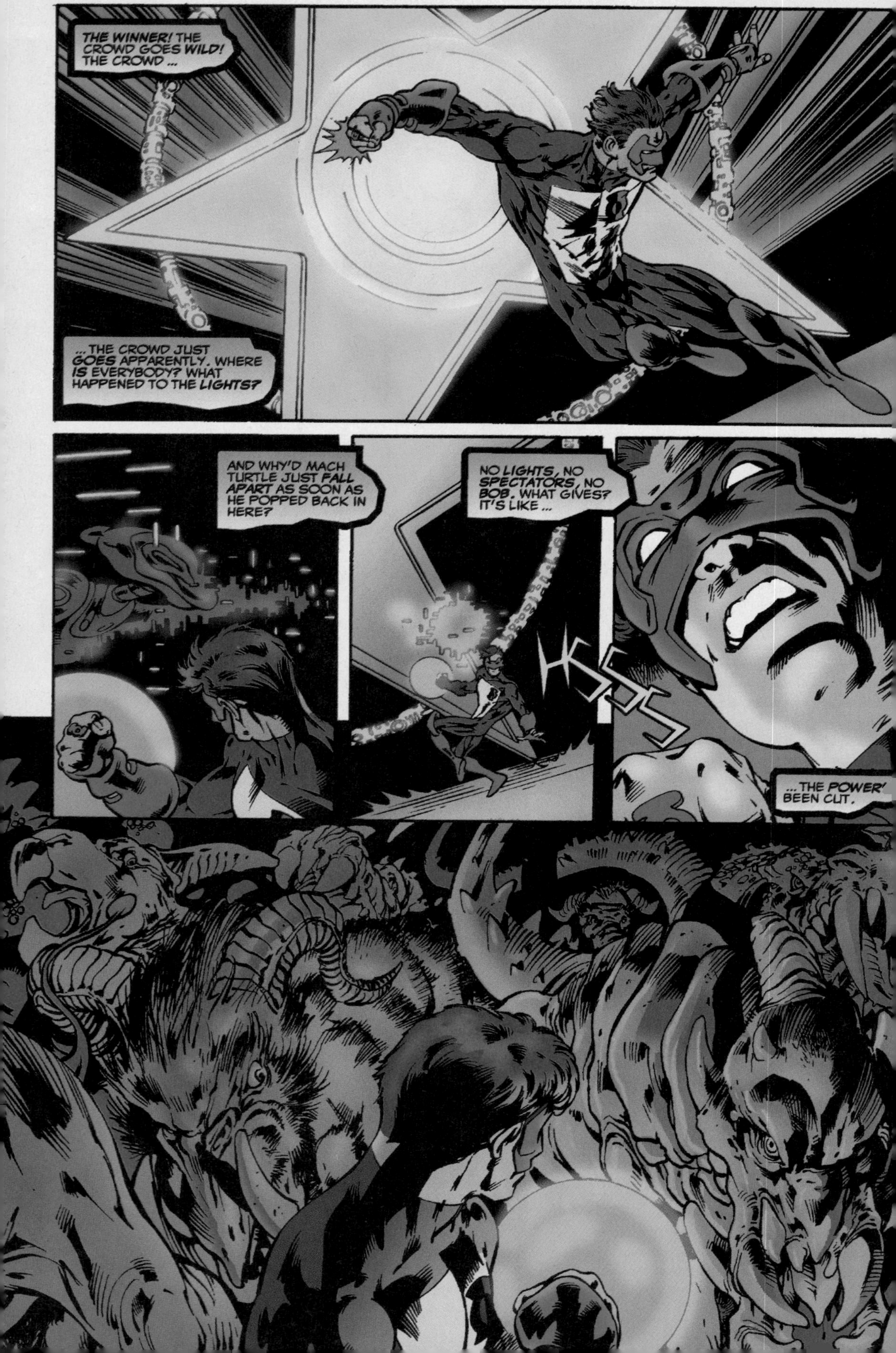

THE WINNER! THE CROWD GOES WILD! THE CROWD ...
... THE CROWD JUST GOES APPARENTLY. WHERE IS EVERYBODY? WHAT HAPPENED TO THE LIGHTS?
AND WHY'D MACH TURTLE JUST FALL APART AS SOON AS HE POPPED BACK IN HERE?
NO LIGHTS, NO SPECTATORS, NO BOB. WHAT GIVES? IT'S LIKE ...
HSSS
... THE POWER' BEEN CUT.

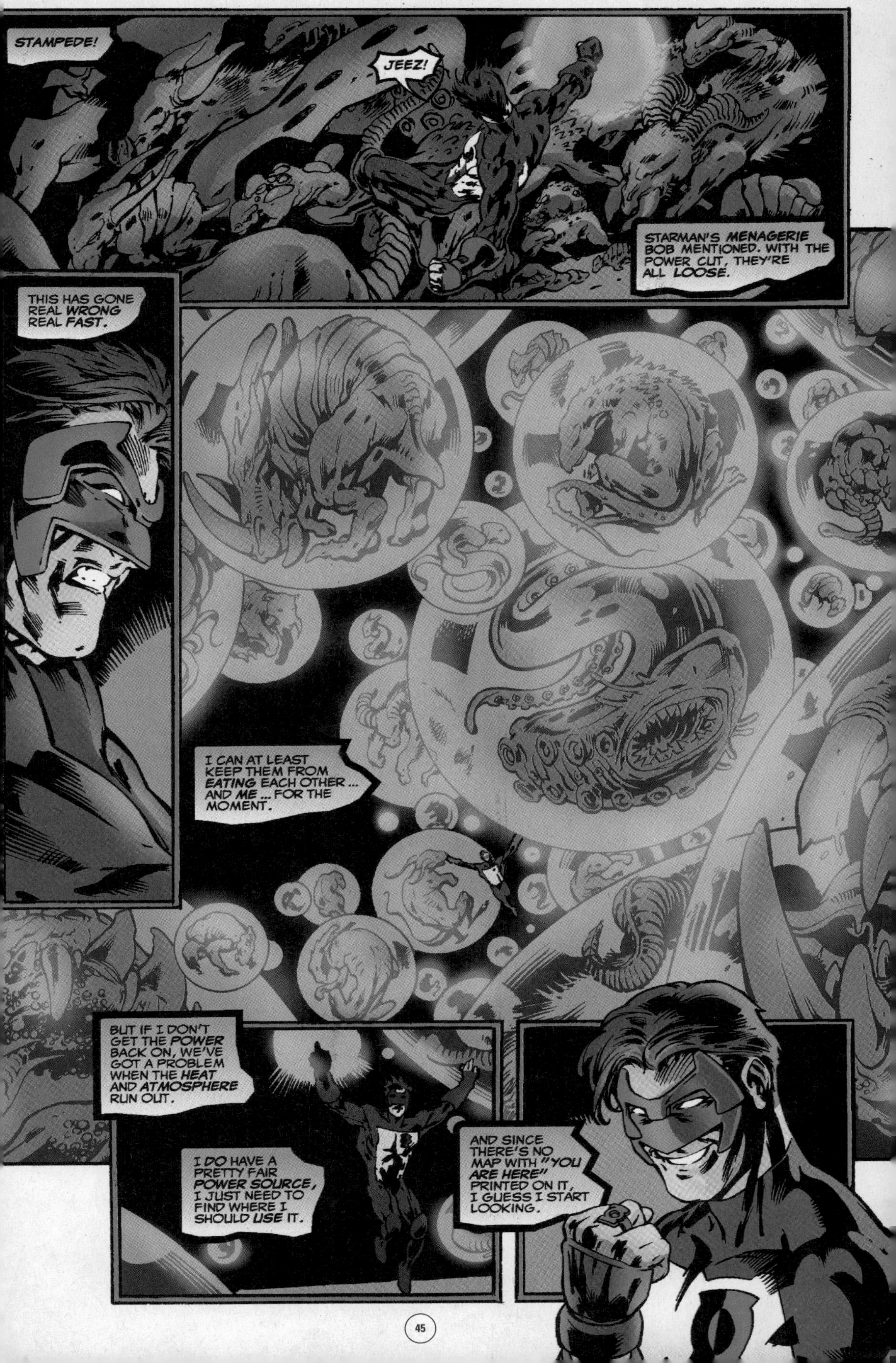
STAMPEDE!
JEEZ!
STARMAN'S MENAGERIE BOB MENTIONED. WITH THE POWER CUT, THEY'RE ALL LOOSE.
THIS HAS GONE REAL WRONG REAL FAST.
I CAN AT LEAST KEEP THEM FROM EATING EACH OTHER ... AND ME ... FOR THE MOMENT.
BUT IF I DON'T GET THE POWER BACK ON, WE'VE GOT A PROBLEM WHEN THE HEAT AND ATMOSPHERE RUN OUT.
I DO HAVE A PRETTY FAIR POWER SOURCE, I JUST NEED TO FIND WHERE I SHOULD USE IT.
AND SINCE THERE'S NO MAP WITH "YOU ARE HERE" PRINTED ON IT, I GUESS I START LOOKING.

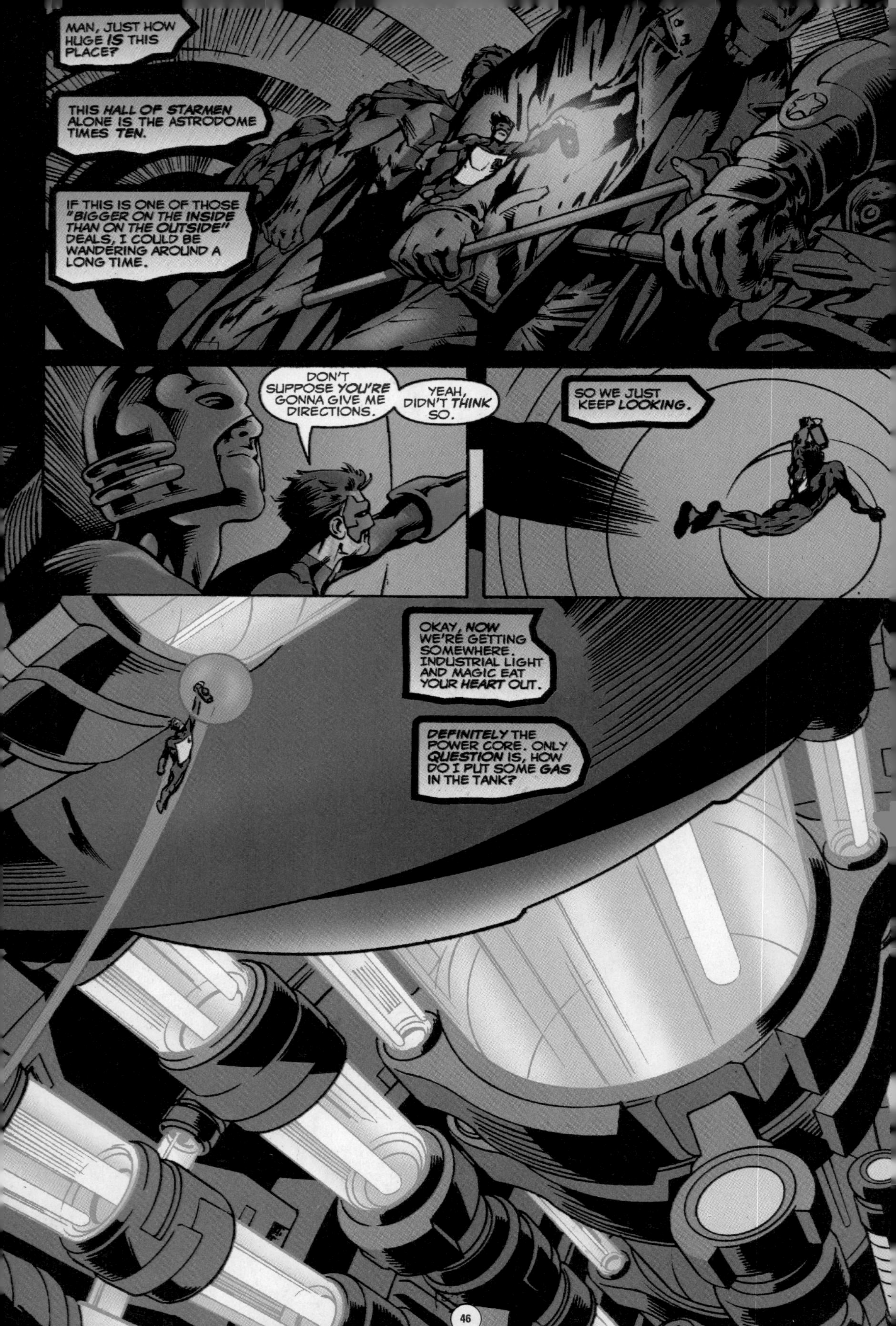
MAN, JUST HOW HUGE IS THIS PLACE?
THIS HALL OF STARMEN ALONE IS THE ASTRODOME TIMES TEN.
IF THIS IS ONE OF THOSE "BIGGER ON THE INSIDE THAN ON THE OUTSIDE" DEALS, I COULD BE WANDERING AROUND A LONG TIME.
DON'T SUPPOSE YOU'RE GONNA GIVE ME DIRECTIONS.
YEAH, DIDN'T THINK SO.
SO WE JUST KEEP LOOKING.
OKAY, NOW WE'RE GETTING SOMEWHERE. INDUSTRIAL LIGHT AND MAGIC EAT YOUR HEART OUT.
DEFINITELY THE POWER CORE. ONLY QUESTION IS, HOW DO I PUT SOME GAS IN THE TANK?

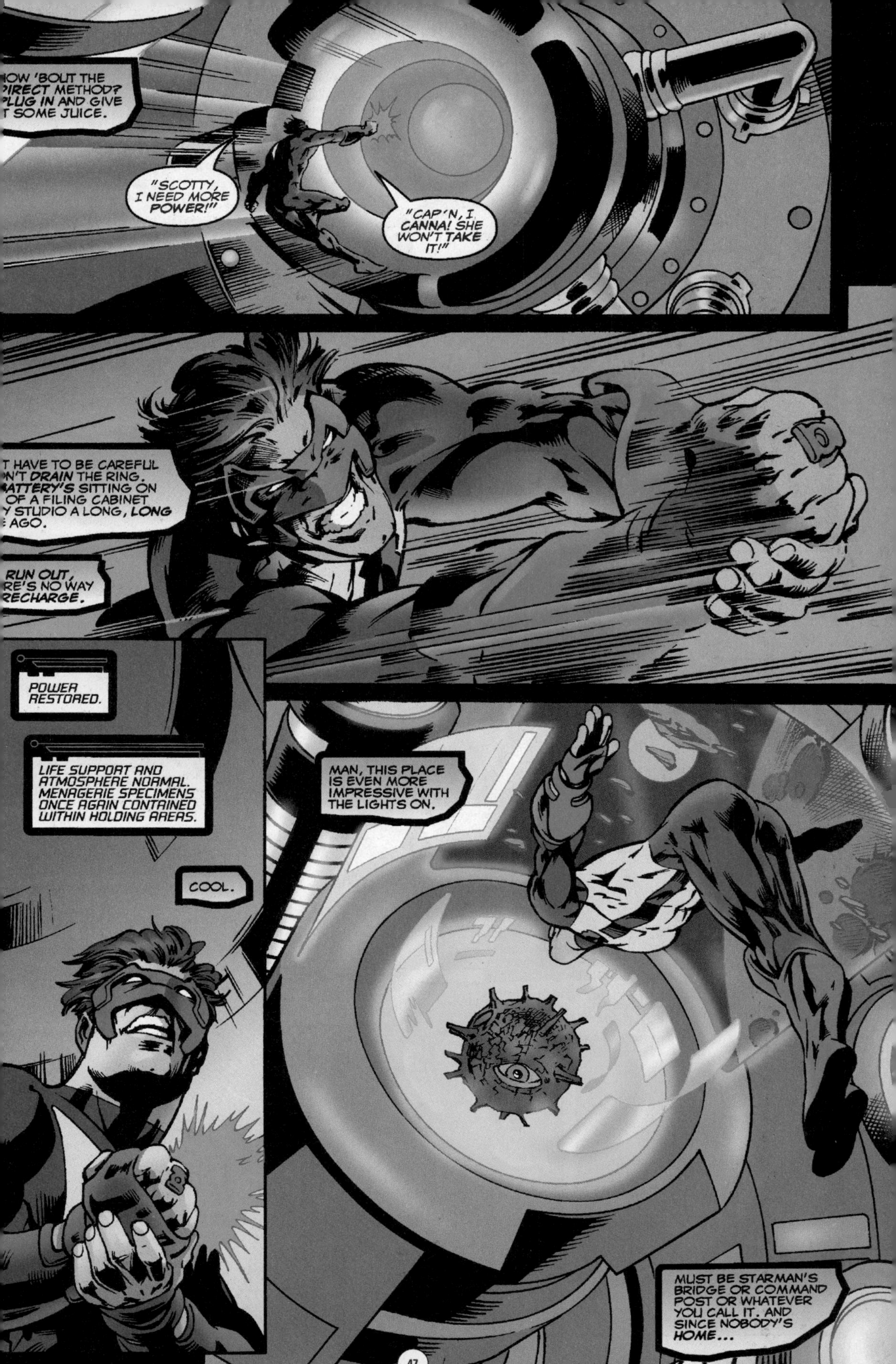
HOW 'BOUT THE DIRECT METHOD? PLUG IN AND GIVE T SOME JUICE.
"SCOTTY, I NEED MORE POWER!"
"CAP'N, I CANNA! SHE WON'T TAKE IT!"
T HAVE TO BE CAREFUL N'T DRAIN THE RING. ATTERY'S SITTING ON OF A FILING CABINET Y STUDIO A LONG, LONG AGO.
RUN OUT, RE'S NO WAY RECHARGE.
POWER RESTORED.
LIFE SUPPORT AND ATMOSPHERE NORMAL. MENAGERIE SPECIMENS ONCE AGAIN CONTAINED WITHIN HOLDING AREAS.
COOL.
MAN, THIS PLACE IS EVEN MORE IMPRESSIVE WITH THE LIGHTS ON.
MUST BE STARMAN'S BRIDGE OR COMMAND POST OR WHATEVER YOU CALL IT. AND SINCE NOBODY'S HOME...

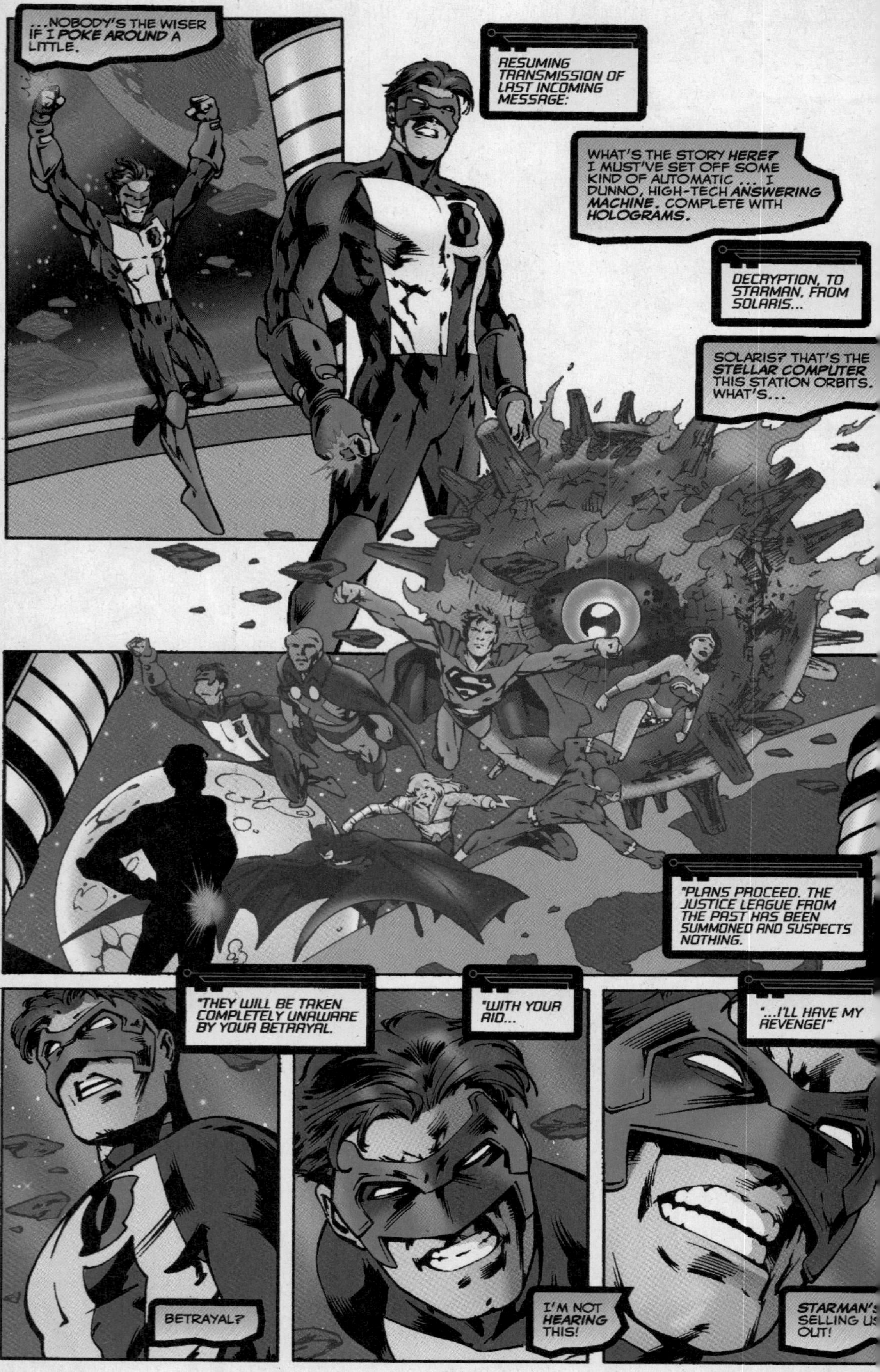
...NOBODY'S THE WISER IF I POKE AROUND A LITTLE.
RESUMING TRANSMISSION OF LAST INCOMING MESSAGE:
WHAT'S THE STORY HERE? I MUST'VE SET OFF SOME KIND OF AUTOMATIC ... I DUNNO, HIGH-TECH ANSWERING MACHINE. COMPLETE WITH HOLOGRAMS.
DECRYPTION, TO STARMAN, FROM SOLARIS...
SOLARIS? THAT'S THE STELLAR COMPUTER THIS STATION ORBITS. WHAT'S...
"PLANS PROCEED. THE JUSTICE LEAGUE FROM THE PAST HAS BEEN SUMMONED AND SUSPECTS NOTHING.
"THEY WILL BE TAKEN COMPLETELY UNAWARE BY YOUR BETRAYAL.
BETRAYAL?
"WITH YOUR AID...
I'M NOT HEARING THIS!
"...I'LL HAVE MY REVENGE!"
STARMAN'S SELLING US OUT!

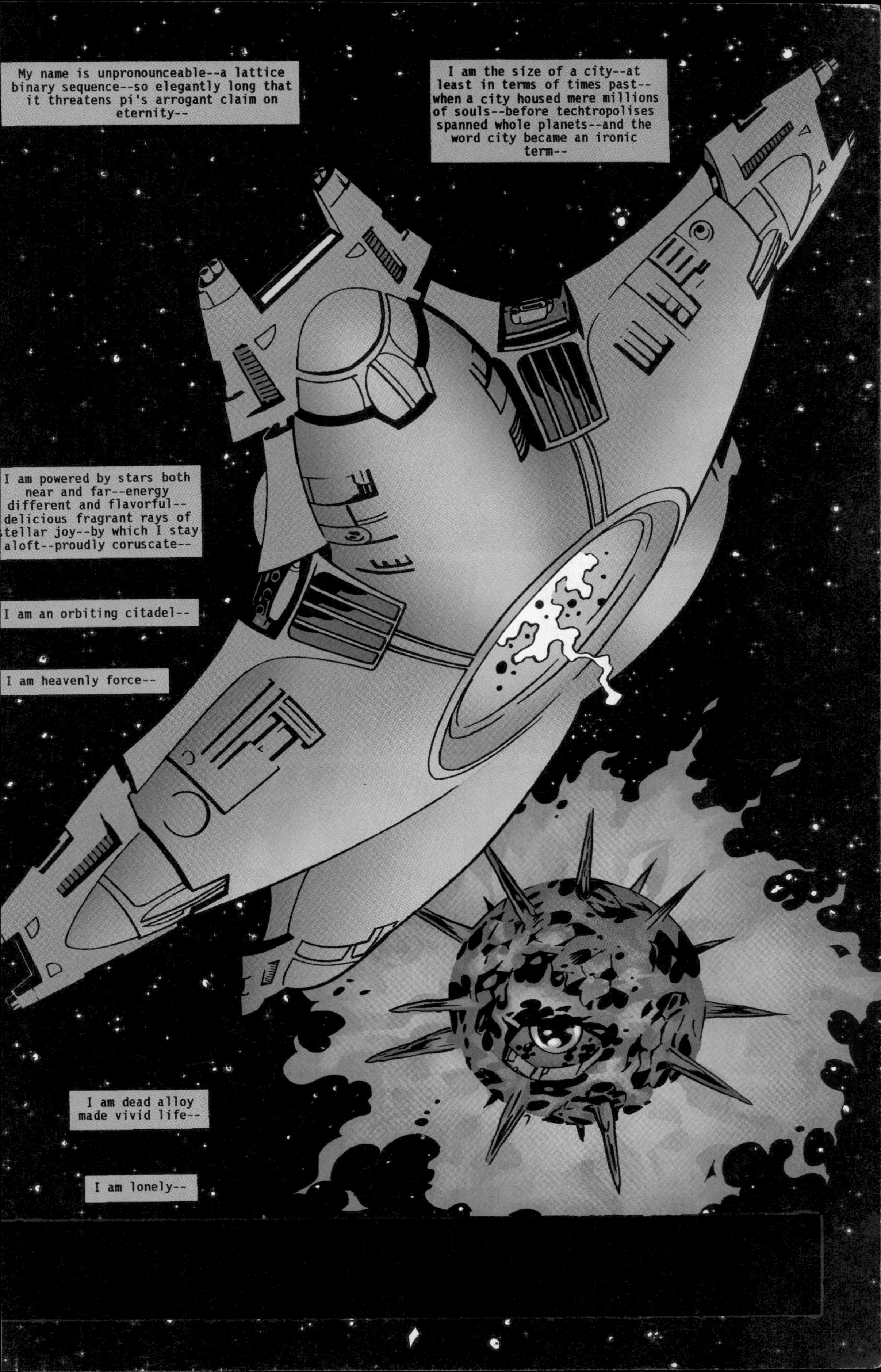
My name is unpronounceable--a lattice binary sequence--so elegantly long that it threatens pi's arrogant claim on eternity--
I am the size of a city--at least in terms of times past--when a city housed mere millions of souls--before techtropolises spanned whole planets--and the word city became an ironic term--
I am powered by stars both near and far--energy different and flavorful--delicious fragrant rays of stellar joy--by which I stay aloft--proudly coruscate--
I am an orbiting citadel--
I am heavenly force--
I am dead alloy made vivid life--
I am lonely--

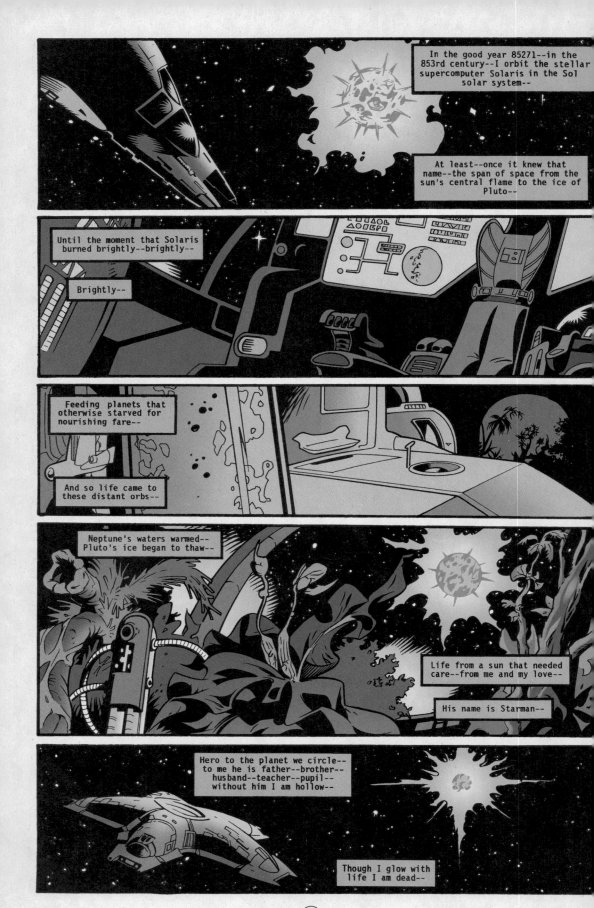

In the good year 85271--in the 853rd century--I orbit the stellar supercomputer Solaris in the Sol solar system--

At least--once it knew that name--the span of space from the sun's central flame to the ice of Pluto--

Until the moment that Solaris burned brightly--brightly--

Brightly--

Feeding planets that otherwise starved for nourishing fare--

And so life came to these distant orbs--

Neptune's waters warmed--Pluto's ice began to thaw--

Life from a sun that needed care--from me and my love--

His name is Starman--

Hero to the planet we circle--to me he is father--brother--husband--teacher--pupil--without him I am hollow--

Though I glow with life I am dead--

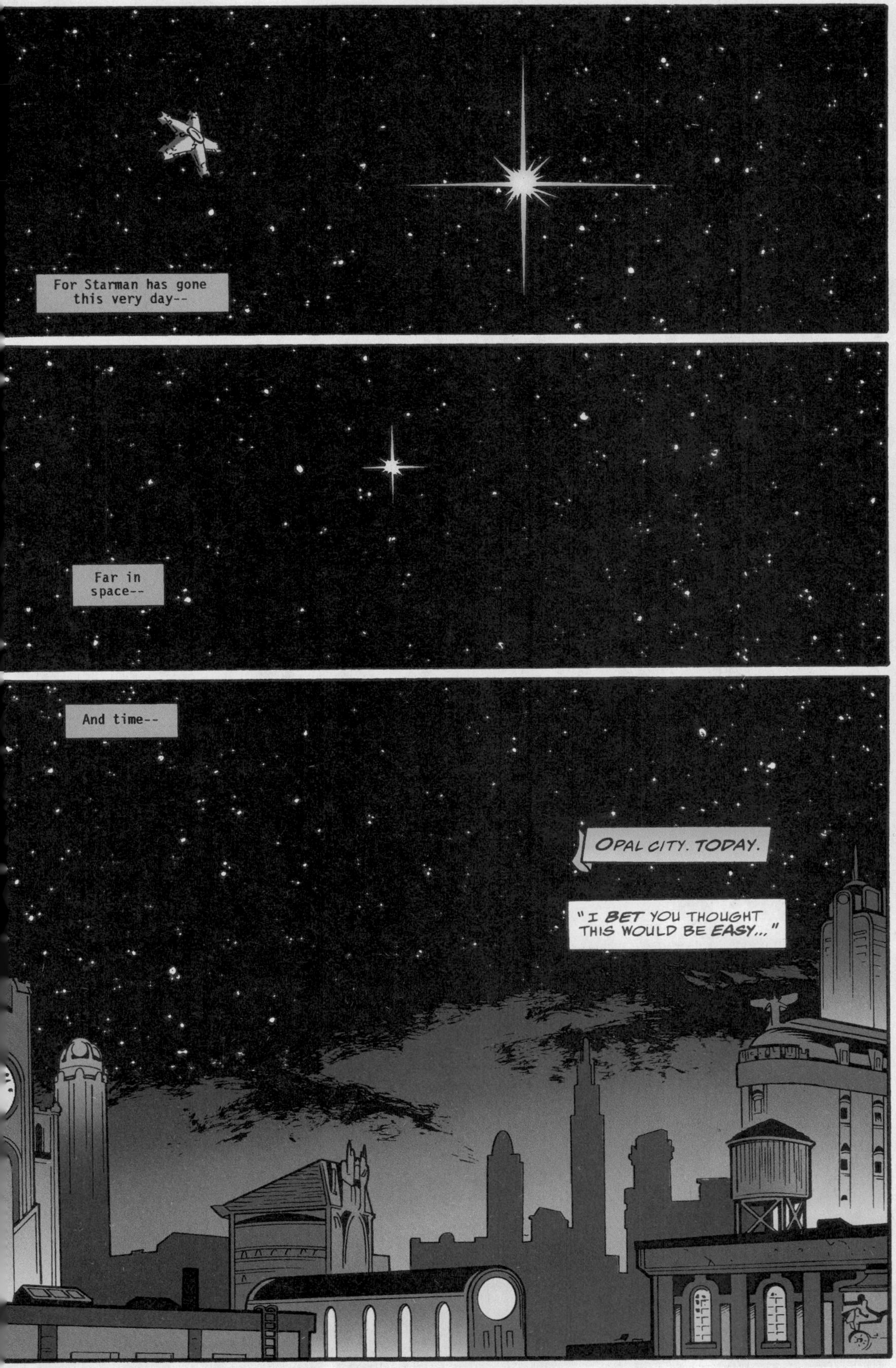
For Starman has gone this very day--
Far in space--
And time--
OPAL CITY. TODAY.
"I BET YOU THOUGHT THIS WOULD BE EASY..."

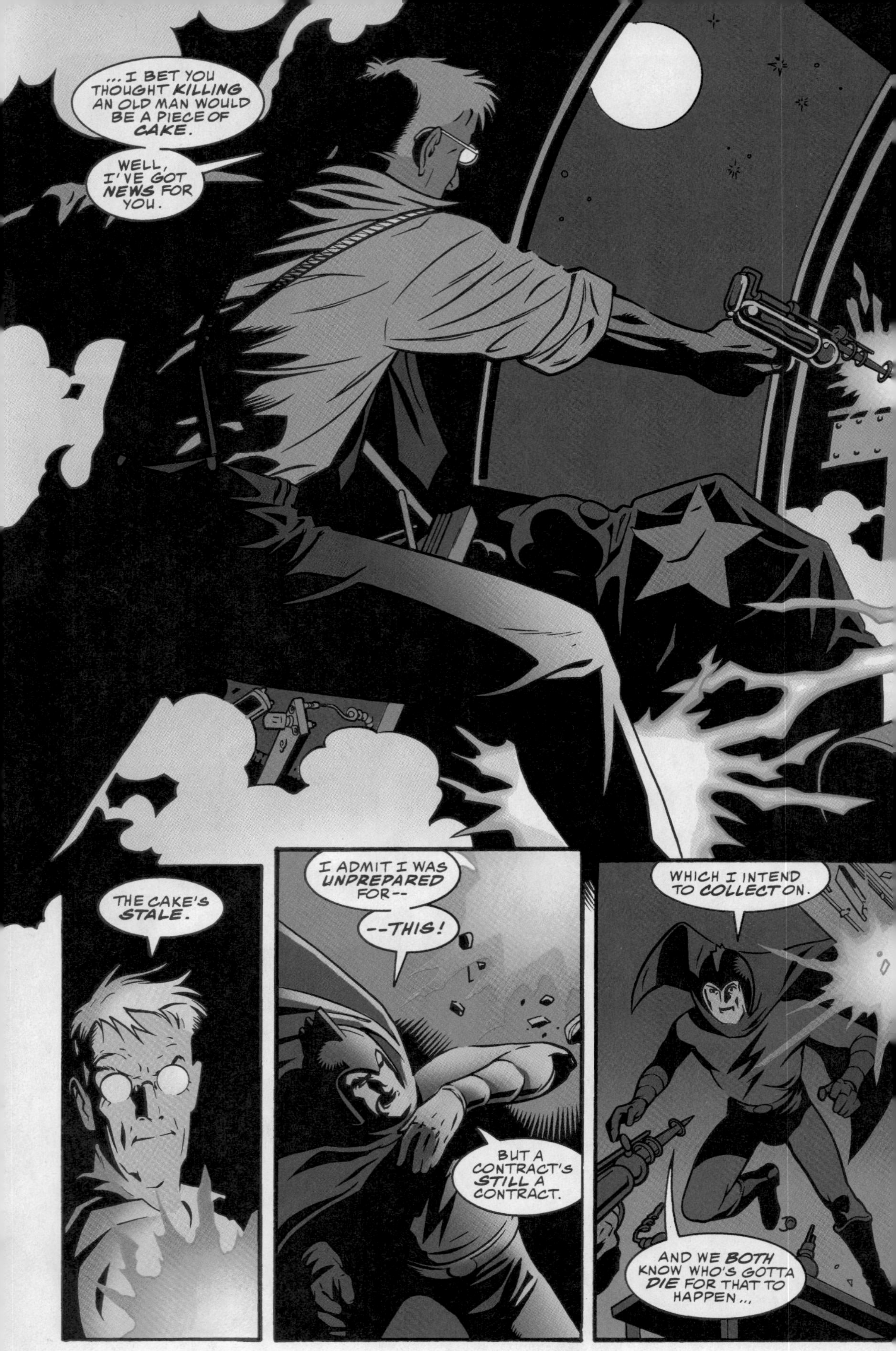
...I BET YOU THOUGHT KILLING AN OLD MAN WOULD BE A PIECE OF CAKE.
WELL, I'VE GOT NEWS FOR YOU.
THE CAKE'S STALE.
I ADMIT I WAS UNPREPARED FOR--
--THIS!
BUT A CONTRACT'S STILL A CONTRACT.
WHICH I INTEND TO COLLECT ON.
AND WE BOTH KNOW WHO'S GOTTA DIE FOR THAT TO HAPPEN...

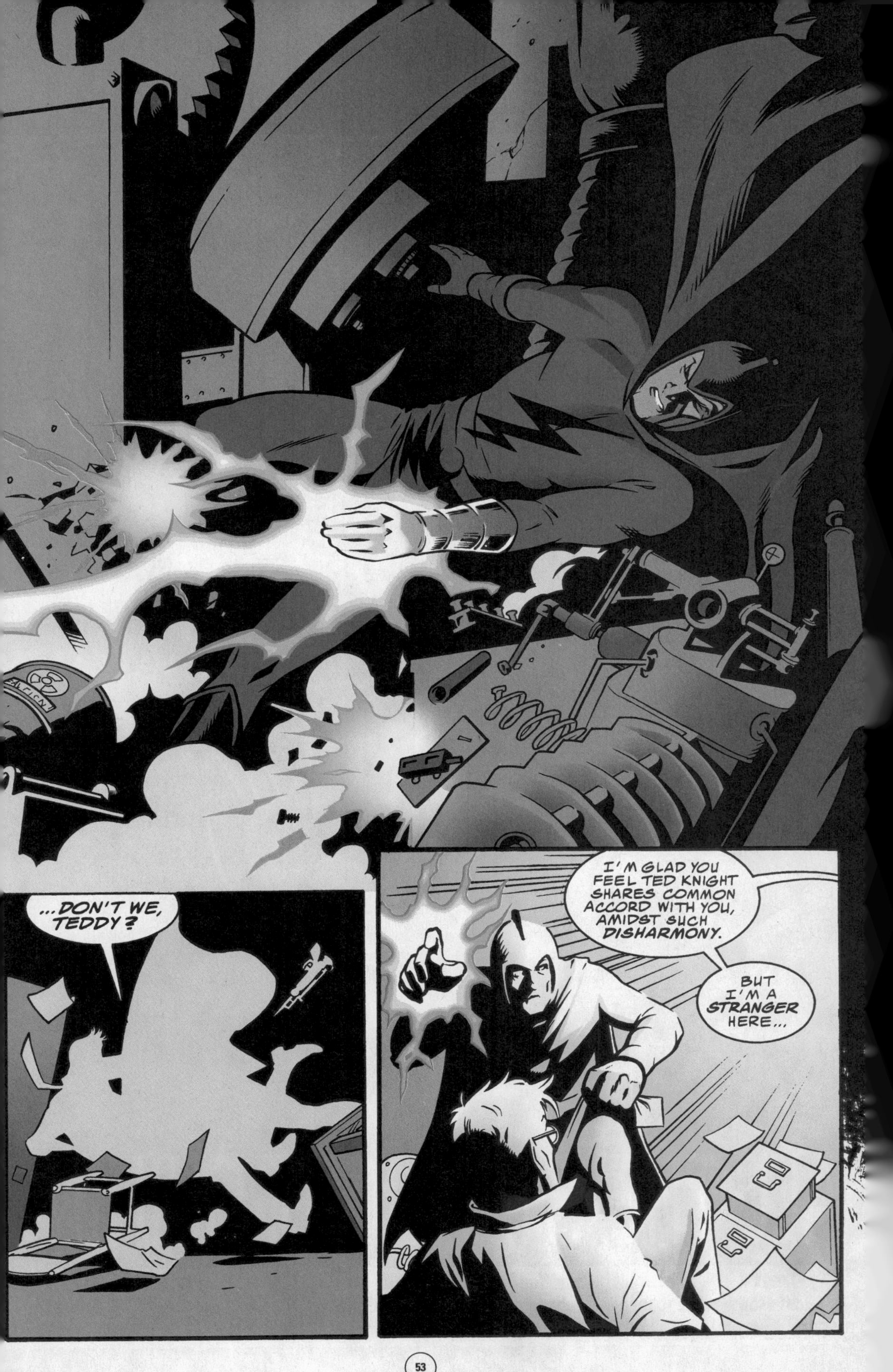
...DON'T WE, TEDDY?
I'M GLAD YOU FEEL TED KNIGHT SHARES COMMON ACCORD WITH YOU, AMIDST SUCH DISHARMONY.
BUT I'M A STRANGER HERE...

ALL THE STARLIGHT SHINING

James Robinson	Peter Snejbjerg	Wade Von Grawbadger	Bill Oakley	Gregory Wright	GCW color	Peter Tomasi	Archie Goodwin
story & words	penciller	inker	letterer	colorist	separation	editor	guiding light

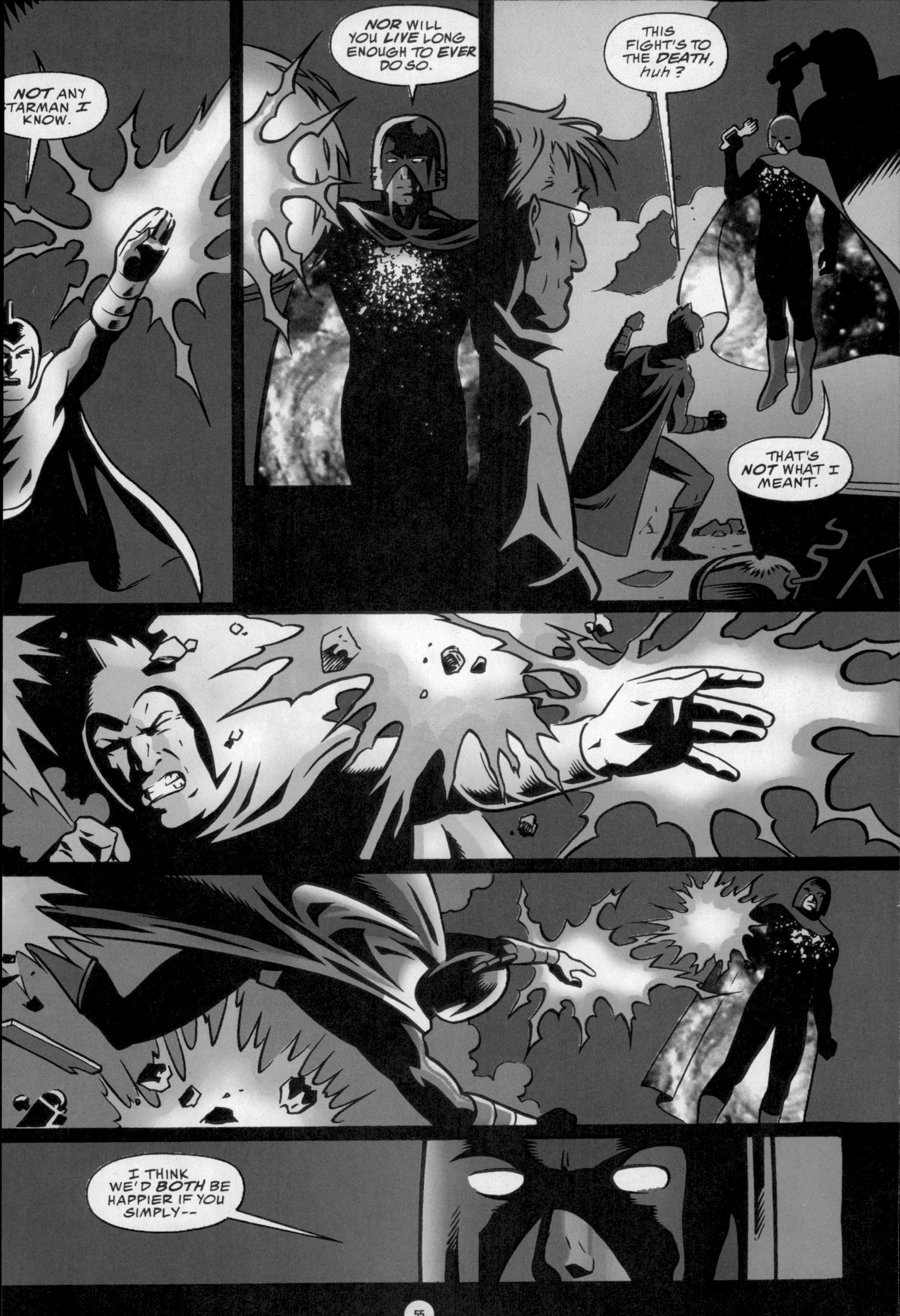
NOT ANY STARMAN I KNOW.
NOR WILL YOU LIVE LONG ENOUGH TO EVER DO SO.
THIS FIGHT'S TO THE DEATH, huh?
THAT'S NOT WHAT I MEANT.
I THINK WE'D BOTH BE HAPPIER IF YOU SIMPLY--

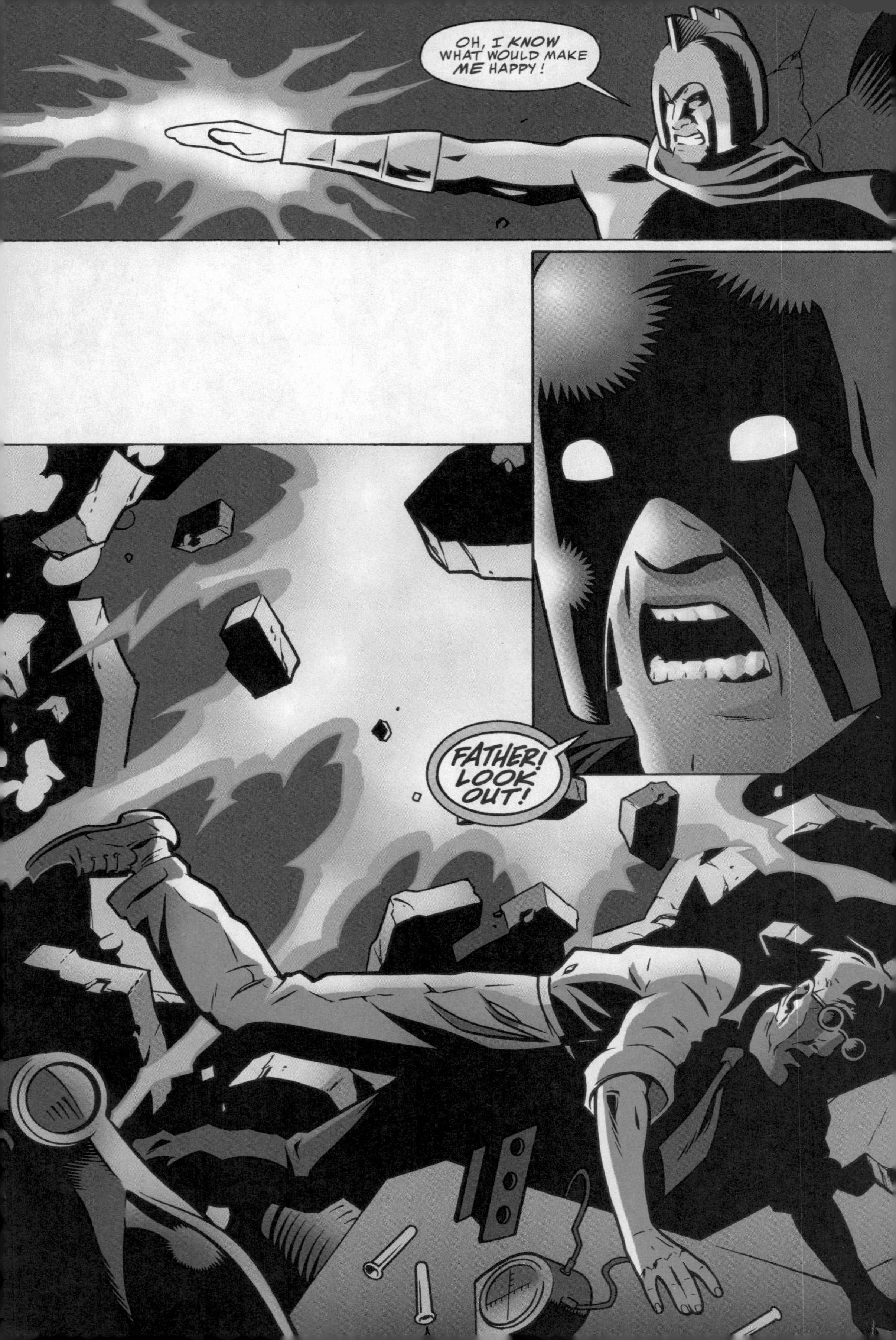
OH, I KNOW WHAT WOULD MAKE ME HAPPY!
FATHER! LOOK OUT!

HE'S GONE. VANISHED.

YES. VILLAINS HAVE A *HABIT* OF DOING THAT.

I'M SORRY.

FOR *WHAT*, SAVING MY LIFE?

FOR *LETTING* HIM ESCAPE.

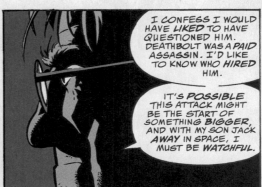

I CONFESS I WOULD HAVE *LIKED* TO HAVE QUESTIONED HIM. DEATHBOLT WAS A *PAID* ASSASSIN. I'D LIKE TO KNOW WHO *HIRED* HIM.

IT'S *POSSIBLE* THIS ATTACK MIGHT BE THE START OF SOMETHING *BIGGER*, AND WITH MY SON JACK *AWAY* IN SPACE, I MUST BE *WATCHFUL*.

ANYWAY, THAT LEAVES *YOU* AND *ME*, DOESN'T IT?

YOU WHO ARE TED KNIGHT. THE FIRST STARMAN.

IS *THAT* WHY YOU CALLED ME "FATHER"? AM I *SEEN* AS SOME KIND OF FATHER TO *ALL* THOSE WHO'LL *BECOME* STARMAN?

I CALLED YOU FATHER BECAUSE YOU ARE *JUST* THAT... MY *FOREFATHER*... MANY GENERATIONS REMOVED, OF COURSE.

I'M *NOT* SURE I FOLLOW YOU.

MY NAME IS *FARRIS KNIGHT*. I'M YOUR *DIRECT* DESCENDANT.

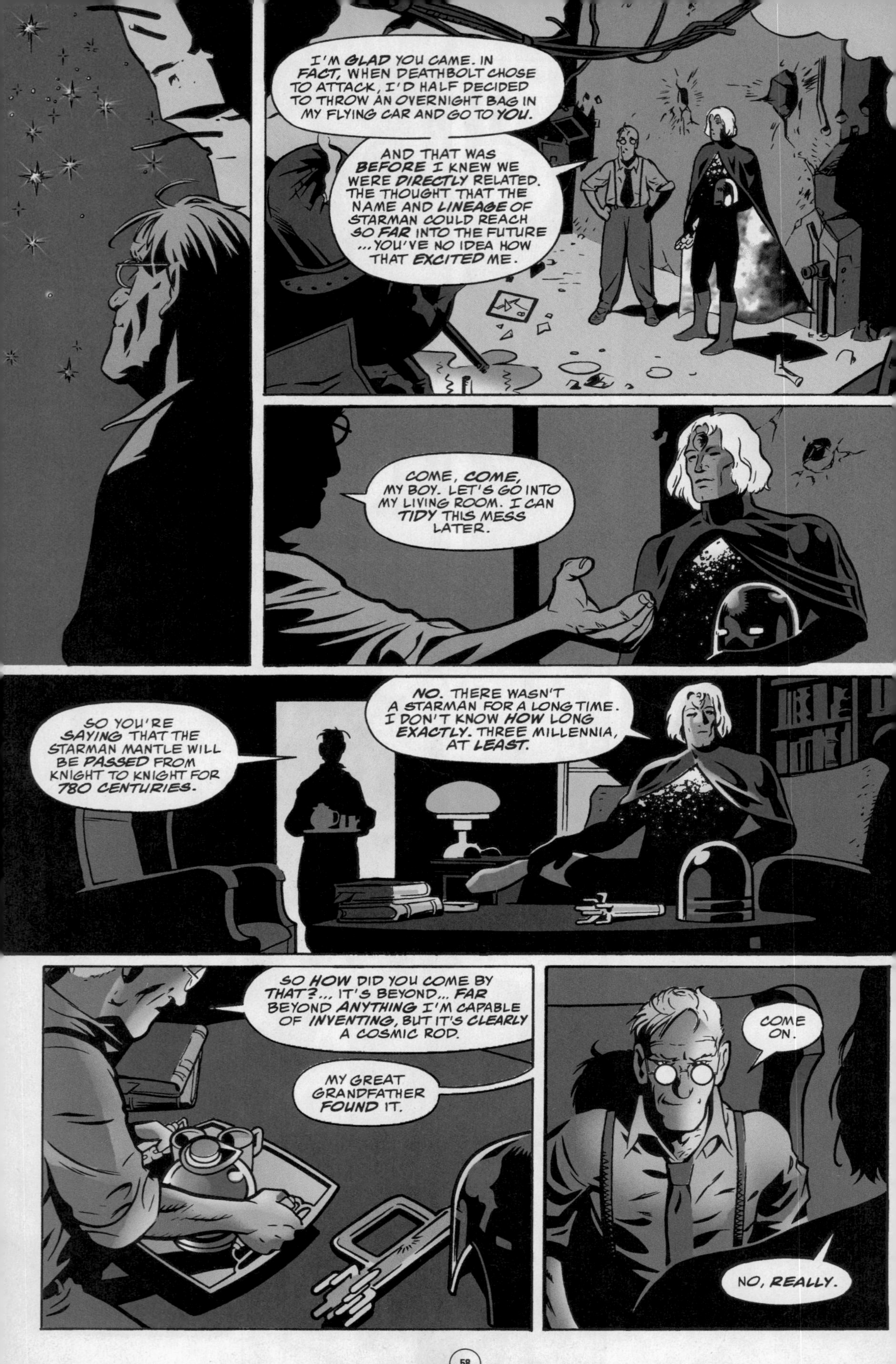

I'M GLAD YOU CAME. IN FACT, WHEN DEATHBOLT CHOSE TO ATTACK, I'D HALF DECIDED TO THROW AN OVERNIGHT BAG IN MY FLYING CAR AND GO TO YOU.
AND THAT WAS BEFORE I KNEW WE WERE DIRECTLY RELATED. THE THOUGHT THAT THE NAME AND LINEAGE OF STARMAN COULD REACH SO FAR INTO THE FUTURE ...YOU'VE NO IDEA HOW THAT EXCITED ME.
COME, COME, MY BOY. LET'S GO INTO MY LIVING ROOM. I CAN TIDY THIS MESS LATER.
SO YOU'RE SAYING THAT THE STARMAN MANTLE WILL BE PASSED FROM KNIGHT TO KNIGHT FOR 780 CENTURIES.
NO. THERE WASN'T A STARMAN FOR A LONG TIME. I DON'T KNOW HOW LONG EXACTLY. THREE MILLENNIA, AT LEAST.
SO HOW DID YOU COME BY THAT?... IT'S BEYOND... FAR BEYOND ANYTHING I'M CAPABLE OF INVENTING, BUT IT'S CLEARLY A COSMIC ROD.
MY GREAT GRANDFATHER FOUND IT.
COME ON.
NO, REALLY.

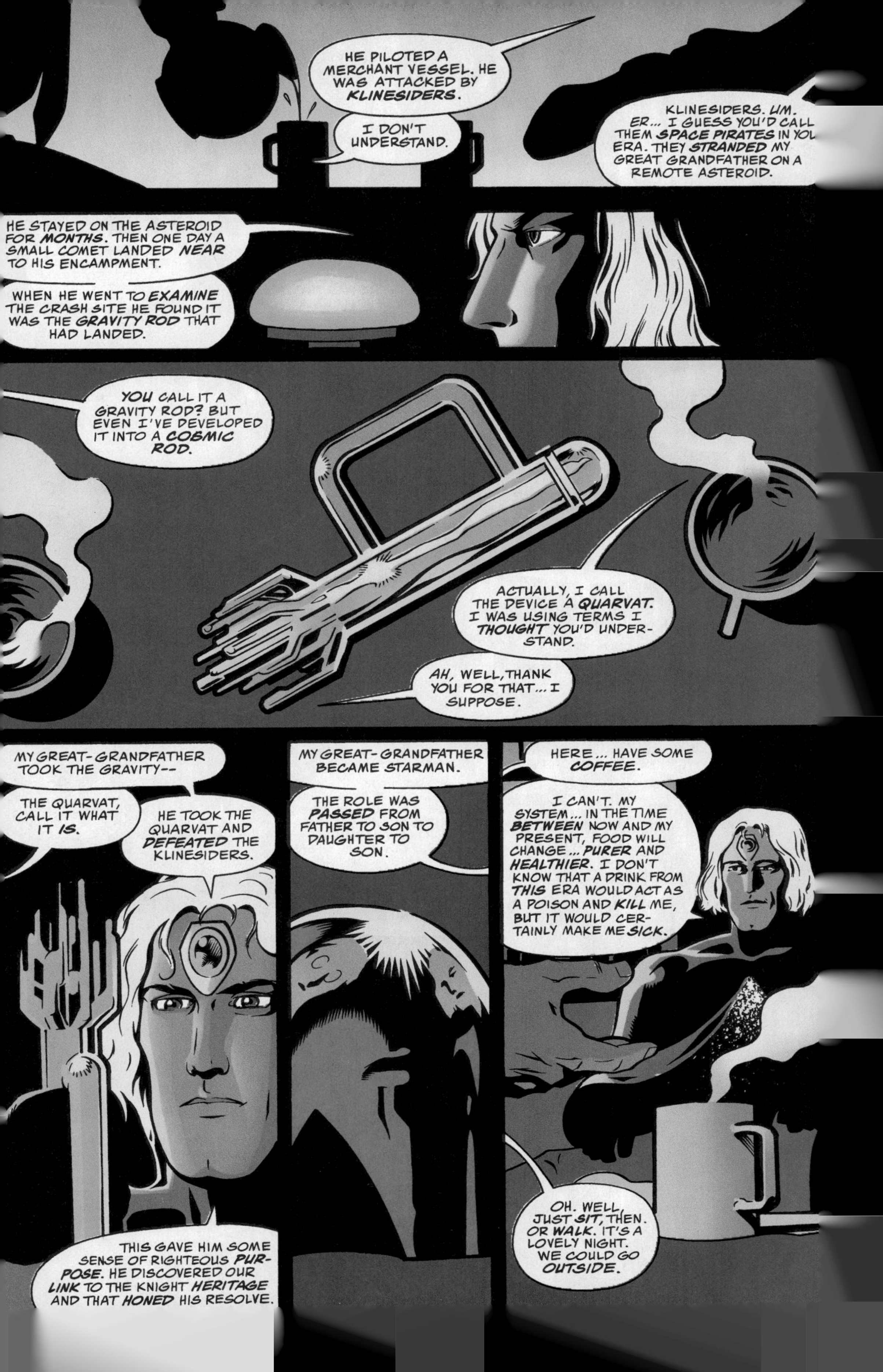
HE PILOTED A MERCHANT VESSEL. HE WAS ATTACKED BY KLINESIDERS.
I DON'T UNDERSTAND.
KLINESIDERS. UM. ER... I GUESS YOU'D CALL THEM SPACE PIRATES IN YOU ERA. THEY STRANDED MY GREAT GRANDFATHER ON A REMOTE ASTEROID.
HE STAYED ON THE ASTEROID FOR MONTHS. THEN ONE DAY A SMALL COMET LANDED NEAR TO HIS ENCAMPMENT.
WHEN HE WENT TO EXAMINE THE CRASH SITE HE FOUND IT WAS THE GRAVITY ROD THAT HAD LANDED.
YOU CALL IT A GRAVITY ROD? BUT EVEN I'VE DEVELOPED IT INTO A COSMIC ROD.
ACTUALLY, I CALL THE DEVICE A QUARVAT. I WAS USING TERMS I THOUGHT YOU'D UNDER-STAND.
AH, WELL, THANK YOU FOR THAT... I SUPPOSE.
MY GREAT-GRANDFATHER TOOK THE GRAVITY--
THE QUARVAT, CALL IT WHAT IT IS.
HE TOOK THE QUARVAT AND DEFEATED THE KLINESIDERS.
THIS GAVE HIM SOME SENSE OF RIGHTEOUS PUR-POSE. HE DISCOVERED OUR LINK TO THE KNIGHT HERITAGE AND THAT HONED HIS RESOLVE.
MY GREAT-GRANDFATHER BECAME STARMAN.
THE ROLE WAS PASSED FROM FATHER TO SON TO DAUGHTER TO SON.
HERE... HAVE SOME COFFEE.
I CAN'T. MY SYSTEM... IN THE TIME BETWEEN NOW AND MY PRESENT, FOOD WILL CHANGE... PURER AND HEALTHIER. I DON'T KNOW THAT A DRINK FROM THIS ERA WOULD ACT AS A POISON AND KILL ME, BUT IT WOULD CER-TAINLY MAKE ME SICK.
OH. WELL, JUST SIT, THEN. OR WALK. IT'S A LOVELY NIGHT. WE COULD GO OUTSIDE.

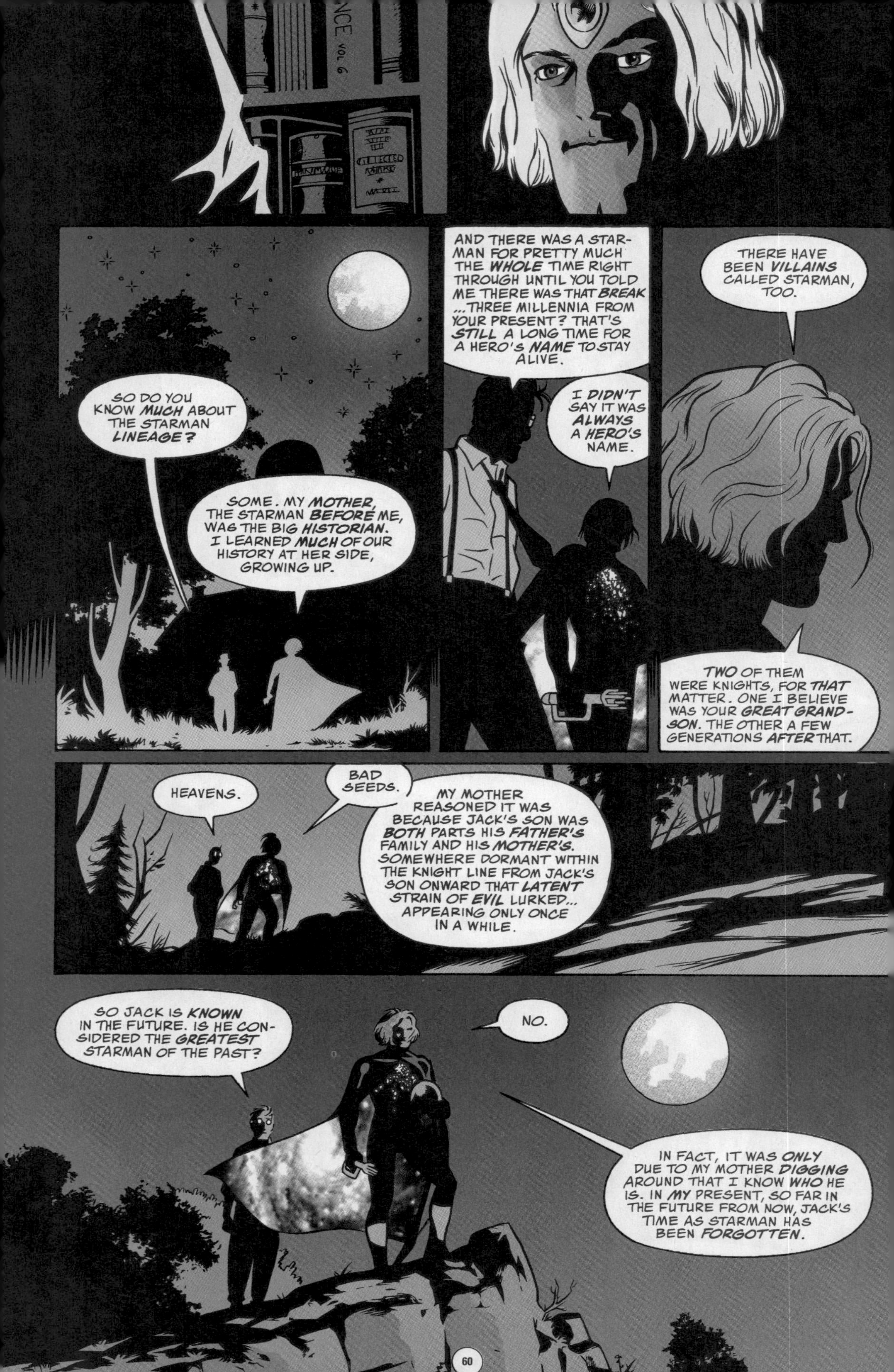
SO DO YOU KNOW MUCH ABOUT THE STARMAN LINEAGE?
SOME. MY MOTHER, THE STARMAN BEFORE ME, WAS THE BIG HISTORIAN. I LEARNED MUCH OF OUR HISTORY AT HER SIDE, GROWING UP.
AND THERE WAS A STARMAN FOR PRETTY MUCH THE WHOLE TIME RIGHT THROUGH UNTIL YOU TOLD ME THERE WAS THAT BREAK ...THREE MILLENNIA FROM YOUR PRESENT? THAT'S STILL A LONG TIME FOR A HERO'S NAME TO STAY ALIVE.
I DIDN'T SAY IT WAS ALWAYS A HERO'S NAME.
THERE HAVE BEEN VILLAINS CALLED STARMAN, TOO.
TWO OF THEM WERE KNIGHTS, FOR THAT MATTER. ONE I BELIEVE WAS YOUR GREAT GRANDSON. THE OTHER A FEW GENERATIONS AFTER THAT.
HEAVENS.
BAD SEEDS.
MY MOTHER REASONED IT WAS BECAUSE JACK'S SON WAS BOTH PARTS HIS FATHER'S FAMILY AND HIS MOTHER'S. SOMEWHERE DORMANT WITHIN THE KNIGHT LINE FROM JACK'S SON ONWARD THAT LATENT STRAIN OF EVIL LURKED... APPEARING ONLY ONCE IN A WHILE.
SO JACK IS KNOWN IN THE FUTURE. IS HE CONSIDERED THE GREATEST STARMAN OF THE PAST?
NO.
IN FACT, IT WAS ONLY DUE TO MY MOTHER DIGGING AROUND THAT I KNOW WHO HE IS. IN MY PRESENT, SO FAR IN THE FUTURE FROM NOW, JACK'S TIME AS STARMAN HAS BEEN FORGOTTEN.

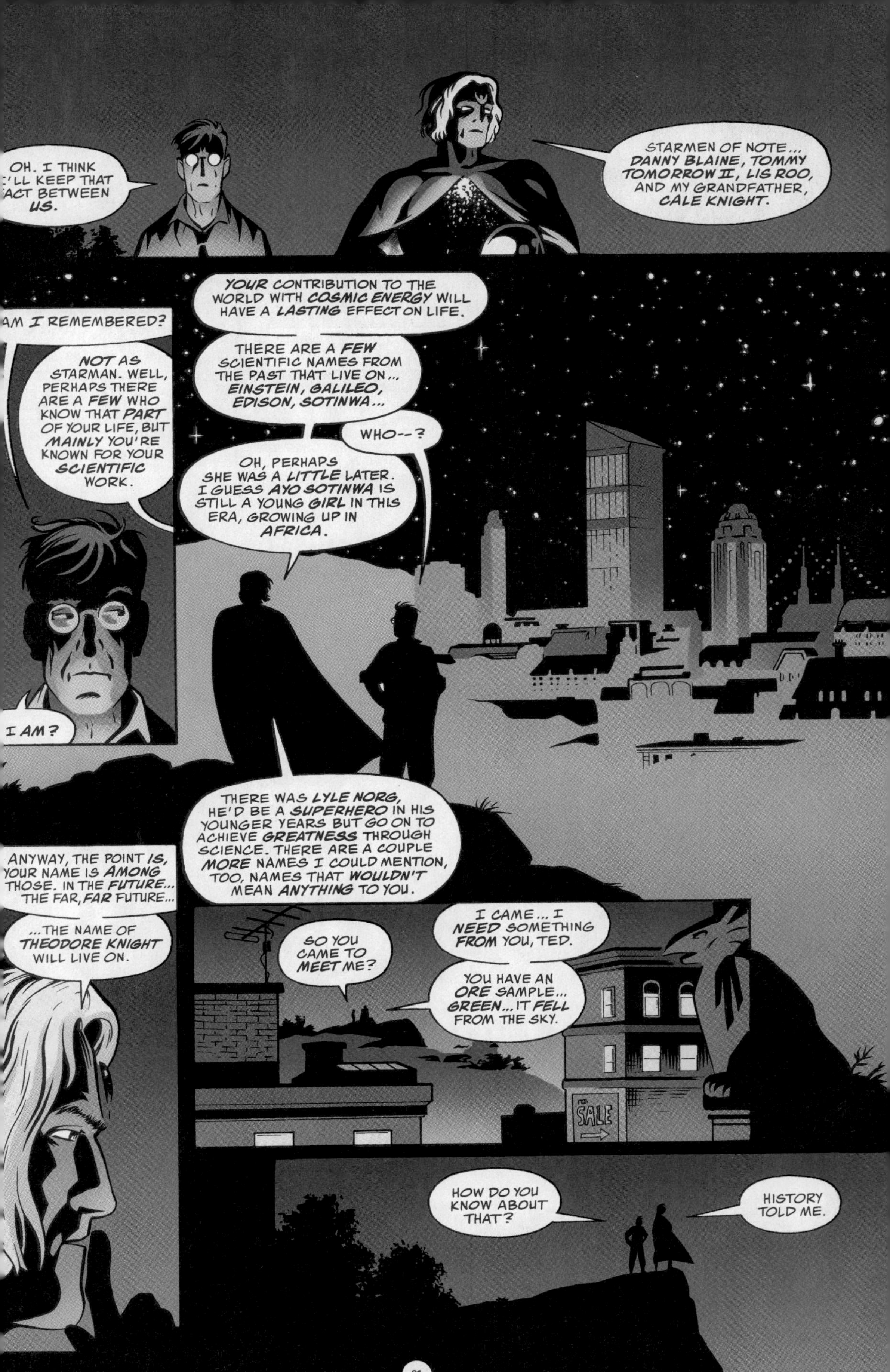

OH. I THINK I'LL KEEP THAT FACT BETWEEN US.
STARMEN OF NOTE... DANNY BLAINE, TOMMY TOMORROW II, LIS ROO, AND MY GRANDFATHER, CALE KNIGHT.
AM I REMEMBERED?
NOT AS STARMAN. WELL, PERHAPS THERE ARE A FEW WHO KNOW THAT PART OF YOUR LIFE, BUT MAINLY YOU'RE KNOWN FOR YOUR SCIENTIFIC WORK.
I AM?
YOUR CONTRIBUTION TO THE WORLD WITH COSMIC ENERGY WILL HAVE A LASTING EFFECT ON LIFE.
THERE ARE A FEW SCIENTIFIC NAMES FROM THE PAST THAT LIVE ON... EINSTEIN, GALILEO, EDISON, SOTINWA...
WHO--?
OH, PERHAPS SHE WAS A LITTLE LATER. I GUESS AYO SOTINWA IS STILL A YOUNG GIRL IN THIS ERA, GROWING UP IN AFRICA.
THERE WAS LYLE NORG, HE'D BE A SUPERHERO IN HIS YOUNGER YEARS BUT GO ON TO ACHIEVE GREATNESS THROUGH SCIENCE. THERE ARE A COUPLE MORE NAMES I COULD MENTION, TOO, NAMES THAT WOULDN'T MEAN ANYTHING TO YOU.
ANYWAY, THE POINT IS, YOUR NAME IS AMONG THOSE. IN THE FUTURE... THE FAR, FAR FUTURE...
...THE NAME OF THEODORE KNIGHT WILL LIVE ON.
SO YOU CAME TO MEET ME?
I CAME... I NEED SOMETHING FROM YOU, TED.
YOU HAVE AN ORE SAMPLE... GREEN... IT FELL FROM THE SKY.
SALE
HOW DO YOU KNOW ABOUT THAT?
HISTORY TOLD ME.

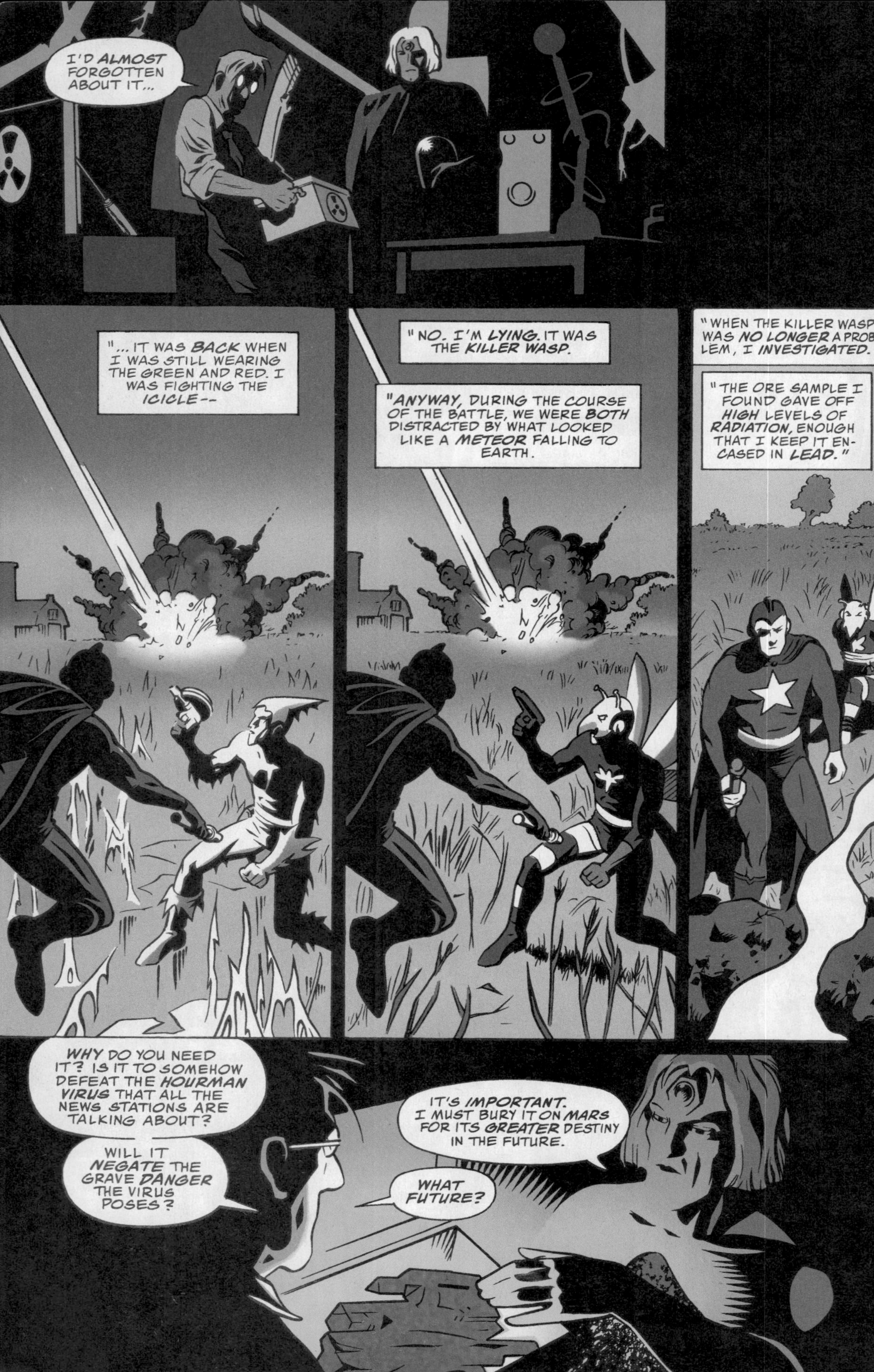
I'D ALMOST FORGOTTEN ABOUT IT...
"... IT WAS BACK WHEN I WAS STILL WEARING THE GREEN AND RED. I WAS FIGHTING THE ICICLE--
"NO. I'M LYING. IT WAS THE KILLER WASP.
"ANYWAY, DURING THE COURSE OF THE BATTLE, WE WERE BOTH DISTRACTED BY WHAT LOOKED LIKE A METEOR FALLING TO EARTH.
"WHEN THE KILLER WASP WAS NO LONGER A PROB-LEM, I INVESTIGATED.
"THE ORE SAMPLE I FOUND GAVE OFF HIGH LEVELS OF RADIATION, ENOUGH THAT I KEEP IT EN-CASED IN LEAD."
WHY DO YOU NEED IT? IS IT TO SOMEHOW DEFEAT THE HOURMAN VIRUS THAT ALL THE NEWS STATIONS ARE TALKING ABOUT?
WILL IT NEGATE THE GRAVE DANGER THE VIRUS POSES?
IT'S IMPORTANT. I MUST BURY IT ON MARS FOR ITS GREATER DESTINY IN THE FUTURE.
WHAT FUTURE?

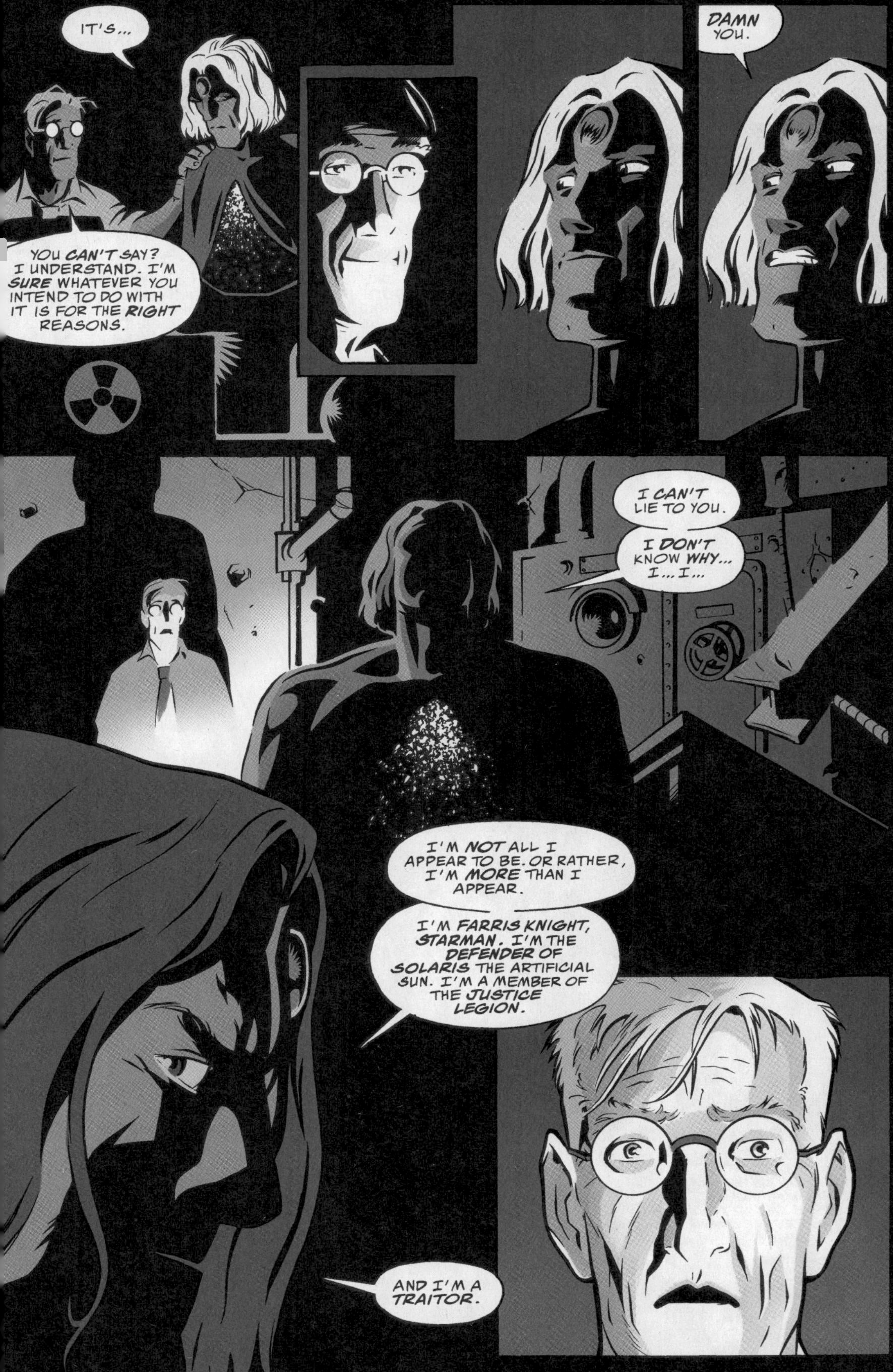
IT'S...
YOU CAN'T SAY? I UNDERSTAND. I'M SURE WHATEVER YOU INTEND TO DO WITH IT IS FOR THE RIGHT REASONS.
DAMN YOU.
I CAN'T LIE TO YOU.
I DON'T KNOW WHY... I... I...
I'M NOT ALL I APPEAR TO BE. OR RATHER, I'M MORE THAN I APPEAR.
I'M FARRIS KNIGHT, STARMAN. I'M THE DEFENDER OF SOLARIS THE ARTIFICIAL SUN. I'M A MEMBER OF THE JUSTICE LEGION.
AND I'M A TRAITOR.

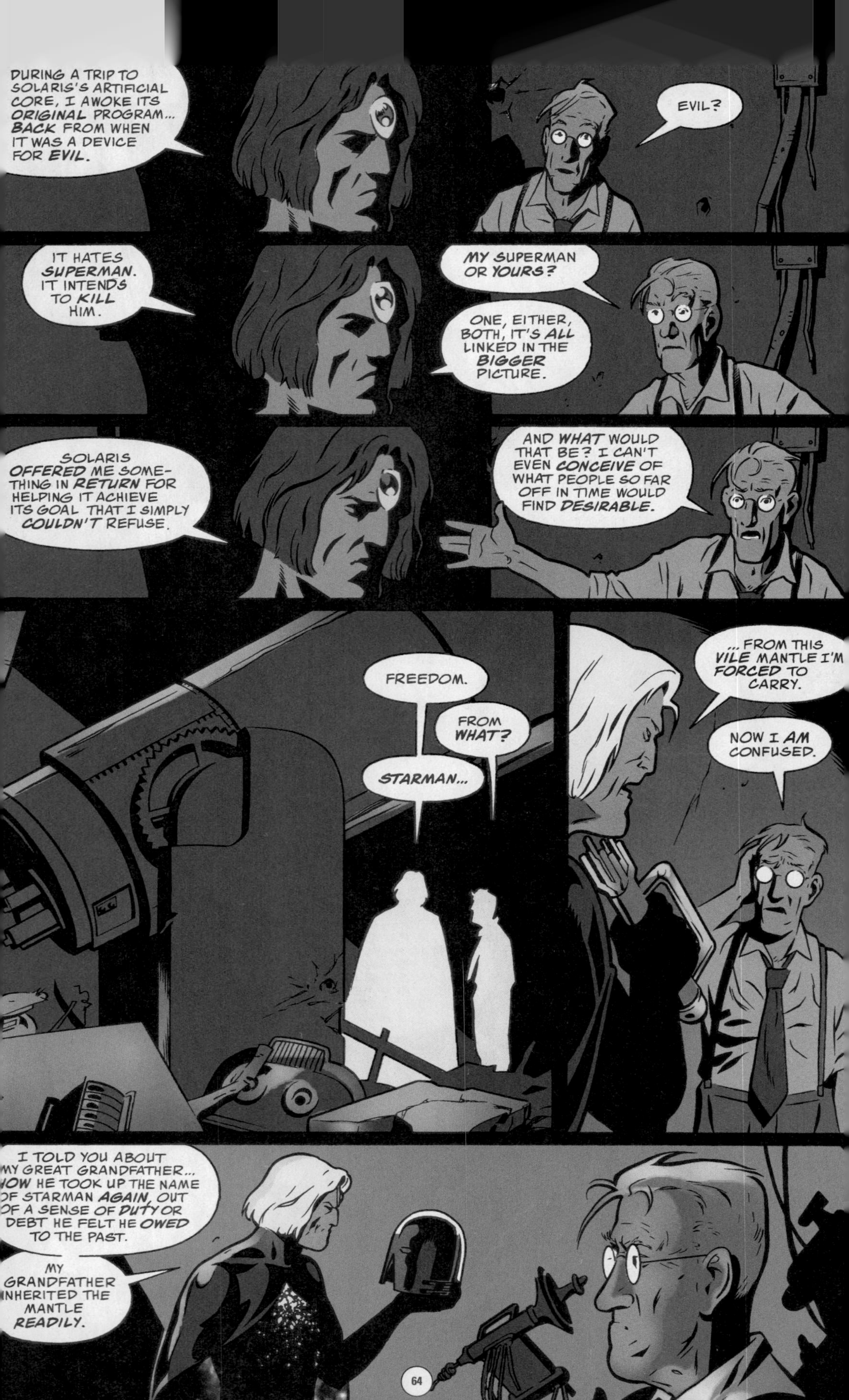
DURING A TRIP TO SOLARIS'S ARTIFICIAL CORE, I AWOKE ITS ORIGINAL PROGRAM... BACK FROM WHEN IT WAS A DEVICE FOR EVIL.
EVIL?
IT HATES SUPERMAN. IT INTENDS TO KILL HIM.
MY SUPERMAN OR YOURS?
ONE, EITHER, BOTH, IT'S ALL LINKED IN THE BIGGER PICTURE.
SOLARIS OFFERED ME SOMETHING IN RETURN FOR HELPING IT ACHIEVE ITS GOAL THAT I SIMPLY COULDN'T REFUSE.
AND WHAT WOULD THAT BE? I CAN'T EVEN CONCEIVE OF WHAT PEOPLE SO FAR OFF IN TIME WOULD FIND DESIRABLE.
FREEDOM.
FROM WHAT?
STARMAN...
...FROM THIS VILE MANTLE I'M FORCED TO CARRY.
NOW I AM CONFUSED.
I TOLD YOU ABOUT MY GREAT GRANDFATHER... HOW HE TOOK UP THE NAME OF STARMAN AGAIN, OUT OF A SENSE OF DUTY OR DEBT HE FELT HE OWED TO THE PAST.
MY GRANDFATHER INHERITED THE MANTLE READILY.

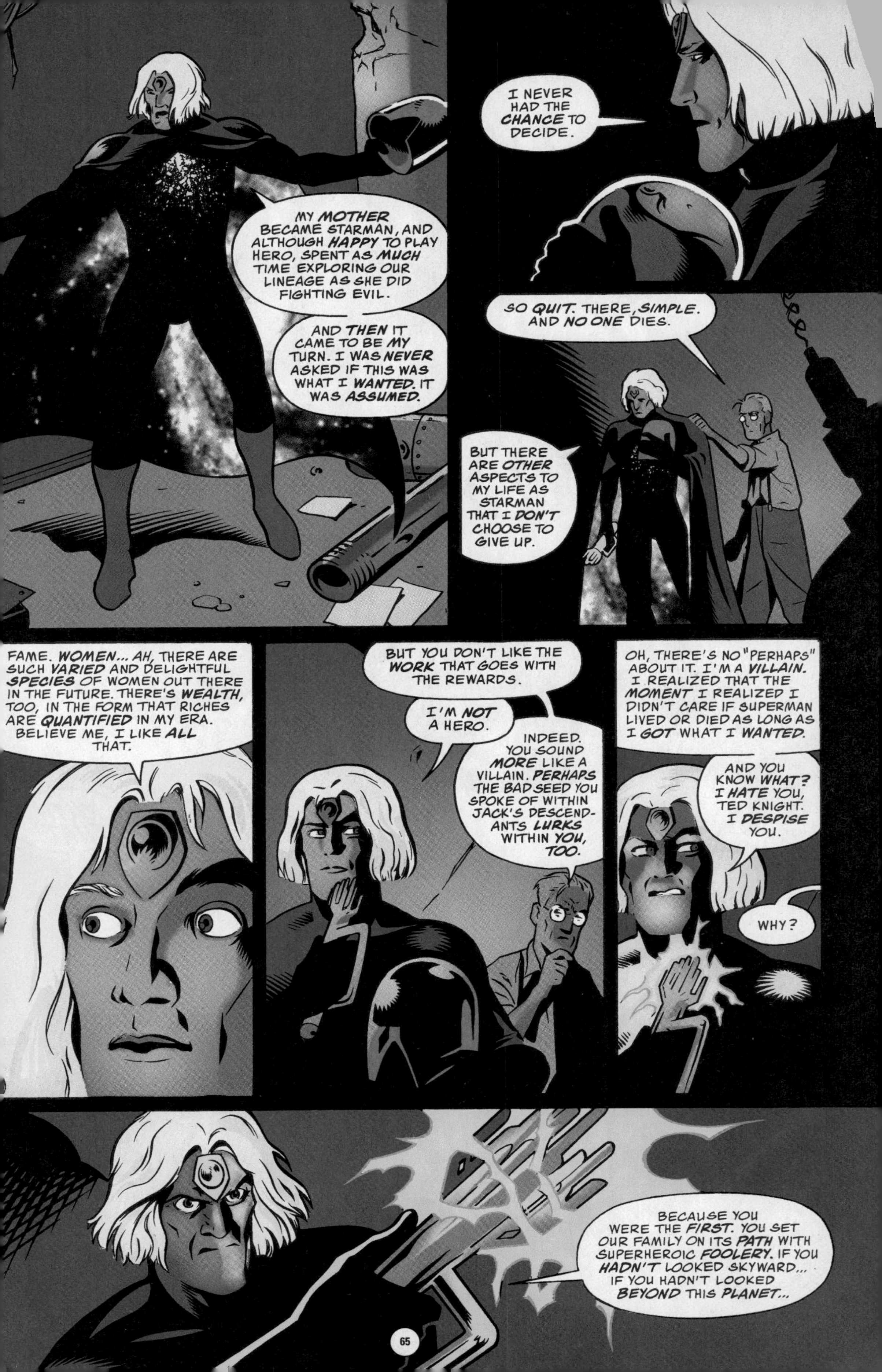

MY MOTHER BECAME STARMAN, AND ALTHOUGH HAPPY TO PLAY HERO, SPENT AS MUCH TIME EXPLORING OUR LINEAGE AS SHE DID FIGHTING EVIL.
AND THEN IT CAME TO BE MY TURN. I WAS NEVER ASKED IF THIS WAS WHAT I WANTED. IT WAS ASSUMED.
I NEVER HAD THE CHANCE TO DECIDE.
SO QUIT. THERE, SIMPLE. AND NO ONE DIES.
BUT THERE ARE OTHER ASPECTS TO MY LIFE AS STARMAN THAT I DON'T CHOOSE TO GIVE UP.
FAME. WOMEN... AH, THERE ARE SUCH VARIED AND DELIGHTFUL SPECIES OF WOMEN OUT THERE IN THE FUTURE. THERE'S WEALTH, TOO, IN THE FORM THAT RICHES ARE QUANTIFIED IN MY ERA. BELIEVE ME, I LIKE ALL THAT.
BUT YOU DON'T LIKE THE WORK THAT GOES WITH THE REWARDS.
I'M NOT A HERO.
INDEED. YOU SOUND MORE LIKE A VILLAIN. PERHAPS THE BAD SEED YOU SPOKE OF WITHIN JACK'S DESCENDANTS LURKS WITHIN YOU, TOO.
OH, THERE'S NO "PERHAPS" ABOUT IT. I'M A VILLAIN. I REALIZED THAT THE MOMENT I REALIZED I DIDN'T CARE IF SUPERMAN LIVED OR DIED AS LONG AS I GOT WHAT I WANTED.
AND YOU KNOW WHAT? I HATE YOU, TED KNIGHT. I DESPISE YOU.
WHY?
BECAUSE YOU WERE THE FIRST. YOU SET OUR FAMILY ON ITS PATH WITH SUPERHEROIC FOOLERY. IF YOU HADN'T LOOKED SKYWARD... IF YOU HADN'T LOOKED BEYOND THIS PLANET...

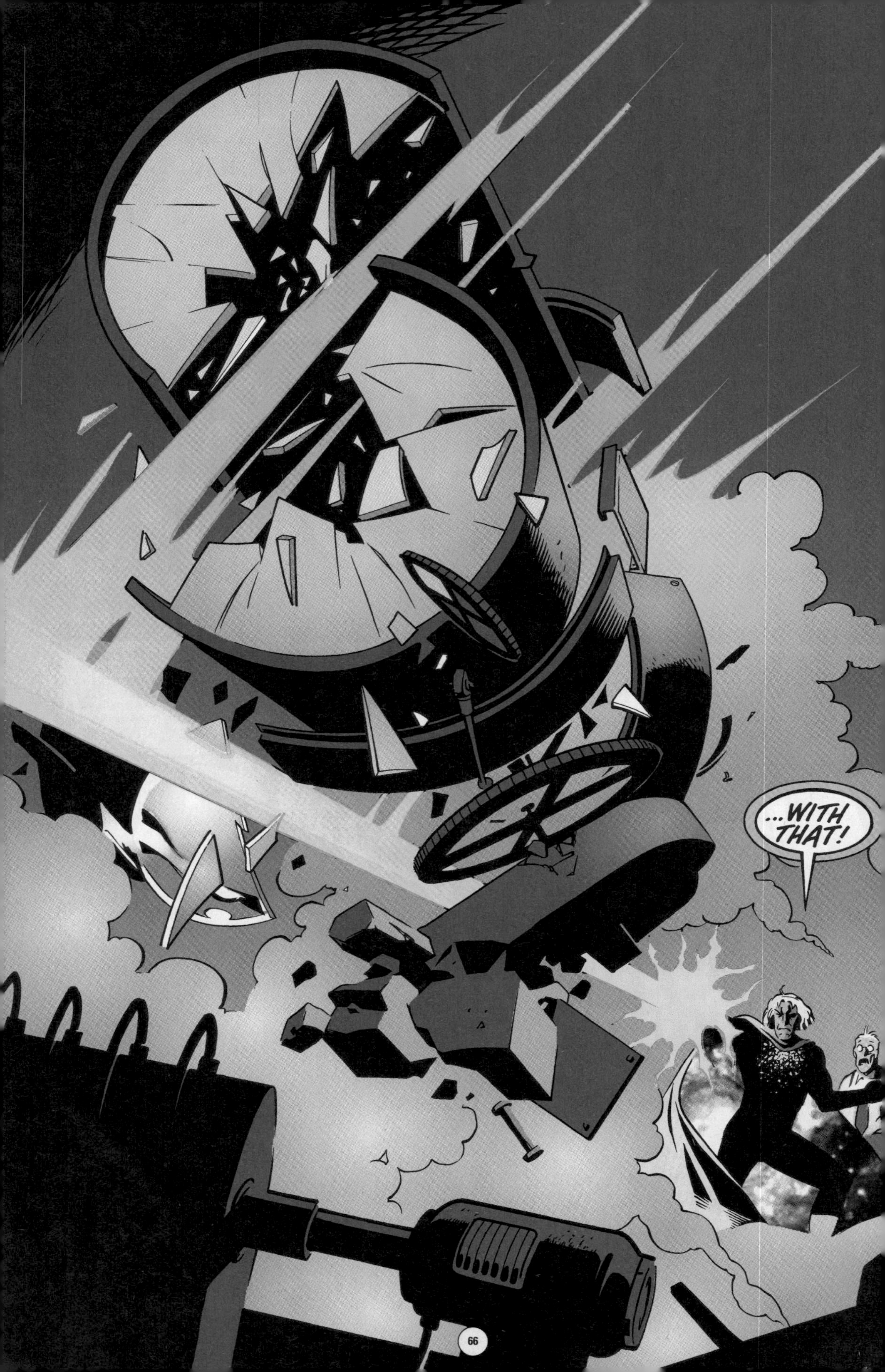
...WITH THAT!

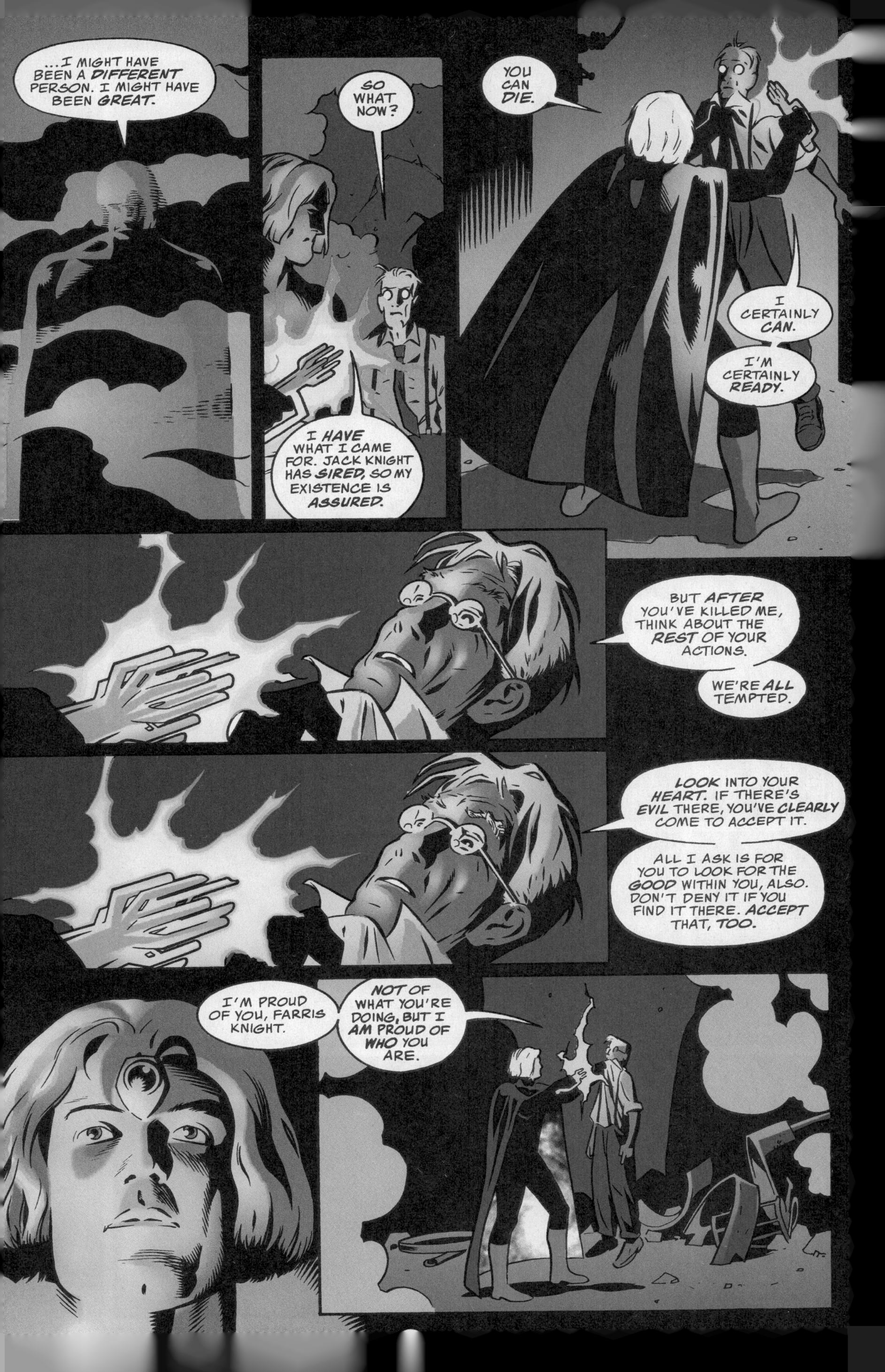

...I MIGHT HAVE BEEN A DIFFERENT PERSON. I MIGHT HAVE BEEN GREAT.
SO WHAT NOW?
I HAVE WHAT I CAME FOR. JACK KNIGHT HAS SIRED, SO MY EXISTENCE IS ASSURED.
YOU CAN DIE.
I CERTAINLY CAN.
I'M CERTAINLY READY.
BUT AFTER YOU'VE KILLED ME, THINK ABOUT THE REST OF YOUR ACTIONS.
WE'RE ALL TEMPTED.
LOOK INTO YOUR HEART. IF THERE'S EVIL THERE, YOU'VE CLEARLY COME TO ACCEPT IT.
ALL I ASK IS FOR YOU TO LOOK FOR THE GOOD WITHIN YOU, ALSO. DON'T DENY IT IF YOU FIND IT THERE. ACCEPT THAT, TOO.
I'M PROUD OF YOU, FARRIS KNIGHT.
NOT OF WHAT YOU'RE DOING, BUT I AM PROUD OF WHO YOU ARE.

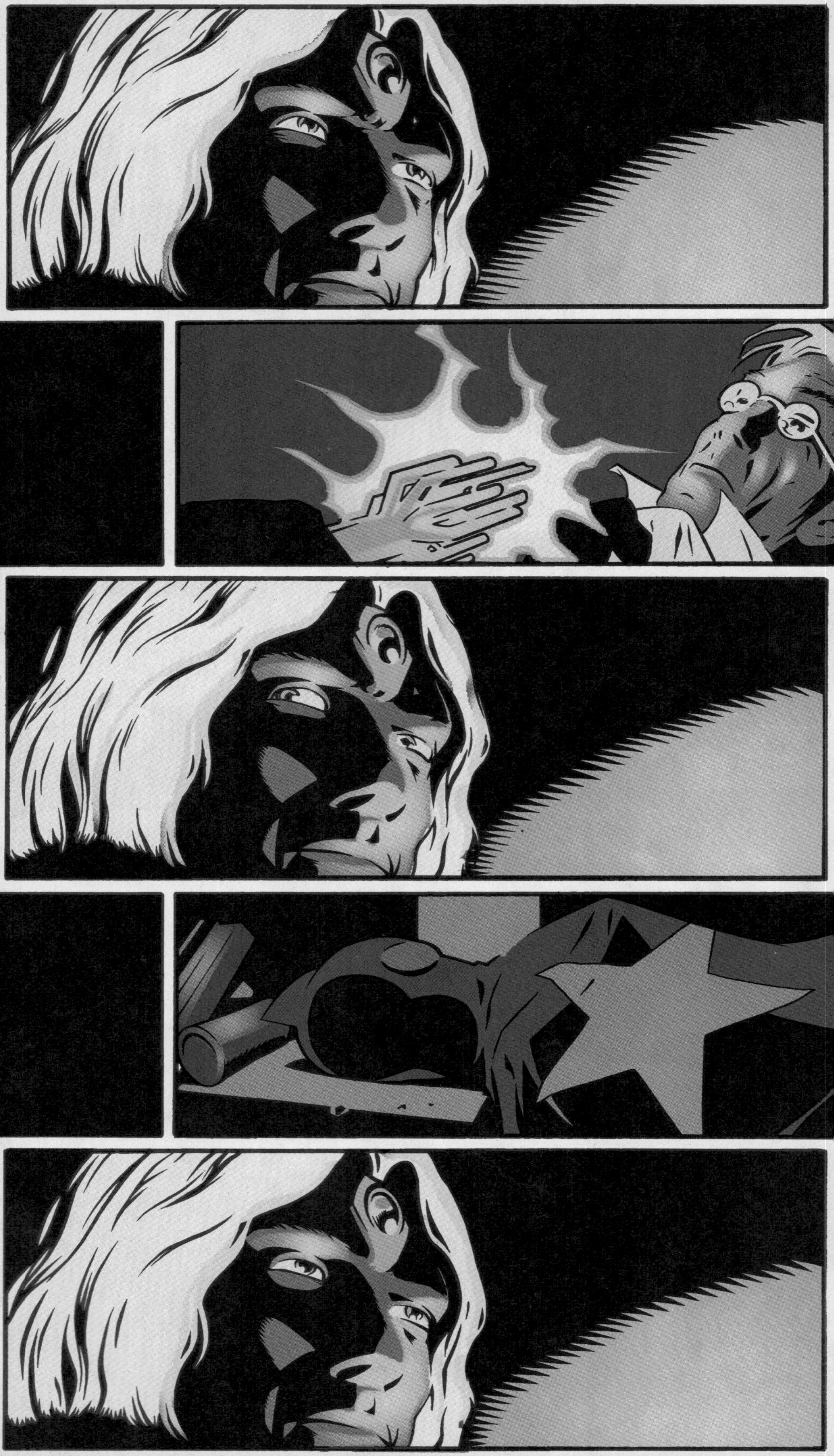

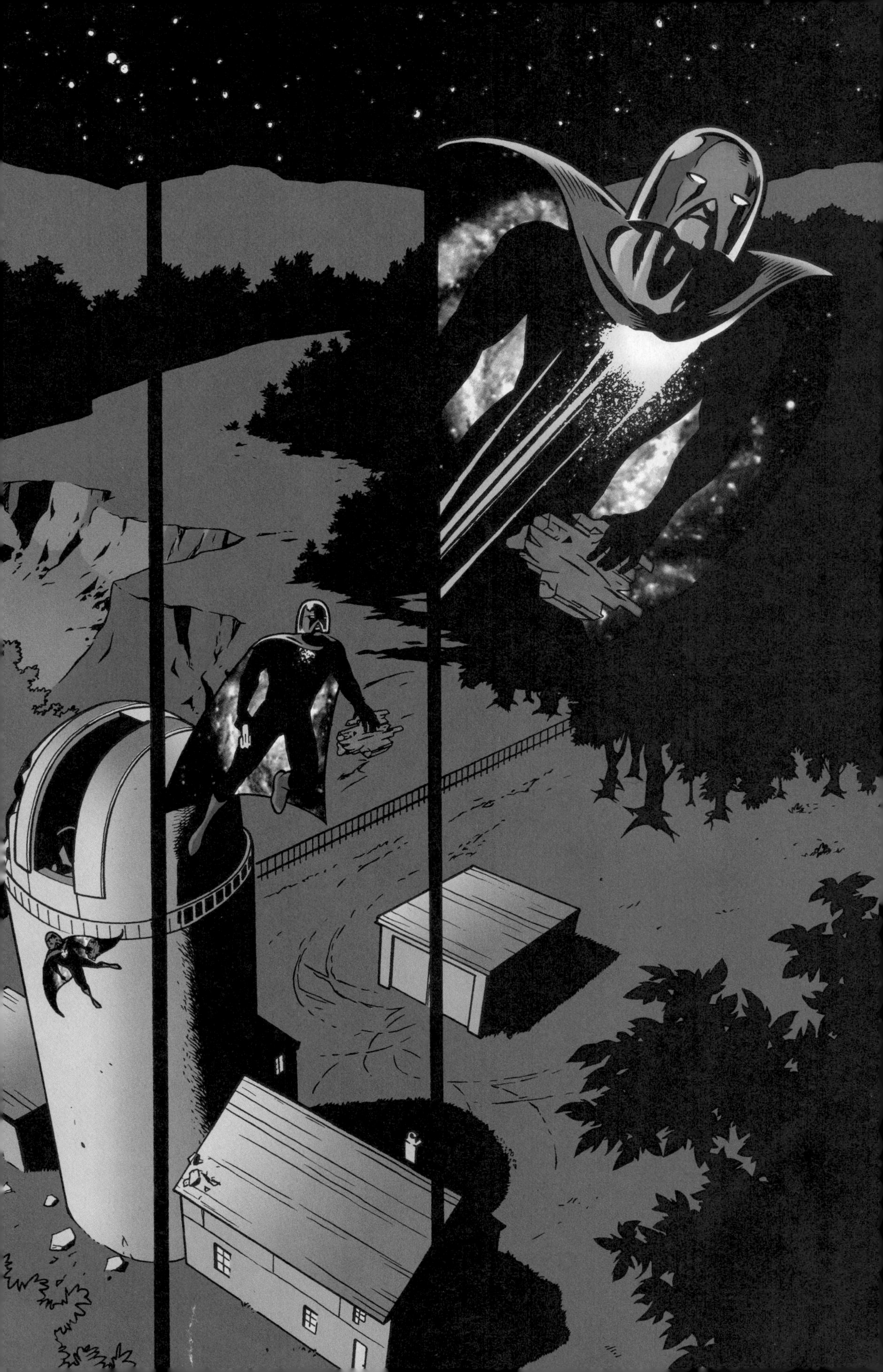

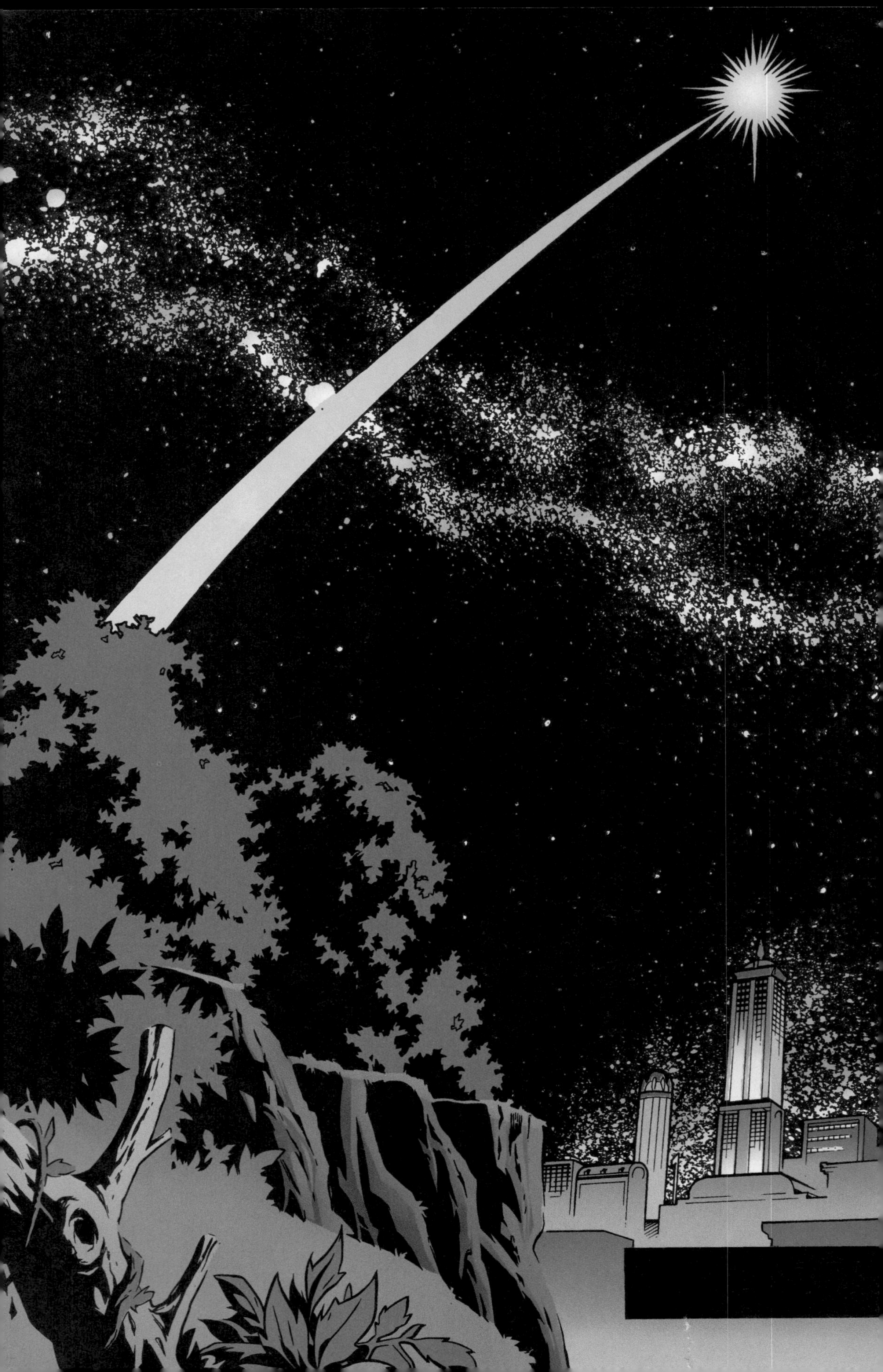

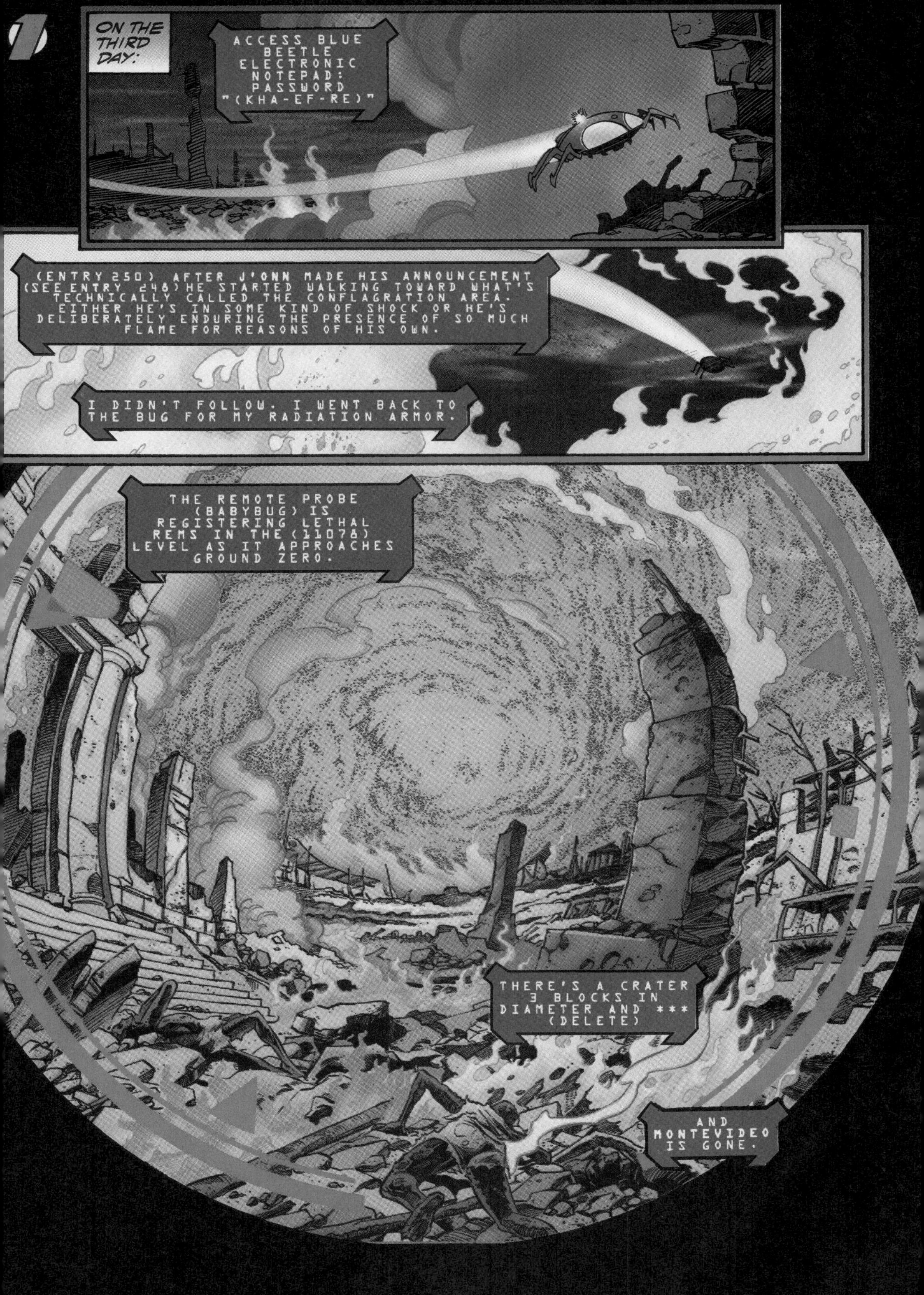
ON THE THIRD DAY:
ACCESS BLUE BEETLE ELECTRONIC NOTEPAD: PASSWORD "(KHA-EF-RE)"
(ENTRY 250) AFTER J'ONN MADE HIS ANNOUNCEMENT (SEE ENTRY 248) HE STARTED WALKING TOWARD WHAT'S TECHNICALLY CALLED THE CONFLAGRATION AREA. EITHER HE'S IN SOME KIND OF SHOCK OR HE'S DELIBERATELY ENDURING THE PRESENCE OF SO MUCH FLAME FOR REASONS OF HIS OWN.
I DIDN'T FOLLOW. I WENT BACK TO THE BUG FOR MY RADIATION ARMOR.
THE REMOTE PROBE (BABYBUG) IS REGISTERING LETHAL REMS IN THE (11078) LEVEL AS IT APPROACHES GROUND ZERO.
THERE'S A CRATER 3 BLOCKS IN DIAMETER AND *** (DELETE)
AND MONTEVIDEO IS GONE.

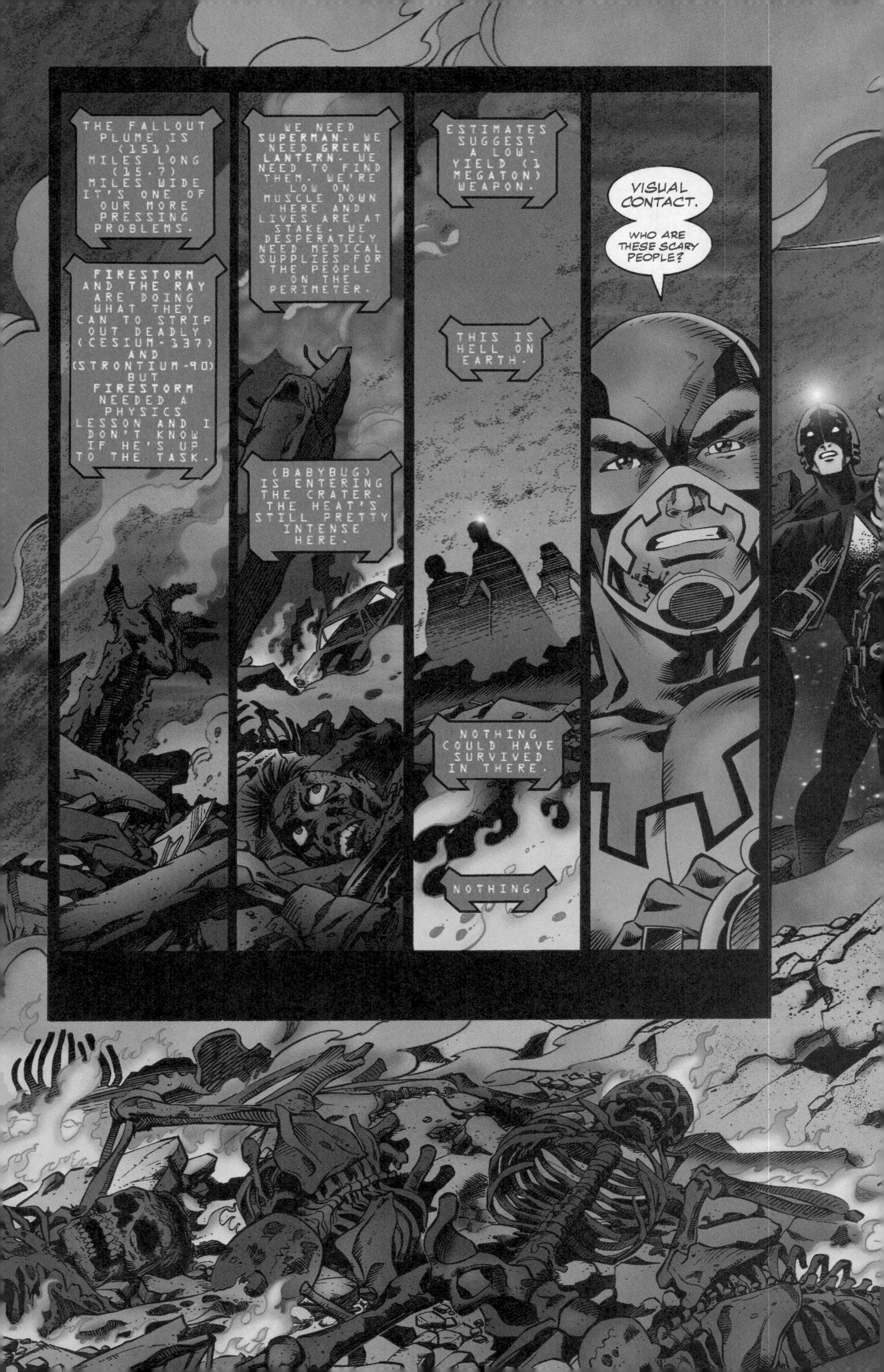
THE FALLOUT PLUME IS (151) MILES LONG (15.7) MILES WIDE IT'S ONE OF OUR MORE PRESSING PROBLEMS.
FIRESTORM AND THE RAY ARE DOING WHAT THEY CAN TO STRIP OUT DEADLY (CESIUM-137) AND (STRONTIUM-90) BUT FIRESTORM NEEDED A PHYSICS LESSON AND I DON'T KNOW IF HE'S UP TO THE TASK.
WE NEED SUPERMAN. WE NEED GREEN LANTERN. WE NEED TO FIND THEM. WE'RE LOW ON MUSCLE DOWN HERE AND LIVES ARE AT STAKE. WE DESPERATELY NEED MEDICAL SUPPLIES FOR THE PEOPLE ON THE PERIMETER.
(BABYBUG) IS ENTERING THE CRATER. THE HEAT'S STILL PRETTY INTENSE HERE.
ESTIMATES SUGGEST A LOW-YIELD (1 MEGATON) WEAPON.
THIS IS HELL ON EARTH.
NOTHING COULD HAVE SURVIVED IN THERE.
NOTHING.
VISUAL CONTACT.
WHO ARE THESE SCARY PEOPLE?

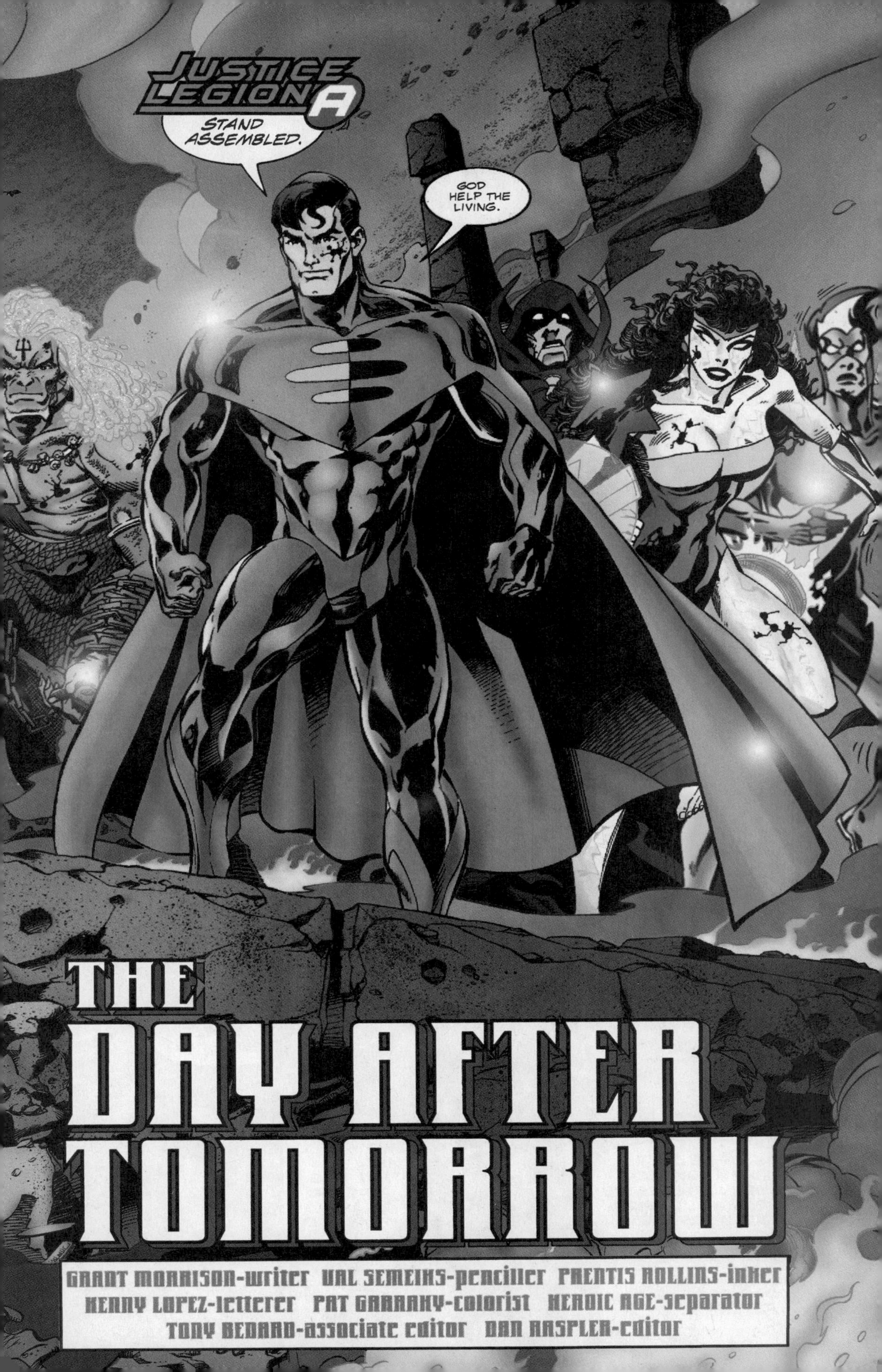
JUSTICE LEGION A
STAND ASSEMBLED.
GOD HELP THE LIVING.
THE DAY AFTER TOMORROW
GRANT MORRISON-writer VAL SEMEIKS-penciller PRENTIS ROLLINS-inker
KENNY LOPEZ-letterer PAT GARRAHY-colorist HEROIC AGE-separator
TONY BEDARD-associate editor DAN RASPLER-editor

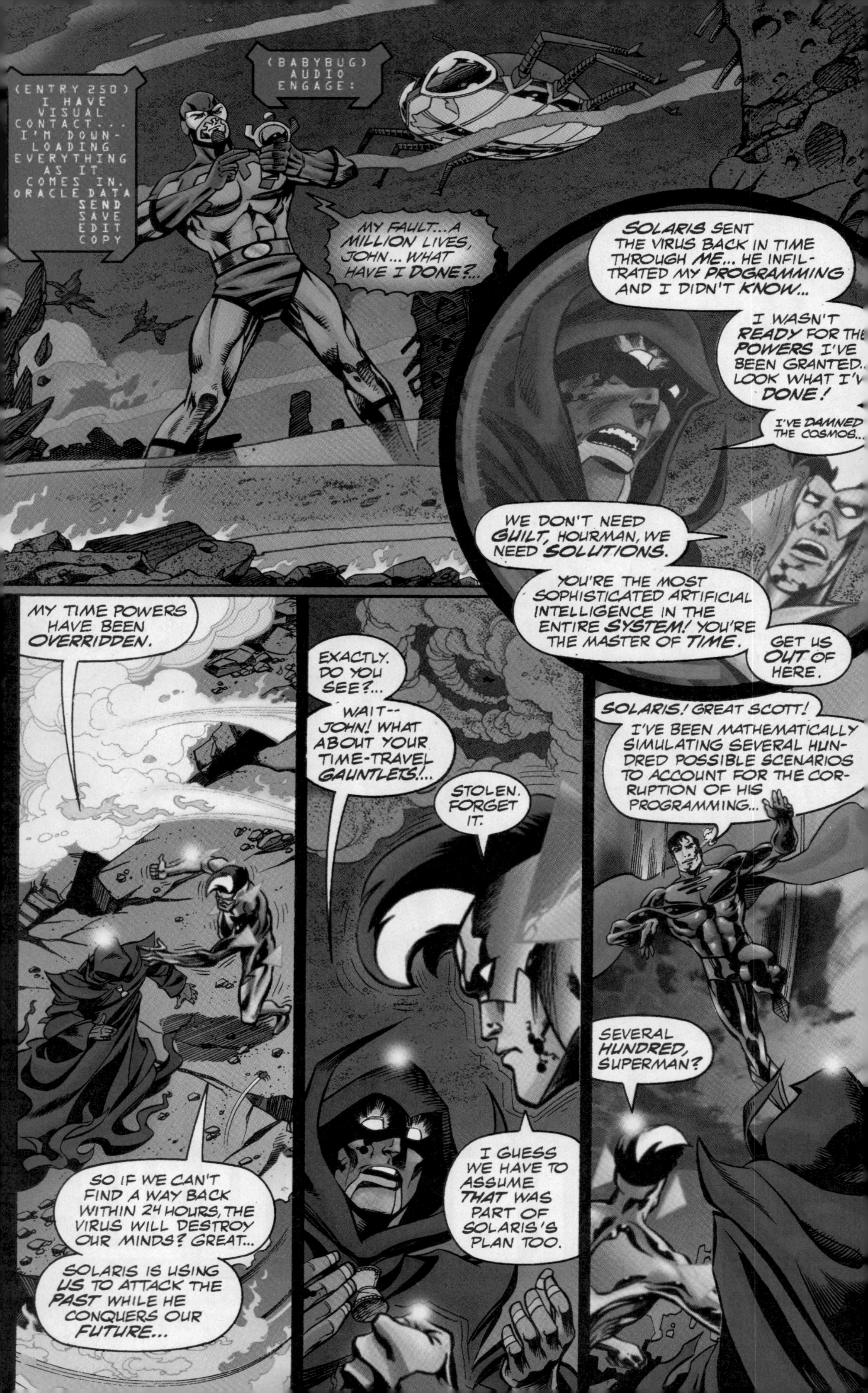
(ENTRY 250) I HAVE VISUAL CONTACT... I'M DOWN-LOADING EVERYTHING AS IT COMES IN. ORACLE DATA SEND SAVE EDIT COPY
(BABYBUG) AUDIO ENGAGE:
MY FAULT...A MILLION LIVES, JOHN... WHAT HAVE I DONE?...
SOLARIS SENT THE VIRUS BACK IN TIME THROUGH ME... HE INFIL-TRATED MY PROGRAMMING AND I DIDN'T KNOW...
I WASN'T READY FOR THE POWERS I'VE BEEN GRANTED... LOOK WHAT I'VE DONE!
I'VE DAMNED THE COSMOS...
WE DON'T NEED GUILT, HOURMAN, WE NEED SOLUTIONS.
YOU'RE THE MOST SOPHISTICATED ARTIFICIAL INTELLIGENCE IN THE ENTIRE SYSTEM! YOU'RE THE MASTER OF TIME.
GET US OUT OF HERE.
MY TIME POWERS HAVE BEEN OVERRIDDEN.
SO IF WE CAN'T FIND A WAY BACK WITHIN 24 HOURS, THE VIRUS WILL DESTROY OUR MINDS? GREAT...
SOLARIS IS USING US TO ATTACK THE PAST WHILE HE CONQUERS OUR FUTURE...
EXACTLY. DO YOU SEE?...
WAIT-- JOHN! WHAT ABOUT YOUR TIME-TRAVEL GAUNTLETS!...
STOLEN. FORGET IT.
I GUESS WE HAVE TO ASSUME THAT WAS PART OF SOLARIS'S PLAN TOO.
SOLARIS! GREAT SCOTT!
I'VE BEEN MATHEMATICALLY SIMULATING SEVERAL HUN-DRED POSSIBLE SCENARIOS TO ACCOUNT FOR THE COR-RUPTION OF HIS PROGRAMMING...
SEVERAL HUNDRED, SUPERMAN?

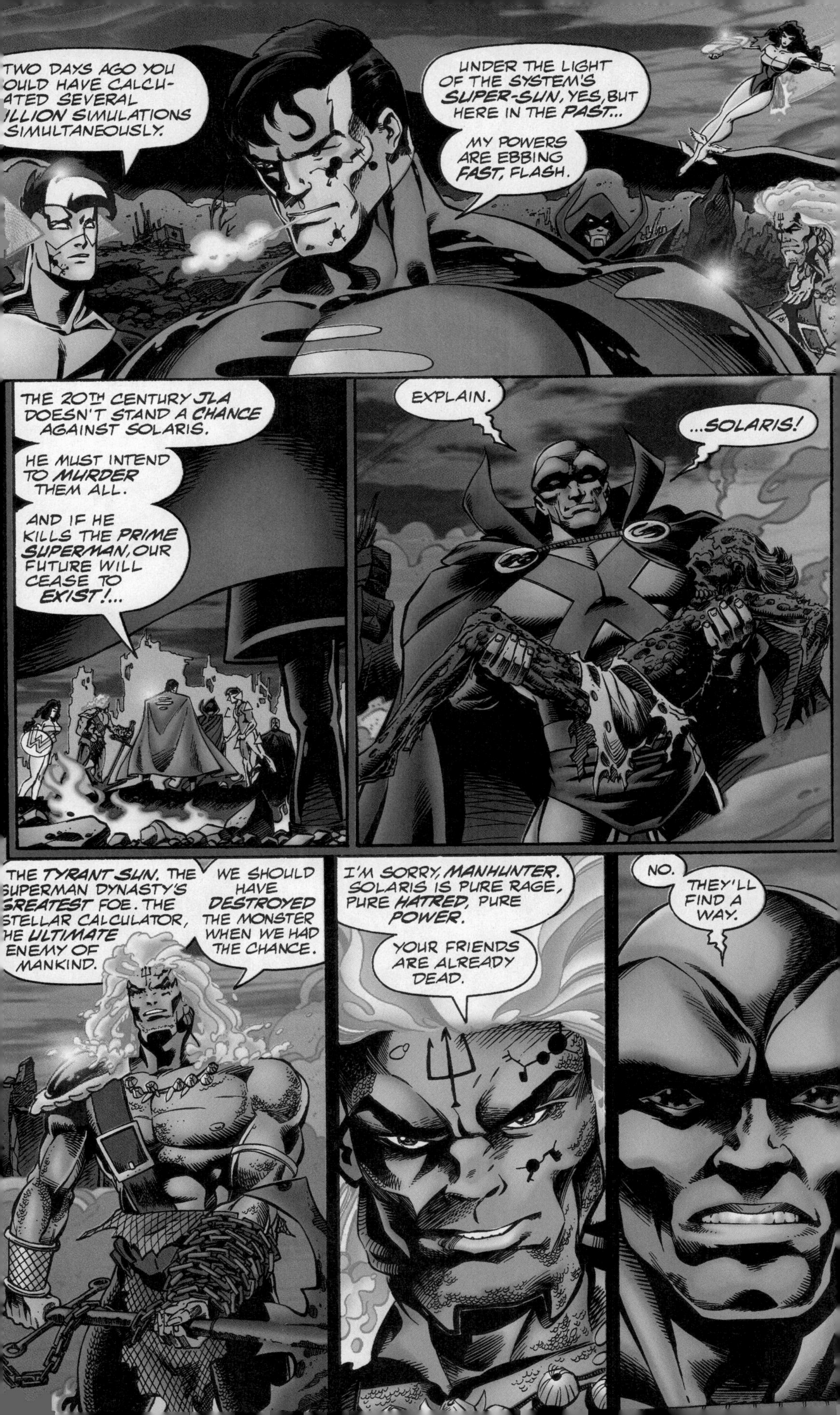

TWO DAYS AGO YOU OULD HAVE CALCU-ATED SEVERAL ILLION SIMULATIONS SIMULTANEOUSLY.
UNDER THE LIGHT OF THE SYSTEM'S SUPER-SUN, YES, BUT HERE IN THE PAST...
MY POWERS ARE EBBING FAST, FLASH.
THE 20TH CENTURY JLA DOESN'T STAND A CHANCE AGAINST SOLARIS.
HE MUST INTEND TO MURDER THEM ALL.
AND IF HE KILLS THE PRIME SUPERMAN, OUR FUTURE WILL CEASE TO EXIST!...
EXPLAIN.
...SOLARIS!
THE TYRANT SUN. THE SUPERMAN DYNASTY'S GREATEST FOE. THE STELLAR CALCULATOR, HE ULTIMATE ENEMY OF MANKIND.
WE SHOULD HAVE DESTROYED THE MONSTER WHEN WE HAD THE CHANCE.
I'M SORRY, MANHUNTER. SOLARIS IS PURE RAGE, PURE HATRED, PURE POWER.
YOUR FRIENDS ARE ALREADY DEAD.
NO.
THEY'LL FIND A WAY.

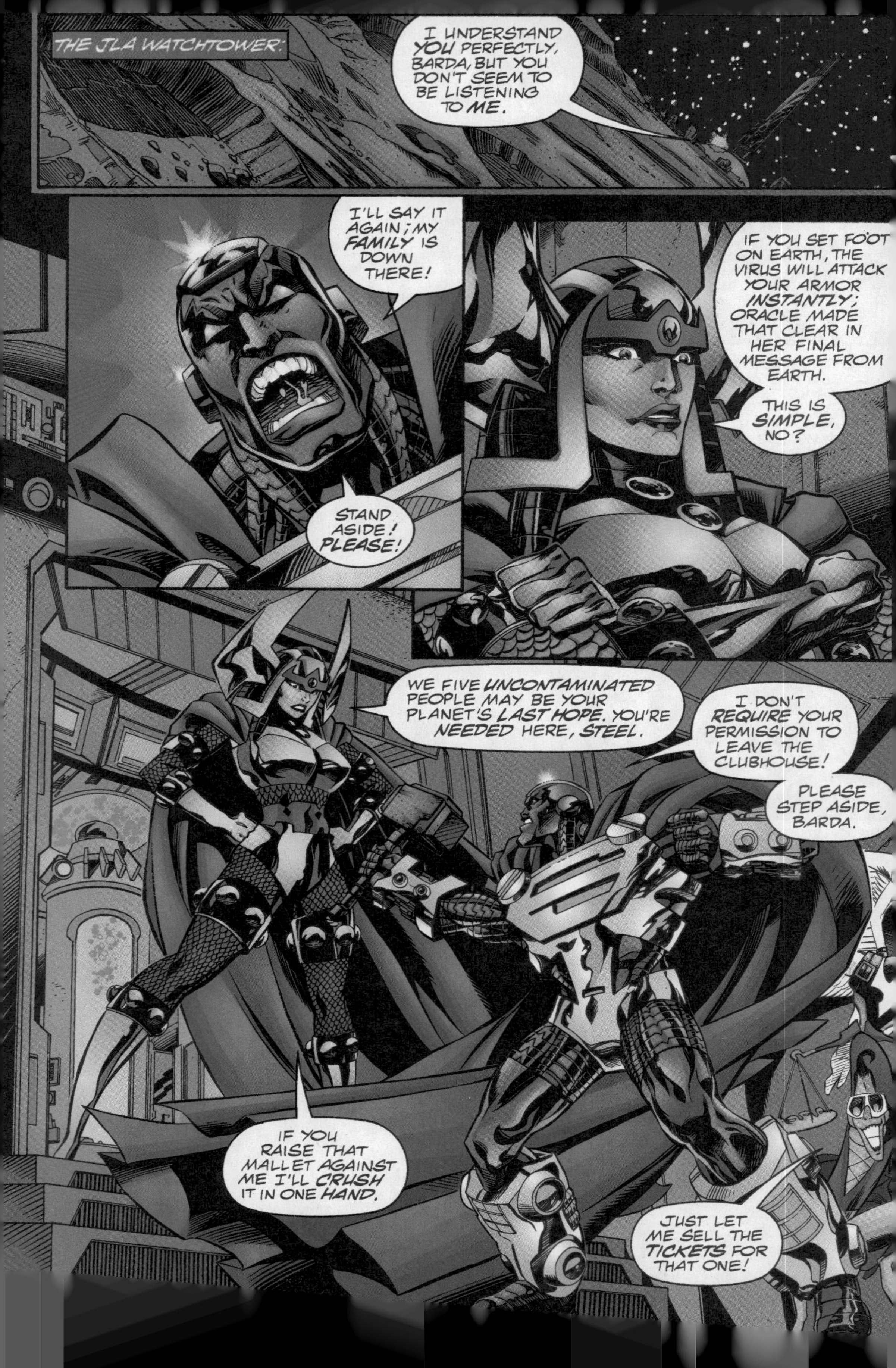
THE JLA WATCHTOWER:
I UNDERSTAND YOU PERFECTLY, BARDA, BUT YOU DON'T SEEM TO BE LISTENING TO ME.
I'LL SAY IT AGAIN; MY FAMILY IS DOWN THERE!
STAND ASIDE! PLEASE!
IF YOU SET FOOT ON EARTH, THE VIRUS WILL ATTACK YOUR ARMOR INSTANTLY; ORACLE MADE THAT CLEAR IN HER FINAL MESSAGE FROM EARTH.
THIS IS SIMPLE, NO?
WE FIVE UNCONTAMINATED PEOPLE MAY BE YOUR PLANET'S LAST HOPE. YOU'RE NEEDED HERE, STEEL.
I DON'T REQUIRE YOUR PERMISSION TO LEAVE THE CLUBHOUSE!
PLEASE STEP ASIDE, BARDA.
IF YOU RAISE THAT MALLET AGAINST ME I'LL CRUSH IT IN ONE HAND.
JUST LET ME SELL THE TICKETS FOR THAT ONE!

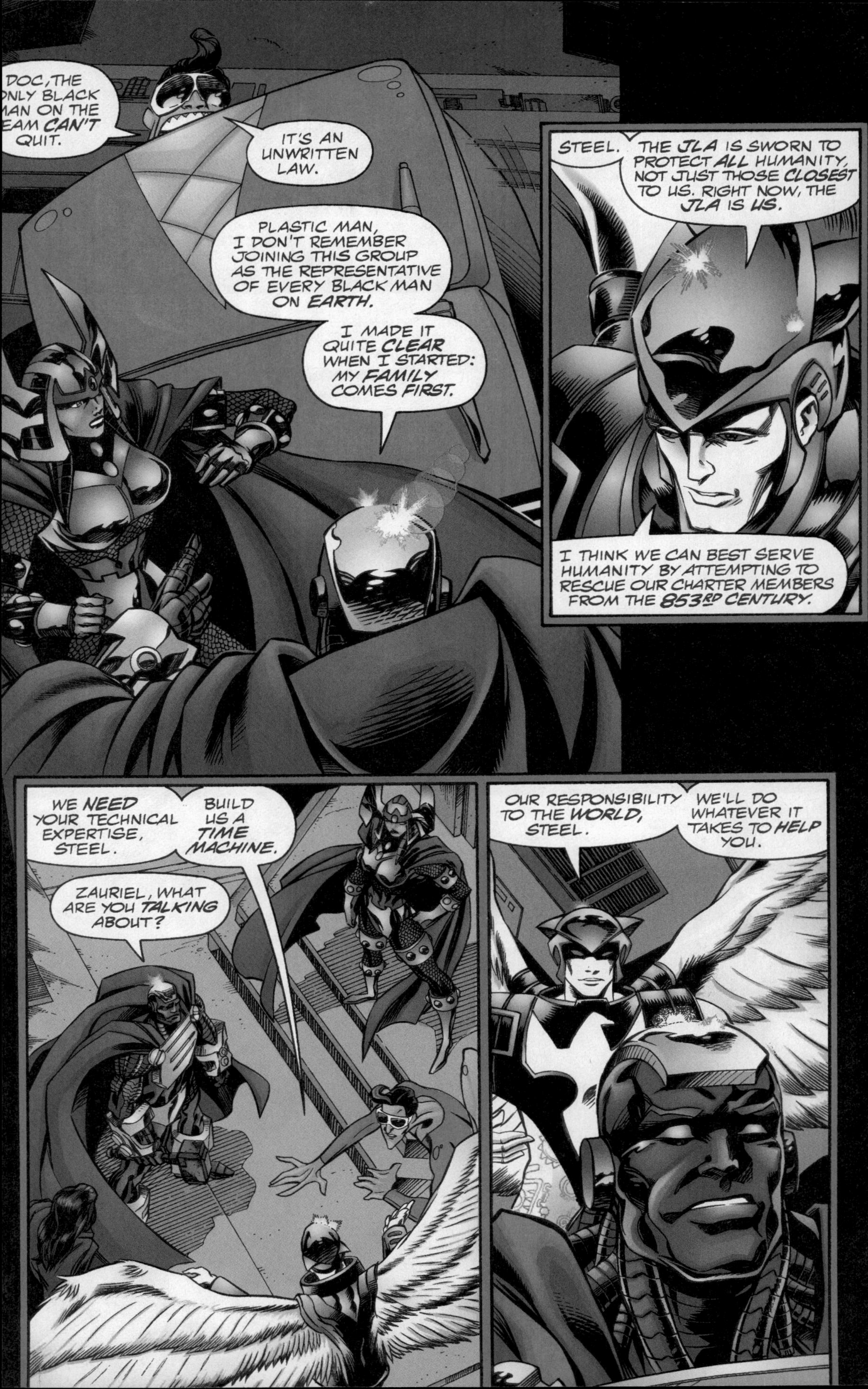
DOC, THE ONLY BLACK MAN ON THE TEAM CAN'T QUIT.
IT'S AN UNWRITTEN LAW.
PLASTIC MAN, I DON'T REMEMBER JOINING THIS GROUP AS THE REPRESENTATIVE OF EVERY BLACK MAN ON EARTH.
I MADE IT QUITE CLEAR WHEN I STARTED: MY FAMILY COMES FIRST.
STEEL.
THE JLA IS SWORN TO PROTECT ALL HUMANITY, NOT JUST THOSE CLOSEST TO US. RIGHT NOW, THE JLA IS US.
I THINK WE CAN BEST SERVE HUMANITY BY ATTEMPTING TO RESCUE OUR CHARTER MEMBERS FROM THE 853RD CENTURY.
WE NEED YOUR TECHNICAL EXPERTISE, STEEL.
BUILD US A TIME MACHINE.
ZAURIEL, WHAT ARE YOU TALKING ABOUT?
OUR RESPONSIBILITY TO THE WORLD, STEEL.
WE'LL DO WHATEVER IT TAKES TO HELP YOU.

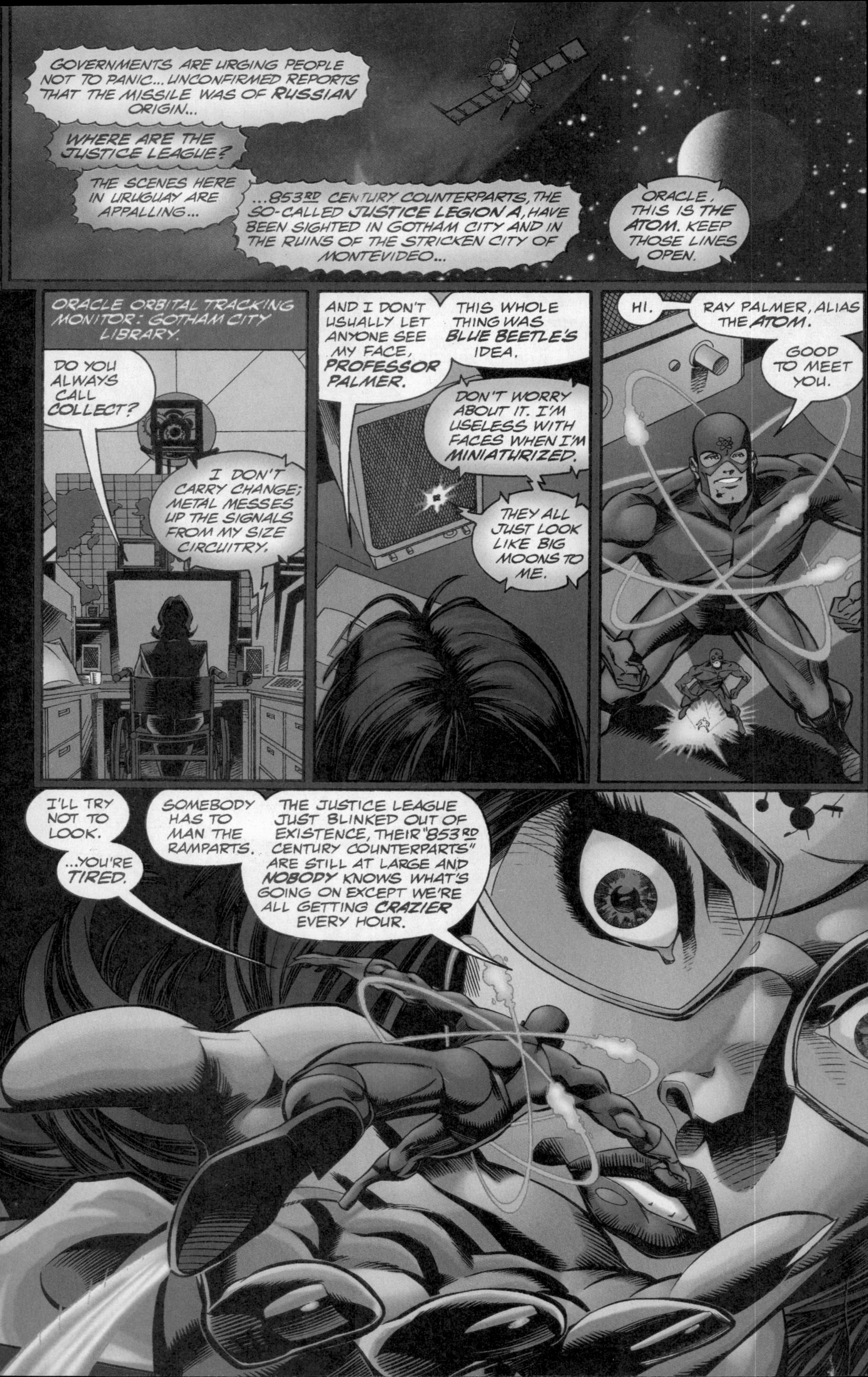
GOVERNMENTS ARE URGING PEOPLE NOT TO PANIC... UNCONFIRMED REPORTS THAT THE MISSILE WAS OF RUSSIAN ORIGIN...
WHERE ARE THE JUSTICE LEAGUE?
THE SCENES HERE IN URUGUAY ARE APPALLING...
...853RD CENTURY COUNTERPARTS, THE SO-CALLED JUSTICE LEGION A, HAVE BEEN SIGHTED IN GOTHAM CITY AND IN THE RUINS OF THE STRICKEN CITY OF MONTEVIDEO...
ORACLE, THIS IS THE ATOM. KEEP THOSE LINES OPEN.
ORACLE ORBITAL TRACKING MONITOR: GOTHAM CITY LIBRARY.
DO YOU ALWAYS CALL COLLECT?
I DON'T CARRY CHANGE; METAL MESSES UP THE SIGNALS FROM MY SIZE CIRCUITRY.
AND I DON'T USUALLY LET ANYONE SEE MY FACE, PROFESSOR PALMER.
THIS WHOLE THING WAS BLUE BEETLE'S IDEA.
DON'T WORRY ABOUT IT. I'M USELESS WITH FACES WHEN I'M MINIATURIZED.
THEY ALL JUST LOOK LIKE BIG MOONS TO ME.
HI.
RAY PALMER, ALIAS THE ATOM.
GOOD TO MEET YOU.
I'LL TRY NOT TO LOOK.
...YOU'RE TIRED.
SOMEBODY HAS TO MAN THE RAMPARTS.
THE JUSTICE LEAGUE JUST BLINKED OUT OF EXISTENCE, THEIR "853RD CENTURY COUNTERPARTS" ARE STILL AT LARGE AND NOBODY KNOWS WHAT'S GOING ON EXCEPT WE'RE ALL GETTING CRAZIER EVERY HOUR.

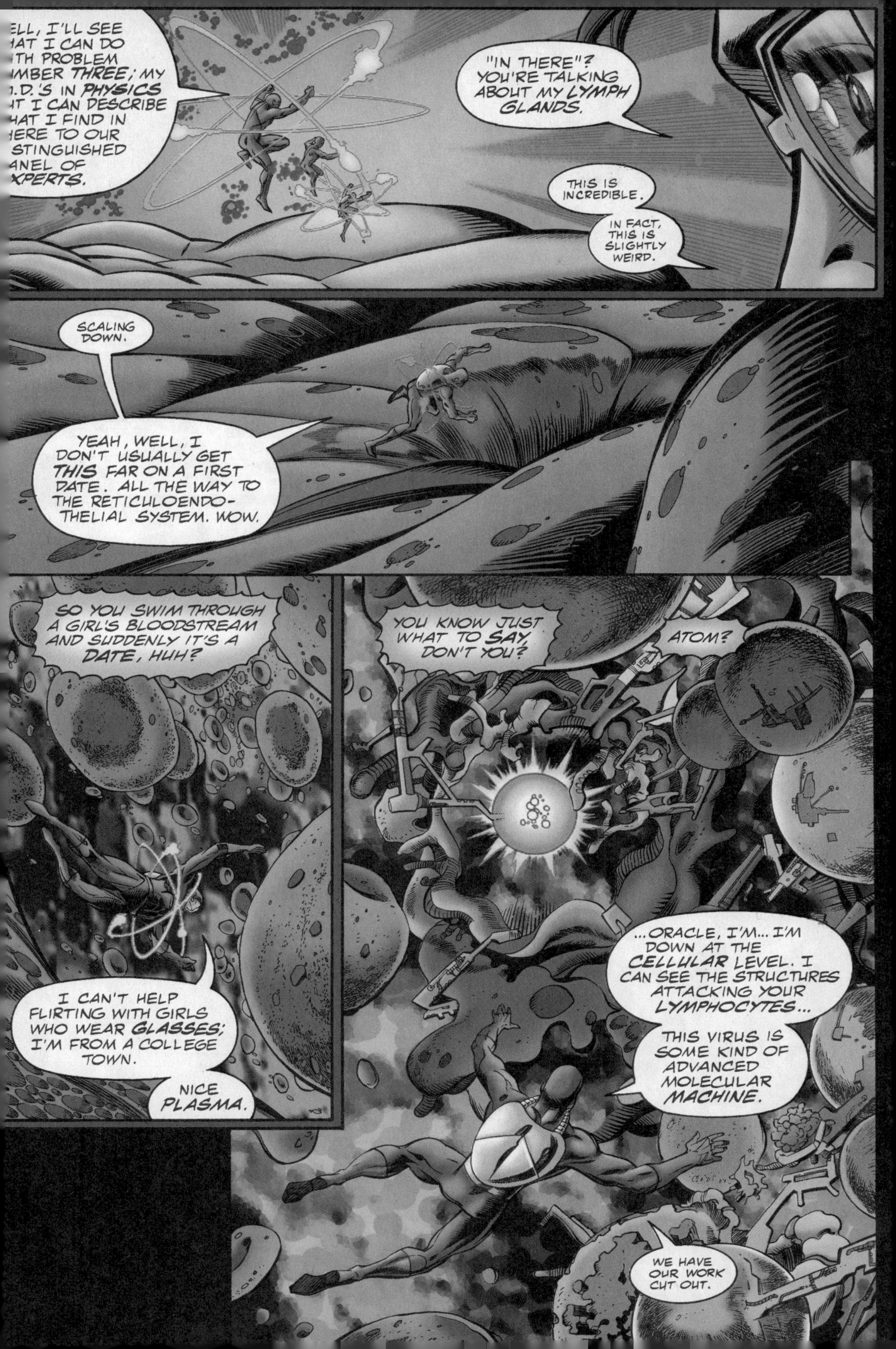
ELL, I'LL SEE HAT I CAN DO ITH PROBLEM UMBER THREE; MY D.D.'S IN PHYSICS HT I CAN DESCRIBE HAT I FIND IN HERE TO OUR STINGUISHED ANEL OF XPERTS.
"IN THERE"? YOU'RE TALKING ABOUT MY LYMPH GLANDS.
THIS IS INCREDIBLE.
IN FACT, THIS IS SLIGHTLY WEIRD.
SCALING DOWN.
YEAH, WELL, I DON'T USUALLY GET THIS FAR ON A FIRST DATE. ALL THE WAY TO THE RETICULOENDO-THELIAL SYSTEM. WOW.
SO YOU SWIM THROUGH A GIRL'S BLOODSTREAM AND SUDDENLY IT'S A DATE, HUH?
I CAN'T HELP FLIRTING WITH GIRLS WHO WEAR GLASSES; I'M FROM A COLLEGE TOWN.
NICE PLASMA.
YOU KNOW JUST WHAT TO SAY, DON'T YOU?
ATOM?
...ORACLE, I'M... I'M DOWN AT THE CELLULAR LEVEL. I CAN SEE THE STRUCTURES ATTACKING YOUR LYMPHOCYTES...
THIS VIRUS IS SOME KIND OF ADVANCED MOLECULAR MACHINE.
WE HAVE OUR WORK CUT OUT.

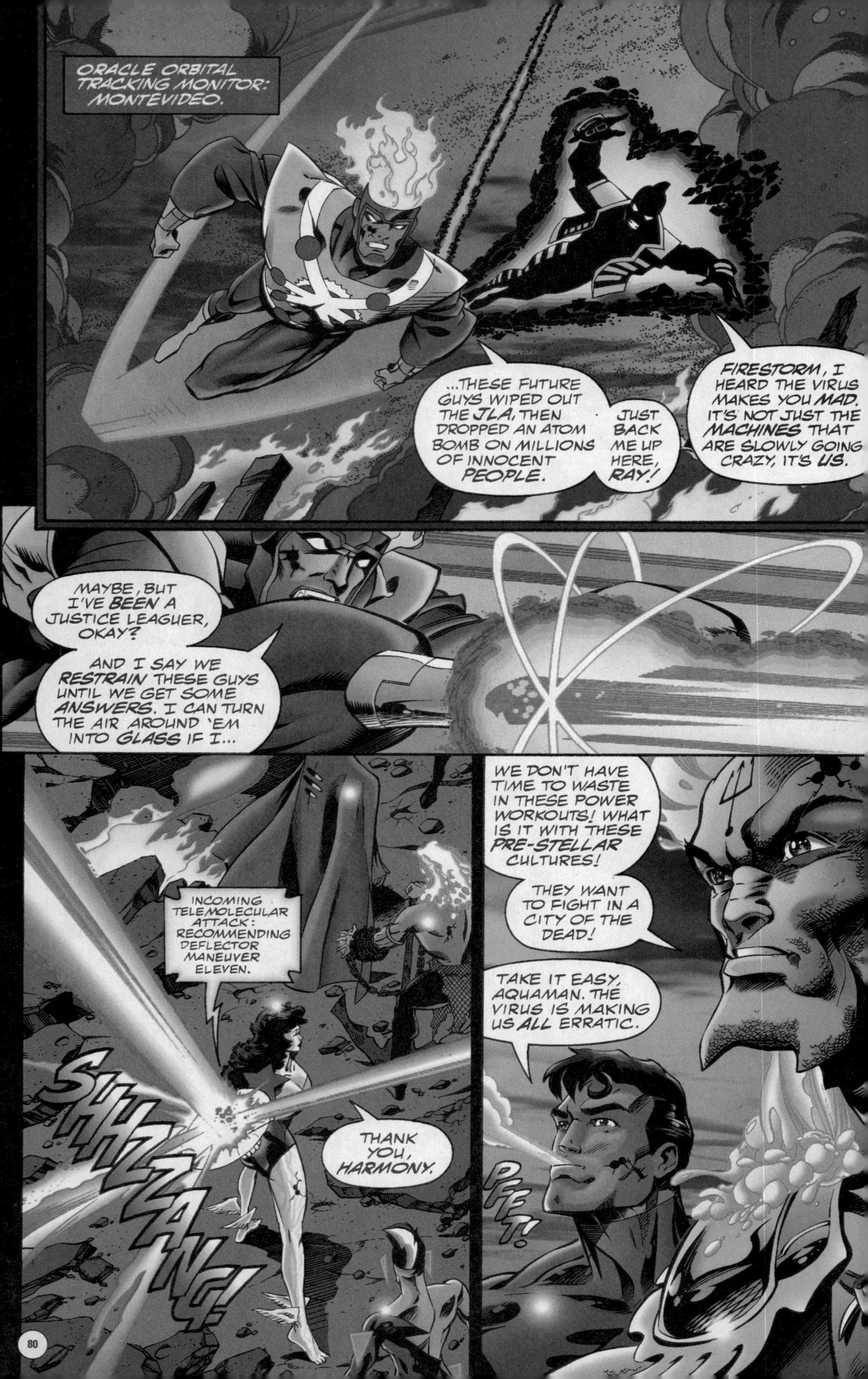

ORACLE ORBITAL TRACKING MONITOR: MONTEVIDEO.
...THESE FUTURE GUYS WIPED OUT THE JLA, THEN DROPPED AN ATOM BOMB ON MILLIONS OF INNOCENT PEOPLE.
JUST BACK ME UP HERE, RAY!
FIRESTORM, I HEARD THE VIRUS MAKES YOU MAD. IT'S NOT JUST THE MACHINES THAT ARE SLOWLY GOING CRAZY, IT'S US.
MAYBE, BUT I'VE BEEN A JUSTICE LEAGUER, OKAY?
AND I SAY WE RESTRAIN THESE GUYS UNTIL WE GET SOME ANSWERS. I CAN TURN THE AIR AROUND 'EM INTO GLASS IF I...
INCOMING TELEMOLECULAR ATTACK: RECOMMENDING DEFLECTOR MANEUVER ELEVEN.
SHHZZANG!
THANK YOU, HARMONY.
WE DON'T HAVE TIME TO WASTE IN THESE POWER WORKOUTS! WHAT IS IT WITH THESE PRE-STELLAR CULTURES!
THEY WANT TO FIGHT IN A CITY OF THE DEAD!
TAKE IT EASY, AQUAMAN. THE VIRUS IS MAKING US ALL ERRATIC.
PFFT!

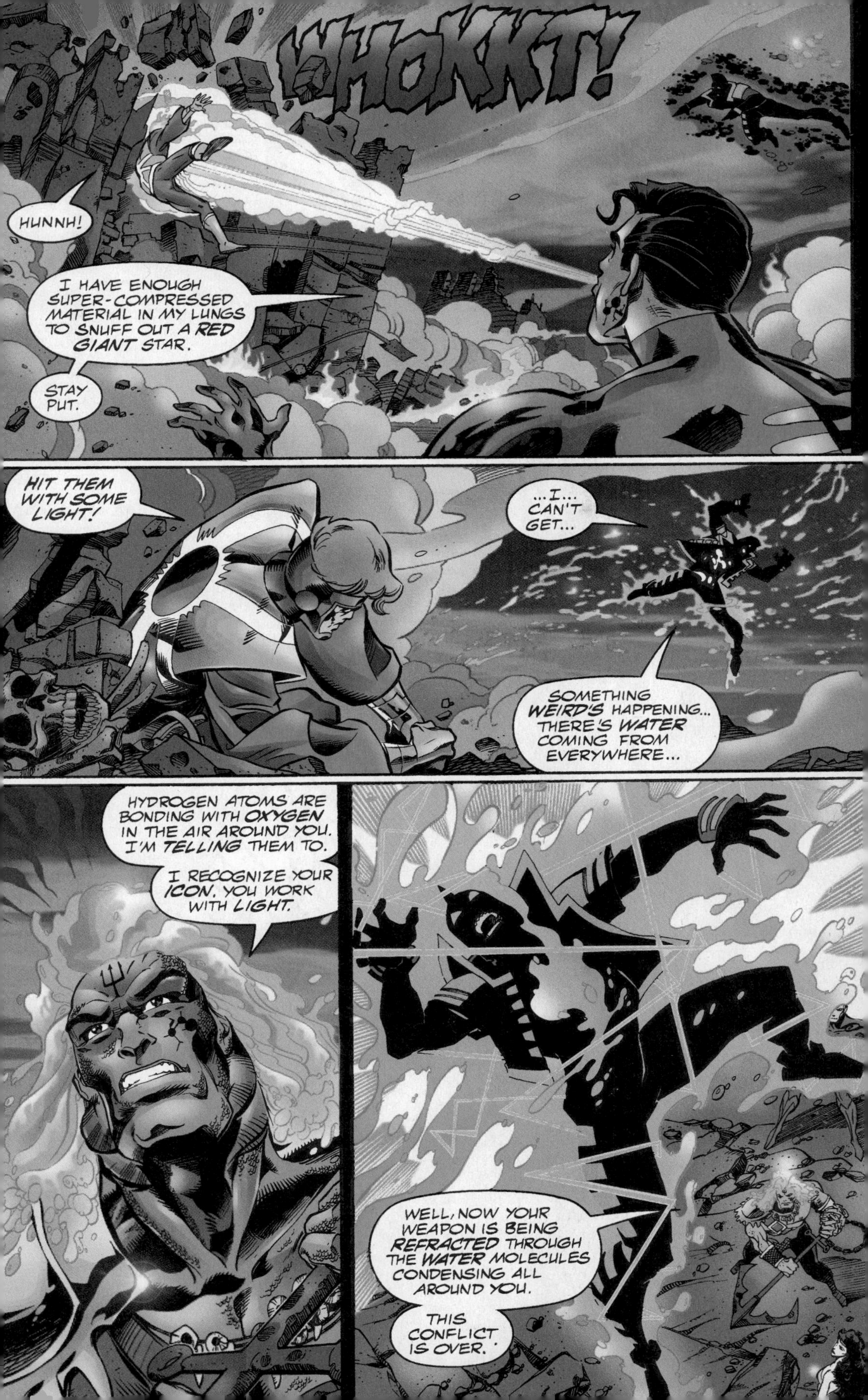
WHOKKT!
HUNNH!
I HAVE ENOUGH SUPER-COMPRESSED MATERIAL IN MY LUNGS TO SNUFF OUT A RED GIANT STAR.
STAY PUT.
HIT THEM WITH SOME LIGHT!
...I... CAN'T GET...
SOMETHING WEIRD'S HAPPENING... THERE'S WATER COMING FROM EVERYWHERE...
HYDROGEN ATOMS ARE BONDING WITH OXYGEN IN THE AIR AROUND YOU. I'M TELLING THEM TO.
I RECOGNIZE YOUR ICON. YOU WORK WITH LIGHT.
WELL, NOW YOUR WEAPON IS BEING REFRACTED THROUGH THE WATER MOLECULES CONDENSING ALL AROUND YOU.
THIS CONFLICT IS OVER.

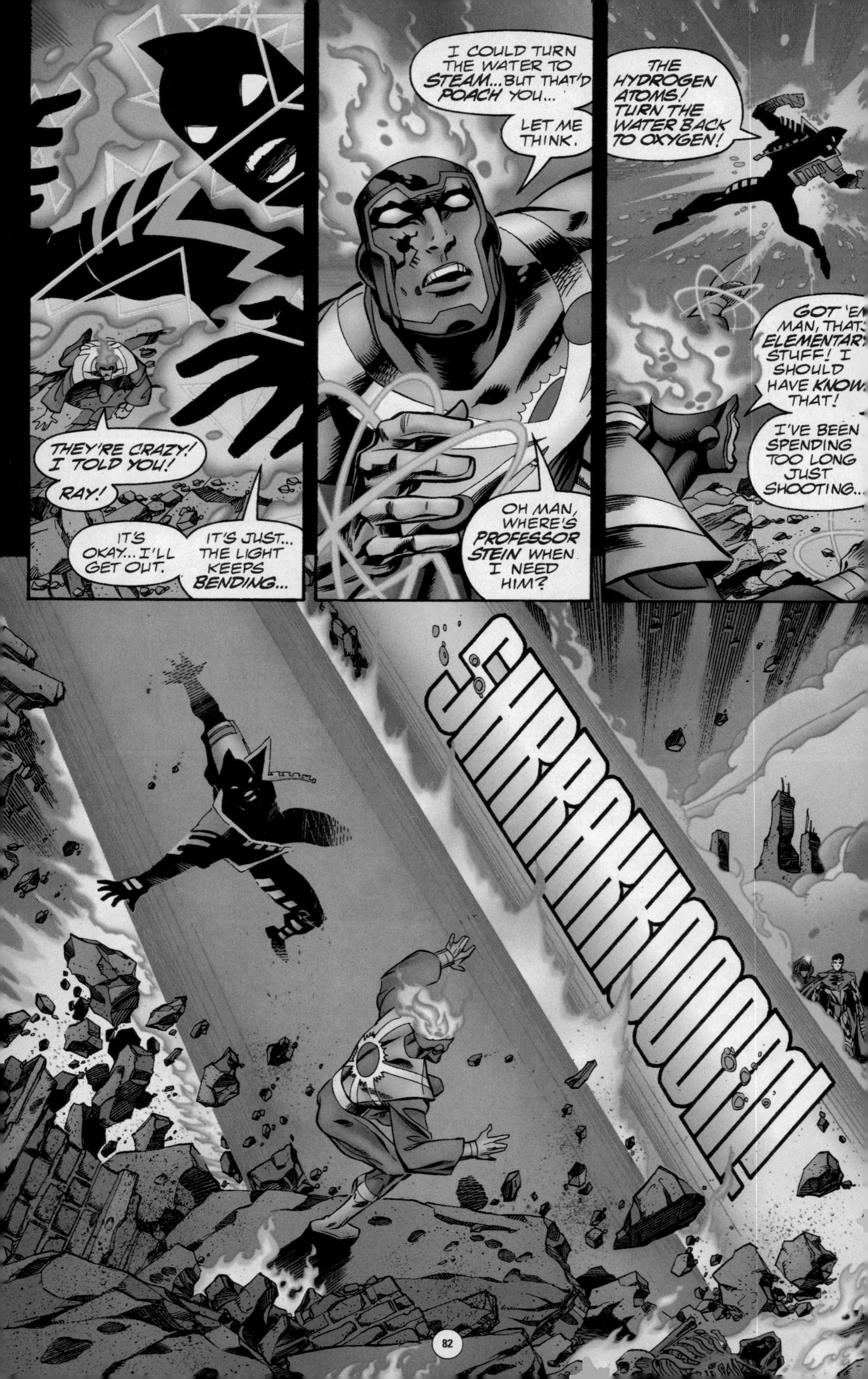
THEY'RE CRAZY! I TOLD YOU!
RAY!
IT'S OKAY...I'LL GET OUT.
IT'S JUST... THE LIGHT KEEPS BENDING...
I COULD TURN THE WATER TO STEAM...BUT THAT'D POACH YOU...
LET ME THINK.
OH MAN, WHERE'S PROFESSOR STEIN WHEN I NEED HIM?
THE HYDROGEN ATOMS! TURN THE WATER BACK TO OXYGEN!
GOT 'EM MAN, THAT'S ELEMENTAR STUFF! I SHOULD HAVE KNOW THAT!
I'VE BEEN SPENDING TOO LONG JUST SHOOTING...
SHRRAKOOOM!

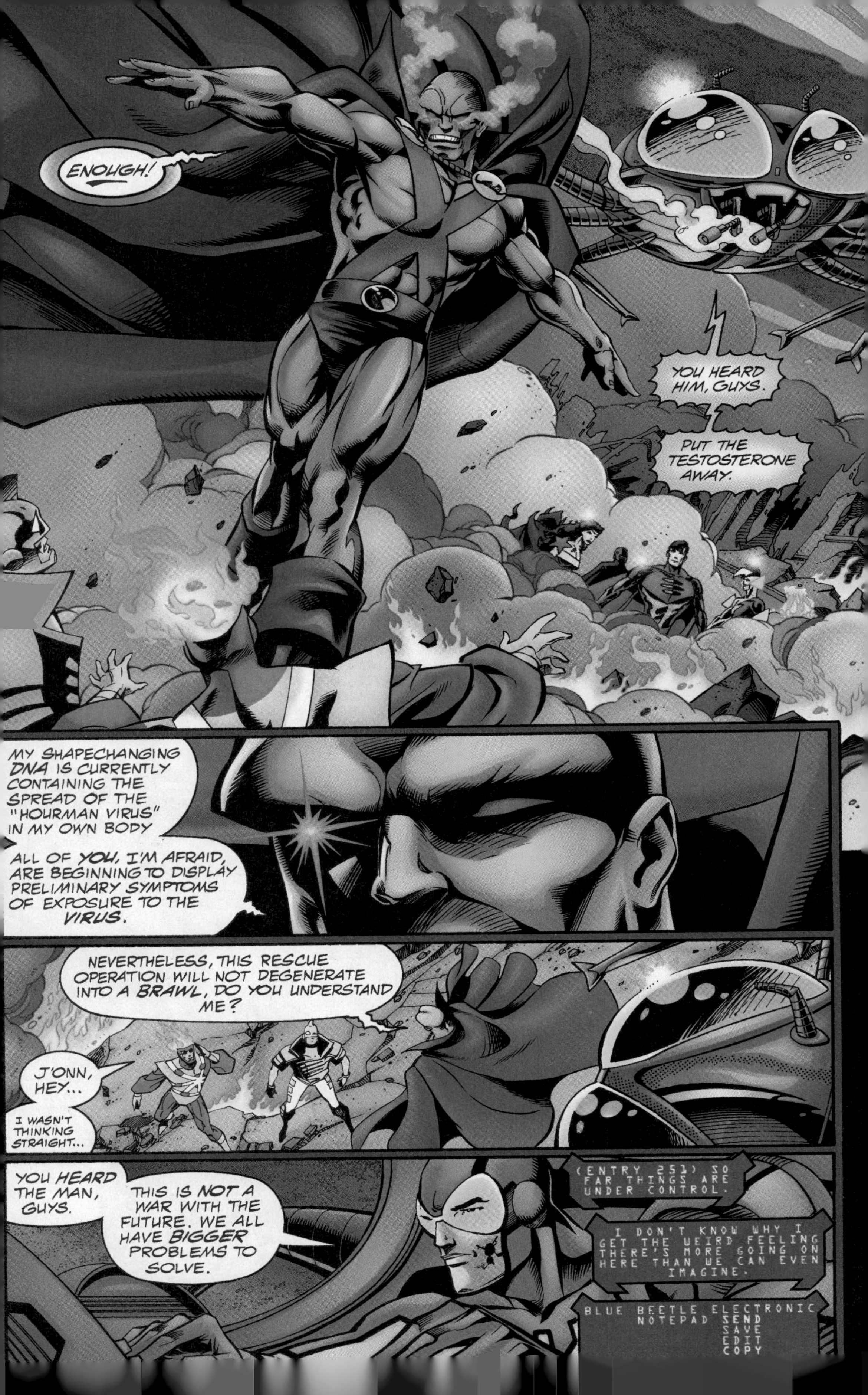
ENOUGH!
YOU HEARD HIM, GUYS.
PUT THE TESTOSTERONE AWAY.
MY SHAPECHANGING DNA IS CURRENTLY CONTAINING THE SPREAD OF THE "HOURMAN VIRUS" IN MY OWN BODY
ALL OF YOU, I'M AFRAID, ARE BEGINNING TO DISPLAY PRELIMINARY SYMPTOMS OF EXPOSURE TO THE VIRUS.
NEVERTHELESS, THIS RESCUE OPERATION WILL NOT DEGENERATE INTO A BRAWL, DO YOU UNDERSTAND ME?
J'ONN, HEY...
I WASN'T THINKING STRAIGHT...
YOU HEARD THE MAN, GUYS.
THIS IS NOT A WAR WITH THE FUTURE. WE ALL HAVE BIGGER PROBLEMS TO SOLVE.
(ENTRY 251) SO FAR THINGS ARE UNDER CONTROL.
I DON'T KNOW WHY I GET THE WEIRD FEELING THERE'S MORE GOING ON HERE THAN WE CAN EVEN IMAGINE.
BLUE BEETLE ELECTRONIC NOTEPAD
SEND
SAVE
EDIT
COPY

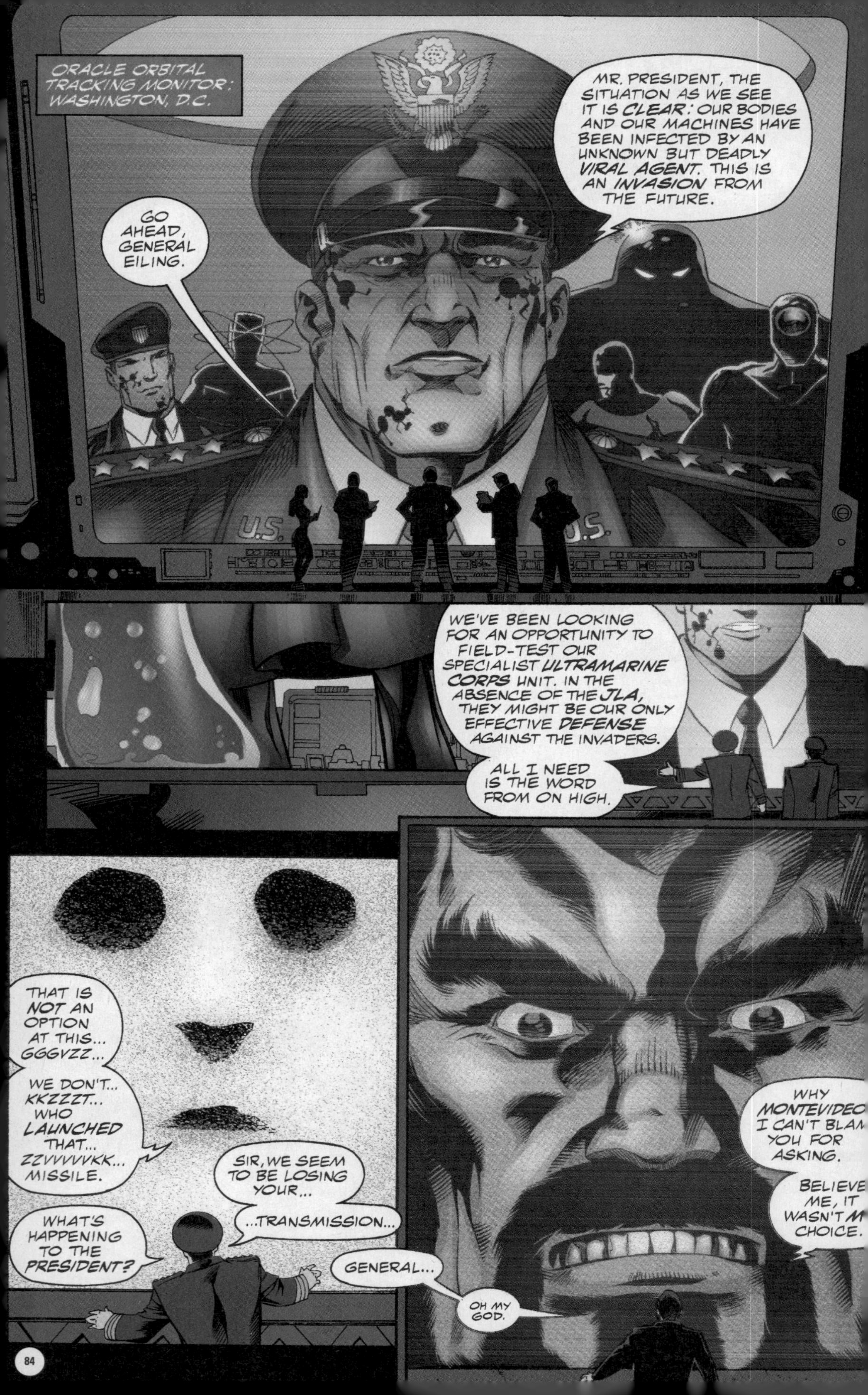
ORACLE ORBITAL TRACKING MONITOR: WASHINGTON, D.C.
GO AHEAD, GENERAL EILING.
MR. PRESIDENT, THE SITUATION AS WE SEE IT IS CLEAR: OUR BODIES AND OUR MACHINES HAVE BEEN INFECTED BY AN UNKNOWN BUT DEADLY VIRAL AGENT. THIS IS AN INVASION FROM THE FUTURE.
WE'VE BEEN LOOKING FOR AN OPPORTUNITY TO FIELD-TEST OUR SPECIALIST ULTRAMARINE CORPS UNIT. IN THE ABSENCE OF THE JLA, THEY MIGHT BE OUR ONLY EFFECTIVE DEFENSE AGAINST THE INVADERS.
ALL I NEED IS THE WORD FROM ON HIGH.
THAT IS NOT AN OPTION AT THIS... GGGVZZ...
WE DON'T... KKZZZT... WHO LAUNCHED THAT... ZZVVVVVKK... MISSILE.
SIR, WE SEEM TO BE LOSING YOUR...
...TRANSMISSION...
WHAT'S HAPPENING TO THE PRESIDENT?
GENERAL...
OH MY GOD.
WHY MONTEVIDEO I CAN'T BLAM YOU FOR ASKING.
BELIEVE ME, IT WASN'T M CHOICE.

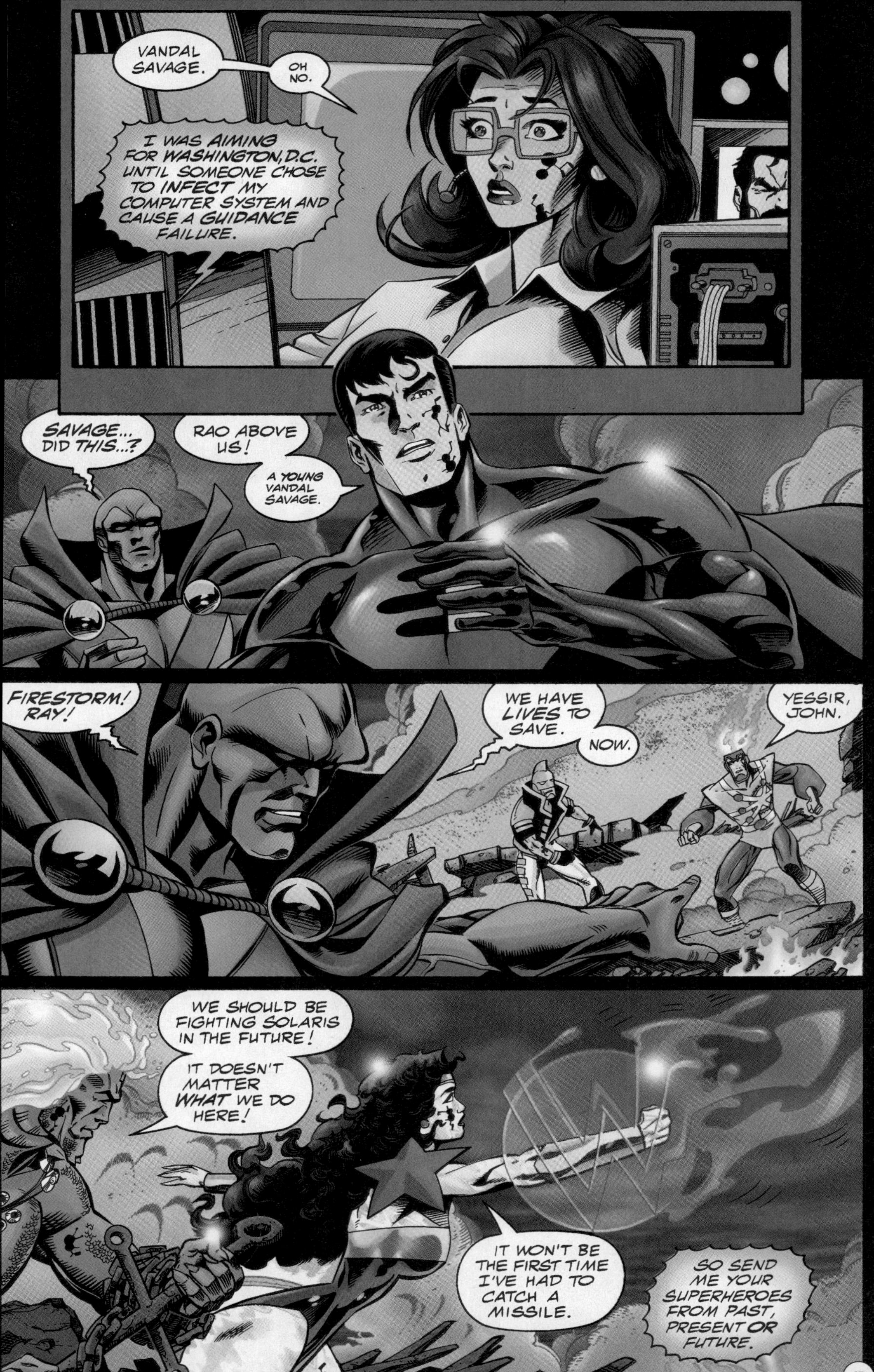
VANDAL SAVAGE.
OH NO.
I WAS AIMING FOR WASHINGTON, D.C. UNTIL SOMEONE CHOSE TO INFECT MY COMPUTER SYSTEM AND CAUSE A GUIDANCE FAILURE.
SAVAGE... DID THIS...?
RAO ABOVE US!
A YOUNG VANDAL SAVAGE.
FIRESTORM! RAY!
WE HAVE LIVES TO SAVE.
NOW.
YESSIR, JOHN.
WE SHOULD BE FIGHTING SOLARIS IN THE FUTURE!
IT DOESN'T MATTER WHAT WE DO HERE!
IT WON'T BE THE FIRST TIME I'VE HAD TO CATCH A MISSILE.
SO SEND ME YOUR SUPERHEROES FROM PAST, PRESENT OR FUTURE.

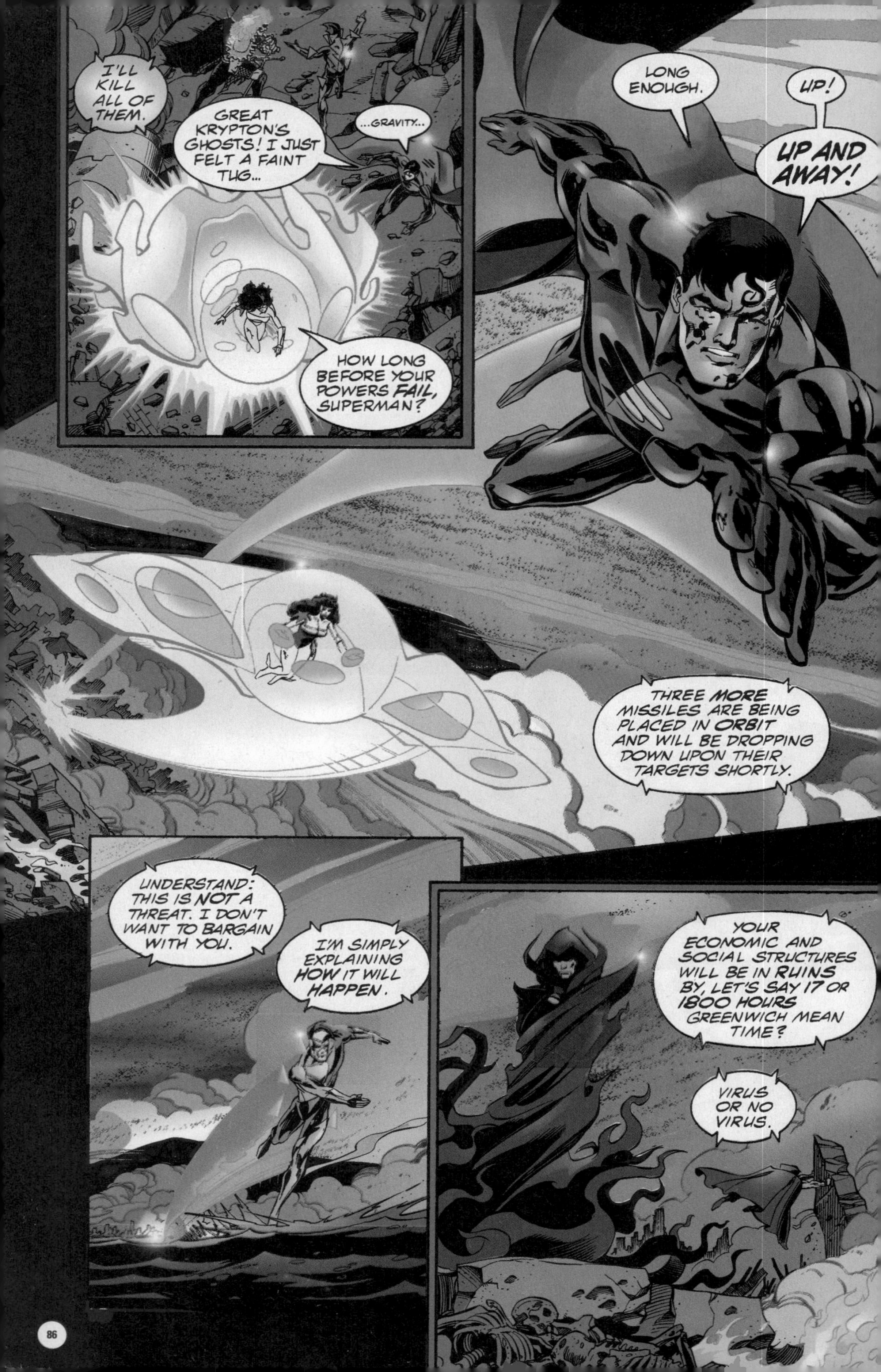
I'LL KILL ALL OF THEM.
GREAT KRYPTON'S GHOSTS! I JUST FELT A FAINT TUG...
...GRAVITY...
HOW LONG BEFORE YOUR POWERS FAIL, SUPERMAN?
LONG ENOUGH.
UP!
UP AND AWAY!
THREE MORE MISSILES ARE BEING PLACED IN ORBIT AND WILL BE DROPPING DOWN UPON THEIR TARGETS SHORTLY.
UNDERSTAND: THIS IS NOT A THREAT. I DON'T WANT TO BARGAIN WITH YOU.
I'M SIMPLY EXPLAINING HOW IT WILL HAPPEN.
YOUR ECONOMIC AND SOCIAL STRUCTURES WILL BE IN RUINS BY, LET'S SAY 17 OR 1800 HOURS GREENWICH MEAN TIME?
VIRUS OR NO VIRUS.

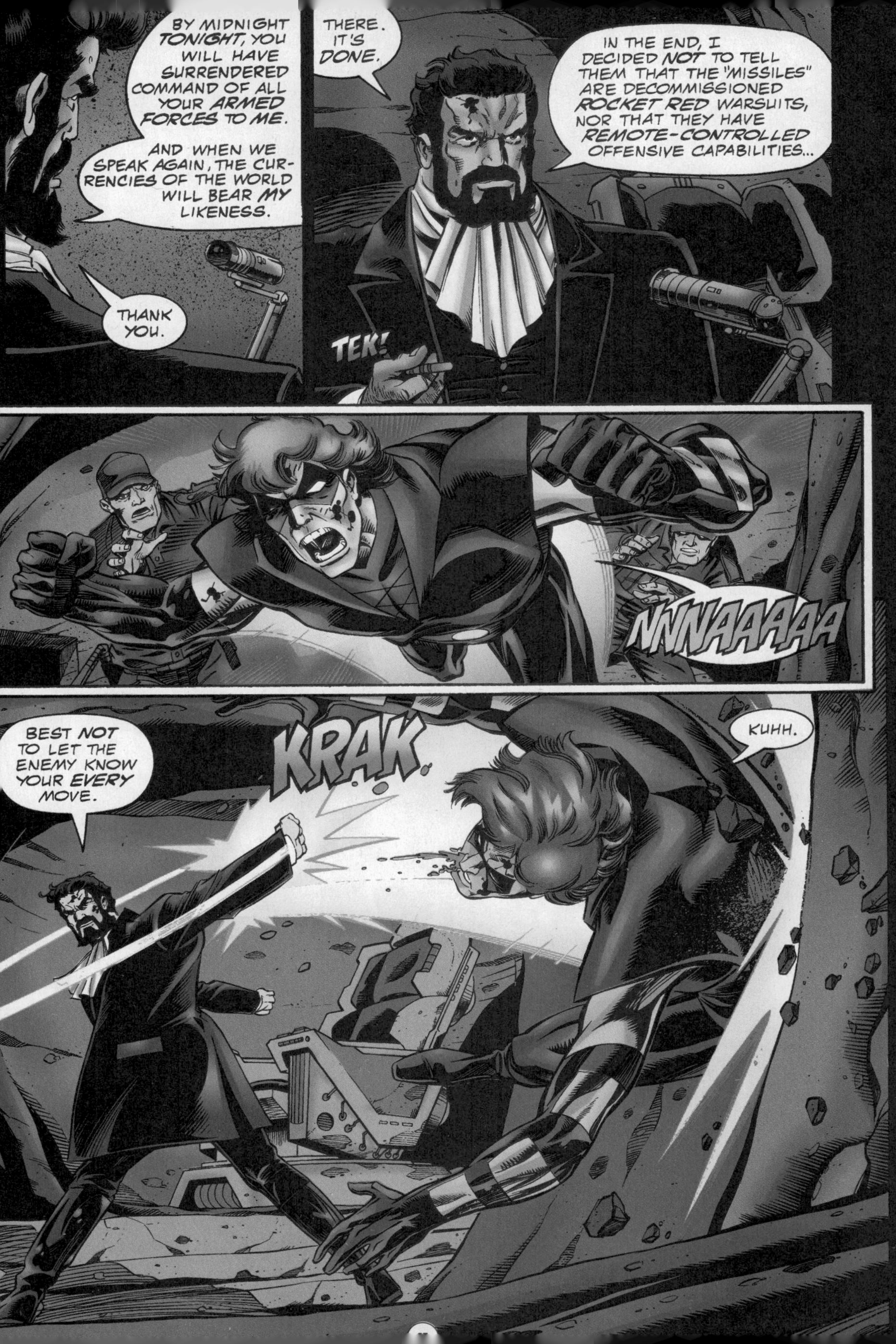
BY MIDNIGHT TONIGHT, YOU WILL HAVE SURRENDERED COMMAND OF ALL YOUR ARMED FORCES TO ME.
AND WHEN WE SPEAK AGAIN, THE CURRENCIES OF THE WORLD WILL BEAR MY LIKENESS.
THANK YOU.
THERE. IT'S DONE.
IN THE END, I DECIDED NOT TO TELL THEM THAT THE "MISSILES" ARE DECOMMISSIONED ROCKET RED WARSUITS, NOR THAT THEY HAVE REMOTE-CONTROLLED OFFENSIVE CAPABILITIES...
TEK!
NNNAAAAAA
BEST NOT TO LET THE ENEMY KNOW YOUR EVERY MOVE.
KRAK
KUHH.

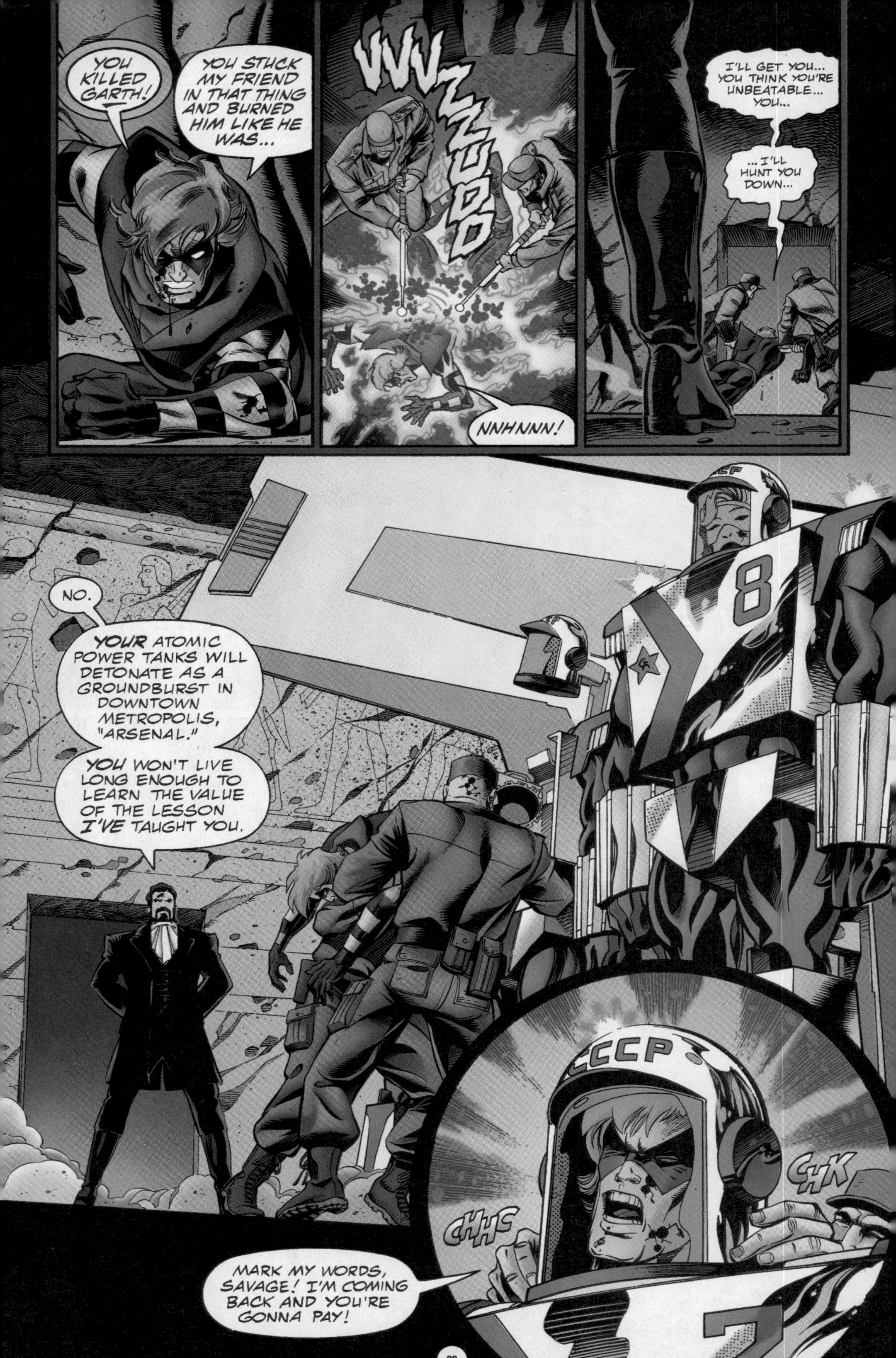
YOU KILLED GARTH!
YOU STUCK MY FRIEND IN THAT THING AND BURNED HIM LIKE HE WAS...
VVVZZZUDD
NNHNNN!
I'LL GET YOU... YOU THINK YOU'RE UNBEATABLE... YOU...
... I'LL HUNT YOU DOWN...
NO.
YOUR ATOMIC POWER TANKS WILL DETONATE AS A GROUNDBURST IN DOWNTOWN METROPOLIS, "ARSENAL."
YOU WON'T LIVE LONG ENOUGH TO LEARN THE VALUE OF THE LESSON I'VE TAUGHT YOU.
CCCP
8
CHHC
CHK
MARK MY WORDS, SAVAGE! I'M COMING BACK AND YOU'RE GONNA PAY!

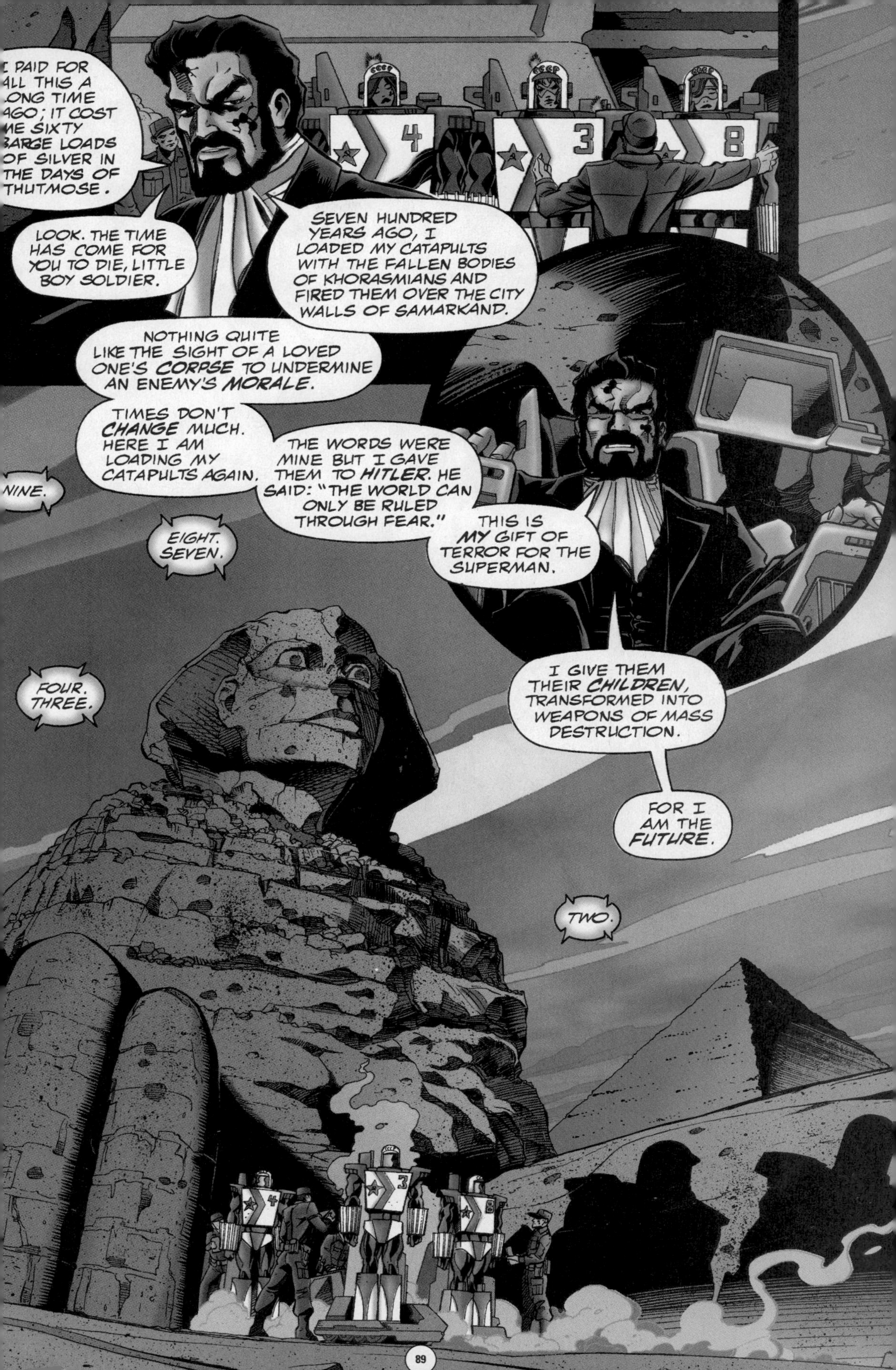
I PAID FOR ALL THIS A LONG TIME AGO; IT COST ME SIXTY BARGE LOADS OF SILVER IN THE DAYS OF THUTMOSE.
LOOK. THE TIME HAS COME FOR YOU TO DIE, LITTLE BOY SOLDIER.
SEVEN HUNDRED YEARS AGO, I LOADED MY CATAPULTS WITH THE FALLEN BODIES OF KHORASMIANS AND FIRED THEM OVER THE CITY WALLS OF SAMARKAND.
NOTHING QUITE LIKE THE SIGHT OF A LOVED ONE'S CORPSE TO UNDERMINE AN ENEMY'S MORALE.
TIMES DON'T CHANGE MUCH. HERE I AM LOADING MY CATAPULTS AGAIN.
THE WORDS WERE MINE BUT I GAVE THEM TO HITLER. HE SAID: "THE WORLD CAN ONLY BE RULED THROUGH FEAR."
NINE.
EIGHT. SEVEN.
THIS IS MY GIFT OF TERROR FOR THE SUPERMAN.
FOUR. THREE.
I GIVE THEM THEIR CHILDREN, TRANSFORMED INTO WEAPONS OF MASS DESTRUCTION.
FOR I AM THE FUTURE.
TWO.

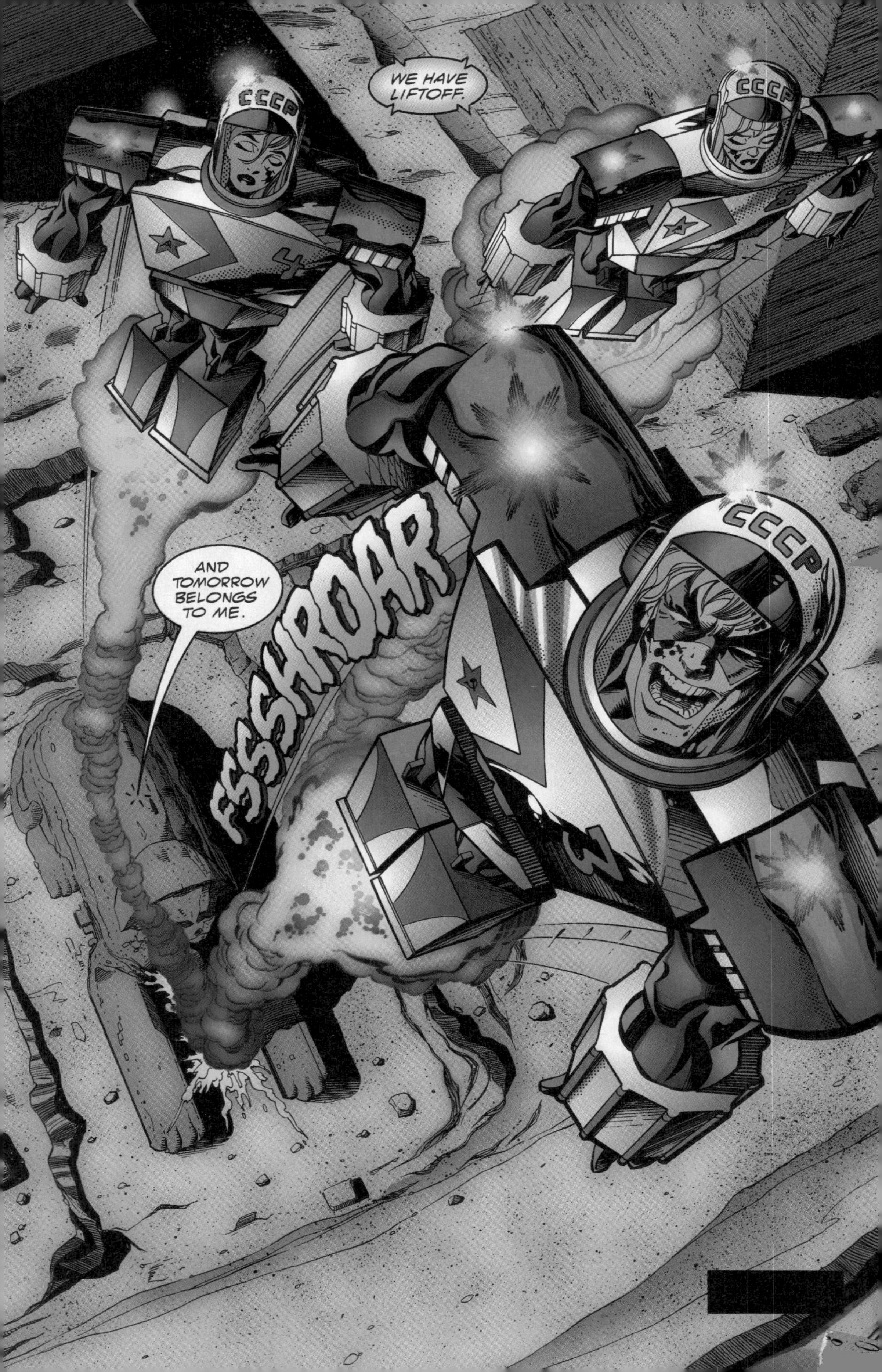
WE HAVE LIFTOFF.
AND TOMORROW BELONGS TO ME.
FSSSHROAR
[redacted]

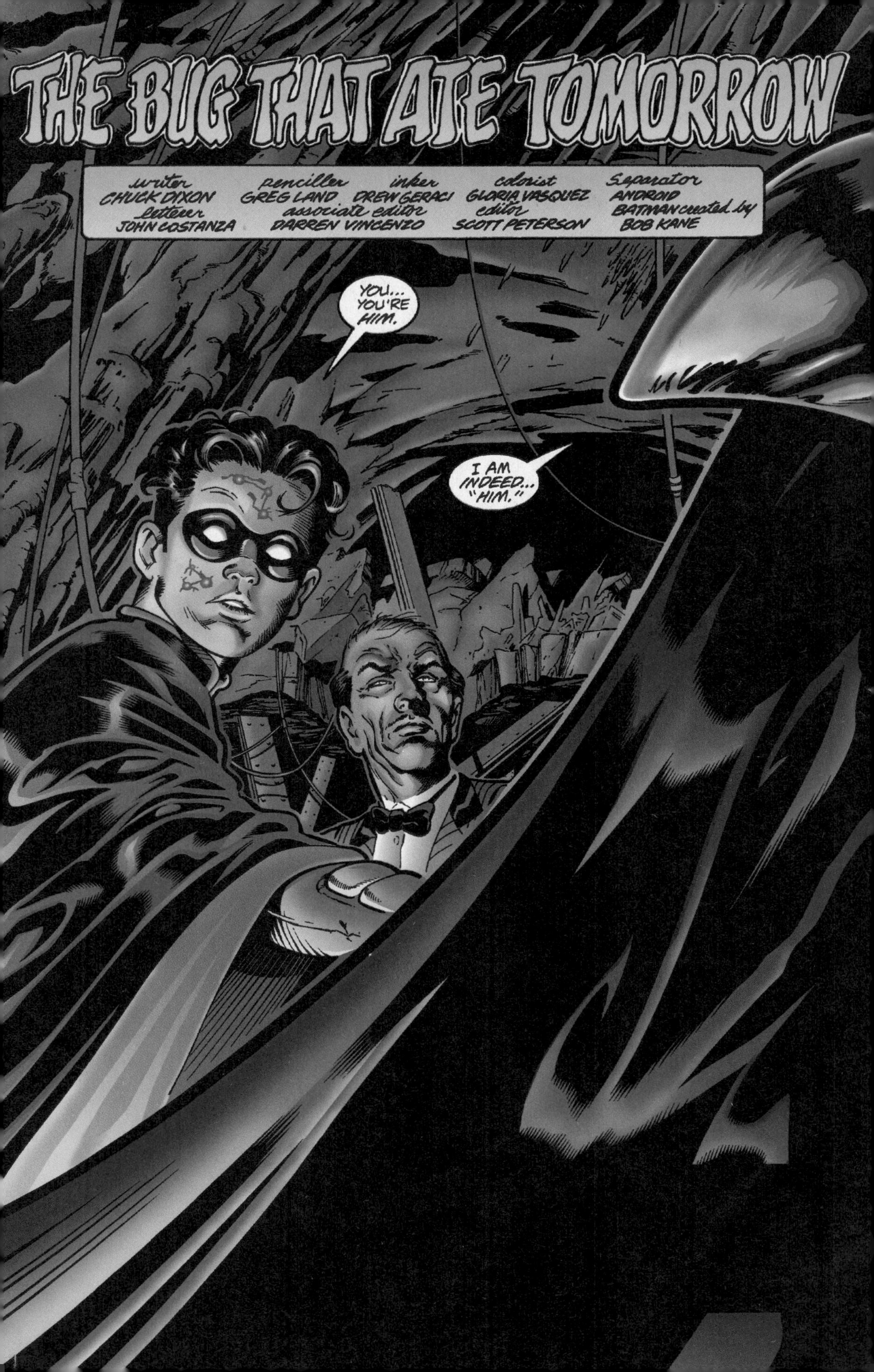
THE BUG THAT ATE TOMORROW
writer CHUCK DIXON penciller GREG LAND inker DREW GERACI colorist GLORIA VASQUEZ separator ANDROID
letterer JOHN COSTANZA associate editor DARREN VINCENZO editor SCOTT PETERSON BATMAN created by BOB KANE
YOU... YOU'RE HIM.
I AM INDEED... "HIM."

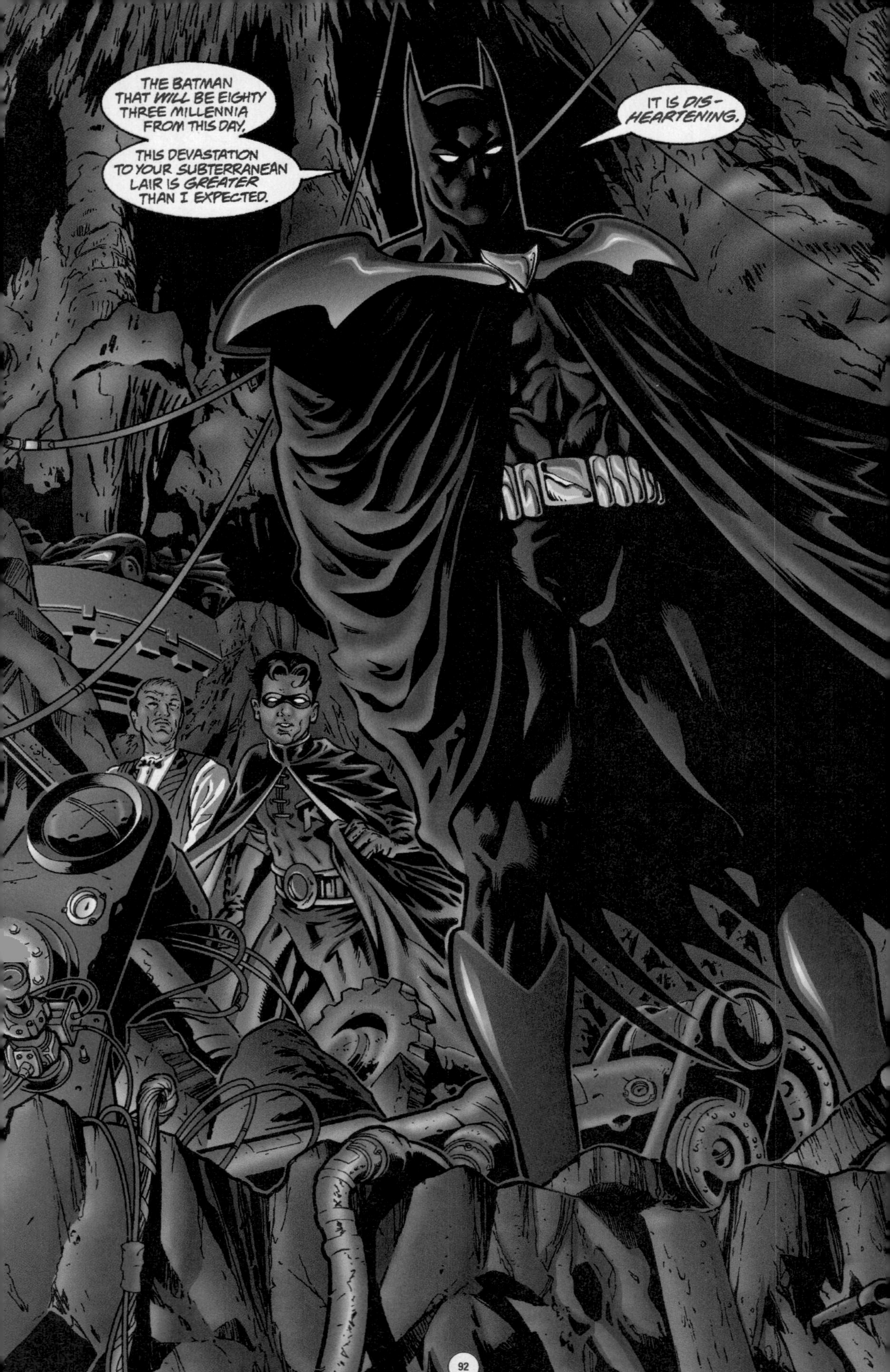
THE BATMAN THAT WILL BE EIGHTY THREE MILLENNIA FROM THIS DAY.
THIS DEVASTATION TO YOUR SUBTERRANEAN LAIR IS GREATER THAN I EXPECTED.
IT IS DIS-HEARTENING.

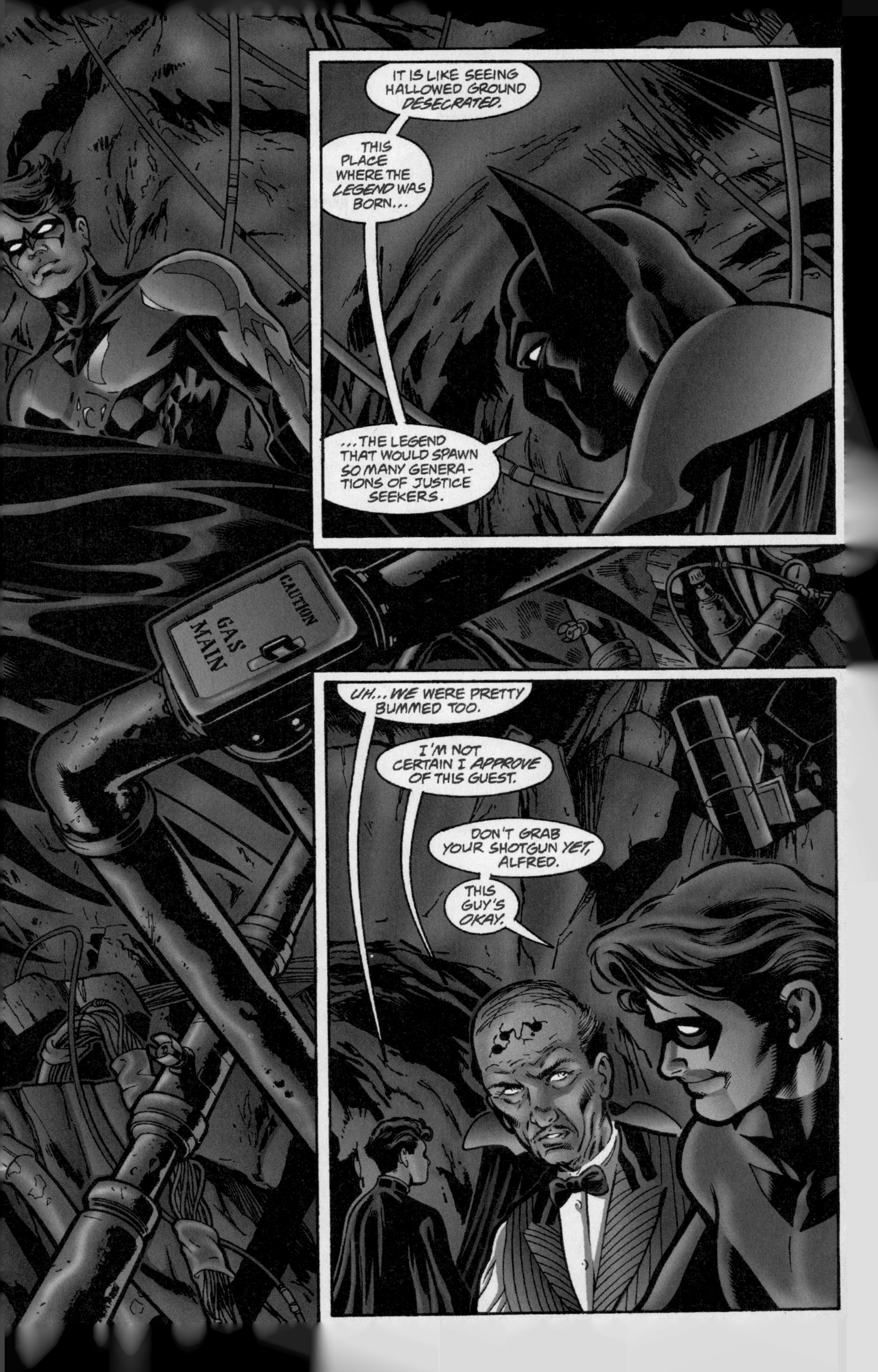

IT IS LIKE SEEING HALLOWED GROUND *DESECRATED.*
THIS PLACE WHERE THE *LEGEND* WAS BORN...
...THE LEGEND THAT WOULD SPAWN SO MANY GENERA-TIONS OF JUSTICE SEEKERS.
CAUTION
GAS MAIN
UH...WE WERE PRETTY BUMMED TOO.
I'M NOT CERTAIN I *APPROVE* OF THIS GUEST.
DON'T GRAB YOUR SHOTGUN *YET,* ALFRED.
THIS GUY'S *OKAY.*

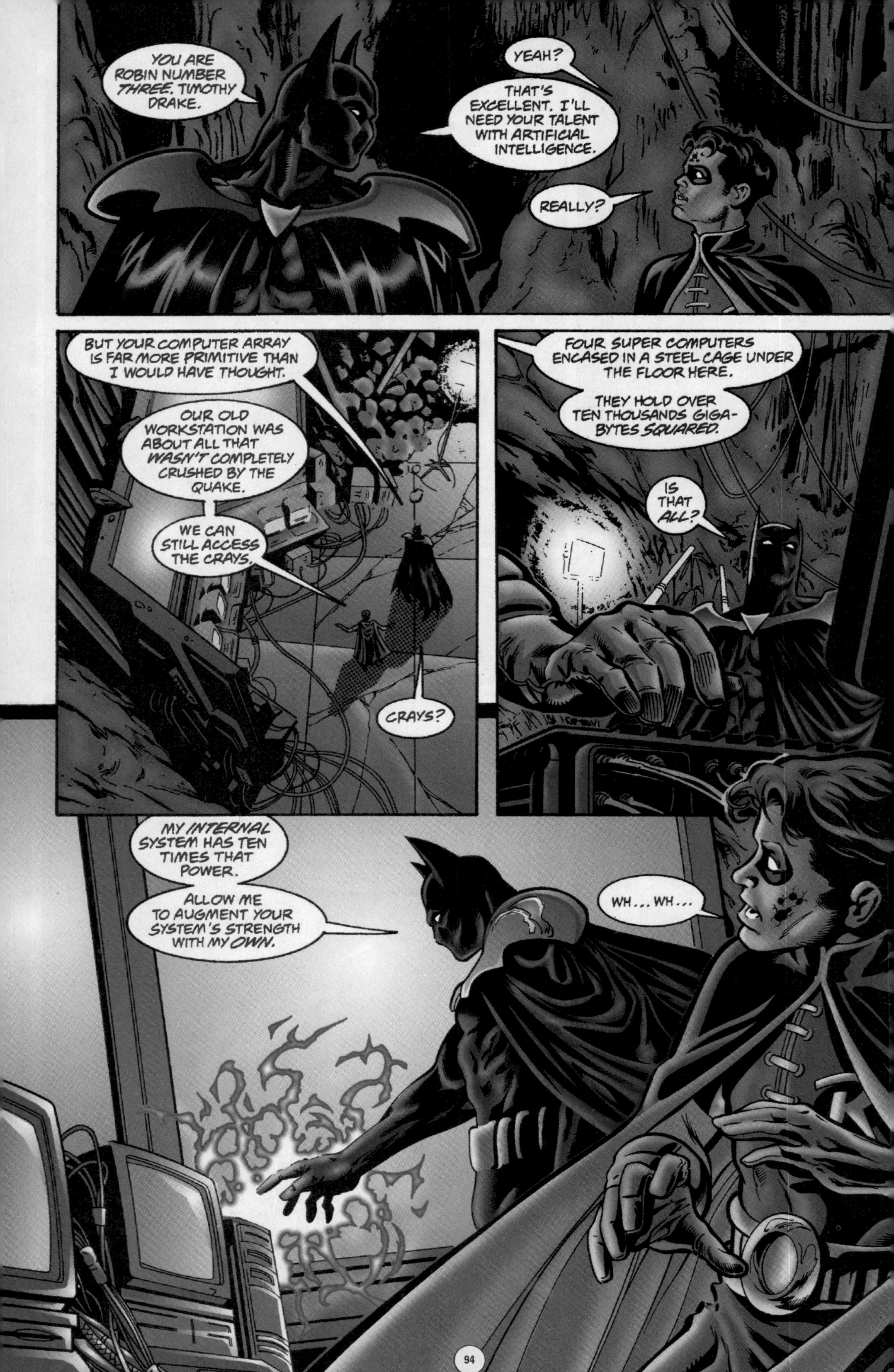
YOU ARE ROBIN NUMBER THREE. TIMOTHY DRAKE.
YEAH?
THAT'S EXCELLENT. I'LL NEED YOUR TALENT WITH ARTIFICIAL INTELLIGENCE.
REALLY?
BUT YOUR COMPUTER ARRAY IS FAR MORE PRIMITIVE THAN I WOULD HAVE THOUGHT.
OUR OLD WORKSTATION WAS ABOUT ALL THAT WASN'T COMPLETELY CRUSHED BY THE QUAKE.
WE CAN STILL ACCESS THE CRAYS.
CRAYS?
FOUR SUPER COMPUTERS ENCASED IN A STEEL CAGE UNDER THE FLOOR HERE.
THEY HOLD OVER TEN THOUSANDS GIGA-BYTES SQUARED.
IS THAT ALL?
MY INTERNAL SYSTEM HAS TEN TIMES THAT POWER.
ALLOW ME TO AUGMENT YOUR SYSTEM'S STRENGTH WITH MY OWN.
WH... WH...

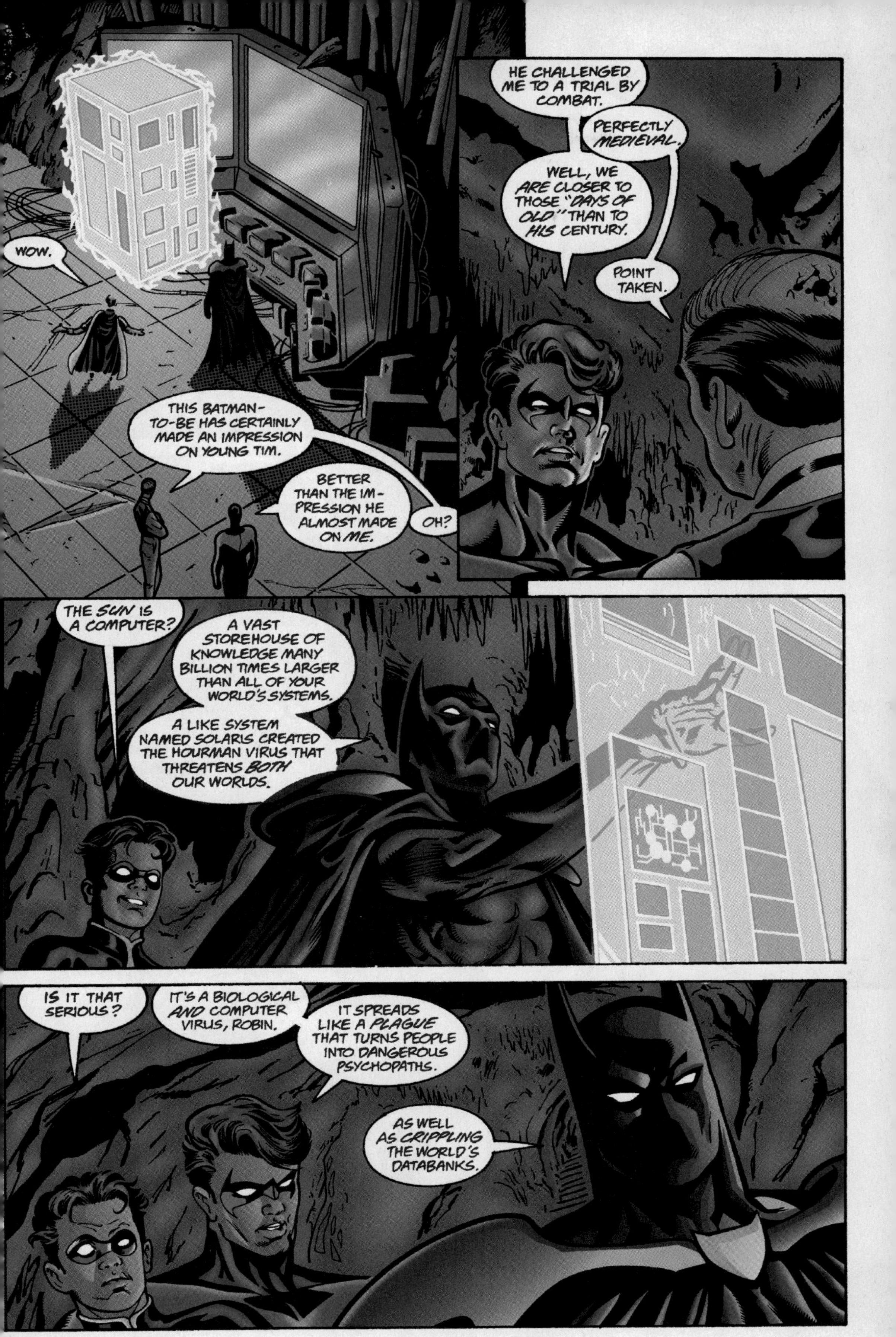
WOW.
THIS BATMAN-TO-BE HAS CERTAINLY MADE AN IMPRESSION ON YOUNG TIM.
BETTER THAN THE IMPRESSION HE ALMOST MADE ON ME.
OH?
HE CHALLENGED ME TO A TRIAL BY COMBAT.
PERFECTLY MEDIEVAL.
WELL, WE ARE CLOSER TO THOSE "DAYS OF OLD" THAN TO HIS CENTURY.
POINT TAKEN.
THE SUN IS A COMPUTER?
A VAST STOREHOUSE OF KNOWLEDGE MANY BILLION TIMES LARGER THAN ALL OF YOUR WORLD'S SYSTEMS.
A LIKE SYSTEM NAMED SOLARIS CREATED THE HOURMAN VIRUS THAT THREATENS BOTH OUR WORLDS.
IS IT THAT SERIOUS?
IT'S A BIOLOGICAL AND COMPUTER VIRUS, ROBIN.
IT SPREADS LIKE A PLAGUE THAT TURNS PEOPLE INTO DANGEROUS PSYCHOPATHS.
AS WELL AS CRIPPLING THE WORLD'S DATABANKS.

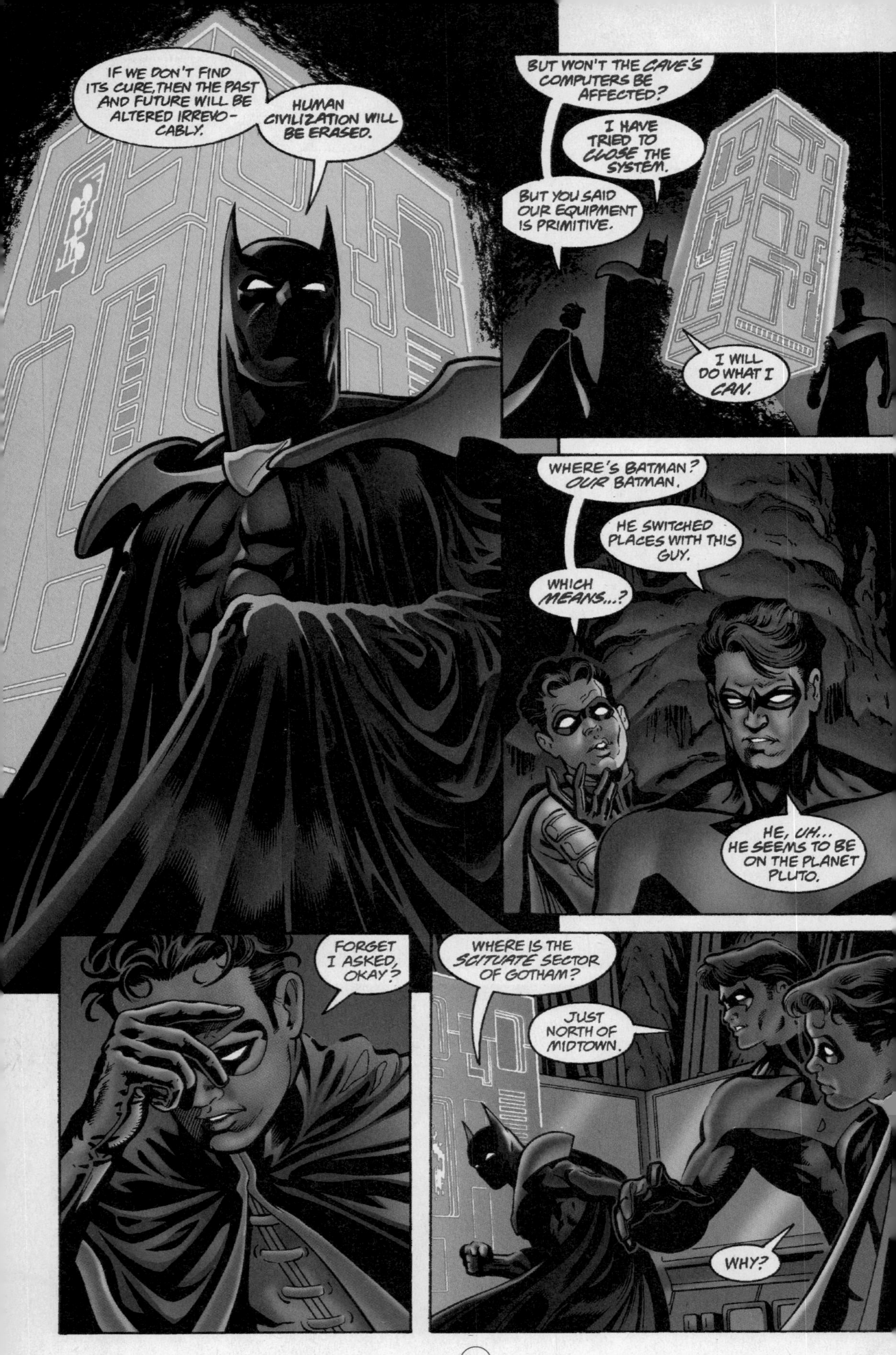
IF WE DON'T FIND ITS CURE, THEN THE PAST AND FUTURE WILL BE ALTERED IRREVOCABLY.
HUMAN CIVILIZATION WILL BE ERASED.
BUT WON'T THE CAVE'S COMPUTERS BE AFFECTED?
I HAVE TRIED TO CLOSE THE SYSTEM.
BUT YOU SAID OUR EQUIPMENT IS PRIMITIVE.
I WILL DO WHAT I CAN.
WHERE'S BATMAN? OUR BATMAN.
HE SWITCHED PLACES WITH THIS GUY.
WHICH MEANS...?
HE, UH... HE SEEMS TO BE ON THE PLANET PLUTO.
FORGET I ASKED, OKAY?
WHERE IS THE SCITUATE SECTOR OF GOTHAM?
JUST NORTH OF MIDTOWN.
WHY?

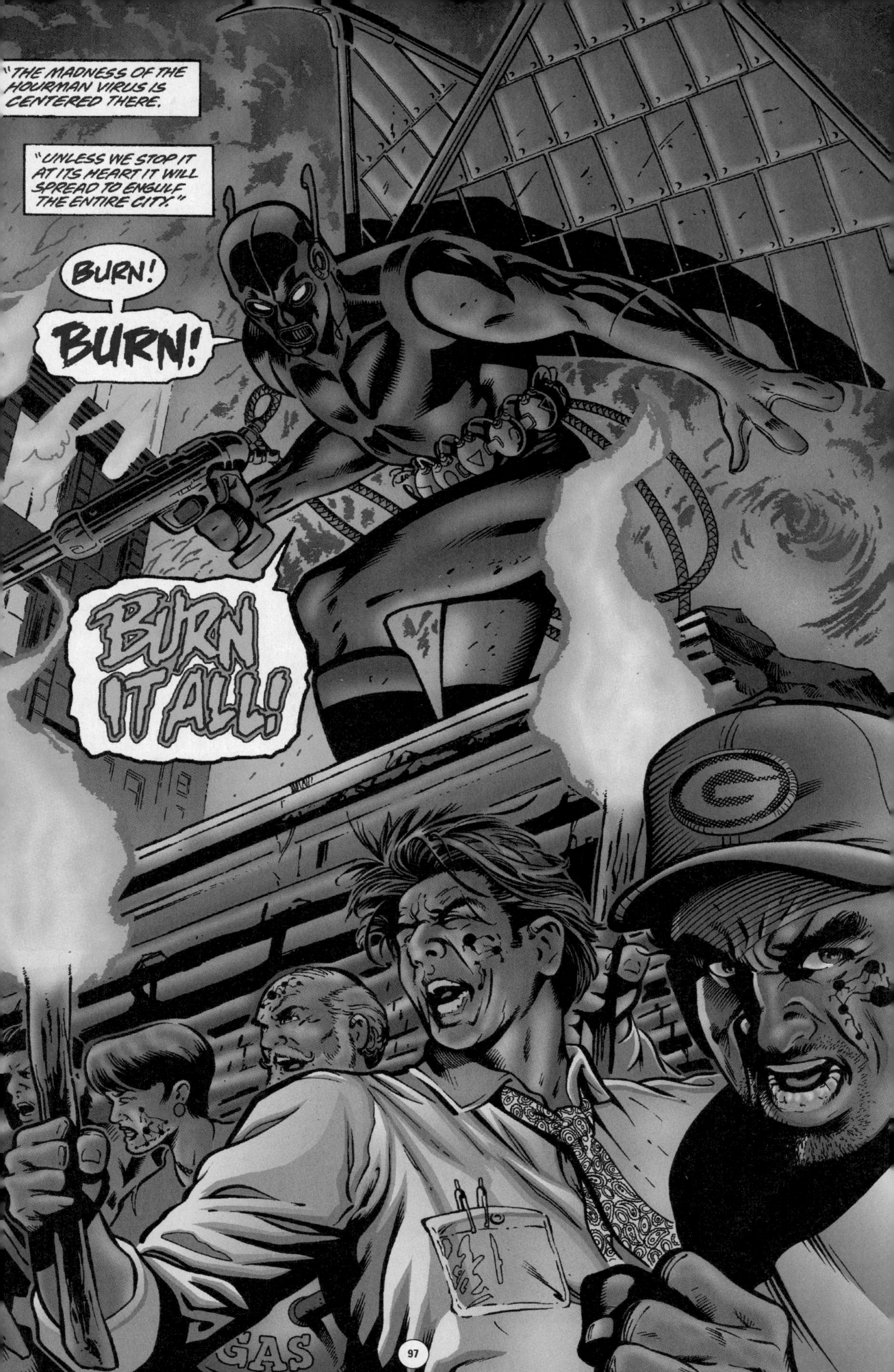
"THE MADNESS OF THE HOURMAN VIRUS IS CENTERED THERE.
"UNLESS WE STOP IT AT ITS HEART IT WILL SPREAD TO ENGULF THE ENTIRE CITY."
BURN!
BURN!
BURN IT ALL!
GAS

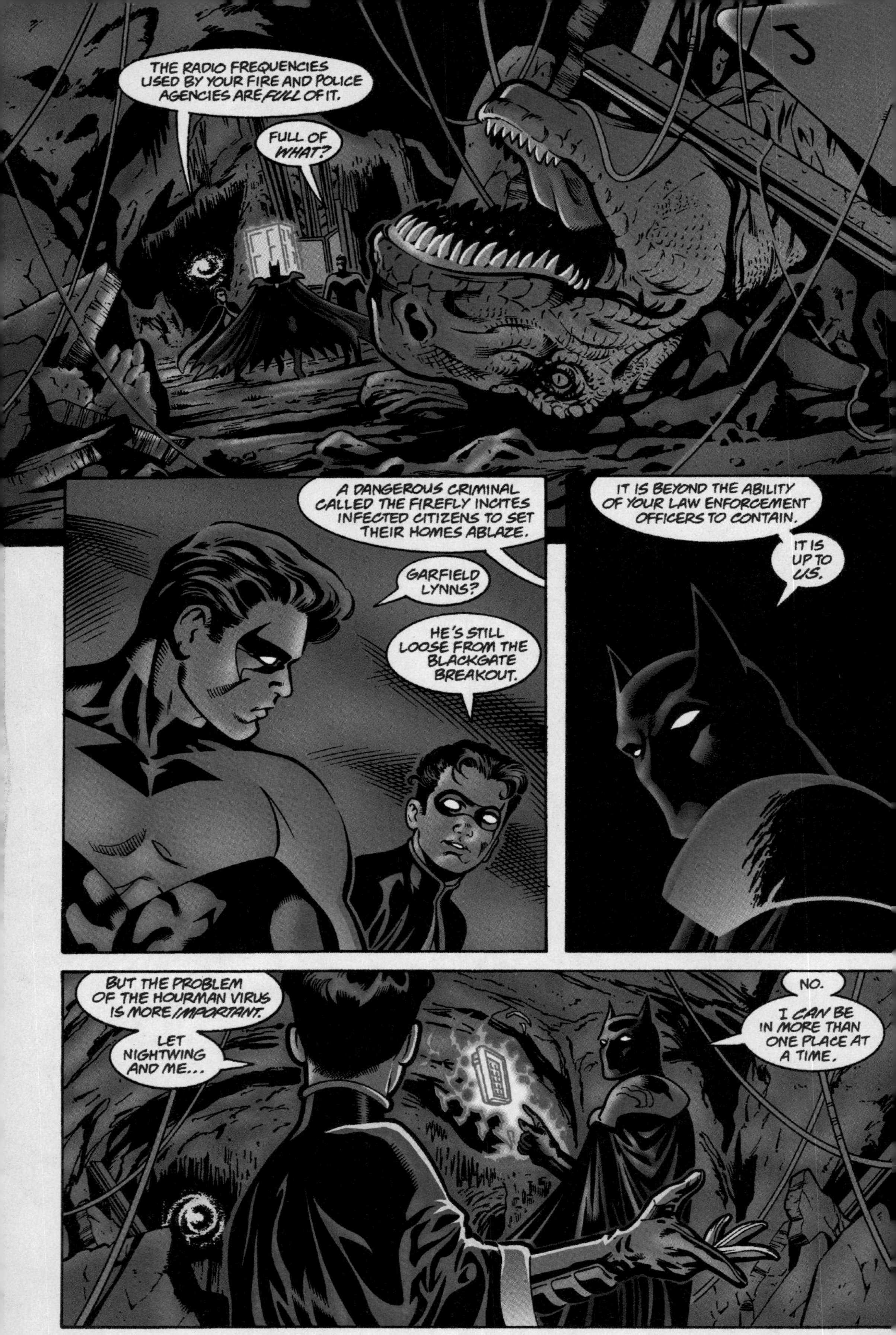
THE RADIO FREQUENCIES USED BY YOUR FIRE AND POLICE AGENCIES ARE FULL OF IT.
FULL OF WHAT?
A DANGEROUS CRIMINAL CALLED THE FIREFLY INCITES INFECTED CITIZENS TO SET THEIR HOMES ABLAZE.
GARFIELD LYNNS?
HE'S STILL LOOSE FROM THE BLACKGATE BREAKOUT.
IT IS BEYOND THE ABILITY OF YOUR LAW ENFORCEMENT OFFICERS TO CONTAIN.
IT IS UP TO US.
BUT THE PROBLEM OF THE HOURMAN VIRUS IS MORE IMPORTANT.
LET NIGHTWING AND ME...
NO.
I CAN BE IN MORE THAN ONE PLACE AT A TIME.

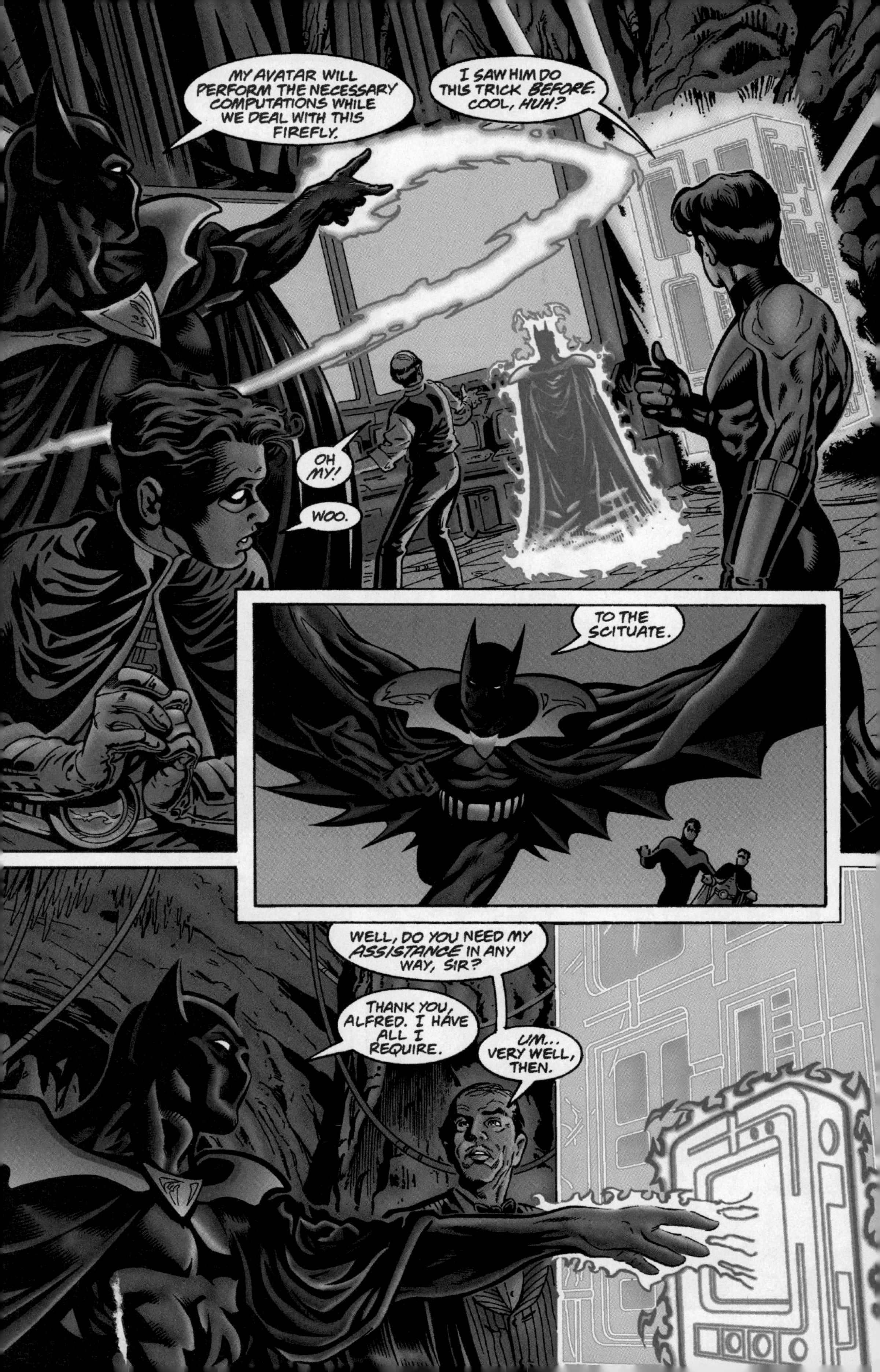
MY AVATAR WILL PERFORM THE NECESSARY COMPUTATIONS WHILE WE DEAL WITH THIS FIREFLY.
I SAW HIM DO THIS TRICK BEFORE. COOL, HUH?
OH MY!
WOO.
TO THE SCITUATE.
WELL, DO YOU NEED MY ASSISTANCE IN ANY WAY, SIR?
THANK YOU, ALFRED. I HAVE ALL I REQUIRE.
UM... VERY WELL, THEN.

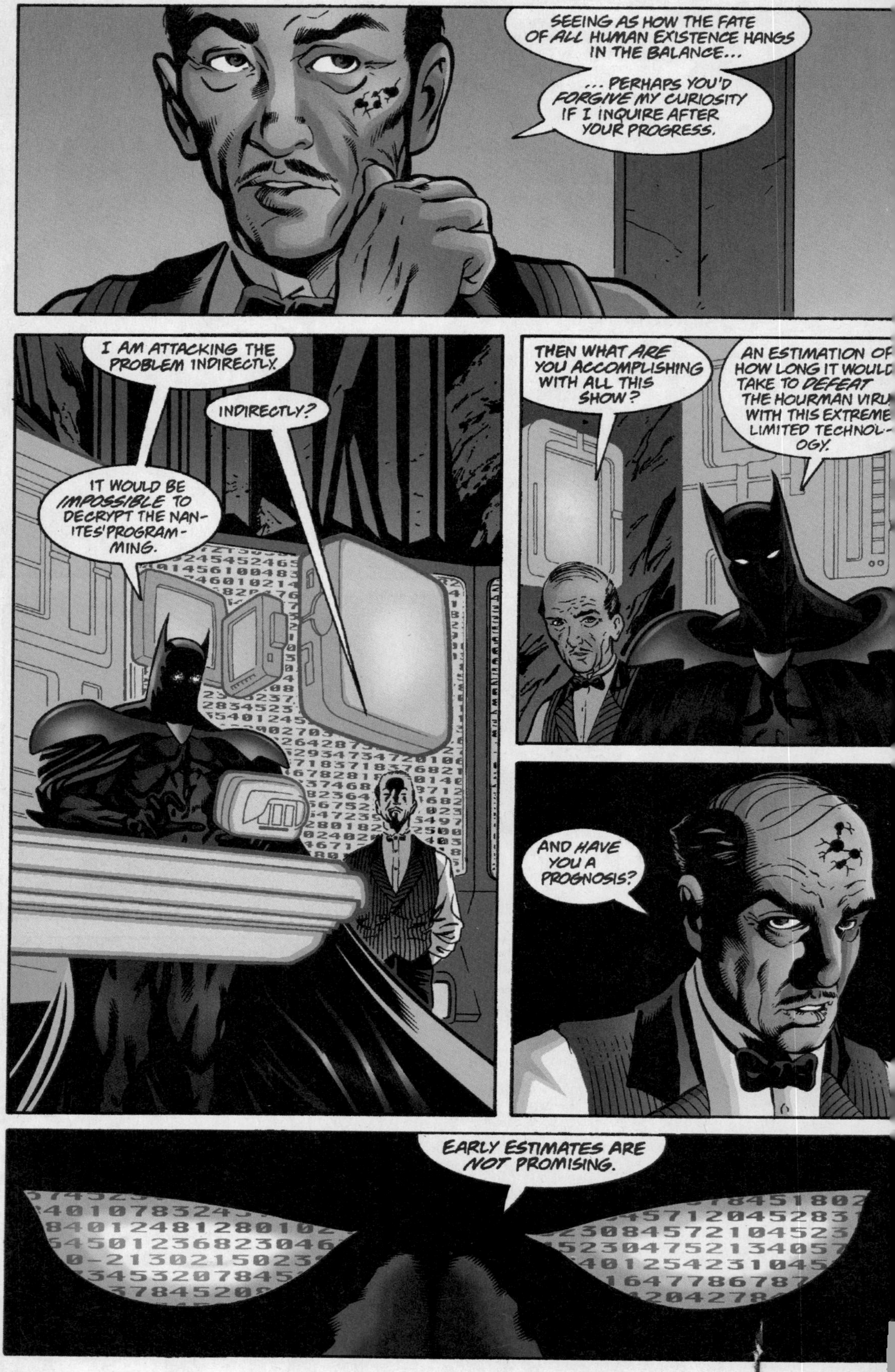
SEEING AS HOW THE FATE OF ALL HUMAN EXISTENCE HANGS IN THE BALANCE...
...PERHAPS YOU'D FORGIVE MY CURIOSITY IF I INQUIRE AFTER YOUR PROGRESS.
I AM ATTACKING THE PROBLEM INDIRECTLY.
INDIRECTLY?
IT WOULD BE IMPOSSIBLE TO DECRYPT THE NANITES' PROGRAMMING.
THEN WHAT ARE YOU ACCOMPLISHING WITH ALL THIS SHOW?
AN ESTIMATION OF HOW LONG IT WOULD TAKE TO DEFEAT THE HOURMAN VIRU WITH THIS EXTREME LIMITED TECHNOLOGY.
AND HAVE YOU A PROGNOSIS?
EARLY ESTIMATES ARE NOT PROMISING.

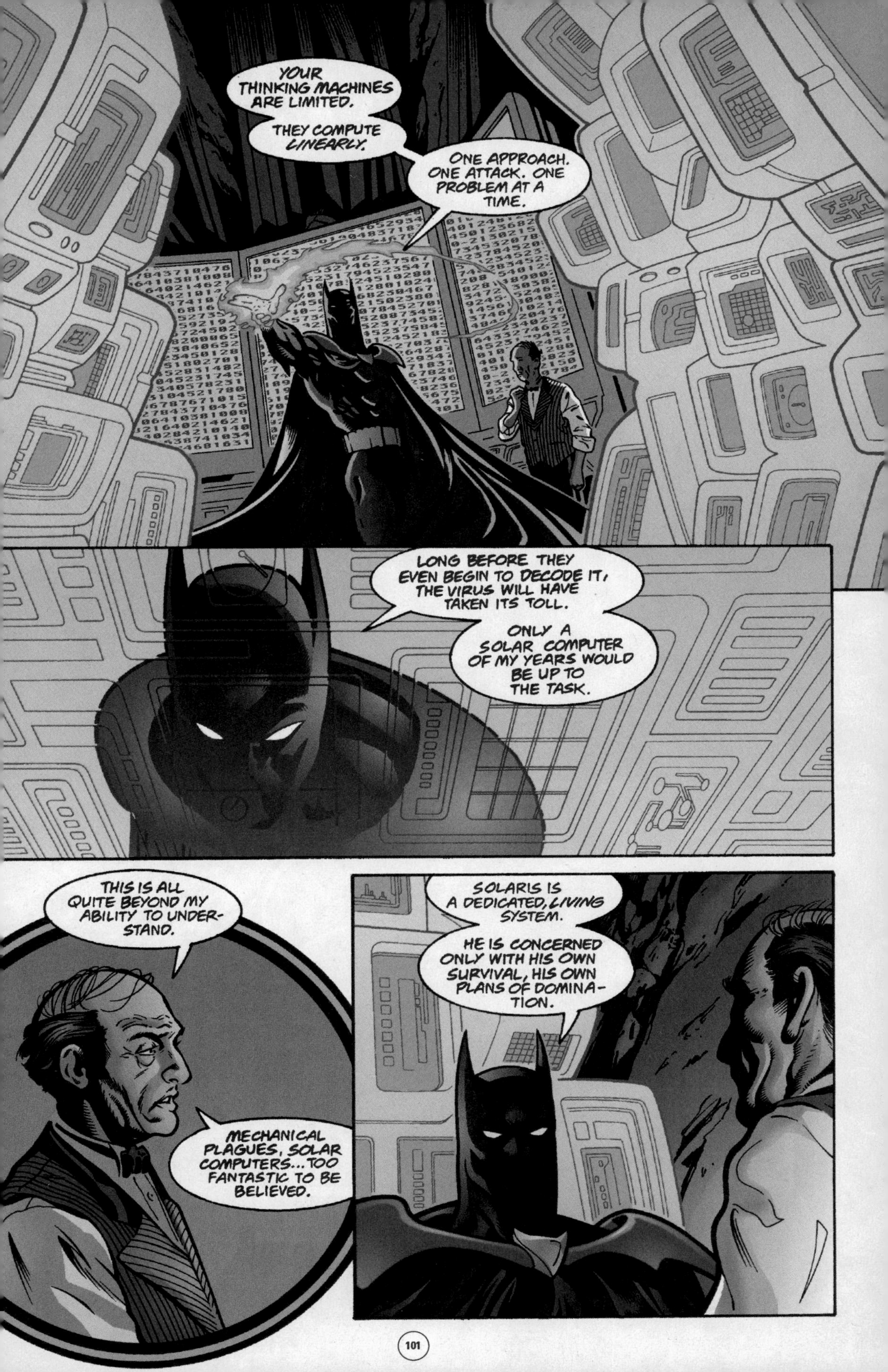
YOUR THINKING MACHINES ARE LIMITED.
THEY COMPUTE LINEARLY.
ONE APPROACH. ONE ATTACK. ONE PROBLEM AT A TIME.
LONG BEFORE THEY EVEN BEGIN TO DECODE IT, THE VIRUS WILL HAVE TAKEN ITS TOLL.
ONLY A SOLAR COMPUTER OF MY YEARS WOULD BE UP TO THE TASK.
THIS IS ALL QUITE BEYOND MY ABILITY TO UNDER-STAND.
MECHANICAL PLAGUES, SOLAR COMPUTERS...TOO FANTASTIC TO BE BELIEVED.
SOLARIS IS A DEDICATED, LIVING SYSTEM.
HE IS CONCERNED ONLY WITH HIS OWN SURVIVAL, HIS OWN PLANS OF DOMINA-TION.

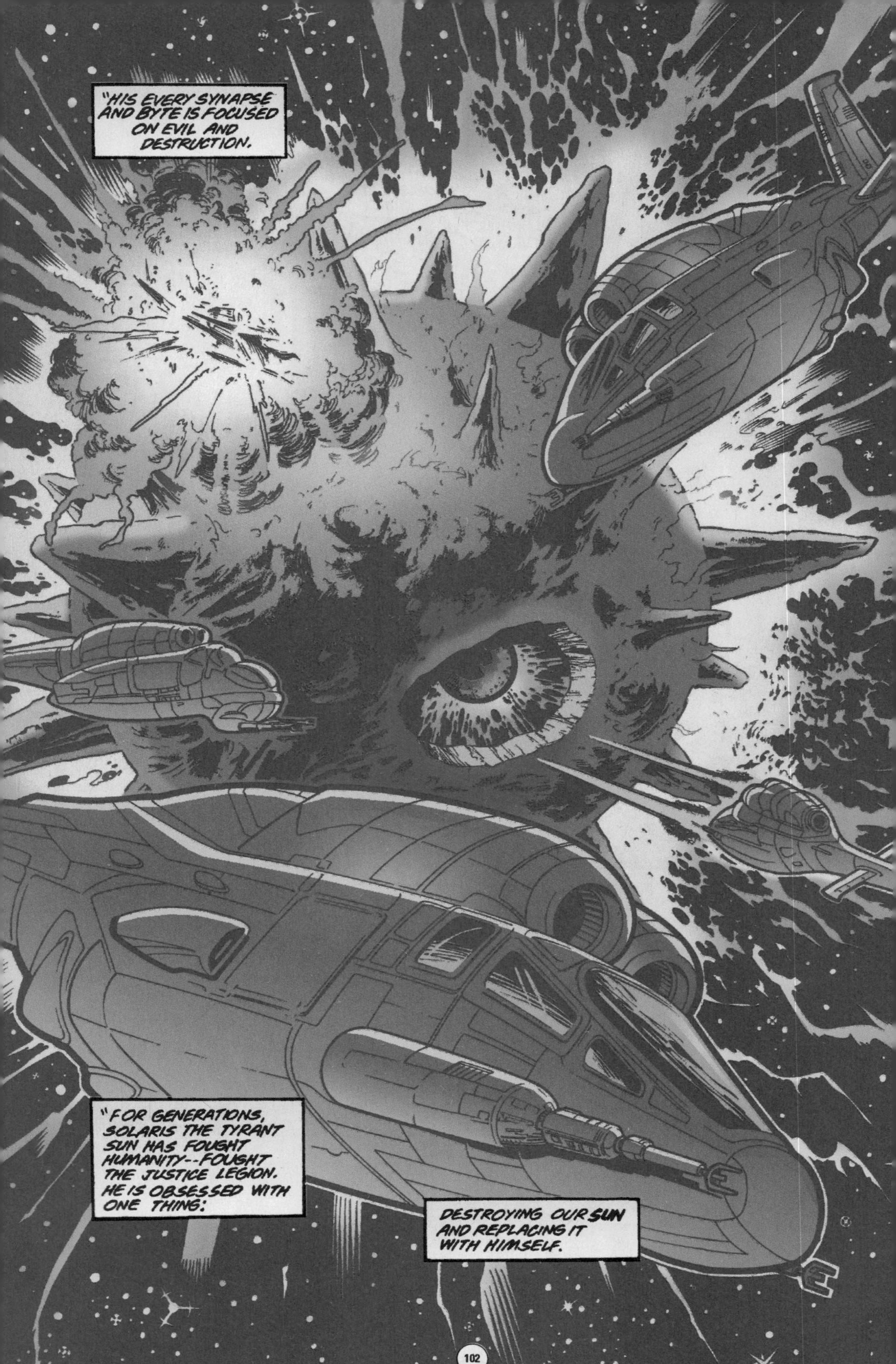
"HIS EVERY SYNAPSE AND BYTE IS FOCUSED ON EVIL AND DESTRUCTION.
"FOR GENERATIONS, SOLARIS THE TYRANT SUN HAS FOUGHT HUMANITY--FOUGHT THE JUSTICE LEGION. HE IS OBSESSED WITH ONE THING:
DESTROYING OUR SUN AND REPLACING IT WITH HIMSELF.

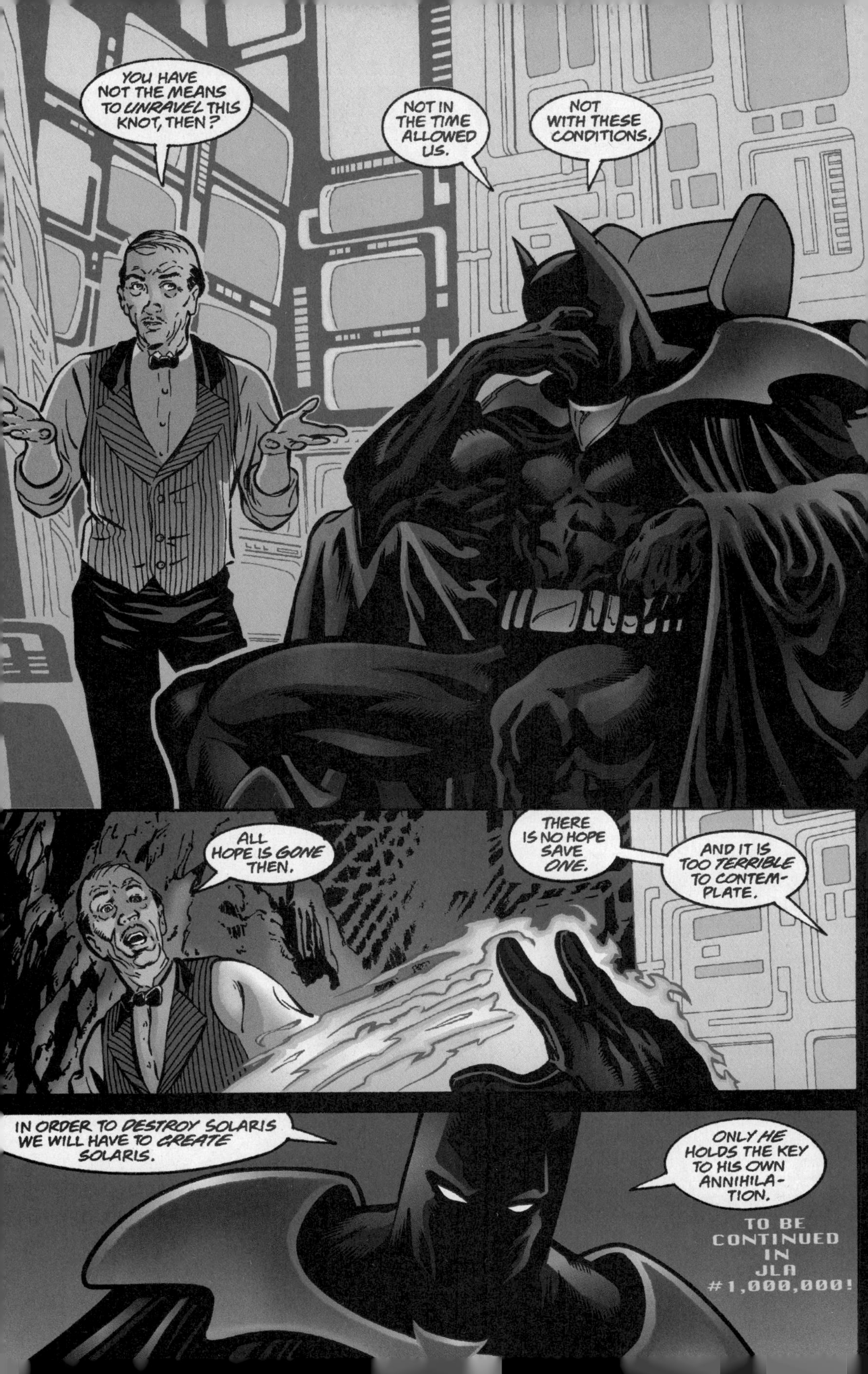
YOU HAVE NOT THE MEANS TO UNRAVEL THIS KNOT, THEN?
NOT IN THE TIME ALLOWED US.
NOT WITH THESE CONDITIONS.
ALL HOPE IS GONE THEN.
THERE IS NO HOPE SAVE ONE.
AND IT IS TOO TERRIBLE TO CONTEMPLATE.
IN ORDER TO DESTROY SOLARIS WE WILL HAVE TO CREATE SOLARIS.
ONLY HE HOLDS THE KEY TO HIS OWN ANNIHILATION.
TO BE CONTINUED IN JLA #1,000,000!

DIGIPRINT

THE BATTLE FOR THE FUTURE WAS NOW WAGED ON TWO FRONTS.

WHILE THE 853RD-CENTURY DARK KNIGHT RACED TO FIND A CURE FOR THE MADDENING "HOURMAN VIRUS," VANDAL SAVAGE'S PLANS FOR ATOMIC ARMAGEDDON MOVED FORWARD AT A FRIGHTENING PACE. THE SALVO OF ROCKET RED WARSUITS LAUNCHED BY SAVAGE, EACH WITH A HELPLESS TITAN TRAPPED INSIDE, BLAZED TOWARD CITIES PARALYZED BY THE NANITE MALADY.

BUT THE HOURMAN VIRUS WAS EXACTLY WHAT DEFEATED THE IMMORTAL CONQUEROR.

SAVAGE'S FIRST ROCKET RED, WHICH LEFT MONTEVIDEO A SMOKING CRATER, WAS MEANT TO RAIN FALLOUT ON WASHINGTON, D.C. WITH THE HOURMAN VIRUS FOULING THE WARSUIT'S GUIDANCE COMPUTER, THE AQUATIC HERO TEMPEST BAILED OUT UNCONSCIOUS OVER THE ATLANTIC OCEAN. WASHINGTON WAS SAVED...THOUGH A MILLION URUGUAYAN CITIZENS PERISHED.

IF NOT FOR THE EFFORTS OF HEROES FROM TWO DISTANT ERAS, THREE MORE CITIES WOULD HAVE KNOWN SAVAGE'S TIMELESS WRATH.

THE SUPERMAN FROM 85,271 A.D. USED HIS ASTOUNDING "FORCE VISION" TO FREE ARSENAL AND CONTAIN A ROCKET RED FROM LAYING WASTE TO METROPOLIS.

SUPERGIRL WAS LIBERATED FROM HER WARSUIT, AIMED AT INCINERATING BRUSSELS, BY THE 853RD-CENTURY WONDER WOMAN.

AND SINGAPORE WAS SPARED NUCLEAR DEVASTATION BY IMPULSE AND THE FUTURE FLASH JOHN FOX, WHOSE COMBINED POWERS DISARMED THE ROCKET RED AND FREED FELLOW SUPER-SPEEDSTER JESSE QUICK.

VICTORY CELEBRATIONS, HOWEVER, WERE SHORT-LIVED.

VANDAL SAVAGE REMAINED AT LARGE, AND THE HOURMAN VIRUS CONTINUED TO RAGE ACROSS THE PLANET, SWIFTLY ERODING THE MINDS OF MAN AND MACHINE...

384500830
JLA WATCHTOWER:
1998

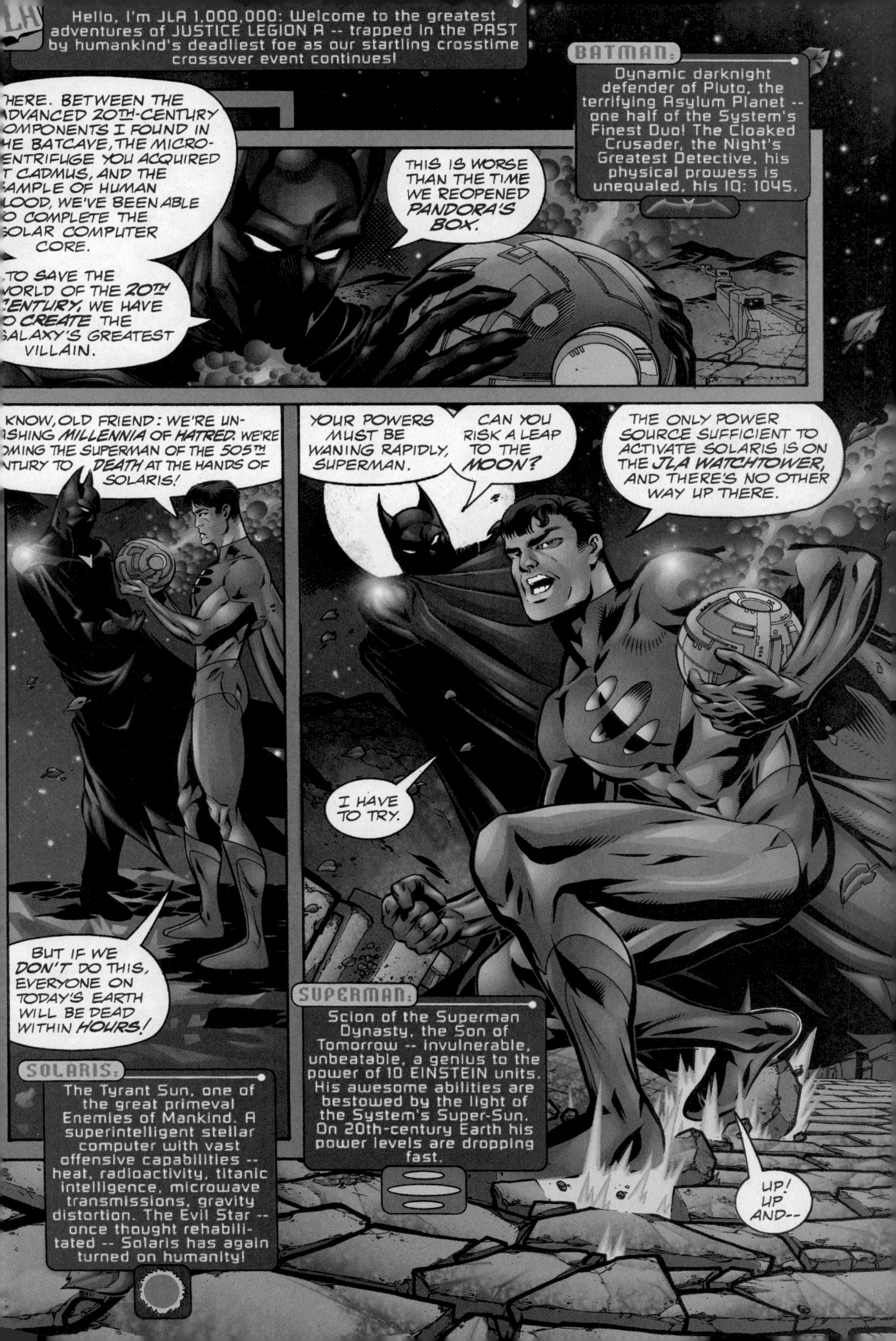
Hello, I'm JLA 1,000,000: Welcome to the greatest adventures of JUSTICE LEGION A -- trapped in the PAST by humankind's deadliest foe as our startling crosstime crossover event continues!
HERE. BETWEEN THE DVANCED 20TH-CENTURY OMPONENTS I FOUND IN HE BATCAVE, THE MICRO-ENTRIFUGE YOU ACQUIRED T CADMUS, AND THE AMPLE OF HUMAN LOOD, WE'VE BEEN ABLE O COMPLETE THE OLAR COMPUTER CORE.
.TO SAVE THE ORLD OF THE 20TH ENTURY, WE HAVE O CREATE THE ALAXY'S GREATEST VILLAIN.
THIS IS WORSE THAN THE TIME WE REOPENED PANDORA'S BOX.
BATMAN:
Dynamic darknight defender of Pluto, the terrifying Asylum Planet -- one half of the System's Finest Duo! The Cloaked Crusader, the Night's Greatest Detective, his physical prowess is unequaled, his IQ: 1045.
KNOW, OLD FRIEND: WE'RE UN-ASHING MILLENNIA OF HATRED. WE'RE OMING THE SUPERMAN OF THE 505TH NTURY TO DEATH AT THE HANDS OF SOLARIS!
BUT IF WE DON'T DO THIS, EVERYONE ON TODAY'S EARTH WILL BE DEAD WITHIN HOURS!
SOLARIS:
The Tyrant Sun, one of the great primeval Enemies of Mankind. A superintelligent stellar computer with vast offensive capabilities -- heat, radioactivity, titanic intelligence, microwave transmissions, gravity distortion. The Evil Star -- once thought rehabilitated -- Solaris has again turned on humanity!
YOUR POWERS MUST BE WANING RAPIDLY, SUPERMAN.
CAN YOU RISK A LEAP TO THE MOON?
THE ONLY POWER SOURCE SUFFICIENT TO ACTIVATE SOLARIS IS ON THE JLA WATCHTOWER, AND THERE'S NO OTHER WAY UP THERE.
I HAVE TO TRY.
SUPERMAN:
Scion of the Superman Dynasty, the Son of Tomorrow -- invulnerable, unbeatable, a genius to the power of 10 EINSTEIN units. His awesome abilities are bestowed by the light of the System's Super-Sun. On 20th-century Earth his power levels are dropping fast.
UP! UP AND--

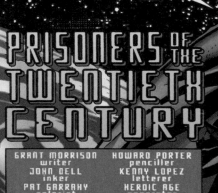

PRISONERS OF THE TWENTIETH CENTURY

GRANT MORRISON
writer

HOWARD PORTER
penciller

JOHN DELL
inker

KENNY LOPEZ
letterer

PAT GARRAHY
colorist

HEROIC AGE
separator

TONY BEDARD
associate editor

DAN RASPLER
editor

FEATURING
THE GREATEST HEROES OF
THE 853rd CENTURY!
SUPERMAN...BATMAN...
FLASH...STARMAN...
WONDER WOMAN...
AQUAMAN...HOURMAN...

AND GUEST-STARRING
THE LEGENDARY JUSTICE
LEAGUE OF AMERICA!
STEEL...HUNTRESS...
PLASTIC MAN...ZAURIEL...
BIG BARDA...MANHUNTER FROM
MARS...BATMAN

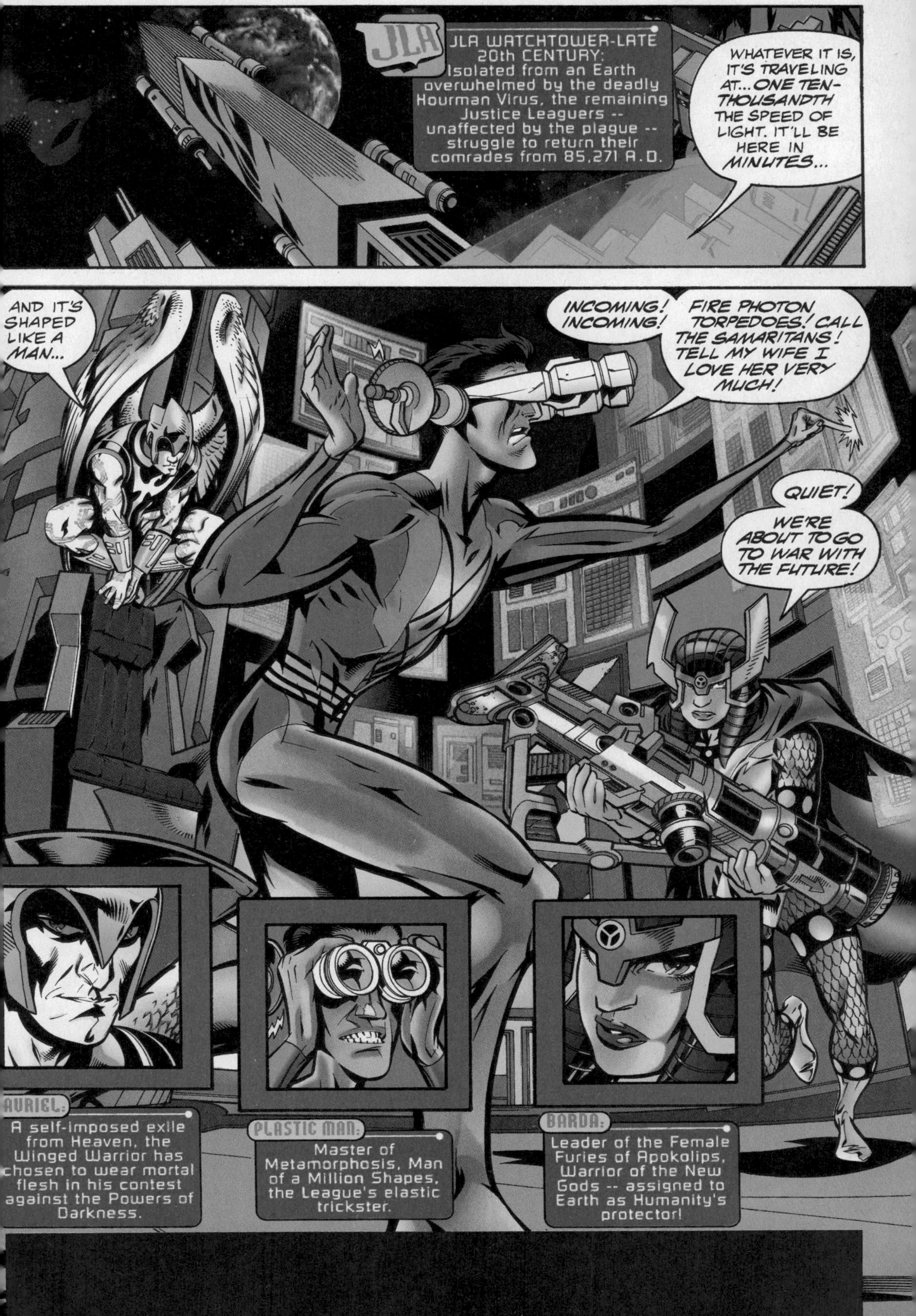
JLA
JLA WATCHTOWER-LATE 20th CENTURY: Isolated from an Earth overwhelmed by the deadly Hourman Virus, the remaining Justice Leaguers -- unaffected by the plague -- struggle to return their comrades from 85,271 A.D.
WHATEVER IT IS, IT'S TRAVELING AT... ONE TEN-THOUSANDTH THE SPEED OF LIGHT. IT'LL BE HERE IN MINUTES...
AND IT'S SHAPED LIKE A MAN...
INCOMING! INCOMING!
FIRE PHOTON TORPEDOES! CALL THE SAMARITANS! TELL MY WIFE I LOVE HER VERY MUCH!
QUIET!
WE'RE ABOUT TO GO TO WAR WITH THE FUTURE!
ZAURIEL:
A self-imposed exile from Heaven, the Winged Warrior has chosen to wear mortal flesh in his contest against the Powers of Darkness.
PLASTIC MAN:
Master of Metamorphosis, Man of a Million Shapes, the League's elastic trickster.
BARDA:
Leader of the Female Furies of Apokolips, Warrior of the New Gods -- assigned to Earth as Humanity's protector!

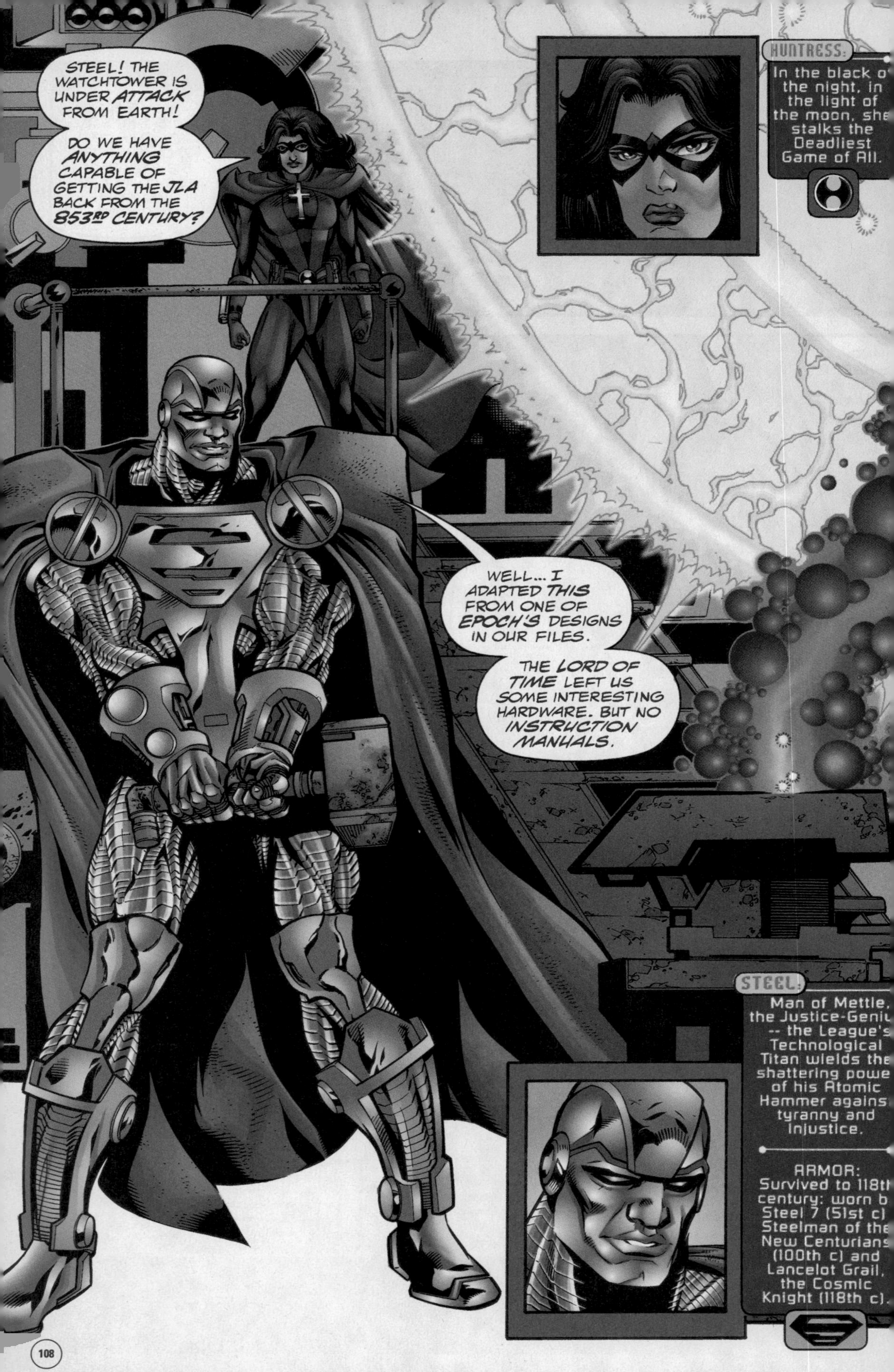

STEEL! THE WATCHTOWER IS UNDER ATTACK FROM EARTH!
DO WE HAVE ANYTHING CAPABLE OF GETTING THE JLA BACK FROM THE 853RD CENTURY?
HUNTRESS:
In the black of the night, in the light of the moon, she stalks the Deadliest Game of All.
WELL... I ADAPTED THIS FROM ONE OF EPOCH'S DESIGNS IN OUR FILES.
THE LORD OF TIME LEFT US SOME INTERESTING HARDWARE. BUT NO INSTRUCTION MANUALS.
STEEL:
Man of Mettle, the Justice-Geniu -- the League's Technological Titan wields the shattering powe of his Atomic Hammer agains tyranny and Injustice.
ARMOR:
Survived to 118th century: worn b Steel 7 (51st c) Steelman of the New Centurians (100th c) and Lancelot Grail, the Cosmic Knight (118th c).

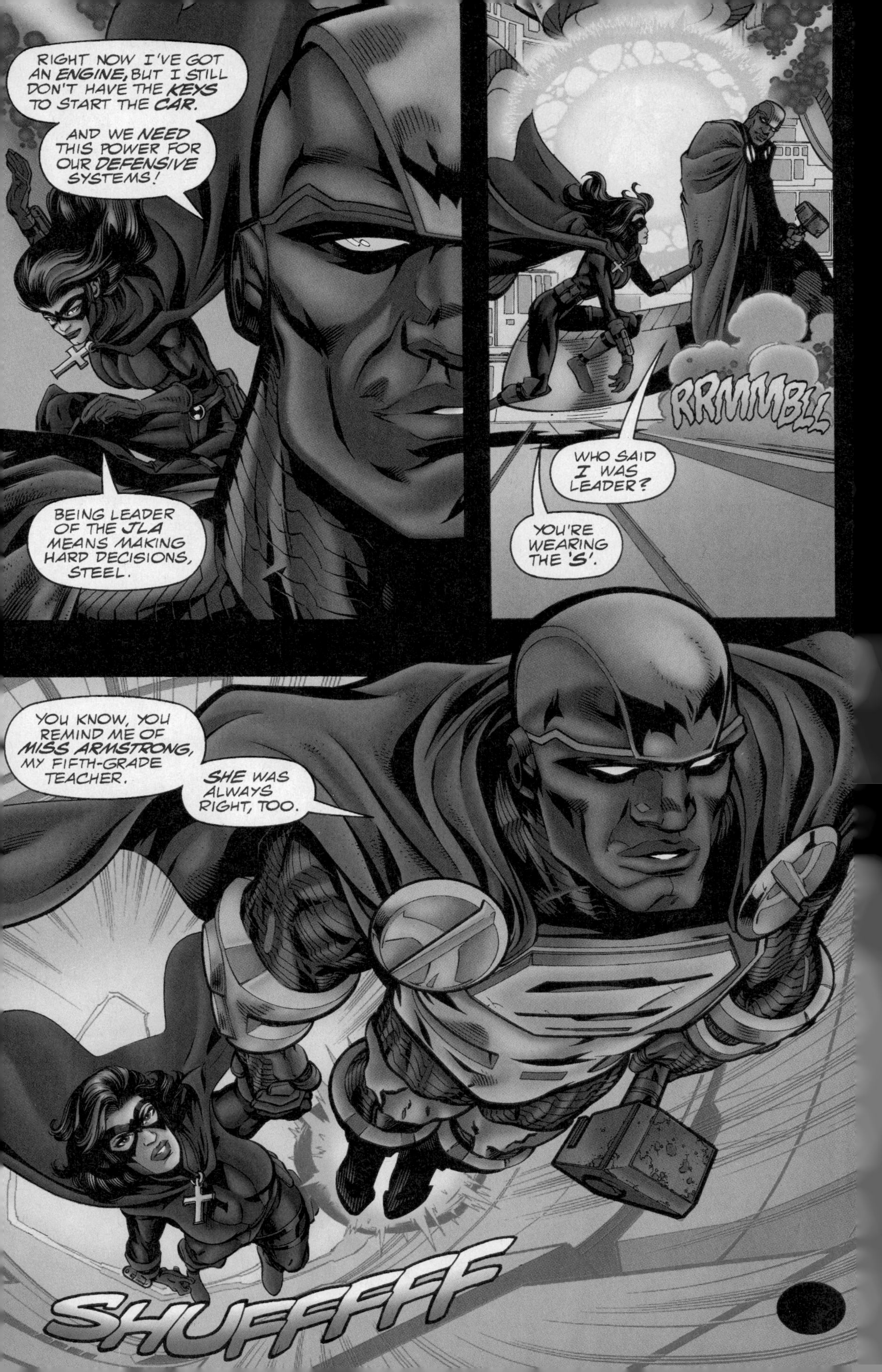
RIGHT NOW I'VE GOT AN ENGINE, BUT I STILL DON'T HAVE THE KEYS TO START THE CAR.
AND WE NEED THIS POWER FOR OUR DEFENSIVE SYSTEMS!
BEING LEADER OF THE JLA MEANS MAKING HARD DECISIONS, STEEL.
RRMMBLL
WHO SAID I WAS LEADER?
YOU'RE WEARING THE 'S'.
YOU KNOW, YOU REMIND ME OF MISS ARMSTRONG, MY FIFTH-GRADE TEACHER.
SHE WAS ALWAYS RIGHT, TOO.
SHUFFFFF

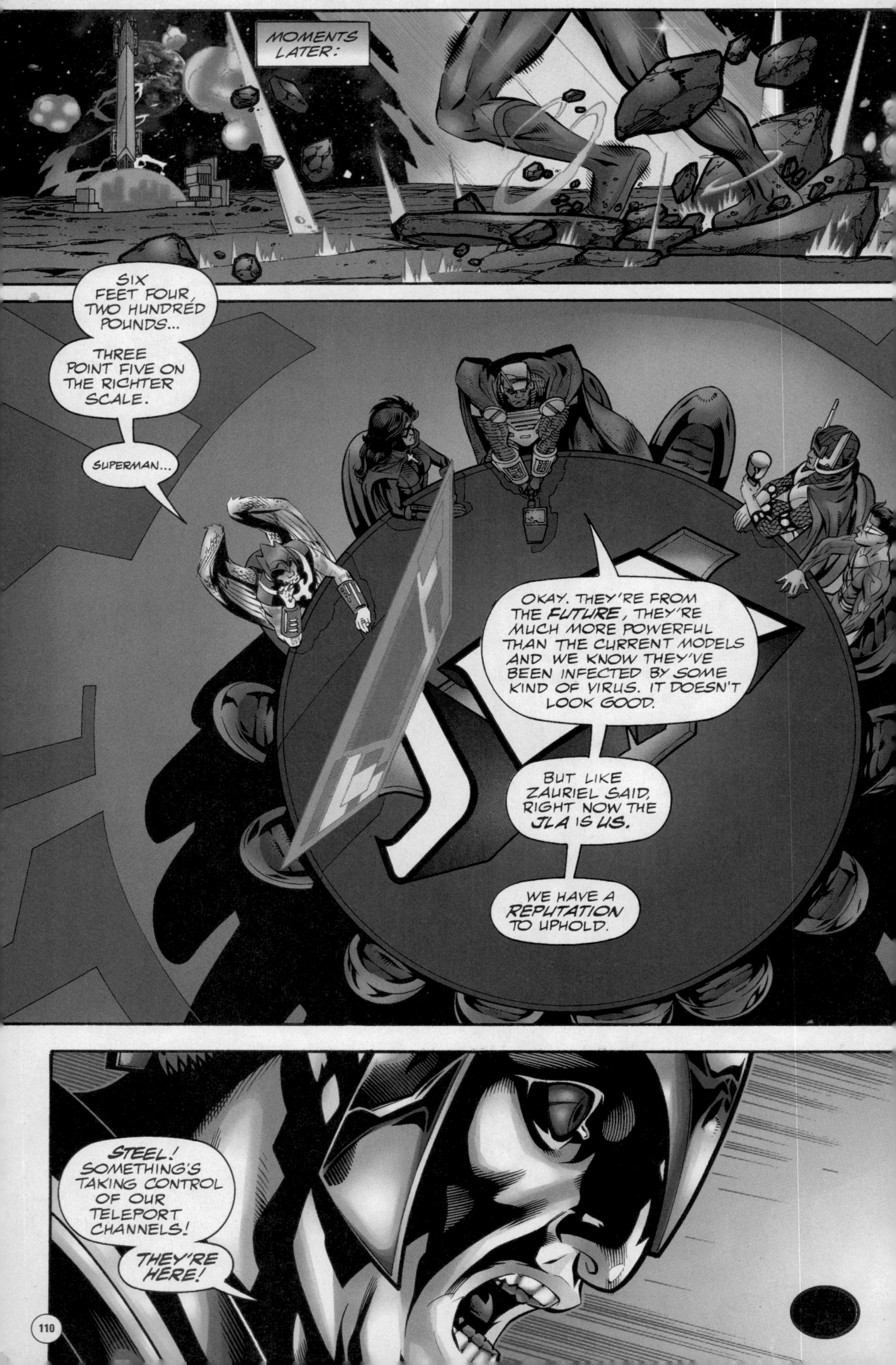

MOMENTS LATER:
SIX FEET FOUR, TWO HUNDRED POUNDS...
THREE POINT FIVE ON THE RICHTER SCALE.
SUPERMAN...
OKAY. THEY'RE FROM THE FUTURE, THEY'RE MUCH MORE POWERFUL THAN THE CURRENT MODELS AND WE KNOW THEY'VE BEEN INFECTED BY SOME KIND OF VIRUS. IT DOESN'T LOOK GOOD.
BUT LIKE ZAURIEL SAID, RIGHT NOW THE JLA IS US.
WE HAVE A REPUTATION TO UPHOLD.
STEEL! SOMETHING'S TAKING CONTROL OF OUR TELEPORT CHANNELS!
THEY'RE HERE!

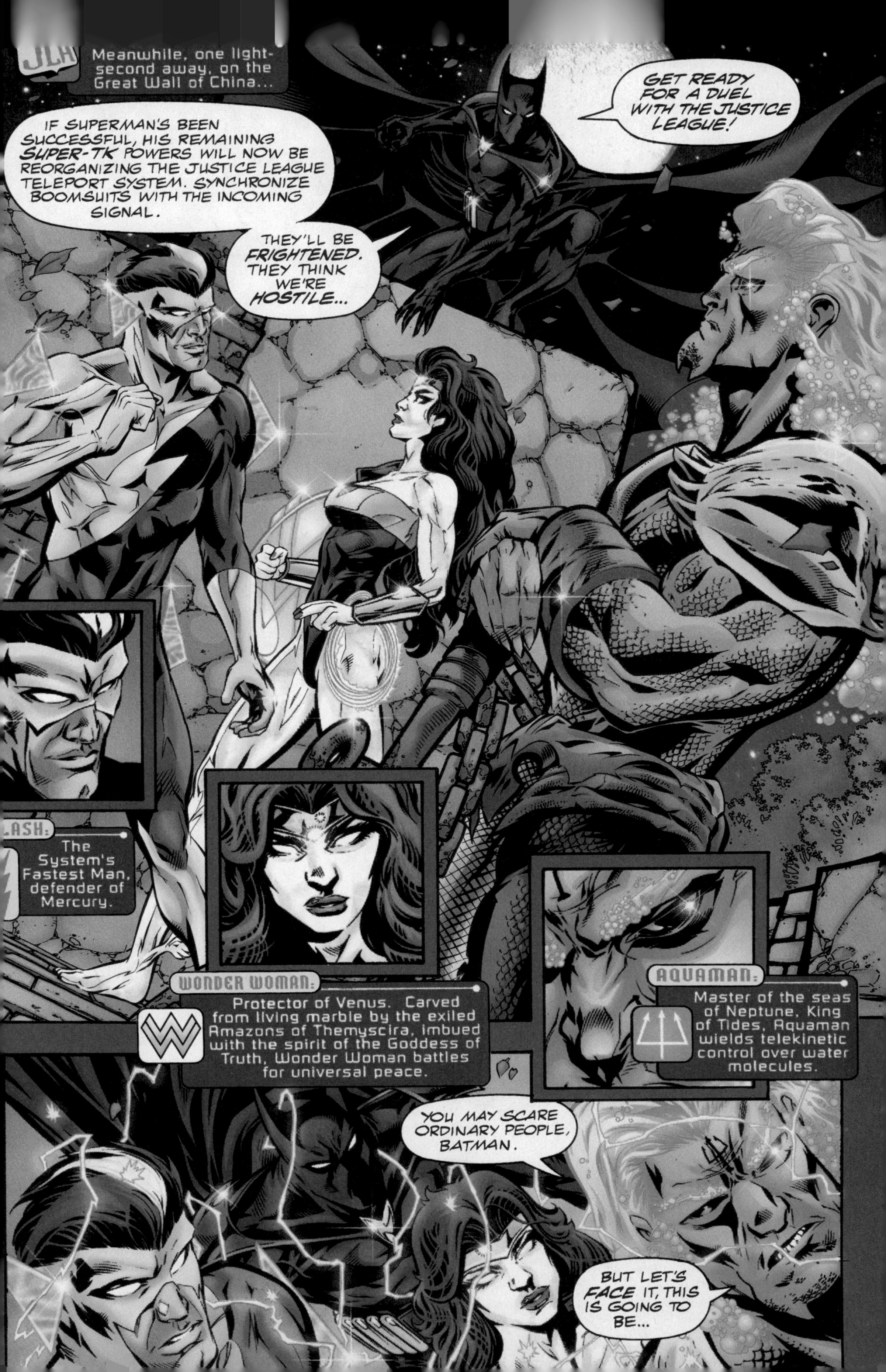
JLA
Meanwhile, one light-second away, on the Great Wall of China...
IF SUPERMAN'S BEEN SUCCESSFUL, HIS REMAINING SUPER-TK POWERS WILL NOW BE REORGANIZING THE JUSTICE LEAGUE TELEPORT SYSTEM. SYNCHRONIZE BOOMSUITS WITH THE INCOMING SIGNAL.
THEY'LL BE FRIGHTENED. THEY THINK WE'RE HOSTILE...
GET READY FOR A DUEL WITH THE JUSTICE LEAGUE!
LASH:
The System's Fastest Man, defender of Mercury.
WONDER WOMAN:
Protector of Venus. Carved from living marble by the exiled Amazons of Themyscira, imbued with the spirit of the Goddess of Truth, Wonder Woman battles for universal peace.
AQUAMAN:
Master of the seas of Neptune, King of Tides, Aquaman wields telekinetic control over water molecules.
YOU MAY SCARE ORDINARY PEOPLE, BATMAN.
BUT LET'S FACE IT, THIS IS GOING TO BE...

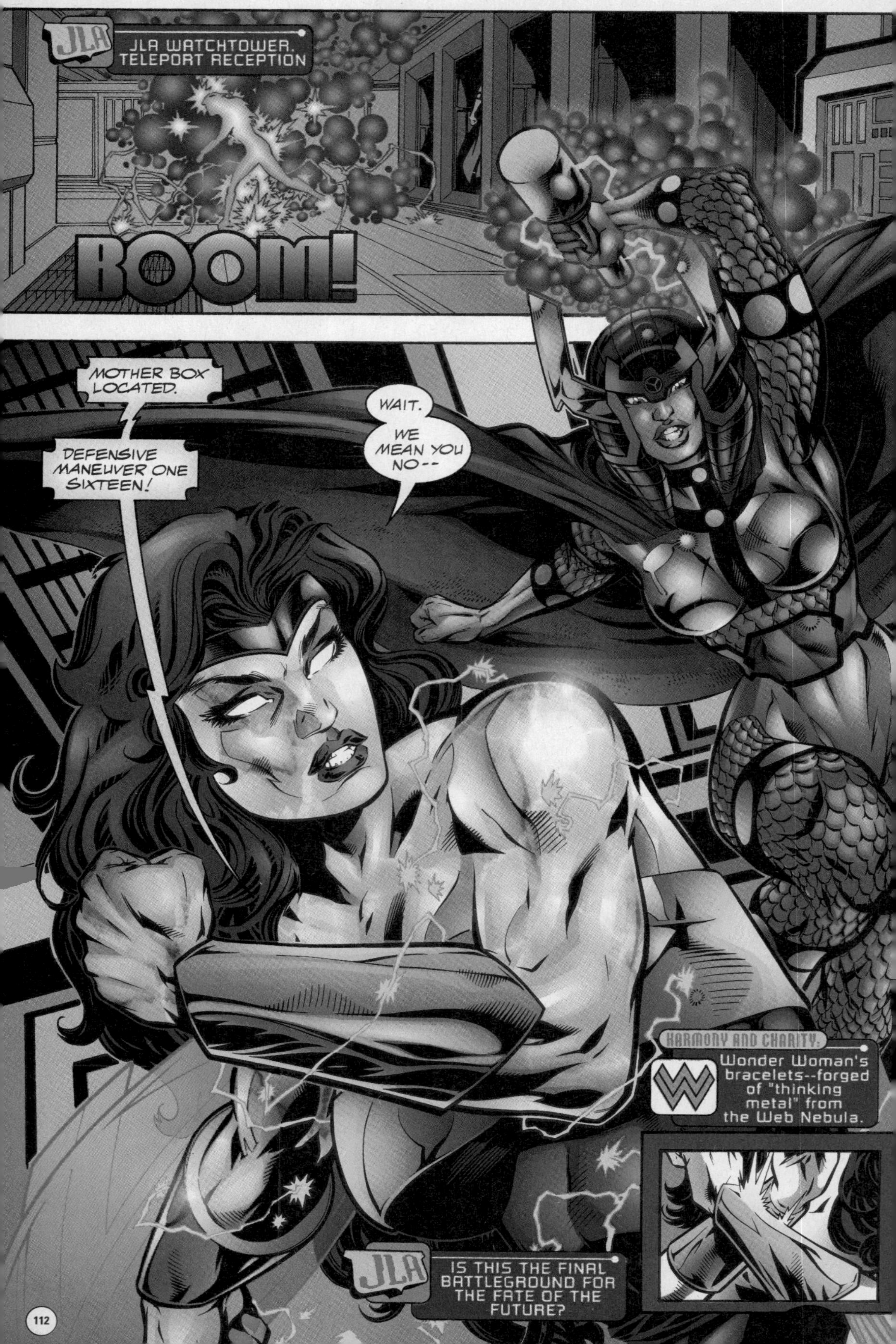
JLA
JLA WATCHTOWER. TELEPORT RECEPTION
BOOM!
MOTHER BOX LOCATED.
DEFENSIVE MANEUVER ONE SIXTEEN!
WAIT.
WE MEAN YOU NO--
HARMONY AND CHARITY.
Wonder Woman's bracelets--forged of "thinking metal" from the Web Nebula.
JLA
IS THIS THE FINAL BATTLEGROUND FOR THE FATE OF THE FUTURE?

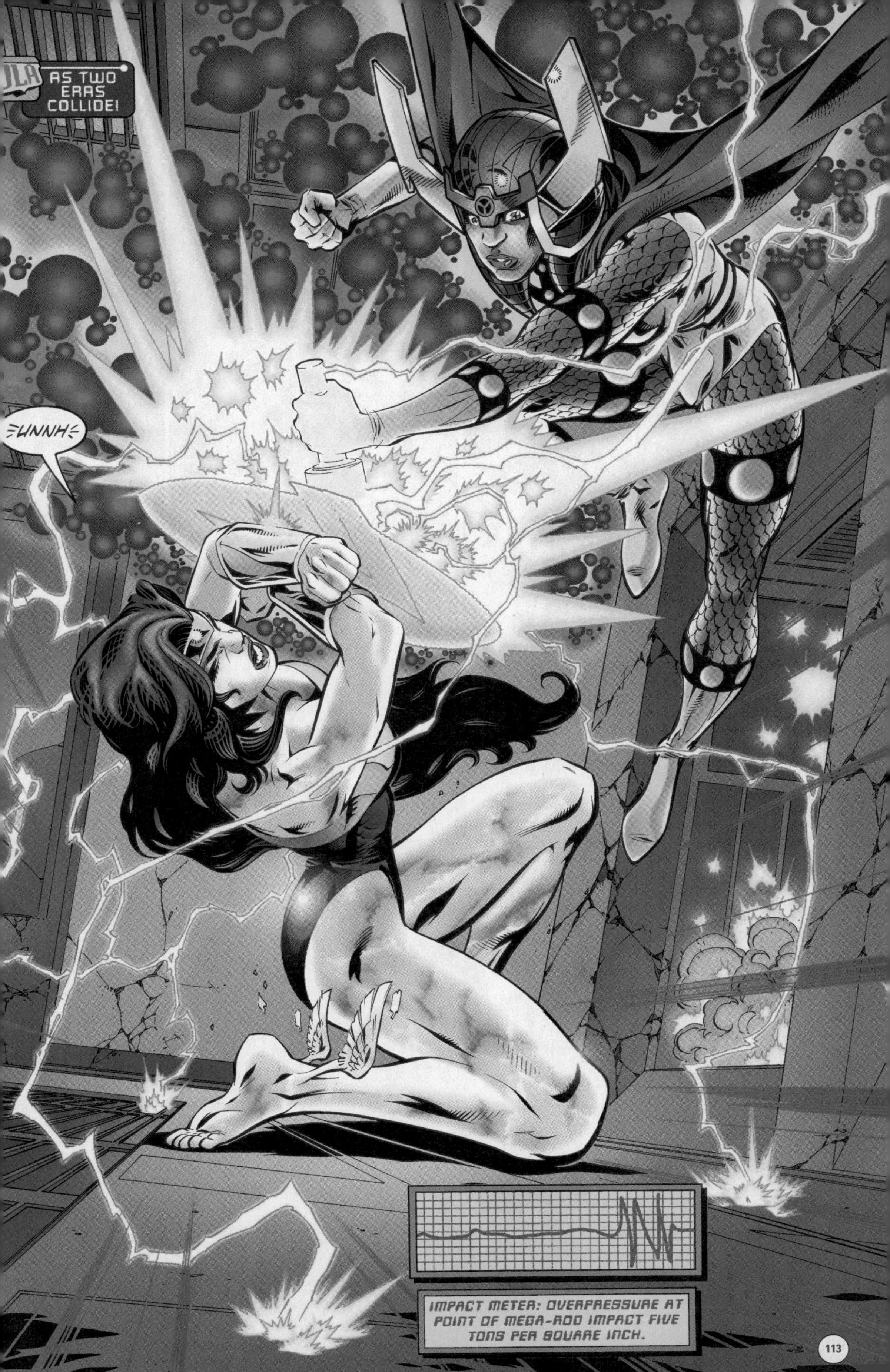
JLA
AS TWO ERAS COLLIDE!
UNNH
IMPACT METER: OVERPRESSURE AT POINT OF MEGA-ROD IMPACT FIVE TONS PER SQUARE INCH.

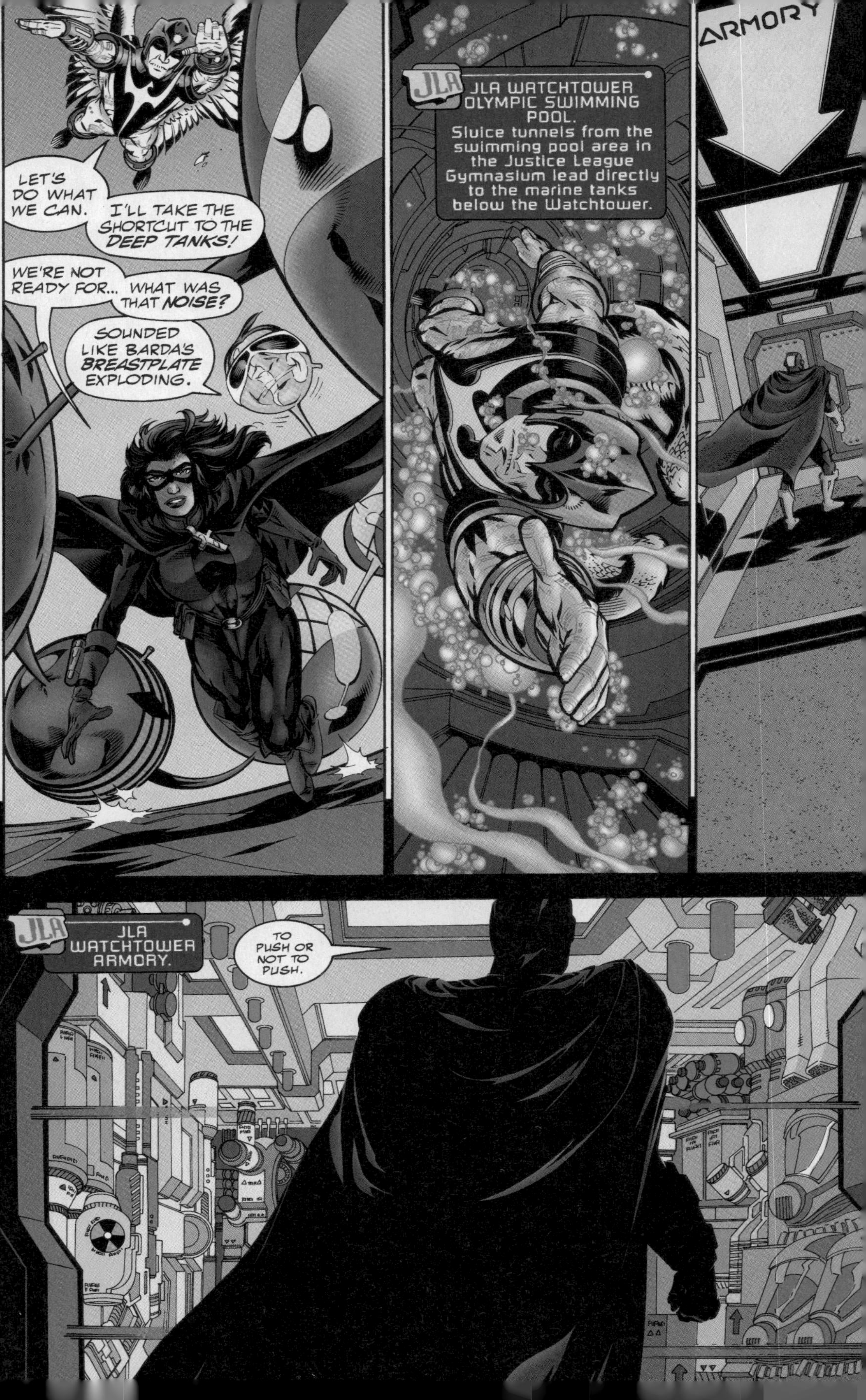
LET'S DO WHAT WE CAN.
I'LL TAKE THE SHORTCUT TO THE DEEP TANKS!
WE'RE NOT READY FOR... WHAT WAS THAT NOISE?
SOUNDED LIKE BARDA'S BREASTPLATE EXPLODING.
JLA
JLA WATCHTOWER OLYMPIC SWIMMING POOL.
Sluice tunnels from the swimming pool area in the Justice League Gymnasium lead directly to the marine tanks below the Watchtower.
ARMORY
JLA
JLA WATCHTOWER ARMORY.
TO PUSH OR NOT TO PUSH.

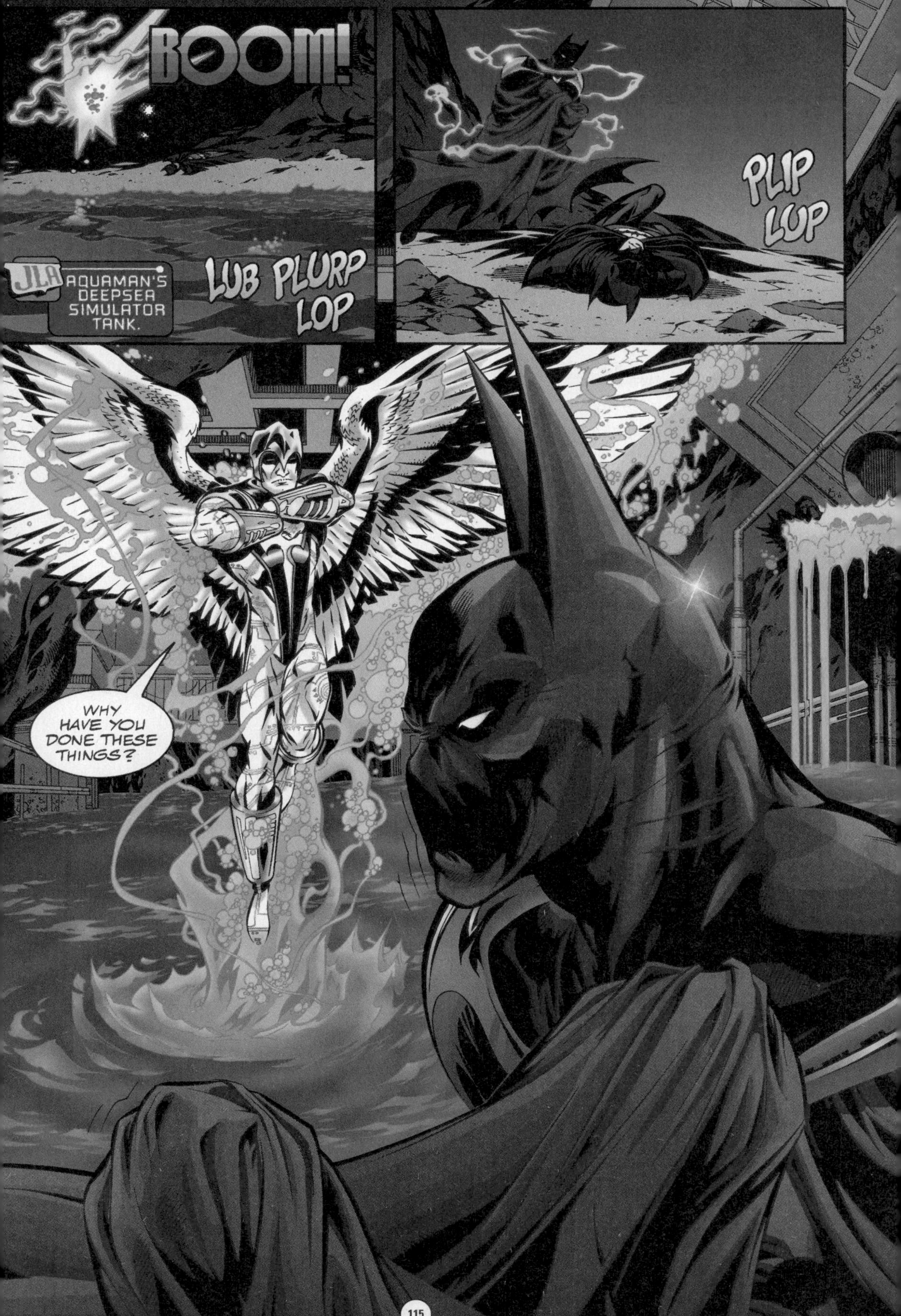
BOOM!
JLA AQUAMAN'S DEEPSEA SIMULATOR TANK.
LUB PLURP LOP
PLIP LOP
WHY HAVE YOU DONE THESE THINGS?

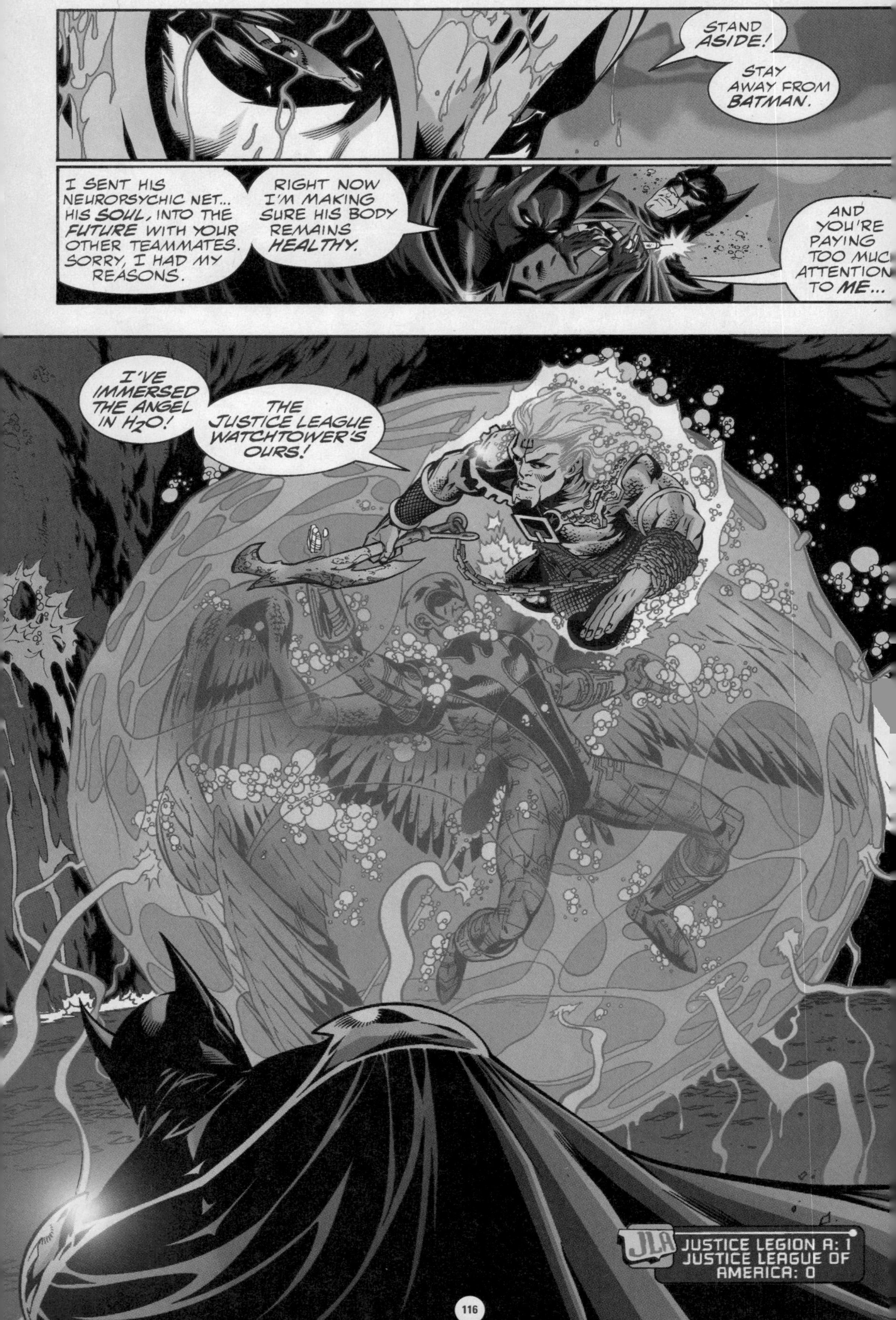
STAND ASIDE!
STAY AWAY FROM BATMAN.
I SENT HIS NEUROPSYCHIC NET... HIS SOUL, INTO THE FUTURE WITH YOUR OTHER TEAMMATES. SORRY, I HAD MY REASONS.
RIGHT NOW I'M MAKING SURE HIS BODY REMAINS HEALTHY.
AND YOU'RE PAYING TOO MUC ATTENTION TO ME...
I'VE IMMERSED THE ANGEL IN H2O!
THE JUSTICE LEAGUE WATCHTOWER'S OURS!
JLA
JUSTICE LEGION A: 1
JUSTICE LEAGUE OF AMERICA: 0

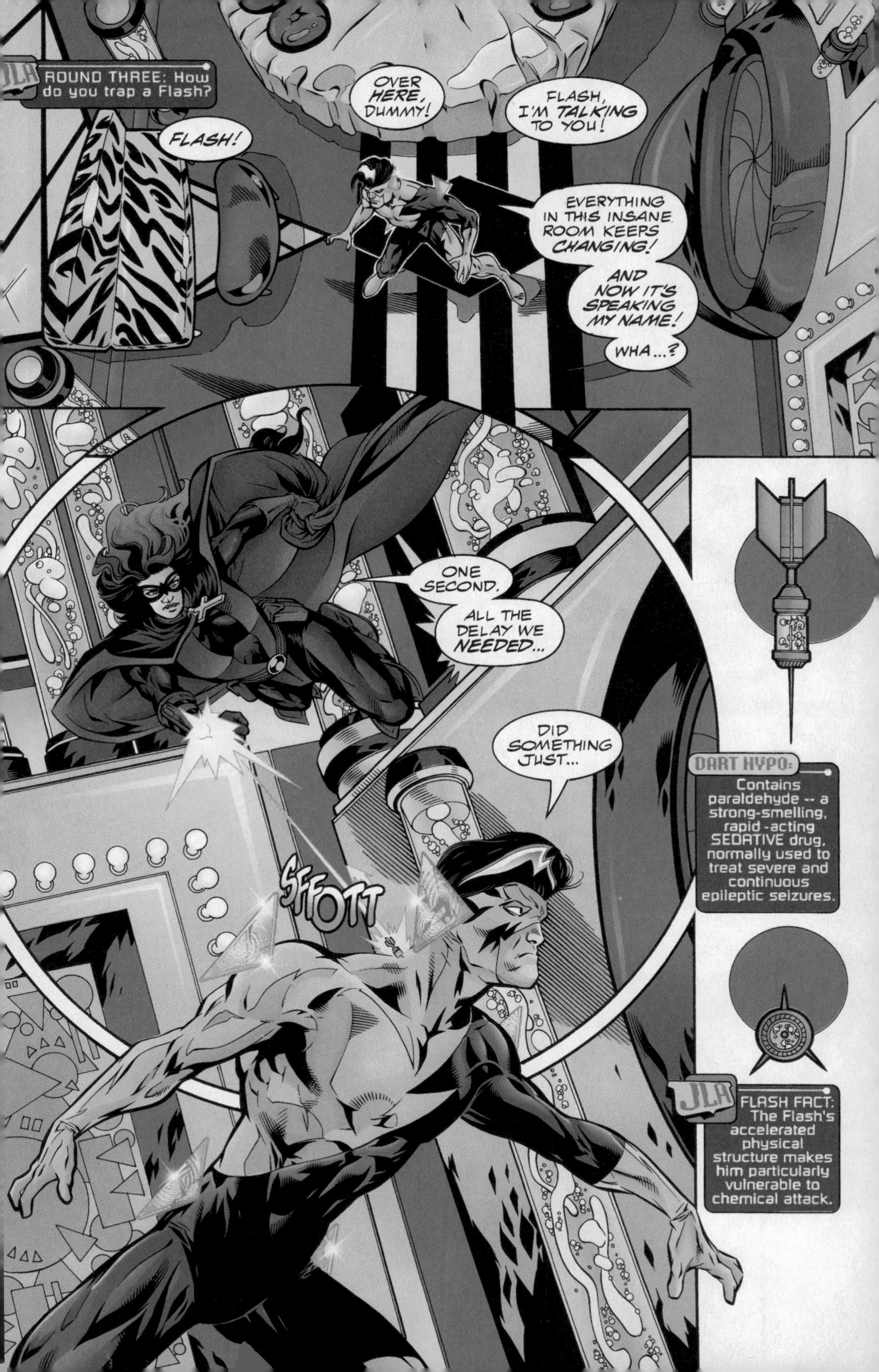
ROUND THREE: How do you trap a Flash?
FLASH!
OVER HERE, DUMMY!
FLASH, I'M TALKING TO YOU!
EVERYTHING IN THIS INSANE ROOM KEEPS CHANGING!
AND NOW IT'S SPEAKING MY NAME!
WHA...?
ONE SECOND.
ALL THE DELAY WE NEEDED...
DID SOMETHING JUST...
SFFOTT
DART HYPO:
Contains paraldehyde -- a strong-smelling, rapid-acting SEDATIVE drug, normally used to treat severe and continuous epileptic seizures.
FLASH FACT: The Flash's accelerated physical structure makes him particularly vulnerable to chemical attack.

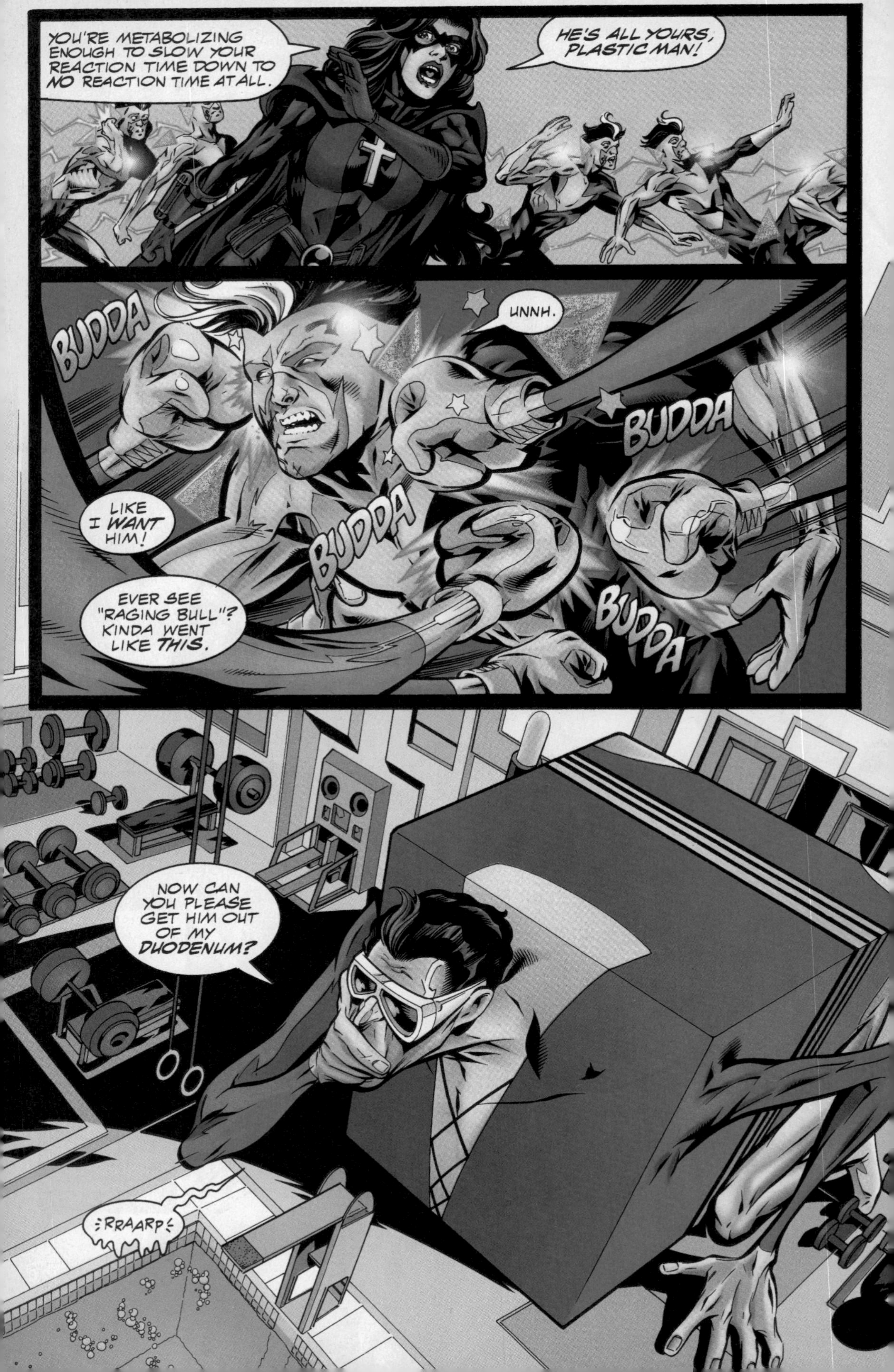
YOU'RE METABOLIZING ENOUGH TO SLOW YOUR REACTION TIME DOWN TO NO REACTION TIME AT ALL.
HE'S ALL YOURS, PLASTIC MAN!
BUDDA
UNNH.
BUDDA
LIKE I WANT HIM!
BUDDA
EVER SEE "RAGING BULL"? KINDA WENT LIKE THIS.
BUDDA
NOW CAN YOU PLEASE GET HIM OUT OF MY DUODENUM?
RRAARP

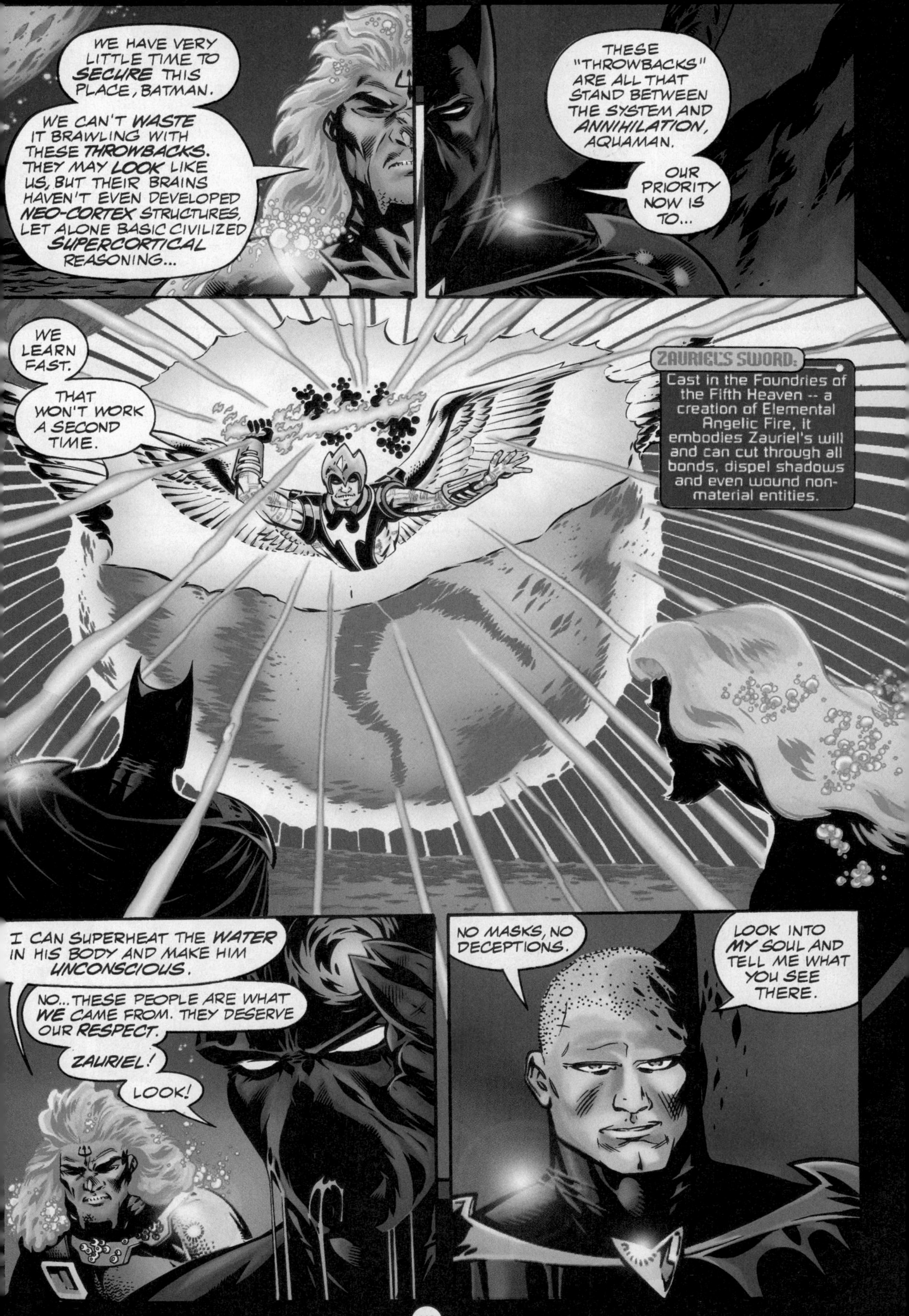
WE HAVE VERY LITTLE TIME TO SECURE THIS PLACE, BATMAN.
WE CAN'T WASTE IT BRAWLING WITH THESE THROWBACKS. THEY MAY LOOK LIKE US, BUT THEIR BRAINS HAVEN'T EVEN DEVELOPED NEO-CORTEX STRUCTURES, LET ALONE BASIC CIVILIZED SUPERCORTICAL REASONING...
THESE "THROWBACKS" ARE ALL THAT STAND BETWEEN THE SYSTEM AND ANNIHILATION, AQUAMAN.
OUR PRIORITY NOW IS TO...
WE LEARN FAST.
THAT WON'T WORK A SECOND TIME.
ZAURIEL'S SWORD:
Cast in the Foundries of the Fifth Heaven -- a creation of Elemental Angelic Fire, it embodies Zauriel's will and can cut through all bonds, dispel shadows and even wound non-material entities.
I CAN SUPERHEAT THE WATER IN HIS BODY AND MAKE HIM UNCONSCIOUS.
NO... THESE PEOPLE ARE WHAT WE CAME FROM. THEY DESERVE OUR RESPECT.
ZAURIEL!
LOOK!
NO MASKS, NO DECEPTIONS.
LOOK INTO MY SOUL AND TELL ME WHAT YOU SEE THERE.

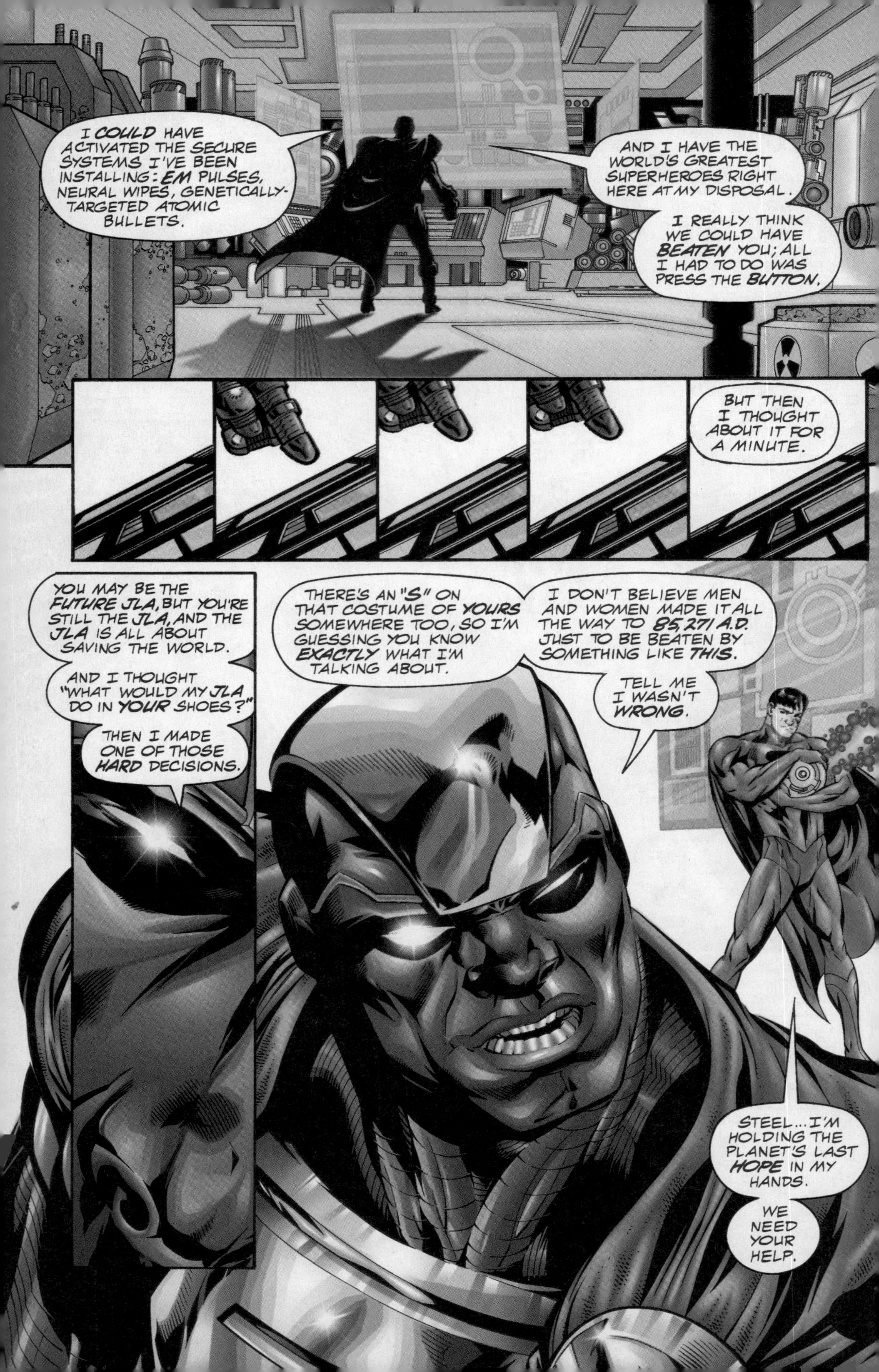
I COULD HAVE ACTIVATED THE SECURE SYSTEMS I'VE BEEN INSTALLING: EM PULSES, NEURAL WIPES, GENETICALLY-TARGETED ATOMIC BULLETS.
AND I HAVE THE WORLD'S GREATEST SUPERHEROES RIGHT HERE AT MY DISPOSAL.
I REALLY THINK WE COULD HAVE BEATEN YOU; ALL I HAD TO DO WAS PRESS THE BUTTON.
BUT THEN I THOUGHT ABOUT IT FOR A MINUTE.
YOU MAY BE THE FUTURE JLA, BUT YOU'RE STILL THE JLA, AND THE JLA IS ALL ABOUT SAVING THE WORLD.
AND I THOUGHT "WHAT WOULD MY JLA DO IN YOUR SHOES?"
THEN I MADE ONE OF THOSE HARD DECISIONS.
THERE'S AN "S" ON THAT COSTUME OF YOURS SOMEWHERE TOO, SO I'M GUESSING YOU KNOW EXACTLY WHAT I'M TALKING ABOUT.
I DON'T BELIEVE MEN AND WOMEN MADE IT ALL THE WAY TO 85,271 A.D. JUST TO BE BEATEN BY SOMETHING LIKE THIS.
TELL ME I WASN'T WRONG.
STEEL... I'M HOLDING THE PLANET'S LAST HOPE IN MY HANDS.
WE NEED YOUR HELP.

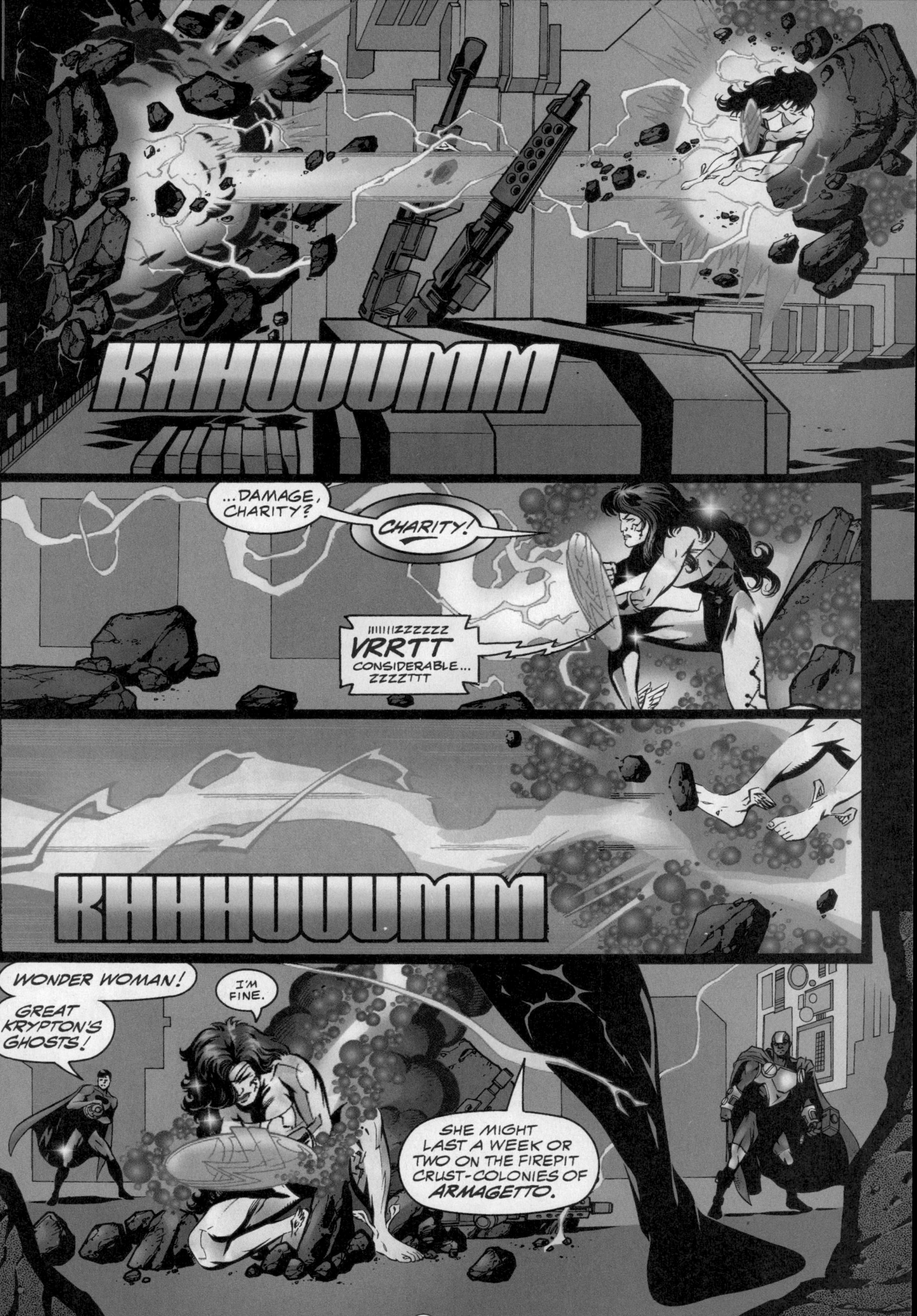
KHHUUUMMM
...DAMAGE, CHARITY?
CHARITY!
IIIIIIIZZZZZZ VRRTT CONSIDERABLE... ZZZZTTT
KHHHUUUMMM
WONDER WOMAN!
GREAT KRYPTON'S GHOSTS!
I'M FINE.
SHE MIGHT LAST A WEEK OR TWO ON THE FIREPIT CRUST-COLONIES OF ARMAGETTO.

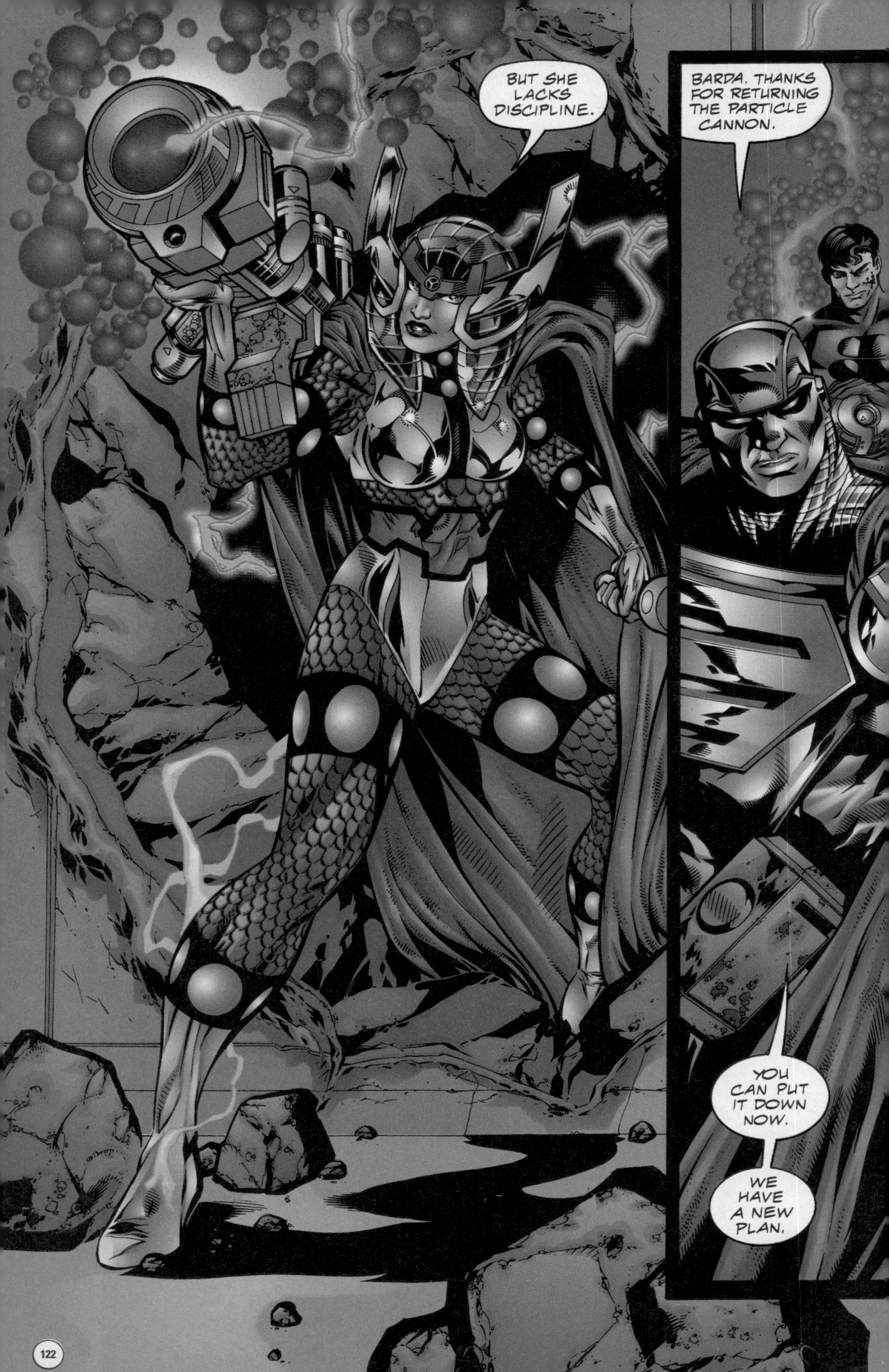
BUT SHE LACKS DISCIPLINE.
BARDA. THANKS FOR RETURNING THE PARTICLE CANNON.
YOU CAN PUT IT DOWN NOW.
WE HAVE A NEW PLAN.

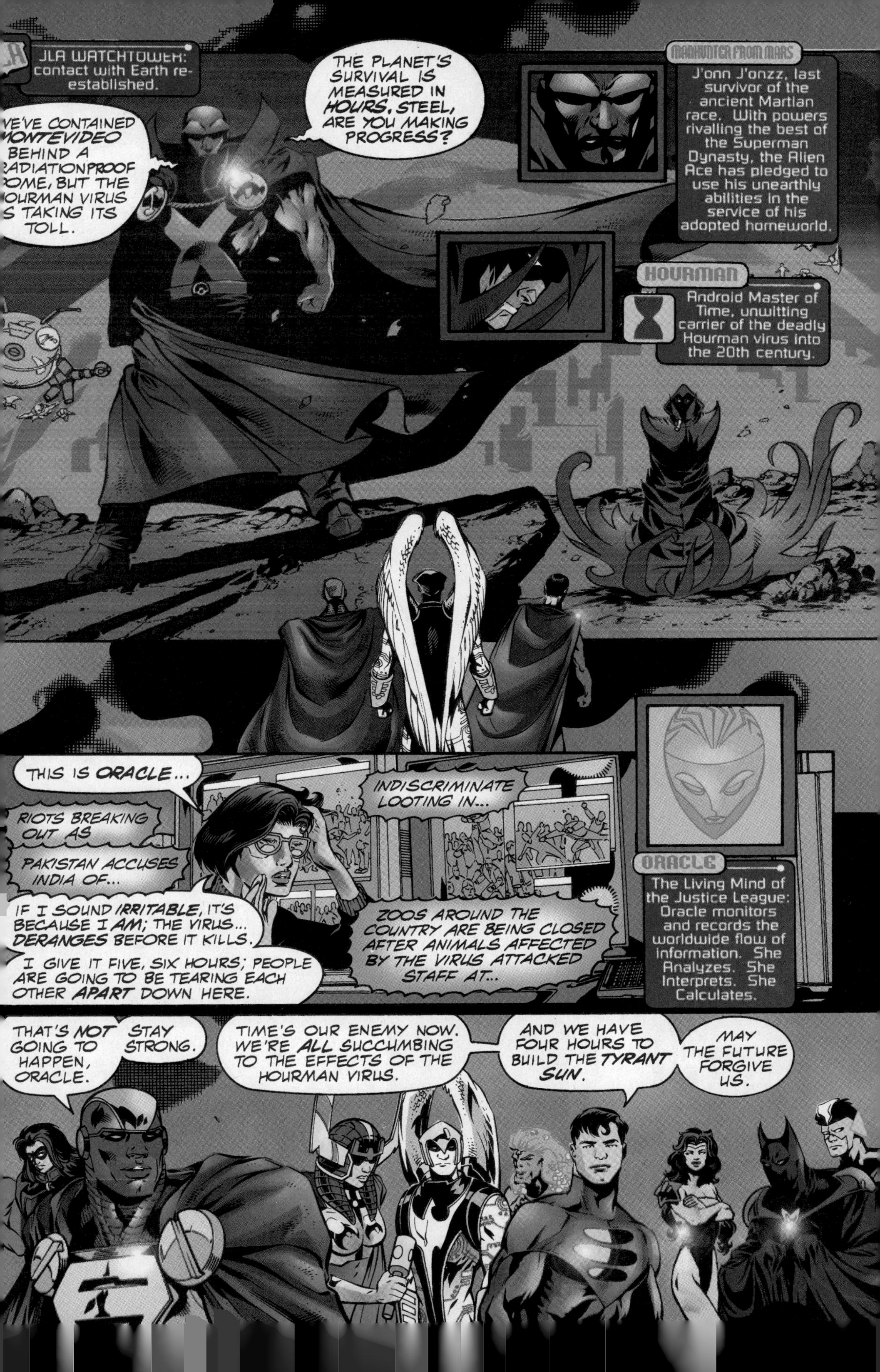
JLA WATCHTOWER: contact with Earth re-established.
WE'VE CONTAINED MONTEVIDEO BEHIND A RADIATIONPROOF DOME, BUT THE HOURMAN VIRUS IS TAKING ITS TOLL.
THE PLANET'S SURVIVAL IS MEASURED IN HOURS. STEEL, ARE YOU MAKING PROGRESS?
MANHUNTER FROM MARS
J'onn J'onzz, last survivor of the ancient Martian race. With powers rivalling the best of the Superman Dynasty, the Alien Ace has pledged to use his unearthly abilities in the service of his adopted homeworld.
HOURMAN
Android Master of Time, unwitting carrier of the deadly Hourman virus into the 20th century.
THIS IS ORACLE...
RIOTS BREAKING OUT AS
PAKISTAN ACCUSES INDIA OF...
INDISCRIMINATE LOOTING IN...
IF I SOUND IRRITABLE, IT'S BECAUSE I AM; THE VIRUS... DERANGES BEFORE IT KILLS.
I GIVE IT FIVE, SIX HOURS; PEOPLE ARE GOING TO BE TEARING EACH OTHER APART DOWN HERE.
ZOOS AROUND THE COUNTRY ARE BEING CLOSED AFTER ANIMALS AFFECTED BY THE VIRUS ATTACKED STAFF AT...
ORACLE
The Living Mind of the Justice League: Oracle monitors and records the worldwide flow of information. She Analyzes. She Interprets. She Calculates.
THAT'S NOT GOING TO HAPPEN, ORACLE.
STAY STRONG.
TIME'S OUR ENEMY NOW. WE'RE ALL SUCCUMBING TO THE EFFECTS OF THE HOURMAN VIRUS.
AND WE HAVE FOUR HOURS TO BUILD THE TYRANT SUN.
MAY THE FUTURE FORGIVE US.

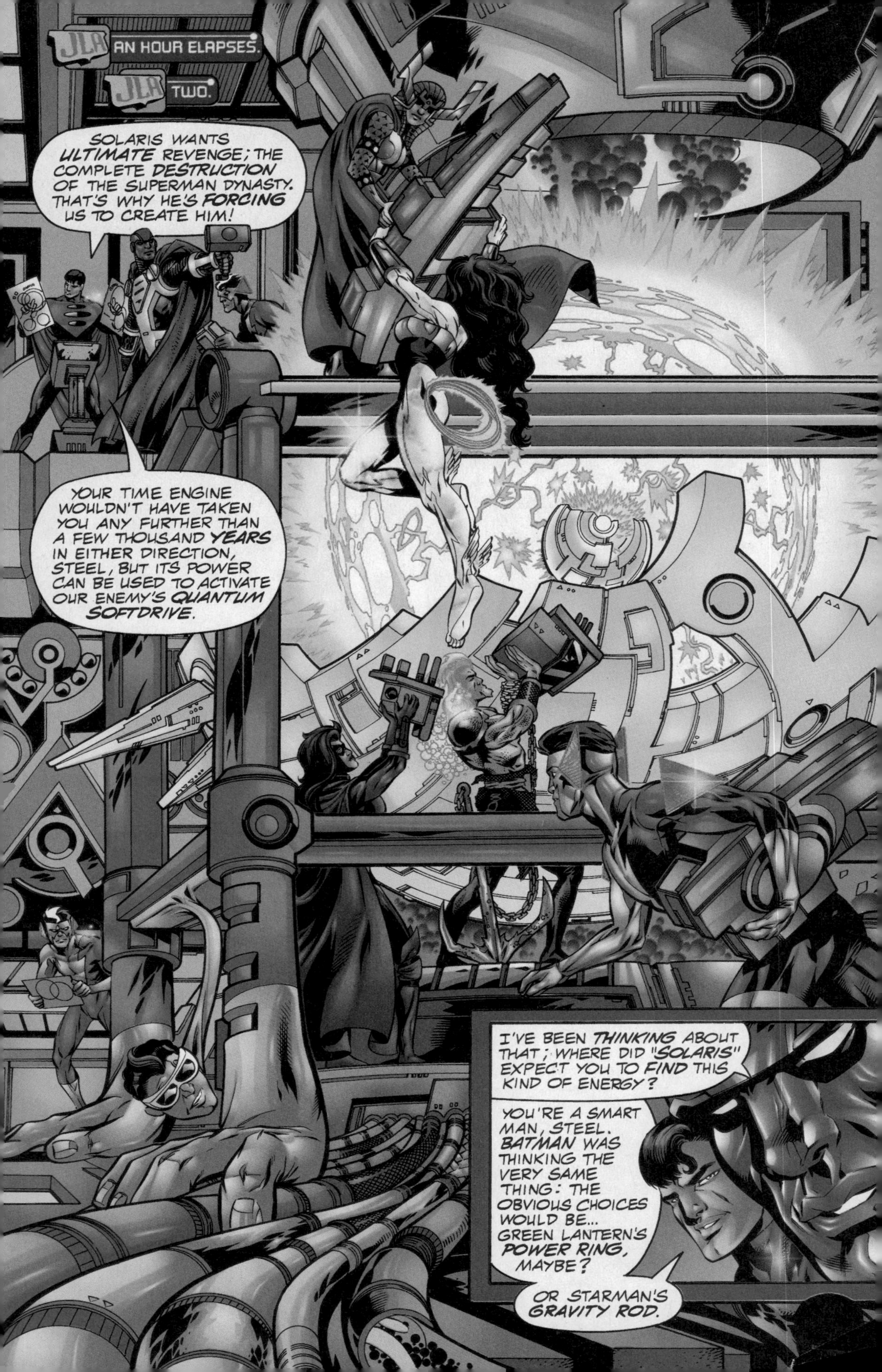
JLA AN HOUR ELAPSES.
JLA TWO.
SOLARIS WANTS ULTIMATE REVENGE; THE COMPLETE DESTRUCTION OF THE SUPERMAN DYNASTY. THAT'S WHY HE'S FORCING US TO CREATE HIM!
YOUR TIME ENGINE WOULDN'T HAVE TAKEN YOU ANY FURTHER THAN A FEW THOUSAND YEARS IN EITHER DIRECTION, STEEL, BUT ITS POWER CAN BE USED TO ACTIVATE OUR ENEMY'S QUANTUM SOFTDRIVE.
I'VE BEEN THINKING ABOUT THAT; WHERE DID "SOLARIS" EXPECT YOU TO FIND THIS KIND OF ENERGY?
YOU'RE A SMART MAN, STEEL. BATMAN WAS THINKING THE VERY SAME THING: THE OBVIOUS CHOICES WOULD BE... GREEN LANTERN'S POWER RING, MAYBE?
OR STARMAN'S GRAVITY ROD.

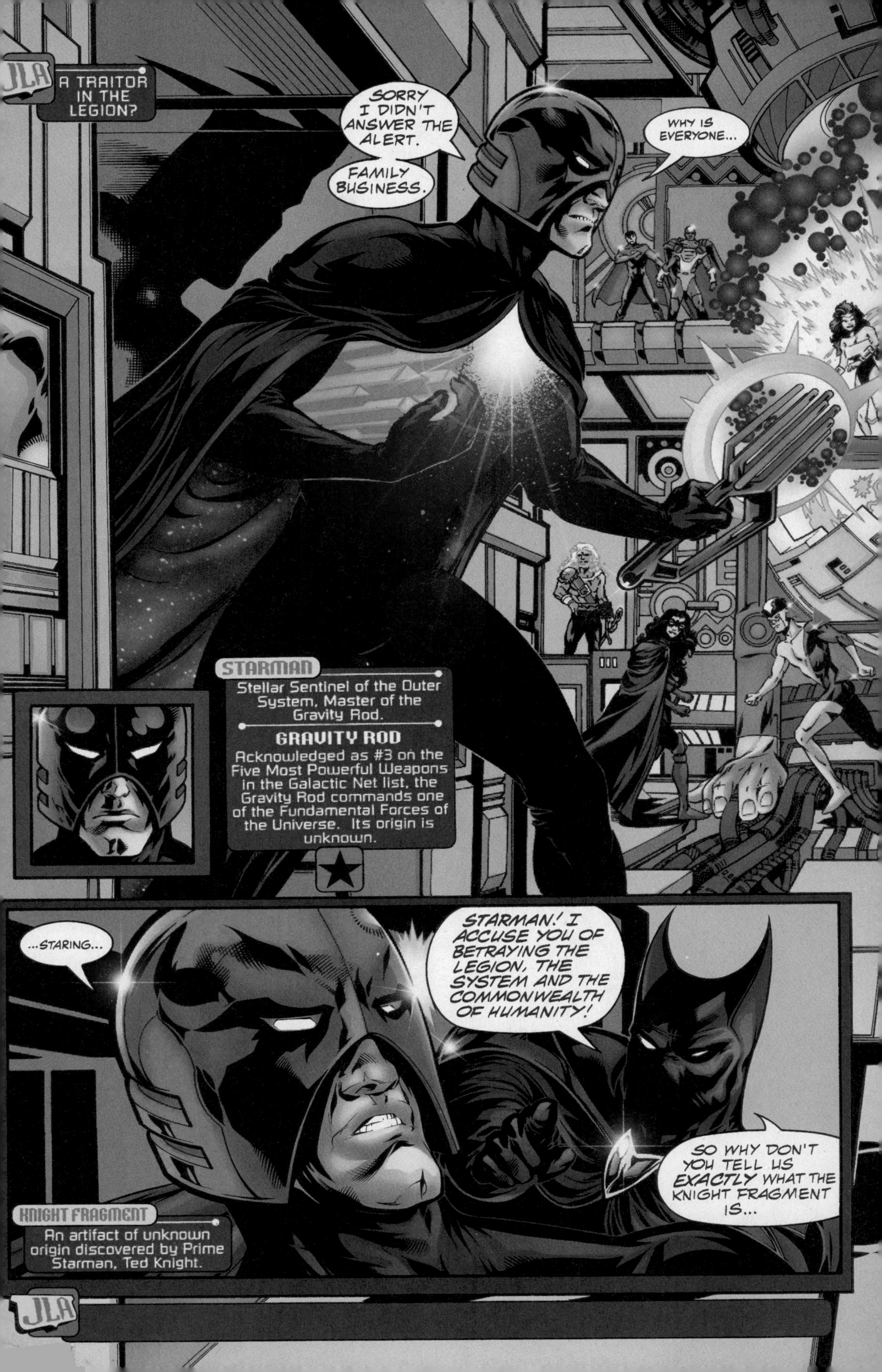
JLA
A TRAITOR IN THE LEGION?
SORRY I DIDN'T ANSWER THE ALERT.
FAMILY BUSINESS.
WHY IS EVERYONE...
STARMAN
Stellar Sentinel of the Outer System, Master of the Gravity Rod.
GRAVITY ROD
Acknowledged as #3 on the Five Most Powerful Weapons in the Galactic Net list, the Gravity Rod commands one of the Fundamental Forces of the Universe. Its origin is unknown.
...STARING...
STARMAN! I ACCUSE YOU OF BETRAYING THE LEGION, THE SYSTEM AND THE COMMONWEALTH OF HUMANITY!
SO WHY DON'T YOU TELL US EXACTLY WHAT THE KNIGHT FRAGMENT IS...
KNIGHT FRAGMENT
An artifact of unknown origin discovered by Prime Starman, Ted Knight.
JLA

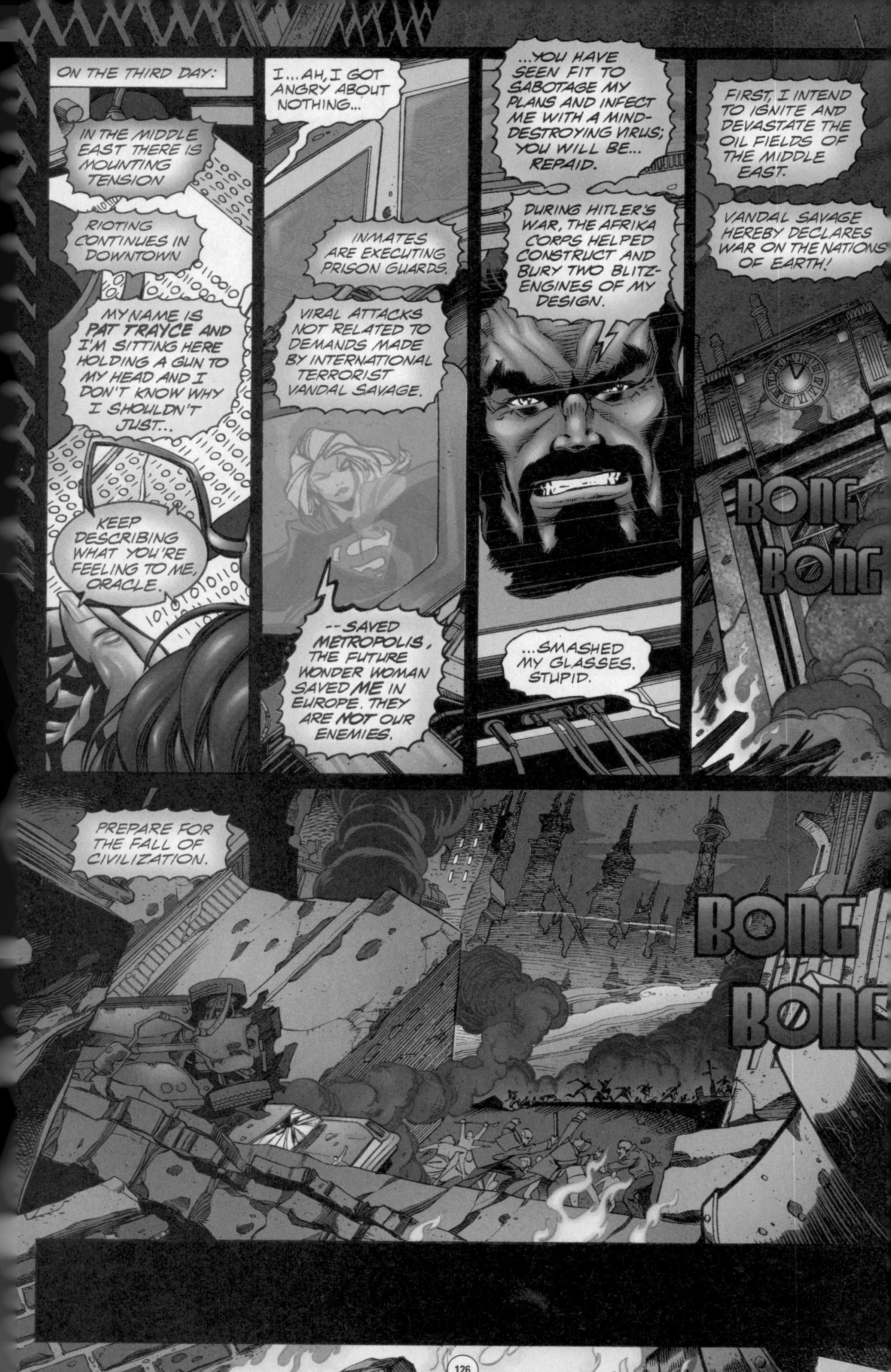

ON THE THIRD DAY:
IN THE MIDDLE EAST THERE IS MOUNTING TENSION
RIOTING CONTINUES IN DOWNTOWN
MY NAME IS PAT TRAYCE AND I'M SITTING HERE HOLDING A GUN TO MY HEAD AND I DON'T KNOW WHY I SHOULDN'T JUST...
KEEP DESCRIBING WHAT YOU'RE FEELING TO ME, ORACLE.
I...AH, I GOT ANGRY ABOUT NOTHING...
INMATES ARE EXECUTING PRISON GUARDS.
VIRAL ATTACKS NOT RELATED TO DEMANDS MADE BY INTERNATIONAL TERRORIST VANDAL SAVAGE.
--SAVED METROPOLIS, THE FUTURE WONDER WOMAN SAVED ME IN EUROPE. THEY ARE NOT OUR ENEMIES.
...YOU HAVE SEEN FIT TO SABOTAGE MY PLANS AND INFECT ME WITH A MIND-DESTROYING VIRUS; YOU WILL BE... REPAID.
DURING HITLER'S WAR, THE AFRIKA CORPS HELPED CONSTRUCT AND BURY TWO BLITZ-ENGINES OF MY DESIGN.
...SMASHED MY GLASSES. STUPID.
FIRST, I INTEND TO IGNITE AND DEVASTATE THE OIL FIELDS OF THE MIDDLE EAST.
VANDAL SAVAGE HEREBY DECLARES WAR ON THE NATIONS OF EARTH!
BONG
BONG
PREPARE FOR THE FALL OF CIVILIZATION.
BONG
BONG

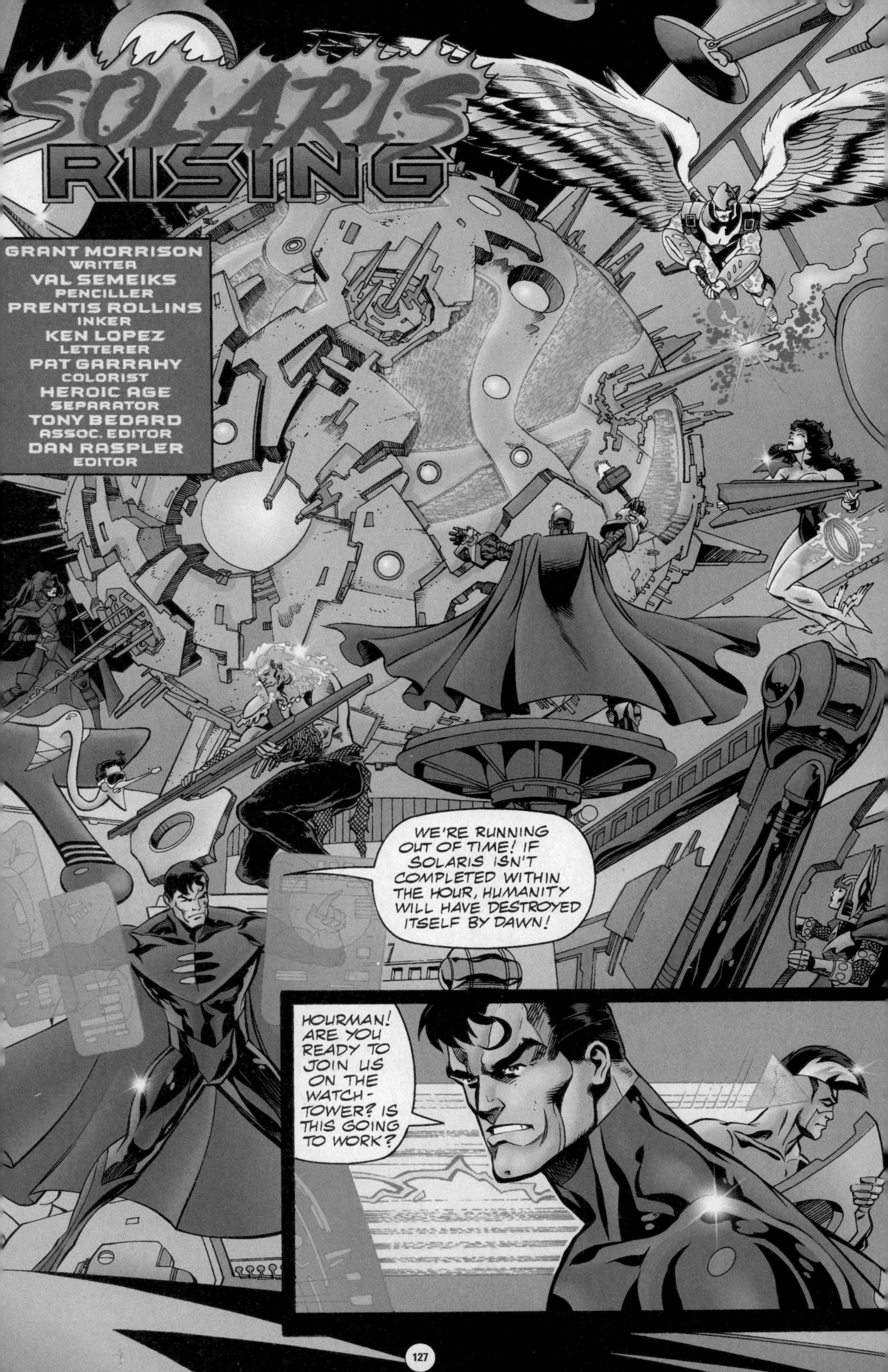
SOLARIS RISING
GRANT MORRISON WRITER
VAL SEMEIKS PENCILLER
PRENTIS ROLLINS INKER
KEN LOPEZ LETTERER
PAT GARRAHY COLORIST
HEROIC AGE SEPARATOR
TONY BEDARD ASSOC. EDITOR
DAN RASPLER EDITOR
WE'RE RUNNING OUT OF TIME! IF SOLARIS ISN'T COMPLETED WITHIN THE HOUR, HUMANITY WILL HAVE DESTROYED ITSELF BY DAWN!
HOURMAN! ARE YOU READY TO JOIN US ON THE WATCH-TOWER? IS THIS GOING TO WORK?

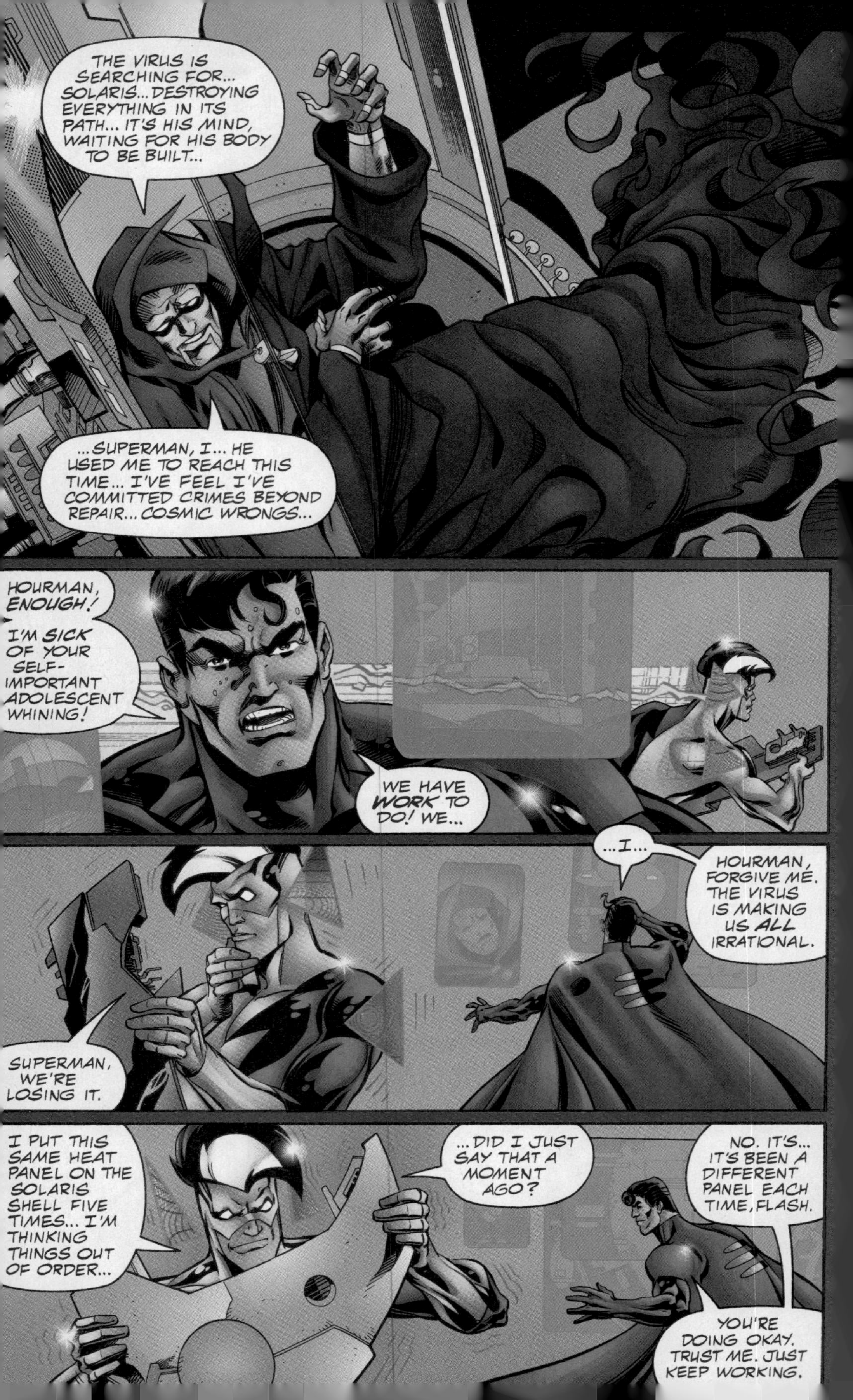
THE VIRUS IS SEARCHING FOR... SOLARIS... DESTROYING EVERYTHING IN ITS PATH... IT'S HIS MIND, WAITING FOR HIS BODY TO BE BUILT...
...SUPERMAN, I... HE USED ME TO REACH THIS TIME... I'VE FEEL I'VE COMMITTED CRIMES BEYOND REPAIR... COSMIC WRONGS...
HOURMAN, ENOUGH!
I'M SICK OF YOUR SELF-IMPORTANT ADOLESCENT WHINING!
WE HAVE WORK TO DO! WE...
...I...
HOURMAN, FORGIVE ME. THE VIRUS IS MAKING US ALL IRRATIONAL.
SUPERMAN, WE'RE LOSING IT.
I PUT THIS SAME HEAT PANEL ON THE SOLARIS SHELL FIVE TIMES... I'M THINKING THINGS OUT OF ORDER...
...DID I JUST SAY THAT A MOMENT AGO?
NO. IT'S... IT'S BEEN A DIFFERENT PANEL EACH TIME, FLASH.
YOU'RE DOING OKAY. TRUST ME. JUST KEEP WORKING.

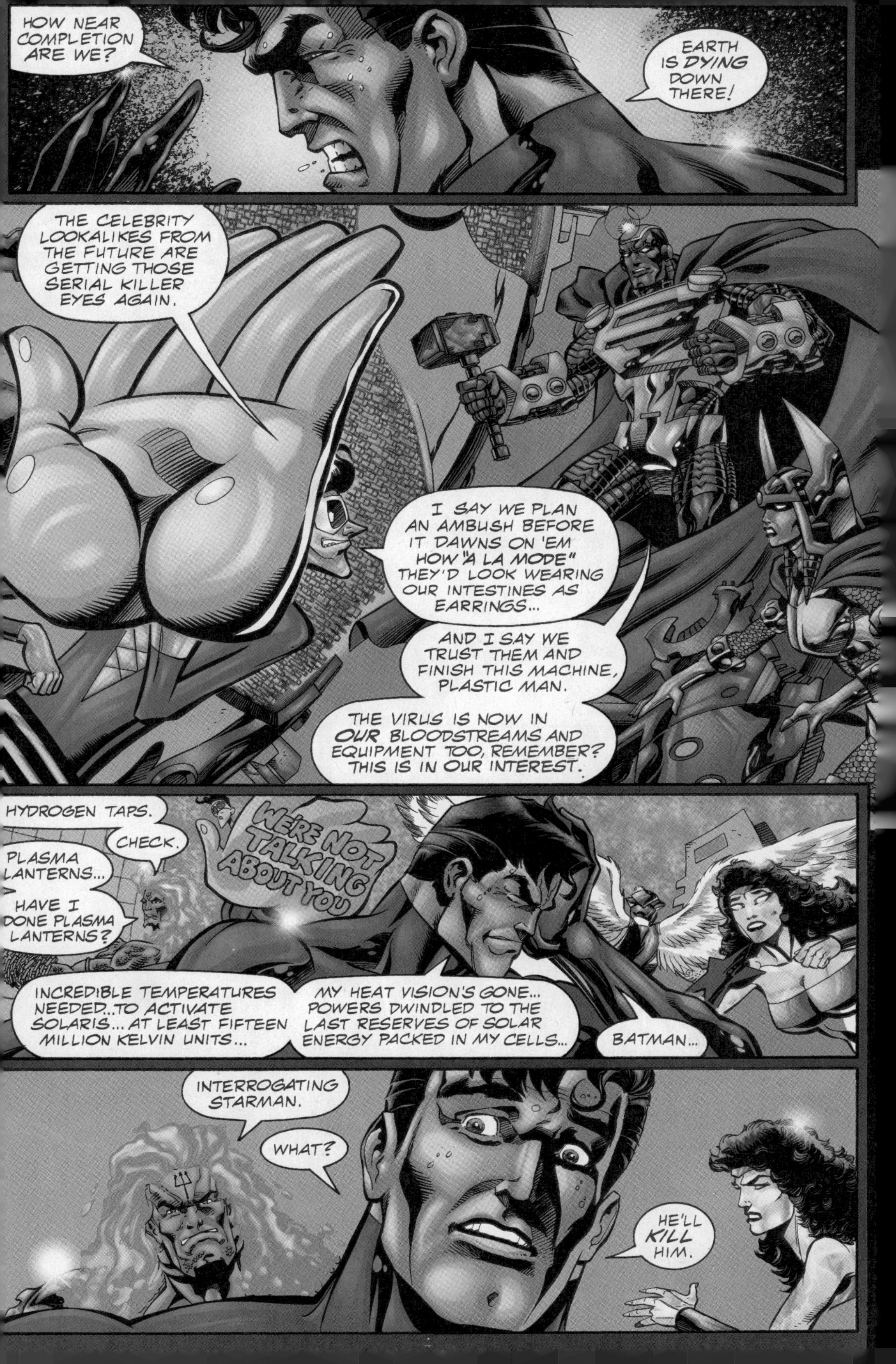
HOW NEAR COMPLETION ARE WE?
EARTH IS DYING DOWN THERE!
THE CELEBRITY LOOKALIKES FROM THE FUTURE ARE GETTING THOSE SERIAL KILLER EYES AGAIN.
I SAY WE PLAN AN AMBUSH BEFORE IT DAWNS ON 'EM HOW "A LA MODE" THEY'D LOOK WEARING OUR INTESTINES AS EARRINGS...
AND I SAY WE TRUST THEM AND FINISH THIS MACHINE, PLASTIC MAN.
THE VIRUS IS NOW IN OUR BLOODSTREAMS AND EQUIPMENT TOO, REMEMBER? THIS IS IN OUR INTEREST.
HYDROGEN TAPS.
CHECK.
WE'RE NOT TALKING ABOUT YOU
PLASMA LANTERNS...
HAVE I DONE PLASMA LANTERNS?
INCREDIBLE TEMPERATURES NEEDED...TO ACTIVATE SOLARIS... AT LEAST FIFTEEN MILLION KELVIN UNITS...
MY HEAT VISION'S GONE... POWERS DWINDLED TO THE LAST RESERVES OF SOLAR ENERGY PACKED IN MY CELLS...
BATMAN...
INTERROGATING STARMAN.
WHAT?
HE'LL KILL HIM.

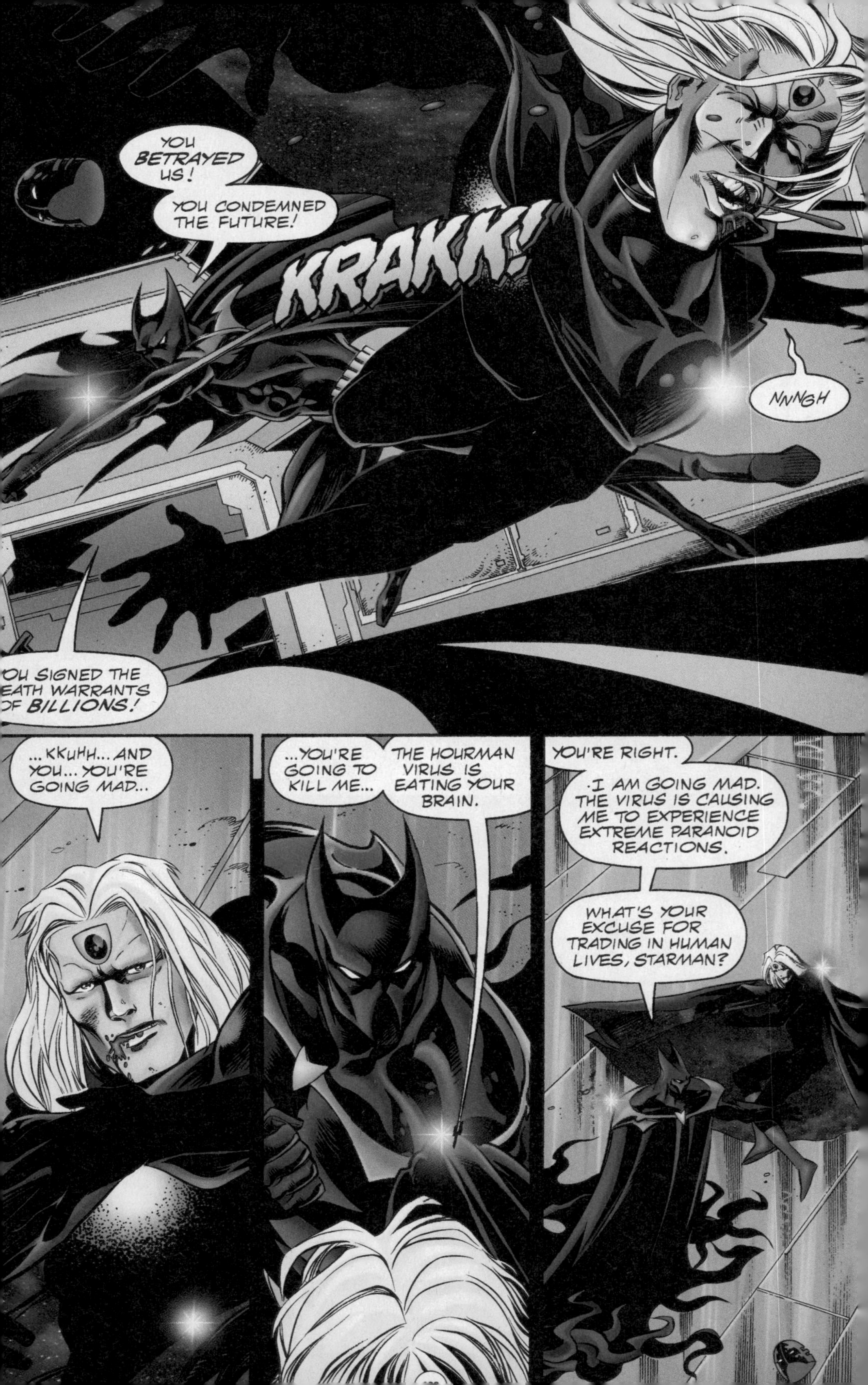

YOU BETRAYED US!
YOU CONDEMNED THE FUTURE!
KRAKK!
NNNGH
OU SIGNED THE EATH WARRANTS OF BILLIONS!
...KKUHH...AND YOU...YOU'RE GOING MAD...
...YOU'RE GOING TO KILL ME...
THE HOURMAN VIRUS IS EATING YOUR BRAIN.
YOU'RE RIGHT.
I AM GOING MAD. THE VIRUS IS CAUSING ME TO EXPERIENCE EXTREME PARANOID REACTIONS.
WHAT'S YOUR EXCUSE FOR TRADING IN HUMAN LIVES, STARMAN?

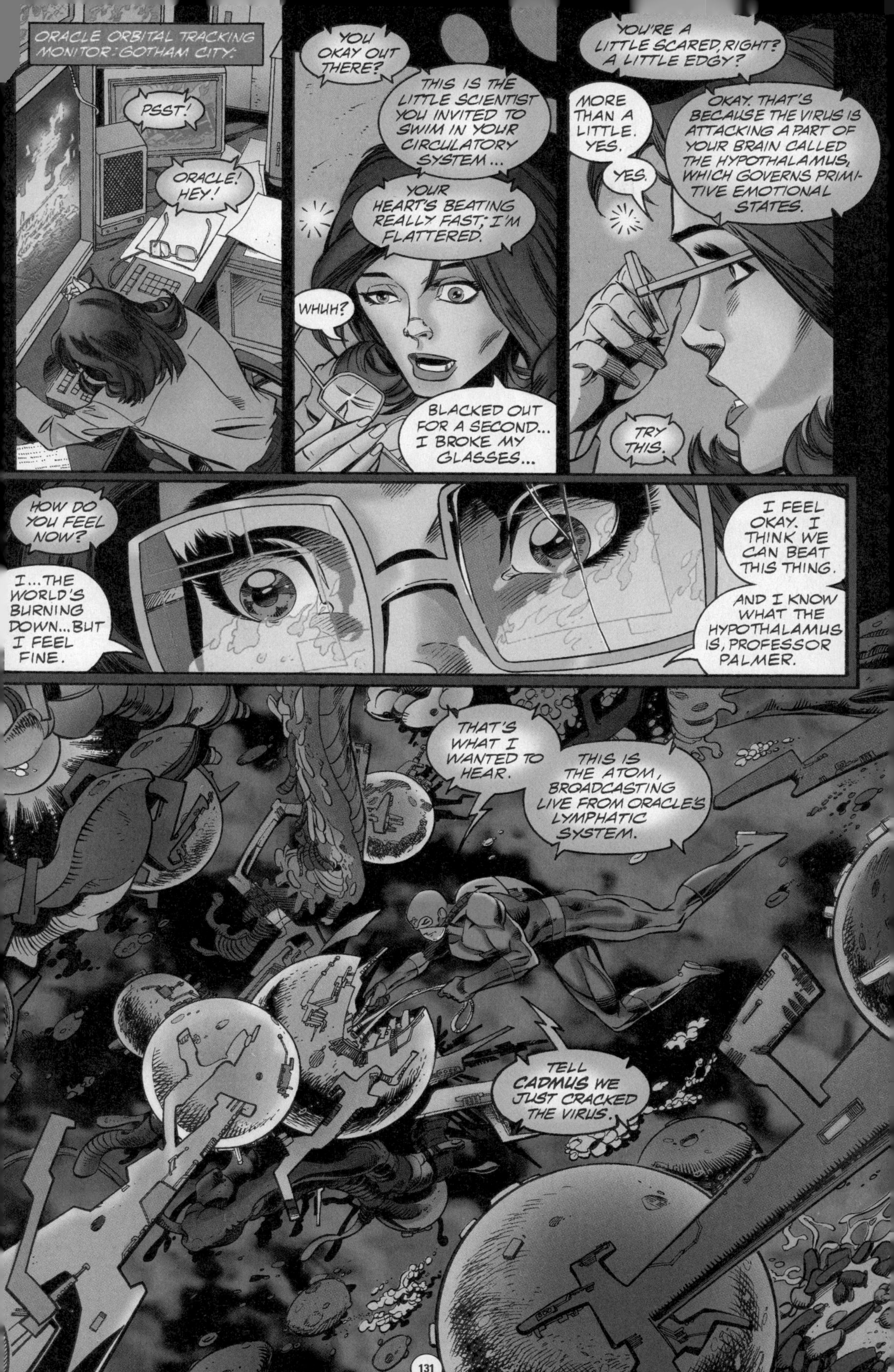
ORACLE ORBITAL TRACKING MONITOR: GOTHAM CITY.
PSST!
ORACLE! HEY!
YOU OKAY OUT THERE?
THIS IS THE LITTLE SCIENTIST YOU INVITED TO SWIM IN YOUR CIRCULATORY SYSTEM...
YOUR HEART'S BEATING REALLY FAST; I'M FLATTERED.
WHUH?
BLACKED OUT FOR A SECOND... I BROKE MY GLASSES...
YOU'RE A LITTLE SCARED, RIGHT? A LITTLE EDGY?
MORE THAN A LITTLE. YES.
YES.
OKAY. THAT'S BECAUSE THE VIRUS IS ATTACKING A PART OF YOUR BRAIN CALLED THE HYPOTHALAMUS, WHICH GOVERNS PRIMITIVE EMOTIONAL STATES.
TRY THIS.
HOW DO YOU FEEL NOW?
I... THE WORLD'S BURNING DOWN... BUT I FEEL FINE.
I FEEL OKAY. I THINK WE CAN BEAT THIS THING.
AND I KNOW WHAT THE HYPOTHALAMUS IS, PROFESSOR PALMER.
THAT'S WHAT I WANTED TO HEAR.
THIS IS THE ATOM, BROADCASTING LIVE FROM ORACLE'S LYMPHATIC SYSTEM.
TELL CADMUS WE JUST CRACKED THE VIRUS.

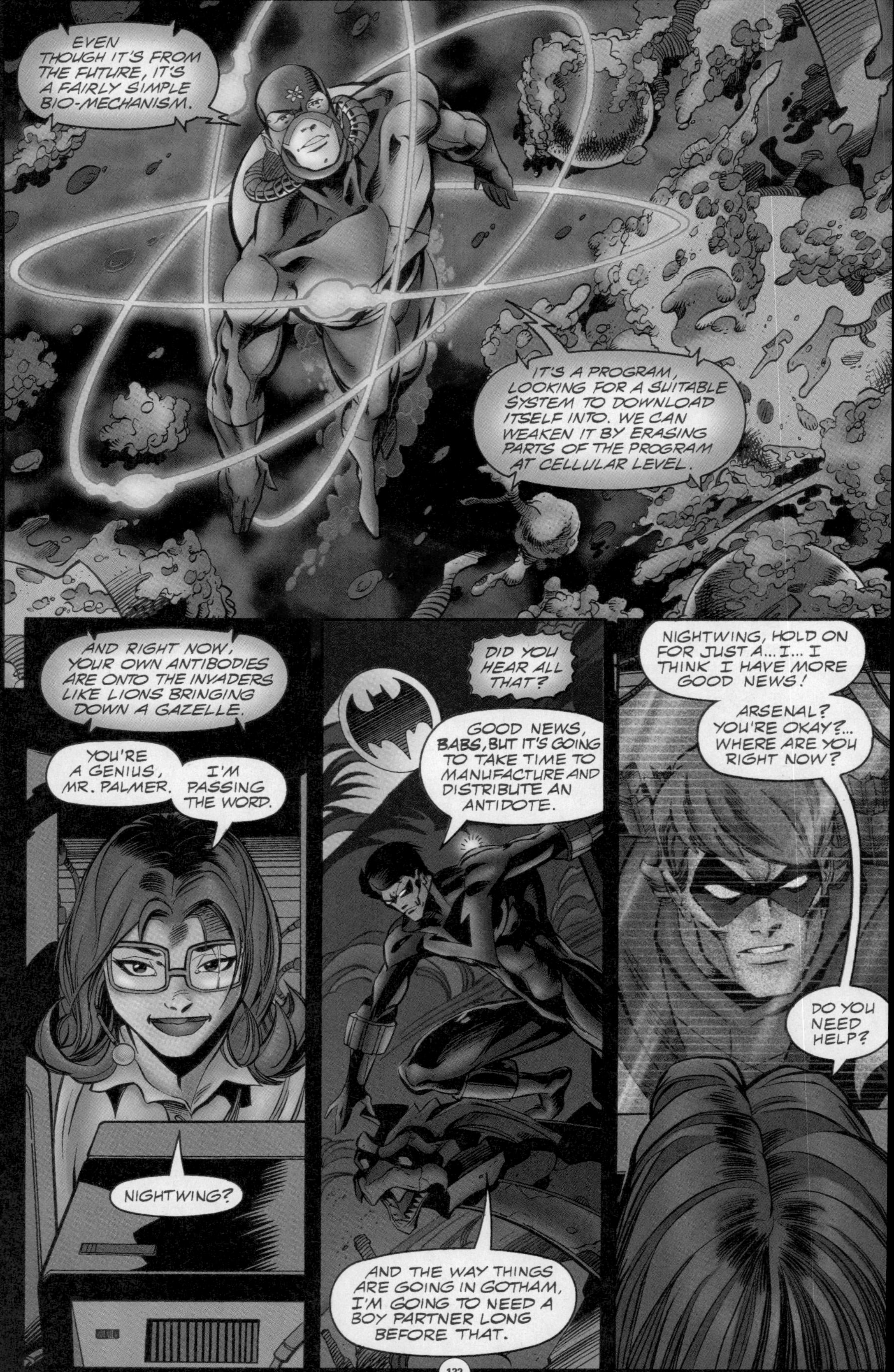
EVEN THOUGH IT'S FROM THE FUTURE, IT'S A FAIRLY SIMPLE BIO-MECHANISM.
IT'S A PROGRAM, LOOKING FOR A SUITABLE SYSTEM TO DOWNLOAD ITSELF INTO. WE CAN WEAKEN IT BY ERASING PARTS OF THE PROGRAM AT CELLULAR LEVEL.
AND RIGHT NOW, YOUR OWN ANTIBODIES ARE ONTO THE INVADERS LIKE LIONS BRINGING DOWN A GAZELLE.
YOU'RE A GENIUS, MR. PALMER.
I'M PASSING THE WORD.
NIGHTWING?
DID YOU HEAR ALL THAT?
GOOD NEWS, BABS, BUT IT'S GOING TO TAKE TIME TO MANUFACTURE AND DISTRIBUTE AN ANTIDOTE.
AND THE WAY THINGS ARE GOING IN GOTHAM, I'M GOING TO NEED A BOY PARTNER LONG BEFORE THAT.
NIGHTWING, HOLD ON FOR JUST A... I... I THINK I HAVE MORE GOOD NEWS!
ARSENAL? YOU'RE OKAY?... WHERE ARE YOU RIGHT NOW?
DO YOU NEED HELP?

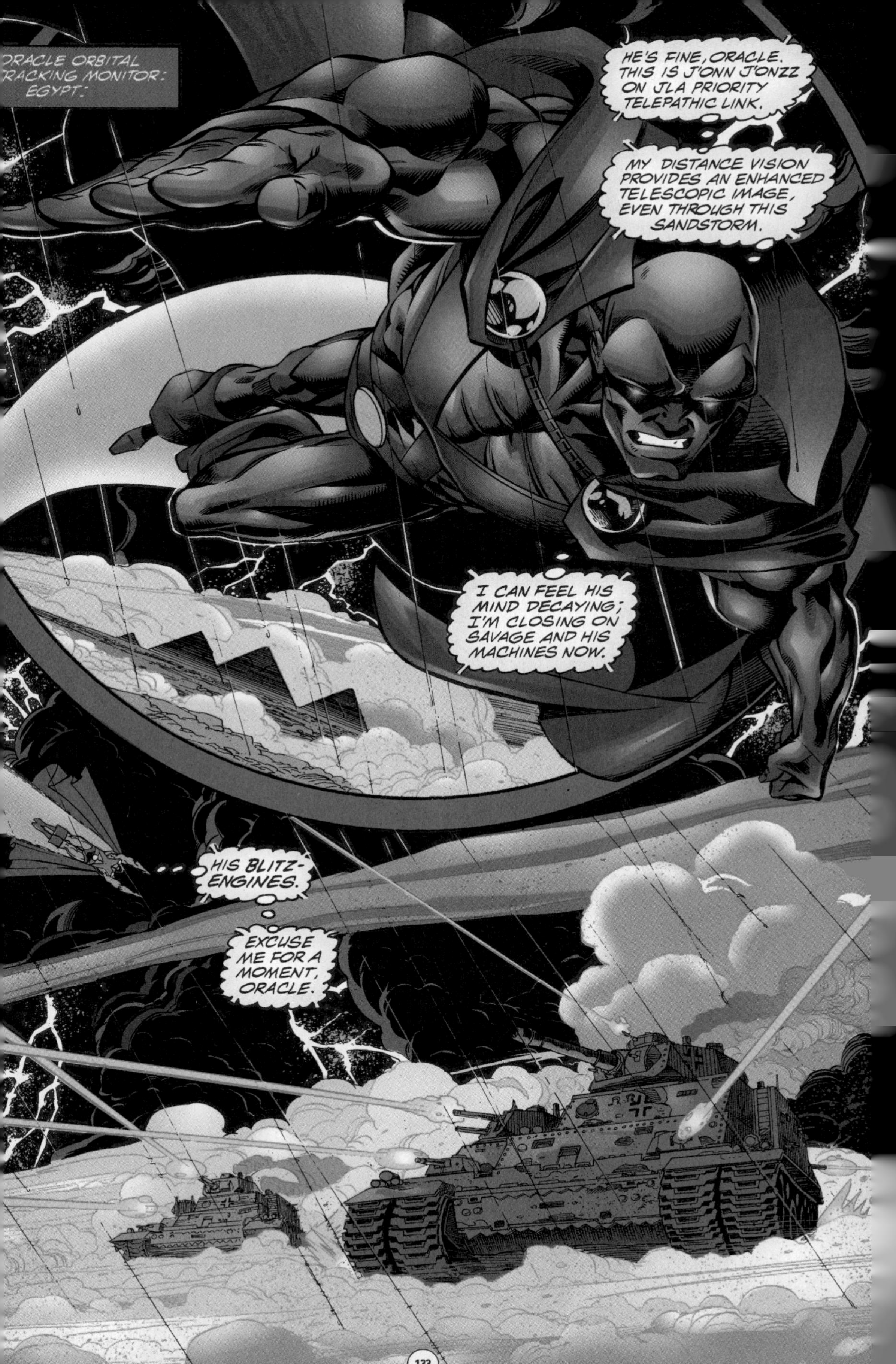
ORACLE ORBITAL TRACKING MONITOR: EGYPT:
HE'S FINE, ORACLE. THIS IS J'ONN J'ONZZ ON JLA PRIORITY TELEPATHIC LINK.
MY DISTANCE VISION PROVIDES AN ENHANCED TELESCOPIC IMAGE, EVEN THROUGH THIS SANDSTORM.
I CAN FEEL HIS MIND DECAYING; I'M CLOSING ON SAVAGE AND HIS MACHINES NOW.
...HIS BLITZ-ENGINES.
EXCUSE ME FOR A MOMENT, ORACLE.

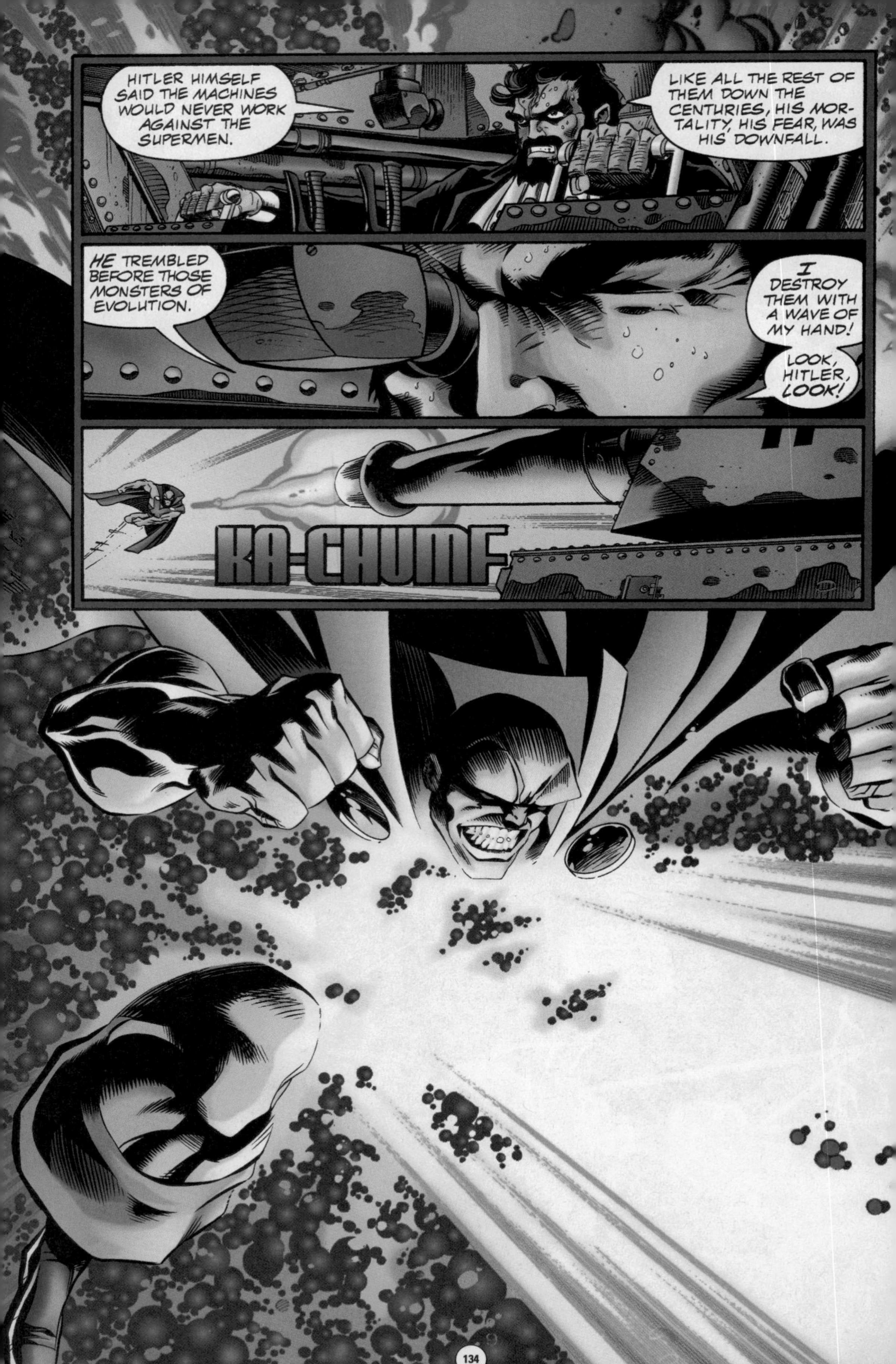
HITLER HIMSELF SAID THE MACHINES WOULD NEVER WORK AGAINST THE SUPERMEN.
LIKE ALL THE REST OF THEM DOWN THE CENTURIES, HIS MORTALITY, HIS FEAR, WAS HIS DOWNFALL.
HE TREMBLED BEFORE THOSE MONSTERS OF EVOLUTION.
I DESTROY THEM WITH A WAVE OF MY HAND!
LOOK, HITLER, LOOK!
KA-CHUMF

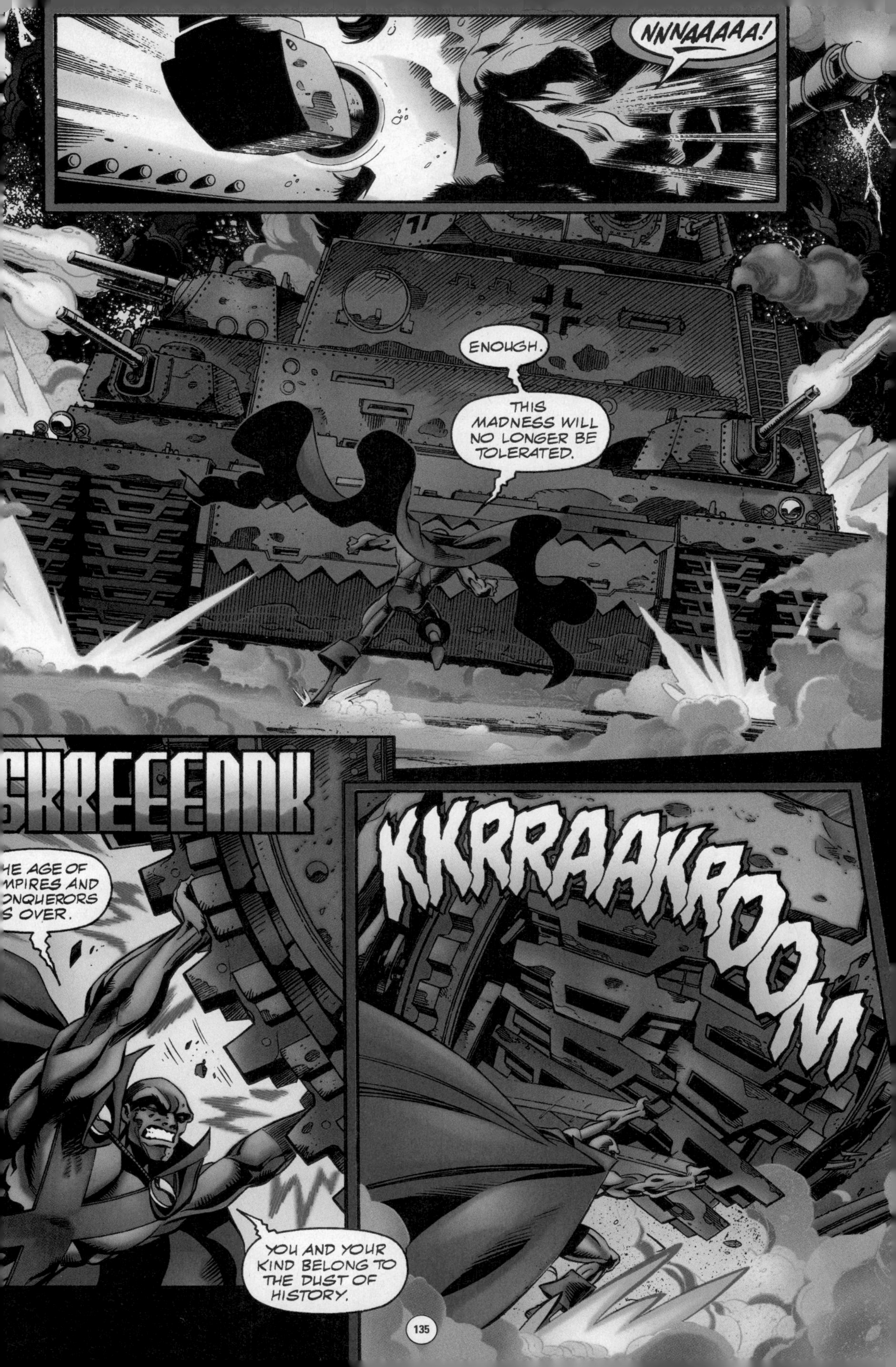
NNNAAAAA!
ENOUGH.
THIS MADNESS WILL NO LONGER BE TOLERATED.
SKREEENNK
HE AGE OF MPIRES AND ONQUERORS S OVER.
KKRRAAKROOM
YOU AND YOUR KIND BELONG TO THE DUST OF HISTORY.

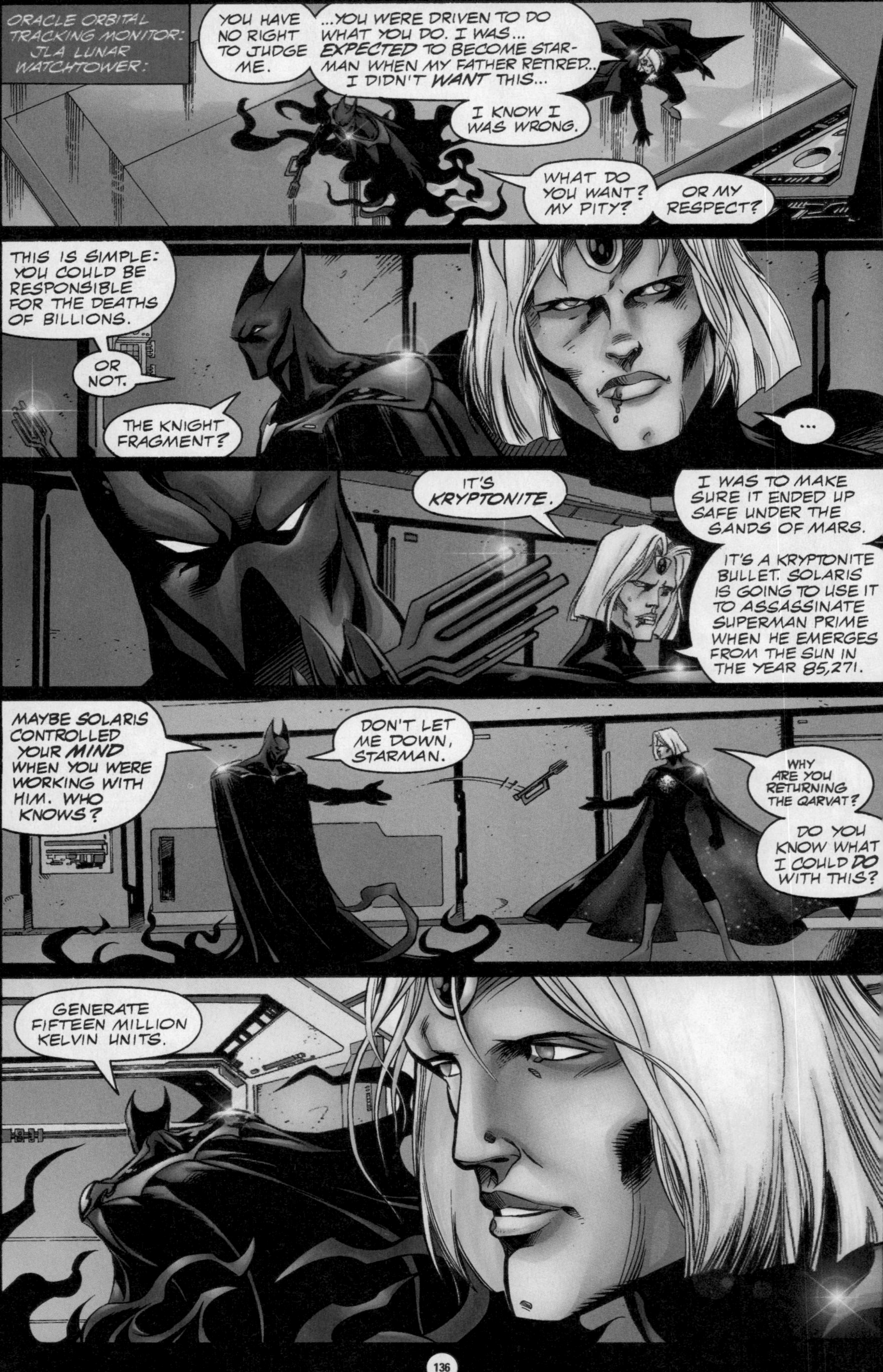
ORACLE ORBITAL TRACKING MONITOR: JLA LUNAR WATCHTOWER:
YOU HAVE NO RIGHT TO JUDGE ME.
...YOU WERE DRIVEN TO DO WHAT YOU DO. I WAS... EXPECTED TO BECOME STARMAN WHEN MY FATHER RETIRED.. I DIDN'T WANT THIS...
I KNOW I WAS WRONG.
WHAT DO YOU WANT? MY PITY?
OR MY RESPECT?
THIS IS SIMPLE: YOU COULD BE RESPONSIBLE FOR THE DEATHS OF BILLIONS.
OR NOT.
THE KNIGHT FRAGMENT?
...
IT'S KRYPTONITE.
I WAS TO MAKE SURE IT ENDED UP SAFE UNDER THE SANDS OF MARS.
IT'S A KRYPTONITE BULLET. SOLARIS IS GOING TO USE IT TO ASSASSINATE SUPERMAN PRIME WHEN HE EMERGES FROM THE SUN IN THE YEAR 85,271.
MAYBE SOLARIS CONTROLLED YOUR MIND WHEN YOU WERE WORKING WITH HIM. WHO KNOWS?
DON'T LET ME DOWN, STARMAN.
WHY ARE YOU RETURNING THE QARVAT?
DO YOU KNOW WHAT I COULD DO WITH THIS?
GENERATE FIFTEEN MILLION KELVIN UNITS.

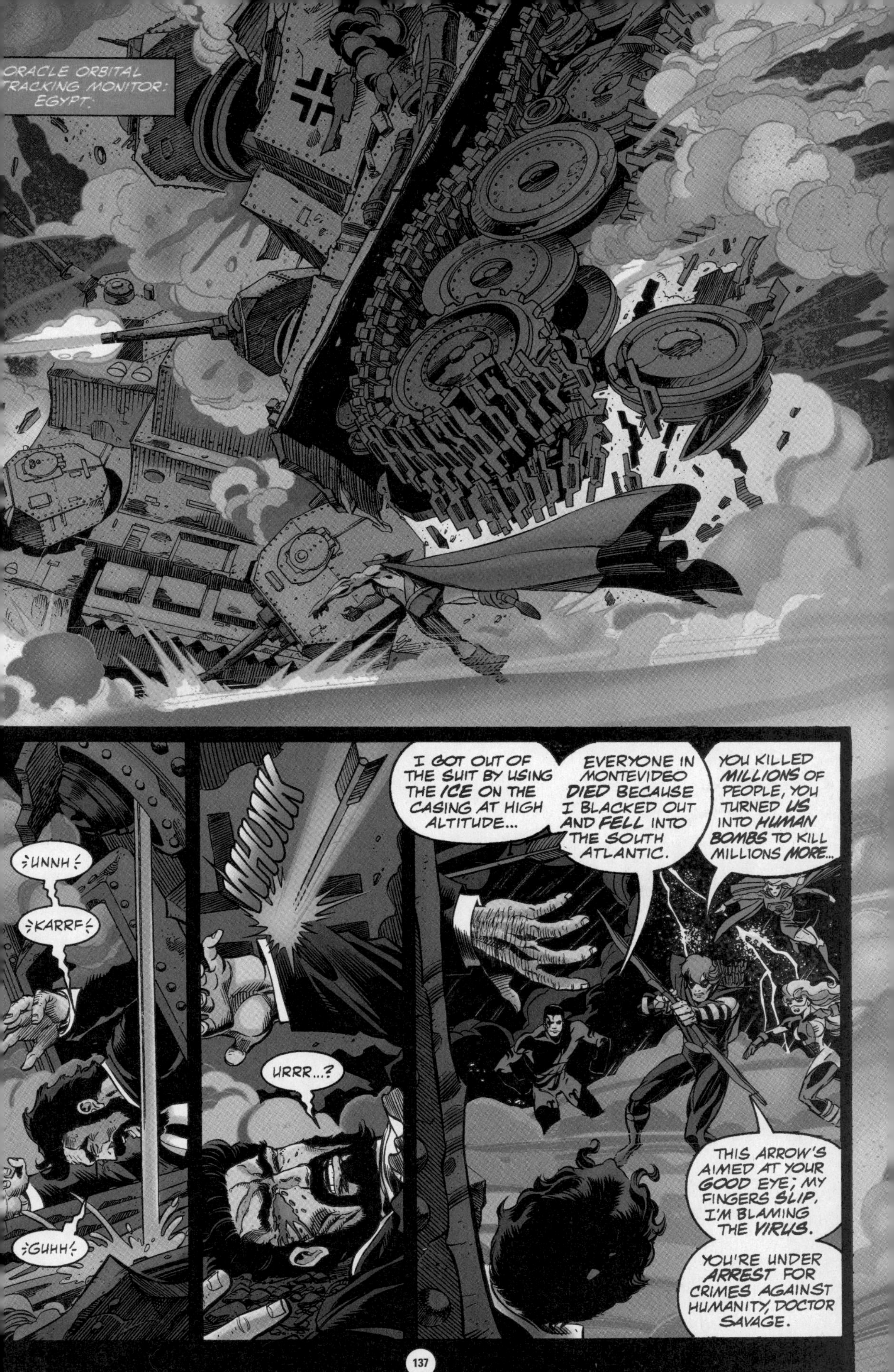
ORACLE ORBITAL TRACKING MONITOR: EGYPT.
UNNH
KARRF
GUHH
WHUNK
URRR...?
I GOT OUT OF THE SUIT BY USING THE ICE ON THE CASING AT HIGH ALTITUDE...
EVERYONE IN MONTEVIDEO DIED BECAUSE I BLACKED OUT AND FELL INTO THE SOUTH ATLANTIC.
YOU KILLED MILLIONS OF PEOPLE, YOU TURNED US INTO HUMAN BOMBS TO KILL MILLIONS MORE...
THIS ARROW'S AIMED AT YOUR GOOD EYE; MY FINGERS SLIP, I'M BLAMING THE VIRUS.
YOU'RE UNDER ARREST FOR CRIMES AGAINST HUMANITY, DOCTOR SAVAGE.

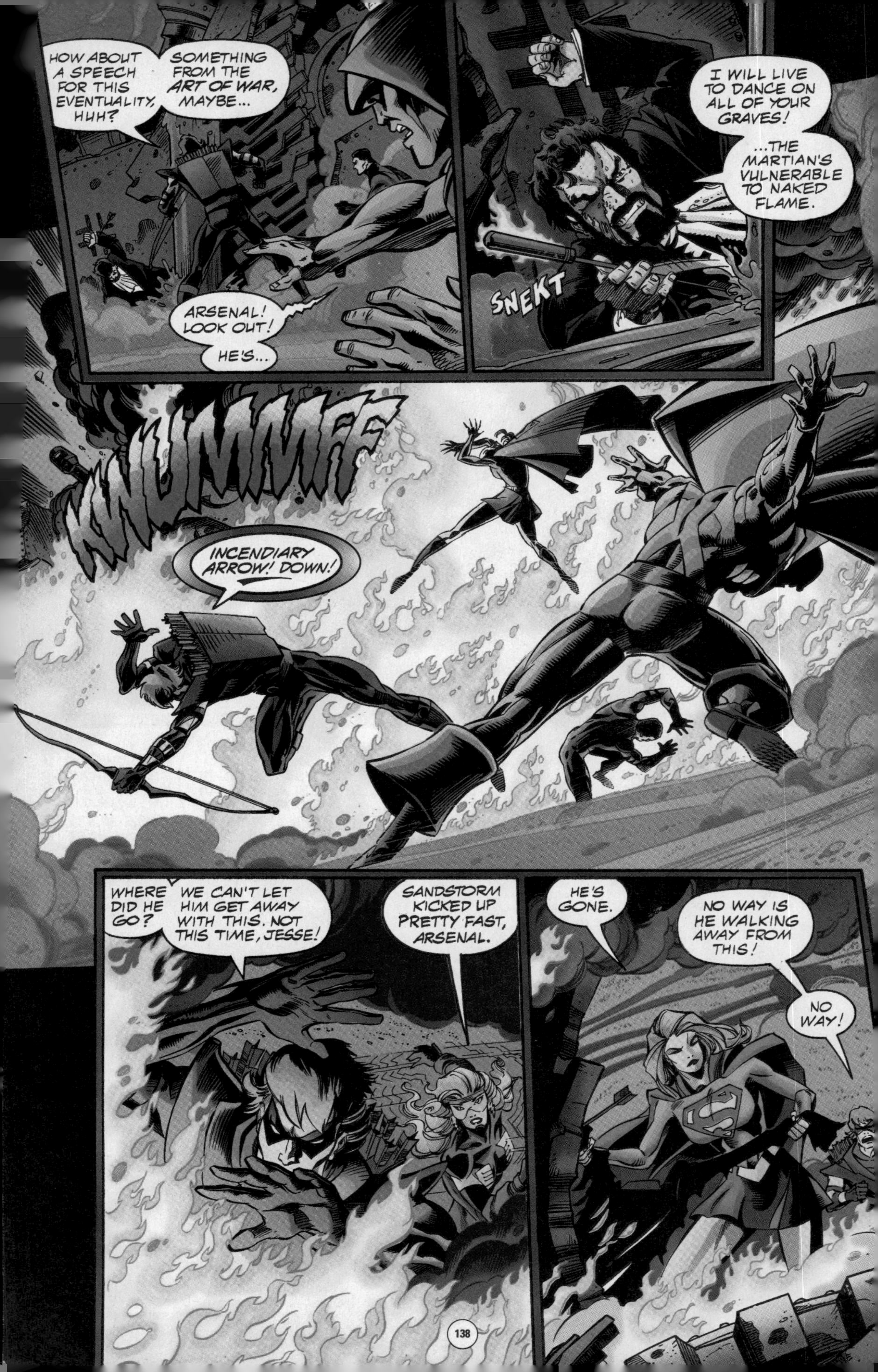
HOW ABOUT A SPEECH FOR THIS EVENTUALITY, HUH?
SOMETHING FROM THE ART OF WAR, MAYBE...
ARSENAL! LOOK OUT!
HE'S...
I WILL LIVE TO DANCE ON ALL OF YOUR GRAVES!
...THE MARTIAN'S VULNERABLE TO NAKED FLAME.
SNEKT
KNUMMF
INCENDIARY ARROW! DOWN!
WHERE DID HE GO?
WE CAN'T LET HIM GET AWAY WITH THIS. NOT THIS TIME, JESSE!
SANDSTORM KICKED UP PRETTY FAST, ARSENAL.
HE'S GONE.
NO WAY IS HE WALKING AWAY FROM THIS!
NO WAY!

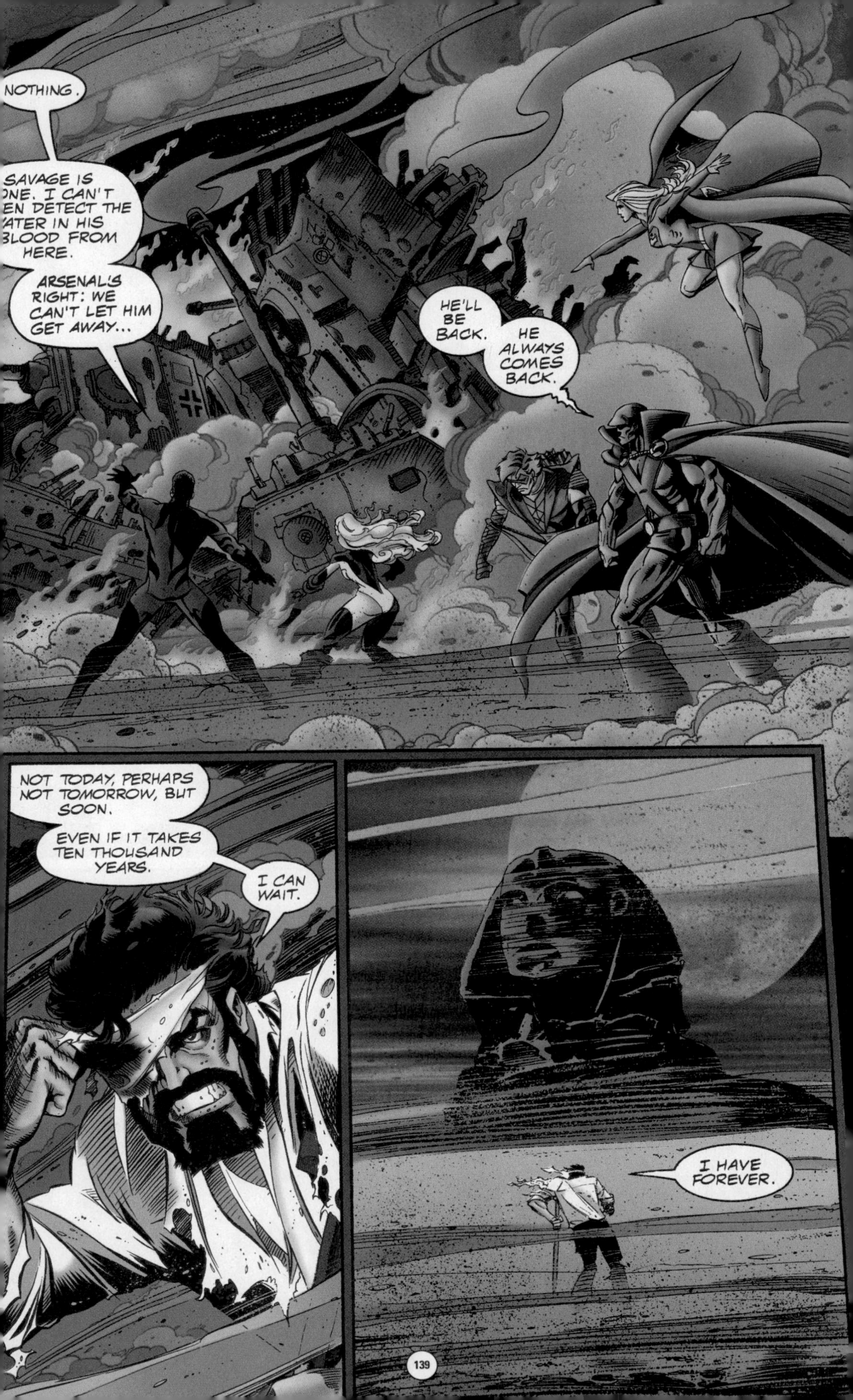
NOTHING.
SAVAGE IS ONE. I CAN'T EN DETECT THE VATER IN HIS BLOOD FROM HERE.
ARSENAL'S RIGHT: WE CAN'T LET HIM GET AWAY...
HE'LL BE BACK.
HE ALWAYS COMES BACK.
NOT TODAY, PERHAPS NOT TOMORROW, BUT SOON.
EVEN IF IT TAKES TEN THOUSAND YEARS.
I CAN WAIT.
I HAVE FOREVER.

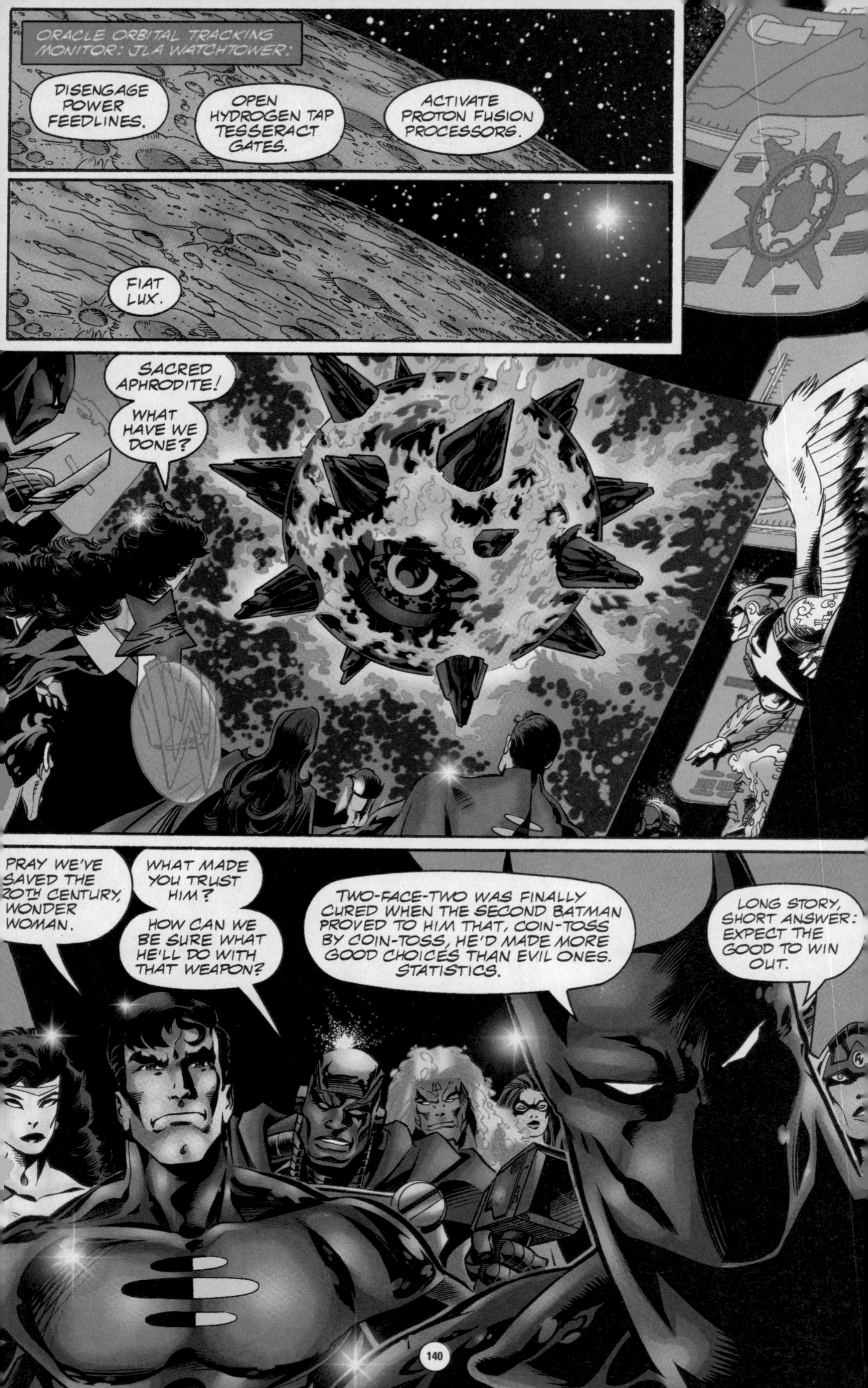
ORACLE ORBITAL TRACKING MONITOR: JLA WATCHTOWER:
DISENGAGE POWER FEEDLINES.
OPEN HYDROGEN TAP TESSERACT GATES.
ACTIVATE PROTON FUSION PROCESSORS.
FIAT LUX.
SACRED APHRODITE!
WHAT HAVE WE DONE?
PRAY WE'VE SAVED THE 20TH CENTURY, WONDER WOMAN.
WHAT MADE YOU TRUST HIM?
HOW CAN WE BE SURE WHAT HE'LL DO WITH THAT WEAPON?
TWO-FACE-TWO WAS FINALLY CURED WHEN THE SECOND BATMAN PROVED TO HIM THAT, COIN-TOSS BY COIN-TOSS, HE'D MADE MORE GOOD CHOICES THAN EVIL ONES. STATISTICS.
LONG STORY, SHORT ANSWER: EXPECT THE GOOD TO WIN OUT.

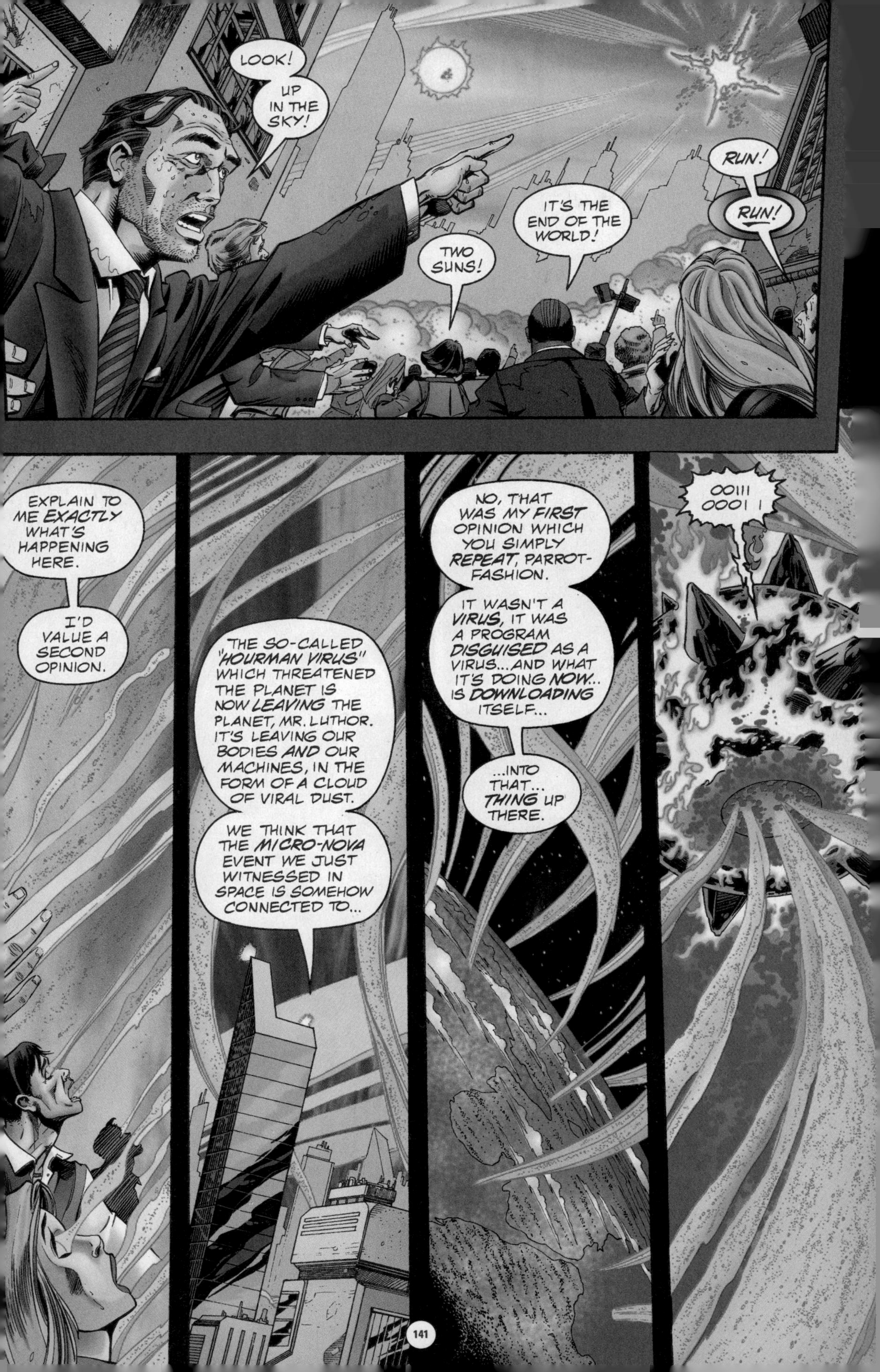
LOOK!
UP IN THE SKY!
RUN!
RUN!
IT'S THE END OF THE WORLD!
TWO SUNS!
EXPLAIN TO ME EXACTLY WHAT'S HAPPENING HERE.
I'D VALUE A SECOND OPINION.
THE SO-CALLED "HOURMAN VIRUS" WHICH THREATENED THE PLANET IS NOW LEAVING THE PLANET, MR. LUTHOR. IT'S LEAVING OUR BODIES AND OUR MACHINES, IN THE FORM OF A CLOUD OF VIRAL DUST.
WE THINK THAT THE MICRO-NOVA EVENT WE JUST WITNESSED IN SPACE IS SOMEHOW CONNECTED TO...
NO, THAT WAS MY FIRST OPINION WHICH YOU SIMPLY REPEAT, PARROT-FASHION.
IT WASN'T A VIRUS, IT WAS A PROGRAM DISGUISED AS A VIRUS... AND WHAT IT'S DOING NOW... IS DOWNLOADING ITSELF...
...INTO THAT... THING UP THERE.
00111 0001 1

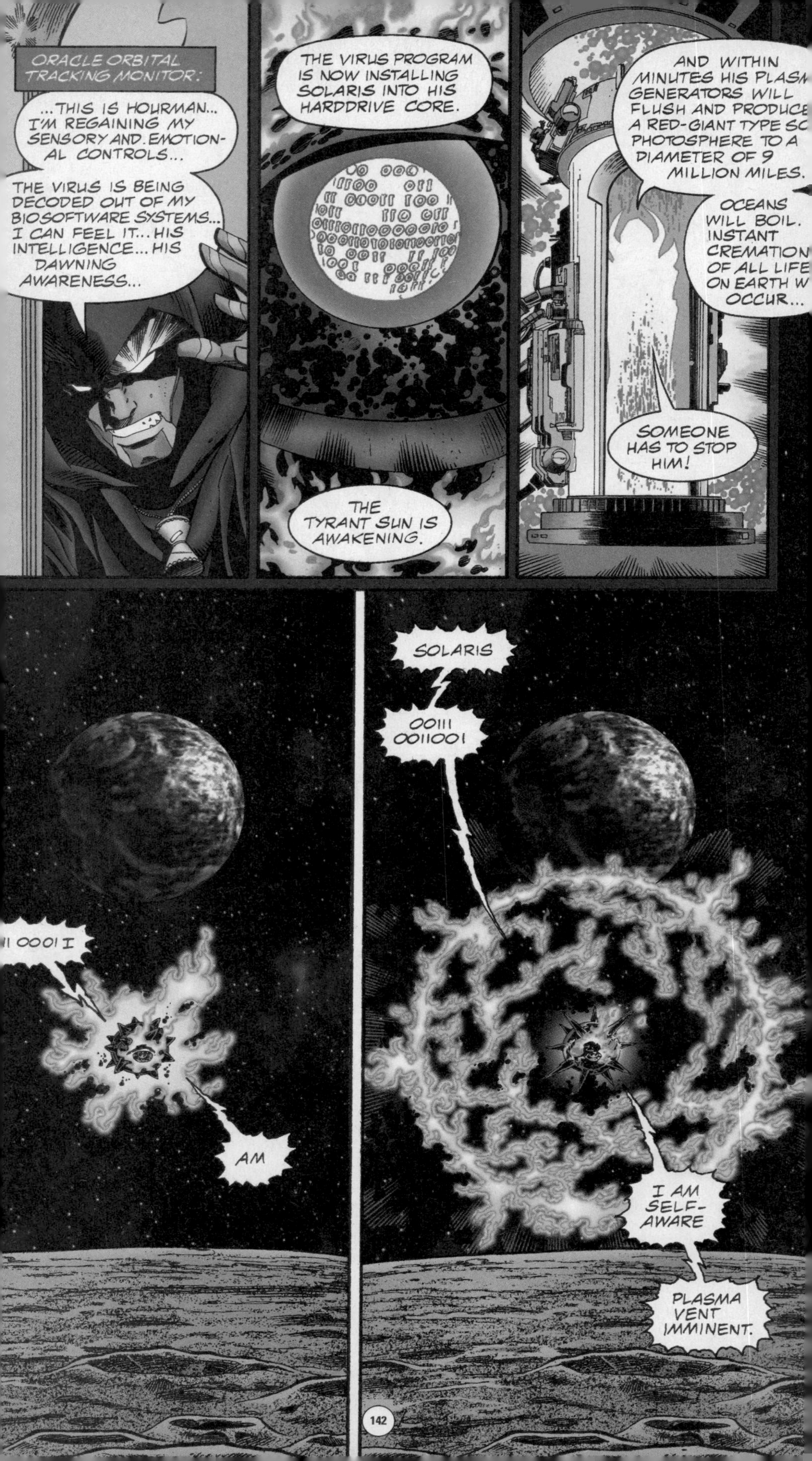
ORACLE ORBITAL TRACKING MONITOR:
...THIS IS HOURMAN... I'M REGAINING MY SENSORY AND EMOTIONAL CONTROLS...
THE VIRUS IS BEING DECODED OUT OF MY BIOSOFTWARE SYSTEMS... I CAN FEEL IT... HIS INTELLIGENCE... HIS DAWNING AWARENESS...
THE VIRUS PROGRAM IS NOW INSTALLING SOLARIS INTO HIS HARDDRIVE CORE.
THE TYRANT SUN IS AWAKENING.
AND WITHIN MINUTES HIS PLASM GENERATORS WILL FLUSH AND PRODUCE A RED-GIANT TYPE SO PHOTOSPHERE TO A DIAMETER OF 9 MILLION MILES.
OCEANS WILL BOIL. INSTANT CREMATION OF ALL LIFE ON EARTH W OCCUR...
SOMEONE HAS TO STOP HIM!
I OOOI I
AM
SOLARIS
OOIII OOIIOOI
I AM SELF-AWARE
PLASMA VENT IMMINENT.

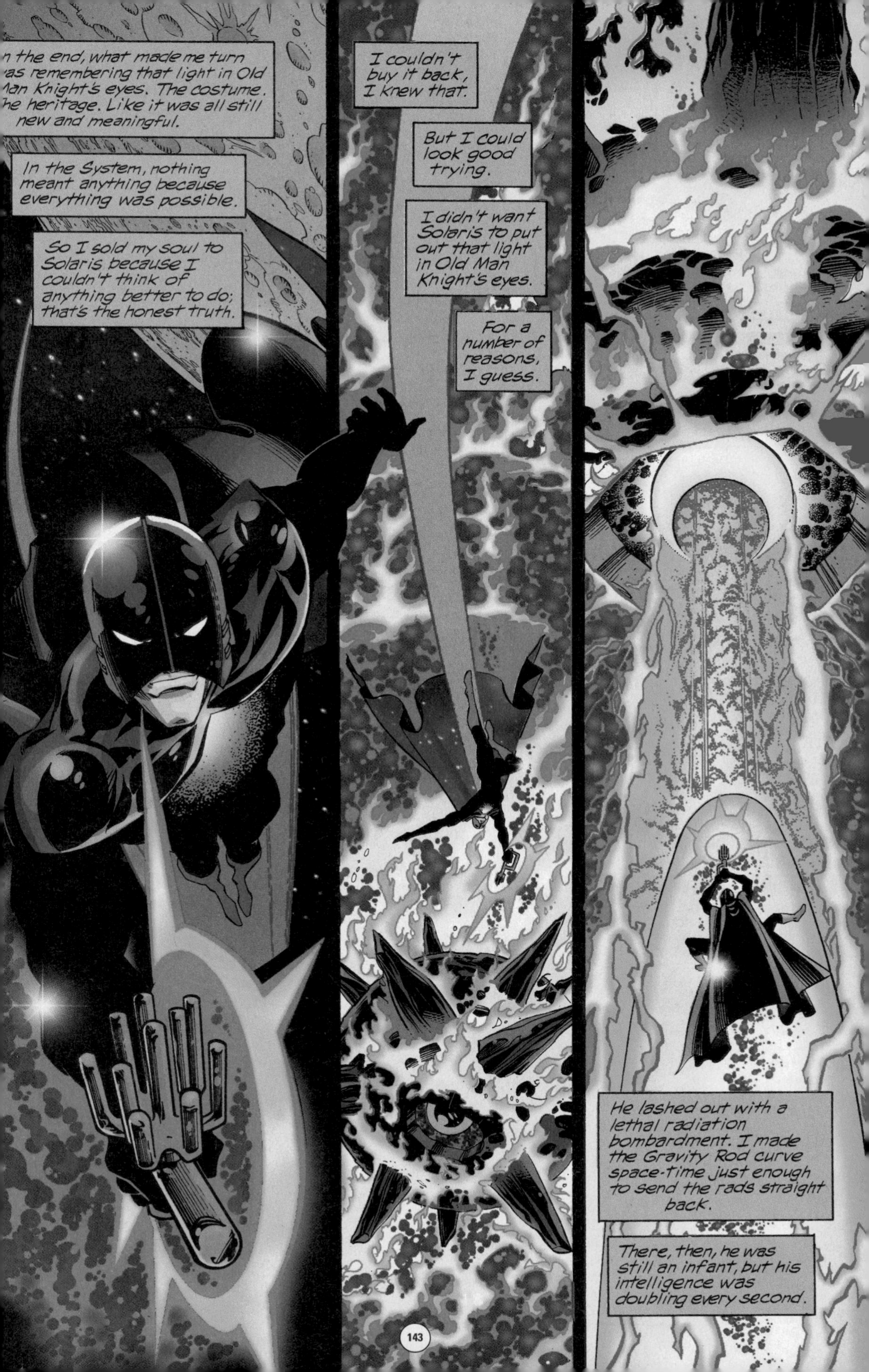
In the end, what made me turn was remembering that light in Old Man Knight's eyes. The costume. The heritage. Like it was all still new and meaningful.
In the System, nothing meant anything because everything was possible.
So I sold my soul to Solaris because I couldn't think of anything better to do; that's the honest truth.
I couldn't buy it back, I knew that.
But I could look good trying.
I didn't want Solaris to put out that light in Old Man Knight's eyes.
For a number of reasons, I guess.
He lashed out with a lethal radiation bombardment. I made the Gravity Rod curve space-time just enough to send the rads straight back.
There, then, he was still an infant, but his intelligence was doubling every second.

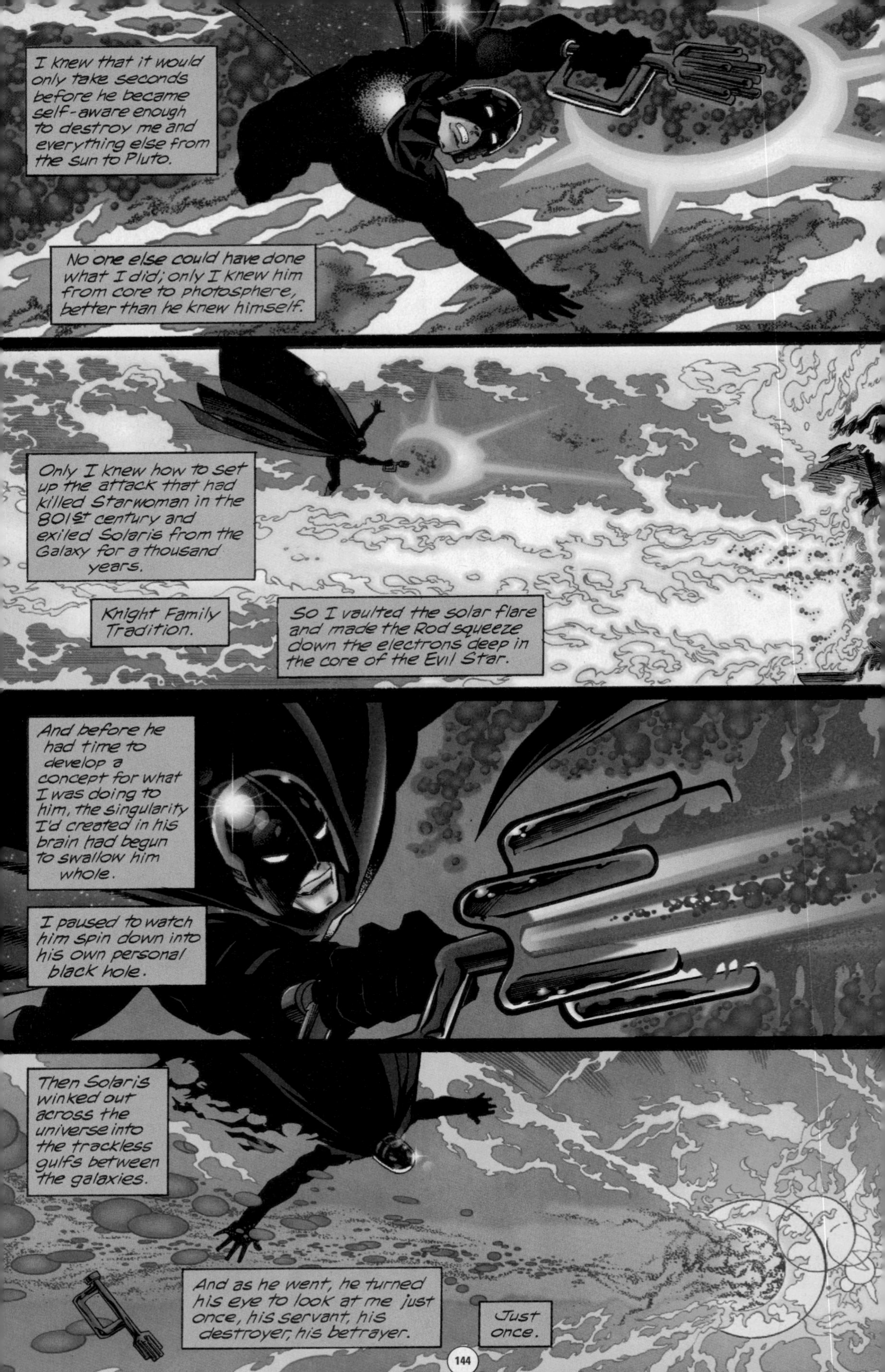

I knew that it would only take seconds before he became self-aware enough to destroy me and everything else from the sun to Pluto.
No one else could have done what I did; only I knew him from core to photosphere, better than he knew himself.
Only I knew how to set up the attack that had killed Starwoman in the 801st century and exiled Solaris from the Galaxy for a thousand years.
Knight Family Tradition.
So I vaulted the solar flare and made the Rod squeeze down the electrons deep in the core of the Evil Star.
And before he had time to develop a concept for what I was doing to him, the singularity I'd created in his brain had begun to swallow him whole.
I paused to watch him spin down into his own personal black hole.
Then Solaris winked out across the universe into the trackless gulfs between the galaxies.
And as he went, he turned his eye to look at me just once, his servant, his destroyer, his betrayer.
Just once.

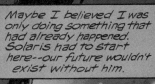

I don't know if I ended up a hero or a villain.

I don't know if Solaris was really controlling my mind back home in 85,271.

Maybe I believed I was only doing something that had already happened. Solaris had to start here--our future wouldn't exist without him.

Everything just falling into place, like an explosion going backwards I once saw.

The Knight Family history. Tradition. Heritage.

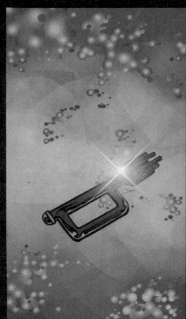

There never seemed to be any place for me in all that.

Always where you least expect it, huh?

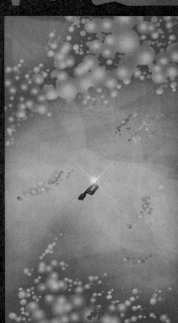

SUIT MERCY-DESTRUCT ENGAGED.

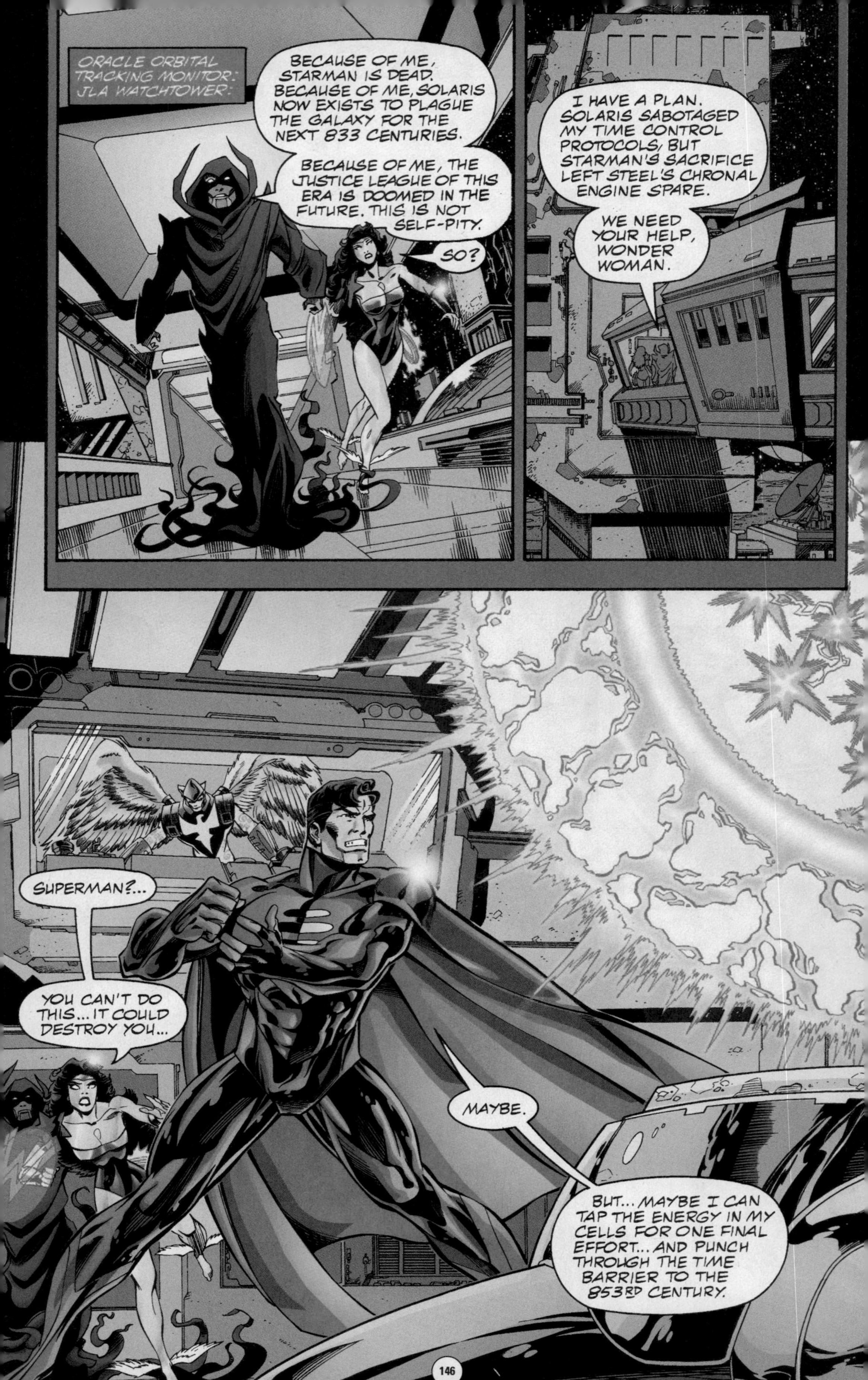
ORACLE ORBITAL TRACKING MONITOR: JLA WATCHTOWER:
BECAUSE OF ME, STARMAN IS DEAD. BECAUSE OF ME, SOLARIS NOW EXISTS TO PLAGUE THE GALAXY FOR THE NEXT 833 CENTURIES.
BECAUSE OF ME, THE JUSTICE LEAGUE OF THIS ERA IS DOOMED IN THE FUTURE. THIS IS NOT SELF-PITY.
SO?
I HAVE A PLAN. SOLARIS SABOTAGED MY TIME CONTROL PROTOCOLS, BUT STARMAN'S SACRIFICE LEFT STEEL'S CHRONAL ENGINE SPARE.
WE NEED YOUR HELP, WONDER WOMAN.
SUPERMAN?...
YOU CAN'T DO THIS... IT COULD DESTROY YOU...
MAYBE.
BUT... MAYBE I CAN TAP THE ENERGY IN MY CELLS FOR ONE FINAL EFFORT... AND PUNCH THROUGH THE TIME BARRIER TO THE 853RD CENTURY.

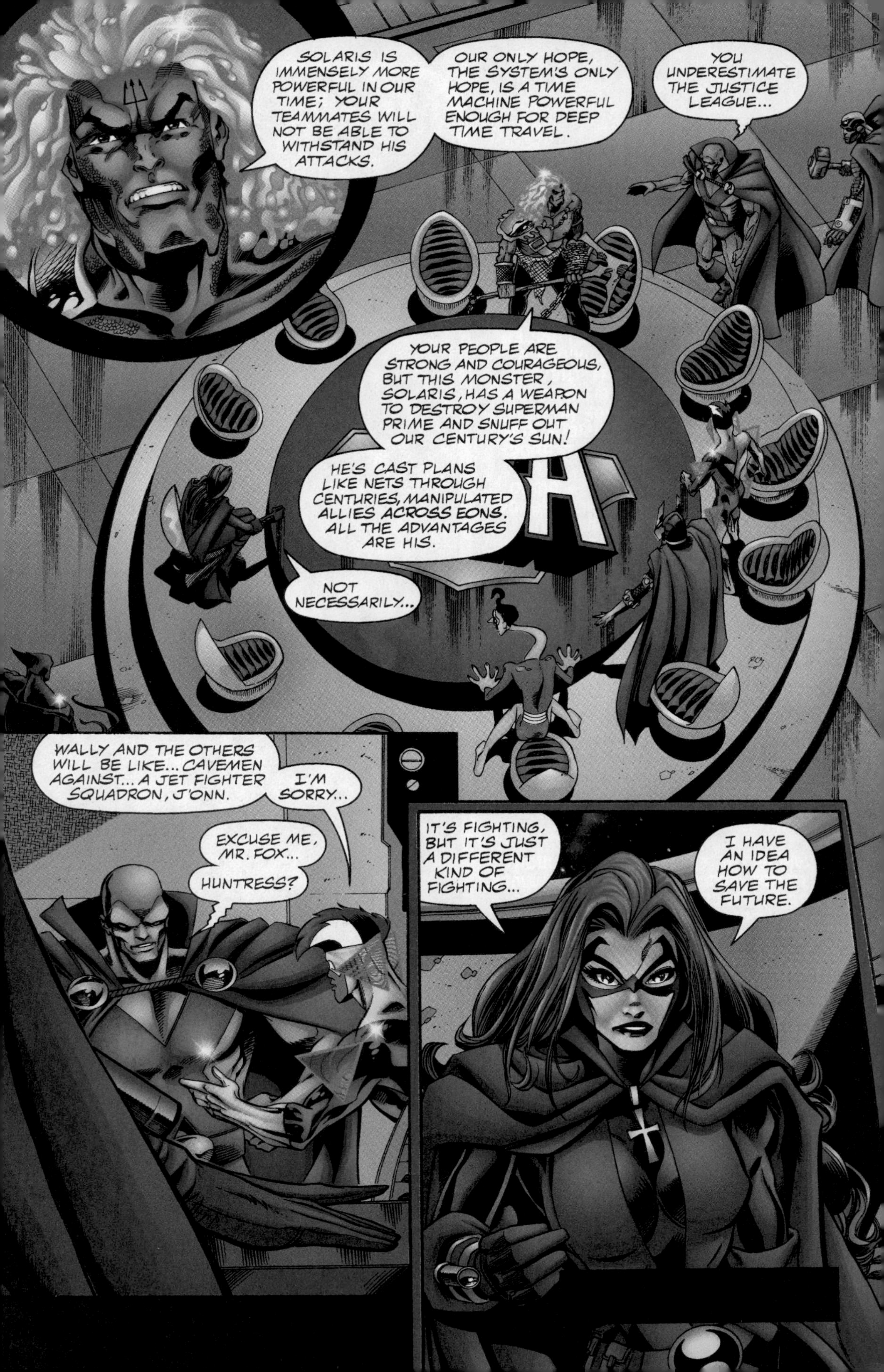
SOLARIS IS IMMENSELY MORE POWERFUL IN OUR TIME; YOUR TEAMMATES WILL NOT BE ABLE TO WITHSTAND HIS ATTACKS.
OUR ONLY HOPE, THE SYSTEM'S ONLY HOPE, IS A TIME MACHINE POWERFUL ENOUGH FOR DEEP TIME TRAVEL.
YOU UNDERESTIMATE THE JUSTICE LEAGUE...
YOUR PEOPLE ARE STRONG AND COURAGEOUS, BUT THIS MONSTER, SOLARIS, HAS A WEAPON TO DESTROY SUPERMAN PRIME AND SNUFF OUT OUR CENTURY'S SUN!
HE'S CAST PLANS LIKE NETS THROUGH CENTURIES, MANIPULATED ALLIES ACROSS EONS. ALL THE ADVANTAGES ARE HIS.
NOT NECESSARILY...
WALLY AND THE OTHERS WILL BE LIKE... CAVEMEN AGAINST... A JET FIGHTER SQUADRON, J'ONN.
I'M SORRY...
EXCUSE ME, MR. FOX...
HUNTRESS?
IT'S FIGHTING, BUT IT'S JUST A DIFFERENT KIND OF FIGHTING...
I HAVE AN IDEA HOW TO SAVE THE FUTURE.

•••INPUT

DIGIPRINT

IN THE EYES OF A TRILLION SENTIENTS, THE JLA WERE IMPOSTORS.

TRAPPED IN THE 853RD CENTURY AND FIGHTING FOR THEIR LIVES, THE 20TH-CENTURY JLA'S FIRST ORDER OF SURVIVAL WAS TO CONVINCE A SKEPTICAL GALAXY THAT THEY WERE NOT IMPERFECT BIZARRO DUPLICATES — RELICS OF A BYGONE PLAGUE RESPONSIBLE FOR CENTURIES OF DEATH AND TERROR.

WALLY WEST, THE FLASH — AIDED BY A POSSIBLE HEIR TO HIS LEGACY IN THE 853RD CENTURY AND AN AGED CAPTAIN MARVEL, STILL ALIVE AFTER CENTURIES IN STASIS ON THE ROCK OF ETERNITY — HELPED DEBUNK THE "BIZARRO PLAGUE" WHILE ROUTING AN ATTACK ON THE PLANET MERCURY'S COMPLEX INFORMATION-BASED ECONONET BY DATA-TERRORISTS COMMANDER COLD AND HEAT WAVE.

THE BIZARRO PLAGUE SCARE...THE SABOTAGE OF THE JLA'S PLANETARY CHALLENGES...THE GALAXYWIDE TURMOIL...WAS QUICKLY REVEALED TO BE ALL THE TYRANT SUN SOLARIS'S DOING.

WHILE THE TIME-LOST JLA FOUGHT TO PREVENT SOLARIS'S MAD SCHEMES FROM SUCCEEDING, ANOTHER HERO WITH ORIGINS IN THE 20TH CENTURY DID HIS PART.

MITCH SHELLEY, THE SO-CALLED RESURRECTION MAN AND ONE OF JUST A HANDFUL OF PRESENT-DAY HEROES TO SURVIVE INTO THE 853RD CENTURY, MADE HIS WAY TO THE RED PLANET MARS, DETERMINED TO CONFRONT SOLARIS'S ALLY AND SHELLEY'S ETERNAL FOE...VANDAL SAVAGE, ALSO VERY MUCH ALIVE IN THE YEAR 85,271 A.D....

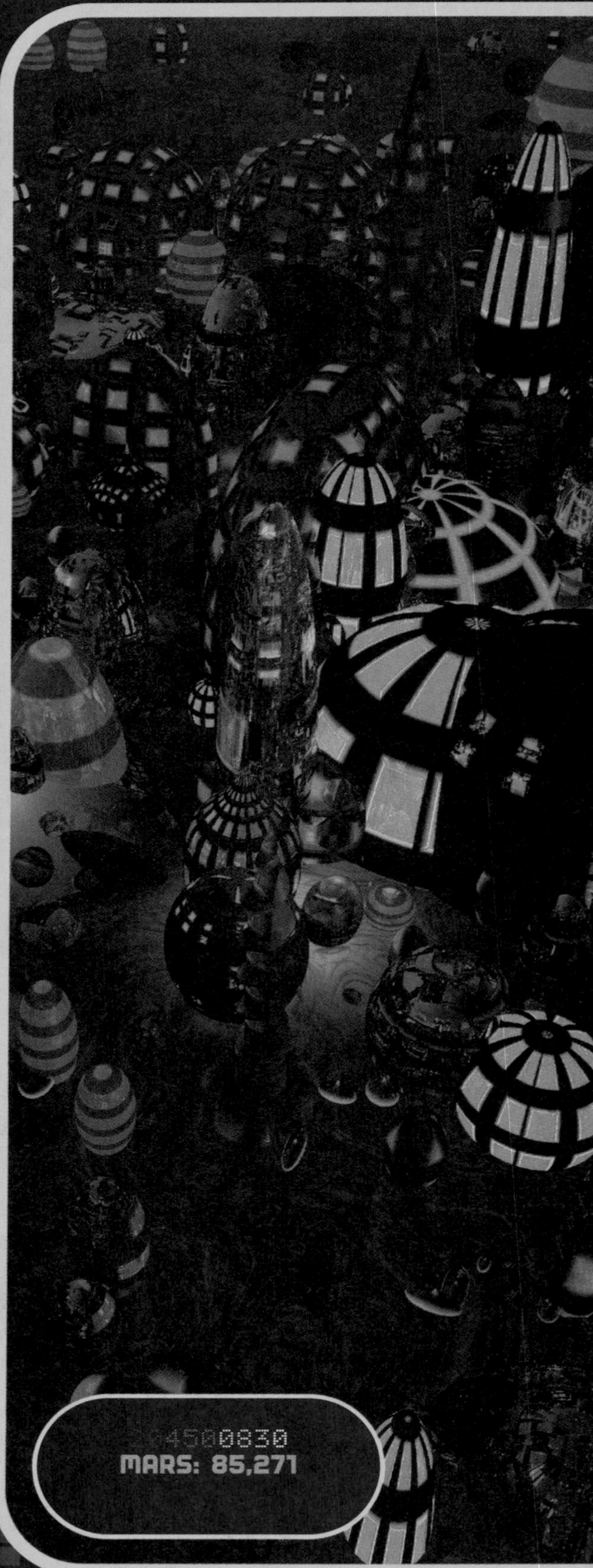
04500830
MARS: 85,271

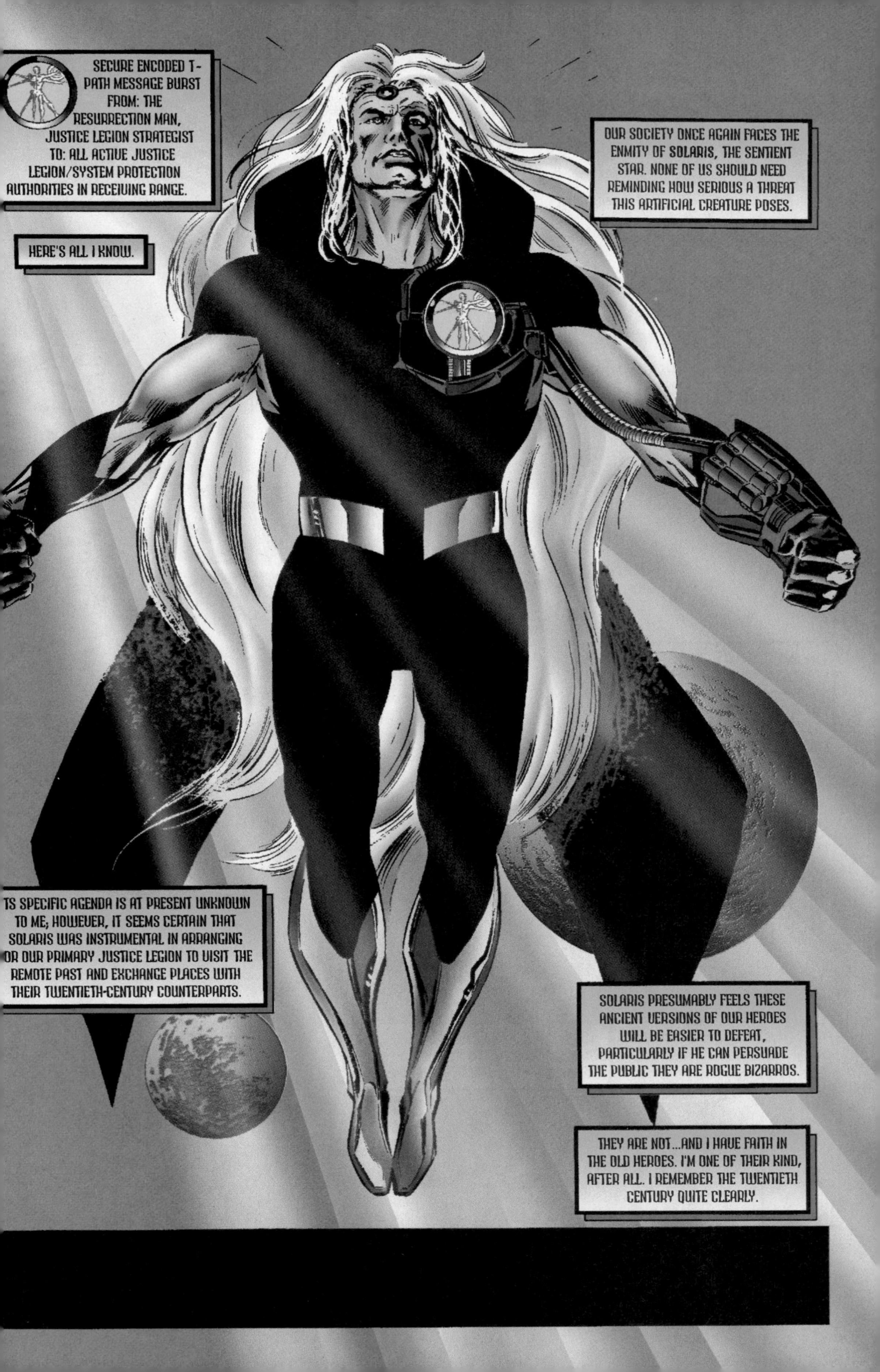

SECURE ENCODED T-PATH MESSAGE BURST FROM: THE RESURRECTION MAN, JUSTICE LEGION STRATEGIST TO: ALL ACTIVE JUSTICE LEGION/SYSTEM PROTECTION AUTHORITIES IN RECEIVING RANGE.
OUR SOCIETY ONCE AGAIN FACES THE ENMITY OF SOLARIS, THE SENTIENT STAR. NONE OF US SHOULD NEED REMINDING HOW SERIOUS A THREAT THIS ARTIFICIAL CREATURE POSES.
HERE'S ALL I KNOW.
TS SPECIFIC AGENDA IS AT PRESENT UNKNOWN TO ME; HOWEVER, IT SEEMS CERTAIN THAT SOLARIS WAS INSTRUMENTAL IN ARRANGING OR OUR PRIMARY JUSTICE LEGION TO VISIT THE REMOTE PAST AND EXCHANGE PLACES WITH THEIR TWENTIETH-CENTURY COUNTERPARTS.
SOLARIS PRESUMABLY FEELS THESE ANCIENT VERSIONS OF OUR HEROES WILL BE EASIER TO DEFEAT, PARTICULARLY IF HE CAN PERSUADE THE PUBLIC THEY ARE ROGUE BIZARROS.
THEY ARE NOT...AND I HAVE FAITH IN THE OLD HEROES. I'M ONE OF THEIR KIND, AFTER ALL. I REMEMBER THE TWENTIETH CENTURY QUITE CLEARLY.

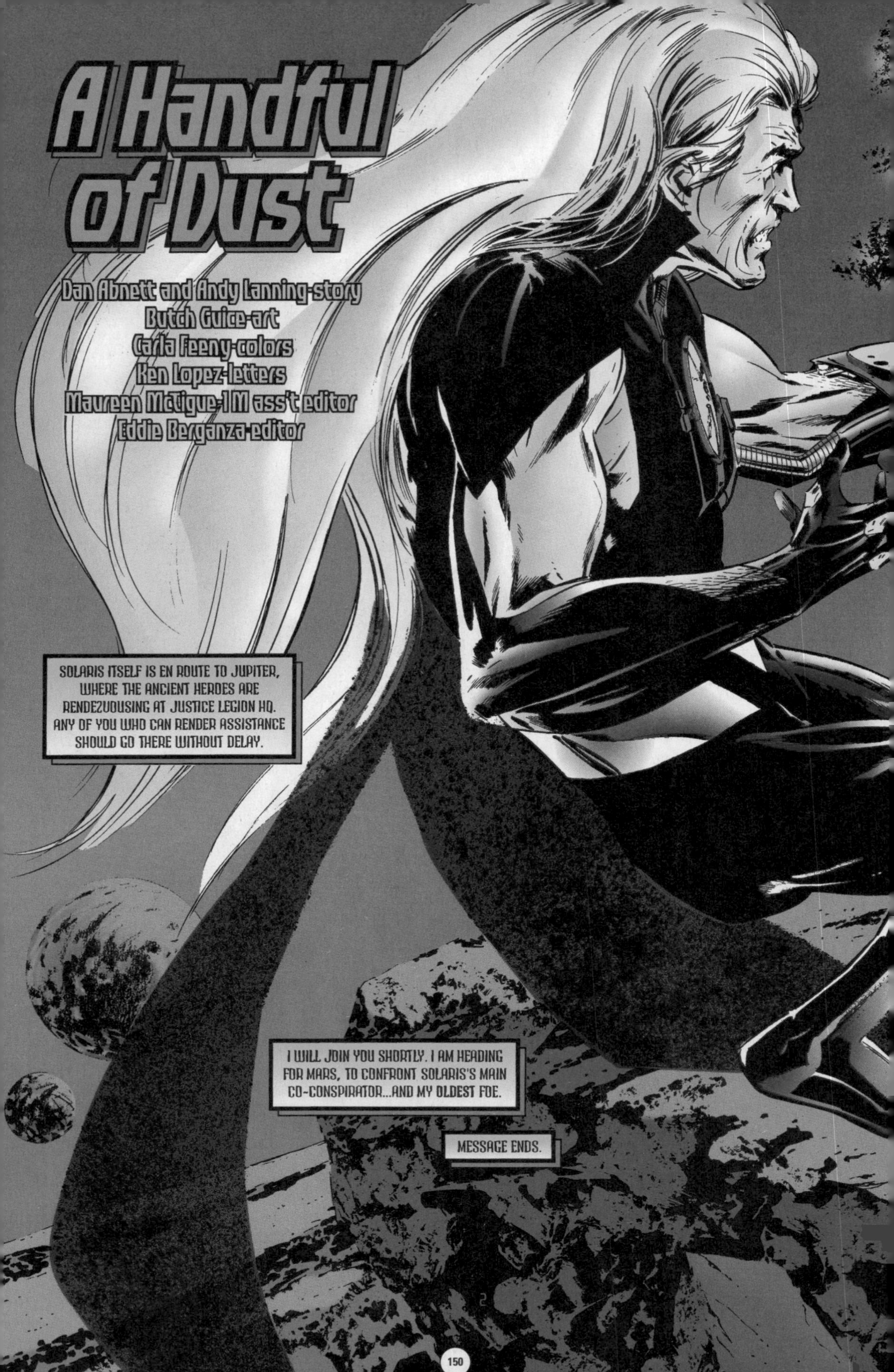
A Handful of Dust
Dan Abnett and Andy Lanning-story
Butch Guice-art
Carla Feeny-colors
Ken Lopez-letters
Maureen McTigue-1M ass't editor
Eddie Berganza-editor
SOLARIS ITSELF IS EN ROUTE TO JUPITER, WHERE THE ANCIENT HEROES ARE RENDEZVOUSING AT JUSTICE LEGION HQ. ANY OF YOU WHO CAN RENDER ASSISTANCE SHOULD GO THERE WITHOUT DELAY.
I WILL JOIN YOU SHORTLY. I AM HEADING FOR MARS, TO CONFRONT SOLARIS'S MAIN CO-CONSPIRATOR...AND MY OLDEST FOE.
MESSAGE ENDS.

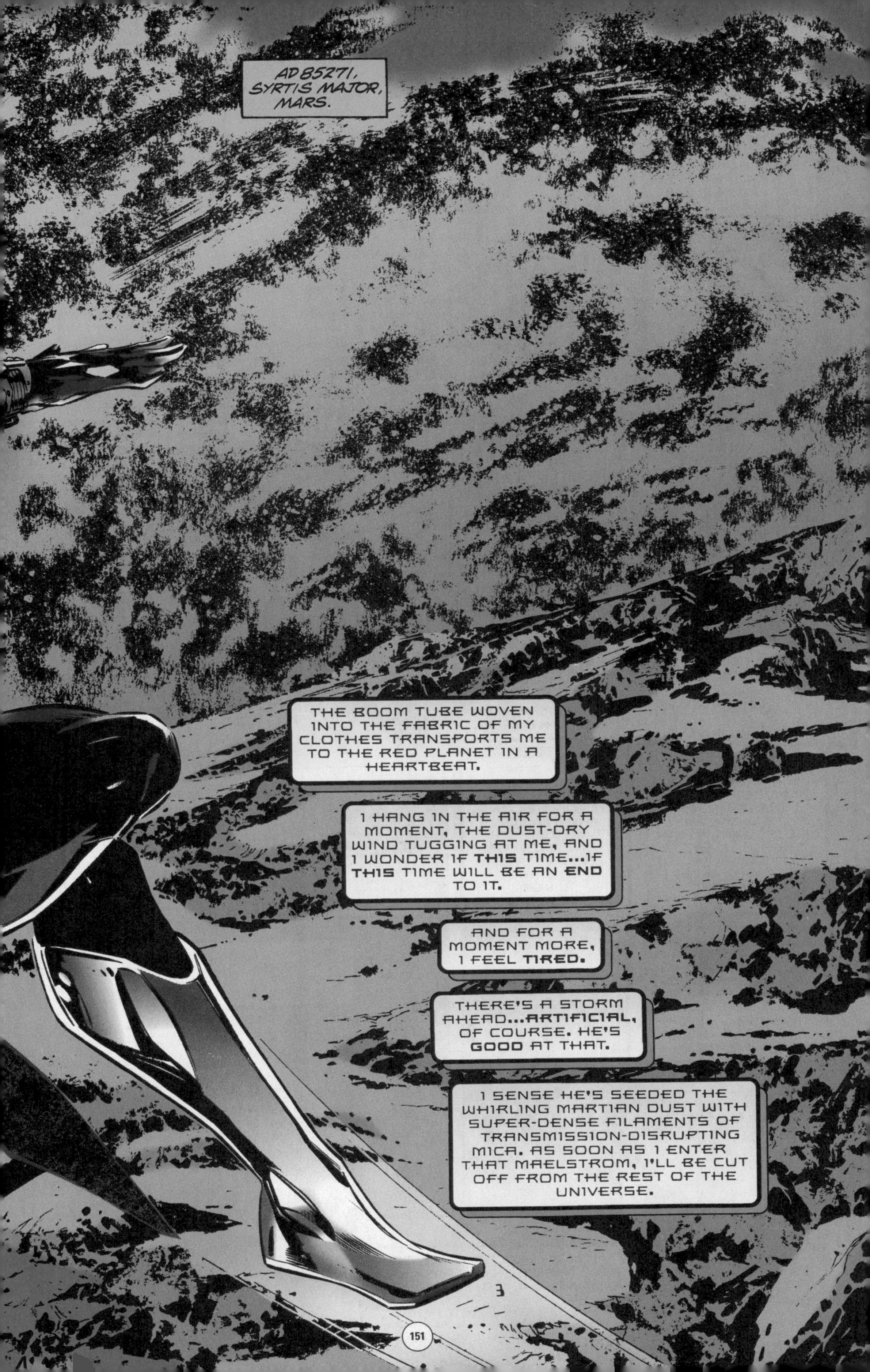
AD 85271, SYRTIS MAJOR, MARS.
THE BOOM TUBE WOVEN INTO THE FABRIC OF MY CLOTHES TRANSPORTS ME TO THE RED PLANET IN A HEARTBEAT.
I HANG IN THE AIR FOR A MOMENT, THE DUST-DRY WIND TUGGING AT ME, AND I WONDER IF **THIS** TIME...IF **THIS** TIME WILL BE AN **END** TO IT.
AND FOR A MOMENT MORE, I FEEL **TIRED.**
THERE'S A STORM AHEAD...**ARTIFICIAL,** OF COURSE. HE'S **GOOD** AT THAT.
I SENSE HE'S SEEDED THE WHIRLING MARTIAN DUST WITH SUPER-DENSE FILAMENTS OF TRANSMISSION-DISRUPTING MICA. AS SOON AS I ENTER THAT MAELSTROM, I'LL BE CUT OFF FROM THE REST OF THE UNIVERSE.

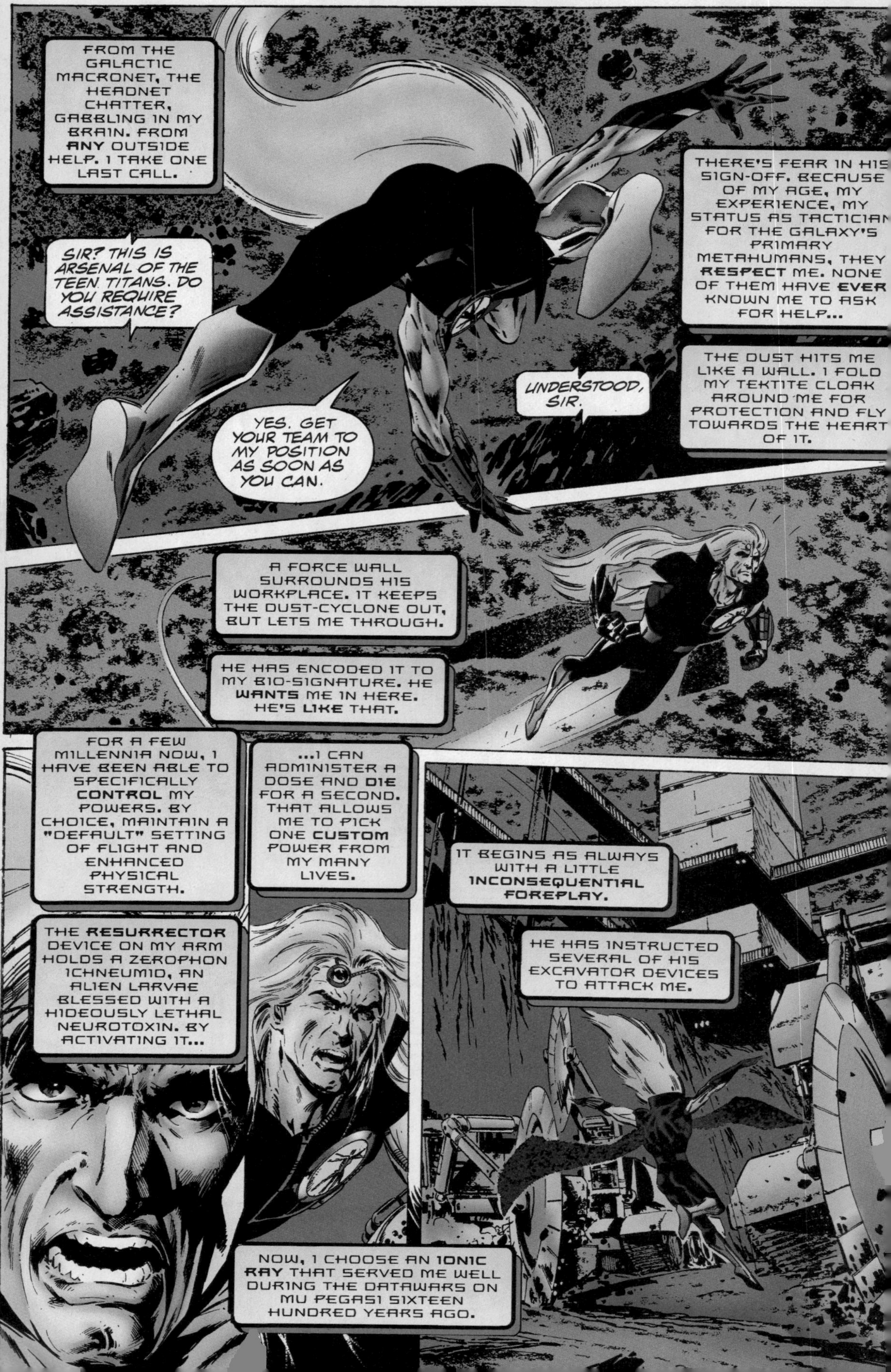
FROM THE GALACTIC MACRONET, THE HEADNET CHATTER, GABBLING IN MY BRAIN. FROM ANY OUTSIDE HELP. I TAKE ONE LAST CALL.
THERE'S FEAR IN HIS SIGN-OFF. BECAUSE OF MY AGE, MY EXPERIENCE, MY STATUS AS TACTICIAN FOR THE GALAXY'S PRIMARY METAHUMANS, THEY RESPECT ME. NONE OF THEM HAVE EVER KNOWN ME TO ASK FOR HELP...
SIR? THIS IS ARSENAL OF THE TEEN TITANS. DO YOU REQUIRE ASSISTANCE?
YES. GET YOUR TEAM TO MY POSITION AS SOON AS YOU CAN.
UNDERSTOOD, SIR.
THE DUST HITS ME LIKE A WALL. I FOLD MY TEKTITE CLOAK AROUND ME FOR PROTECTION AND FLY TOWARDS THE HEART OF IT.
A FORCE WALL SURROUNDS HIS WORKPLACE. IT KEEPS THE DUST-CYCLONE OUT, BUT LETS ME THROUGH.
HE HAS ENCODED IT TO MY BIO-SIGNATURE. HE WANTS ME IN HERE. HE'S LIKE THAT.
FOR A FEW MILLENNIA NOW, I HAVE BEEN ABLE TO SPECIFICALLY CONTROL MY POWERS. BY CHOICE, MAINTAIN A "DEFAULT" SETTING OF FLIGHT AND ENHANCED PHYSICAL STRENGTH.
THE RESURRECTOR DEVICE ON MY ARM HOLDS A ZEROPHON ICHNEUMID, AN ALIEN LARVAE BLESSED WITH A HIDEOUSLY LETHAL NEUROTOXIN. BY ACTIVATING IT...
...I CAN ADMINISTER A DOSE AND DIE FOR A SECOND. THAT ALLOWS ME TO PICK ONE CUSTOM POWER FROM MY MANY LIVES.
IT BEGINS AS ALWAYS WITH A LITTLE INCONSEQUENTIAL FOREPLAY.
HE HAS INSTRUCTED SEVERAL OF HIS EXCAVATOR DEVICES TO ATTACK ME.
NOW, I CHOOSE AN IONIC RAY THAT SERVED ME WELL DURING THE DATAWARS ON MU PEGASI SIXTEEN HUNDRED YEARS AGO.

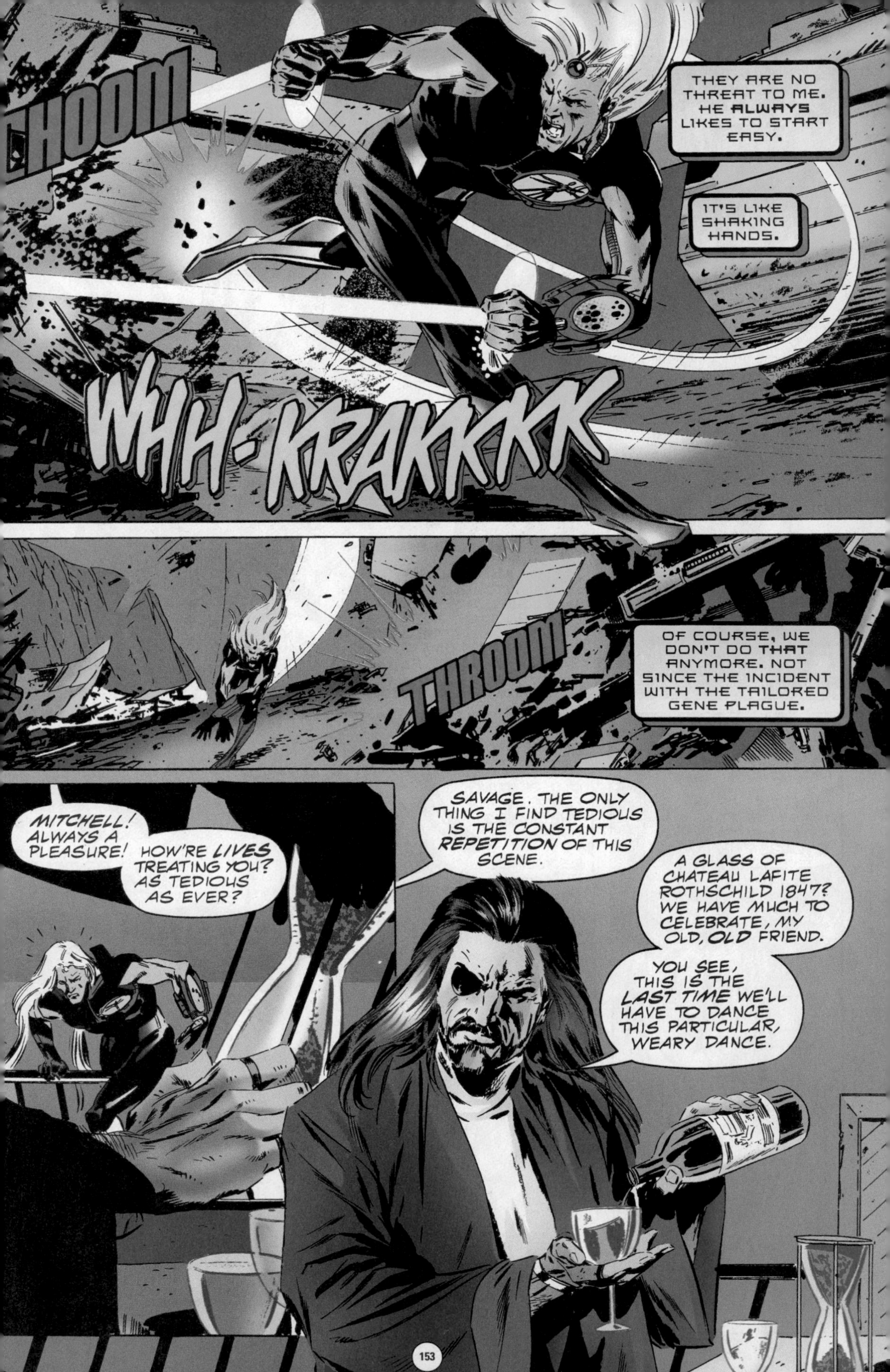
CHOOM
THEY ARE NO THREAT TO ME. HE ALWAYS LIKES TO START EASY.
IT'S LIKE SHAKING HANDS.
WHH-KRAKKKK
THROOM
OF COURSE, WE DON'T DO THAT ANYMORE. NOT SINCE THE INCIDENT WITH THE TAILORED GENE PLAGUE.
MITCHELL! ALWAYS A PLEASURE!
HOW'RE LIVES TREATING YOU? AS TEDIOUS AS EVER?
SAVAGE. THE ONLY THING I FIND TEDIOUS IS THE CONSTANT REPETITION OF THIS SCENE.
A GLASS OF CHATEAU LAFITE ROTHSCHILD 1847? WE HAVE MUCH TO CELEBRATE, MY OLD, OLD FRIEND.
YOU SEE, THIS IS THE LAST TIME WE'LL HAVE TO DANCE THIS PARTICULAR, WEARY DANCE.

ACCOUNT FOR YOUR CORDIALITY, SAVAGE. THIS IS THE BEING YOU DESCRIBED AS OUR GREATEST THREAT.

THE TACTICAL ADVISOR OF THE JUSTICE LEGION.

YOU'RE A *STAR*, SOLARIS. I DON'T *EXPECT* YOU TO APPRECIATE *HUMAN* SOCIAL GRACES.

MITCHELL IS MY OLDEST FRIEND. WE'VE BOTH BEEN AROUND FOR AN *AWFUL* LOT LONGER THAN YOU.

END THIS. BRING THE KNIGHT FRAGMENT TO ME WITHOUT DELAY.

ALL IN GOOD TIME. MITCHELL AND I WILL BE DONE HERE SOON ENOUGH. *THEN* I'LL COURIER THE *KNIGHT FRAGMENT* TO YOU MYSELF.

END COMMUNI-CATION.

SENTIENT STARS, HUH? NO SENSE OF *OCCASION*.

WHAT'S THE *KNIGHT FRAGMENT*, SAVAGE?

THIS. I'VE JUST SUCCESSFULLY EXCAVATED IT FROM ITS AGE-OLD RESTING PLACE UNDER THE SANDS HERE.

RECOGNIZE IT? GREEN... *DEADLY...?*

MY GOD... *KRYPTONITE...?*

THE *LAST* PIECE IN THE UNIVERSE! AND THE ONE THING THAT WILL *END* THE SUPERMAN DYNASTY *FOREVER*.

I DON'T DO THINGS BY *HALF MEASURES*, MITCHELL.

AND I *LOVE* MY WORK.

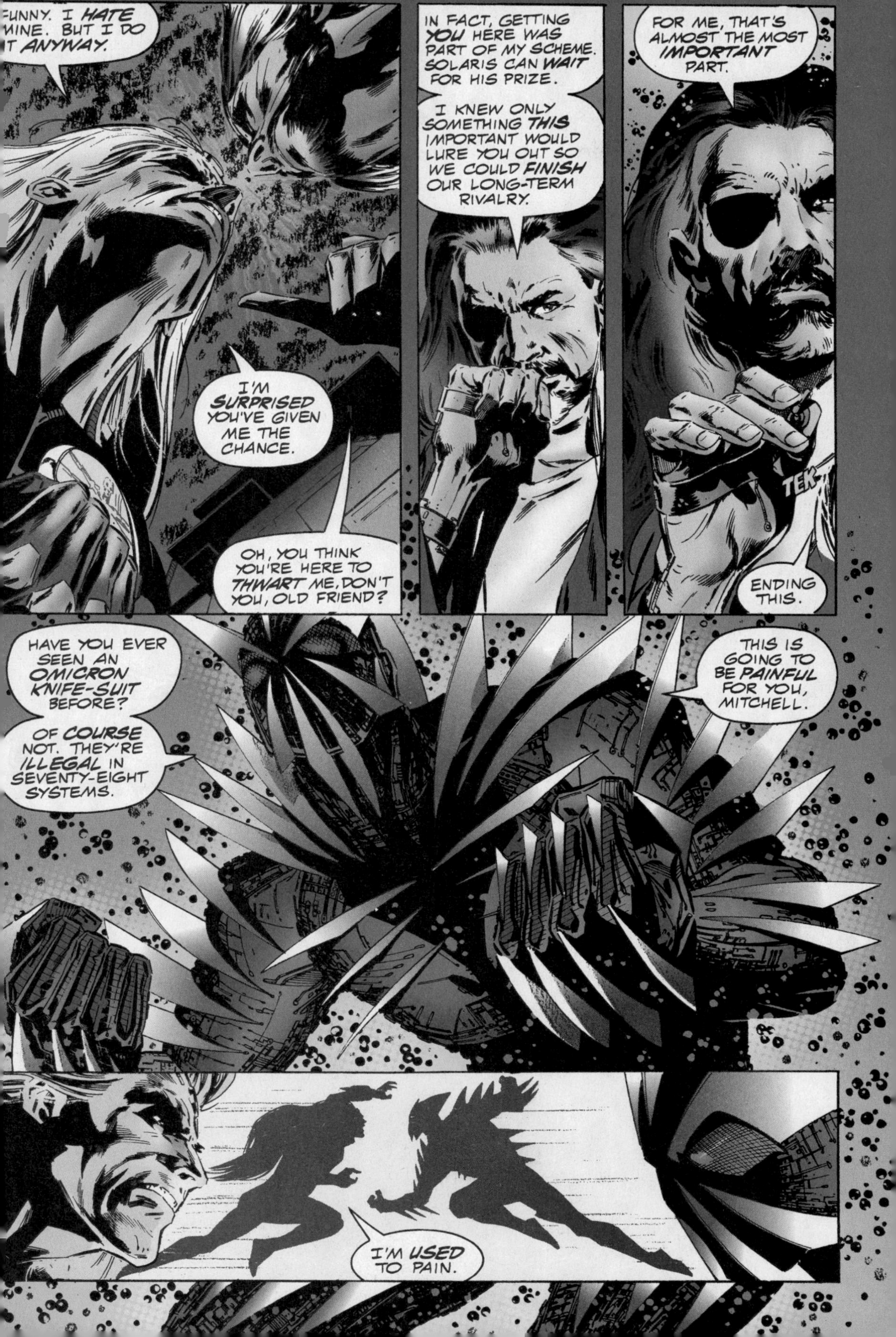
FUNNY. I HATE
MINE. BUT I DO
T ANYWAY.
I'M SURPRISED YOU'VE GIVEN ME THE CHANCE.
OH, YOU THINK YOU'RE HERE TO THWART ME, DON'T YOU, OLD FRIEND?
IN FACT, GETTING YOU HERE WAS PART OF MY SCHEME. SOLARIS CAN WAIT FOR HIS PRIZE.
I KNEW ONLY SOMETHING THIS IMPORTANT WOULD LURE YOU OUT SO WE COULD FINISH OUR LONG-TERM RIVALRY.
FOR ME, THAT'S ALMOST THE MOST IMPORTANT PART.
TEK
ENDING THIS.
HAVE YOU EVER SEEN AN OMICRON KNIFE-SUIT BEFORE?
OF COURSE NOT. THEY'RE ILLEGAL IN SEVENTY-EIGHT SYSTEMS.
THIS IS GOING TO BE PAINFUL FOR YOU, MITCHELL.
I'M USED TO PAIN.

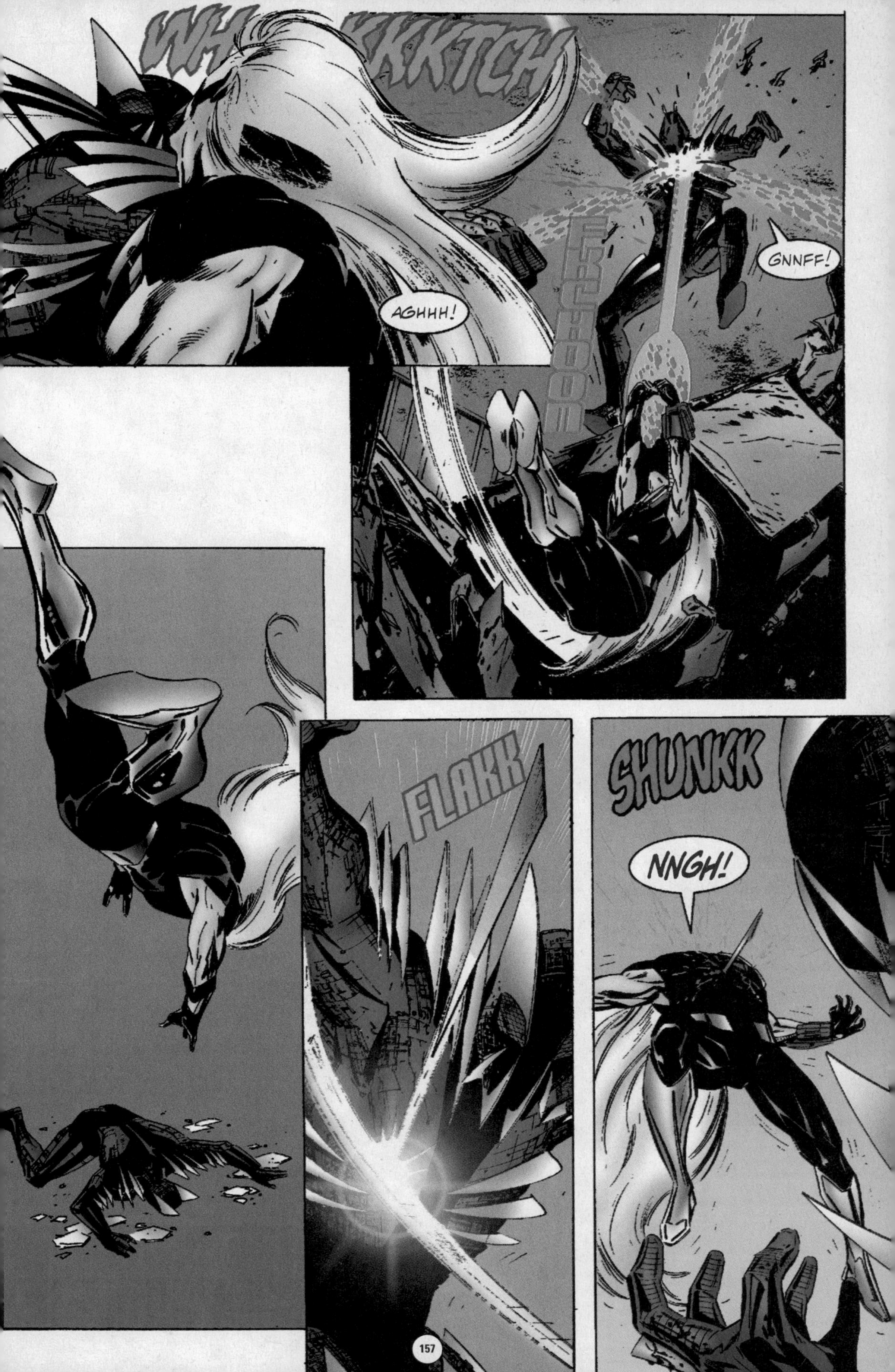
AGHHH!
GNNFF!
FLAKK
SHUNKK
NNGH!

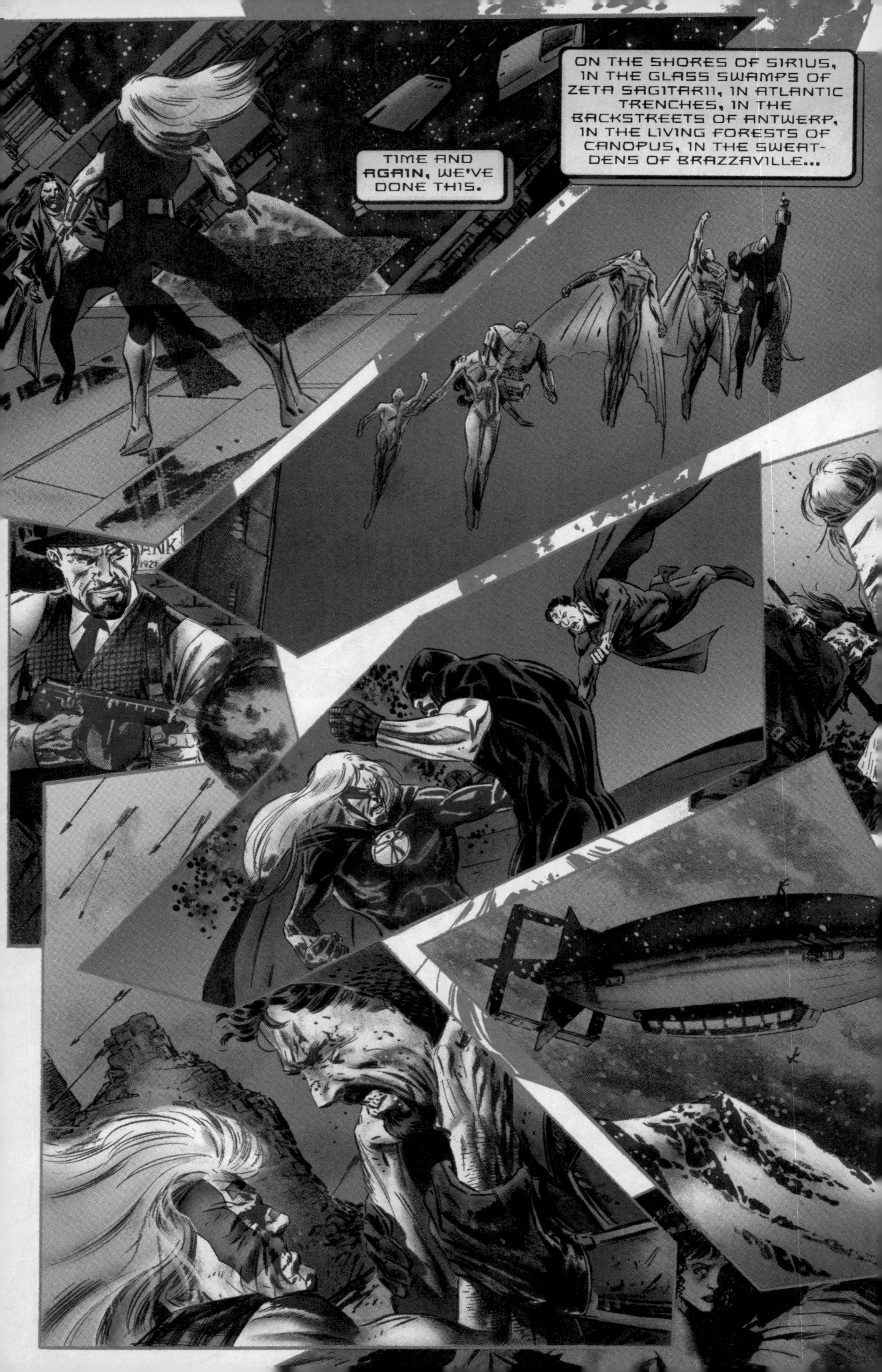
TIME AND AGAIN, WE'VE DONE THIS.
ON THE SHORES OF SIRIUS, IN THE GLASS SWAMPS OF ZETA SAGITARII, IN ATLANTIC TRENCHES, IN THE BACKSTREETS OF ANTWERP, IN THE LIVING FORESTS OF CANOPUS, IN THE SWEAT-DENS OF BRAZZAVILLE...

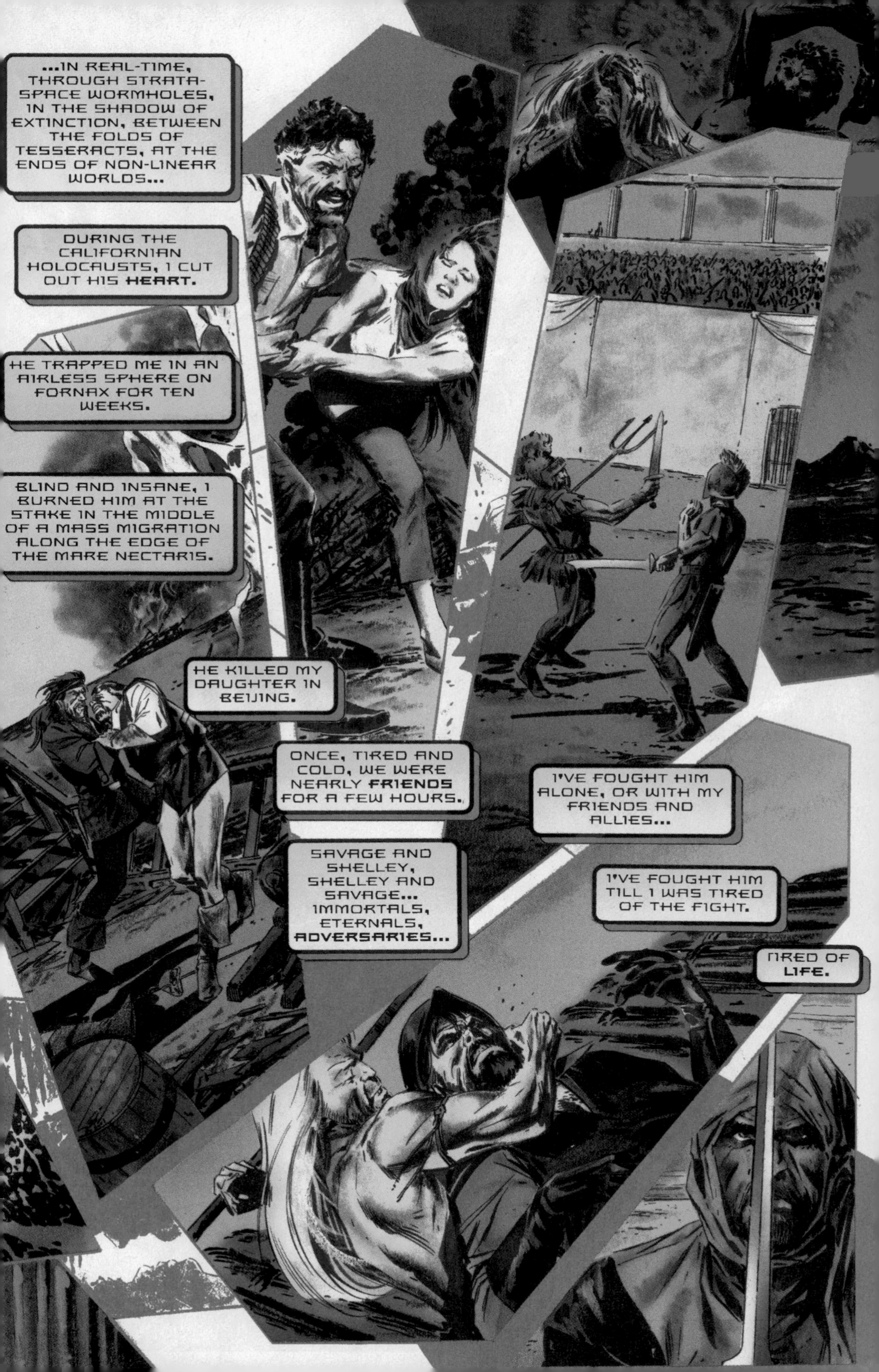
...IN REAL-TIME, THROUGH STRATA-SPACE WORMHOLES, IN THE SHADOW OF EXTINCTION, BETWEEN THE FOLDS OF TESSERACTS, AT THE ENDS OF NON-LINEAR WORLDS...
DURING THE CALIFORNIAN HOLOCAUSTS, I CUT OUT HIS HEART.
HE TRAPPED ME IN AN AIRLESS SPHERE ON FORNAX FOR TEN WEEKS.
BLIND AND INSANE, I BURNED HIM AT THE STAKE IN THE MIDDLE OF A MASS MIGRATION ALONG THE EDGE OF THE MARE NECTARIS.
HE KILLED MY DAUGHTER IN BEIJING.
ONCE, TIRED AND COLD, WE WERE NEARLY FRIENDS FOR A FEW HOURS.
I'VE FOUGHT HIM ALONE, OR WITH MY FRIENDS AND ALLIES...
SAVAGE AND SHELLEY, SHELLEY AND SAVAGE... IMMORTALS, ETERNALS, ADVERSARIES...
I'VE FOUGHT HIM TILL I WAS TIRED OF THE FIGHT.
TIRED OF LIFE.

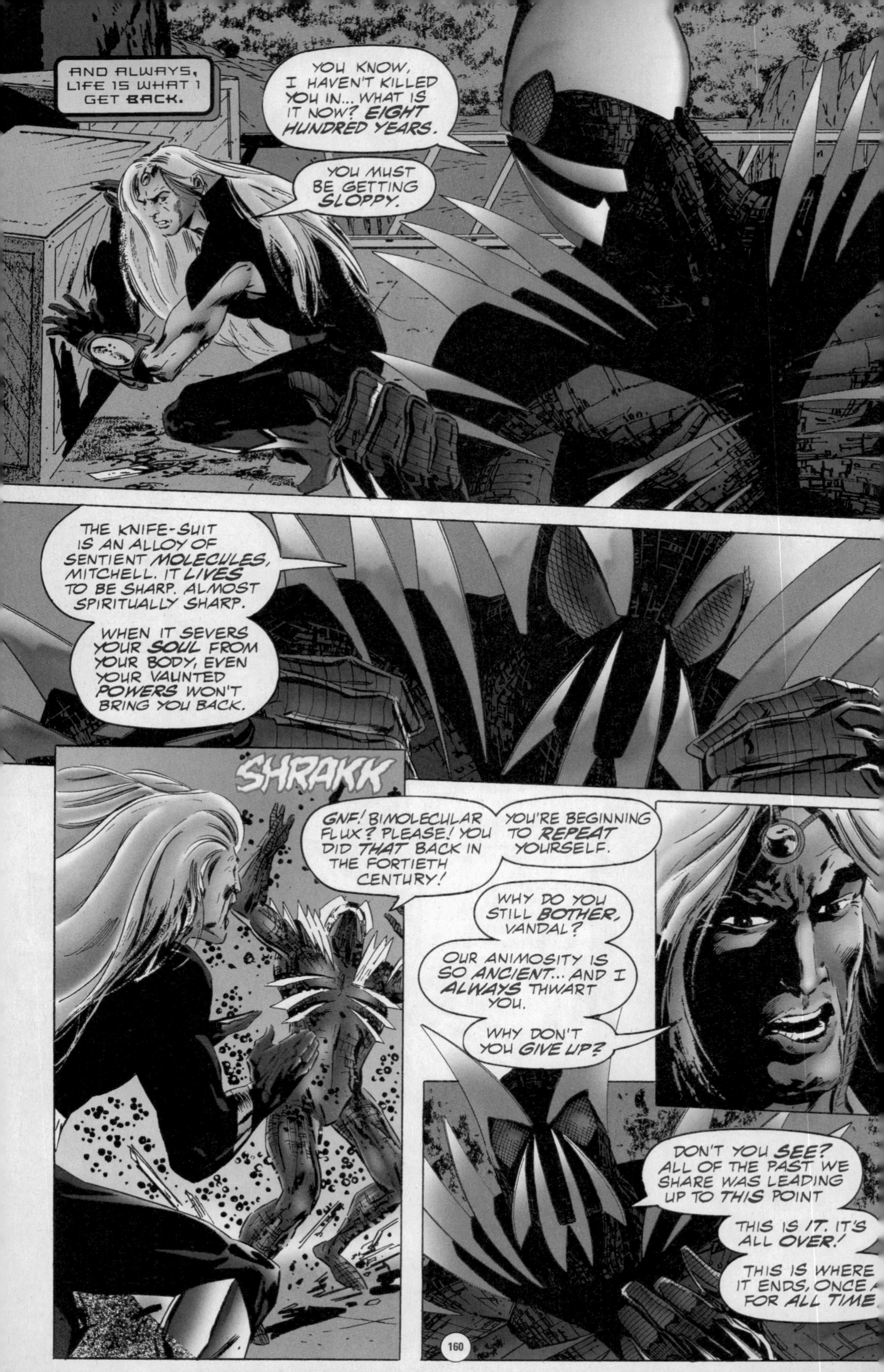
AND ALWAYS, LIFE IS WHAT I GET BACK.
YOU KNOW, I HAVEN'T KILLED YOU IN... WHAT IS IT NOW? EIGHT HUNDRED YEARS.
YOU MUST BE GETTING SLOPPY.
THE KNIFE-SUIT IS AN ALLOY OF SENTIENT MOLECULES, MITCHELL. IT LIVES TO BE SHARP. ALMOST SPIRITUALLY SHARP.
WHEN IT SEVERS YOUR SOUL FROM YOUR BODY, EVEN YOUR VAUNTED POWERS WON'T BRING YOU BACK.
SHRAKK
GNF! BIMOLECULAR FLUX? PLEASE! YOU DID THAT BACK IN THE FORTIETH CENTURY!
YOU'RE BEGINNING TO REPEAT YOURSELF.
WHY DO YOU STILL BOTHER, VANDAL?
OUR ANIMOSITY IS SO ANCIENT... AND I ALWAYS THWART YOU.
WHY DON'T YOU GIVE UP?
DON'T YOU SEE? ALL OF THE PAST WE SHARE WAS LEADING UP TO THIS POINT
THIS IS IT. IT'S ALL OVER!
THIS IS WHERE IT ENDS, ONCE FOR ALL TIME

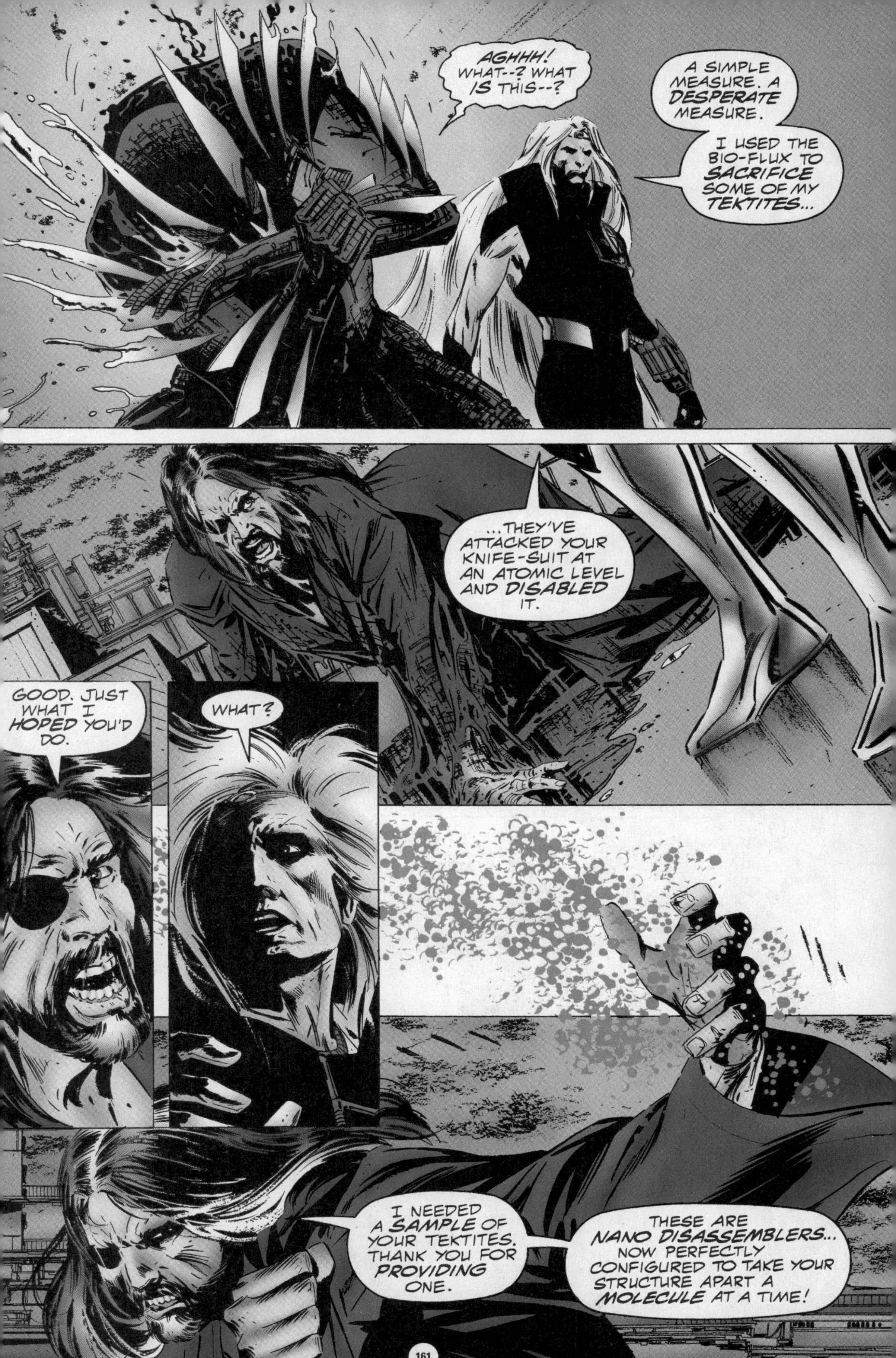
AGHHH! WHAT--? WHAT IS THIS--?
A SIMPLE MEASURE. A DESPERATE MEASURE.
I USED THE BIO-FLUX TO SACRIFICE SOME OF MY TEKTITES...
...THEY'VE ATTACKED YOUR KNIFE-SUIT AT AN ATOMIC LEVEL AND DISABLED IT.
GOOD. JUST WHAT I HOPED YOU'D DO.
WHAT?
I NEEDED A SAMPLE OF YOUR TEKTITES. THANK YOU FOR PROVIDING ONE.
THESE ARE NANO DISASSEMBLERS... NOW PERFECTLY CONFIGURED TO TAKE YOUR STRUCTURE APART A MOLECULE AT A TIME!

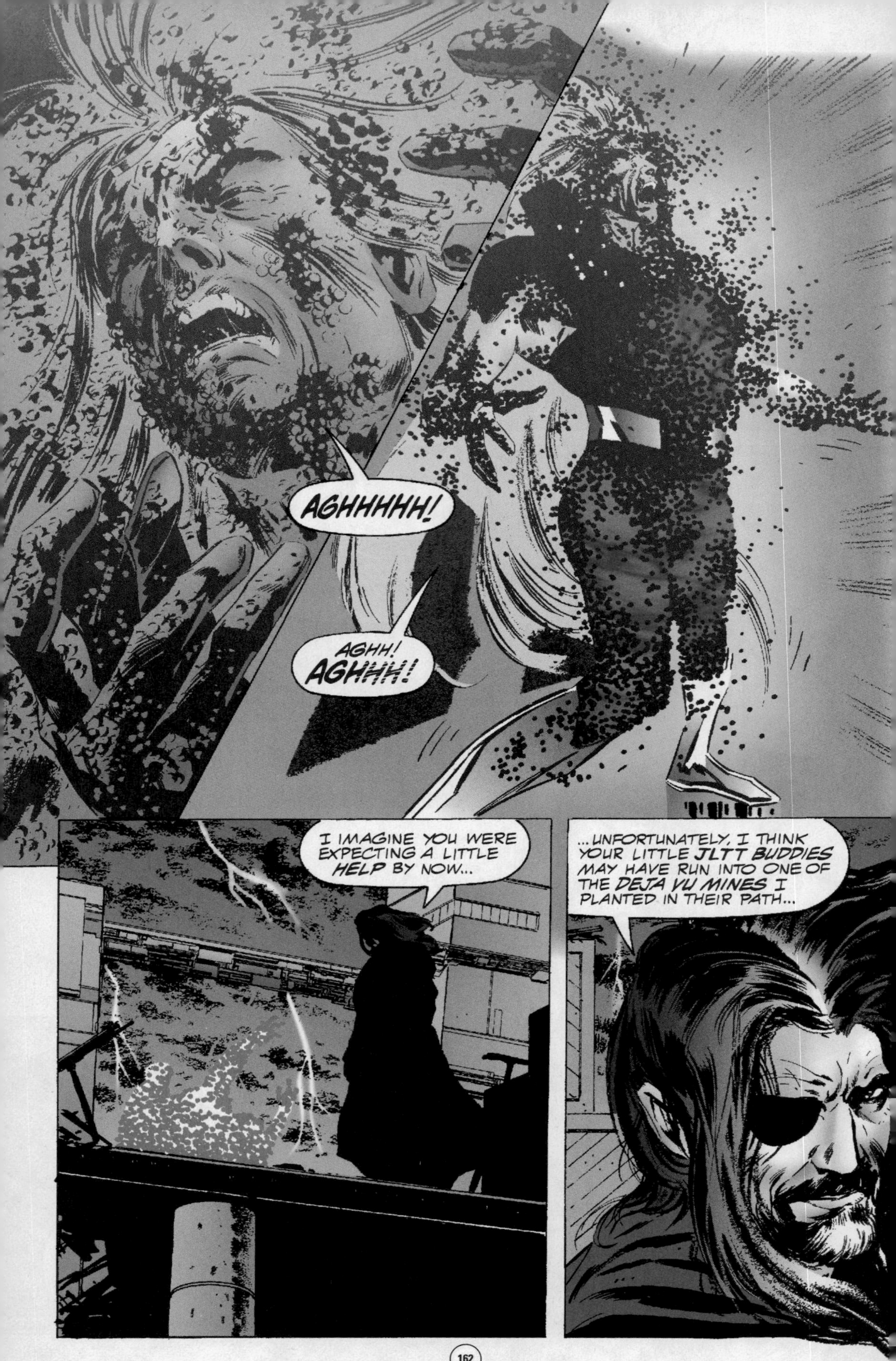
AGHHHHH!
AGHH! AGHHH!
I IMAGINE YOU WERE EXPECTING A LITTLE HELP BY NOW...
...UNFORTUNATELY, I THINK YOUR LITTLE JLTT BUDDIES MAY HAVE RUN INTO ONE OF THE DEJA VU MINES I PLANTED IN THEIR PATH...

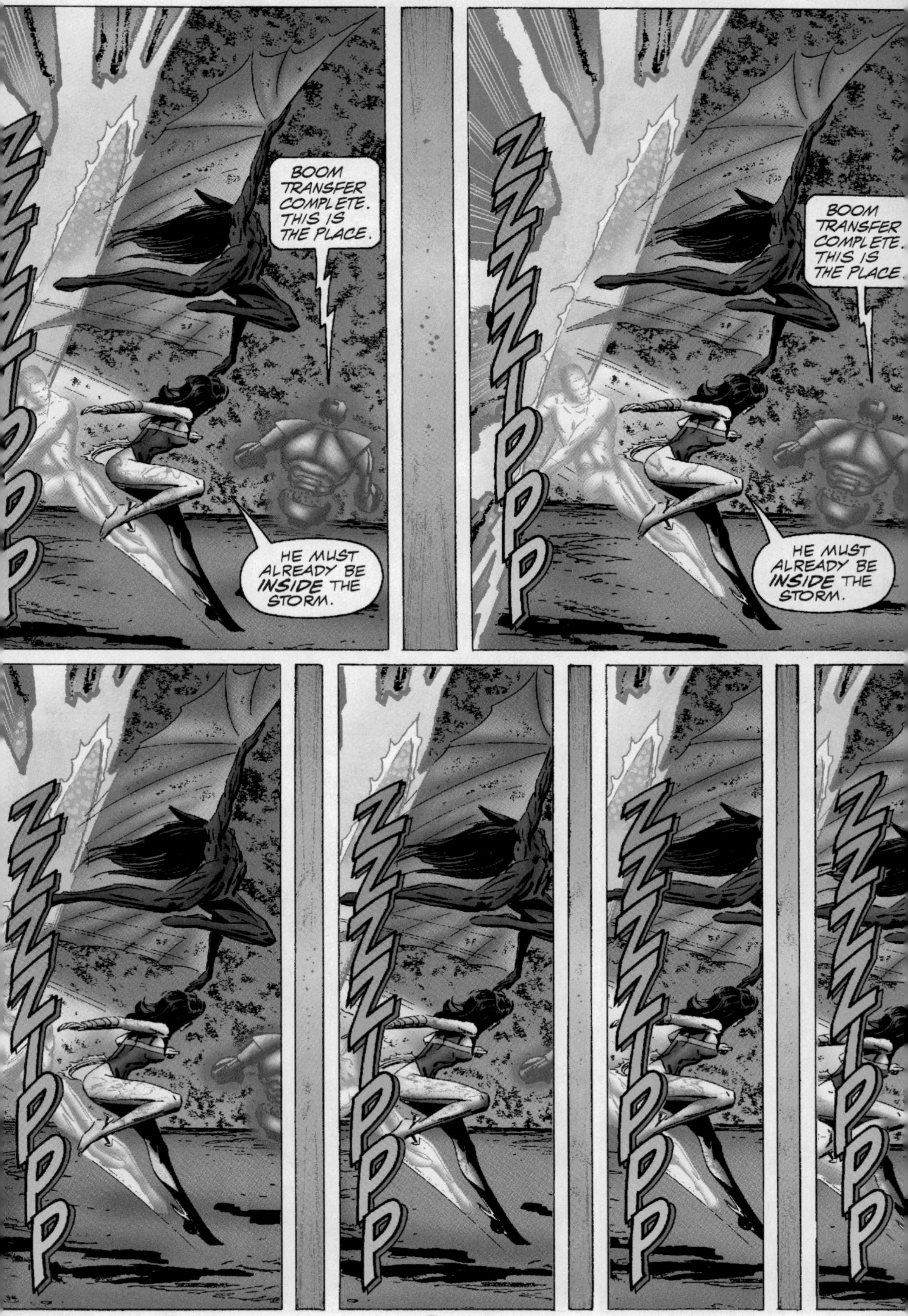
ZZZZZZZIPPP
BOOM TRANSFER COMPLETE. THIS IS THE PLACE.
HE MUST ALREADY BE INSIDE THE STORM.
ZZZZZIPPP
BOOM TRANSFER COMPLETE. THIS IS THE PLACE.
HE MUST ALREADY BE INSIDE THE STORM.
ZZZZZIPPP
ZZZZZIPPP
ZZZZZIPPP
ZZZZZIPPP

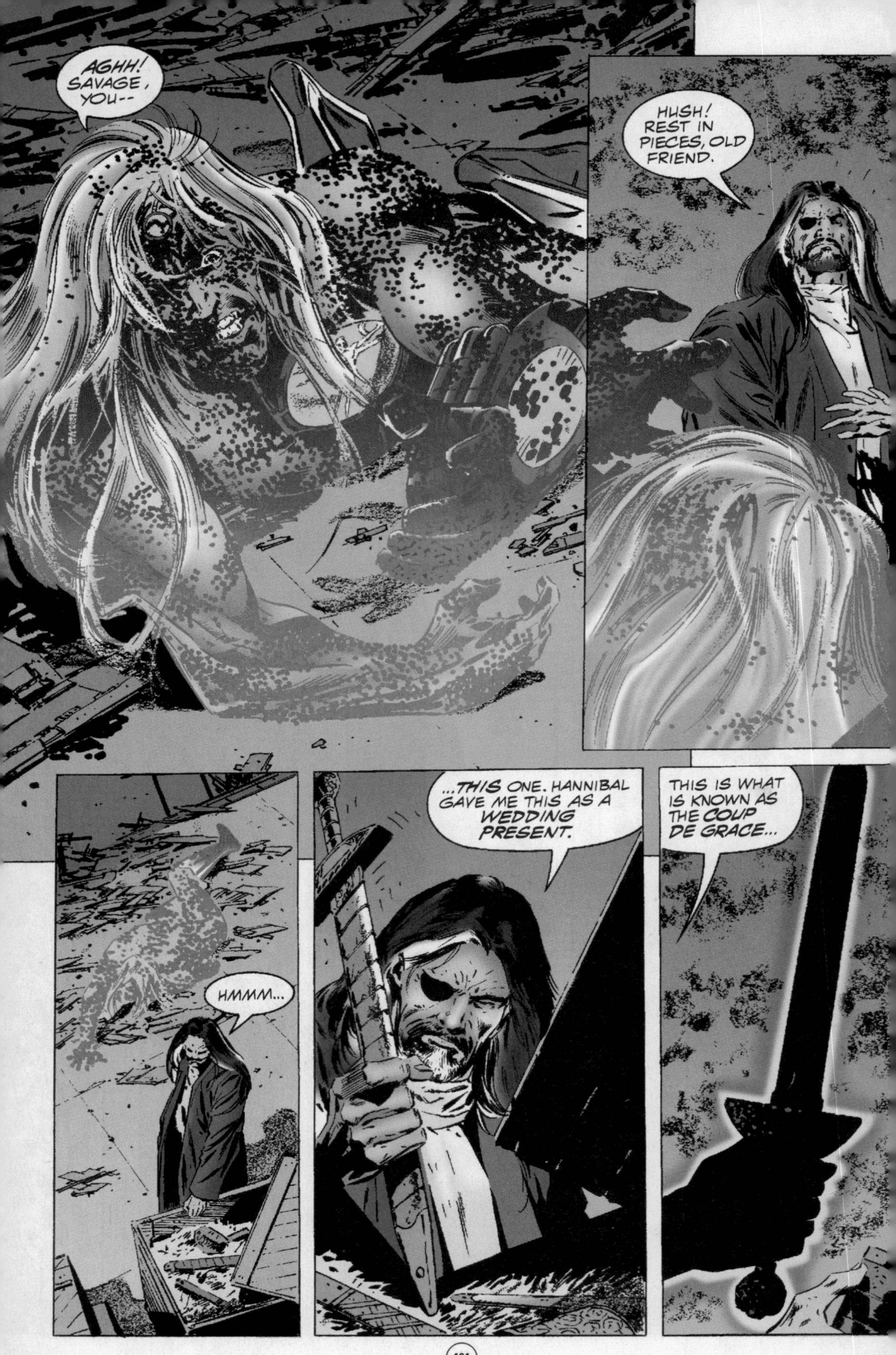

AGHH! SAVAGE, YOU--
HUSH! REST IN PIECES, OLD FRIEND.
HMMM...
...THIS ONE. HANNIBAL GAVE ME THIS AS A WEDDING PRESENT.
THIS IS WHAT IS KNOWN AS THE COUP DE GRACE...

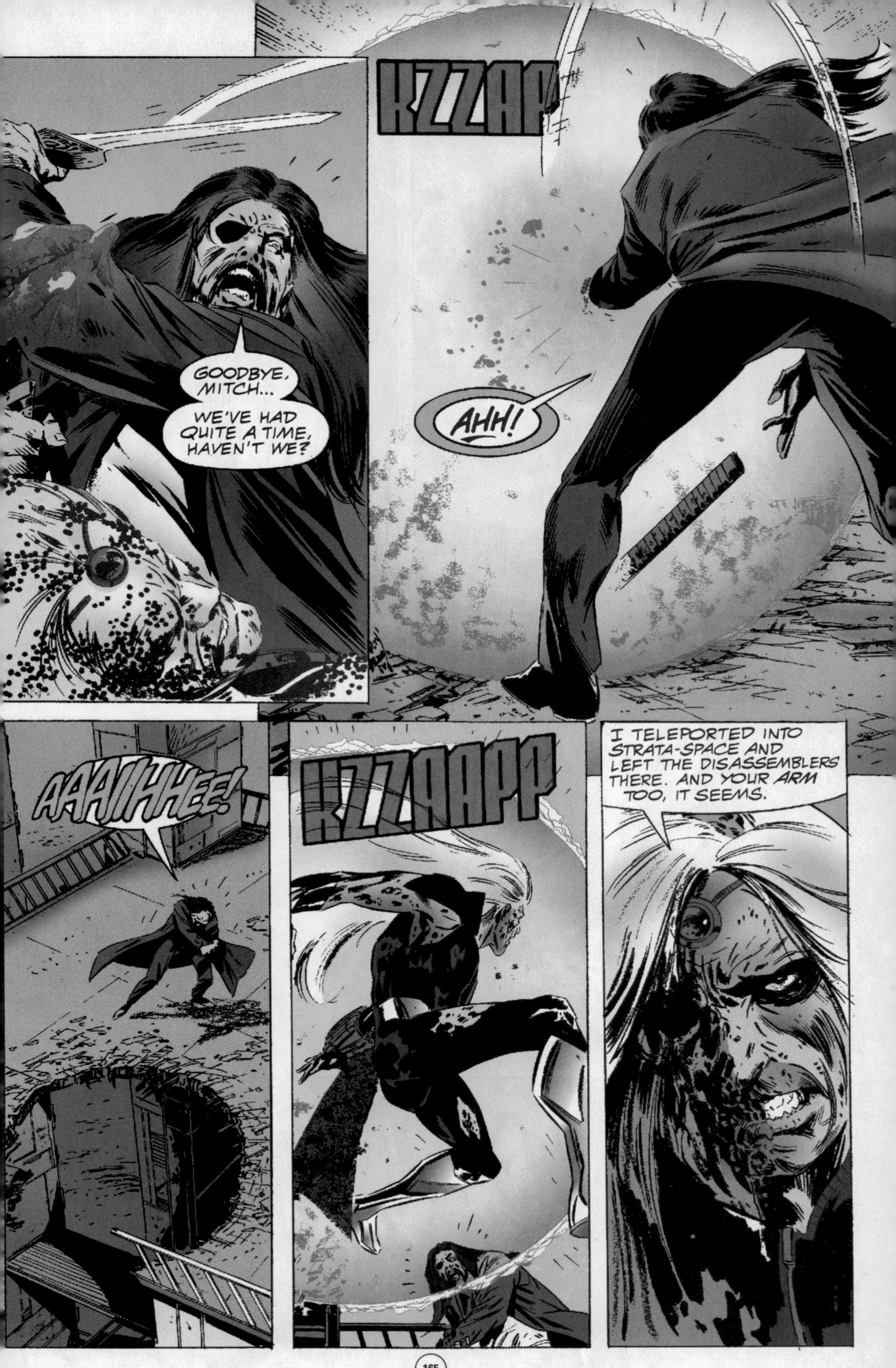
KZZAP
GOODBYE, MITCH...
WE'VE HAD QUITE A TIME, HAVEN'T WE?
AHH!
AAAIIHHEE!
KZZAAPP
I TELEPORTED INTO STRATA-SPACE AND LEFT THE DISASSEMBLERS THERE. AND YOUR ARM TOO, IT SEEMS.

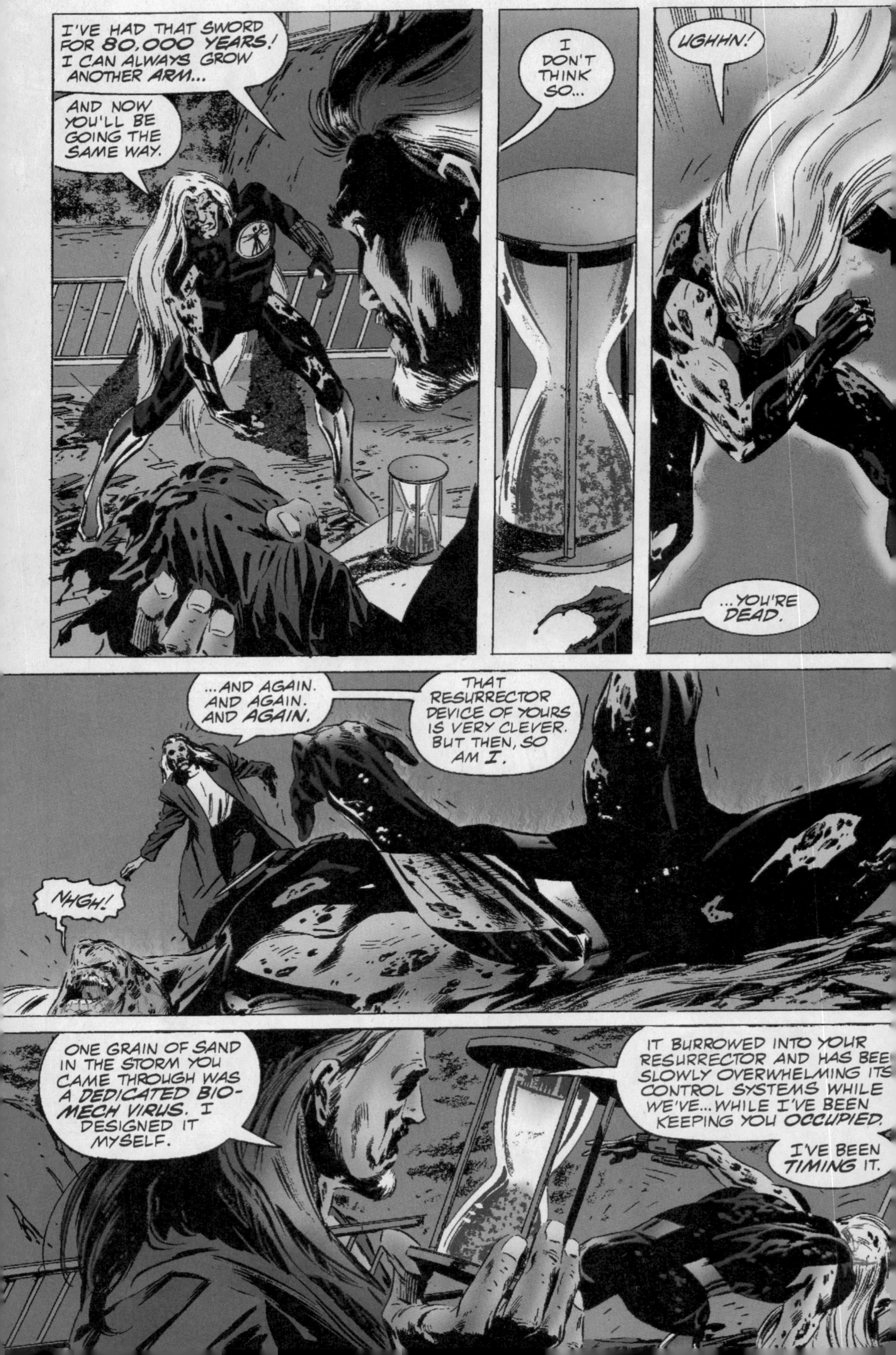
I'VE HAD THAT SWORD FOR 80,000 YEARS! I CAN ALWAYS GROW ANOTHER ARM...
AND NOW YOU'LL BE GOING THE SAME WAY.
I DON'T THINK SO...
UGHHN!
...YOU'RE DEAD.
...AND AGAIN. AND AGAIN. AND AGAIN.
THAT RESURRECTOR DEVICE OF YOURS IS VERY CLEVER. BUT THEN, SO AM I.
NHGH!
ONE GRAIN OF SAND IN THE STORM YOU CAME THROUGH WAS A DEDICATED BIO-MECH VIRUS. I DESIGNED IT MYSELF.
IT BURROWED INTO YOUR RESURRECTOR AND HAS BEE SLOWLY OVERWHELMING ITS CONTROL SYSTEMS WHILE WE'VE...WHILE I'VE BEEN KEEPING YOU OCCUPIED.
I'VE BEEN TIMING IT.

I KNEW I COULDN'T KILL YOU *OUTRIGHT*, SO I FIGURED I KILL YOU *FOREVER* INSTEAD.

THE VIRUS WILL MAKE SURE THE *RESURRECTOR* KEEPS KILLING YOU, OVER AND *OVER.*

THIS IS AS *CLOSE* TO *DEATH* AS YOU'RE EVER GOING TO SEE. GET USED TO IT.

ANYWAY, HAVEN'T I JUST DONE YOU A *FAVOR*?

GOTTA GO.

NOW HAVE I GOT EVERYTHING?

KNIGHT FRAGMENT?

KEYS?

OKAY THEN... VOICE COMMAND SAVAGE, VANDAL.

ACTIVATE BOOM TUBE TRANSFER AND OPEN THE FORCE SHIELD.

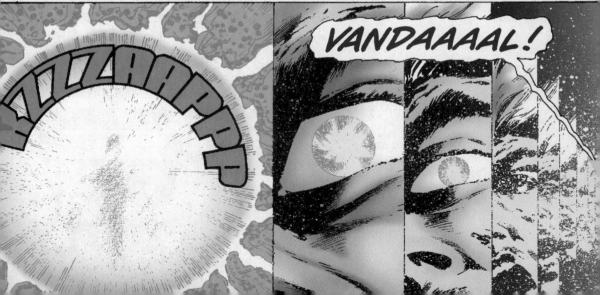

KZZZAAPPP

VANDAAAAL!

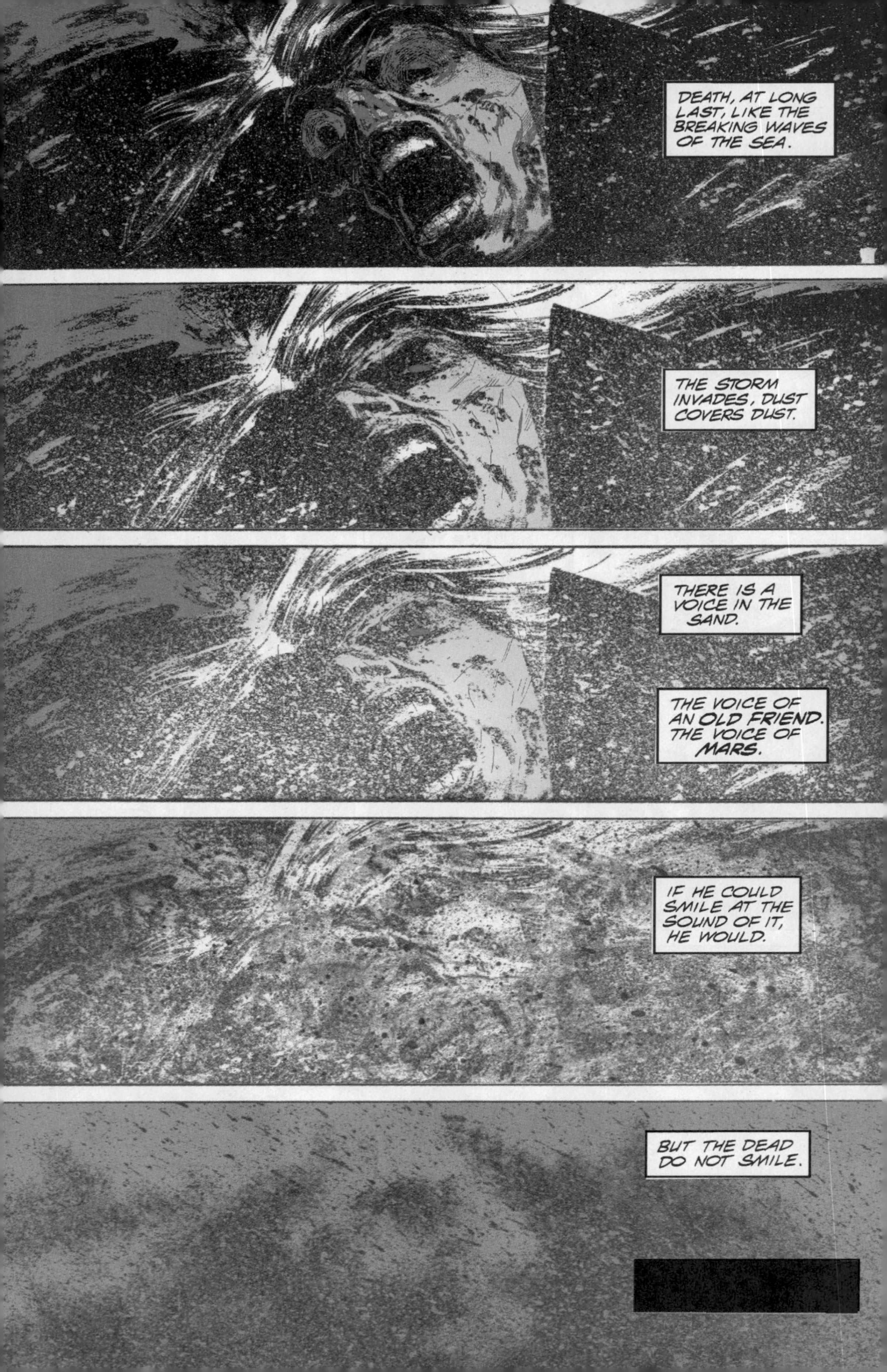
DEATH, AT LONG LAST, LIKE THE BREAKING WAVES OF THE SEA.
THE STORM INVADES, DUST COVERS DUST.
THERE IS A VOICE IN THE SAND.
THE VOICE OF AN OLD FRIEND. THE VOICE OF MARS.
IF HE COULD SMILE AT THE SOUND OF IT, HE WOULD.
BUT THE DEAD DO NOT SMILE.
[redacted]

•••INPUT

DIGIPRINT

TO SAVE PAST AND FUTURE, THE JLA ROCKETED TO JUPITER!

PREVAILING AGAINST INSURMOUNTABLE ODDS IN A TIME WHERE EVERYONE HAS SUPER-POWERS, THE 20TH CENTURY JLA FINALLY REGROUPED TO COMBAT THE THREAT OF THE MALEVOLENT STELLAR-SUN SOLARIS.

BUT ARE THEIR EFFORTS TOO LATE?

TO THWART SOLARIS'S PLANS TO MURDER THE PRIME-SUPERMAN WITH THE KRYPTONITE FRAGMENT HE UNEARTHED ON MARS, THE LEAGUE NOW SPEEDS TO THE JOVIAN HEADQUARTERS OF THE JUSTICE LEGION A IN ORDER TO RETURN TO THEIR OWN ERA AND REUNITE WITH THEIR 853RD-CENTURY COUNTERPARTS TRAPPED IN THE PAST.

MEANWHILE, THE 20TH-CENTURY SUPERMAN JOURNEYS TO LEARN THE ORIGINS OF SOLARIS'S BOUNDLESS HATRED, AN ENMITY LINKING THE TYRANT SUN AND THE MAN OF STEEL'S PROGENY IN THE SUPERMAN DYNASTY FOR MILLENNIA.

IN AN 853RD-CENTURY JUNKYARD TESSERACT, HOME TO HUMANKIND'S CENTURIES OF WASTE AND CASTOFFS, THE KRYPTONIAN HERO HEADS TOWARD A REUNION WITH AN OLD AND BEAUTIFUL FRIEND, THE LAST SURVIVOR OF THE FABULOUS ROBOTIC METAL MEN...

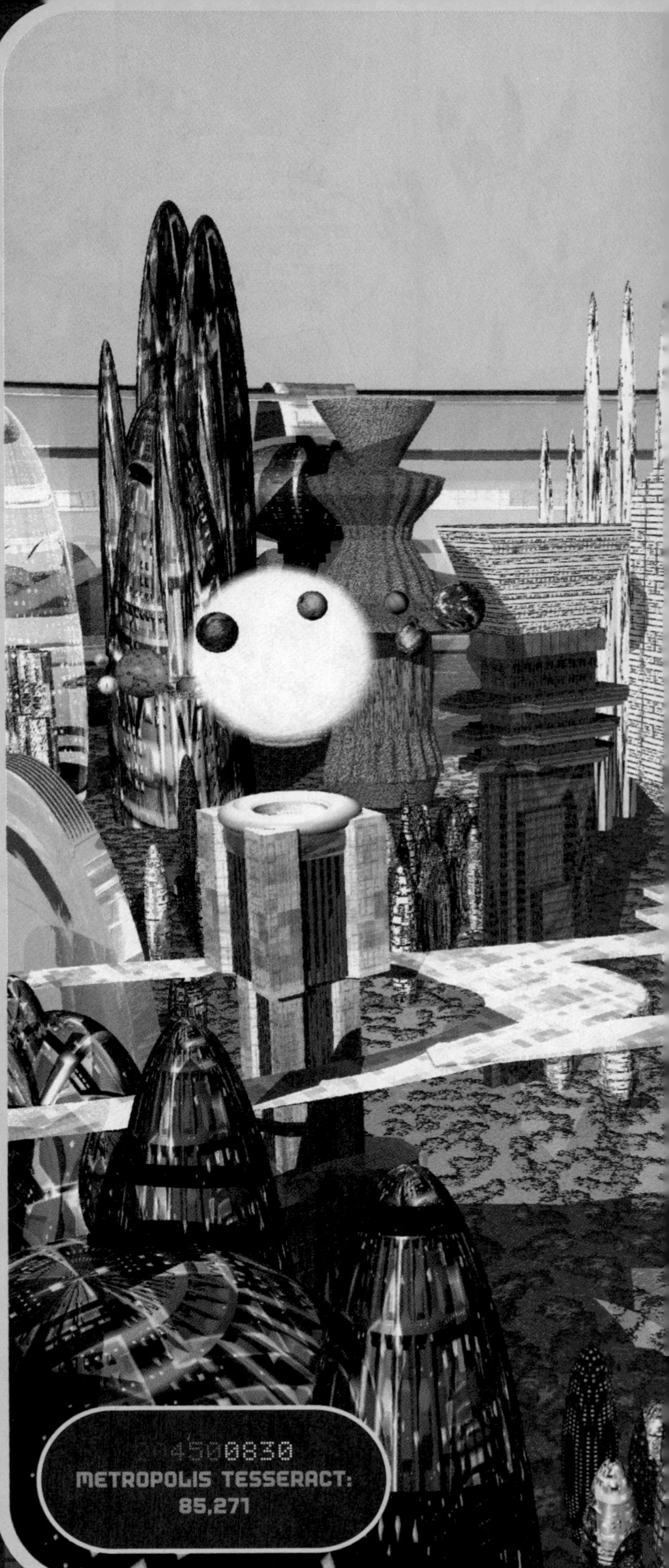
4500830
METROPOLIS TESSERACT:
85,271

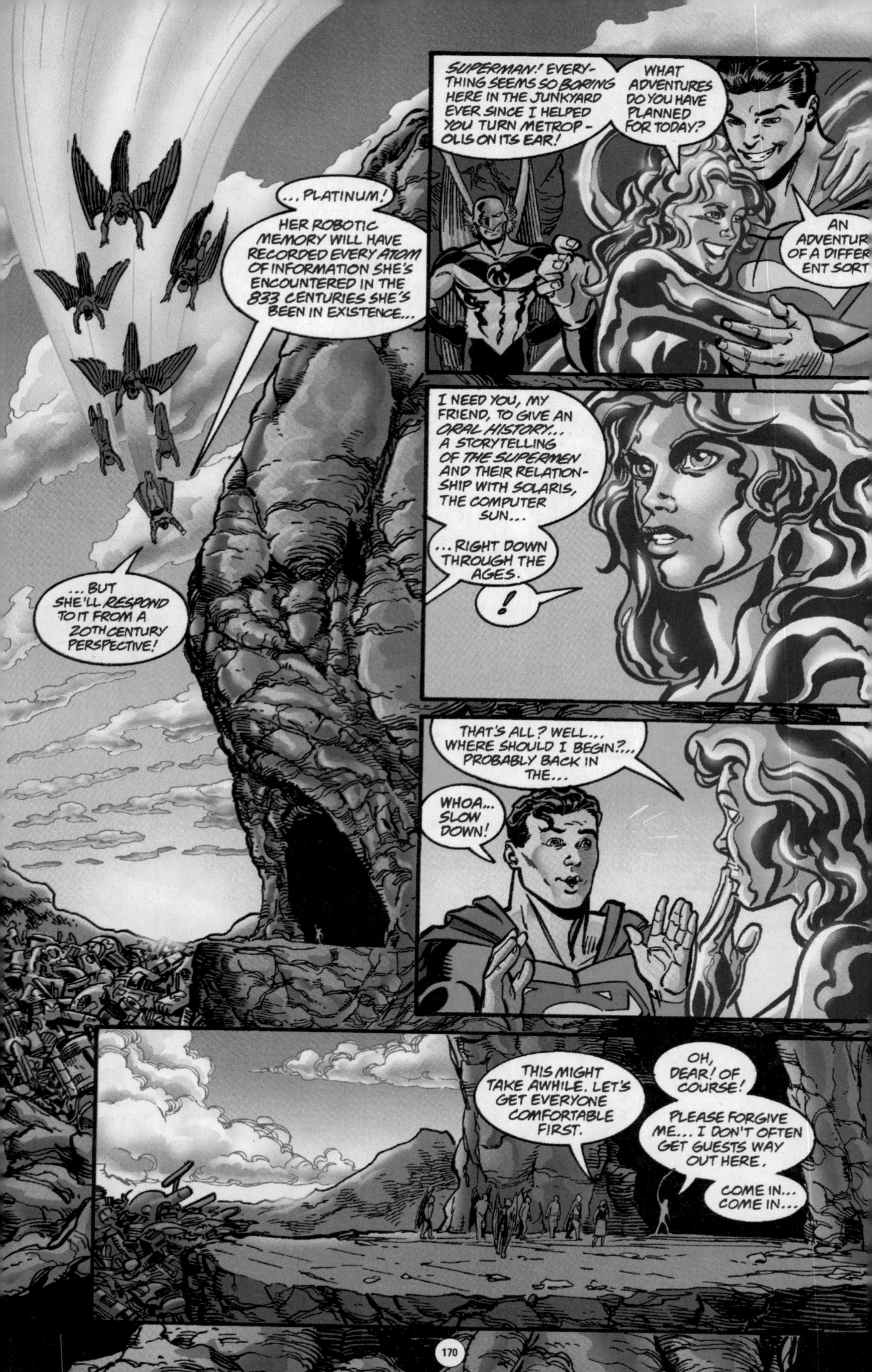

...PLATINUM!
HER ROBOTIC MEMORY WILL HAVE RECORDED EVERY ATOM OF INFORMATION SHE'S ENCOUNTERED IN THE 833 CENTURIES SHE'S BEEN IN EXISTENCE...
...BUT SHE'LL RESPOND TO IT FROM A 20TH CENTURY PERSPECTIVE!
SUPERMAN! EVERYTHING SEEMS SO BORING HERE IN THE JUNKYARD EVER SINCE I HELPED YOU TURN METROPOLIS ON ITS EAR!
WHAT ADVENTURES DO YOU HAVE PLANNED FOR TODAY?
AN ADVENTUR OF A DIFFER ENT SORT
I NEED YOU, MY FRIEND, TO GIVE AN ORAL HISTORY... A STORYTELLING OF THE SUPERMEN AND THEIR RELATIONSHIP WITH SOLARIS, THE COMPUTER SUN...
...RIGHT DOWN THROUGH THE AGES.
!
THAT'S ALL? WELL... WHERE SHOULD I BEGIN?... PROBABLY BACK IN THE...
WHOA... SLOW DOWN!
THIS MIGHT TAKE AWHILE. LET'S GET EVERYONE COMFORTABLE FIRST.
OH, DEAR! OF COURSE!
PLEASE FORGIVE ME... I DON'T OFTEN GET GUESTS WAY OUT HERE.
COME IN... COME IN...

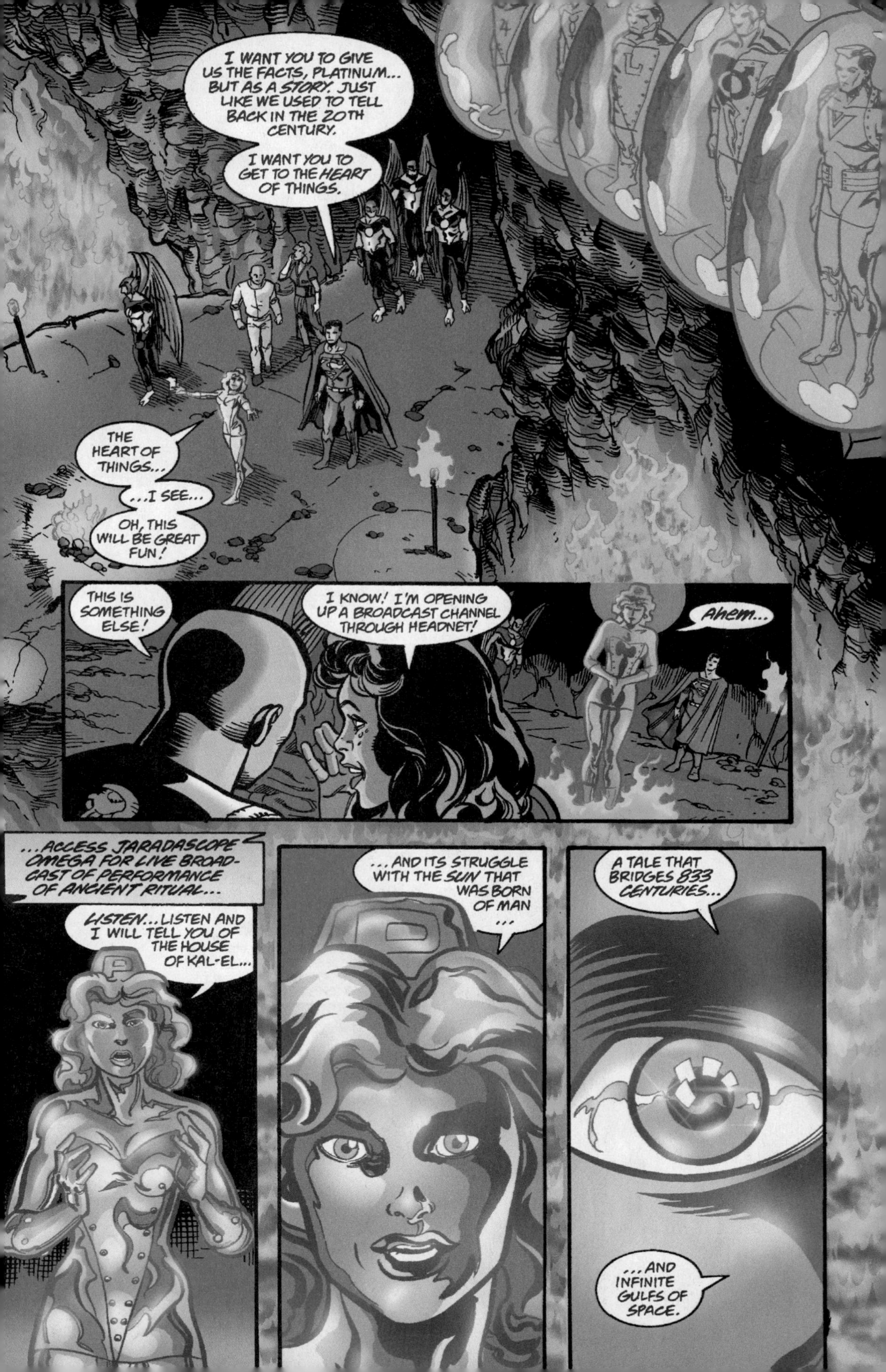

I WANT YOU TO GIVE US THE FACTS, PLATINUM... BUT AS A STORY. JUST LIKE WE USED TO TELL BACK IN THE 20TH CENTURY.
I WANT YOU TO GET TO THE HEART OF THINGS.
THE HEART OF THINGS...
...I SEE...
OH, THIS WILL BE GREAT FUN!
THIS IS SOMETHING ELSE!
I KNOW! I'M OPENING UP A BROADCAST CHANNEL THROUGH HEADNET!
Ahem...
...ACCESS JARADASCOPE OMEGA FOR LIVE BROAD-CAST OF PERFORMANCE OF ANCIENT RITUAL...
LISTEN... LISTEN AND I WILL TELL YOU OF THE HOUSE OF KAL-EL...
...AND ITS STRUGGLE WITH THE SUN THAT WAS BORN OF MAN...
A TALE THAT BRIDGES 833 CENTURIES...
...AND INFINITE GULFS OF SPACE.

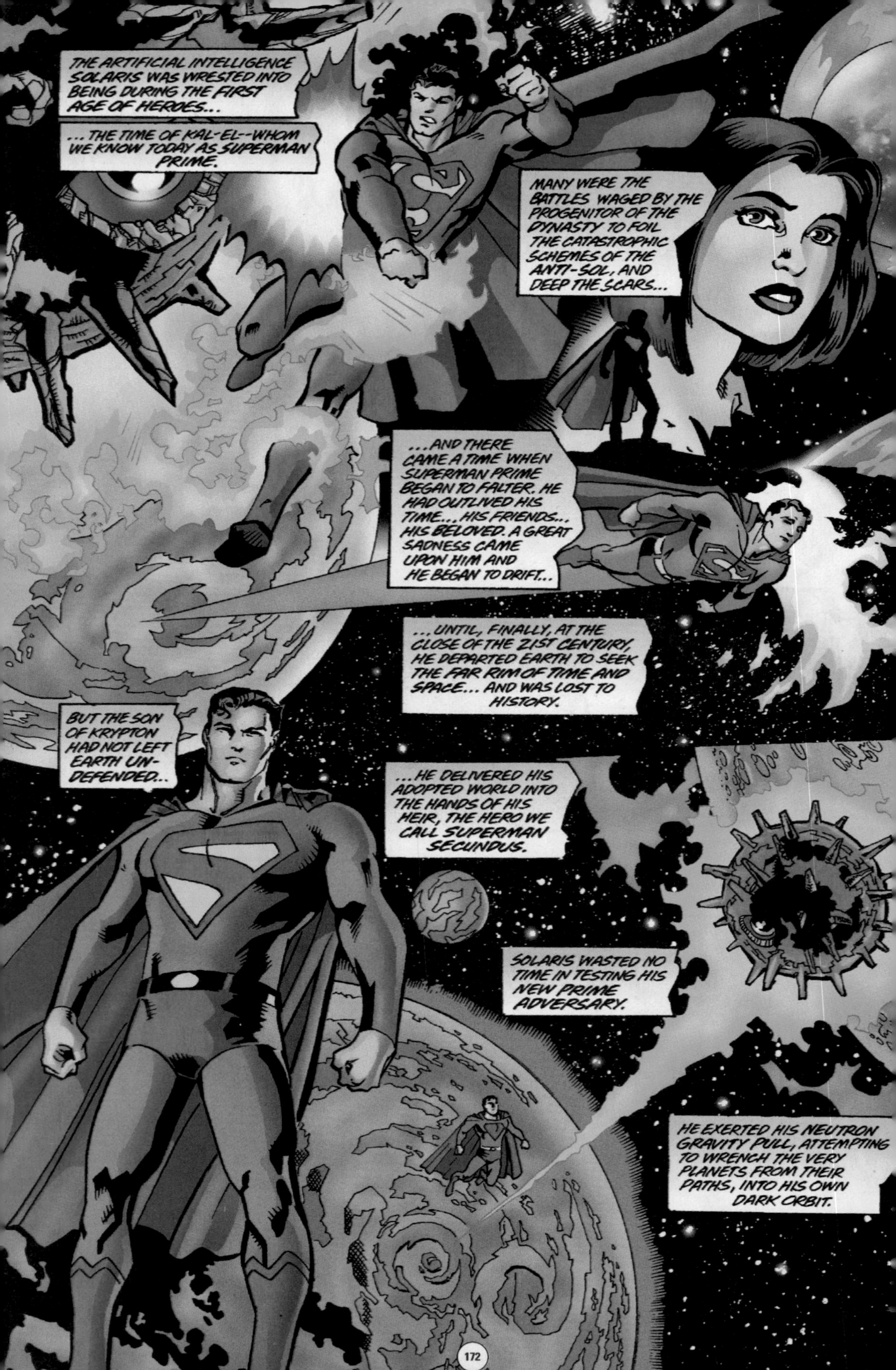
THE ARTIFICIAL INTELLIGENCE SOLARIS WAS WRESTED INTO BEING DURING THE FIRST AGE OF HEROES...
...THE TIME OF KAL-EL--WHOM WE KNOW TODAY AS SUPERMAN PRIME.
MANY WERE THE BATTLES WAGED BY THE PROGENITOR OF THE DYNASTY TO FOIL THE CATASTROPHIC SCHEMES OF THE ANTI-SOL, AND DEEP THE SCARS...
...AND THERE CAME A TIME WHEN SUPERMAN PRIME BEGAN TO FALTER. HE HAD OUTLIVED HIS TIME... HIS FRIENDS... HIS BELOVED. A GREAT SADNESS CAME UPON HIM AND HE BEGAN TO DRIFT...
...UNTIL, FINALLY, AT THE CLOSE OF THE 21ST CENTURY, HE DEPARTED EARTH TO SEEK THE FAR RIM OF TIME AND SPACE... AND WAS LOST TO HISTORY.
BUT THE SON OF KRYPTON HAD NOT LEFT EARTH UN-DEFENDED...
...HE DELIVERED HIS ADOPTED WORLD INTO THE HANDS OF HIS HEIR, THE HERO WE CALL SUPERMAN SECUNDUS.
SOLARIS WASTED NO TIME IN TESTING HIS NEW PRIME ADVERSARY.
HE EXERTED HIS NEUTRON GRAVITY PULL, ATTEMPTING TO WRENCH THE VERY PLANETS FROM THEIR PATHS, INTO HIS OWN DARK ORBIT.

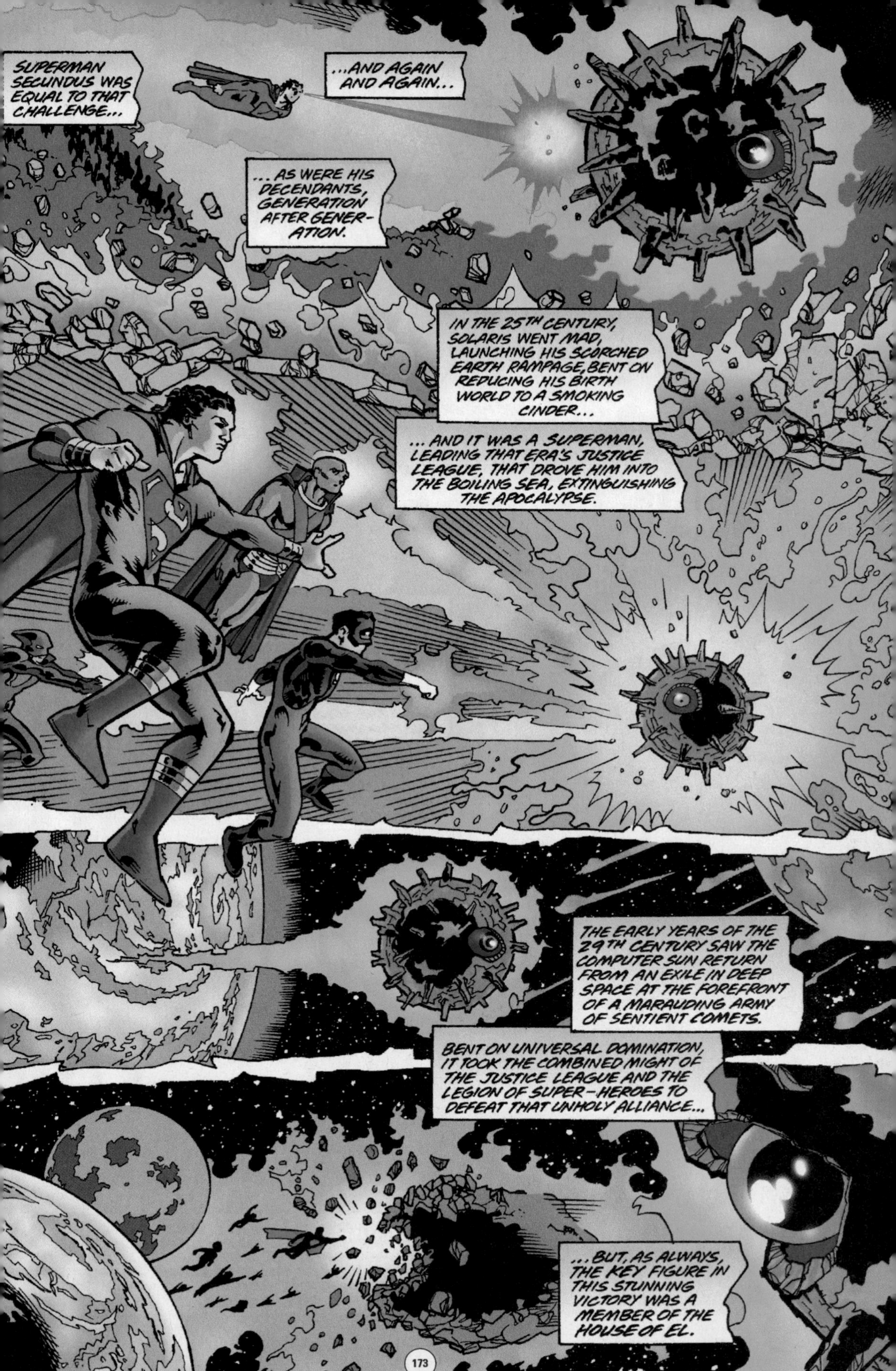
SUPERMAN SECUNDUS WAS EQUAL TO THAT CHALLENGE...
...AND AGAIN AND AGAIN...
...AS WERE HIS DECENDANTS, GENERATION AFTER GENERATION.
IN THE 25TH CENTURY, SOLARIS WENT MAD, LAUNCHING HIS SCORCHED EARTH RAMPAGE, BENT ON REDUCING HIS BIRTH WORLD TO A SMOKING CINDER...
...AND IT WAS A SUPERMAN, LEADING THAT ERA'S JUSTICE LEAGUE, THAT DROVE HIM INTO THE BOILING SEA, EXTINGUISHING THE APOCALYPSE.
THE EARLY YEARS OF THE 29TH CENTURY SAW THE COMPUTER SUN RETURN FROM AN EXILE IN DEEP SPACE AT THE FOREFRONT OF A MARAUDING ARMY OF SENTIENT COMETS.
BENT ON UNIVERSAL DOMINATION, IT TOOK THE COMBINED MIGHT OF THE JUSTICE LEAGUE AND THE LEGION OF SUPER-HEROES TO DEFEAT THAT UNHOLY ALLIANCE...
...BUT, AS ALWAYS, THE KEY FIGURE IN THIS STUNNING VICTORY WAS A MEMBER OF THE HOUSE OF EL.

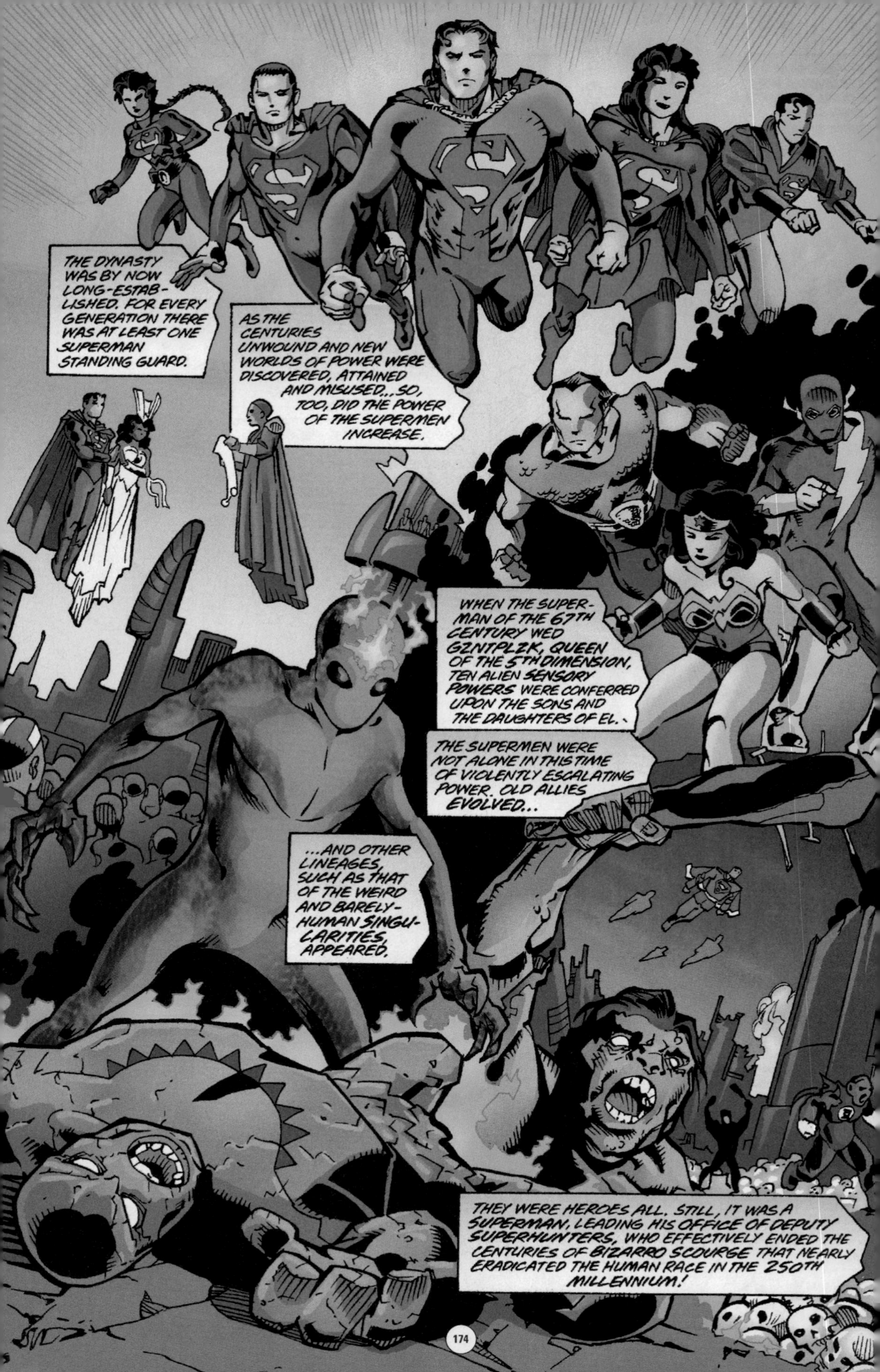
THE DYNASTY WAS BY NOW LONG-ESTABLISHED. FOR EVERY GENERATION THERE WAS AT LEAST ONE SUPERMAN STANDING GUARD.
AS THE CENTURIES UNWOUND AND NEW WORLDS OF POWER WERE DISCOVERED, ATTAINED AND MISUSED... SO, TOO, DID THE POWER OF THE SUPERMEN INCREASE.
WHEN THE SUPERMAN OF THE 67TH CENTURY WED GZNTPLZK, QUEEN OF THE 5TH DIMENSION, TEN ALIEN SENSORY POWERS WERE CONFERRED UPON THE SONS AND THE DAUGHTERS OF EL.
THE SUPERMEN WERE NOT ALONE IN THIS TIME OF VIOLENTLY ESCALATING POWER. OLD ALLIES EVOLVED...
...AND OTHER LINEAGES, SUCH AS THAT OF THE WEIRD AND BARELY-HUMAN SINGULARITIES, APPEARED.
THEY WERE HEROES ALL. STILL, IT WAS A SUPERMAN, LEADING HIS OFFICE OF DEPUTY SUPERHUNTERS, WHO EFFECTIVELY ENDED THE CENTURIES OF BIZARRO SCOURGE THAT NEARLY ERADICATED THE HUMAN RACE IN THE 250TH MILLENNIUM!

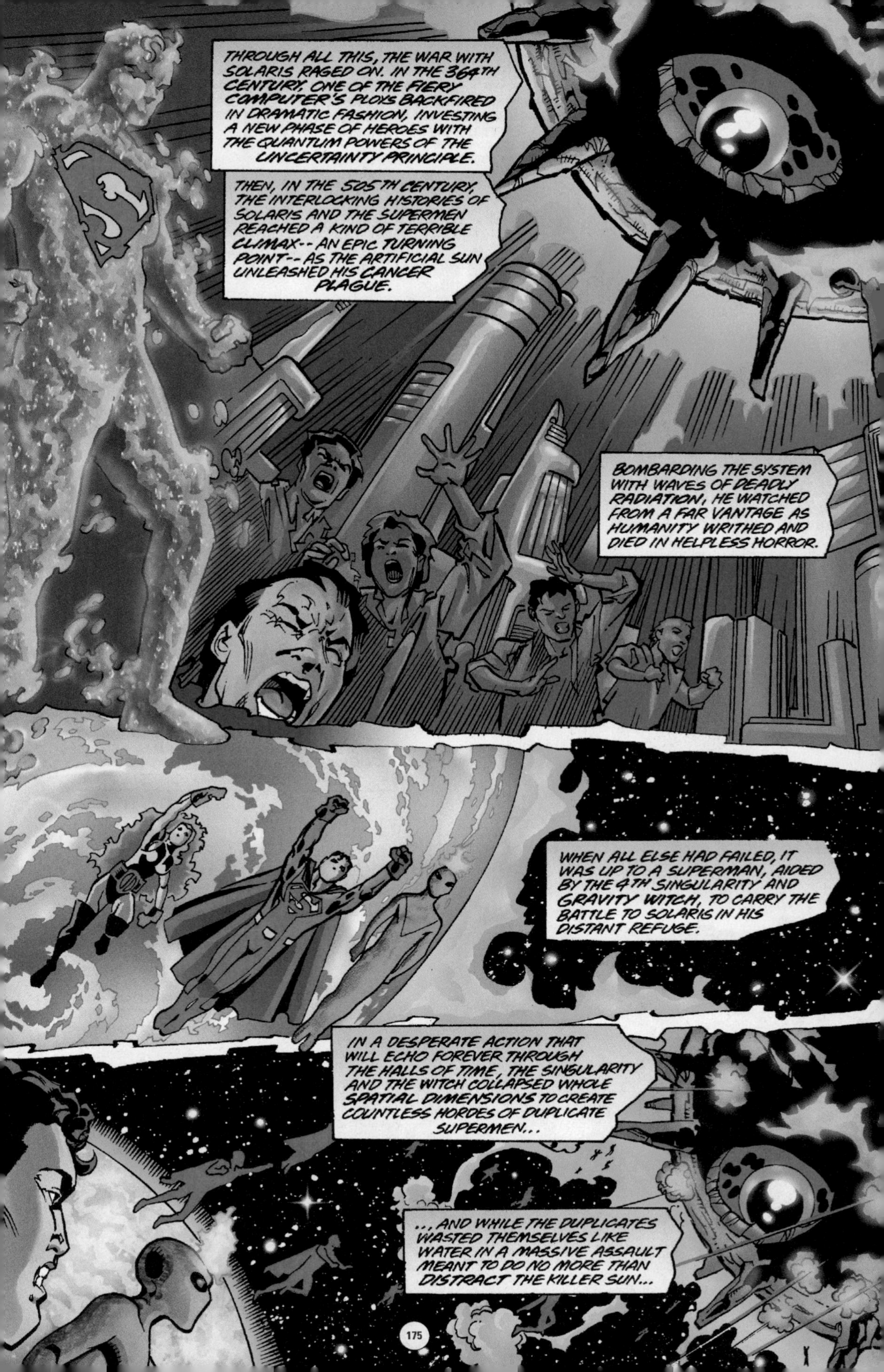
THROUGH ALL THIS, THE WAR WITH SOLARIS RAGED ON. IN THE 364TH CENTURY, ONE OF THE FIERY COMPUTER'S PLOYS BACKFIRED IN DRAMATIC FASHION, INVESTING A NEW PHASE OF HEROES WITH THE QUANTUM POWERS OF THE UNCERTAINTY PRINCIPLE.
THEN, IN THE 505TH CENTURY, THE INTERLOCKING HISTORIES OF SOLARIS AND THE SUPERMEN REACHED A KIND OF TERRIBLE CLIMAX-- AN EPIC TURNING POINT-- AS THE ARTIFICIAL SUN UNLEASHED HIS CANCER PLAGUE.
BOMBARDING THE SYSTEM WITH WAVES OF DEADLY RADIATION, HE WATCHED FROM A FAR VANTAGE AS HUMANITY WRITHED AND DIED IN HELPLESS HORROR.
WHEN ALL ELSE HAD FAILED, IT WAS UP TO A SUPERMAN, AIDED BY THE 4TH SINGULARITY AND GRAVITY WITCH, TO CARRY THE BATTLE TO SOLARIS IN HIS DISTANT REFUGE.
IN A DESPERATE ACTION THAT WILL ECHO FOREVER THROUGH THE HALLS OF TIME, THE SINGULARITY AND THE WITCH COLLAPSED WHOLE SPATIAL DIMENSIONS TO CREATE COUNTLESS HORDES OF DUPLICATE SUPERMEN...
...AND WHILE THE DUPLICATES WASTED THEMSELVES LIKE WATER IN A MASSIVE ASSAULT MEANT TO DO NO MORE THAN DISTRACT THE KILLER SUN...

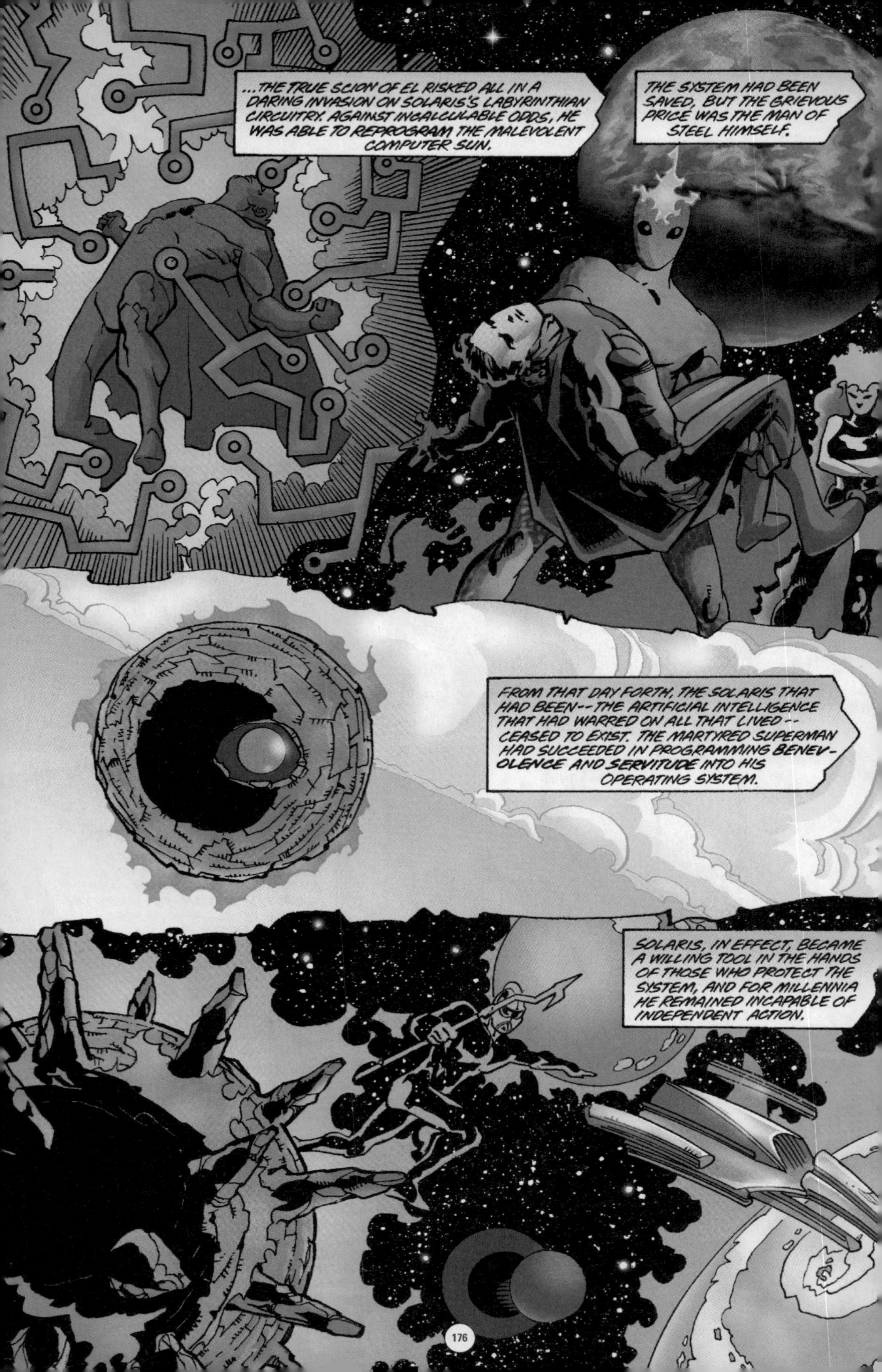
...THE TRUE SCION OF EL RISKED ALL IN A DARING INVASION ON SOLARIS'S LABYRINTHIAN CIRCUITRY. AGAINST INCALCULABLE ODDS, HE WAS ABLE TO REPROGRAM THE MALEVOLENT COMPUTER SUN.
THE SYSTEM HAD BEEN SAVED, BUT THE GRIEVOUS PRICE WAS THE MAN OF STEEL HIMSELF.
FROM THAT DAY FORTH, THE SOLARIS THAT HAD BEEN--THE ARTIFICIAL INTELLIGENCE THAT HAD WARRED ON ALL THAT LIVED--CEASED TO EXIST. THE MARTYRED SUPERMAN HAD SUCCEEDED IN PROGRAMMING BENEVOLENCE AND SERVITUDE INTO HIS OPERATING SYSTEM.
SOLARIS, IN EFFECT, BECAME A WILLING TOOL IN THE HANDS OF THOSE WHO PROTECT THE SYSTEM, AND FOR MILLENNIA HE REMAINED INCAPABLE OF INDEPENDENT ACTION.

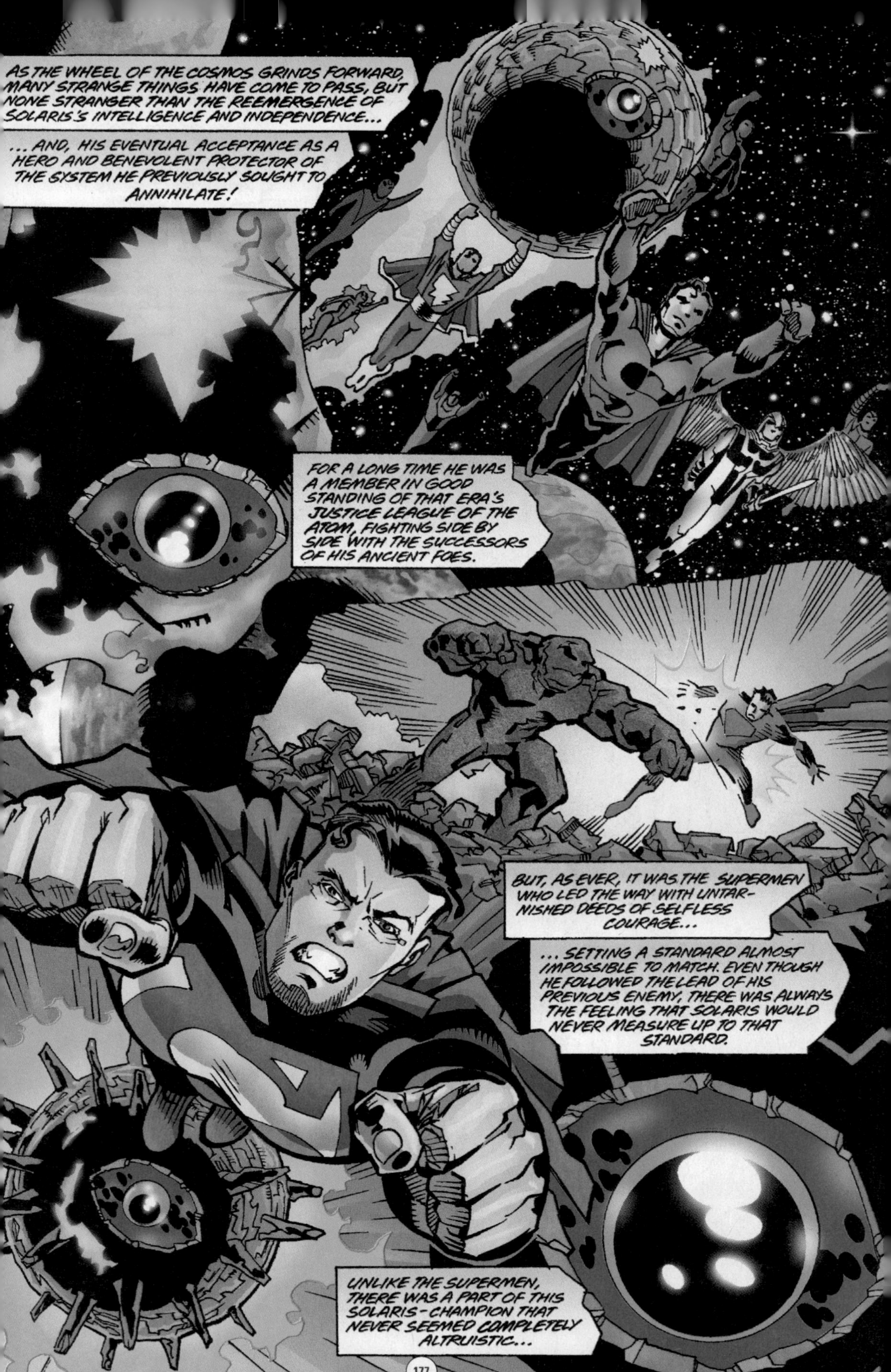
AS THE WHEEL OF THE COSMOS GRINDS FORWARD, MANY STRANGE THINGS HAVE COME TO PASS, BUT NONE STRANGER THAN THE REEMERGENCE OF SOLARIS'S INTELLIGENCE AND INDEPENDENCE...
...AND, HIS EVENTUAL ACCEPTANCE AS A HERO AND BENEVOLENT PROTECTOR OF THE SYSTEM HE PREVIOUSLY SOUGHT TO ANNIHILATE!
FOR A LONG TIME HE WAS A MEMBER IN GOOD STANDING OF THAT ERA'S JUSTICE LEAGUE OF THE ATOM, FIGHTING SIDE BY SIDE WITH THE SUCCESSORS OF HIS ANCIENT FOES.
BUT, AS EVER, IT WAS THE SUPERMEN WHO LED THE WAY WITH UNTAR-NISHED DEEDS OF SELFLESS COURAGE...
...SETTING A STANDARD ALMOST IMPOSSIBLE TO MATCH. EVEN THOUGH HE FOLLOWED THE LEAD OF HIS PREVIOUS ENEMY, THERE WAS ALWAYS THE FEELING THAT SOLARIS WOULD NEVER MEASURE UP TO THAT STANDARD.
UNLIKE THE SUPERMEN, THERE WAS A PART OF THIS SOLARIS-CHAMPION THAT NEVER SEEMED COMPLETELY ALTRUISTIC...

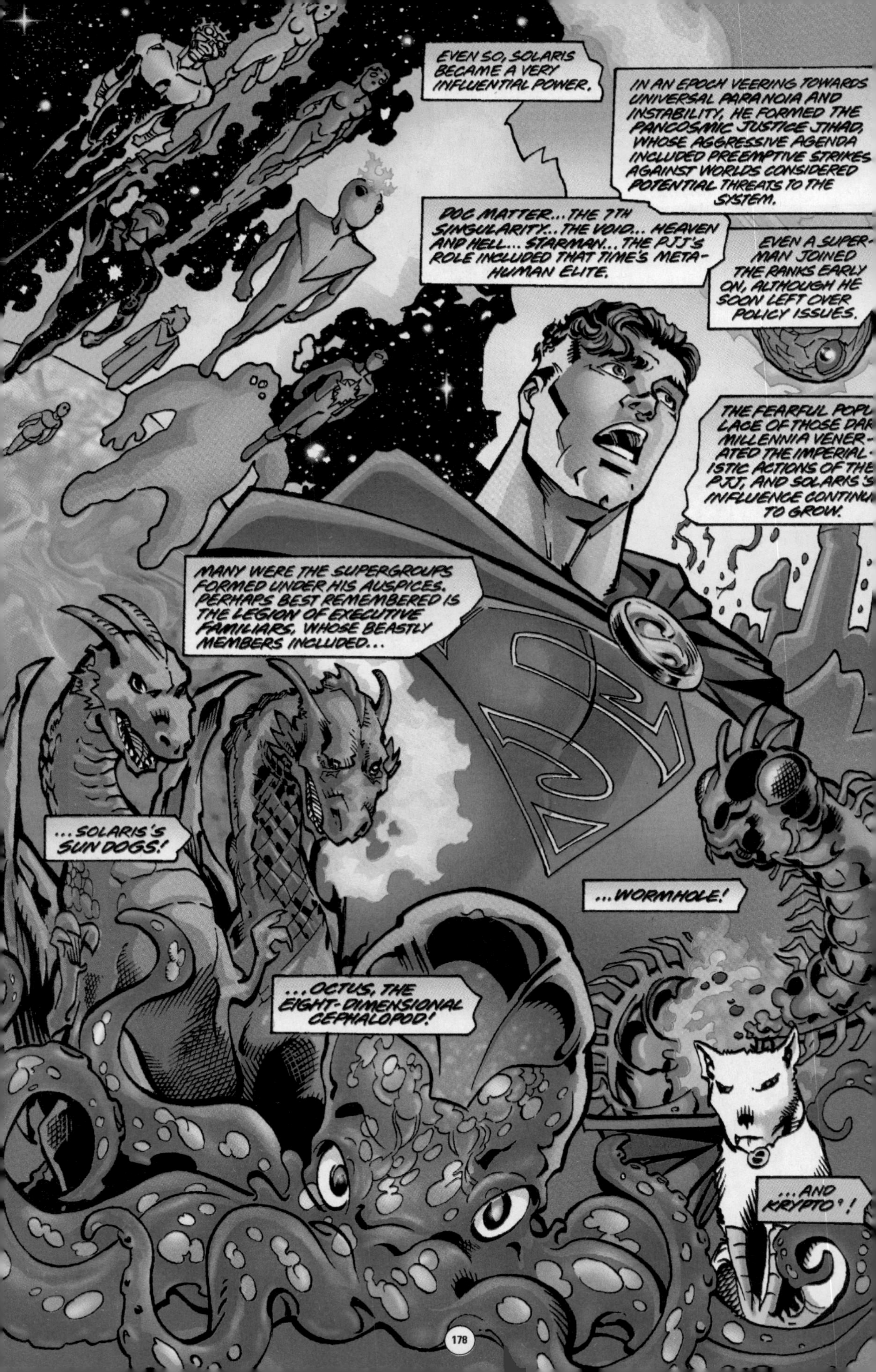

EVEN SO, SOLARIS BECAME A VERY INFLUENTIAL POWER.
IN AN EPOCH VEERING TOWARDS UNIVERSAL PARANOIA AND INSTABILITY, HE FORMED THE PANCOSMIC JUSTICE JIHAD, WHOSE AGGRESSIVE AGENDA INCLUDED PREEMPTIVE STRIKES AGAINST WORLDS CONSIDERED POTENTIAL THREATS TO THE SYSTEM.
DOC MATTER... THE 7TH SINGULARITY... THE VOID... HEAVEN AND HELL... STARMAN... THE PJJ'S ROLE INCLUDED THAT TIME'S META-HUMAN ELITE.
EVEN A SUPER-MAN JOINED THE RANKS EARLY ON, ALTHOUGH HE SOON LEFT OVER POLICY ISSUES.
THE FEARFUL POPU LACE OF THOSE DAR MILLENNIA VENER-ATED THE IMPERIAL-ISTIC ACTIONS OF THE PJJ, AND SOLARIS'S INFLUENCE CONTINU TO GROW.
MANY WERE THE SUPERGROUPS FORMED UNDER HIS AUSPICES. PERHAPS BEST REMEMBERED IS THE LEGION OF EXECUTIVE FAMILIARS, WHOSE BEASTLY MEMBERS INCLUDED...
...SOLARIS'S SUN DOGS!
...WORMHOLE!
...OCTUS, THE EIGHT-DIMENSIONAL CEPHALOPOD!
...AND KRYPTO⁹!

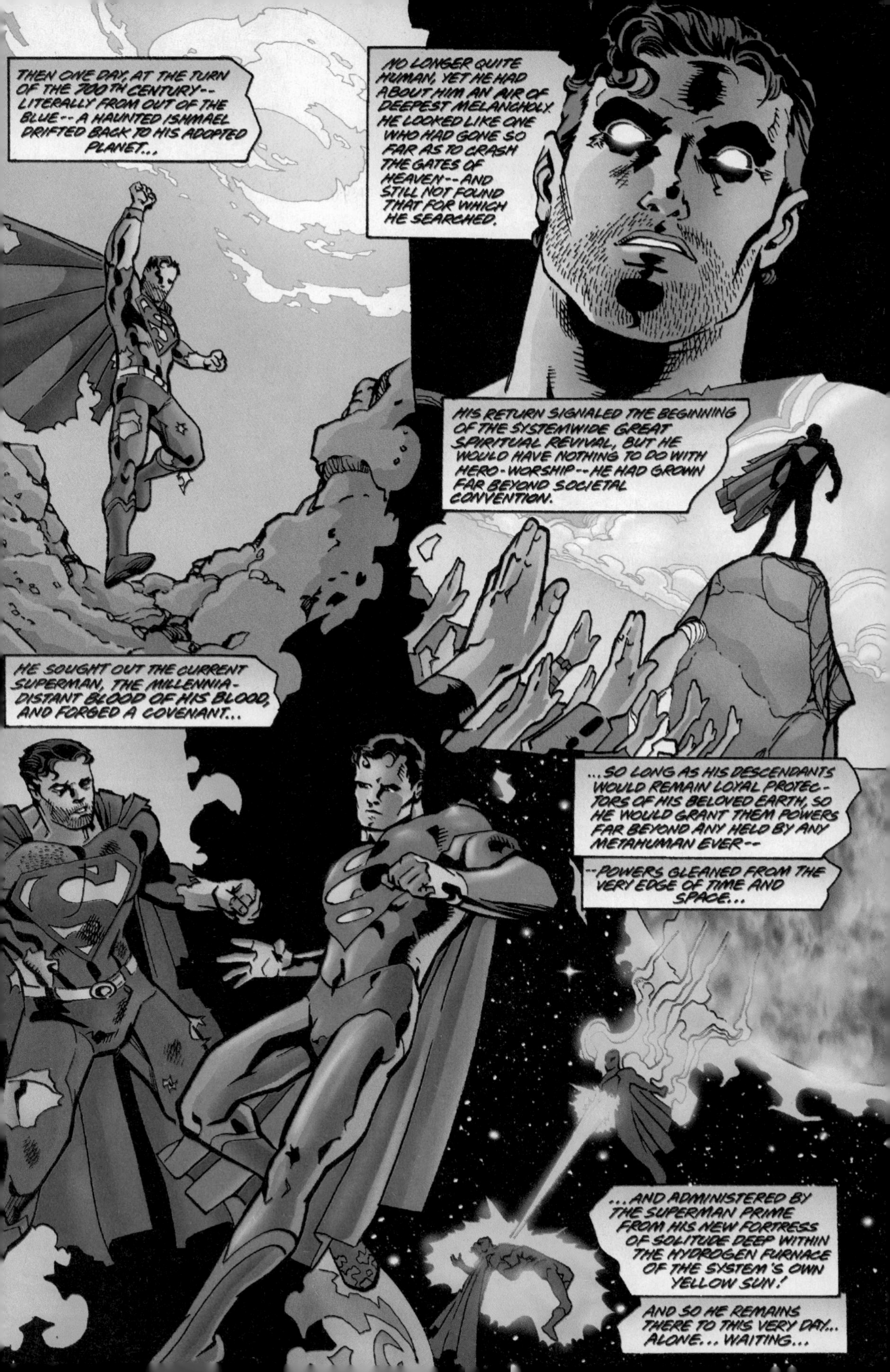
THEN ONE DAY, AT THE TURN OF THE 700TH CENTURY-- LITERALLY FROM OUT OF THE BLUE-- A HAUNTED ISHMAEL DRIFTED BACK TO HIS ADOPTED PLANET...
NO LONGER QUITE HUMAN, YET HE HAD ABOUT HIM AN AIR OF DEEPEST MELANCHOLY. HE LOOKED LIKE ONE WHO HAD GONE SO FAR AS TO CRASH THE GATES OF HEAVEN--AND STILL NOT FOUND THAT FOR WHICH HE SEARCHED.
HIS RETURN SIGNALED THE BEGINNING OF THE SYSTEMWIDE GREAT SPIRITUAL REVIVAL, BUT HE WOULD HAVE NOTHING TO DO WITH HERO-WORSHIP--HE HAD GROWN FAR BEYOND SOCIETAL CONVENTION.
HE SOUGHT OUT THE CURRENT SUPERMAN, THE MILLENNIA-DISTANT BLOOD OF HIS BLOOD, AND FORGED A COVENANT...
...SO LONG AS HIS DESCENDANTS WOULD REMAIN LOYAL PROTECTORS OF HIS BELOVED EARTH, SO HE WOULD GRANT THEM POWERS FAR BEYOND ANY HELD BY ANY METAHUMAN EVER--
--POWERS GLEANED FROM THE VERY EDGE OF TIME AND SPACE...
...AND ADMINISTERED BY THE SUPERMAN PRIME FROM HIS NEW FORTRESS OF SOLITUDE DEEP WITHIN THE HYDROGEN FURNACE OF THE SYSTEM'S OWN YELLOW SUN!
AND SO HE REMAINS THERE TO THIS VERY DAY... ALONE... WAITING...

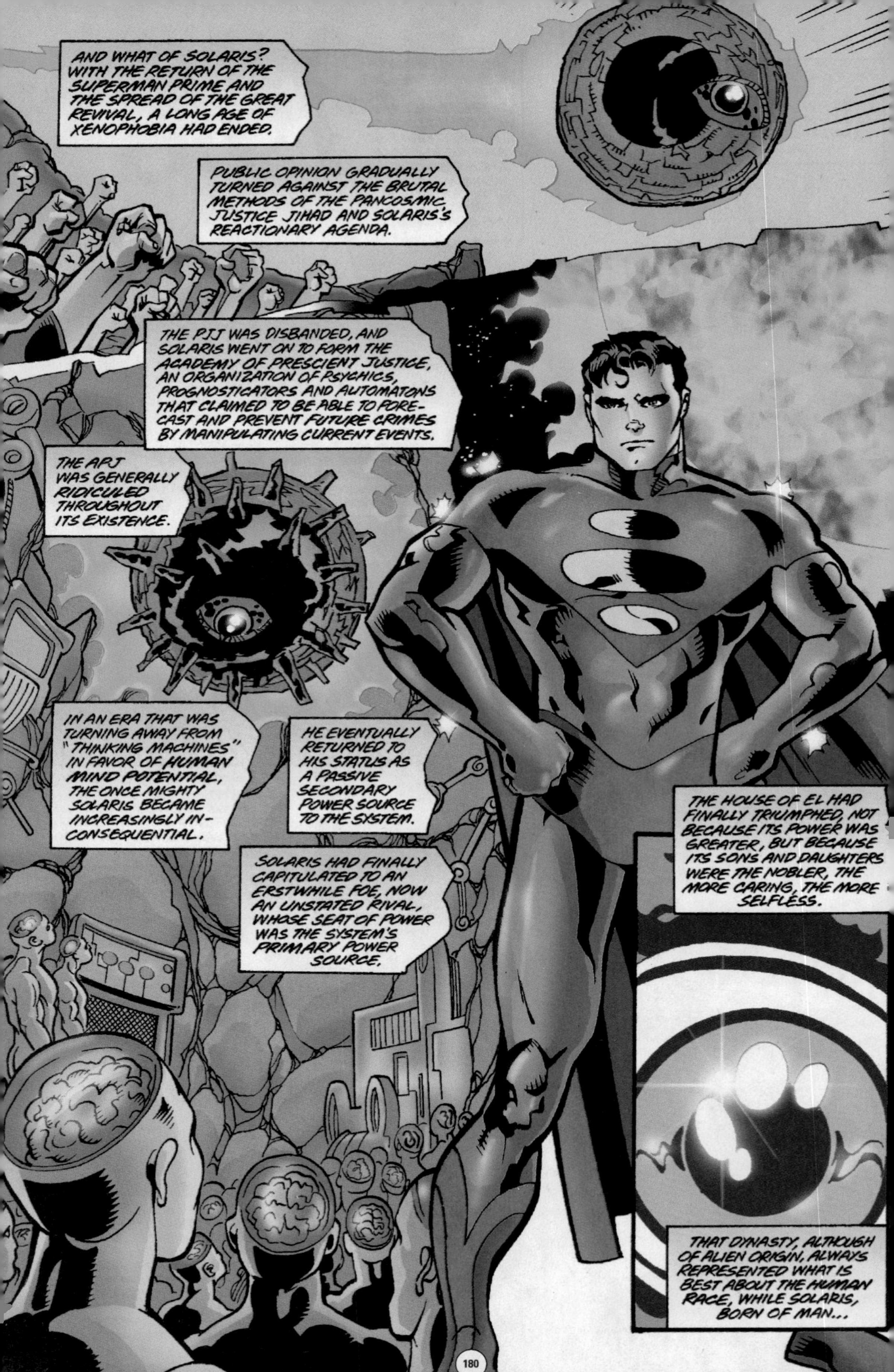
AND WHAT OF SOLARIS? WITH THE RETURN OF THE SUPERMAN PRIME AND THE SPREAD OF THE GREAT REVIVAL, A LONG AGE OF XENOPHOBIA HAD ENDED.
PUBLIC OPINION GRADUALLY TURNED AGAINST THE BRUTAL METHODS OF THE PANCOSMIC JUSTICE JIHAD AND SOLARIS'S REACTIONARY AGENDA.
THE PJJ WAS DISBANDED, AND SOLARIS WENT ON TO FORM THE ACADEMY OF PRESCIENT JUSTICE, AN ORGANIZATION OF PSYCHICS, PROGNOSTICATORS AND AUTOMATONS THAT CLAIMED TO BE ABLE TO FORECAST AND PREVENT FUTURE CRIMES BY MANIPULATING CURRENT EVENTS.
THE APJ WAS GENERALLY RIDICULED THROUGHOUT ITS EXISTENCE.
IN AN ERA THAT WAS TURNING AWAY FROM "THINKING MACHINES" IN FAVOR OF HUMAN MIND POTENTIAL, THE ONCE MIGHTY SOLARIS BECAME INCREASINGLY INCONSEQUENTIAL.
HE EVENTUALLY RETURNED TO HIS STATUS AS A PASSIVE SECONDARY POWER SOURCE TO THE SYSTEM.
SOLARIS HAD FINALLY CAPITULATED TO AN ERSTWHILE FOE, NOW AN UNSTATED RIVAL, WHOSE SEAT OF POWER WAS THE SYSTEM'S PRIMARY POWER SOURCE.
THE HOUSE OF EL HAD FINALLY TRIUMPHED, NOT BECAUSE ITS POWER WAS GREATER, BUT BECAUSE ITS SONS AND DAUGHTERS WERE THE NOBLER, THE MORE CARING, THE MORE SELFLESS.
THAT DYNASTY, ALTHOUGH OF ALIEN ORIGIN, ALWAYS REPRESENTED WHAT IS BEST ABOUT THE HUMAN RACE, WHILE SOLARIS, BORN OF MAN...

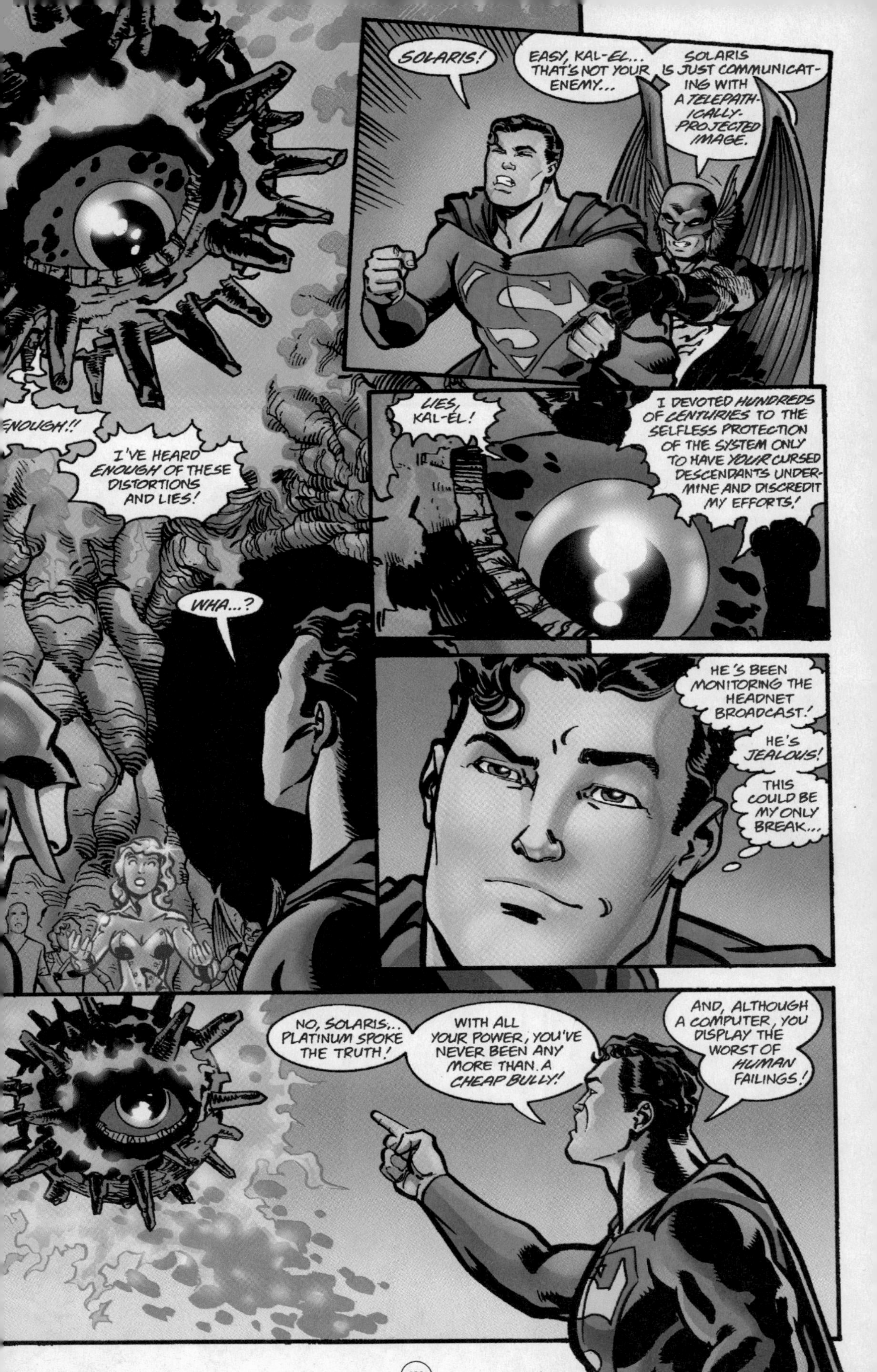
SOLARIS!
EASY, KAL-EL... THAT'S NOT YOUR ENEMY...
SOLARIS IS JUST COMMUNICATING WITH A TELEPATHICALLY-PROJECTED IMAGE.
LIES, KAL-EL!
I DEVOTED HUNDREDS OF CENTURIES TO THE SELFLESS PROTECTION OF THE SYSTEM ONLY TO HAVE YOUR CURSED DESCENDANTS UNDERMINE AND DISCREDIT MY EFFORTS!
ENOUGH!!
I'VE HEARD ENOUGH OF THESE DISTORTIONS AND LIES!
WHA...?
HE'S BEEN MONITORING THE HEADNET BROADCAST!
HE'S JEALOUS!
THIS COULD BE MY ONLY BREAK...
NO, SOLARIS... PLATINUM SPOKE THE TRUTH!
WITH ALL YOUR POWER, YOU'VE NEVER BEEN ANY MORE THAN A CHEAP BULLY!
AND, ALTHOUGH A COMPUTER, YOU DISPLAY THE WORST OF HUMAN FAILINGS!

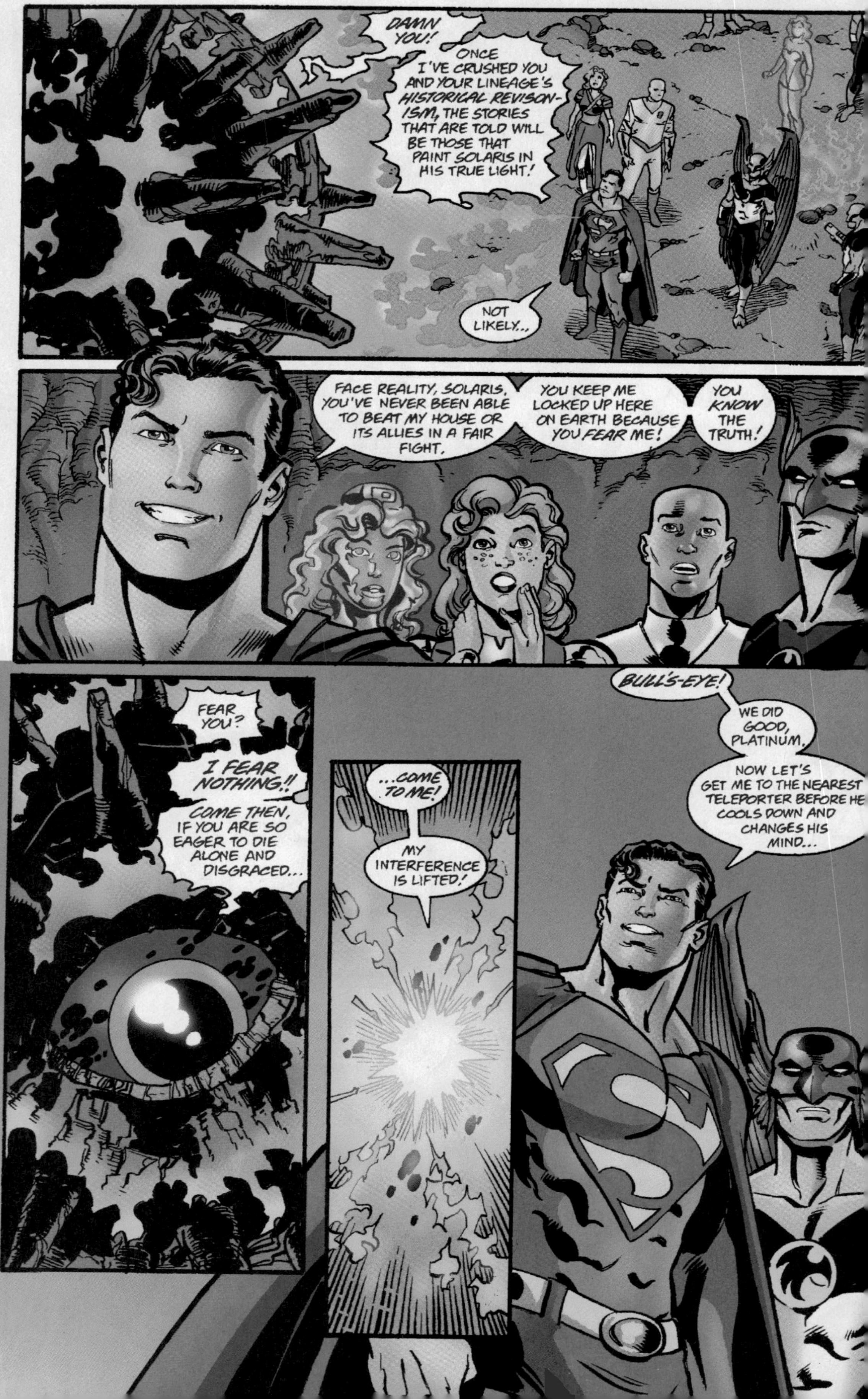
DAMN YOU!
ONCE I'VE CRUSHED YOU AND YOUR LINEAGE'S HISTORICAL REVISON-ISM, THE STORIES THAT ARE TOLD WILL BE THOSE THAT PAINT SOLARIS IN HIS TRUE LIGHT!
NOT LIKELY...
FACE REALITY, SOLARIS, YOU'VE NEVER BEEN ABLE TO BEAT MY HOUSE OR ITS ALLIES IN A FAIR FIGHT.
YOU KEEP ME LOCKED UP HERE ON EARTH BECAUSE YOU FEAR ME!
YOU KNOW THE TRUTH!
FEAR YOU?
I FEAR NOTHING!!
COME THEN, IF YOU ARE SO EAGER TO DIE ALONE AND DISGRACED...
...COME TO ME!
MY INTERFERENCE IS LIFTED!
BULL'S-EYE!
WE DID GOOD, PLATINUM.
NOW LET'S GET ME TO THE NEAREST TELEPORTER BEFORE HE COOLS DOWN AND CHANGES HIS MIND...

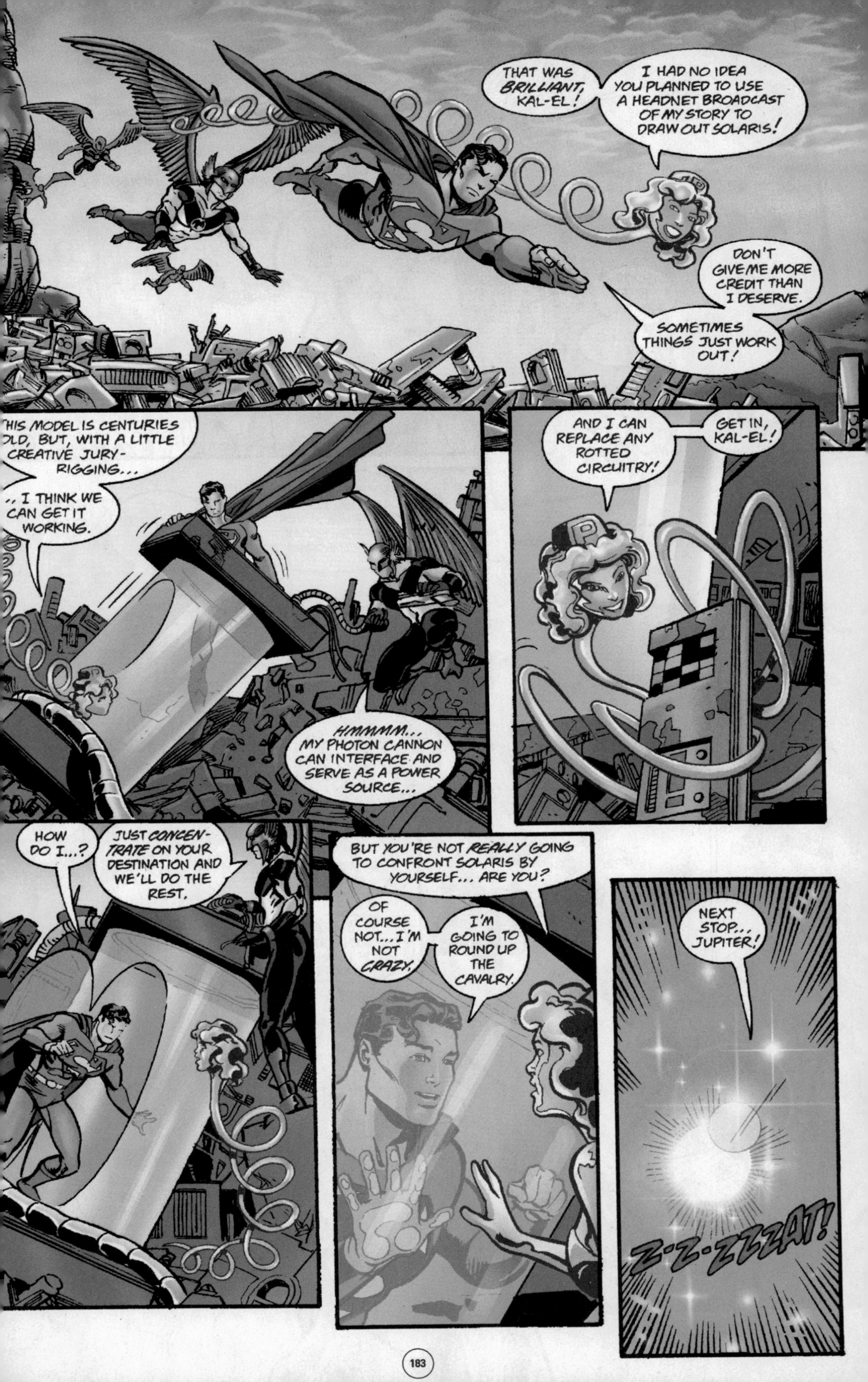
THAT WAS BRILLIANT, KAL-EL!
I HAD NO IDEA YOU PLANNED TO USE A HEADNET BROADCAST OF MY STORY TO DRAW OUT SOLARIS!
DON'T GIVE ME MORE CREDIT THAN I DESERVE.
SOMETIMES THINGS JUST WORK OUT!
THIS MODEL IS CENTURIES OLD, BUT, WITH A LITTLE CREATIVE JURY-RIGGING...
.., I THINK WE CAN GET IT WORKING.
HMMMM... MY PHOTON CANNON CAN INTERFACE AND SERVE AS A POWER SOURCE...
AND I CAN REPLACE ANY ROTTED CIRCUITRY!
GET IN, KAL-EL!
HOW DO I...?
JUST CONCENTRATE ON YOUR DESTINATION AND WE'LL DO THE REST.
BUT YOU'RE NOT REALLY GOING TO CONFRONT SOLARIS BY YOURSELF... ARE YOU?
OF COURSE NOT... I'M NOT CRAZY.
I'M GOING TO ROUND UP THE CAVALRY.
NEXT STOP... JUPITER!
Z-Z-ZZZAT!

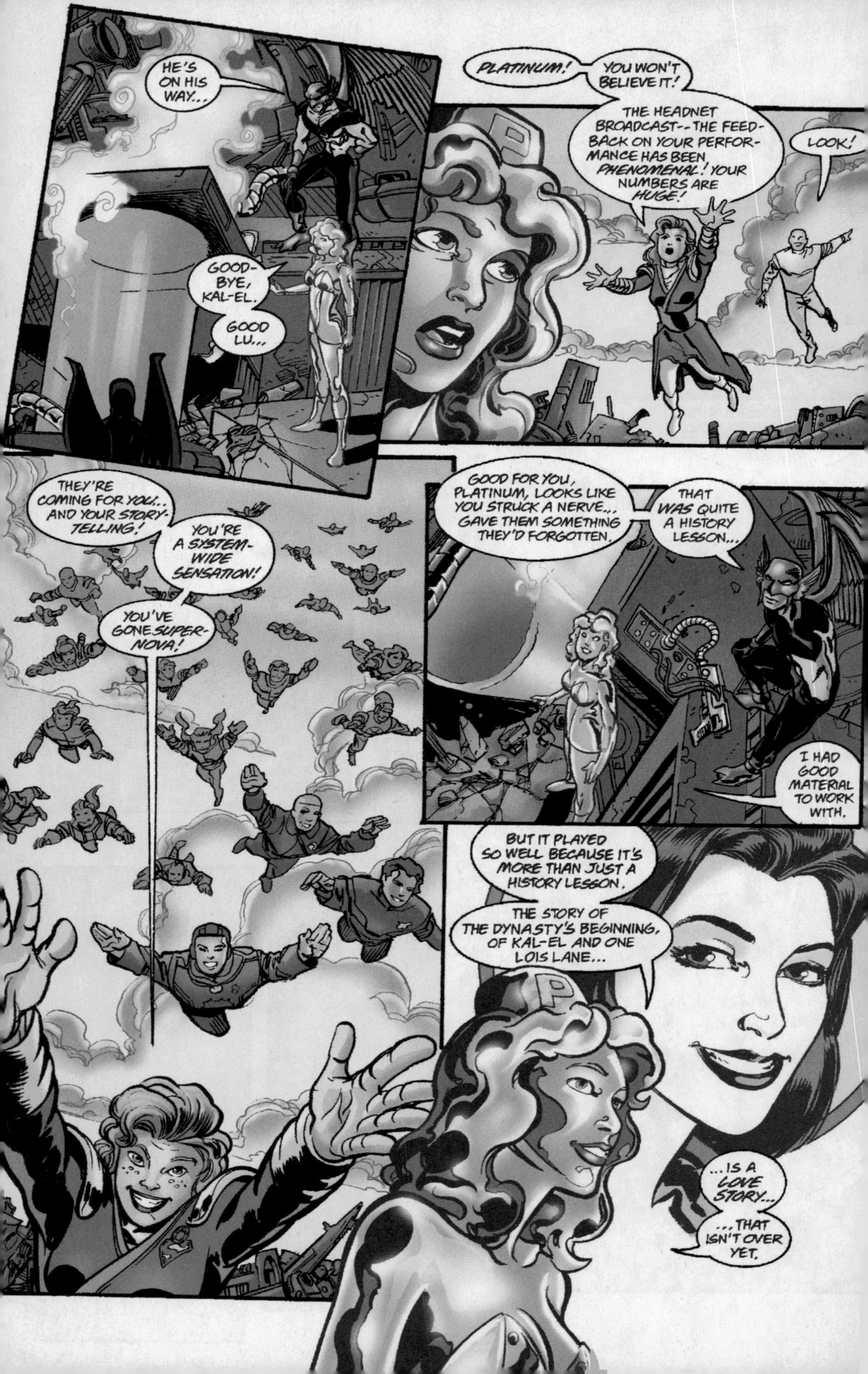
HE'S ON HIS WAY...
GOOD-BYE, KAL-EL.
GOOD LU...
PLATINUM!
YOU WON'T BELIEVE IT!
THE HEADNET BROADCAST--THE FEED-BACK ON YOUR PERFORMANCE HAS BEEN PHENOMENAL! YOUR NUMBERS ARE HUGE!
LOOK!
THEY'RE COMING FOR YOU... AND YOUR STORY-TELLING!
YOU'RE A SYSTEM-WIDE SENSATION!
YOU'VE GONE SUPER-NOVA!
GOOD FOR YOU, PLATINUM, LOOKS LIKE YOU STRUCK A NERVE... GAVE THEM SOMETHING THEY'D FORGOTTEN.
THAT WAS QUITE A HISTORY LESSON...
I HAD GOOD MATERIAL TO WORK WITH.
BUT IT PLAYED SO WELL BECAUSE IT'S MORE THAN JUST A HISTORY LESSON.
THE STORY OF THE DYNASTY'S BEGINNING, OF KAL-EL AND ONE LOIS LANE...
...IS A LOVE STORY...
...THAT ISN'T OVER YET.

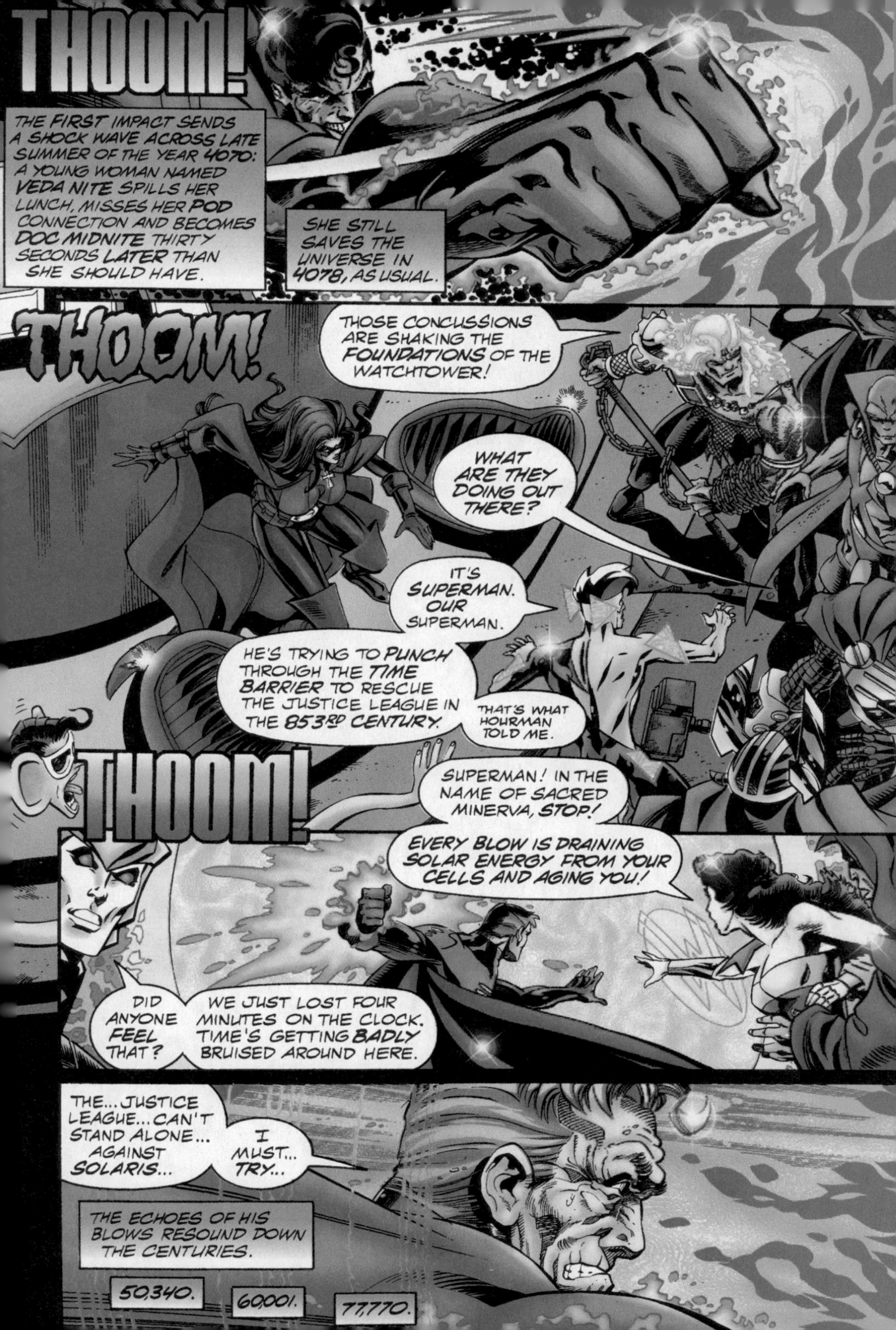
THOOM!
THE FIRST IMPACT SENDS A SHOCK WAVE ACROSS LATE SUMMER OF THE YEAR 4070: A YOUNG WOMAN NAMED VEDA NITE SPILLS HER LUNCH, MISSES HER POD CONNECTION AND BECOMES DOC MIDNITE THIRTY SECONDS LATER THAN SHE SHOULD HAVE.
SHE STILL SAVES THE UNIVERSE IN 4078, AS USUAL.
THOOM!
THOSE CONCUSSIONS ARE SHAKING THE FOUNDATIONS OF THE WATCHTOWER!
WHAT ARE THEY DOING OUT THERE?
IT'S SUPERMAN. OUR SUPERMAN.
HE'S TRYING TO PUNCH THROUGH THE TIME BARRIER TO RESCUE THE JUSTICE LEAGUE IN THE 853RD CENTURY.
THAT'S WHAT HOURMAN TOLD ME.
THOOM!
SUPERMAN! IN THE NAME OF SACRED MINERVA, STOP!
EVERY BLOW IS DRAINING SOLAR ENERGY FROM YOUR CELLS AND AGING YOU!
DID ANYONE FEEL THAT?
WE JUST LOST FOUR MINUTES ON THE CLOCK. TIME'S GETTING BADLY BRUISED AROUND HERE.
THE... JUSTICE LEAGUE... CAN'T STAND ALONE... AGAINST SOLARIS...
I MUST... TRY...
THE ECHOES OF HIS BLOWS RESOUND DOWN THE CENTURIES.
50,340.
60,001.
77,770.

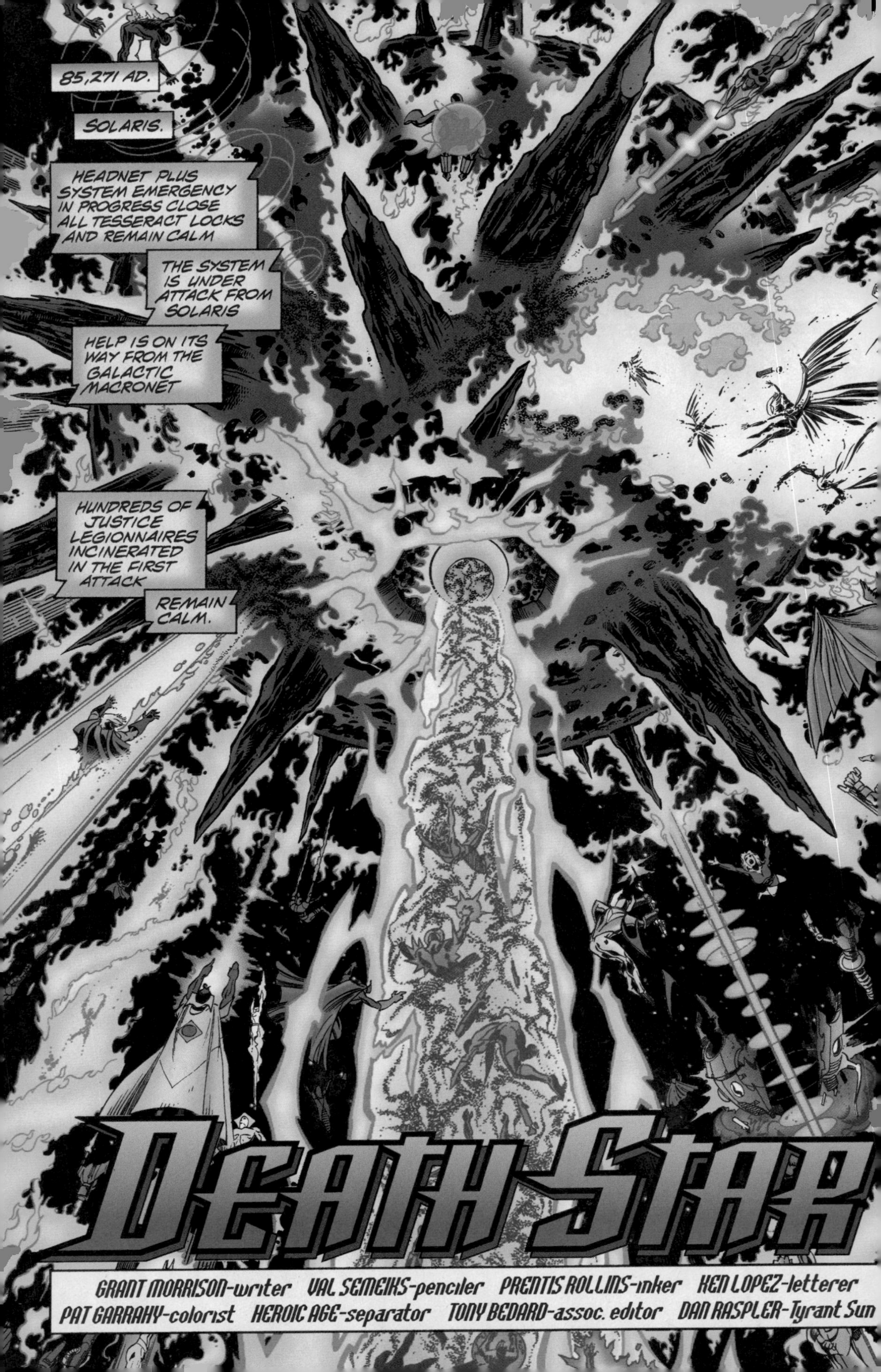
85,271 AD.
SOLARIS.
HEADNET PLUS SYSTEM EMERGENCY IN PROGRESS CLOSE ALL TESSERACT LOCKS AND REMAIN CALM
THE SYSTEM IS UNDER ATTACK FROM SOLARIS
HELP IS ON ITS WAY FROM THE GALACTIC MACRONET
HUNDREDS OF JUSTICE LEGIONNAIRES INCINERATED IN THE FIRST ATTACK
REMAIN CALM.
DEATH STAR
GRANT MORRISON-writer VAL SEMEIKS-penciler PRENTIS ROLLINS-inker KEN LOPEZ-letterer
PAT GARRAHY-colorist HEROIC AGE-separator TONY BEDARD-assoc. editor DAN RASPLER-Tyrant Sun

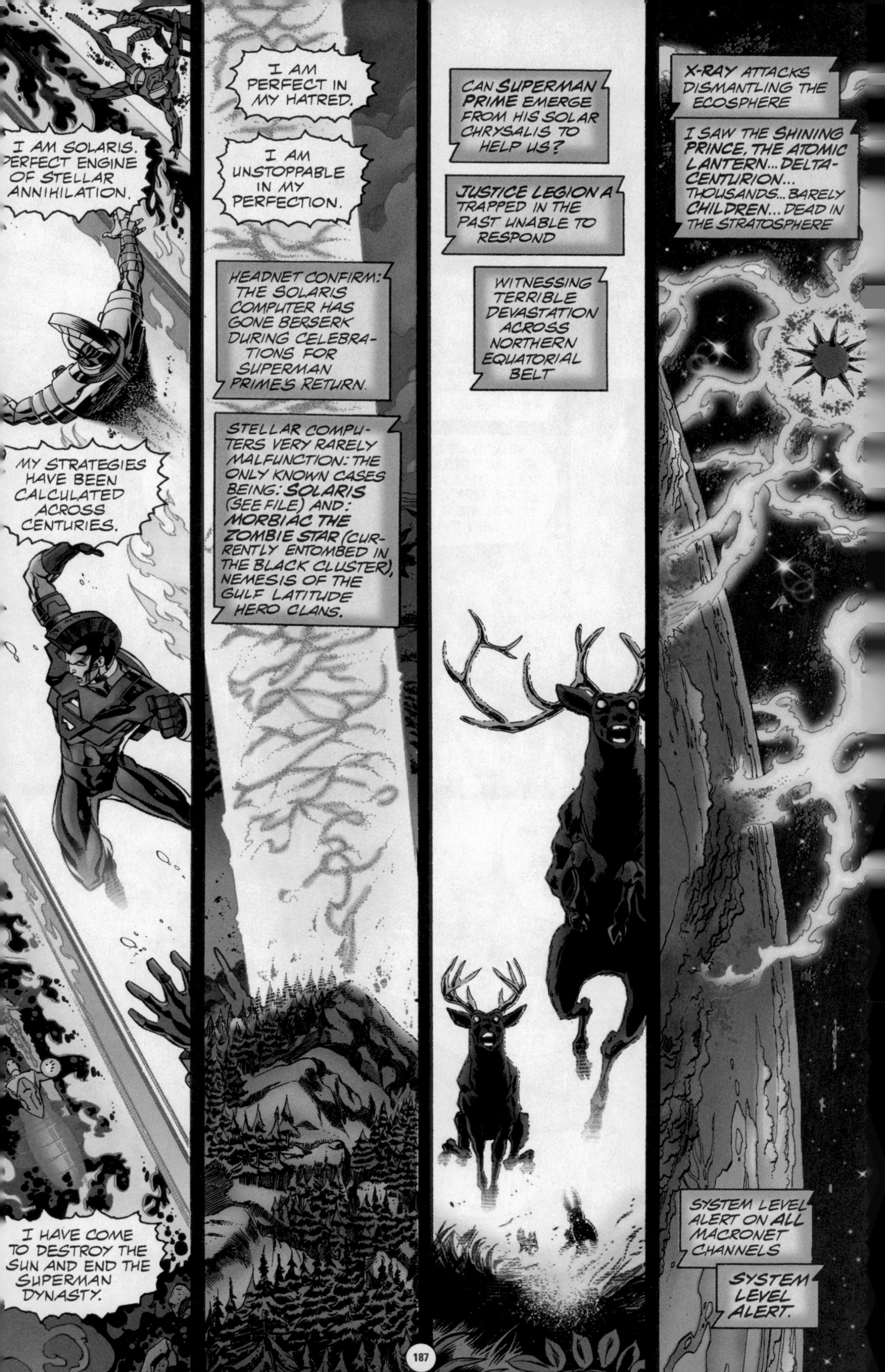
I AM SOLARIS. PERFECT ENGINE OF STELLAR ANNIHILATION.
MY STRATEGIES HAVE BEEN CALCULATED ACROSS CENTURIES.
I HAVE COME TO DESTROY THE SUN AND END THE SUPERMAN DYNASTY.
I AM PERFECT IN MY HATRED.
I AM UNSTOPPABLE IN MY PERFECTION.
HEADNET CONFIRM: THE SOLARIS COMPUTER HAS GONE BERSERK DURING CELEBRATIONS FOR SUPERMAN PRIME'S RETURN.
STELLAR COMPUTERS VERY RARELY MALFUNCTION: THE ONLY KNOWN CASES BEING: SOLARIS (SEE FILE) AND: MORBIAC THE ZOMBIE STAR (CURRENTLY ENTOMBED IN THE BLACK CLUSTER), NEMESIS OF THE GULF LATITUDE HERO CLANS.
CAN SUPERMAN PRIME EMERGE FROM HIS SOLAR CHRYSALIS TO HELP US?
JUSTICE LEGION A TRAPPED IN THE PAST UNABLE TO RESPOND
WITNESSING TERRIBLE DEVASTATION ACROSS NORTHERN EQUATORIAL BELT
X-RAY ATTACKS DISMANTLING THE ECOSPHERE
I SAW THE SHINING PRINCE, THE ATOMIC LANTERN... DELTA-CENTURION... THOUSANDS... BARELY CHILDREN... DEAD IN THE STRATOSPHERE
SYSTEM LEVEL ALERT ON ALL MACRONET CHANNELS
SYSTEM LEVEL ALERT.

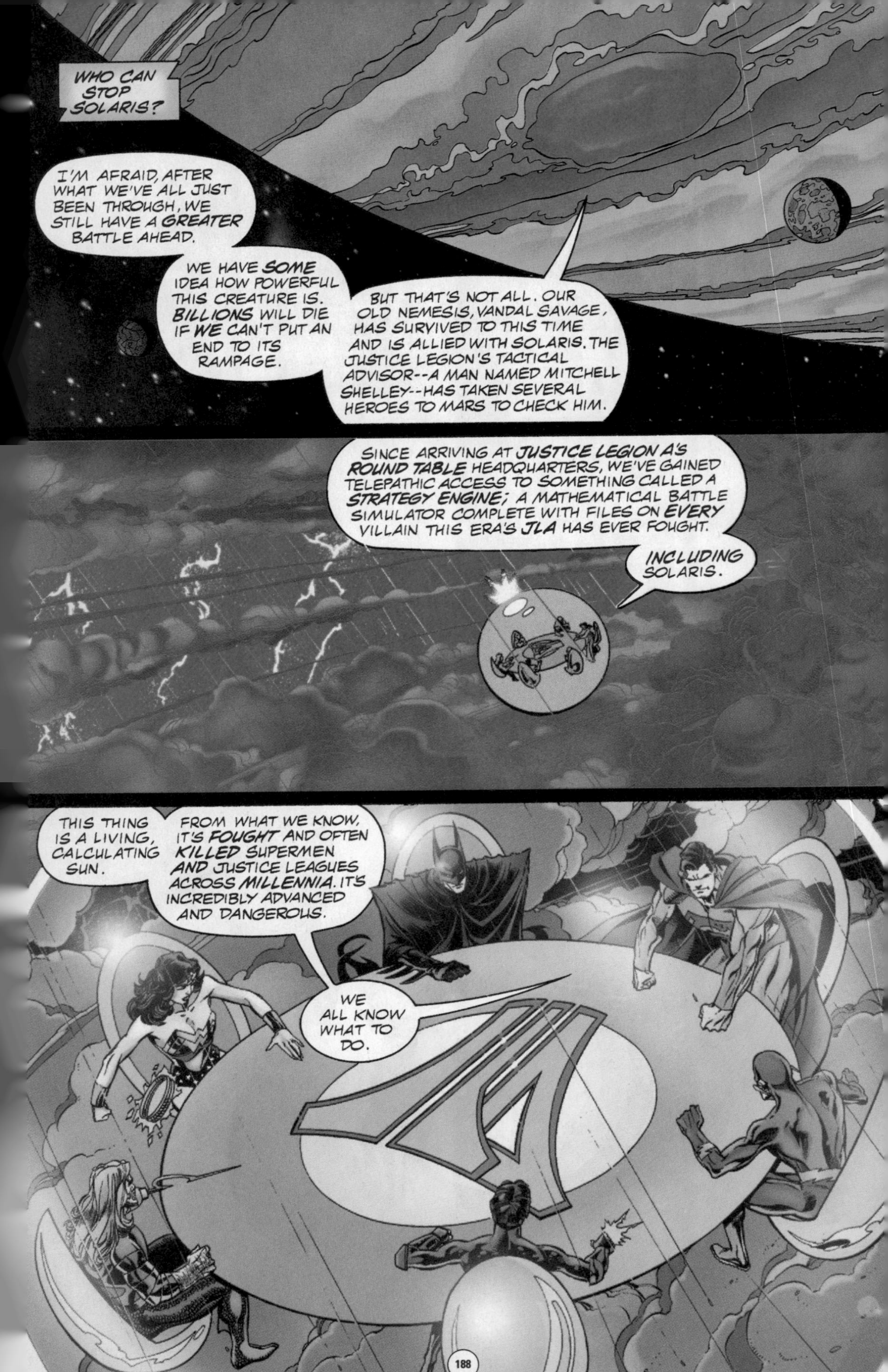
WHO CAN STOP SOLARIS?
I'M AFRAID, AFTER WHAT WE'VE ALL JUST BEEN THROUGH, WE STILL HAVE A GREATER BATTLE AHEAD.
WE HAVE SOME IDEA HOW POWERFUL THIS CREATURE IS. BILLIONS WILL DIE IF WE CAN'T PUT AN END TO ITS RAMPAGE.
BUT THAT'S NOT ALL. OUR OLD NEMESIS, VANDAL SAVAGE, HAS SURVIVED TO THIS TIME AND IS ALLIED WITH SOLARIS. THE JUSTICE LEGION'S TACTICAL ADVISOR--A MAN NAMED MITCHELL SHELLEY--HAS TAKEN SEVERAL HEROES TO MARS TO CHECK HIM.
SINCE ARRIVING AT JUSTICE LEGION A'S ROUND TABLE HEADQUARTERS, WE'VE GAINED TELEPATHIC ACCESS TO SOMETHING CALLED A STRATEGY ENGINE; A MATHEMATICAL BATTLE SIMULATOR COMPLETE WITH FILES ON EVERY VILLAIN THIS ERA'S JLA HAS EVER FOUGHT.
INCLUDING SOLARIS.
THIS THING IS A LIVING, CALCULATING SUN.
FROM WHAT WE KNOW, IT'S FOUGHT AND OFTEN KILLED SUPERMEN AND JUSTICE LEAGUES ACROSS MILLENNIA. IT'S INCREDIBLY ADVANCED AND DANGEROUS.
WE ALL KNOW WHAT TO DO.

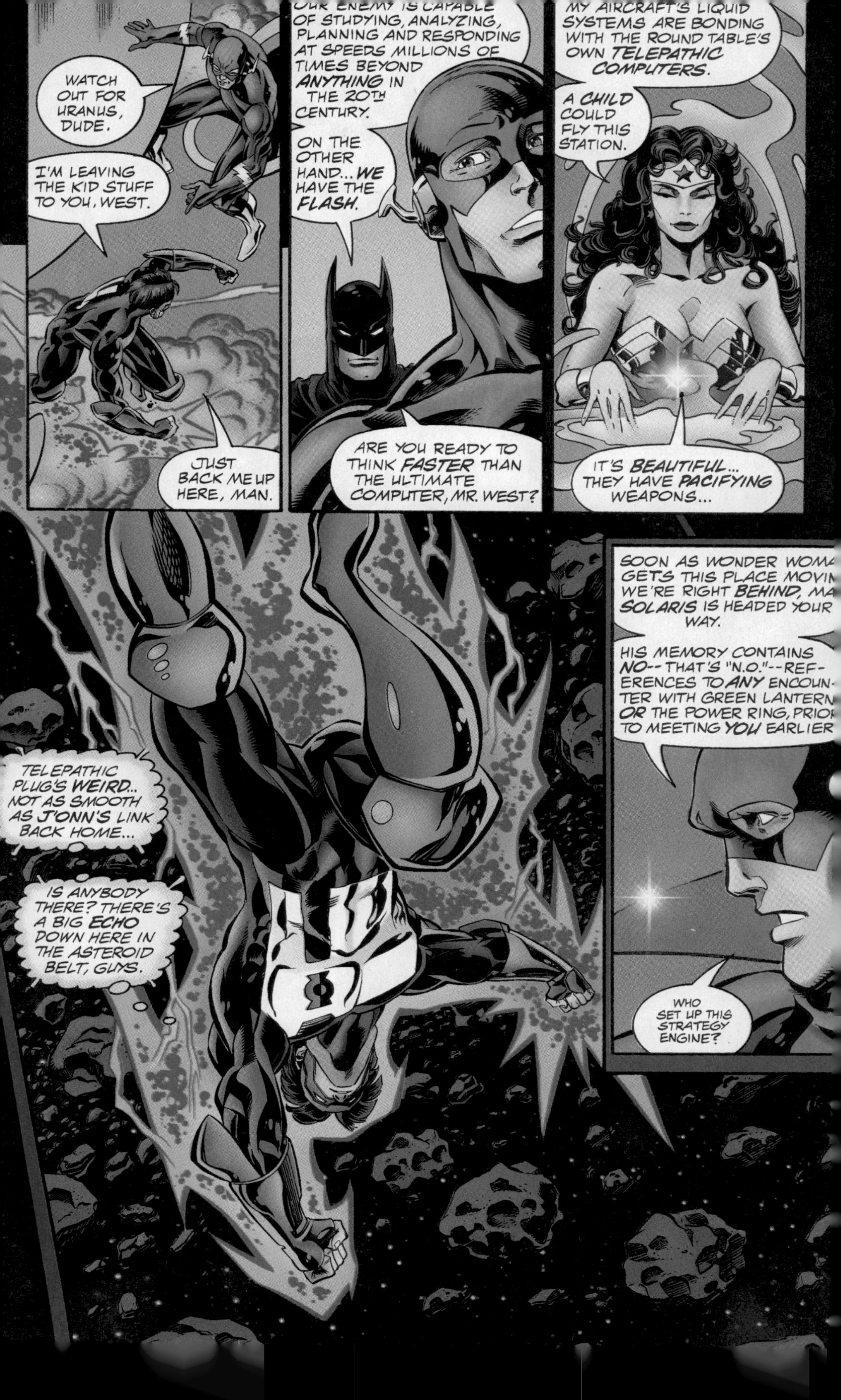

WATCH OUT FOR URANUS, DUDE.
I'M LEAVING THE KID STUFF TO YOU, WEST.
JUST BACK ME UP HERE, MAN.
OF STUDYING, ANALYZING, PLANNING AND RESPONDING AT SPEEDS MILLIONS OF TIMES BEYOND ANYTHING IN THE 20TH CENTURY.
ON THE OTHER HAND... WE HAVE THE FLASH.
ARE YOU READY TO THINK FASTER THAN THE ULTIMATE COMPUTER, MR. WEST?
SYSTEMS ARE BONDING WITH THE ROUND TABLE'S OWN TELEPATHIC COMPUTERS.
A CHILD COULD FLY THIS STATION.
IT'S BEAUTIFUL... THEY HAVE PACIFYING WEAPONS...
TELEPATHIC PLUG'S WEIRD... NOT AS SMOOTH AS J'ONN'S LINK BACK HOME...
IS ANYBODY THERE? THERE'S A BIG ECHO DOWN HERE IN THE ASTEROID BELT, GUYS.
SOON AS WONDER WOMA GETS THIS PLACE MOVIN WE'RE RIGHT BEHIND, MA SOLARIS IS HEADED YOUR WAY.
HIS MEMORY CONTAINS NO-- THAT'S "N.O."--REFERENCES TO ANY ENCOUNTER WITH GREEN LANTERN OR THE POWER RING, PRIOR TO MEETING YOU EARLIER
WHO SET UP THIS STRATEGY ENGINE?

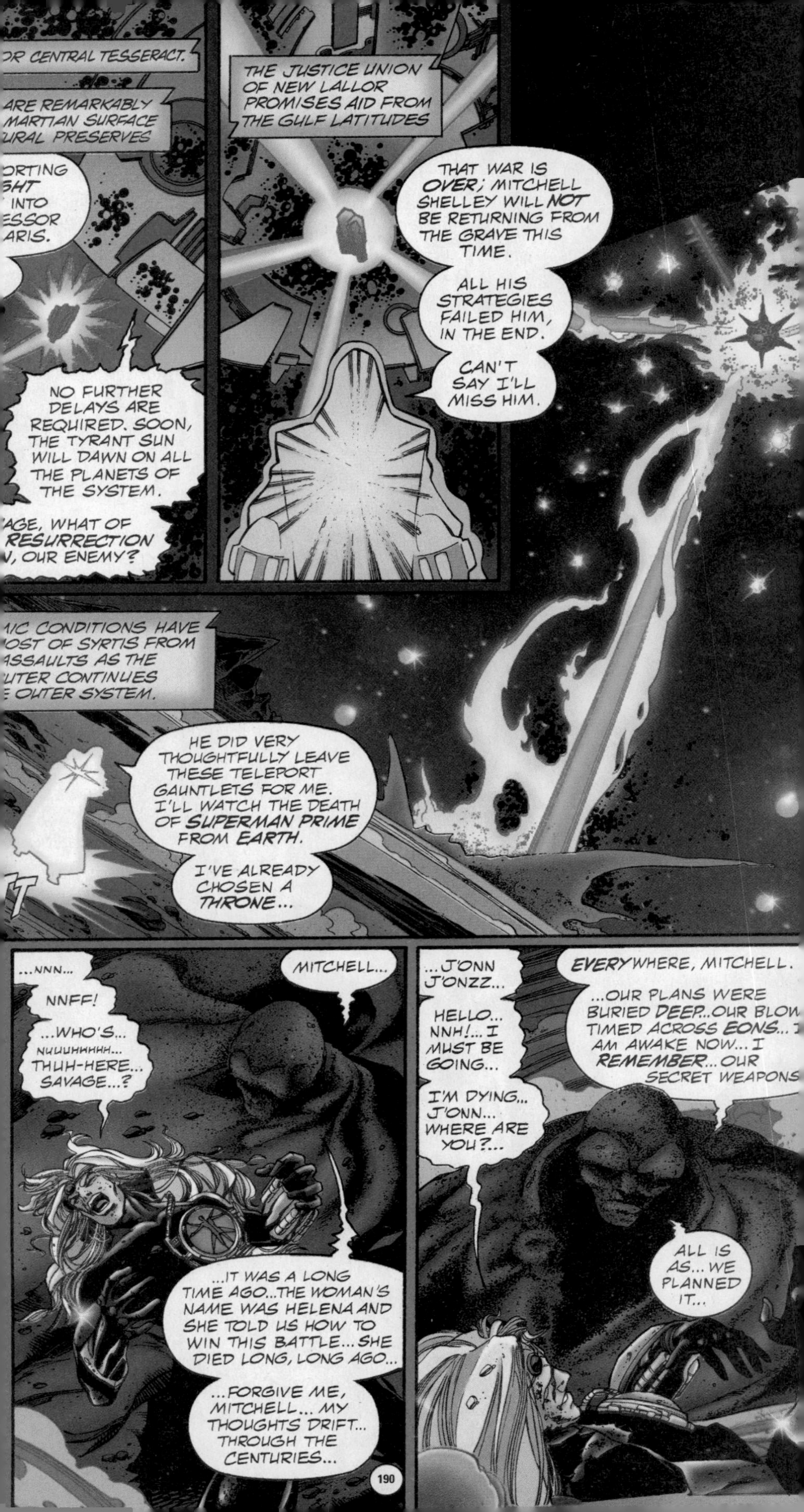

OR CENTRAL TESSERACT.
ARE REMARKABLY
MARTIAN SURFACE
URAL PRESERVES
ORTING
GHT
INTO
ESSOR
ARIS.
NO FURTHER DELAYS ARE REQUIRED. SOON, THE TYRANT SUN WILL DAWN ON ALL THE PLANETS OF THE SYSTEM.
AGE, WHAT OF
RESURRECTION
, OUR ENEMY?
THE JUSTICE UNION OF NEW LALLOR PROMISES AID FROM THE GULF LATITUDES
THAT WAR IS OVER; MITCHELL SHELLEY WILL NOT BE RETURNING FROM THE GRAVE THIS TIME.
ALL HIS STRATEGIES FAILED HIM, IN THE END.
CAN'T SAY I'LL MISS HIM.
MIC CONDITIONS HAVE
OST OF SYRTIS FROM
ASSAULTS AS THE
UTER CONTINUES
E OUTER SYSTEM.
HE DID VERY THOUGHTFULLY LEAVE THESE TELEPORT GAUNTLETS FOR ME. I'LL WATCH THE DEATH OF SUPERMAN PRIME FROM EARTH.
I'VE ALREADY CHOSEN A THRONE...
...NNN...
NNFF!
...WHO'S... NUUUHHHHH... THUH-HERE... SAVAGE...?
MITCHELL...
...IT WAS A LONG TIME AGO...THE WOMAN'S NAME WAS HELENA AND SHE TOLD US HOW TO WIN THIS BATTLE... SHE DIED LONG, LONG AGO...
...FORGIVE ME, MITCHELL... MY THOUGHTS DRIFT... THROUGH THE CENTURIES...
...J'ONN J'ONZZ...
HELLO... NNH!... I MUST BE GOING...
I'M DYING... J'ONN... WHERE ARE YOU?...
EVERYWHERE, MITCHELL.
...OUR PLANS WERE BURIED DEEP...OUR BLOW TIMED ACROSS EONS... I AM AWAKE NOW... I REMEMBER... OUR SECRET WEAPONS
ALL IS AS... WE PLANNED IT...

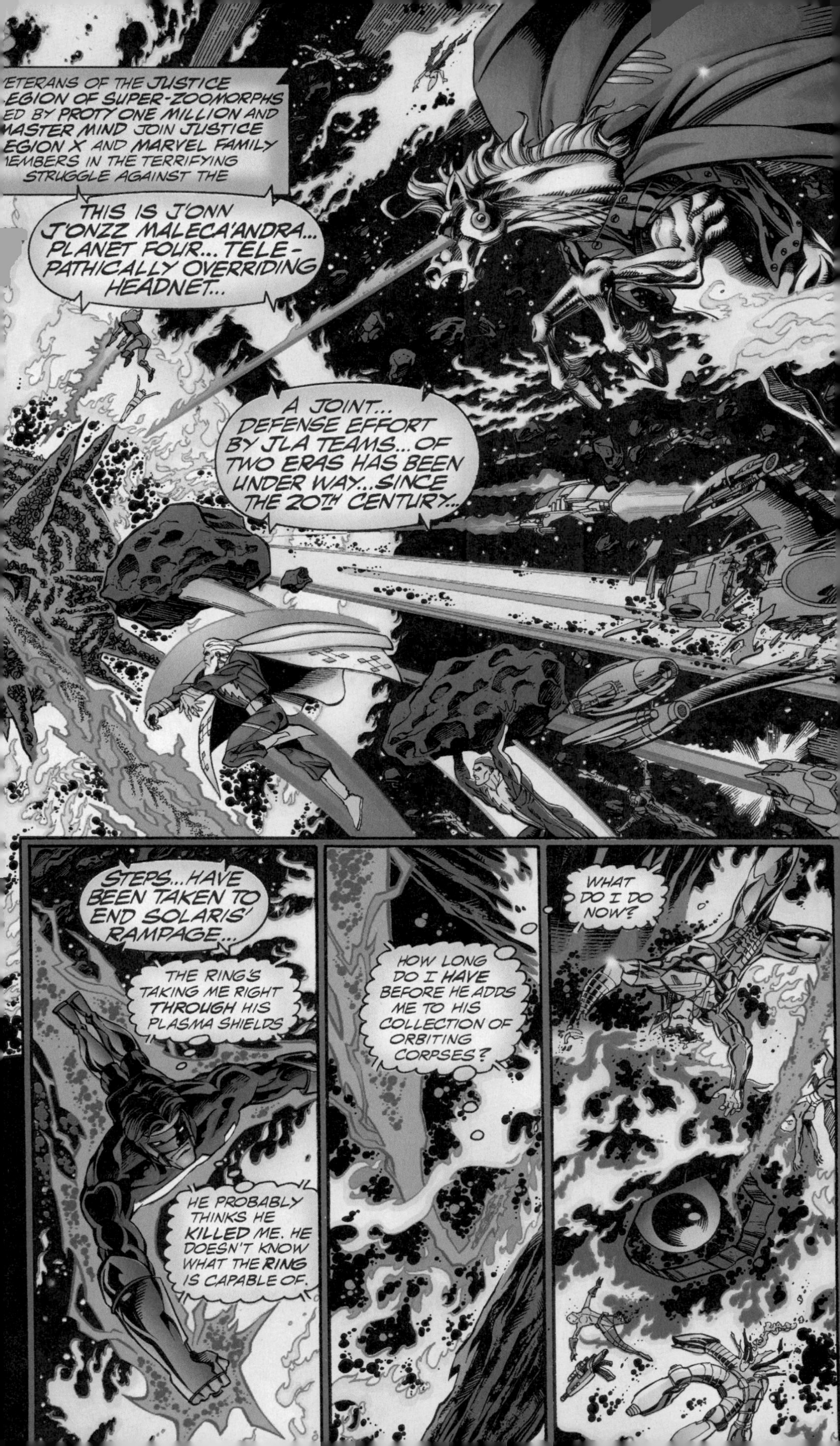

ETERANS OF THE JUSTICE
EGION OF SUPER-ZOOMORPHS
ED BY PROTY ONE MILLION AND
ASTER MIND JOIN JUSTICE
EGION X AND MARVEL FAMILY
EMBERS IN THE TERRIFYING
STRUGGLE AGAINST THE
THIS IS J'ONN J'ONZZ MALECA'ANDRA... PLANET FOUR... TELE-PATHICALLY OVERRIDING HEADNET...
A JOINT... DEFENSE EFFORT BY JLA TEAMS... OF TWO ERAS HAS BEEN UNDER WAY...SINCE THE 20TH CENTURY...
STEPS...HAVE BEEN TAKEN TO END SOLARIS' RAMPAGE...
THE RING'S TAKING ME RIGHT THROUGH HIS PLASMA SHIELDS
HE PROBABLY THINKS HE KILLED ME. HE DOESN'T KNOW WHAT THE RING IS CAPABLE OF.
HOW LONG DO I HAVE BEFORE HE ADDS ME TO HIS COLLECTION OF ORBITING CORPSES?
WHAT DO I DO NOW?

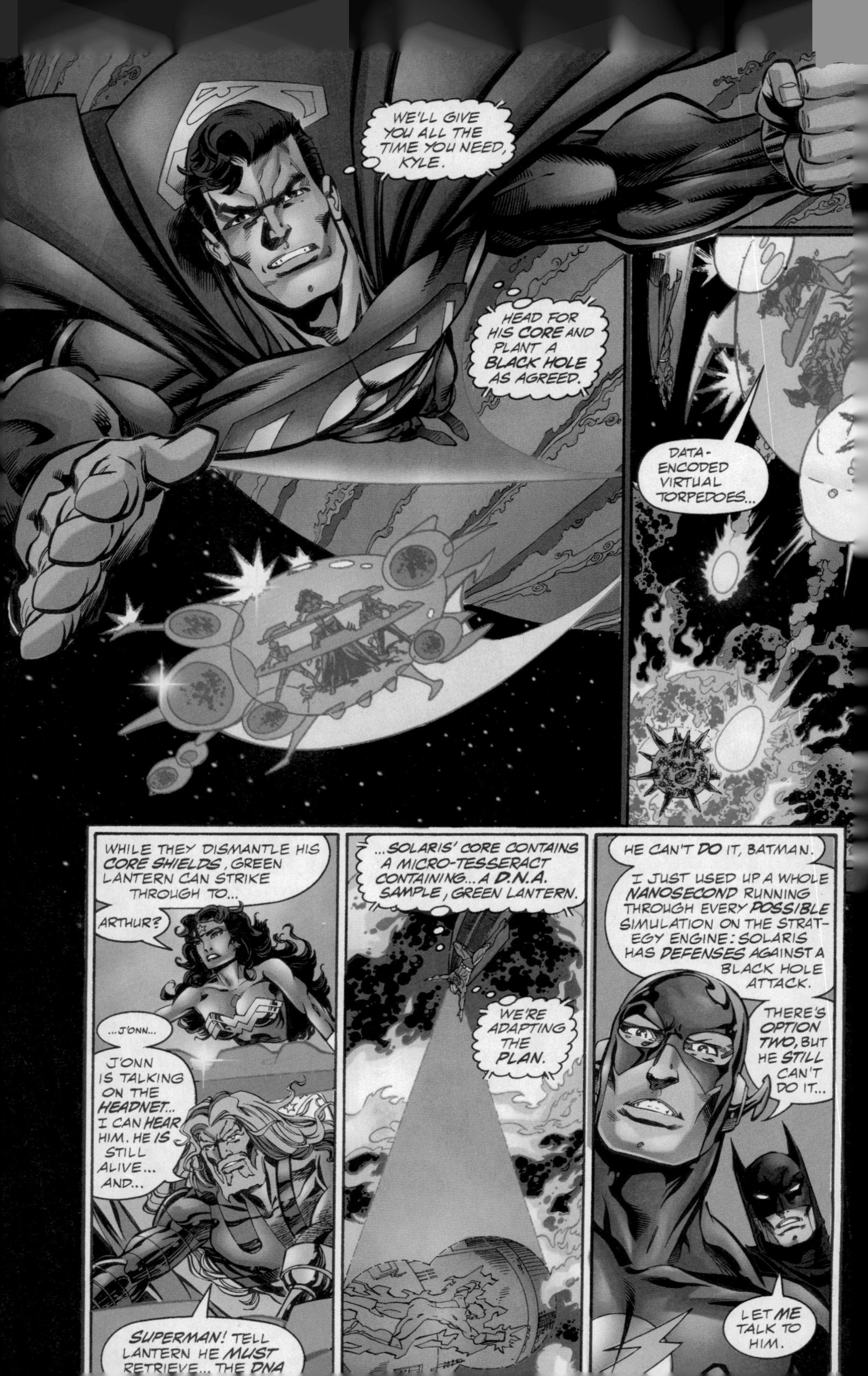
WE'LL GIVE YOU ALL THE TIME YOU NEED, KYLE.
HEAD FOR HIS CORE AND PLANT A BLACK HOLE AS AGREED.
DATA-ENCODED VIRTUAL TORPEDOES...
WHILE THEY DISMANTLE HIS CORE SHIELDS, GREEN LANTERN CAN STRIKE THROUGH TO...
ARTHUR?
...J'ONN...
J'ONN IS TALKING ON THE HEADNET... I CAN HEAR HIM. HE IS STILL ALIVE... AND...
SUPERMAN! TELL LANTERN HE MUST RETRIEVE... THE DNA
...SOLARIS' CORE CONTAINS A MICRO-TESSERACT CONTAINING... A D.N.A. SAMPLE, GREEN LANTERN.
WE'RE ADAPTING THE PLAN.
HE CAN'T DO IT, BATMAN.
I JUST USED UP A WHOLE NANOSECOND RUNNING THROUGH EVERY POSSIBLE SIMULATION ON THE STRATEGY ENGINE: SOLARIS HAS DEFENSES AGAINST A BLACK HOLE ATTACK.
THERE'S OPTION TWO, BUT HE STILL CAN'T DO IT...
LET ME TALK TO HIM.

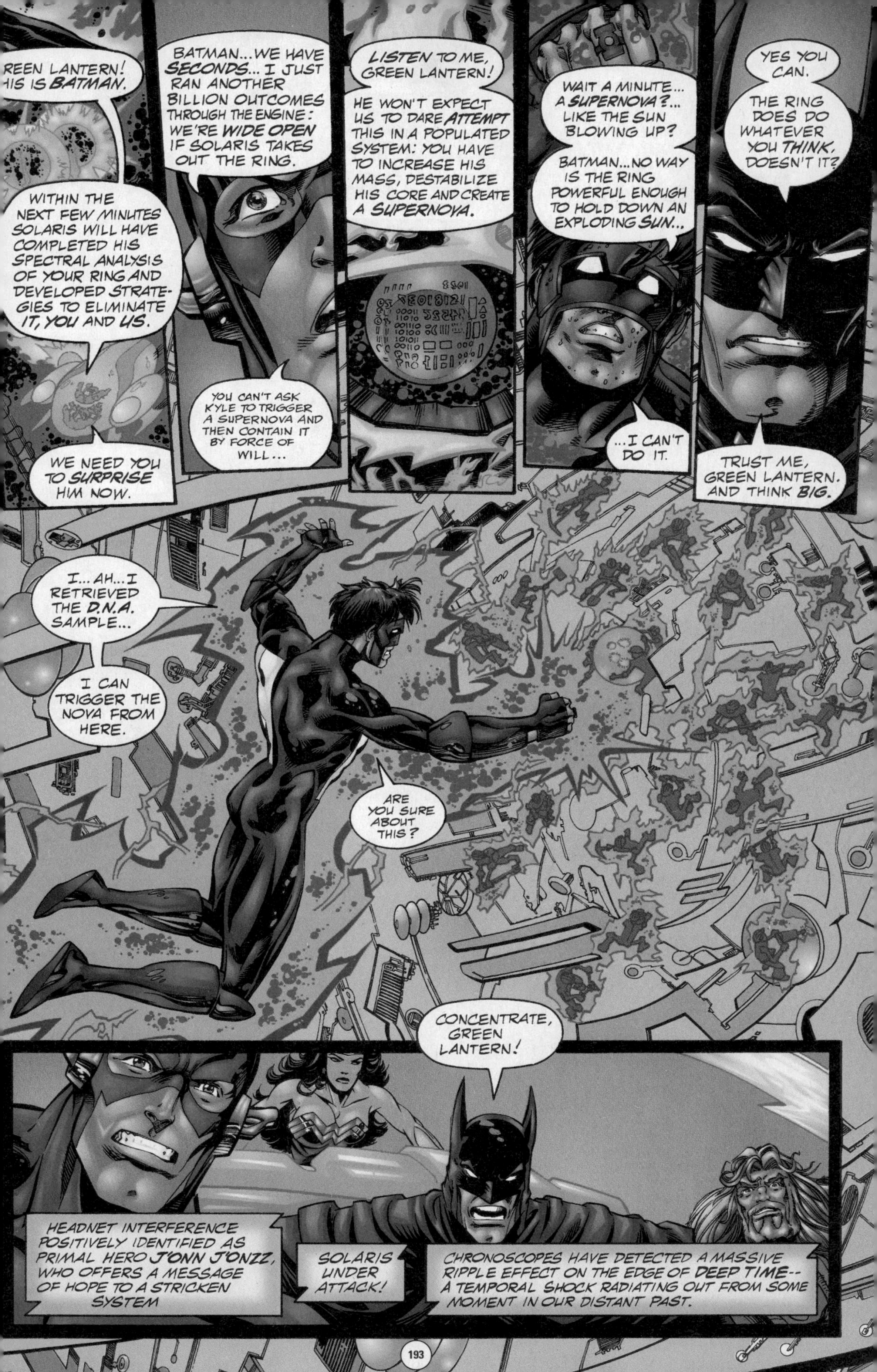
REEN LANTERN! HIS IS BATMAN.
WITHIN THE NEXT FEW MINUTES SOLARIS WILL HAVE COMPLETED HIS SPECTRAL ANALYSIS OF YOUR RING AND DEVELOPED STRATEGIES TO ELIMINATE IT, YOU AND US.
WE NEED YOU TO SURPRISE HIM NOW.
BATMAN... WE HAVE SECONDS... I JUST RAN ANOTHER BILLION OUTCOMES THROUGH THE ENGINE: WE'RE WIDE OPEN IF SOLARIS TAKES OUT THE RING.
YOU CAN'T ASK KYLE TO TRIGGER A SUPERNOVA AND THEN CONTAIN IT BY FORCE OF WILL...
LISTEN TO ME, GREEN LANTERN!
HE WON'T EXPECT US TO DARE ATTEMPT THIS IN A POPULATED SYSTEM: YOU HAVE TO INCREASE HIS MASS, DESTABILIZE HIS CORE AND CREATE A SUPERNOVA.
WAIT A MINUTE... A SUPERNOVA?... LIKE THE SUN BLOWING UP?
BATMAN... NO WAY IS THE RING POWERFUL ENOUGH TO HOLD DOWN AN EXPLODING SUN...
...I CAN'T DO IT.
YES YOU CAN.
THE RING DOES DO WHATEVER YOU THINK, DOESN'T IT?
TRUST ME, GREEN LANTERN. AND THINK BIG.
I... AH... I RETRIEVED THE D.N.A. SAMPLE...
I CAN TRIGGER THE NOVA FROM HERE.
ARE YOU SURE ABOUT THIS?
CONCENTRATE, GREEN LANTERN!
HEADNET INTERFERENCE POSITIVELY IDENTIFIED AS PRIMAL HERO J'ONN J'ONZZ, WHO OFFERS A MESSAGE OF HOPE TO A STRICKEN SYSTEM
SOLARIS UNDER ATTACK!
CHRONOSCOPES HAVE DETECTED A MASSIVE RIPPLE EFFECT ON THE EDGE OF DEEP TIME-- A TEMPORAL SHOCK RADIATING OUT FROM SOME MOMENT IN OUR DISTANT PAST.

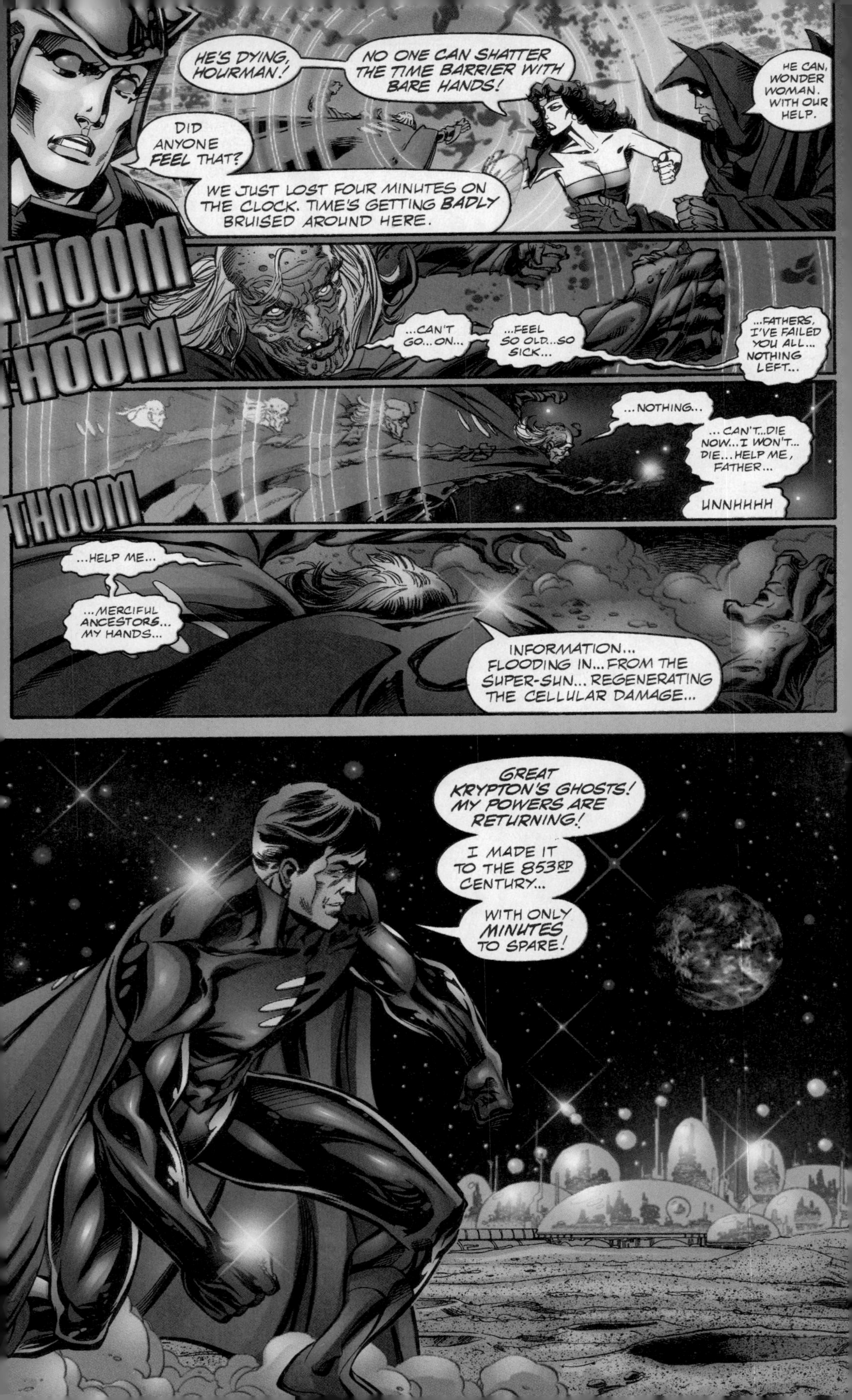
HE'S DYING, HOURMAN!
NO ONE CAN SHATTER THE TIME BARRIER WITH BARE HANDS!
HE CAN, WONDER WOMAN. WITH OUR HELP.
DID ANYONE FEEL THAT?
WE JUST LOST FOUR MINUTES ON THE CLOCK. TIME'S GETTING BADLY BRUISED AROUND HERE.
THOOM
THOOM
...CAN'T GO...ON...
...FEEL SO OLD...SO SICK...
...FATHERS, I'VE FAILED YOU ALL... NOTHING LEFT...
...NOTHING...
...CAN'T...DIE NOW...I WON'T... DIE...HELP ME, FATHER...
UNNHHHH
THOOM
...HELP ME...
...MERCIFUL ANCESTORS... MY HANDS...
INFORMATION... FLOODING IN...FROM THE SUPER-SUN... REGENERATING THE CELLULAR DAMAGE...
GREAT KRYPTON'S GHOSTS! MY POWERS ARE RETURNING!
I MADE IT TO THE 853RD CENTURY...
WITH ONLY MINUTES TO SPARE!

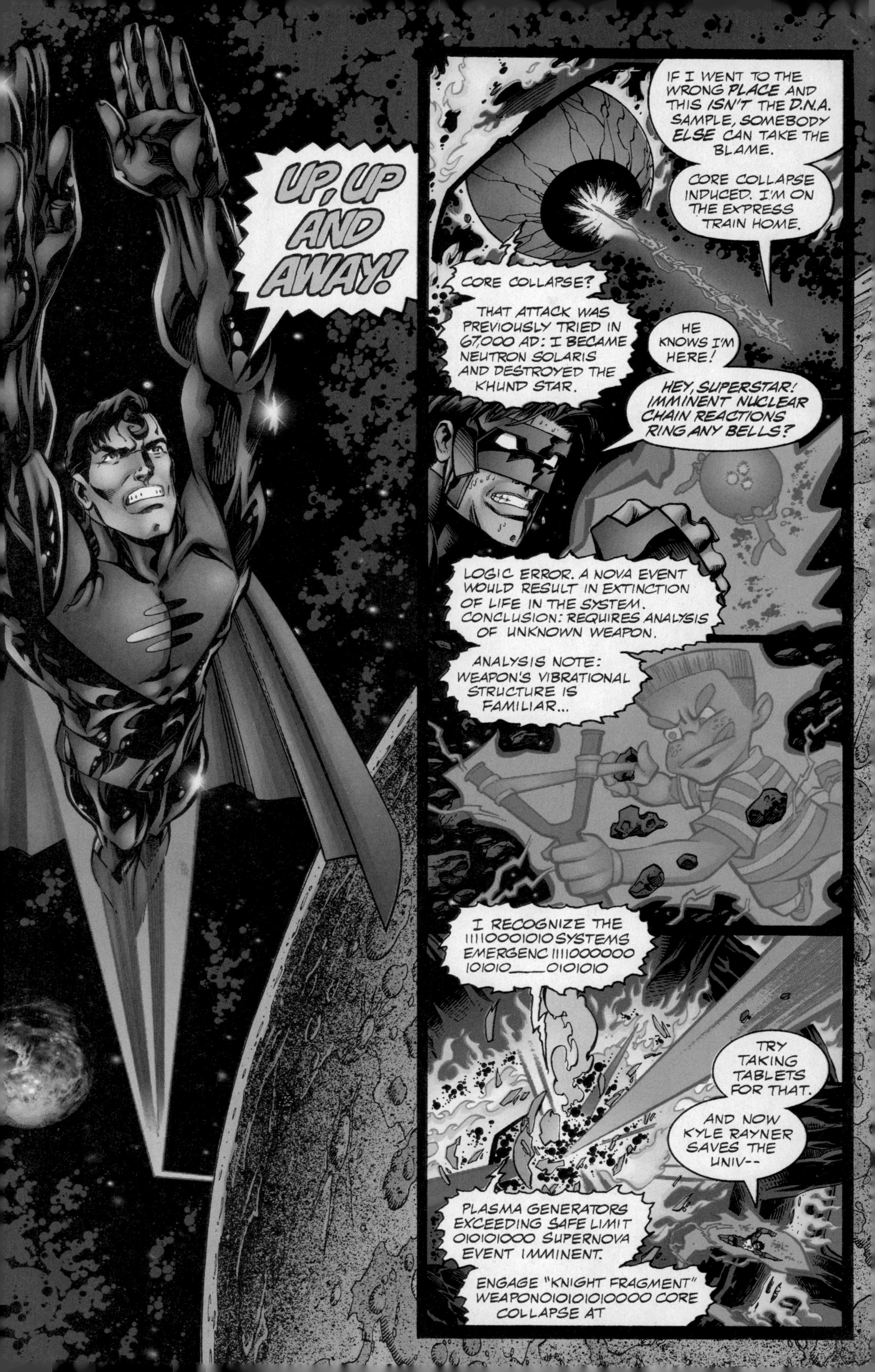
UP, UP AND AWAY!
IF I WENT TO THE WRONG PLACE AND THIS ISN'T THE D.N.A. SAMPLE, SOMEBODY ELSE CAN TAKE THE BLAME.
CORE COLLAPSE INDUCED. I'M ON THE EXPRESS TRAIN HOME.
CORE COLLAPSE?
THAT ATTACK WAS PREVIOUSLY TRIED IN 67,000 AD: I BECAME NEUTRON SOLARIS AND DESTROYED THE KHUND STAR.
HE KNOWS I'M HERE!
HEY, SUPERSTAR! IMMINENT NUCLEAR CHAIN REACTIONS RING ANY BELLS?
LOGIC ERROR. A NOVA EVENT WOULD RESULT IN EXTINCTION OF LIFE IN THE SYSTEM. CONCLUSION: REQUIRES ANALYSIS OF UNKNOWN WEAPON.
ANALYSIS NOTE: WEAPON'S VIBRATIONAL STRUCTURE IS FAMILIAR...
I RECOGNIZE THE 1111000101010 SYSTEMS EMERGENC 11110000000 101010____0101010
TRY TAKING TABLETS FOR THAT.
AND NOW KYLE RAYNER SAVES THE UNIV--
PLASMA GENERATORS EXCEEDING SAFE LIMIT 010101000 SUPERNOVA EVENT IMMINENT.
ENGAGE "KNIGHT FRAGMENT" WEAPON0101010100000 CORE COLLAPSE AT

AH.

IT... IT JUST HAPPENED!... I... *GOT* HIM...

SOMETHING GOT *THROUGH*... HE FIRED SOMETHING THAT WAS ABLE TO GO RIGHT THROUGH MY *SHIELD*... BUT I *GOT* HIM...

SO... WHAT DO I *DO* WITH HIM?

I HAVE IOIOIO POISONED OIOIOIOOOO THE SUN OIOIOIIIIOIO 1000 I WILL REORGANIZE OIOIO 0010

SUPERMAN PRIME OIOIO 00010 IS ALREADY 01001 110 DEAD 101000 0010 DEAD OIOIO 11

KRYPTONIT... HE WAS MANEUVERING HIMSELF INTO POSITION TO ATTACK THE *SUN* WITH THAT MISSILE!

196

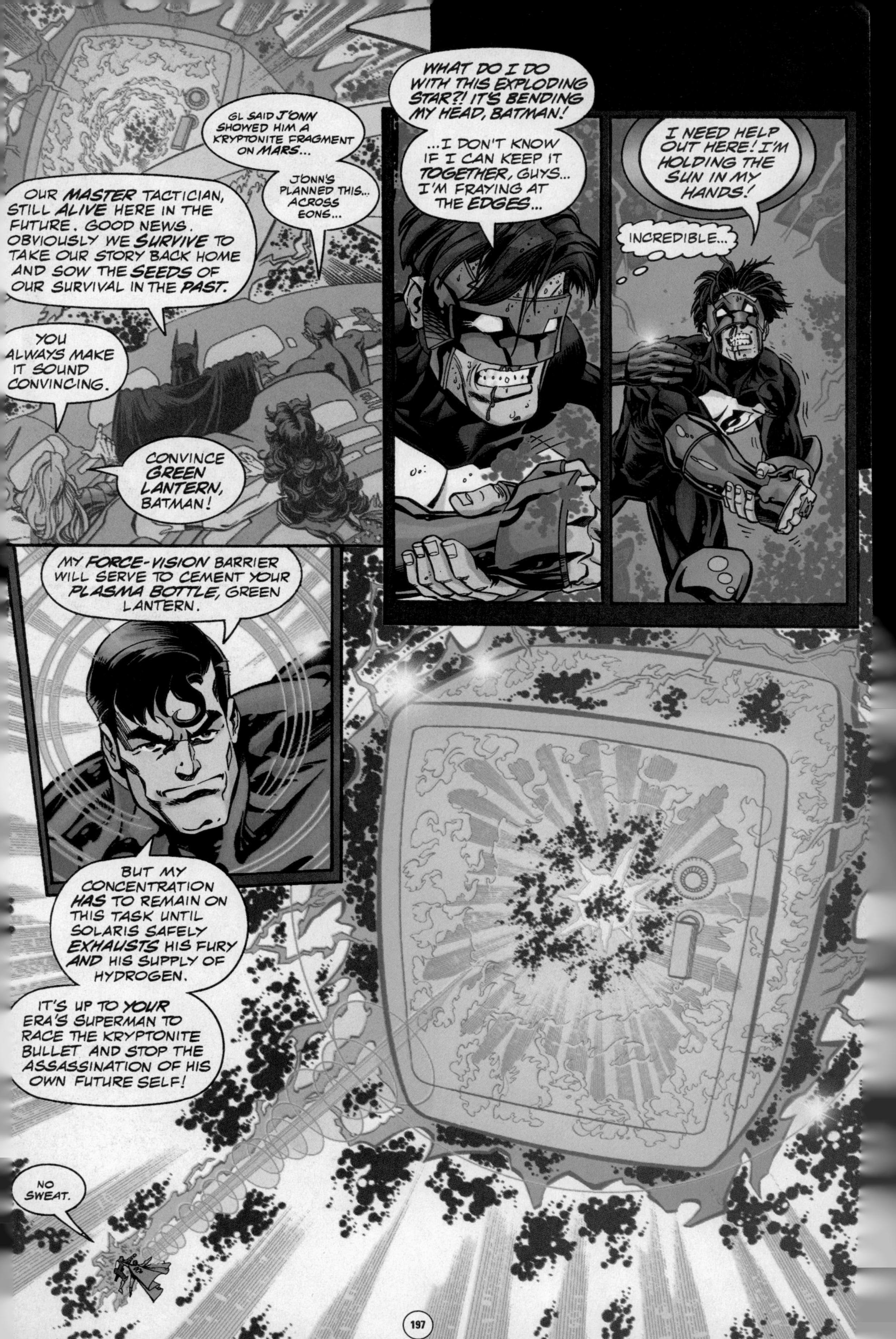
GL SAID J'ONN SHOWED HIM A KRYPTONITE FRAGMENT ON MARS...
J'ONN'S PLANNED THIS... ACROSS EONS...
OUR MASTER TACTICIAN, STILL ALIVE HERE IN THE FUTURE. GOOD NEWS. OBVIOUSLY WE SURVIVE TO TAKE OUR STORY BACK HOME AND SOW THE SEEDS OF OUR SURVIVAL IN THE PAST.
YOU ALWAYS MAKE IT SOUND CONVINCING.
CONVINCE GREEN LANTERN, BATMAN!
WHAT DO I DO WITH THIS EXPLODING STAR?! IT'S BENDING MY HEAD, BATMAN!
...I DON'T KNOW IF I CAN KEEP IT TOGETHER, GUYS... I'M FRAYING AT THE EDGES...
I NEED HELP OUT HERE! I'M HOLDING THE SUN IN MY HANDS!
INCREDIBLE...
MY FORCE-VISION BARRIER WILL SERVE TO CEMENT YOUR PLASMA BOTTLE, GREEN LANTERN.
BUT MY CONCENTRATION HAS TO REMAIN ON THIS TASK UNTIL SOLARIS SAFELY EXHAUSTS HIS FURY AND HIS SUPPLY OF HYDROGEN.
IT'S UP TO YOUR ERA'S SUPERMAN TO RACE THE KRYPTONITE BULLET AND STOP THE ASSASSINATION OF HIS OWN FUTURE SELF!
NO SWEAT.

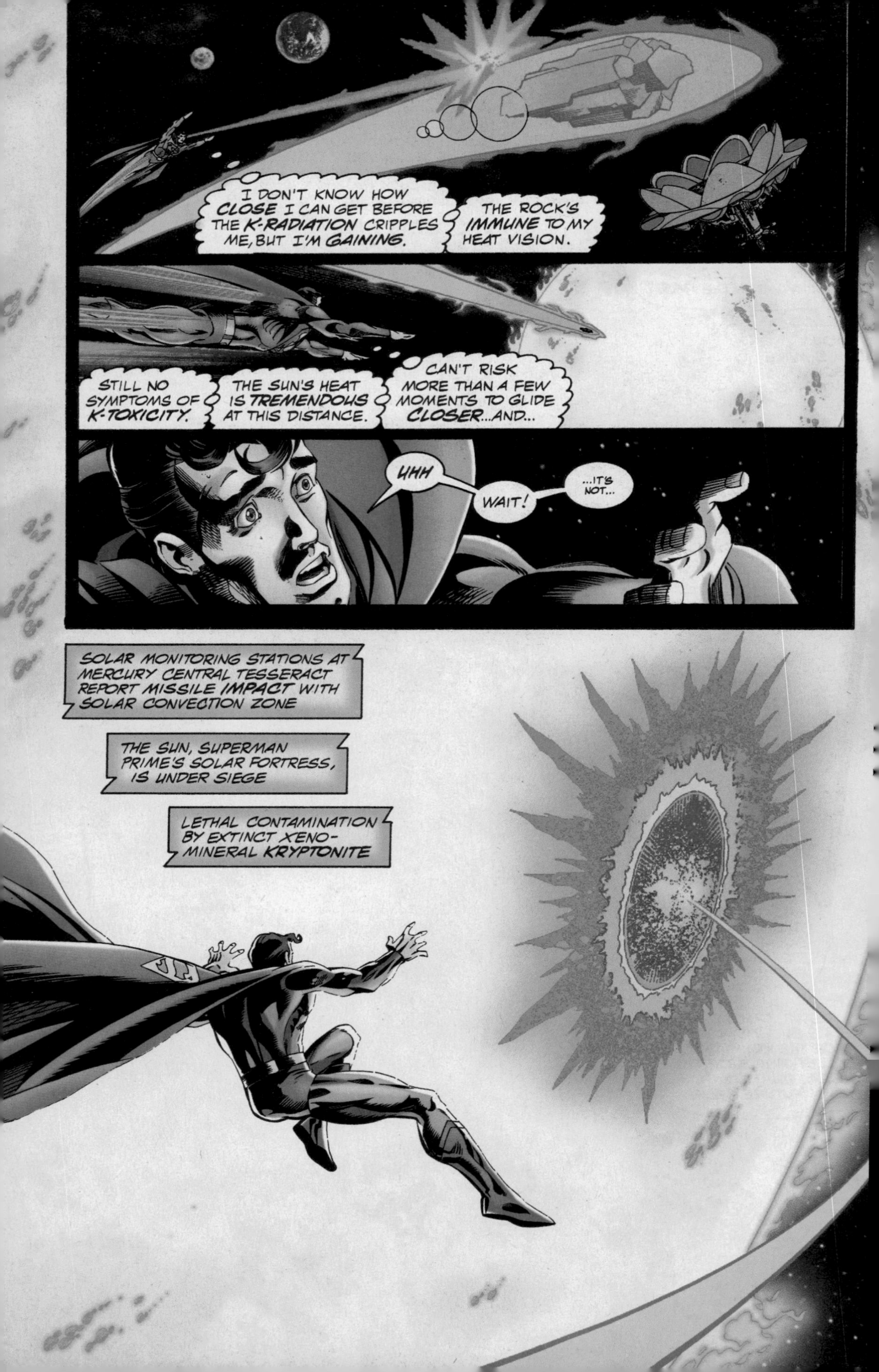
I DON'T KNOW HOW CLOSE I CAN GET BEFORE THE K-RADIATION CRIPPLES ME, BUT I'M GAINING.
THE ROCK'S IMMUNE TO MY HEAT VISION.
STILL NO SYMPTOMS OF K-TOXICITY.
THE SUN'S HEAT IS TREMENDOUS AT THIS DISTANCE.
CAN'T RISK MORE THAN A FEW MOMENTS TO GLIDE CLOSER...AND...
UHH
WAIT!
...IT'S NOT...
SOLAR MONITORING STATIONS AT MERCURY CENTRAL TESSERACT REPORT MISSILE IMPACT WITH SOLAR CONVECTION ZONE
THE SUN, SUPERMAN PRIME'S SOLAR FORTRESS, IS UNDER SIEGE
LETHAL CONTAMINATION BY EXTINCT XENO-MINERAL KRYPTONITE

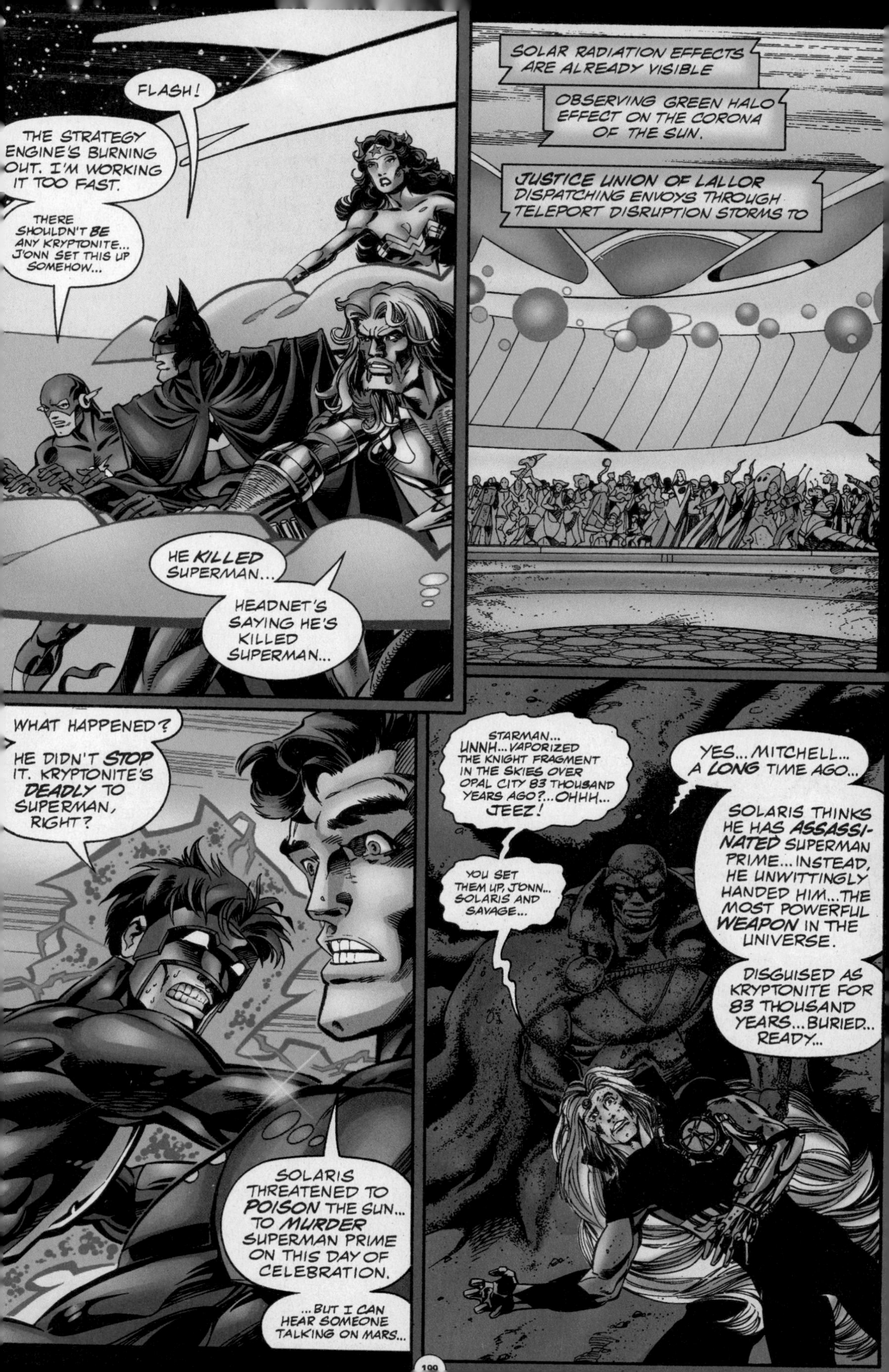

FLASH!
THE STRATEGY ENGINE'S BURNING OUT. I'M WORKING IT TOO FAST.
THERE SHOULDN'T BE ANY KRYPTONITE... J'ONN SET THIS UP SOMEHOW...
HE KILLED SUPERMAN...
HEADNET'S SAYING HE'S KILLED SUPERMAN...
SOLAR RADIATION EFFECTS ARE ALREADY VISIBLE
OBSERVING GREEN HALO EFFECT ON THE CORONA OF THE SUN.
JUSTICE UNION OF LALLOR DISPATCHING ENVOYS THROUGH TELEPORT DISRUPTION STORMS TO
WHAT HAPPENED?
HE DIDN'T STOP IT. KRYPTONITE'S DEADLY TO SUPERMAN, RIGHT?
SOLARIS THREATENED TO POISON THE SUN... TO MURDER SUPERMAN PRIME ON THIS DAY OF CELEBRATION.
...BUT I CAN HEAR SOMEONE TALKING ON MARS...
STARMAN... UNNH...VAPORIZED THE KNIGHT FRAGMENT IN THE SKIES OVER OPAL CITY 83 THOUSAND YEARS AGO?...OHHH... JEEZ!
YES... MITCHELL... A LONG TIME AGO...
YOU SET THEM UP, J'ONN... SOLARIS AND SAVAGE...
SOLARIS THINKS HE HAS ASSASSINATED SUPERMAN PRIME... INSTEAD, HE UNWITTINGLY HANDED HIM...THE MOST POWERFUL WEAPON IN THE UNIVERSE.
DISGUISED AS KRYPTONITE FOR 83 THOUSAND YEARS...BURIED... READY...

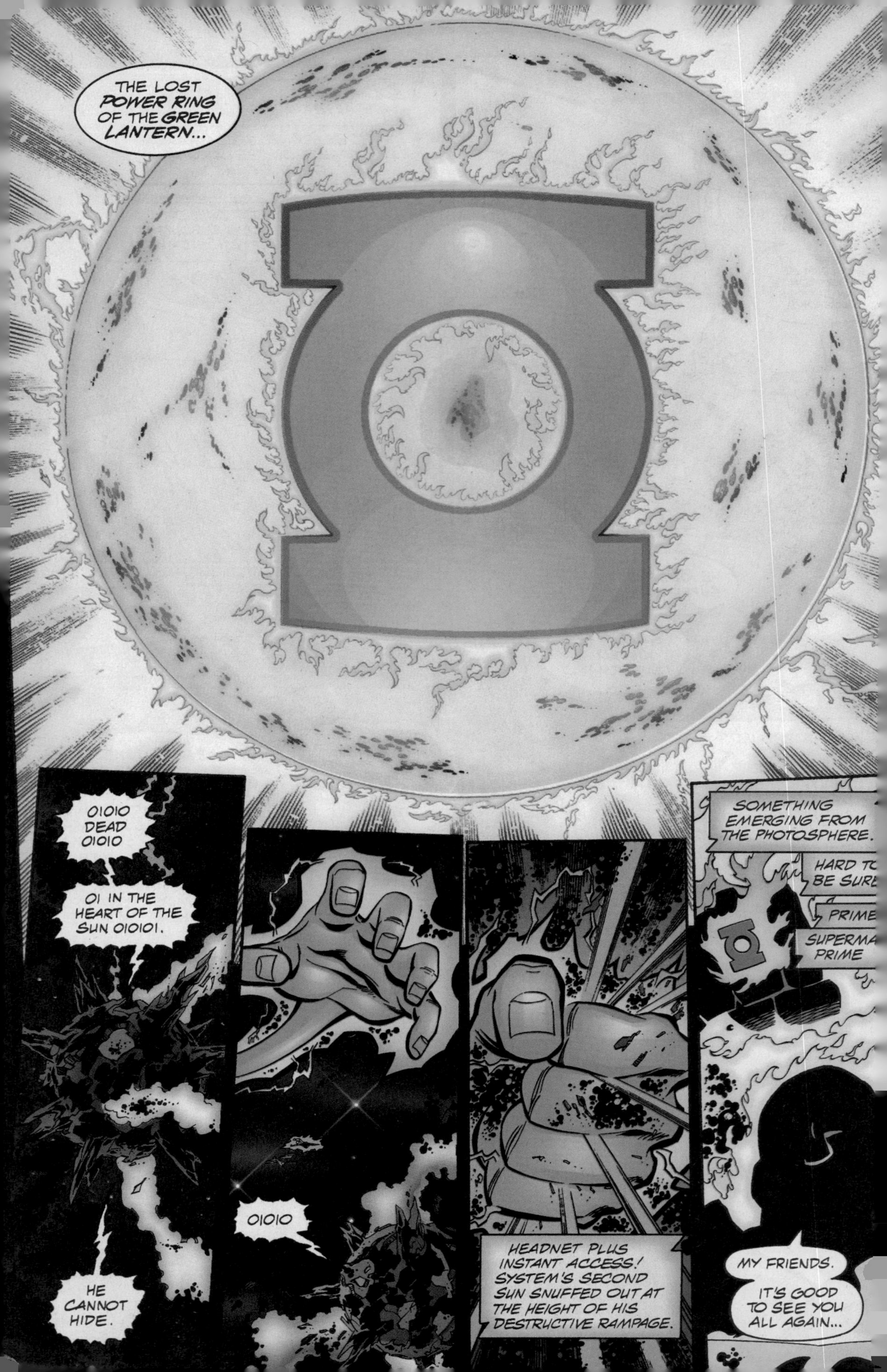
THE LOST POWER RING OF THE GREEN LANTERN...
01010 DEAD 01010
01 IN THE HEART OF THE SUN 010101.
HE CANNOT HIDE.
01010
HEADNET PLUS INSTANT ACCESS! SYSTEM'S SECOND SUN SNUFFED OUT AT THE HEIGHT OF HIS DESTRUCTIVE RAMPAGE.
SOMETHING EMERGING FROM THE PHOTOSPHERE.
MY FRIENDS.
IT'S GOOD TO SEE YOU ALL AGAIN...

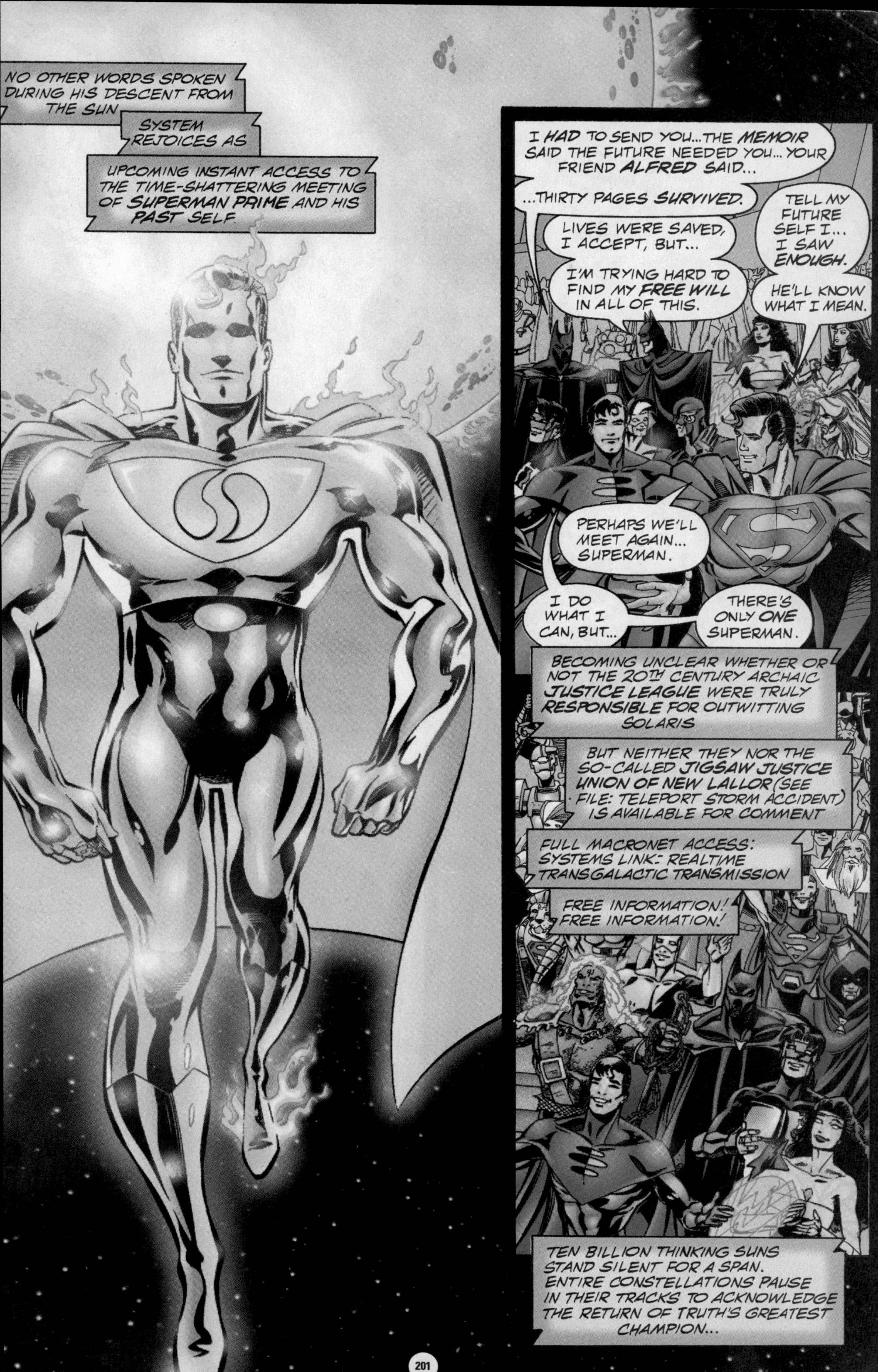

NO OTHER WORDS SPOKEN DURING HIS DESCENT FROM THE SUN.
SYSTEM REJOICES AS
UPCOMING INSTANT ACCESS TO THE TIME-SHATTERING MEETING OF SUPERMAN PRIME AND HIS PAST SELF.
I HAD TO SEND YOU... THE MEMOIR SAID THE FUTURE NEEDED YOU... YOUR FRIEND ALFRED SAID...
...THIRTY PAGES SURVIVED.
LIVES WERE SAVED, I ACCEPT, BUT...
I'M TRYING HARD TO FIND MY FREE WILL IN ALL OF THIS.
TELL MY FUTURE SELF I... I SAW ENOUGH.
HE'LL KNOW WHAT I MEAN.
PERHAPS WE'LL MEET AGAIN... SUPERMAN.
I DO WHAT I CAN, BUT...
THERE'S ONLY ONE SUPERMAN.
BECOMING UNCLEAR WHETHER OR NOT THE 20TH CENTURY ARCHAIC JUSTICE LEAGUE WERE TRULY RESPONSIBLE FOR OUTWITTING SOLARIS
BUT NEITHER THEY NOR THE SO-CALLED JIGSAW JUSTICE UNION OF NEW LALLOR (SEE FILE: TELEPORT STORM ACCIDENT) IS AVAILABLE FOR COMMENT
FULL MACRONET ACCESS: SYSTEMS LINK: REALTIME TRANSGALACTIC TRANSMISSION
FREE INFORMATION! FREE INFORMATION!
TEN BILLION THINKING SUNS STAND SILENT FOR A SPAN. ENTIRE CONSTELLATIONS PAUSE IN THEIR TRACKS TO ACKNOWLEDGE THE RETURN OF TRUTH'S GREATEST CHAMPION...

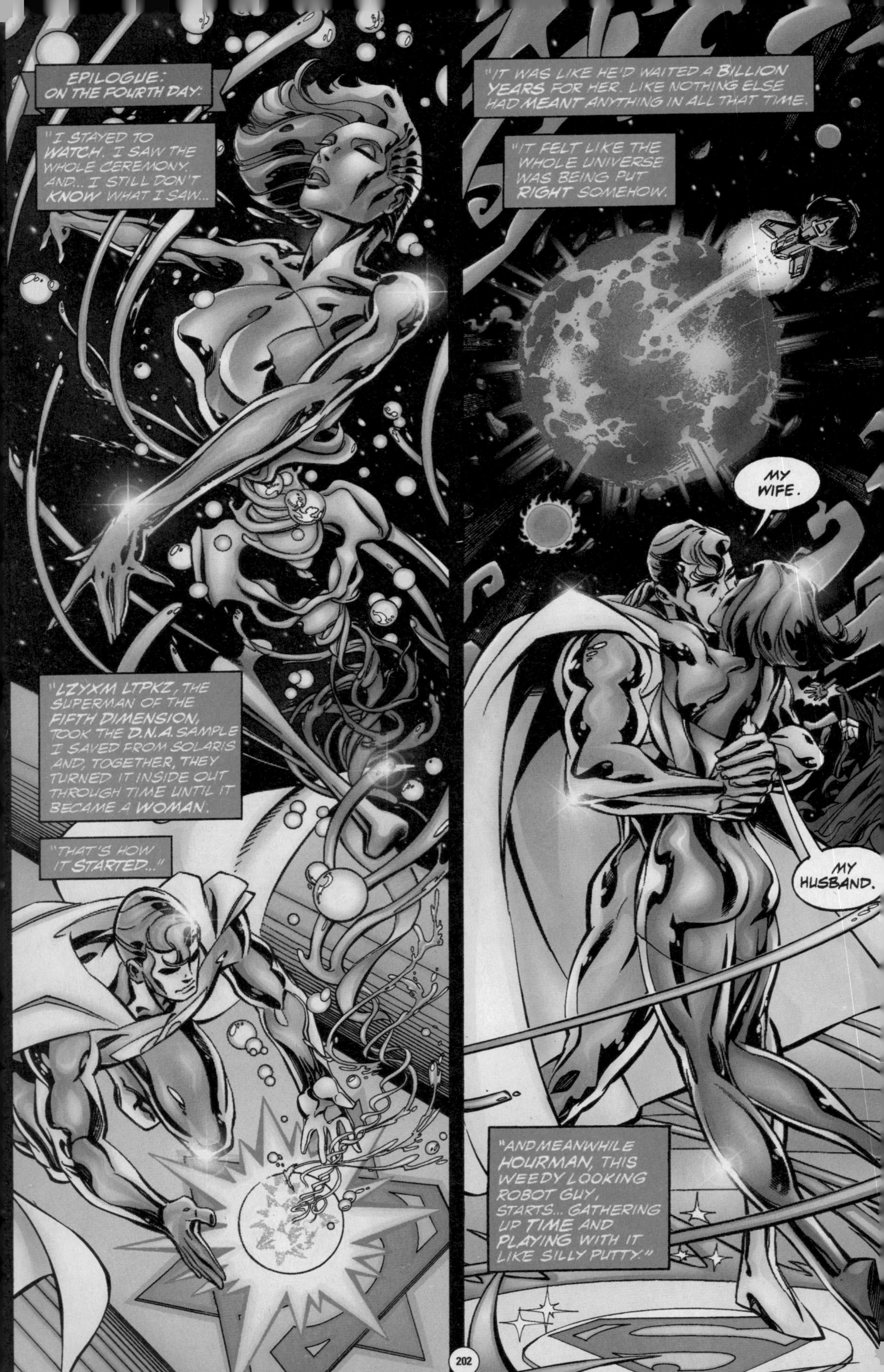
EPILOGUE: ON THE FOURTH DAY:
"I STAYED TO WATCH. I SAW THE WHOLE CEREMONY. AND... I STILL DON'T KNOW WHAT I SAW...
"LZYXM LTPKZ, THE SUPERMAN OF THE FIFTH DIMENSION, TOOK THE D.N.A. SAMPLE I SAVED FROM SOLARIS AND, TOGETHER, THEY TURNED IT INSIDE OUT THROUGH TIME UNTIL IT BECAME A WOMAN.
"THAT'S HOW IT STARTED..."
"IT WAS LIKE HE'D WAITED A BILLION YEARS FOR HER. LIKE NOTHING ELSE HAD MEANT ANYTHING IN ALL THAT TIME.
"IT FELT LIKE THE WHOLE UNIVERSE WAS BEING PUT RIGHT SOMEHOW.
MY WIFE.
MY HUSBAND.
"AND MEANWHILE HOURMAN, THIS WEEDY LOOKING ROBOT GUY, STARTS... GATHERING UP TIME AND PLAYING WITH IT LIKE SILLY PUTTY."

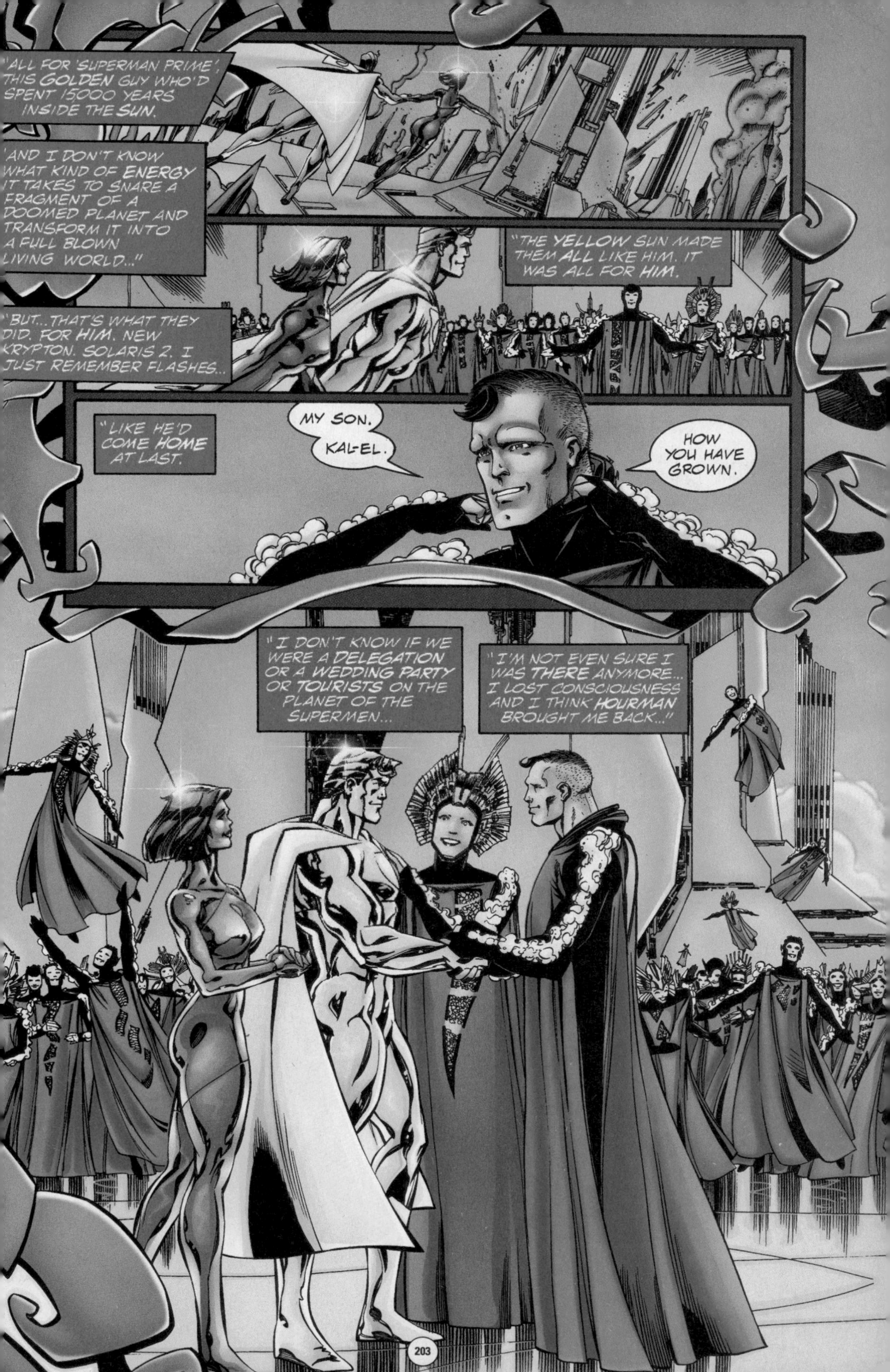
"ALL FOR 'SUPERMAN PRIME', THIS GOLDEN GUY WHO'D SPENT 15,000 YEARS INSIDE THE SUN.
"AND I DON'T KNOW WHAT KIND OF ENERGY IT TAKES TO SNARE A FRAGMENT OF A DOOMED PLANET AND TRANSFORM IT INTO A FULL BLOWN LIVING WORLD..."
"THE YELLOW SUN MADE THEM ALL LIKE HIM. IT WAS ALL FOR HIM.
"BUT...THAT'S WHAT THEY DID. FOR HIM. NEW KRYPTON. SOLARIS 2. I JUST REMEMBER FLASHES...
"LIKE HE'D COME HOME AT LAST.
MY SON. KAL-EL.
HOW YOU HAVE GROWN.
"I DON'T KNOW IF WE WERE A DELEGATION OR A WEDDING PARTY OR TOURISTS ON THE PLANET OF THE SUPERMEN...
"I'M NOT EVEN SURE I WAS THERE ANYMORE... I LOST CONSCIOUSNESS AND I THINK HOURMAN BROUGHT ME BACK..."

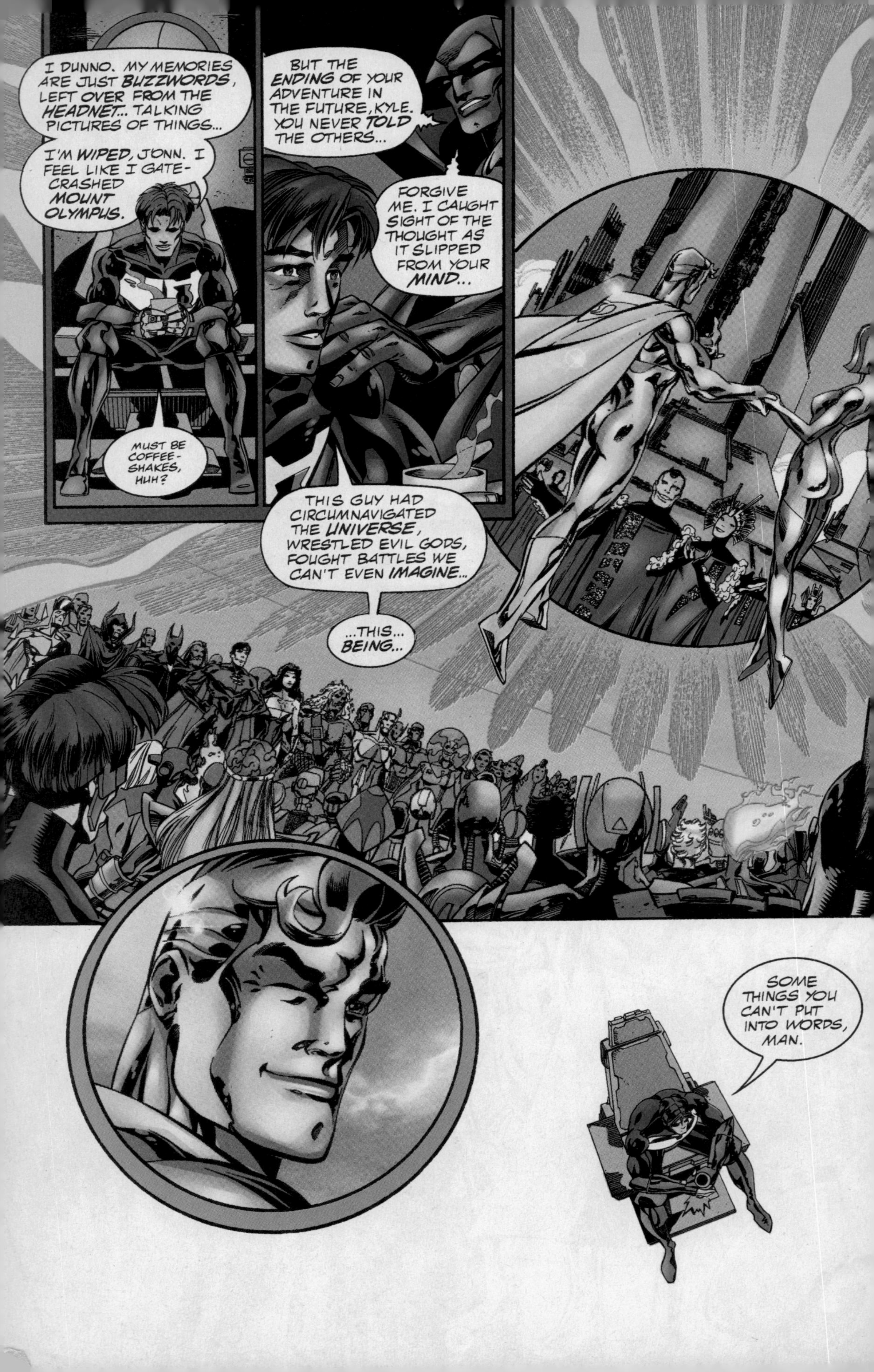
I DUNNO. MY MEMORIES ARE JUST BUZZWORDS, LEFT OVER FROM THE HEADNET... TALKING PICTURES OF THINGS...
I'M WIPED, J'ONN. I FEEL LIKE I GATE-CRASHED MOUNT OLYMPUS.
MUST BE COFFEE-SHAKES, HUH?
BUT THE ENDING OF YOUR ADVENTURE IN THE FUTURE, KYLE. YOU NEVER TOLD THE OTHERS...
FORGIVE ME. I CAUGHT SIGHT OF THE THOUGHT AS IT SLIPPED FROM YOUR MIND...
THIS GUY HAD CIRCUMNAVIGATED THE UNIVERSE, WRESTLED EVIL GODS, FOUGHT BATTLES WE CAN'T EVEN IMAGINE...
...THIS... BEING...
SOME THINGS YOU CAN'T PUT INTO WORDS, MAN.

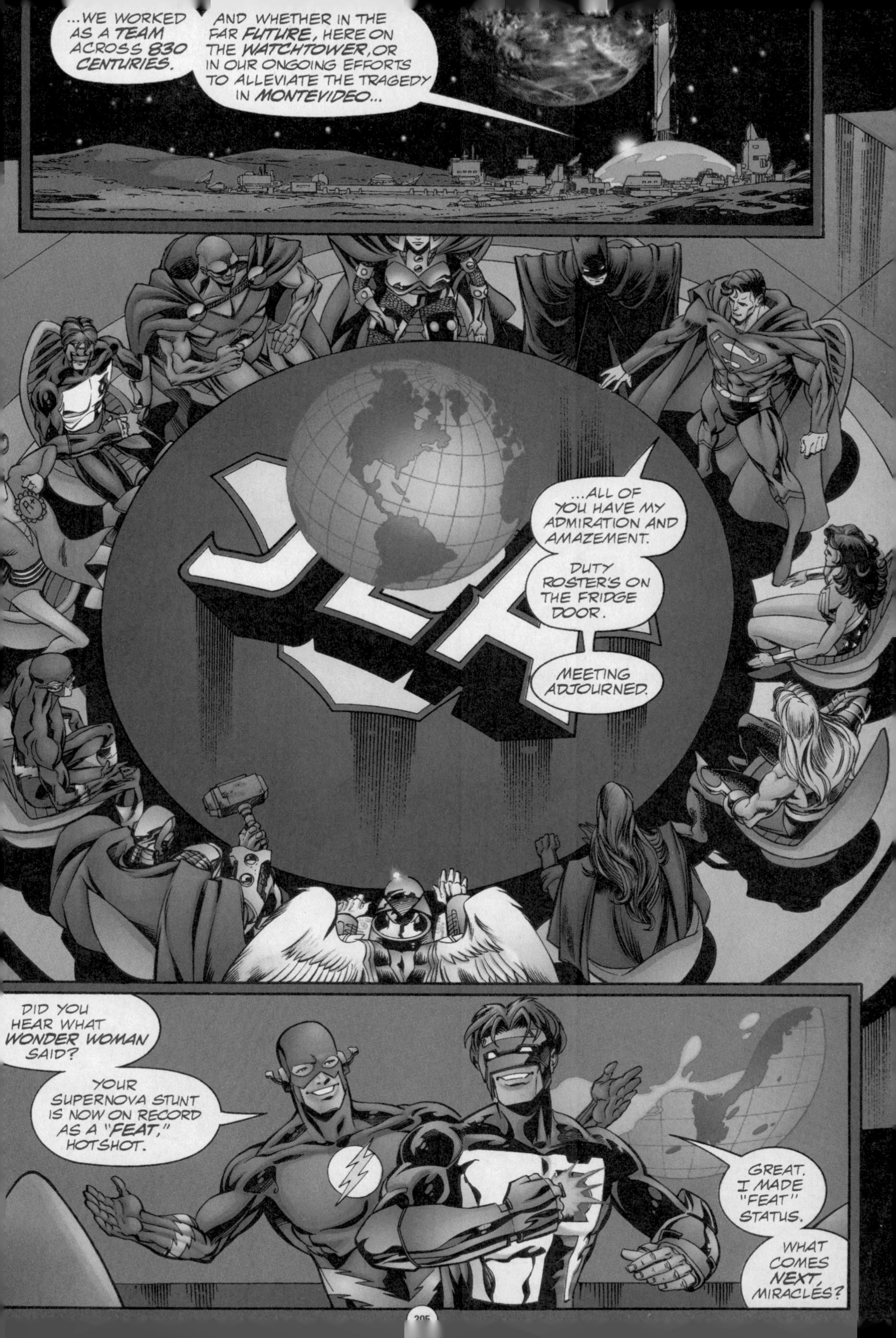
...WE WORKED AS A TEAM ACROSS 830 CENTURIES.
AND WHETHER IN THE FAR FUTURE, HERE ON THE WATCHTOWER, OR IN OUR ONGOING EFFORTS TO ALLEVIATE THE TRAGEDY IN MONTEVIDEO...
...ALL OF YOU HAVE MY ADMIRATION AND AMAZEMENT.
DUTY ROSTER'S ON THE FRIDGE DOOR.
MEETING ADJOURNED.
DID YOU HEAR WHAT WONDER WOMAN SAID?
YOUR SUPERNOVA STUNT IS NOW ON RECORD AS A "FEAT," HOTSHOT.
GREAT. I MADE "FEAT" STATUS.
WHAT COMES NEXT, MIRACLES?

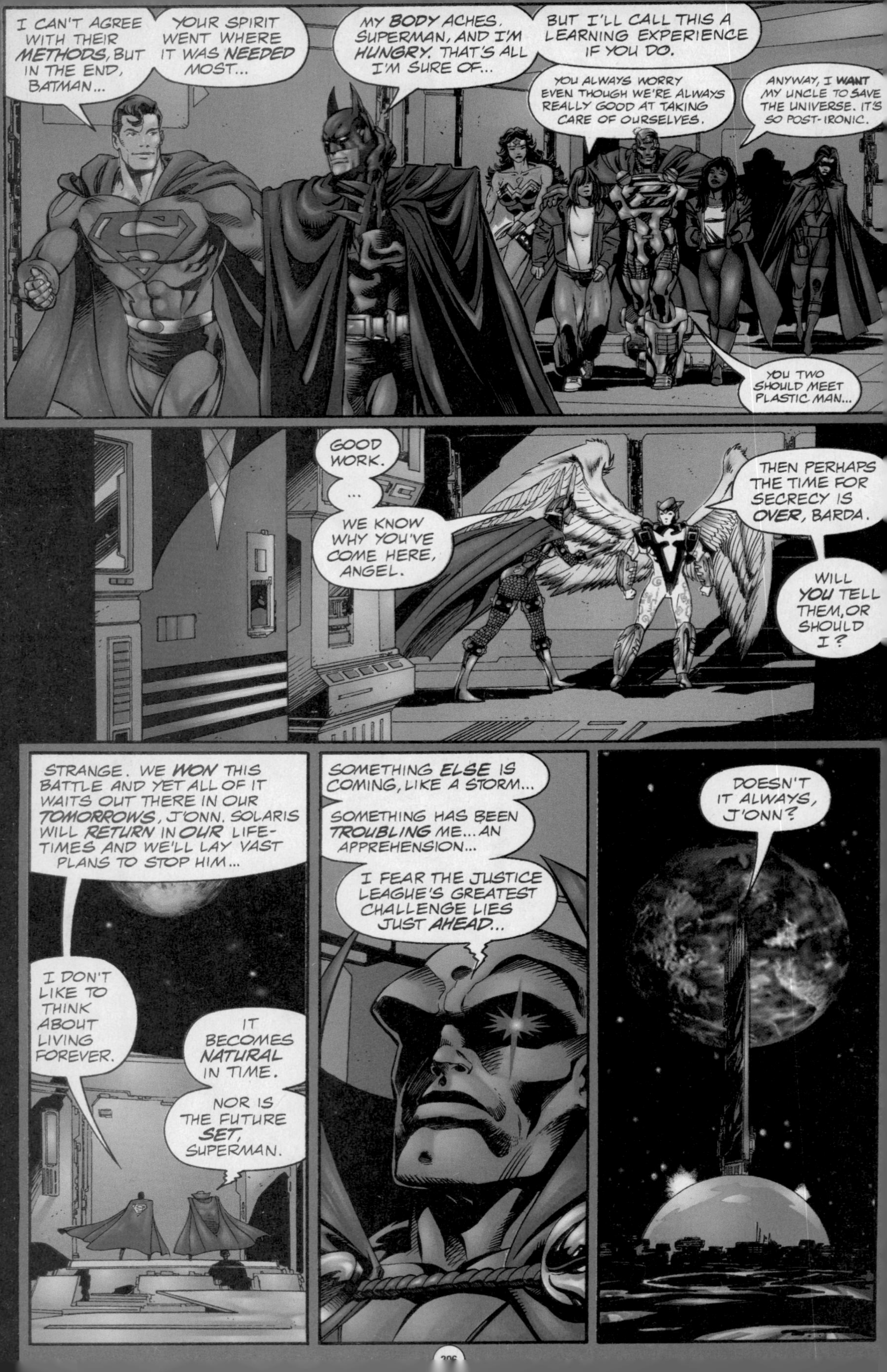

I CAN'T AGREE WITH THEIR METHODS, BUT IN THE END, BATMAN...
YOUR SPIRIT WENT WHERE IT WAS NEEDED MOST...
MY BODY ACHES, SUPERMAN, AND I'M HUNGRY. THAT'S ALL I'M SURE OF...
BUT I'LL CALL THIS A LEARNING EXPERIENCE IF YOU DO.
YOU ALWAYS WORRY EVEN THOUGH WE'RE ALWAYS REALLY GOOD AT TAKING CARE OF OURSELVES.
ANYWAY, I WANT MY UNCLE TO SAVE THE UNIVERSE. IT'S SO POST-IRONIC.
YOU TWO SHOULD MEET PLASTIC MAN...
GOOD WORK.
...
WE KNOW WHY YOU'VE COME HERE, ANGEL.
THEN PERHAPS THE TIME FOR SECRECY IS OVER, BARDA.
WILL YOU TELL THEM, OR SHOULD I?
STRANGE. WE WON THIS BATTLE AND YET ALL OF IT WAITS OUT THERE IN OUR TOMORROWS, J'ONN. SOLARIS WILL RETURN IN OUR LIFETIMES AND WE'LL LAY VAST PLANS TO STOP HIM...
I DON'T LIKE TO THINK ABOUT LIVING FOREVER.
IT BECOMES NATURAL IN TIME.
NOR IS THE FUTURE SET, SUPERMAN.
SOMETHING ELSE IS COMING, LIKE A STORM...
SOMETHING HAS BEEN TROUBLING ME... AN APPREHENSION...
I FEAR THE JUSTICE LEAGUE'S GREATEST CHALLENGE LIES JUST AHEAD...
DOESN'T IT ALWAYS, J'ONN?

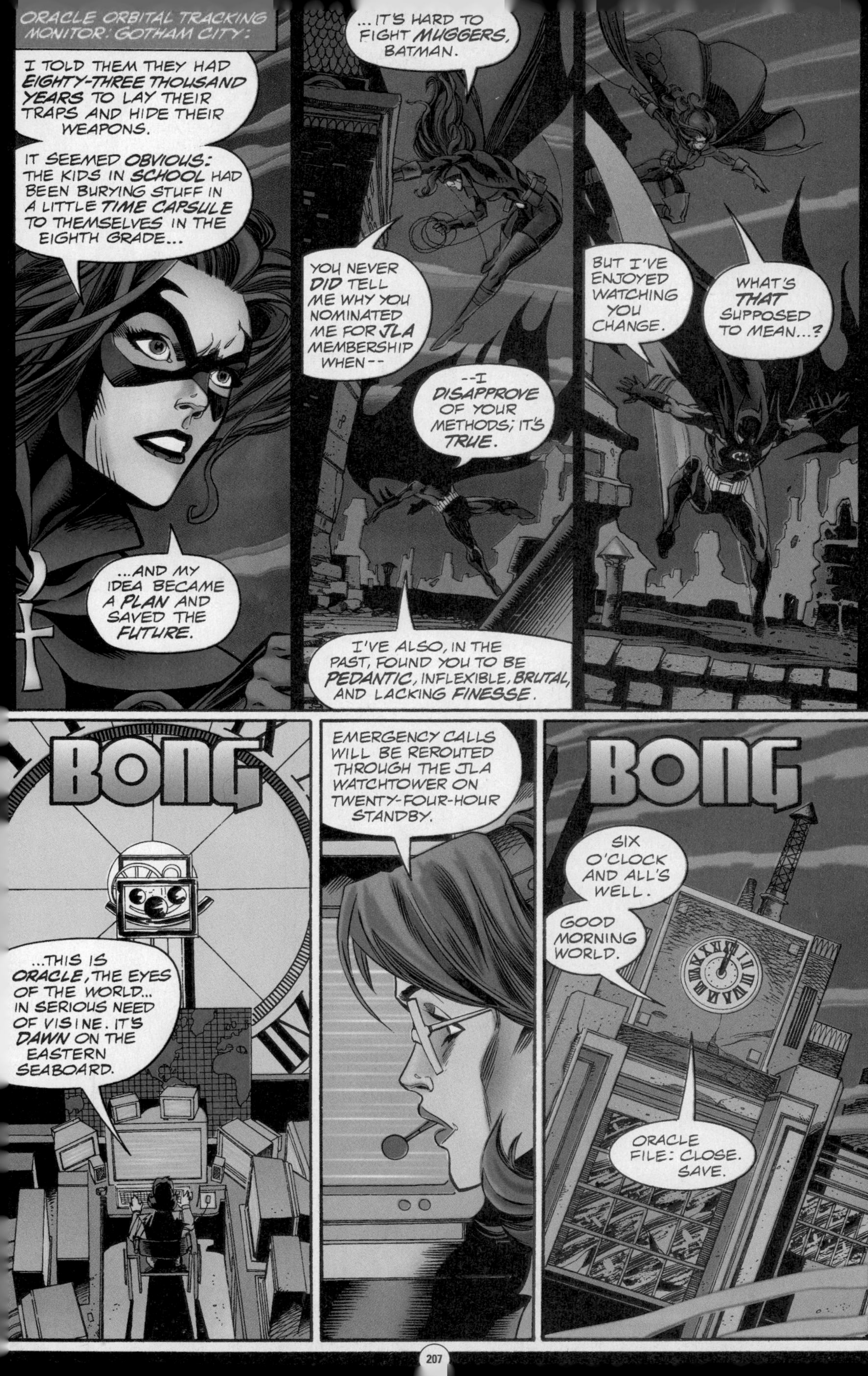
ORACLE ORBITAL TRACKING MONITOR: GOTHAM CITY:
I TOLD THEM THEY HAD EIGHTY-THREE THOUSAND YEARS TO LAY THEIR TRAPS AND HIDE THEIR WEAPONS.
IT SEEMED OBVIOUS: THE KIDS IN SCHOOL HAD BEEN BURYING STUFF IN A LITTLE TIME CAPSULE TO THEMSELVES IN THE EIGHTH GRADE...
...AND MY IDEA BECAME A PLAN AND SAVED THE FUTURE.
...IT'S HARD TO FIGHT MUGGERS, BATMAN.
YOU NEVER DID TELL ME WHY YOU NOMINATED ME FOR JLA MEMBERSHIP WHEN--
--I DISAPPROVE OF YOUR METHODS; IT'S TRUE.
I'VE ALSO, IN THE PAST, FOUND YOU TO BE PEDANTIC, INFLEXIBLE, BRUTAL, AND LACKING FINESSE.
BUT I'VE ENJOYED WATCHING YOU CHANGE.
WHAT'S THAT SUPPOSED TO MEAN...?
BONG
...THIS IS ORACLE, THE EYES OF THE WORLD... IN SERIOUS NEED OF VISINE. IT'S DAWN ON THE EASTERN SEABOARD.
EMERGENCY CALLS WILL BE REROUTED THROUGH THE JLA WATCHTOWER ON TWENTY-FOUR-HOUR STANDBY.
BONG
SIX O'CLOCK AND ALL'S WELL.
GOOD MORNING WORLD.
ORACLE FILE: CLOSE. SAVE.

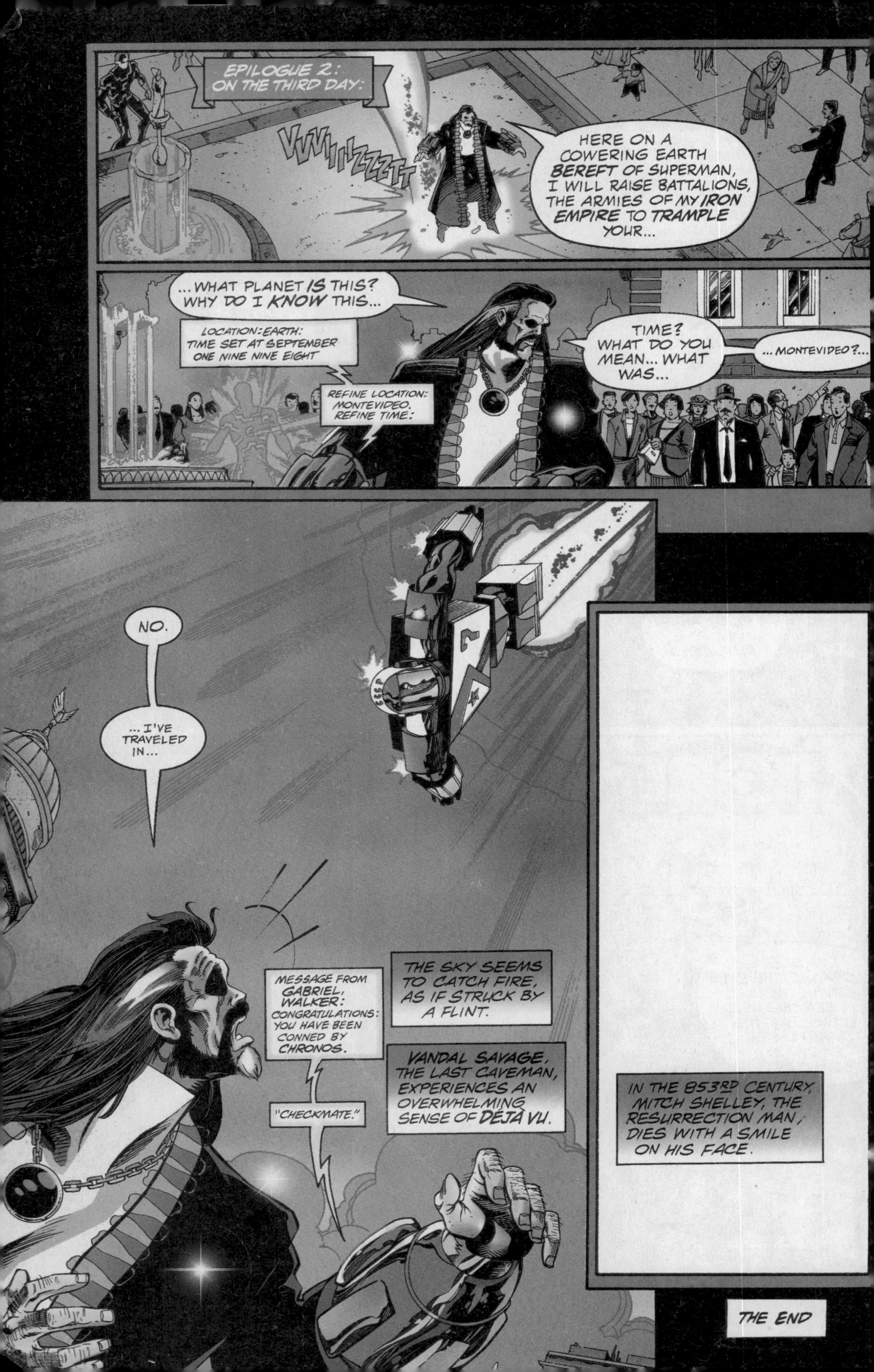
EPILOGUE 2: ON THE THIRD DAY:
VVVIIIIZZZZTTT
HERE ON A COWERING EARTH BEREFT OF SUPERMAN, I WILL RAISE BATTALIONS, THE ARMIES OF MY IRON EMPIRE TO TRAMPLE YOUR...
...WHAT PLANET IS THIS? WHY DO I KNOW THIS...
LOCATION: EARTH: TIME SET AT SEPTEMBER ONE NINE NINE EIGHT
REFINE LOCATION: MONTEVIDEO. REFINE TIME:
TIME? WHAT DO YOU MEAN... WHAT WAS...
...MONTEVIDEO?...
NO.
...I'VE TRAVELED IN...
MESSAGE FROM GABRIEL WALKER: CONGRATULATIONS: YOU HAVE BEEN CONNED BY CHRONOS.
"CHECKMATE."
THE SKY SEEMS TO CATCH FIRE, AS IF STRUCK BY A FLINT.
VANDAL SAVAGE, THE LAST CAVEMAN, EXPERIENCES AN OVERWHELMING SENSE OF DÉJÀ VU.
IN THE 853RD CENTURY, MITCH SHELLEY, THE RESURRECTION MAN, DIES WITH A SMILE ON HIS FACE.
THE END